D1603401

KING SOLOMON'S MINES

AND OTHER ADVENTURE CLASSICS

KING SOLOMON'S MINES

AND OTHER ADVENTURE CLASSICS

FALL RIVER PRESS

New York

FALL RIVER PRESS

New York

An Imprint of Sterling Publishing Co., Inc.
1166 Avenue of the Americas
New York, NY 10036

Fall River Press and the distinctive Fall River Press logo are registered trademarks
of Barnes & Noble, Inc.

Compilation © 2016 by Sterling Publishing Co., Inc.

All rights reserved. No part of this publication may be reproduced, stored in a retrieval system,
or transmitted in any form or by any means (including electronic, mechanical, photocopying,
recording, or otherwise) without prior written permission from the publisher.

ISBN 978-1-4351-6289-1

For information about custom editions, special sales, and premium and corporate purchases,
please contact Sterling Special Sales at 800-805-5489 or specialsales@sterlingpublishing.com.

Manufactured in the United States of America

2 4 6 8 10 9 7 5 3 1

www.sterlingpublishing.com

CONTENTS

CONTENTS

In the South Seas

In Terra Incognita

INTRODUCTION

I<small>N NOVEMBER OF</small> 1910, <small>A NEW PULP FICTION MAGAZINE APPEARED ON NEWS-</small>
stands across the country bearing the simple title *Adventure*. It featured fourteen
stories and the first installments of two serialized novels that would run to com-
pletion in the next three to four issues. Over the next few years, the magazine would
feature stories of virtually every conceivable adventure type: jungle adventures,
desert adventures, nautical adventures, Wild West adventures, war adventures, his-
torical adventures, pirate adventures, South Sea adventures, airborne adventures,
lost world adventures, even adventures with a macabre or supernatural twist. To say
that *Adventure* was a success with readers would be an understatement. In 1917, the
magazine changed from monthly to twice monthly publication. From 1921 to 1926, its
publishing frequency increased to three issues per month. *Adventure* outlasted virtually all of the pulp magazines it shared newsstand space with, most of which had died
off by the end of the 1950s. By the time it breathed its last gasp as a men's magazine in
1971, it had published just shy of 900 issues and close to 10,000 stories.

The enormous popularity of *Adventure* and other magazines of its kind in the first
half of the twentieth century was not a surprise phenomenon. Rather, it was a validation
of what publishers recognized as the reading public's voracious appetite for stories that
would transport them by armchair to strange and exotic locales where thrill-packed
adventures awaited. *King Solomon's Mines and Other Adventure Classics* celebrates the
long history of adventure fiction with twenty-five stories set where adventure naturally
seemed to ferment: in the desert, the jungle, the South Sea islands, the American west,
the sea, and terra incognita, that vast uncharted terrain where any number of lost
worlds and forgotten empires could be found.

The earliest story in this book, Edgar Allan Poe's "A Descent into the Maelström,"
dates to 1841. Although Poe is not generally thought of in terms of adventure fiction,
this account of its narrator's white-knuckle ride through a deadly whirlpool was a
forerunner of many later tales of adventure narrated as first-person brushes with danger.
Robert Louis Stevenson's "The Beach of Falesá" (1893) and Rudyard Kipling's "The
Man Who Would Be King" (1899) are both examples of another popular adventure
fiction type: the story of westerners who find themselves out of their depth in lands
and cultures alien to their own.

The early twentieth century was the golden age of adventure fiction, when travel
and trade opened up foreign lands that had once seemed secret and inscrutable to

westerners and stimulated the imaginations of writers eager to fill their every corner with intrigues and escapades. Some of the legendary heroes and heroines of adventure fiction emerged at this time. In "The Caballero's Way" (1904), O. Henry introduced the Cisco Kid, soon to be immortalized in movies, television, and comic books. Likewise, in 1919, Johnston McCulley published his novel *The Curse of Capistrano*, the first of several dozen tales of the masked vigilante known as Zorro. It would eventually be retitled *The Mark of Zorro* to capitalize on the renown of the 1920 film adaptation of the same name featuring Douglas Fairbanks. In between these two publishing events, in 1912, Edgar Rice Burroughs conceived Tarzan the Apeman in his now-classic novel *Tarzan of the Apes*. "The Capture of Tarzan" (1916) is one of a handful of short stories that Burroughs collected in *Jungle Tales of Tarzan* (1919). Tarzan's direct descendant, Sheena, Queen of the Jungle, is the heroine of Joseph W. Musgrave's "Sword of Gimshai" (1954), the last of four published stories about her exploits. Allan Quatermain, the hero of *King Solomon's Mines* and other stories by H. Rider Haggard, may not be as well known as these other iconic characters, but his adventures helped to popularize the Lost World genre, whose stories tell of fabled lands and forgotten civilizations lost to time and memory.

Adventure fiction flourished in the pulp fiction magazines that were ubiquitous at newsstands for the first half of the twentieth century. L. Patrick Greene's "Tools" (1921), featuring his gentleman diamond buyer "the Major," William Hope Hodgson's "The Albatross" (1911), and Lynn Montross's "A Gulp of Water" (1920) all come from the pages of *Adventure*. Elmer Brown Mason's "The Golden Anaconda" (1916), one of the best-known adventure stories to appear in *The Popular Magazine*, is proof that top-notch tales of adventure were surfacing in other publications of the day.

The world is a much smaller place today than it was when the stories in this book were written. Globalization, war, travel, and the Internet's erosion of once-impenetrable boundaries have exposed most of its once-unknown territories and reduced the possibilities for thrill-packed exploits within them. Fortunately for readers, the stories in this book harken back to a time when the unexplored worlds of the not-too-distant past were more colorful and full of imaginative potential, and adventures could be found to wherever a writer's fancy led him.

IN THE SUN
AND DESERT

THE MAN WHO WOULD BE KING

Rudyard Kipling

Brother to a Prince and fellow to a beggar if he be found worthy.

THE LAW, AS QUOTED, LAYS DOWN A FAIR CONDUCT OF LIFE, AND ONE NOT easy to follow. I have been fellow to a beggar again and again under circumstances which prevented either of us finding out whether the other was worthy. I have still to be brother to a Prince, though I once came near to kinship with what might have been a veritable King and was promised the reversion of a Kingdom—army, law-courts, revenue and policy all complete. But, to-day, I greatly fear that my King is dead, and if I want a crown I must go hunt it for myself.

The beginning of everything was in a railway train upon the road to Mhow from Ajmir. There had been a Deficit in the Budget, which necessitated travelling, not Second-class, which is only half as dear as First-class, but by Intermediate, which is very awful indeed. There are no cushions in the Intermediate class, and the population are either Intermediate, which is Eurasian, or native, which for a long night journey is nasty, or Loafer, which is amusing though intoxicated. Intermediates do not buy from refreshment-rooms. They carry their food in bundles and pots, and buy sweets from the native sweetmeat-sellers, and drink the roadside water. That is why in hot weather Intermediates are taken out of the carriages dead, and in all weathers are most properly looked down upon.

My particular Intermediate happened to be empty till I reached Nasirabad, when a big black-browed gentleman in shirtsleeves entered, and, following the custom of Intermediates, passed the time of day. He was a wanderer and a vagabond like myself, but with an educated taste for whiskey. He told tales of things he had seen and done, of out-of-the-way corners of the Empire into which he had penetrated, and of adventures in which he risked his life for a few days' food.

"If India was filled with men like you and me, not knowing more than the crows where they'd get their next day's rations, it isn't seventy millions of revenue the land would be paying—its seven hundred millions," said he; and as I looked at his mouth and chin I was disposed to agree with him.

We talked politics—the politics of Loaferdom that sees things from the underside where the lath and plaster is not smoothed off—and we talked postal arrangements because my friend wanted to send a telegram back from the next station to Ajmir, the turning-off place from the Bombay to the Mhow line as you travel westward. My friend had no money beyond eight annas which he wanted for dinner, and I had no money at all, owing to the hitch in the Budget before mentioned. Further, I was going into a wilderness where, though I should resume touch with the Treasury, there were no telegraph offices. I was, therefore, unable to help him in any way.

"We might threaten a Stationmaster, and make him send a wire on tick," said my friend, "but that'd mean enquiries for you and for me, and I've got my hands full these days. Did you say you were travelling back along this line within any days?"

"Within ten," I said.

"Can't you make it eight?" said he. "Mine is rather urgent business."

"I can send your telegram within ten days if that will serve you," I said.

I couldn't trust the wire to fetch him now I think of it. It's this way. He leaves Delhi on the 23rd for Bombay. That means he'll be running through Ajmir about the night of the 23rd."

"But I'm going into the Indian Desert," I explained.

"Well *and* good," said he. "You'll be changing at Marwar Junction to get into Jodhpore territory—you must do that—and he'll be coming through Marwar Junction in the early morning of the 24th by the Bombay Mail. Can you be at Marwar Junction on that time? 'T won't be inconveniencing you because I know that there's precious few pickings to be got out of these Central India States—even though you pretend to be correspondent of the *Backwoodsman*."

"Have you ever tried that trick?" I asked.

"Again and again, but the Residents find you out, and then you get escorted to the Border before you've time to get your knife into them. But about my friend here. I *must* give him a word o' mouth to tell him what's come to me or else he won't know where to go. I would take it more than kind of you if you was to come out of Central India in time to catch him at Marwar Junction, and say to him: 'He has gone South for the week.' He'll know what that means. He's a big man with a red beard, and a great swell he is. You'll find him sleeping like a gentleman with all his luggage round him in a Second-class apartment. But don't you be afraid. Slip down the window and say: 'He has gone South for the week,' and he'll tumble. It's only cutting your time of stay in those parts by two days. I ask you as a stranger—going to the West," he said with emphasis.

"Where have *you* come from?"

"From the East," said he, "and I am hoping that you will give him the message on the Square—for the sake of my Mother as well as your own."

Englishmen are not usually softened by appeals to the memory of their mothers; but for certain reasons, which will be fully apparent, I saw fit to agree.

"It's more than a little matter," said he, "and that's why I asked you to do it—and now I know that I can depend on you doing it. A Second-class carriage at Marwar Junction, and a red-haired man asleep in it. You'll be sure to remember. I get out at the next station, and I must hold on there till he comes or sends me what I want."

"I'll give the message if I catch him," I said, "and for the sake of your Mother as well as mine I'll give you a word of advice. Don't try to run the Central India States just now as the correspondent of the *Backwoodsman*. There's a real one knocking about here, and it might lead to trouble."

"Thank you," said he simply, "and when will the swine be gone? I can't starve because he's ruining my work. I wanted to get hold of the Degumber Rajah down here about his father's widow, and give him a jump."

"What did he do to his father's widow, then?"

"Filled her up with red pepper and slippered her to death as she hung from a beam. I found that out myself and I'm the only man that would dare going into the State to get hush-money for it. They'll try to poison me, same as they did in Chortumna when I went on the loot there. But you'll give the man at Marwar Junction my message?"

He got out at a little roadside station, and I reflected. I had heard, more than once, of men personating correspondents of newspapers and bleeding small Native States with threats of exposure, but I had never met any of the caste before. They lead a hard life, and generally die with great suddenness. The Native States have a wholesome horror of English newspapers, which may throw light on their peculiar methods of government, and do their best to choke correspondents with champagne, or drive them out of their mind with four-inhand barouches. They do not understand that nobody cares a straw for the internal administration of Native States so long as oppression and crime are kept within decent limits, and the ruler is not drugged, drunk, or diseased from one end of the year to the other. They are the dark places of the earth, full of unimaginable cruelty, touching the Railway and the Telegraph on one side, and, on the other, the days of Harun-al-Raschid. When I left the train I did business with divers Kings, and in eight days passed through many changes of life. Sometimes I wore dress-clothes and consorted with Princes and Politicals, drinking from crystal and eating from silver. Sometimes I lay out upon the ground and devoured what I could get, from a plate made of leaves, and drank the running water, and slept under the same rug as my servant. It was all in the day's work.

Then I headed for the Great Indian Desert upon the proper date, as I had promised, and the night Mail set me down at Marwar Junction, where a funny little, happy-go-lucky, native-managed railway runs to Jodhpore. The Bombay Mail from Delhi makes a short halt at Marwar. She arrived as I got in, and I had just time to hurry to her platform and go down the carriages. There was only one Second-class on the train. I slipped the window and looked down upon a flaming red beard, half covered by a railway rug. That was my man, fast asleep, and I dug him gently in the ribs. He woke with a grunt, and I saw his face in the light of the lamps. It was a great and shining face.

"Tickets again?" said he.

"No," said I. "I am to tell you that he is gone South for the week. He has gone South for the week!"

The train had begun to move out. The red man rubbed his eyes. "He has gone South for the week," he repeated. "Now that's just like his impidence. Did he say that I was to give you anything? 'Cause I won't."

"He didn't," I said and dropped away, and watched the red lights die out in the dark. It was horribly cold because the wind was blowing off the sands. I climbed into my own train—not an Intermediate carriage this time—and went to sleep.

If the man with the beard had given me a rupee I should have kept it as a memento of a rather curious affair. But the consciousness of having done my duty was my only reward.

Later on I reflected that two gentlemen like my friends could not do any good if they foregathered and personated correspondents of newspapers, and might, if they black-mailed one of the little rat-trap states of Central India or Southern Rajputana, get themselves into serious difficulties. I therefore took some trouble to describe them as accurately as I could remember to people who would be interested in deporting them: and succeeded, so I was later informed, in having them headed back from the Degumber borders.

Then I became respectable, and returned to an Office where there were no Kings and no incidents outside the daily manufacture of a newspaper. A newspaper office seems to attract every conceivable sort of person, to the prejudice of discipline. Zenana mission ladies arrive, and beg that the Editor will instantly abandon all his duties to describe a Christian prize-giving in a backslum of a perfectly inaccessible village; Colonels who have been overpassed for command sit down and sketch the outline of a series of ten, twelve, or twenty-four leading articles on Seniority *versus* Selection; missionaries wish to know why they have not been permitted to escape from their regular vehicles of abuse and swear at a brother-missionary under special patronage of the editorial We; stranded theatrical companies troop up to explain that they cannot pay for their advertisements, but on their return from New Zealand or Tahiti will do so with interest; inventors of patent punkah-pulling machines, carriage couplings and unbreakable swords and axletrees call with specifications in their pockets and hours at their disposal; tea-companies enter and elaborate their prospectuses with the office pens; secretaries of ball-committees clamour to have the glories of their last dance more fully described; strange ladies rustle in and say: "I want a hundred lady's cards printed at once, please," which is manifestly part of an Editor's duty; and every dissolute ruffian that ever tramped the Grand Trunk Road makes it his business to ask for employment as a proof-reader. And, all the time, the telephone-bell is ringing madly, and Kings are being killed on the Continent, and Empires are saying—"You're another," and Mister Gladstone is calling down brimstone upon the British Dominions, and the little black copy-boys are whining, "*kaa-pi chay-ha-yeh*" (copy wanted) like tired bees, and most of the paper is as black as Modred's shield.

But that is the amusing part of the year. There are six other months when none ever come to call, and the thermometer walks inch by inch up to the top of the glass, and the office is darkened just above reading-light, and the press machines are red-hot of touch, and nobody writes anything but accounts of amusements in the Hill-stations or obituary notices. Then the telephone becomes a tinkling terror, because it tells you of the sudden deaths of men and women that you knew intimately, and the prickly-heat covers you with a garment, and you sit down and write: "A slight increase of sickness is reported from the Khuda Janta Khan District. The outbreak is purely sporadic in its nature, and, thanks to the energetic efforts of the District authorities, is now almost at an end. It is, however, with deep regret we record the death," etc.

Then the sickness really breaks out, and the less recording and reporting the better for the peace of the subscribers. But the Empires and the Kings continue to divert themselves as selfishly as before, and the Foreman thinks that a daily paper really ought to come out once in twenty-four hours, and all the people at the Hill-stations in the middle of their amusements say: "Good gracious! Why can't the paper be sparkling? I'm sure there's plenty going on up here."

That is the dark half of the moon, and, as the advertisements say, "must be experienced to be appreciated."

It was in that season, and a remarkably evil season, that the paper began running the last issue of the week on Saturday night, which is to say Sunday morning, after the custom of a London paper. This was a great convenience, for immediately after the paper was put to bed, the dawn would lower the thermometer from 96° to almost 84° for half an hour, and in that chill—you have no idea how cold is 84° on the grass until you begin to pray for it—a very tired man could get off to sleep ere the heat roused him.

One Saturday night it was my pleasant duty to put the paper to bed alone. A King or courtier or a courtesan or a Community was going to die or get a new Constitution, or do something that was important on the other side of the world, and the paper was to be held open till the latest possible minute in order to catch the telegram.

It was a pitchy black night, as stifling as a June night can be, and the *loo*, the red-hot wind from the westward, was booming among the tinder-dry trees and pretending that the rain was on its heels. Now and again a spot of almost boiling water would fall on the dust with the flop of a frog, but all our weary world knew that was only pretence. It was a shade cooler in the pressroom than the office, so I sat there, while the type ticked and clicked, and the night-jars hooted at the windows, and the all but naked compositors wiped the sweat from their foreheads, and called for water. The thing that was keeping us back, whatever it was, would not come off, though the *loo* dropped and the last type was set, and the whole round earth stood still in the choking heat, with its finger on its lip, to wait the event. I drowsed, and wondered whether the telegraph was a blessing, and whether this dying man, or struggling people, might be aware of the inconvenience the delay was causing. There was no special reason beyond the heat and worry to make tension, but, as the clock-hands crept up to three o'clock and the machines spun their fly-wheels two and three times to see that all was in order, before I said the word that would set them off, I could have shrieked aloud.

Then the roar and rattle of the wheels shivered the quiet into little bits. I rose to go away, but two men in white clothes stood in front of me. The first one said: "It's him!" The second said: "So it is!" And they both laughed almost as loudly as the machinery roared, and mopped their foreheads. "We seed there was a light burning across the road and we were sleeping in that ditch there for coolness, and I said to my friend here, The office is open. Let's come along and speak to him as turned us back from the Degumber State," said the smaller of the two. He was the man I had met in the Mhow train, and his fellow was the red-bearded man of Marwar Junction. There was no mistaking the eyebrows of the one or the beard of the other.

I was not pleased, because I wished to go to sleep, not to squabble with loafers. "What do you want?" I asked.

"Half an hour's talk with you, cool and comfortable, in the office," said the red-bearded man. "We'd *like* some drink—the Contrack doesn't begin yet, Peachey, so you needn't look—but what we really want is advice. We don't want money. We ask you as a favour, because we found out you did us a bad turn about Degumber State."

I led from the press-room to the stifling office with the maps on the walls, and the red-haired man rubbed his hands. "That's something like," said he. "This was the proper shop to come to. Now, Sir, let me introduce to you Brother Peachey Carnehan, that's him, and Brother Daniel Dravot, that is *me*, and the less said about our professions the better, for we have been most things in our time. Soldier, sailor, compositor, photographer, proof-reader, street-preacher, and correspondents of the *Backwoodsman* when we thought the paper wanted one. Carnehan is sober, and so am I. Look at us first, and see that's sure. It will save you cutting into my talk. We'll take one of your cigars apiece, and you shall see us light up."

I watched the test. The men were absolutely sober, so I gave them each a tepid whiskey and soda.

"Well *and* good," said Carnehan of the eyebrows, wiping the froth from his moustache. "Let me talk now, Dan. We have been all over India, mostly on foot. We have been boiler-fitters, engine-drivers, petty contractors, and all that, and we have decided that India isn't big enough for such as us."

They certainly were too big for the office. Dravot's beard seemed to fill half the room and Carnehan's shoulders the other half, as they sat on the big table. Carnehan continued: "The country isn't half worked out because they that governs it won't let you touch it. They spend all their blessed time in governing it, and you can't lift a spade, nor chip a rock, nor look for oil, nor anything like that without all the Government saying: 'Leave it alone, and let us govern.' Therefore, such *as* it is, we will let it alone, and go away to some other place where a man isn't crowded, and can come to his own. We are not little men, and there is nothing that we are afraid of except drink, and we have signed a Contrack on that. *Therefore*, we are going away to be Kings."

"Kings in our own right," muttered Dravot.

"Yes, of course," I said. "You've been tramping in the sun, and it's a very warm night, and hadn't you better sleep over the notion? Come tomorrow."

"Neither drunk nor sunstruck," said Dravot. "We have slept over the notion half a year, and require to see Books and Atlases, and we have decided that there is only one place now in the world that two strong men can Sar-a-*whack*. They call it Kafiristan. By my reckoning it's the top right-hand corner of Afghanistan, not more than three hundred miles from Peshawar. They have two-and-thirty heathen idols there, and we'll be the thirty-third and fourth. It's a mountainous country, and the women of those parts are very beautiful."

"But that is provided against in the Contrack," said Carnehan. "Neither women nor Liqu-or, Daniel."

"And that's all we know, except that no one has gone there, and they fight, and in any place where they fight a man who knows how to drill men can always be a King. We shall go to those parts and say to any King we find—'D'you want to vanquish your foes?' and we will show him how to drill men; for that we know better than anything else. Then we will subvert that King and seize his Throne and establish a Dynasty."

"You'll be cut to pieces before you're fifty miles across the Border," I said. "You have to travel through Afghanistan to get to that country. It's one mass of mountains and peaks and glaciers, and no Englishman has been through it. The people are utter brutes, and even if you reached them you couldn't do anything."

"That's more like," said Carnehan. "If you could think us a little more mad we would be more pleased. We have come to you to know about this country, to read a book about it, and be shown maps. We want you to tell us that we are fools and to show us your books." He turned to the bookcases.

"Are you at all in earnest?" I said.

"A little," said Dravot sweetly. "As big a map as you have got, even if it's all blank where Kafiristan is, and any books you've got. We can read, though we aren't very educated."

I uncased the big thirty-two miles-to-the-inch map of India, and two smaller Frontier maps, hauled down volume INF-KAN of the *Encyclopædia Britannica*, and the men consulted them.

"See here!" said Dravot, his thumb on the map. "Up to Jagdallak, Peachey and me know the road. We was there with Roberts' Army. We'll have to turn off to the right at Jagdallak through Laghmann territory. Then we get among the hills—fourteen thousand feet—fifteen thousand—it will be cold work there, but it don't look very far on the map."

I handed him Wood on the *Sources of the Oxus*. Carnehan was deep in the *Encyclopædia*.

"They're a mixed lot," said Dravot reflectively; "and it won't help us to know the names of their tribes. The more tribes the more they'll fight, and the better for us. From Jagdallak to Ashang. H'mm!"

"But all the information about the country is as sketchy and inaccurate as can be," I protested. "No one knows anything about it really. Here's the file of the *United Services' Institute*. Read what Bellew says."

"Blow Bellew!" said Carnehan. "Dan, they're a stinkin' lot of heathens, but this book here says they think they're related to us English."

I smoked while the men pored over *Raverty*, *Wood*, the maps, and the *Encyclopædia*.

"There is no use your waiting," said Dravot politely. "It's about four o'clock now. We'll go before six o'clock if you want to sleep, and we won't steal any of the papers. Don't you sit up. We're two harmless lunatics, and if you come to-morrow evening down to the Serai we'll say goodbye to you."

"You *are* two fools," I answered. "You'll be turned back at the Frontier or cut up the minute you set foot in Afghanistan. Do you want any money or a recommendation down-country? I can help you to the chance of work next week."

"Next week we shall be hard at work ourselves, thank you," said Dravot. "It isn't so easy being a King as it looks. When we've got our Kingdom in going order we'll let you know, and you can come up and help us to govern it."

"Would two lunatics make a Contrack like that?" said Carnehan, with subdued pride, showing me a greasy half-sheet of notepaper on which was written the following. I copied it, then and there, as a curiosity—

This Contract between me and you pursuing witnesseth in the name of God —Amen and so forth.

(One) That me and you will settle this matter together; i.e., to be Kings of Kafiristan.

(Two) That you and me will not, while this matter is being settled, look at any Liquor, nor any Woman black, white, or brown, so as to get mixed up with one or the other harmful.

(Three) That we conduct ourselves with Dignity and Discretion, and if one of, us gets into trouble the other will stay by him.

Signed by you and me this day.
          Peachey Taliaferro Carnehan.
          Daniel Dravot.
          Both Gentlemen at Large

"There was no need for the last article," said Carnehan, blushing modestly; "but it looks regular. Now you know the sort of men that loafers are—we *are* loafers, Dan, until we get out of India—and *do* you think that we would sign a Contrack like that unless we was in earnest? We have kept away from the two things that make life worth having."

"You won't enjoy your lives much longer if you are going to try this idiotic adventure. Don't set the office on fire," I said, "and go away before nine o'clock."

I left them still poring over the maps and making notes on the back of the "Contrack." "Be sure to come down to the Serai to-morrow," were their parting words.

The Kumharsen Serai is the great four-square sink of humanity where the strings of camels and horses from the North load and unload. All the nationalities of Central Asia may be found there, and most of the folk of India proper. Balkh and Bokhara there meet Bengal and Bombay, and try to draw eyeteeth. You can buy ponies, turquoises, Persian pussy-cats, saddle-bags, fat-tailed sheep, and musk in the Kumharsen Serai, and get many strange things for nothing. In the afternoon I went down to see whether my friends intended to keep their word or were lying there drunk.

A priest attired in fragments of ribbons and rags stalked up to me, gravely twisting a child's paper whirligig. Behind him was his servant bending under the load of a crate of mud toys. The two were loading up two camels, and the inhabitants of the Serai watched them with shrieks of laughter.

"The priest is mad," said a horse-dealer to me. "He is going up to Kabul to sell toys to the Amir. He will either be raised to honour or have his head cut off. He came in here this morning and has been behaving madly ever since."

"The witless are under the protection of God," stammered a flat-cheeked Usbeg in broken Hindi. "They foretell future events."

"Would they could have foretold that my caravan would have been cut up by the Shinwaris almost within shadow of the Pass!" grunted the Eusufzai agent of a Raj putana trading-house whose goods had been diverted into the hands of other robbers just across the Border, and whose misfortunes were the laughingstock of the bazar. "Ohé, priest, whence come you, and whither do you go?"

"From Roum have I come," shouted the priest, waving his whirligig; "from Roum, blown by the breath of a hundred devils across the sea! O thieves, robbers, liars, the blessing of Pir Khan on pigs, dogs, and perjurers! Who will take the Protected of God to the North to sell charms that are never still to the Amir? The camels shall not gall, the sons shall not fall sick, and the wives shall remain faithful while they are away, of the men who give me place in their caravan. Who will assist me to slipper the King of the Roos with a golden slipper with a silver heel? The protection of Pir Khan be upon his labours!" He spread out the skirts of his gaberdine and pirouetted between the lines of tethered horses.

"There starts a caravan from Peshawar to Kabul in twenty days, *Huzrut,*" said the Eusufzai trader. "My camels go therewith. Do thou also go and bring us good-luck."

"I will go even now!" shouted the priest. "I will depart upon my winged camels, and be at Peshawar in a day! Ho! Hazar Mir Khan," he yelled to his servant, "drive out the camels, but let me first mount my own."

He leaped on the back of his beast as it knelt, and, turning round to me, cried: "Come thou also, Sahib, a little along the road, and I will sell thee a charm—an amulet that shall make thee King of Kafiristan."

Then the light broke upon me, and I followed the two camels out of the Serai till we reached open road and the priest halted.

"What d'you think o' that?" said he in English. "Carnehan can't talk their patter, so I've made him my servant. He makes a handsome servant. 'Tisn't for nothing that I've been knocking about the country for fourteen years. Didn't I do that talk neat? We'll hitch on to a caravan at Peshawar till we get to Jagdallak, and then we'll see if we can get donkeys for our camels, and strike into Kafiristan. Whirligigs for the Amir, O Lor! Put your hand under the camelbags and tell me what you feel."

I felt the butt of a Martini, and another and another.

"Twenty of 'em," said Dravot placidly. "Twenty of 'em and ammunition to correspond, under the whirligigs and the mud dolls."

"Heaven help you if you are caught with those things!" I said. "A Martini is worth her weight in silver among the Pathans."

"Fifteen hundred rupees of capital—every rupee we could beg, borrow, or steal—are invested on these two camels," said Dravot. "We won't get caught. We're going through the Khaiber with a regular caravan. Who'd touch a poor mad priest?"

"Have you got everything you want?" I asked, overcome with astonishment.

"Not yet, but we shall soon. Give us a memento of your kindness, *Brother*. You did me a service, yesterday, and that time in Marwar. Half my kingdom shall you have, as the saying is." I slipped a small charm compass from my watch chain and handed it up to the priest.

"Good-bye," said Dravot, giving me hand cautiously. "It's the last time we'll shake hands with an Englishman these many days. Shake hands with him, Carnehan," he cried, as the second camel passed me.

Carnehan leaned down and shook hands. Then the camels passed away along the dusty road, and I was left alone to wonder. My eye could detect no failure in the disguises. The scene in the Serai proved that they were complete to the native mind. There was just the chance, therefore, that Carnehan and Dravot would be able to wander through Afghanistan without detection. But, beyond, they would find death—certain and awful death.

Ten days later a native correspondent, giving me the news of the day from Peshawar, wound up his letter with: "There has been much laughter here on account of a certain mad priest who is going in his estimation to sell petty gauds and insignificant trinkets which he ascribes as great charms to H. H. the Amir of Bokhara. He passed through Peshawar and associated himself to the Second Summer caravan that goes to Kabul. The merchants are pleased because through superstition they imagine that such mad fellows bring good-fortune."

The two, then, were beyond the Border. I would have prayed for them, but, that night, a real King died in Europe, and demanded an obituary notice.

The wheel of the world swings through the same phases again and again. Summer passed and winter thereafter, and came and passed again. The daily paper continued and I with it, and upon the third summer there fell a hot night, a night-issue, and a strained waiting for something to be telegraphed from the other side of the world, exactly as had happened before. A few great men had died in the past two years, the machines worked with more clatter, and some of the trees in the Office garden were a few feet taller. But that was all the difference.

I passed over to the press-room, and went through just such a scene as I have already described. The nervous tension was stronger than it had been two years before, and I felt the heat more acutely. At three o'clock I cried, "Print off" and turned to go, when there crept to my chair what was left of a man. He was bent into a circle, his head was sunk between his shoulders, and he moved his feet one over the other like a bear. I could hardly see whether he walked or crawled— this rag-wrapped, whining cripple who addressed me by name, crying that he was come back. "Can you give me a drink?" he whimpered. "For the Lord's sake give me a drink!"

I went back to the office, the man following with groans of pain, and I turned up the lamp.

"Don't you know me?" he gasped, dropping into a chair, and he turned his drawn face, surmounted by a shock of gray hair, to the light.

I looked at him intently. Once before had I seen eyebrows that met over the nose in an inch-broad black band, but for the life of me I could not tell where.

"I don't know you," I said, handing him the whiskey. "What can I do for you?"

He took a gulp of the spirit raw, and shivered in spite of the suffocating heat.

"I've come back," he repeated; "and I was the King of Kafiristan—me and Dravot—crowned Kings we was! In this office we settled it—you setting there and giving us the books; I am Peachey—Peachey Taliaferro Carnehan, and you've been setting here ever since—O Lord!"

I was more than a little astonished, and expressed my feelings accordingly.

"It's true," said Carnehan, with a dry cackle, nursing his feet, which were wrapped in rags. "True as gospel. Kings we were, with crowns upon our heads—me and Dravot—poor Dan oh, poor, poor Dan, that would never take advice, not though I begged of him!"

"Take the whiskey," I said, "and take your own time. Tell me all you can recollect of everything from beginning to end. You got across the border on your camels, Dravot dressed as a mad priest and you his servant. Do you remember that?"

"I ain't mad—yet, but I shall be that way soon. Of course I remember. Keep looking at me, or maybe my words will all go to pieces. Keep looking at me in my eyes and don't say anything."

I leaned forward and looked into his face as steadily as I could. He dropped one hand upon the table and I grasped it by the wrist. It was twisted like a bird's claw, and upon the back was a ragged, red, diamond-shaped scar.

"No, don't look there. Look at *me*," said Carnehan. "That comes afterwards, but for the Lord's sake don't distrack me. We left with that caravan, me and Dravot playing all sorts of antics to amuse the people we were with. Dravot used to make us laugh in the evenings when all the people was cooking their dinners—cooking their dinners, and . . . what did they do then? They lit little fires with sparks that went into Dravot's beard, and we all laughed—fit to die. Little red fires they was, going into Dravot's big red beard—so funny." His eyes left mine and he smiled foolishly.

"You went as far as Jagdallak with that caravan," I said at a venture, "after you had lit those fires. To Jagdallak, where you turned off to try to get into Kafiristan."

"No, we didn't neither. What are you talking about? We turned off before Jagdallak, because we heard the roads was good. But they wasn't good enough for our two camels—mine and Dravot's. When we left the caravan, Dravot took off all his clothes and mine too, and said we would be heathen, because the Kafirs didn't allow Mohammedans to talk to them. So we dressed betwixt and between, and such a sight as Daniel Dravot I never saw yet nor expect to see again. He burned half his beard, and slung a sheepskin over his shoulder, and shaved his head into patterns. He shaved mine, too, and made me wear outrageous things to look like a heathen. That was in a most mountaineous country, and our camels couldn't go along any more because of the mountains. They were tall and black, and coming home I saw them fight like wild goats—there are lots of goats in Kafiristan. And these mountains, they never keep still, no more than the goats. Always fighting they are, and don't let you sleep at night."

"Take some more whiskey," I said very slowly. "What did you and Daniel Dravot do when the camels could go no further because of the rough roads that led into Kafiristan?"

"What did which do? There was a party called Peachey Taliaferro Carnehan that was with Dravot. Shall I tell you about him? He died out there in the cold. Slap from the bridge fell old Peachey, turning and twisting in the air like a penny whirlgig that you can sell to the Amir.—No; they was two for three ha'pence, those whirligigs, or I am much mistaken and woeful sore. . . . And then these camels were no use, and Peachey said to Dravot—'For the Lord's sake let's get out of this before our heads are chopped off,' and with that they killed the camels all among the mountains, not having anything in particular to eat, but first they took off the boxes with the guns and the ammunition, till two men came along driving four mules. Dravot up and dances in front of them, singing—'Sell me four mules.' Says the first man—'If you are rich enough to buy you are rich enough to rob'; but before ever he could put his hand to his knife, Dravot breaks his neck over his knee, and the other party runs away. So Carnehan loaded the mules with the rifles that was taken off the camels, and together we starts forward into those bitter cold mountaineous parts, and never a road broader than the back of your hand."

He paused for a moment, while I asked him if he could remember the nature of the country through which he had journeyed.

"I am telling you as straight as I can, but my head isn't as good as it might be. They drove nails through it to make me hear better how Dravot died. The country was mountaineous and the mules were most contrary, and the inhabitants was dispersed and solitary. They went up and up, and down and down, and that other party, Carnehan, was imploring of Dravot not to sing and whistle so loud, for fear of bringing down the tremenjus avalanches. But Dravot says that if a King couldn't sing it wasn't worth being King, and whacked the mules over the rump, and never took no heed for ten cold days. We came to a big level valley all among the mountains, and the mules were near dead, so we killed them, not having anything in special for them or us to eat. We sat upon the boxes, and played odd and even with the cartridges that was jolted out.

"Then ten men with bows and arrows ran down that valley, chasing twenty men with bows and arrows, and the row was tremenjus. They was fair men—fairer than you or me—with yellow hair and remarkable well built. Says Dravot, unpacking the guns—'This is the beginning of the business. We'll fight for the ten men,' and with that he fires two rifles at the twenty men, and drops one of them at two hundred yards from the rock where he was sitting. The other men began to run, but Carnehan and Dravot sits on the boxes picking them off at all ranges, up and down the valley. Then we goes up to the ten men that had run across the snow too, and they fires a footy little arrow at us. Dravot he shoots above their heads and they all falls down flat. Then he walks over them and kicks them, and then he lifts them up and shakes hands all round to make them friendly like. He calls them and gives them the boxes to carry, and waves his hand for all the world as though he was King already. They takes the boxes and him across the valley and up the hill into a pine wood on the top, where there was half a dozen big stone idols. Dravot he goes to the biggest—a fellow they call Imbra—and lays a rifle and a cartridge at his feet, rubbing his nose respectful with his own nose, patting him on the head, and saluting in front of it. He turns round to the men and nods his head, and says 'That's all right. I'm in the know too, and all these old jim-jams are my friends.' Then he opens his mouth and points down it, and when the first man brings him food, he says—'No'; and when the second man brings him food he says—'No'; but when one of the old priests and the boss of the village brings him food, he says—'Yes'; very haughty and eats it slow. That was how we came to our first village, without any trouble, just as though we had tumbled from the skies. But we tumbled from one of those damned rope-bridges, you see, and—you couldn't expect a man to laugh much after that?"

"Take some more whiskey and go on," I said. "That was the first village you came into. How did you get to be King?"

"I wasn't King," said Carnehan. "Dravot he was the King, and a handsome man he looked with the gold crown on his head and all. Him and the other party stayed in that village, and every morning Dravot sat by the side of old Imbra, and the people came and worshipped. That was Dravot's order. Then a lot of men came into the valley, and Carnehan Dravot picks them off with the rifles before they knew where they was, and runs down into the valley and up again the other side and finds another village, same as the first one, and the people all falls down flat on their faces, and Dravot says—'Now what is the trouble between you two villages?' and the people points to a woman, as fair as you or me, that was carried off, and Dravot takes her back to the first village and counts up the dead—eight there was. For each dead man Dravot pours a little milk on the ground and waves his arms like a whirligig and 'That's all right,' says he. Then he and Carnehan takes the big boss of each village by the arm and walks them down into the valley, and shows them how to scratch a line with a spear right down the valley, and gives each a sod of turf from both sides of the line. Then all the people comes down and shouts like the devil and all, and Dravot says—'Go and dig the land, and be fruitful and multiply,' which they did, though they didn't understand. Then we asks the names of things in their lingo—bread and water and fire and idols and such—and Dravot leads the priest of each village up to the idol, and says he must sit there and judge the people, and if anything goes wrong he is to be shot.

"Next week they was all turning up the land in the valley as quiet as bees and much prettier, and the priests heard all the complaints and told Dravot in dumb show what it was about. 'That's just the beginning,' says Dravot. 'They think we're Gods.' He and Carnehan picks out twenty good men and shows them how to click off a rifle, and form fours, and advance in line, and they was very pleased to do so, and clever to see the hang of it. Then he takes out his pipe and his baccy-pouch and leaves one at one village, and one at the other, and off we two goes to see what was to be done in the next valley. That was all rock, and there was a little village there, and Carnehan says—'Send 'em to the old valley to plant,' and takes 'em there and gives 'em some land that wasn't took before. They were a poor lot, and we blooded 'em with a kid before letting 'em into the new Kingdom. That was to impress the people, and then they settled down quiet, and Carnehan went back to Dravot, who had got into another valley, all snow and ice and most mountaineous. There was no people there and the Army got afraid, so Dravot shoots one of them, and goes on till he finds some people in a village, and the Army explains that unless the people wants to be killed they had better not shoot their little matchlocks; for they had matchlocks. We makes friends with the priest and I stays there alone with two of the Army, teaching the men how to drill, and a thundering big Chief comes across the snow with kettle-drums and horns twanging, because he heard there was a new God kicking about. Carnehan sights for the brown of the men half a mile across the snow and wings one of them. Then he sends a message to the Chief that, unless he wished to be killed, he must come and shake hands with me and leave his arms behind. The Chief comes alone first, and Carnehan shakes hands with him and whirls his arms about, same as Dravot used, and very much surprised that Chief was, and strokes my eyebrows. Then Carnehan goes alone to the Chief, and asks him in dumb show if he had an enemy he hated. 'I have,' says the Chief. So Carnehan weeds out the pick of his men, and sets the two of the Army to show them drill and at the end of two weeks the men can manœuvre about as well as Volunteers. So he marches with the Chief to a great big plain on the top of a mountain, and the Chief's men rushes into a village and takes it; we three Martinis firing into the brown of the enemy. So we took that village too, and I gives the Chief a rag from my coat and says, 'Occupy till I come'; which was scriptural. By way of a reminder, when me and the Army was eighteen hundred yards away, I drops a bullet near him standing on the snow, and all the people falls flat on their faces. Then I sends a letter to Dravot wherever he be by land or by sea."

At the risk of throwing the creature out of train I interrupted—"How could you write a letter up yonder?"

"The letter?—Oh!—The letter! Keep looking at me between the eyes, please. It was a string-talk letter, that we'd learned the way of it from a blind beggar in the Punjab."

I remember that there had once come to the office a blind man with a knotted twig and a piece of string which he wound round the twig according to some cipher of his own. He could, after the lapse of days or hours, repeat the sentence which he had reeled up. He had reduced the alphabet to eleven primitive sounds; and tried to teach me his method, but I could not understand.

"I sent that letter to Dravot," said Carnehan; "and told him to come back because this Kingdom was growing too big for me to handle, and then I struck for the first valley, to see how the priests were working. They called the village we took along with the Chief, Bashkai, and the first village we took, Er-Heb. The priests at Er-Heb was doing all right, but they had a lot of pending cases about land to show me, and some men from another village had been firing arrows at night. I went out and looked for that village, and fired four rounds at it from a thousand yards. That used all the cartridges I cared to spend, and I waited for Dravot, who had been away two or three months, and I kept my people quiet.

"One morning I heard the devil's own noise of drums and horns, and Dan Dravot marches down the hill with his Army and a tail of hundreds of men, and, which was the most amazing, a great gold crown on his head. 'My Gord, Carnehan,' says Daniel, 'this is a tremenjus business, and we've got the whole country as far as it's worth having. I am the son of Alexander by Queen Semiramis, and you're my younger brother and a God too! It's the biggest thing we've ever seen. I've been marching and fighting for six weeks with the Army, and every footy little village for fifty miles has come in rejoiceful; and more than that, I've got the key of the whole show, as you'll see, and I've got a crown for you! I told 'em to make two of 'em at a place called Shu, where the gold lies in the rock like suet in mutton. Gold I've seen, and turquoise I've kicked out of the cliffs, and there's garnets in the sands of the river, and here's a chunk of amber that a man brought me. Call up all the priests and, here, take your crown.'

"One of the men opens a black hair bag, and I slips the crown on. It was too small and too heavy, but I wore it for the glory. Hammered gold it was—five pound weight, like a hoop of a barrel.

"'Peachey,' says Dravot, 'we don't want to fight no more. The Craft's the trick, so help me!' and he brings forward that same Chief that I left at Bashkai—Billy Fish we called him afterwards, because he was so like Billy Fish that drove the big tank-engine at Mach on the Bolan in the old days. 'Shake hands with him,' says Dravot, and I shook hands and nearly dropped, for Billy Fish gave me the Grip. I said nothing, but tried him with the Fellow Craft Grip. He answers, all right, and I tried the Master's Grip, but that was a slip. 'A Fellow Craft he is!' I says to Dan. 'Does he know the word?'—'He does,' says Dan, 'and all the priests know. It's a miracle! The Chiefs and the priests can work a Fellow Craft Lodge in a way that's very like ours, and they've cut the marks on the rocks, but they don't know the Third Degree, and they've come to find out. It's

Gord's Truth. I've known these long years that the Afghans knew up to the Fellow Craft Degree, but this is a miracle. A God and a Grand-Master of the Craft am I, and a Lodge in the Third Degree I will open, and we'll raise the head priests and the Chiefs of the villages.'

" 'It's against all the law,' I says, 'holding a Lodge without warrant from any one; and you know we never held office in any Lodge.' "

" 'It's a master-stroke o' policy,' says Dravot. 'It means running the country as easy as a four-wheeled bogie on a down grade. We can't stop to enquire now, or they'll turn against us. I've forty Chiefs at my heel, and passed and raised according to their merit they shall be. Billet these men on the villages, and see that we run up a Lodge of some kind. The temple of Imbra will do for the Lodge-room. The women must make aprons as you show them. I'll hold a levee of Chiefs to-night and Lodge to-morrow.'

"I was fair run off my legs, but I wasn't such a fool as not to see what a pull this Craft business gave us. I showed the priests' families how to make aprons of the degrees, but for Dravot's apron the blue border and marks was made of turquoise lumps on white hide, not cloth. We took a great square stone in the temple for the Master's chair, and little stones for the officers' chairs, and painted the black pavement with white squares, and did what we could to make things regular.

"At the levee which was held that night on the hill-side with big bonfires, Dravot gives out that him and me were Gods and sons of Alexander, and Past Grand-Masters in the Craft, and was come to make Kafiristan a country where every man should eat in peace and drink in quiet, and specially obey us. Then the Chiefs come round to shake hands, and they were so hairy and white and fair it was just shaking hands with old friends. We gave them names according as they was like men we had known in India—Billy Fish, Holly Dilworth, Pikky Kergan, that was Bazar-master when I was at Mhow, and so on, and so on.

"*The* most amazing miracles was at Lodge next night. One of the old priests was watching us continuous, and I felt uneasy, for I knew we'd have to fudge the Ritual, and I didn't know what the men knew. The old priest was a stranger come in from beyond the village of Bashkai. The minute Dravot puts on the Master's apron that the girls had made for him, the priest fetches a whoop and a howl, and tries to overturn the stone that Dravot was sitting on. 'It's all up now,' I says. 'That comes of meddling with the Craft without warrant!' Dravot never winked an eye, not when ten priests took and tilted over the Grand-Master's chair—which was to say the stone of, Imbra. The priest begins rubbing the bottom end of it to clear the black dirt, and presently he shows all the other priests the Master's Mark, same as was on Dravot's apron, cut into the stone. Not even the priests of the temple of Imbra knew it was there. The old chap falls flat on his face at Dravot's feet and kisses 'em. 'Luck again,' says Dravot, across the Lodge to me, 'they say it's the missing Mark that no one could understand the why of. We're more than safe now.' Then he bangs the butt of his gun for a gavel and says: 'By virtue of the authority vested in me by my own right hand and the help of Peachey, I declare myself Grand-Master of all Freemasonry in Kafiristan in this the Mother Lodge o' the country, and King of Kafiristan equally with Peachey!' At that he puts on his crown and I puts on mine—I was doing Senior Warden—and we opens the Lodge in most ample form. It was a amazing miracle! The priests moved in Lodge through the first two degrees almost without telling, as if the memory was coming back to them. After that, Peachey and Dravot raised such as was worthy—high priests and Chiefs of far-off villages. Billy Fish was the first, and I can tell you we scared the soul out of him. It was not in any way according to Ritual, but it served our turn. We didn't raise more than ten of the biggest men, because we didn't want to make the Degree common. And they was clamouring to be raised.

"'In another six months,' says Dravot, 'we'll hold another Communication, and see how you are working.' Then he asks them about their villages, and learns that they was fighting one against the other, and were sick and tired of it. And when they wasn't doing that they was fighting with the Mohammedans. 'You can fight those when they come into our country,' says Dravot. 'Tell off every tenth man of your tribes for a Frontier guard, and send two hundred at a time to this valley to be drilled. Nobody is going to be shot or speared any more so long as he does well, and I know that you won't cheat me, because you're white people—sons of Alexander—and not like common black Mohammedans. You are *my* people, and by God,' says he, running off into English at the end—'I'll make a damned fine Nation of you, or I'll die in the making!'

"I can't tell all we did for the next six months, because Dravot did a lot I couldn't see the hang of, and he learned their lingo in a way I never could. My work was to help the people plough, and now and again go out with some of the Army and see what the other villages were doing, and make 'em throw rope-bridges across the ravines which cut up the country horrid. Dravot was very kind to me, but when he walked up and down in the pine wood pulling that bloody red beard of his with both fists I knew he was thinking plans I could not advise about, and I just waited for orders.

"But Dravot never showed me disrespect before the people. They were afraid of me and the Army, but they loved Dan. He was the best of friends with the priests and the Chiefs; but any one could come across the hills with a complaint and Dravot would hear him out fair, and call four priests together and say what was to be done. He used to call in Billy Fish from Bashkai, and Pikky Kergan from Shu, and an old Chief we called Kafuzelum—it was like enough to his real name—and hold councils with 'em when there was any fighting to be done in small villages. That was his Council of War, and the four priests of Bashkai, Shu, Khawak, and Madora was his Privy Council. Between the lot of 'em they sent me, with forty men and twenty rifles, and sixty men carrying turquoises, into the Ghorband country to buy those hand-made Martini rifles, that come out of the Amir's workshops at Kabul, from one of the Amir's Herati regiments that would have sold the very teeth out of their mouths for turquoises.

"I stayed in Ghorband a month, and gave the Governor there the pick of my baskets for hush-money, and bribed the Colonel of the regiment some more, and between the two and the tribespeople, we got more than a hundred hand-made Martinis, a hundred good Kohat Jezails that'll throw to six hundred yards, and forty man-loads of very bad ammunition for the rifles. I came back with what I had, and distributed 'em among the men that the Chiefs sent in to me to drill. Dravot was too busy to attend to those things, but the old Army that we first made helped me, and we turned out five hundred men that could drill, and two hundred that knew how to hold arms pretty straight. Even those cork-screwed handmade guns was a miracle to them. Dravot talked big about powder-shops and factories, walking up and down in the pine wood when the winter was coming on.

"'I won't make a Nation,' says he. 'I'll make an Empire! These men aren't niggers; they're English! Look at their eyes—look at their mouths. Look at the way they stand up. They sit on chairs in their own houses. They're the Lost Tribes, or something like it, and they've grown to be English. I'll take a census in the spring if the priests don't get frightened. There must be a fair two million of 'em in these hills. The villages are full o' little children. Two million people—two hundred and fifty thousand fighting men—and all English! They only want the rifles and a little drilling. Two hundred and fifty thousand men, ready to cut in on Russia's right flank when she tries for India! Peachey, man,' he says, chewing his beard in great hunks, 'we shall be Emperors—Emperors of the Earth! Rajah Brooke will be a suckling to us. I'll treat with the Viceroy on equal terms. I'll ask him to send me twelve picked English—twelve that I know of—to help us govern a bit. There's Mackray, Sergeantpensioner at Segowli—many's the good dinner he's given me, and his wife a pair of trousers. There's Donkin, the Warder of Tounghoo Jail; there's hundreds that I could lay my hand on if I was in India. The Viceroy shall do it for me, I'll send a man through in the spring for those men, and I'll write for a dispensation from the Grand Lodge for what I've done as Grand-Master. That—and all the Sniders that'll be thrown out when the native troops in India take up the Martini. They'll be worn smooth, but they'll do for fighting in these hills. Twelve English, a hundred thousand Sniders run through the Amir's country in driblets—I'd be content with twenty thousand in one year—and we'd be an Empire. When everything was shipshape, I'd hand over the crown—this crown I'm wearing now—to Queen Victoria on my knees, and she'd say: "Rise up, Sir Daniel Dravot." Oh, it's big! It's big, I tell you! But there's so much to be done in every place—Bashkai, Khawak, Shu, and everywhere else.'

" 'What is it?' I says. 'There are no more men coming in to be drilled this autumn. Look at those, fat, black clouds. They're bringing the snow.'

" 'It isn't that,' says Daniel, putting his hand very hard on my shoulder; 'and I don't wish to say anything that's against you, for no other living man would have followed me and made me what I am as you have done. You're a first-class Commander-in-Chief, and the people know you; but—it's a big country, and somehow you can't help me, Peachey, in the way I want to be helped.'

" 'Go to your blasted priests, then!' I said, and I was sorry when I made that remark, but it did hurt me sore to find Daniel talking so superior when I'd drilled all the men, and done all he told me.

" 'Don't let's quarrel, Peachey,' says Daniel without cursing. 'You're a King too, and the half of this Kingdom is yours; but can't you see, Peachey, we want cleverer men than us now—three or four of 'em, that we can scatter about for our Deputies. It's a hugeous great State, and I can't always tell the right thing to do, and I haven't time for all I want to do, and here's the winter coming on and all.' He put half his beard into his mouth, all red like the gold of his crown.

" 'I'm sorry, Daniel,' says I. 'I've done all I could. I've drilled the men and shown the people how to stack their oats better; and I've brought in those tinware rifles from Ghorand—but I know what you're driving at. I take it Kings always feel oppressed that way.'

" 'There's another thing too,' says Dravot, walking up and down. 'The winter's coming and these people won't be giving much trouble, and if they do we can't move about. I want a wife.'

" 'For Gord's sake leave the women alone!' I says. 'We've both got all the work we can, though I *am* a fool. Remember the Contrack, and keep clear o' women.'

" 'The Contrack only lasted till such time as we was Kings; and Kings we have been these months past,' says Dravot, weighing his crown in his hand. 'You go get a wife too, Peachey—a nice, strapping plump girl that'll keep you warm in the winter. They're prettier than English girls, and we can take the pick of 'em. Boil 'em once or twice in hot water, and they'll come out like chicken and ham.'

" 'Don't tempt me!' I says. 'I will not have any dealings with a woman, not till we are a dam' side more settled than we are now. I've been doing the work o' two men, and you've been doing the work o' three. Let's lie off a bit, and see if we can get some better tobacco from Afghan country and run in some good liquor; but no women.'

" 'Who's talking o' *women?*' says Dravot. 'I said *wife*—a Queen to breed a King's son for the King. A Queen out of the strongest tribe, that'll make them your blood-brothers, and that'll lie by your side and tell you all the people thinks about you and their own affairs. That's what I want.'

" 'Do you remember that Bengali woman I kept at Mogul Serai when I was a plate-layer?' says I. 'A fat lot o' good she was to me. She taught me the lingo and one or two other things; but what happened? She ran away with the Station Master's servant and half my month's pay. Then she turned up at Dadur Junction in tow of a half-caste, and had the impidence to say I was her husband—all among the drivers in the running-shed, too!'

" 'We've done with that,' says Dravot, 'these women are whiter than you or me, and a Queen I will have for the winter months.'

" 'For the last time o' asking, Dan, do *not*,' I says. 'It'll only bring us harm. The Bible says that Kings ain't to waste their strength on women, 'specially when they've got a new raw Kingdom to work over.'

" 'For the last time of answering, I will,' said Dravot, and he went away through the pine-trees looking like a big red devil, the sun being on his crown and beard and all.

"But getting a wife was not as easy as Dan thought. He put it before the Council, and there was no answer till Billy Fish said that he'd better ask the girls. Dravot damned them all round. 'What's wrong with me?' he shouts, standing by the idol Imbra. 'Am I a dog or am I not enough of a man for your wenches? Haven't I put the shadow of my hand over this country? Who stopped the last Afghan raid?' It was me really, but Dravot was too angry to remember. 'Who bought your guns? Who repaired the bridges? Who's the Grand-Master of the sign cut in the stone?' says he, and he thumped his hand on the block that he used to sit on in Lodge, and at Council, which opened like Lodge always. Billy Fish said nothing and no more did the others. 'Keep your hair on, Dan,' said I; 'and ask the girls. That's how it's done at Home, and these people are quite English.'

" 'The marriage of the King is a matter of State,' says Dan, in a white-hot rage, for he could feel, I hope, that he was going against his better mind. He walked out of the Council-room, and the others sat still, looking at the ground.

" 'Billy Fish,' says I to the Chief of Bashkai, 'what's the difficulty here? A straight answer to a true friend.'

" 'You know,' says Billy Fish. 'How should a man tell you who knows everything? How can daughters of men marry Gods or Devils? It's not proper.'

"I remembered something like that in the Bible; but if, after seeing us as long as they had, they still believed we were Gods, it wasn't for me to undeceive them.

"'A God can do anything,' says I. 'If the King is fond of a girl he'll not let her die.'—'She'll have to,' said Billy Fish. 'There are all sorts of Gods and Devils in these mountains, and now and again a girl marries one of them and isn't seen any more. Besides, you two know the Mark cut in the stone. Only the Gods know that. We thought you were men till you showed the sign of the Master.'

"I wished then that we had explained about the loss of the genuine secrets of a Master-Mason at the first go-off; but I said nothing. All that night there was a blowing of horns in a little dark temple half-way down the hill, and I heard a girl crying fit to die. One of the priests told us that she was being prepared to marry the King.

"'I'll have no nonsense of that kind,' says Dan. 'I don't want to interfere with your customs, but I'll take my own wife.'—'The girl's a little bit afraid,' says the priest. 'She thinks she's going to die, and they are a-heartening of her up down in the temple.'

"'Hearten her very tender, then,' says Dravot, 'or I'll hearten you with the butt of a gun so you'll never want to be heartened again.' He licked his lips, did Dan, and stayed up walking about more than half the night, thinking of the wife that he was going to get in the morning. I wasn't any means comfortable, for I knew that dealings with a woman in foreign parts, though you was a crowned King twenty times over, could not but be risky. I got up very early in the morning while Dravot was asleep, and I saw the priests talking together in whispers, and the Chiefs talking together too, and they looked at me out of the corners of their eyes.

"'What is up, Fish?' I says to the Bashkai man, who was wrapped up in his furs and looking splendid to behold.

"'I can't rightly say,' says he; 'but if you can make the King drop all this nonsense about marriage, you'll be doing him and me and yourself a great service.'

"'That I do believe,' says I. 'But sure, you know, Billy, as well as me, having fought against and for us, that the King and me are nothing more than two of the finest men that God Almighty ever made. Nothing more, I do assure you.'

"'That may be,' says Billy Fish, 'and yet I should be sorry if it was.' He sinks his head upon his great fur cloak for a minute and thinks. 'King,' says he, 'be you man or God or Devil, I'll stick by you to-day. I have twenty of my men with me, and they will follow me. We'll go to Bashkai until the storm blows over.'

"A little snow had fallen in the night, and everything was white except the greasy fat clouds that blew down and down from the north. Dravot came out with his crown on his head, swinging his arms and stamping his feet, and looking more pleased than Punch.

"'For the last time, drop it, Dan,' says I in a whisper. 'Billy Fish here says that there will be a row.'

"'A row among my people!' says Dravot. 'Not much. Peachey, you're a fool not to get a wife too. Where's the girl?' says he with a voice as loud as the braying of a jackass. 'Call up all the Chiefs and priests, and let the Emperor see if his wife suits him.'

"There was no need to call any one. They were all there leaning on their guns and spears round the clearing in the centre of the pine wood. A lot of priests went down to the little temple to bring up the girl, and the horns blew fit to wake the dead. Billy Fish saunters round and gets as close to Daniel as he could, and behind him stood his twenty men with matchlocks. Not a man of them under six feet. I was next to Dravot, and behind me was twenty men of the regular Army. Up comes the girl, and a strapping wench she was, covered with silver and turquoises but white as death, and looking back every minute at the priests.

"'She'll do,' said Dan, looking her over. 'What's to be afraid of, lass? Come and kiss me.' He puts his arm round her. She shuts her eyes, gives a bit of a squeak, and down goes her face in the side of Dan's flaming red beard.

"'The slut's bitten me!' says he, clapping his hand to his neck, and, sure enough, his hand was red with blood. Billy Fish and two of his matchlock-men catches hold of Dan by the shoulders and drags him into the Bashkai lot, while the priests howls in their lingo,—'Neither God nor Devil but a man!' I was all taken aback, for a priest cut at me in front, and the Army behind began firing into the Bashkai men.

"'God A'mighty!' says Dan. 'What is the meaning o' this?'

"'Come back! Come away!' says Billy Fish. 'Ruin and Mutiny is the matter. We'll break for Bashkai if we can.'

"I tried to give some sort of orders to my men—the men o' the regular Army—but it was no use, so I fired into the brown of 'em with an English Martini and drilled three beggars in a line. The valley was full of shouting, howling creatures, and every soul was shrieking, 'Not a God nor a Devil but only a man!' The Bashkai troops stuck to Billy Fish all they were worth, but their matchlocks wasn't half as good as the Kabul breech-loaders, and four of them dropped. Dan was bellowing like a bull, for he was very wrath; and Billy Fish had a hard job to prevent him running out at the crowd.

"'We can't stand,' says Billy Fish. 'Make a run for it down the valley! The whole place is against us.' The matchlock-men ran, and we went down the valley in spite of Dravot. He was swearing horrible and crying out he was a King. The priests rolled great stones on us, and the regular Army fired hard, and there wasn't more than six men, not counting Dan, Billy Fish, and Me, that came down to the bottom of the valley alive.

"Then they stopped firing and the horns in the temple blew again. 'Come away—for Gord's sake come away!' says Billy Fish. 'They ll send runners out to all the villages before ever we get to Bashkai. I can protect you there, but I can't do anything now.'

"My own notion is that Dan began to go mad in his head from that hour. He stared up and down like a stuck pig. Then he was all for walking back alone and killing the priests with his bare hands; which he could have done. 'An Emperor am I,' says Daniel, 'and next year I shall be a Knight of the Queen.'

"'All right, Dan,' says I; 'but come along now while there's time.'

"'It's your fault,' says he, 'for not looking after your Army better. There was mutiny in the midst, and you didn't know—you damned engine-driving, plate-laying, missionary's-pass-hunting hound!' He sat upon a rock and called me every foul name he could lay tongue to. I was too heart-sick to care, though it was all his foolishness that brought the smash.

"'I'm sorry, Dan,' says I, 'but there's no accounting for natives. This business is our Fifty-Seven. Maybe we'll make something out of it yet, when we've got to Bashkai.'

"'Let's get to Bashkai, then,' says Dan, 'and, by God, when I come back here again I'll sweep the valley so there isn't a bug in a blanket left!'

"We walked all that day, and all that night Dan was stumping up and down on the snow, chewing his beard and muttering to himself.

"'There's no hope o' getting clear,' said Billy Fish. 'The priests will have sent runners to the villages to say that you are only men. Why didn't you stick on as Gods till things was more settled; I'm a dead man,' says Billy Fish, and he throws himself down on the snow and begins to pray to his Gods.

"Next morning we was in a cruel bad country—all up and down, no level ground at all, and no food either. The six Bashkai men looked at Billy Fish hungry-way as if they wanted to ask something, but they said never a word. At noon we came to the top of a flat mountain all covered with snow, and when we climbed up into it, behold, there was an Army in position waiting in the middle!

"'The runners have been very quick,' says Billy Fish, with a little bit of a laugh. 'They are waiting for us.'

"Three or four men began to fire from the enemy's side, and a chance shot took Daniel in the calf of the leg. That brought him to his senses. He looks across the snow at the Army, and sees the rifles that we had brought into the country.

"'We're done for,' says he. 'They are Englishmen, these people,—and it's my blasted nonsense that has brought you to this. Get back, Billy Fish, and take your men away; you've done what you could, and now cut for it. Carnehan,' says he, 'shake hands with me and go along with Billy. Maybe they won't kill you. I'll go and meet 'em alone. It's me that did it. Me, the King!'

"'Go!' says I. 'Go to Hell, Dan. I'm with you here. Billy Fish, you clear out, and we two will meet those folk.'

"'I'm a Chief,' says Billy Fish, quite quiet. 'I stay with you. My men can go.'

"The Bashkai fellows didn't wait for a second word but ran off, and Dan and Me and Billy Fish walked across to where the drums were drumming and the horns were horning. It was cold—awful cold. I've got that cold in the back of my head now. There's a lump of it there."

The Punkah-coolies had gone to sleep. Two kerosene lamps were blazing in the office, and the perspiration poured down my face and splashed on the blotter as I leaned forward. Carnehan was shivering, and I feared that his mind might go. I wiped my face, took a fresh grip of the piteously mangled hands, and said: 'What happened after that?'

The momentary shift of my eyes had broken the clear current.

"What was you pleased to say?" whined Carnehan. "They took them without any sound. Not a little whisper all along the snow, not though the King knocked down the first man that set hand on him—not though old Peachey fired his last cartridge into the brown of 'em. Not a single solitary sound did those swines make. They just closed up tight, and I tell you their furs stunk. There was a man called Billy Fish, a good friend of us all, and they cut his throat, Sir, then and there, like a pig; and the King kicks up the bloody snow and says: 'We've had a dashed fine run for our money. What's coming next?' But Peachey, Peachey Taliaferro, I tell you, Sir, in confidence as betwixt two friends, he lost his head, Sir. No, he didn't neither. The King lost his head, so he did, all along o' one of those cunning rope-bridges. Kindly let me have the paper-cutter, Sir. It tilted this way. They marched him a mile across the snow to a rope-bridge over a ravine with a river at the bottom. You may have seen such. They prodded him behind like an ox. 'Damn your eyes!' says the King. 'D'you suppose I can't die like a gentleman?' He turns to Peachey—Peachey that was crying like a child. 'I've brought you to this, Peachey,' says he. 'Brought you out of your happy life to be killed in Kafiristan, where you was late Commander-in-Chief of the Emperor's forces. Say you forgive me, Peachey.'—'I do,' says Peachey. 'Fully and freely do I forgive you, Dan.'—'Shake hands, Peachey,' says he. 'I'm going now.' Out he goes, looking neither right nor left, and when he was plumb in the middle of those dizzy dancing ropes,—'Cut, you beggars,' he shouts; and they cut, and old Dan fell, turning round and round and round, twenty thousand miles, for he took half an hour to fall till he struck the water, and I could see his body caught on a rock with the gold crown close beside.

"But do you know what they did to Peachey between two pine-trees? They crucified him, Sir, as Peachey's hand will show. They used wooden pegs for his hands and his feet; and he didn't die. He hung there and screamed, and they took him down next day, and said it was a miracle that he wasn't dead. They took him down—poor old Peachey that hadn't done them any harm—that hadn't done them any—"

He rocked to and fro and wept bitterly, wiping his eyes with the back of his scarred hands and moaning like a child for some ten minutes.

"They was cruel enough to feed him up in the temple, because they said he was more of a God than old Daniel that was a man. Then they turned him out on the snow, and told him to go home, and Peachey came home in about a year, begging along the roads quite safe; for Daniel Dravot he walked before and said: 'Come along, Peachey. It's a big thing we're doing.' The mountains they danced at night, and the mountains they tried to fall on Peachey's head, but Dan he held up his hand, and Peachy came along bent double. He never let go of Dan's hand, and he never let go of Dan's head. They gave it to him as a present in the temple, to remind him not to come again, and though the crown was pure gold, and Peachey was starving, never would Peachey sell the same. You knew Dravot, Sir! You knew Right Worshipful Brother Dravot! Look at me now!"

He fumbled in the mass of rags round his bent waist; brought out a black horsehair bag embroidered with silver thread; and shook therefrom on to my table—the dried, withered head of Daniel Dravot! The morning sun that had long been paling the lamps struck the red beard and blind sunken eyes; struck, too, a heavy circlet of gold studded with raw turquoises, that Carnehan placed tenderly on the battered temples.

"You be'old now," said Carnehan, "the Emperor in his 'abit as he lived—the King of Kafiristan with his crown upon his head. Poor old Daniel that was a monarch once!"

I shuddered, for, in spite of defacements manifold, I recognised the head of the man of Marwar Junction. Carnehan rose to go. I attempted to stop him. He was not fit to walk abroad. "Let me take away the whiskey, and give me a little money," he gasped. "I was a King once. I'll go to the Deputy Commissioner and ask to set in the Poorhouse till I get my health. No, thank you, I can't wait till you get a carriage for me. I've urgent private affairs—in the south—at Marwar."

He shambled out of the office and departed in the direction of the Deputy Commissioner's house. That day at noon I had occasion to go down the blinding hot Mall, and I saw a crooked man crawling along the white dust of the roadside, his hat in his hand, quavering dolorously after the fashion of street-singers at Home. There was not a soul in sight, and he was out of all possible earshot of the houses. And he sang through his nose, turning his head from right to left:—

> "The Son of Man goes forth to war,
>
> A golden crown to gain;
>
> His blood-red banner streams afar—
>
> Who follows in his train?"

I waited to hear no more, but put the poor wretch into my carriage and drove him off to the nearest missionary for eventual transfer to the Asylum. He repeated the hymn twice while he was with me whom he did not in the least recognise, and I left him singing it to the missionary.

Two days later I enquired after his welfare of the Superintendent of the Asylum.

"He was admitted suffering from sun-stroke. He died early yesterday morning," said the Superintendent. "Is it true that he was half an hour bareheaded in the sun at midday?"

"Yes," said I, "but do you happen to know if he had anything upon him by any chance when he died?"

"Not to my knowledge," said the Superintendent.

And there the matter rests.

TEN LITTLE LEGIONARIES

P. C. Wren

A T THE DEPOT AT SIDI BEL-ABBES, SERGEANT-MAJOR SUICIDE-MAKER WAS a devil, but at a little frontier outpost in the desert, he was *the* devil, the increase in his degree being commensurate with the increase in his opportunities. When the Seventh Company of the First Battalion of the First Regiment of the Foreign Legion of France, stationed at Aïnargoula in the Sahara, learned that Lieutenant Roberte was in hospital with a broken leg, it realized that, Captain d'Armentières being absent with the Mule Company, chasing Touaregs to the south, it would be commanded for a space by Sergeant-Major Suicide-Maker—in other words by The Devil.

Not only would it be commanded by him, it would be harried, harassed, hounded, bullied, brow-beaten, and be-deviled; it would be unable to call its soul its own and loth so to call its body.

On realizing the ugly truth, the Seventh Company gasped unanimously and then swore diversely in all the languages of Europe and a few of those of Asia and Africa. It realized that it was about to learn, as the Bucking Bronco remarked to his friend John Bull (once Sir Montague Merline, of the Queen's African Rifles), that it had been wrong in guessing it was already on the ground-floor of hell. Or, if it had been there heretofore, it was now about to have a taste of the cellars.

Sergeant-Major Suicide-Maker had lived well up to his reputation, even under the revisional jurisdiction and faintly restraining curb of Captain d'Armentières and then of Lieutenant Roberte.

Each of these was a strong man and a just, and though anything in the world but mild and indulgent, would not permit really unbridled vicious tyranny such as the Sergeant-Major's unsupervised, unhampered sway would be. Under their command, he would always be limited to the surreptitious abuse of his very considerable legitimate powers. With no one above him, the mind shrank from contemplating the life of a Legionary in Aïnargoula, and from conceiving this worthy as absolute monarch and arbitrary autocrat.

The number of men undergoing *cellule* punishment would be limited only by standing room in the cells—each a miniature Black Hole of Calcutta with embellishments. The time spent in drilling at the *pas gymnastique*[*] and, worse, standing at "attention" in the hottest corner of the red-hot barrack-yard would be only limited by the physical capacity of the Legionaries to run and to stand at "attention." Never would there be "*Rompez*"[†] until some one had been carried to hospital, suffering from heatstroke or collapse. The alternatives to the maddening agony of life would be suicide, desertion (and death from thirst or at the hands of the Arabs), or revolt and the Penal Battalions—the one thing on earth worse than Legion life in a desert station, under a half-mad bully whose monomania was driving men to suicide. *Le Cafard*, the desert madness of the Legion, was rampant and chronic. Ten legionaries under the leadership of a Frenchman calling himself Blondin, and who spoke perfect English and German, had formed a secret society and hatched a plot. They were going to "remove" Sergeant-Major Suicide-Maker and "go on pump," as the legionary calls deserting.

Blondin (a pretty, black-eyed, black-moustached Provençal, who looked like a blue-jowled porcelain doll) was an educated man, brilliantly clever, and of considerable personality and force of character. Also he was a finished and heartless scoundrel. His nine adherents were Ramon Diego, a grizzled Spaniard, a man of tremendous physical strength and weak mind; Fritz Bauer, a Swiss, also much stronger of muscle than of brain; a curious Franco-Berber half-caste called Jean Kebir, who spoke perfect Arabic and knew the Koran by heart *(Kebir* is Arabic for "lion," and a lion Jean Kebir was, and Blondin had been very glad indeed to win him over, as he would be an invaluable interpreter and adviser in the journey Blondin meant to take); Jacques Lejaune, a domineering, violent ruffian, a former merchant-captain, who could steer by the stars and use a compass; Fritz Schlantz, a wonderful marksman; Karl Anderssen, who had won the *médaille* for bravery; Mohamed the Turk—just plain Mohamed *(very* plain); Georges Grondin, the musician, who was a fine cook; and finally the big Moorish negro, Hassan Moghrabi, who understood camels and horses.

The Society had been larger, but Franz Joseph Meyr the Austrian had killed Dimitropoulos the Greek, had deserted alone, and been filleted by the Touaregs. Also Alexandre Bac, late of Montmartre, had hanged himself, and La Cigale had gone too hopelessly mad.

It had been for a grief unto Monsieur Blondin that he could by no means persuade old Jean Boule to join. On being sworn to secrecy and "approached" on the subject, ce bon Jean had replied that he did not desire to quit the Legion (*Bon sang de Dieu!*), and, moreover, that if he went "on pump," his friends les Légionnaires

---

Rupert, 'Erbiggin, and le Bouckaing Bronceau would go too—and he did not wish to drag them into so perilous a venture as an attempt to reach the Moroccan coast across the desert from Aïnargoula. Moreover, if he came to know anything of the plot to kill the Sergeant-Major he would certainly warn him, if it were to be a mere stab-in-the-back assassination affair, some dark night. A fair fight is a different thing. If Blondin met the Sergeant-Major alone, when both had their sword-bayonets—that was a different matter. . . .

Monsieur Blondin sheered off, and decided that the less Jean Boule knew of the matter, the better for the devoted Ten. . . .

> "Ten little Légionnaires
> Going 'on pump,'
> Got away safely
> And gave *les autres* the 'ump,"

sang Monsieur Blondin, who was very fond of airing his really remarkable knowledge of colloquial English, British slang, clichés, rhymes, and *guinguette* songs. Not for nothing had he been a Crédit Lyonnais bank-clerk in London for six years. Being a Provençal, he added a pronounced *galégeade* wit to his *macabre* Legion-humour.

One terrible day the Sergeant-Major excelled himself—but it was not, as it happened, one of the Ten who attempted to "remove" him.

Having drilled the parade of "defaulters" almost to death, he halted the unfortunate wretches with their faces to a red-hot wall and their backs to the smiting sun, and kept them at "attention" until Tou-tou Boil-the-Cat, an evil liver, collapsed and fell. He was allowed to lie. When, with a crash, old Tant-de-Soif went prone upon his face, paying his dues to Alcohol, the Sergeant-Major gave the order to turn about, and then to prepare to fire. When the line stood, with empty rifles to the shoulder, as in the act of firing, he kept it in the arduous strain of this attitude that he might award severe punishment to the owner of the first rifle that began to quiver or sink downward. As he did so, he lashed and goaded his victims mercilessly and skilfully.

At last, the rifle of poor young Jean Brecque began to sway and droop, and the Sergeant-Major concentrated upon the half-fainting lad the virulent stream of his poisonous vituperation. Having dealt with the subject of Jean, he began upon that of Jean's mother, and with such horrible foulness of insult that Jean, whose mother was his saint, sprang forward and swung his rifle up to brain the cowardly brute with the butt. As he bounded forward and sprang at the Sergeant-Major, that officer coolly drew his automatic pistol and shot Jean between the eyes.

Had Blondin acted then, his followers, and the bulk of the parade, would have leapt from their places and clubbed the Sergeant-Major to a jelly. But Monsieur Blondin knew that the Sergeant-Major had seven more bullets in his automatic, also that the first man who moved would get one of them, and suicide formed no part of his programme.

"Not just anyhow and anywhere in the trunk, you will observe, *scélérats,* " remarked the Suicide-Maker coolly, turning Jean over with his foot, "but neatly in the centre of the face, just between the eyes. My favourite spot. *Cessez le feu! Attention! Par files de quatre. Pas gymnastique. . . . En avant. . . . Marche!"* . . .

The plan was that the Ten, stark naked—so as to avoid any incriminating stains, rents, or other marks upon their garments—should, bayonet in hand, await the passing of the "Suicide-Maker" along a dark corridor that evening. Having dealt with him quietly, but faithfully, they would dress, break out of the post, and set their faces for Morocco at the *pas gymnastique.*

As for Monsieur Blondin, he was determined that this should be no wretched abortive stroll into the desert, ending in ignominious return and surrender for food and water; in capture by *goums*[*] in search of the 25 franc reward for the return of a dead or alive deserter; nor in torture and death at the hands of the first party of nomad Arabs that should see fit to fall upon them. Blondin had read the *Anabasis* of one Xenophon, and an *Anabasis* to Maroc he intended to achieve on the shoulders, metaphorically speaking, of the faithful nine. Toward the setting sun would he lead them, across the Plain of the Shott, through the country of the Beni Guil, toward the Haut Atlas range, along the southern slopes to the Adrar Ndren, and so to Marakesh and service with the Sultan, or to escape by Mogador, Mazagan, or Dar-el-Beida. No more difficult really than toward Algiers or Oran, and, whereas capture in that direction was certain, safety, once in Morocco, was almost equally sure. For trained European soldiers were worth their weight in silver to the Sultan, and, in his service, might amass their weight in gold. A Moorish villa (and a harem) surrounded by fig-orchards, olive-fields, vineyards, palm-groves, and a fragrant garden of pepper-trees, eucalyptus, walnut, almond, oleander, orange and lemon, would suit Monsieur Blondin well. Oh, but yes! And the Ouled-Nael dancing-girls, Circassian slaves, Spanish beauties. . . .

The first part of the plan failed, for *ce vieux sale cochon* of a Jean Boule came along the corridor, struck a match to light his cigarette, saw the crouching, staring, naked Ten, and, being a mad Englishman and an accursed dog's-tail, saved the life of the

---

[*] Arab gens d'armes.

Sergeant-Major. That the Ten took no vengeance upon Jean Boule was due to their lack of desire for combat with the mighty *Americain*, le Bouckaing Bronceau, and with those tough and determined fighters, les Légionnaires Rupert and 'Erbiggin. All four were masters of *le boxe*, and, if beaten, knew it not. . . .

The Ten went "on pump" with their wrongs unavenged, save that Blondin stole the big automatic-pistol of the Sergeant-Major from its nail on the wall of the orderly-room.

They took their Lebel rifles and bayonets, an accumulated store of bread and biscuits, water, and, each man, such few cartridges as he had been able to steal and secrete when on the rifle-range, or marching with "sharp" ammunition.

Getting away was a matter of very small difficulty; it would be staying away that would be the trouble. One by one, they went over the wall of the fort, and hid in ditches, beneath culverts, or behind cactus-bushes.

At the appointed rendezvous in the *village Négre*, the Ten assembled, fell in, and marched off at the *pas gymnastique*, Blondin at their head. After travelling for some hours, with only a cigarette-space halt in every hour, and ere the stars began to pale, Blondin gave the order *"Campeẓ!"*, and the little company sank to the ground, cast off accoutrements and capotes, removed boots, and fell asleep. Before dawn Blondin woke them and made a brief speech. If they obeyed him implicitly and faithfully, he would lead them to safety and prosperity; if any man disobeyed him in the slightest particular, he would shoot him dead. If he were to be their leader, as they wished, he must have the promptest and most willing service and subordination from all. There was a terrible time before them ere they win to the Promised Land, but there was an infinitely worse one behind them—so let all who hoped to attain safety and wealth look to it that his least word be their law.

And the Ten Bad Men, desperate, unscrupulous, their hand against every man's, knowing no restraint nor law but Expedience, set forth on their all but hopeless venture, trusting ce cher Blondin (who intended to clamber from this Slime-pit of Siddim on their carcases, and had chosen them for their various utilities to his purpose).

At dawn, Blondin leading, caught sight of a fire as he topped a ridge, sank to earth, and was at once imitated by the others.

He issued clear orders quickly, and the band skirmished toward the fire, *en tirailleur*, in a manner that would have been creditable to the Touaregs themselves. It was a small Arab *douar*, or encampment, of a few *felidj* (low camel-hair tents), and a camel-enclosure. Blondin's shot, to kill the camel-sentry and bring the Arabs running from their tents, was followed by the steady, independent-firing which disposed of these unfortunates.

His whistle was followed by the charge, which also disposed of the remainder and the wounded, and left the Ten in possession of camels, women, food, weapons, tents, Arab clothing, and money. Fortune was favouring the brave! But the Ten were now Nine, for, as they charged, the old sheikh, sick and weak though he was, fired his long gun into the chest of Karl Anderssen at point-blank range. . . .

An hour later the *djemels* were loaded up with what Blondin decided to take, the women were killed, and the Nine were again *en route* for Maroc, enheartened beyond words. There is a great difference between marching and riding, between carrying one's kit and being carried oneself, and between having a little dry bread and having a fine stock of goat-flesh, rice, raisins, barley, and dates when one is crossing the desert.

In addition to the *djemels*, the baggage-camels, there were five *mehara* or swift riding-camels, and, on four of these, Monsieur Blondin had mounted the four men he considered most useful to his purposes—to wit, Jean Kebir, the Berber half-caste who spoke perfect Arabic as well as the *sabir* or lingua-franca of Northern Africa, and knew the Koran by heart; Hassan Moghrabi, the Moorish negro, who understood camels and horses; Mohamed the Turk, who also would look very convincing in native dress; and Jacques Lejaune, who could use a compass and steer by the stars, and who was a very brave and determined scoundrel.

When allotting the *mehara* to these four, after choosing the best for himself, Blondin, hand on pistol, had looked for any signs of discontent from Ramon Diego, Fritz Bauer, Fritz Schlantz, or Georges Grondin, and had found none. Also when he ordered that each man should cut the throat of his own woman, and Hassan Moghrabi should dispose of the three superfluous ones, no man demurred. The Bad Men were the less disposed to refuse to commit cold-blooded murder because the stories of the tortures inflicted upon the stragglers and the wounded of the Legion are horrible beyond words—though not more horrible than the authentic photographs of the tortured remains of these carved and jointed victims, that hang, as terrible warnings to deserters, in every *chambrée* of the *casernes* of the Legion. They killed these women at the word of Blondin—but they knew that the women would not have been content with the mere killing of *them*, had they fallen into the hands of this party of Arabs.

As, clad in complete Arab dress, they rode away in high spirits, le bon Monsieur Blondin sang in English, in his droll way—

> "Ten little Légionnaires
> Charging all in line—
> A naughty Arab shot one
> And then—there were *Nine*."

The Nine rode the whole of that day and, at evening, Blondin led them into a *wadi* or canyon, deep enough for concealment and wide enough for comfort. Here they camped, lit fires, and Georges Grondin made a right savoury stew of kid, rice, raisins, barley, dates, and bread in an Arab *couscous* pot. The Nine slept the sleep of the just and, in the morning, arose and called ce bon Blondin blessed. With camels, food, cooking-pots, sleeping-rugs, tents, clothing, extra weapons, and much other useful loot, hope sprang strong as well as eternal in their more or less human breasts.

Blondin led them on that day until they had made another fifty miles of westing, and halted at a little oasis where there was a well, a *kuba* (or tomb of some marabout or other holy person), and a small *fondouk* or caravan rest-house. Jean Kebir having reconnoitred and declared the *fondouk* empty, and the place safe, they watered their camels, occupied the *fondouk,* and, after a pleasant evening and a good supper, slept beneath its hospitable and verminous shelter—four of the party being on sentry-go, for two hours each, throughout the night.

At this place, the only human beings they encountered were a horrible disintegrating lump of disease that hardly ranked as a human being at all, and an ancient half-witted person who appeared to combine the duties of verger and custodian of the *kuba* with those of caretaker and host of the *fondouk*. Him, Jean Kebir drove into the former building with horrible threats. Fortunately for himself, the aged party strictly conformed with the orders of Kebir, for Blondin had given the Berber instructions to dispatch him forthwith to the joys of Paradise if he were seen outside the tomb. Next day, as the party jogged wearily along, Blondin heard an exclamation from Jean Kebir and, turning, saw him rein in his *mehari* and stare long and earnestly beneath his hand toward the furthermost sand-hills of the southern horizon. On one of these, Blondin could make out a speck. He raised his hand, and the little cavalcade halted.

"What is it?" he asked of Kebir.

"A Targui scout," was the reply. "We shall be attacked by Touaregs—*now* if they are the stronger party, to-night in any case—unless we reach some *ksar** and take refuge. . . . That might be more dangerous than waiting for the Touaregs, though."

"How do you know the man is a Targui?" asked Blondin.

"I do not know *how* I know, but I *do* know," was the reply. "Who else would sit all day motionless on a *mehari* on top of a sand-hill but a Targui? The Touareg system is to camp in a likely place and keep their horses fresh while a chain of slaves covers a wide area around them. In bush country they sit up in trees, and in the desert they sit on camels, as that fellow is doing. Directly they spot anything, they rush off and warn

* Fortified village.

their masters, who then gallop to the attack on horseback if they are in overwhelming strength, or wait until night if they are not."

Even as he spoke the watcher disappeared.

"Push on hard," ordered Blondin, and debated as to whether it would be better for the *mehari*-mounted five to desert the *djemel*-mounted four and escape, leaving them to their fate, or to remain, a band of nine determined rifles. Union is strength, and there is safety in numbers—so he decided that the speed of the party should be that of the well-flogged *djemels*.

"Goad them on, *mes enfants*," cried he to Diego, Bauer, Schlantz, and Grondin. "I will never desert you—but you must put your best leg foremost. We are nine, and they may be ninety or nine hundred, these *sacrés chiens* of Touaregs." An hour of hard riding, another—with decreasing anxiety, and suddenly Blondin's sharp, clear order:

"*Halte! . . . Formez le carré! . . . Attention pour les feux de salve!*" as, with incredible rapidity, an avalanche of horsemen appeared over a ridge and bore down upon them in a cloud of dust, with wild howls of "*Allah Akbar!*" . . . "*Lah illah il Allah!*" and a rising united chant. "*Ul-ul-ul-ul Ullah Akbar.*"

Swiftly the trained legionaries dismounted, knelt their camels in a ring, took cover behind them, and, with loaded rifles, awaited their leader's orders. Coolly Blondin estimated the number of this band of The-Forgotten-of-God, the blue-clad, Veiled Men of the desert. . . . Not more than twenty or thirty. They would never have attacked had not their scout taken the little caravan to be one of traders, some portion of a migrating tribe, or, perchance, a little gang of smugglers, traders of the Ouled-Ougouni or the Ouled-Sidi-Sheikhs, or possibly gun-running Chambaa taking German rifles from Tripoli to Morocco—a rich prey, indeed, if this were so. Each Chambi would fight like Ibliss himself though, if Chambaa they were, for such are fiends and devils, betrayers of hospitality, slayers of guests, defilers of salt, spawn of Jehannum, who were the sons and fathers of murderers and liars. Moreover, they would be doubly watchful, suspicious, and resolute if they, French subjects, were smuggling German guns across French territory into Morocco under the very nose of the Bureau Arabe. . . . However, there were but nine of them, in any case, so *Ul-ul-ul-ul-ul Ullah Akbar!*

"Don't fire till I do—and then at the horses, and don't miss," shouted Blondin.

The avalanche swept down, and lances were lowered, two-handed swords raised, and guns and pistols presented—for the Touareg fire from the saddle at full gallop.

Blondin waited.

Blondin fired. . . . The leading horse and rider crashed to the ground and rolled like shot rabbits. Eight rifles spoke almost simultaneously, and seven more men and horses spun in the dust. At the second volley from the Nine, the Touaregs broke, bent their horses outward from the centre of the line, and fled. All save one, who either could not, or would not, check his maddened horse. Him Blondin shot as his great sword split the skull of Fritz Bauer, whose poor shooting, for which he was notorious, had cost him his life. "*Cessez le feu,*" cried Blondin, as one or two shots were fired after the retreating Arabs. "They won't come back, so don't waste cartridges. . . . See what hero can catch me a horse."

As he coolly examined the ghastly wound of the dying Fritz Bauer, he observed to the faithful Jean Kebir "*Habet!*" and added—

> "Nine little Légionnaires—
> But one fired late
> When a Touareg cut at him—
> And so there were *Eight*."

"*Eh bien, mon Capitaine?*" inquired Kebir.

"*N'importe, mon enfant!*" smiled Monsieur Blondin, and turned his attention to the property and effects of the dying man. . . .

"We shall hear more of these Forsaken-of-God before long," observed Jean Kebir when the eight were once more upon their way.

They did. Just before sunset, as they were silhouetted against the fiery sky in crossing a sandhill ridge, there was a single shot, and Georges Grondin, the cook, grunted, swayed, observed "*Je suis bien touché,*" and fell from his camel.

Gazing round, Blondin saw no signs of the enemy. The plain was empty of life—but there might be hundreds of foemen behind the occasional aloes, palmettos, and Barbary cacti; crouching in the *driss,* or the thickets of lentisks and arbutus and thuyas. Decidedly a place to get out of. If a party of Touareg had ambushed them there, they might empty every saddle without showing a Targui nose. . . .

A ragged volley was fired from the right flank.

"Ride for your lives," he shouted, and set an excellent example to the other seven.

"What of Grondin?" asked Kebir, bringing his *mehari* alongside that of Blondin.

"Let the dead bury their dead," was the reply. (Evidently the fool had not realized that the *raison d'être* of this expedition was to get one, Jean Blondin, safe to Maroc!)

An hour or so later, in a kind of little natural fortress of stones, boulders, and rocks, they encamped for the night, a sharp watch being kept. But while Monsieur Blondin slept, Jean Kebir, who was attached to Georges Grondin, partly on account of his music and partly on account of his cookery, crept out, an hour or so before dawn, and stole back along the track, in the direction from which they had come.

He found his friend at dawn, still alive; but as he had been neatly disembowelled and the abdominal cavity filled with salt and sand and certain other things, he did not attempt to move him. He embraced his cher Georges, bade him farewell, shot him, and returned to the little camp.

As the cavalcade proceeded on its way, Monsieur Blondin, stimulated by the brilliance and coolness of the glorious morning, and by high hopes of escape, burst into song.

> "Eight little Légionnaires
> Riding from 'ell to 'eaven,
> A wicked Targui shot one—
> And then there were *Seven,*"

improvised he. . . .

Various reasons, shortness of food and water being the most urgent, made it desirable that they should reach and enter a small *ksar* that day.

Towards evening, the Seven beheld what was either an oasis or a mirage—a veritable eye-feast in any case, after hours of burning desolate desert, the home only of the hornéd viper, the lizard, and the scorpion.

It proved to be a small palm-forest, with wells, irrigating-ditches, cultivation, pigeons, and inhabitants. Cultivators were hoeing, blindfolded asses were wheeling round and round *noria* wells, veiled women with red *babooshes* on their feet bore brightly coloured water-vases on their heads. Whitewashed houses came into view, and the cupola of an adobe-walled *kuba*.

Jean Kebir was sent on to reconnoitre and prospect, and to use his judgment as to whether his six companions—good men and true, under a pious vow of silence— might safely enter the oasis, and encamp.

While they awaited his return, naked children came running towards them clamouring for gifts. They found the riders dumb, but eloquent of gesture—and the gestures discouraging.

Some women brought clothes and commenced to wash them in an irrigation stream, on some flat stones by a bridge of palm trunks. The six sat motionless on their camels.

A jet-black Haratin boy brought a huge basket of Barbary figs and offered it—as a gift that should bring a reward. At a sign from Blondin, Mohamed the Turk took it and threw the boy a *mitkal.*

"Salaam," said he.

"*Ya, Sidi, Salaam aleikoum,*" answered the boy, with a flash of perfect teeth.

Blondin glared at Mohamed. Could not the son of a camel remember that the party was dumb—pious men under a vow of silence? It was their only chance of avoiding discovery and exposure as accursed Roumis[*] when they were near the habitations of men.

A burst of music from tom-tom, derbukha, and raita broke the heavy silence, and then a solo on the raita, the "Muezzin of Devil," the instrument of the provocative wicked note. Some one was getting born, married, or buried, apparently.

Fritz Schlantz, staring open-mouthed at cyclamens, anemones, asphodels, irises, lilies, and crocuses between a little cemetery and a stream, was, for the moment, back in his Tyrolese village. He shivered. . . .

Jean Kebir returned. He recommended camping on the far side of the village at a spot he had selected. There were strangers, heavily armed with yataghans, lances, horse-pistols, flissas, and *moukalas* in the *fondouk*. In addition to the flint-lock *moukalas* there were several repeating rifles. They were all clad in *burnous* and *chechia*, and appeared to be half-trader, half-brigand Arabs of the Tableland, perhaps Ouled-Ougouni or possibly Aït-Jellal. Anyhow, the best thing to do with them was to give them a wide berth.

The Seven passed through the oasis and, camping on the other side, fed full upon the proceeds of Kebir's foraging and shopping.

That night, Fritz Schlantz was seized with acute internal pains, and was soon obviously and desperately ill.

"Cholera!" said Monsieur Blondin on being awakened by the sufferer's cries and groans. "Saddle up and leave him."

Within the hour the little caravan had departed, Jacques Lejaune steering by the stars. To keep up the spirits of his followers Monsieur Blondin sang aloud.

First he sang—

> "Des marches d'Afrique
> J'en ai pleine le dos.
> On y va trop vite.
> On n'y boit que de l'eau.
> Des lauriers, des victoires,
> De ce songe illusoire
> Que l'on nomme 'la gloire,'
> J'en ai plein le dos,"

---

[*] Europeans.

and then *Derrière l'Hôtel-Dieu,* and *Père Dupanloup en chemin de fer.* In a fine tenor voice, and with great feeling, he next rendered *L'Amour m'a rendu fou,* and then, to a tune of his own composition, sang in English—

> "Seven little Légionnaires
> Eating nice green figs,
> A greedy German ate too much—
> And then there were *Six."*

Day after day, and week after week, the legionaries pushed on, sometimes starving, often thirsty, frequently hunted, sometimes living like the proverbial *coq en pâte,* or, as Blondin said, "Wee peegs in clover," after ambushing and looting a caravan.

Between Amang and Illigh lie the bones of Jacques Lejaune, who was shot by Blondin. As they passed out of the dark and gloomy shade of a great cedar forest, there was a sudden roar, and a lioness flung herself from a rock upon Lejaune's camel. Lejaune was leading as the sun had set. Blondin, who was behind him, fired quickly, and the bullet struck him in the spine and passed out through his shattered breast-bone. He had been getting "difficult" and too fond of giving himself airs on the strength of his navigating ability, and, moreover, Monsieur Blondin had learnt to steer by the stars, having located the polar star by means of the Great Bear.

It was a sad "accident" but Blondin had evidently recovered his spirits by morning, as he was singing again.

He sang—

> "Six little Légionnaires
> Still all live,
> But one grew *indiscipliné*—
> And then there were *Five."* . . .

Distinctly of a *galégeade* wit and a *macabre* humour was Monsieur Blondin, and even as his eye roamed over the scrubby hill-sides and he thought fondly of the *mussu-gues,* the cistus-scrub hillocks of his dear Provence, he calculated the total sum of money now divided among the said Five, and reflected that division, where money is concerned, is deplorable. Also, as he gazed upon the tracts of thorn that recalled the *argeras* of Hyères, he decided that, all things considered, it would be as well for him to reach Marakesh alone. He understood the principle of rarity-value, and knew that either one of two new-comers would not fetch a quarter of the price of a single newcomer to a war-harassed Sultan whose crying need was European drill-sergeants and centurions.

Jean Blondin would rise to be a second Kaid McLeod, and would amass vast wealth to boot. . . .

At Aït-Ashsba, bad luck overtook Ramon Diego. At the *fondouk* he smote a burly negro of Sokoto who jostled him. The negro, one of a band of departing wayfarers, was a master of the art of *rabah*, the native version of *la savate*, and landed Ramon a most terrible kick beneath the breast-bone. As he lay gasping and groaning for breath, the negro whipped out his razor-edged yataghan and bent over the prostrate man. Holding aloof, Blondin saw the negro spit on the back of Ramon Diego's neck, and with his finger draw a line thereon. Stepping swiftly back, the gigantic black then smote with all his strength, and the head of Ramon Diego rolled through the doorway and down the stony slope leading from the *fondouk*. As the negro mounted his swift Filali camel, Blondin investigated the contents of a leather bag which Ramon always wore at the girdle, beneath his *haik*. On being told of the mishap, Jean Kebir was all for pursuit and vengeance. This, Blondin vetoed sternly. There were now only four of them, and henceforth they must walk delicately and be *miskeen*, modest, humble men. Only four now!

> "Five little Légionnaires,
> Each man worth a score;
> But a big nigger 'it one—
> And then there were *Four*,"

sang Monsieur Blondin.

But what a four! Jean Kebir, the genuine local article, more or less; Hassan Moghrabi, near his native heath and well in the picture; Mohamed the Turk, a genuine Mussulman, able to enter any mosque or *kuba* and display his orthodoxy; and himself, a pious man hooded to the eyes, under a vow of silence.

In due course, the Four reached the Adrar highlands, and tasted of the hospitality of this grim spot, with its brigands' *agadirs* or castles of stone. Having no *mezrag*, no token of protection from some Chief of Many Tents, and the thrifty Blondin refusing Kebir's request to be permitted to buy one, they had to trust to speed and secrecy. As it was, a band swooping down upon them from an *agadir* (obviously of Phœnician origin), pursued them so closely and successfully, that Mohamed, the worst mounted, bringing up the rear, was also brought to earth by a lance-thrust through his back, and ended his career hanging by the flesh of his thigh from a huge hook which protruded from the wall above the door of the *agadir*.

Though greatly incensed at the loss of the Turk's camel and cash, Monsieur Blondin was soon able to sing again.

"Four Little Légionnaires
Out upon the spree,
The Adrar robbers caught one—
And soon there were *Three*," . . .

he chanted merrily.

As the Three watched some hideous Aïssa dervishes dancing on glowing charcoal, skewering their limbs and cheeks and tongues, eating fire, and otherwise demonstrating their virtue one night, near Bouzen, a *djemel*, thrusting forth his head and twisting his snaky neck, neatly removed the right knee-cap of Hassan Moghrabi, and he was of no further use to Monsieur Blondin. He was left behind, and died in a ditch some three days later, of loss of blood, starvation, gangrene, and grief.

Clearly Jean Blondin was reserved for great things. Here were the Ten reduced to Two, and of those two he was one—and intended to be the only one when he was safe in Maroc. Singing blithely, he declared that—

"Three little Légionnaires
Nearly travelled through,
When a hungry camel ate one—
And now there are but *Two*." . . .

On through the beautiful Adrar, past its forests of arbutus, lentisk, thuya, figs, pines, and palmettos to its belt of olive groves, walnut, and almond; on toward Djebel Tagharat, the Lord of the Peaks, the Two-Headed. On through the Jibali country, called the "Country of the Gun" by the Arabs, as it produces little else for visitors, toward the Bled-el-Maghzen, the "Government's Territory," experiencing many and strange adventures and hair-breadth escapes. And, all the way, Jean Kebir served his colleague and leader well, and often saved him by his ready wit, knowledge of the country and the *sabir*, and his good advice.

And in time they reached the gorge of Wad Nafiz, and rode over a carpet of pimpernels, larkspur, gladiolus, hyacinths, crocuses, wasp-orchids, asphodels, cyclamens, irises and musk-balsams; and Blondin realized that it was time for Jean Kebir to die, if he were to ride to Marakesh alone and to inherit the whole of what remained of the money looted in the fifteen-hundred-mile journey, that was now within fifteen hours of its end. . . .

He felt quite sad as he shot the sleeping Jean Kebir that night, but by morning was able to sing—

> "Two little Légionnaires
> Travelling with the sun,
> Two was one too many—
> So now there is but *One*,"

and remarked to his camel, " '*Finis coronat opus,*' *mon gars.*". . .

Even as he caught sight, upon the horizon, of the sea of palms in which Marakesh is bathed, he was aware of a rush of yelling, gun-firing, white-clad lunatics bearing down upon him. . . . A Moorish *harka!* Was this a *lab-el-baroda*, a powder-play game—or what? They couldn't be shooting at *him*. . . . What was that Kebir had said? . . . "The Moors are the natural enemies of the Arabs. We must soon get Moorish garb or hide"—when . . . a bullet struck his camel and it sprawled lumberingly to earth. Others threw up spouts of dust. Blondin sprang to his feet and shouted. Curse the fools for thinking him an Arab! *Oh, for the faithful Jean Kebir to shout to them in the* sabir *lingua franca!* . . . A bullet struck him in the chest. Another in the shoulder. He fell.

As the Moors gathered round to slice him in strips with flissa, yataghan and sword, they found that their prey was apparently expending his last breath in prayers and pæans to Allah. He gasped:

> "One little Légionnaire,
> To provide *le bon Dieu* fun,
> Was killed because he killed his friend—
> And now there is *None*." . . .

There were.

Decidedly of a *galégeade* wit and a *macabre* humour to the very last—ce bon Jean Blondin.

"*Que voulez-vous? C'est la Légion!*" . . .

FOR THE SALT WHICH HE HAD EATEN

Talbot Mundy

PROLOGUE

To the northward of Hanadra, blue in the sweltering heat-haze, lay Siroeh, walled in with sun-baked mud and listless. Through a wooden gate at one end of the village filed a string of women with their water-pots. Oxen, tethered underneath the thatched eaves or by the thirsty-looking trees, lay chewing the cud, almost too lazy to flick the flies away. Even the village goats seemed overcome with lassitude. Here and there a pariah dog sneaked in and out among the shadows or lay and licked his sores beside an offal-heap; but there seemed to be no energy in anything. The bone-dry, hot-weather wind had shriveled up verdure and ambition together.

But in the mud-walled cottages, where men were wont to doze through the long, hot days, there were murmurings and restless movement. Men lay on thong-strung beds, and talked instead of dreaming, and the women listened and said nothing—which is the reverse of custom. Hanadra was what it always had been, thatched, sun-baked lassitude; but underneath the thatch there thrummed a beehive atmosphere of tension.

In the center of the village, where the one main road that led from the main gate came to an abrupt end at a low mud wall, stood a house that was larger than the others and somewhat more neatly kept; there had been an effort made at sweeping the enclosure that surrounded it on all four sides, and there was even whitewash, peeling off in places but still comparatively white, smeared on the sun-cracked walls.

Here, besides murmurings and movement, there was evidence of real activity. Tethered against the wall on one side of the house stood a row of horses, saddled and bridled and bearing evidence of having traveled through the heat; through the open doorway the sunshine glinted on a sword-hilt and amid the sound of many voices rang the jingling of a spur as some one sat cornerwise on a wooden table and struck his toe restlessly against the leg.

Another string of women started for the water-hole, with their picturesque brass jars perched at varying angles on their heads; and as each one passed the doorway of this larger house she turned and scowled. A Rajput, lean and black-bearded and swaggering, came to the door and watched them, standing proudly with his arms folded across his breast. As the last woman showed her teeth at him, he laughed aloud.

"Nay!" said a voice inside. "Have done with that! Is noticing the Hindu women fit sport for a Rajput?"

The youngster turned and faced the old, black-bearded veteran who spoke.

"If I had my way," he answered, "I would ride roughshod through this village, and fire the thatch. They fail to realize the honor that we pay them by a visit!"

"Aye, hothead! And burn thy brother's barn with what is in it! The Hindus here are many, and we are few, and there will be burnings and saberings a-plenty before a week is past, if I read the signs aright! Once before have I heard such murmurings. Once before I have seen *chupatties* sent from house to house at sunset—and that time blood ran red along the roadside for a month to follow! Keep thy sword sharp a while and wait the day!"

"But why," growled another deep-throated Rajput voice, "does the Sirkar wait? Why not smite first and swiftly?"

Mahommed Khan moved restlessly and ran his fingers through his beard.

"I know not!" he answered. "In the days when I was Risaldar in the Rajput Horse, and Bellairs sahib was colonel, things were different! But we conquered, and after conquest came security. The English have grown overconfident; they think that Mussulman will always war with Hindu, the one betraying the other; they will not understand that this lies deeper than jealousy—they will not listen! Six months ago I rode to Jundhra and whispered to the general sahib what I thought; but he laughed back at me. He said 'Wolf! wolf!' to me and drew me inside his bungalow and bade me eat my fill."

"Well—what matters it! This land has always been the playground of new conquerors!"

"There will be no new conquerors," growled the old Risaldar, "so long as I and mine have swords to wield for the Raj!"

"But what have the English done for thee or us?"

"This, forgetful one! They have treated us with honor, as surely no other conquerors had done! At thy age, I too measured my happiness in cattle and coin and women, but then came Bellairs sahib, and raised the Rajput Horse, and I enlisted. What came of that was better than all the wealth of Ind!"

He spread his long legs like a pair of scissors and caught a child between them and lifted him.

"Thou ruffian, thou!" he chuckled. "See how he fights! A true Rajput! Nay, beat me not. Some day thou too shalt bear a sword for England, great-grandson mine. Ai-ee! But I grow old."

"For England or the next one!"

"Nay! But for England!" said the Risaldar, setting the child down on his knee. "And thou too, hot-head. Before a week is past! Think you I called my sons and grandsons all together for the fun of it? Think you I rode here through the heat because I needed the exercise or to chatter like an ape or to stand in the doorway making faces at a Hindu woman or to watch thee do it? Here I am, and here I stay until yet more news comes!"

"Then are we to wait here? Are we to swelter in Siroeh, eating up our brother's hospitality, until thy messengers see fit to come and tell us that this scare of thine is past?"

"Nay!" said the Risaldar. "I said that I wait here! Return now to your own homes, each of you. But be in readiness. I am old, but I can ride still. I can round you up. Has any a better horse than mine? If he has, let him make exchange."

"There will be horses for the looting if this revolt of thine breaks out!"

"True! There will be horses for the looting! Well, I wait here then and, when the trouble comes, I can count on thirteen of my blood to carry swords behind me?"

"Aye, when the trouble comes!"

There was a chorus of assent, and the Risaldar arose to let his sons and grandsons file past him. He, who had beggared himself to give each one of them a start in life, felt a little chagrined that they should now refuse to exchange horses with him; but his eye glistened none the less at the sight of their stalwart frames and at the thought of what a fighting unit he could bring to serve the Raj.

"All, then, for England!" he exclaimed.

"Nay, all for thee!" said his eldest-born. "We fight on whichever side thou sayest!"

"Disloyal one!" growled the Risaldar with a scowl. But he grinned into his beard. "Well, to your homes, then—but be ready!"

I

The midnight jackals howled their discontent while heat-cracked India writhed in stuffy torment that was only one degree less than unendurable. Through the stillness and the blackness of the night came every now and then the high-pitched undulating wails of women, that no one answered—for, under that Tophet-lid of blackness, punctured by the low-hung, steel-white stars, men neither knew nor cared whose child had died. Life and hell-hot torture and indifference—all three were one.

There was no moon, nothing to make the inferno visible, except that here and there an oil lamp on some housetop glowed like a blood-spot against the blackness. It was a sensation, rather than sight or sound, that betrayed the neighborhood of thousands upon thousands of human beings, sprawling, writhing, twisting upon the roofs, in restless suffering.

There was no pity in the dry, black vault of heaven, nor in the bone-dry earth, nor in the hearts of men, during that hot weather of '57. Men waited for the threatened wrath to come and writhed and held their tongues. And while they waited in sullen Asiatic patience, through the restless silence and the smell—the suffocating, spice-fed, filth-begotten smell of India—there ran an undercurrent of even deeper mystery than India had ever known.

Priest-ridden Hanadra, that had seen the downfall of a hundred kings, watched through heat-wearied eyes for another whelming the blood-soaked, sudden flood that was to burst the dam of servitude and rid India of her latest horde of conquerors. But eight hundred yards from where her high brick walls lifted their age-scars in the stifling reek, gun-chains jingled in a courtyard, and, sharp-clicking on age-old flagstones, rose the ring of horses' feet.

Section Number One of a troop of Bengal Horse Artillery was waiting under arms. Sabered and grim and ready stood fifty of the finest men that England could produce, each man at his horse's head; and blacker even than the night loomed the long twelve-pounders, in tow behind their limbers. Sometimes a trace-chain jingled as a wheel-horse twitched his flank; and sometimes a man spoke in a low voice, or a horse stamped on the pavement; but they seemed like black graven images of war-gods, half-smothered in the reeking darkness. And above them, from a window that overlooked the courtyard, shone a solitary lamp that glistened here and there upon the sleek black guns and flickered on the saber-hilts, and deepened the already dead-black atmosphere of mystery.

From the room above, where the lamp shone behind gauze curtains came the sound of voices; and in the deepest, death-darkest shadow of the door below there stood a man on guard whose fingers clutched his sword-hilt and whose breath came heavily. He stood motionless, save for his heaving breast; between his fierce, black mustache and his up-brushed, two-pointed beard, his white teeth showed through parted lips. But he gave no other sign that he was not some Rajput princeling's image carved out of the night.

He was an old man, though, for all his straight back and military carriage. The night concealed his shabbiness; but it failed to hide the medals on his breast, one bronze, one silver, that told of campaigns already a generation gone. And his patience was another sign of age; a younger man of his blood and training would have been pacing to and fro instead of standing still.

He stood still even when footsteps resounded on the winding stair above and a saber-ferrule clanked from step to step. The gunners heard and stood squarely to their horses. There was a rustling and a sound of shifting feet, and, a "Whoa,—you!" to an irritated horse; but the Rajput stayed motionless until the footsteps reached the door. Then he took one step forward, faced about and saluted.

"Salaam, Bellairs sahib!" boomed his deep-throated voice, and Lieutenant Bellairs stepped back with a start into the doorway again—one hand on his sword-hilt. The Indian moved sidewise to where the lamplight from the room above could fall upon his face.

"Salaam, Bellairs sahib!" he boomed again.

Then the lieutenant recognized him.

"You, Mahommed Khan!" he exclaimed. "You old war-dog, what brought you here? Heavens, how you startled me! What good wind brought you?"

"Nay! It seems it was an ill wind, sahib!"

"What ill wind? I'm glad to see you!"

"The breath of rumor, sahib!"

"What rumor brought you?"

"Where a man's honor lies, there is he, in the hour of danger! Is all well with the Raj, sahib?"

"With the Raj? How d'you mean, Risaldar?"

Mahommed Khan pointed to the waiting guns and smiled.

"In my days, sahib," he answered, "men seldom exercised the guns at night!"

"I received orders more than three hours ago to bring my section in to Jundhra immediately—immediately—and not a word of explanation!"

"Orders, sahib? And you wait?"

"They seem to have forgotten that I'm married, and by the same token, so do you! What else could I do but wait? My wife can't ride with the section; she isn't strong enough, for one thing; and besides, there's no knowing what this order means; there might be trouble to face of some kind. I've sent into Hanadra to try to drum up an escort for her and I'm waiting here until it comes."

The Risaldar stroked at his beard reflectively.

"We of the service, sahib," he answered, "obey orders at the gallop when they come. When orders come to ride, we ride!"'

Bellairs winced at the thrust.

"That's all very fine, Risaldar. But how about my wife? What's going to happen to her, if I leave her here alone and unprotected?"

"Or to me, sahib? Is my sword-arm withered? Is my saber rusted home?"

"You, old friend! D'you mean to tell me—"

The Risaldar saluted him again.

"Will you stay here and guard her?"

"Nay, sahib! Being not so young as thou art, I know better!"

"What in Tophet do you mean, Mahommed Khan?"

"I mean, sahib,"—the Indian's voice was level and deep, but it vibrated strangely, and his eyes glowed as though war-lights were being born again behind them—"that not for nothing am I come! I heard what thy orders were and—"

"How did you hear what my orders were?"

"My half-brother came hurrying with the news, sahib. I hastened! My horse lies dead one kos from Hanadra here!"

The lieutenant laughed.

"At last, Mahommed? That poor old screw of yours? So he's dead at last, eh? So his time had come at last!"

"We be not all rich men who serve the Raj!" said the Risaldar with dignity. "Ay, sahib, his time was come! And when our time comes may thou and I, sahib, die as he did, with our harness on! What said thy orders, sahib? Haste? Then yonder lies the road, through the archway!"

"But, tell me, Risaldar, what brought you here in such a hurry?"

"A poor old screw, sahib, whose time was come—even as thou hast said!"

"Mahommed Khan, I'm sorry—very sorry, if I insulted you! I—I'm worried— I didn't stop to think. I—old friend, I—"

"It is forgotten, sahib!"

"Tell me—what are these rumors you have heard?"

"But one rumor, sahib—war! Uprising—revolution—treachery—all India waits the word to rise, sahib!"

"You mean—?"

"Mutiny among the troops, and revolution north, south, east and west!"

"Here, too, in Hanadra?"

"Here, too, in Hanadra, sahib! Here they will be among the first to rise!"

"Oh, come! I can't believe that! How was it that my orders said nothing of it then?"

"That, sahib, I know not—not having written out thy orders! I heard that thy orders came. I knew, as I have known this year past, what storm was brewing. I knew, too, that the heaven-born, thy wife, is here. I am thy servant, sahib, as I was thy father's servant—we serve one Queen; thy honor is my honor. Entrust thy memsahib to my keeping!"

"You will guard her?"

"I will bring her in to Jundhra!"

"You alone?"

"Nay, sahib! I, and my sons, and my sons' sons—thirteen men all told!"

"That is good of you, Mahommed Khan. Where are your sons?"

"Leagues from here, sahib. I must bring them. I need a horse."

"And while you are gone?"

"My half-brother, sahib—he is here for no other purpose—he will answer to me for her safety!"

"All right, Mahommed Khan, and thank you! Take my second charger, if you care to; he is a little saddle-sore, but your light weight—"

"Sahib—listen! Between here and Siroeh, where my eldest-born and his three sons live, lie seven leagues. And on from there to Lungra, where the others live, are three more leagues. I need a *horse* this night!"

"What need of thirteen men, Mahommed? You are sufficient by yourself, unless a rebellion breaks out. If it did, why, you and thirteen others would be swamped as surely as you alone!"

"Thy father and I, sahib, rode through the guns at Dera thirteen strong! Alone, I am an old man—not without honor, but of little use; with twelve young blades behind me, though, these Hindu rabble—"

"Do you really mean, Mahommed Khan, that you think Hanadra here will rise?"

"The moment you are gone, sahib!"

"Then, that settles it! The memsahib rides with me!"

"Nay, listen, sahib! Of a truth, thou art a hot-head as thy father was before thee! Thus will it be better. If the heavenborn, thy wife, stays behind, these rabble here will think that the section rides out to exercise, because of the great heat of the sun by day; they will watch for its return, and wait for the parking of the guns before they put torch to the mine that they have laid!"

"The mine? D'you mean they've—"

"Who knows, sahib? But I speak in metaphor. When the guns are parked again and the horses stabled and the men asleep, the rabble, being many, might dare anything!"

"You mean, you think that they—"

"I mean, sahib, that they will take no chances while they think the guns are likely to return!"

"But, if I take the memsahib with me?"

"They will know then, sahib, that the trap is open and the bird flown! Know you how fast news travels? Faster than the guns, Sahib! There will be an ambuscade, from which neither man, nor gun, nor horse, nor memsahib will escape!"

"But if you follow later, it will mean the same thing! When they see you ride off on a spent horse, with twelve swords and the memsahib—d'you mean that they won't ambuscade you?"

"They might, sahib—and again, they might not! Thirteen men and a woman ride faster than a section of artillery, and ride where the guns would jam hub-high against a tree-trunk! And thy orders, sahib—are thy orders nothing?"

"Orders! Yes, confound it! But they know I'm married. They know—"

"Sahib, listen! When the news came to me I was at Siroeh, dangling a great-grandson on my knee. There were no orders, but it seemed the Raj had need of me. I rode! Thou, sahib, hast orders. I am here to guard thy wife—my honor is thy honor—take thou the guns. Yonder lies the road!"

The grim old warrior's voice thrilled with the throb of loyalty, as he stood erect and pointed to the shadowy archway through which the road wound to the plain beyond.

"Sahib, I taught thy father how to use his sword! I nursed thee when thou wert little. Would I give thee false counsel now? Ride, sahib—ride!"

Bellairs turned away and looked at his charger, a big, brown Khaubuli stallion, named for the devil and true in temper and courage to his name; two men were holding him, ten paces off.

"Such a horse I need this night, Sahib! Thy second charger can keep pace with the guns!"

Bellairs gave a sudden order, and the men led the brute back into his stable.

"Change the saddle to my second charger!" he ordered.

Then he turned to the Risaldar again, with hand outstretched.

"I'm ashamed of myself, Mahommed Khan!" he said, with a vain attempt to smile. "I should have gone an hour ago! Please take my horse Shaitan, and make such disposition for my wife's safety as you see fit. Follow as and when you can; I trust you, and I shall be grateful to you whatever happens!"

"Well spoken, Sahib! I knew thou wert a man! We who serve the Raj have neither sons, nor wives, nor sweethearts! Allah guard you, Sahib! The section waits—and the Service can not wait!"

"One moment while I tell my wife!"

"Halt, sahib! Thou hast said good-by a thousand times! A woman's tears—are they heart-meat for a soldier when the bits are champing? Nay! See, sahib; they bring thy second charger! Mount! I will bring thy wife to Jundhra for thee! *The Service waits!*"

The lieutenant turned and mounted.

"Very well, Mahommed Khan!" he said. "I know you're right! Section! Prepare to mount!" he roared, and the stirrups rang in answer to him. "Mount! Good-by, Mahommed Khan! Good luck to you! Section, right! Trot, march!"

With a crash and the clattering of iron shoes on stone the guns jingled off into the darkness, were swallowed by the gaping archway and rattled out on the plain.

The Risaldar stood grimly where he was until the last hoof-beat and bump of gun-wheel had died away into the distance; then he turned and climbed the winding stairway to the room where the lamp still shone through gauzy curtains.

On a dozen roof-tops, where men lay still and muttered, brown eyes followed the movements of the section and teeth that were betel-stained grinned hideously.

From a nearby temple, tight-packed between a hundred crowded houses, came a wailing, high-pitched solo sung to Siva—the Destroyer. And as it died down to a quavering finish it was followed by a ghoulish laugh that echoed and reechoed off the age-old city-wall.

Proud as a Royal Rajput—and there is nothing else on God's green earth that is even half as proud—true to his salt, and stout of heart even if he was trembling at the knees, Mahommed Khan, two-medal man and Risaldar, knocked twice on the door of Mrs. Lellairs' room, and entered.

And away in the distance rose the red reflection of a fire ten leagues away. The Mutiny of '57 had blazed out of sullen mystery already, the sepoys were burning their barracks half-way on the road to Jundhra!

And down below, to the shadow where the Risaldar had stood, crept a giant of a man who had no military bearing. He listened once, and sneaked into the deepest black within the doorway and crouched and waited.

II

Hanadra reeks of history, blood-soaked and mysterious. Temples piled on the site of olden temples; palaces where half-forgotten kings usurped the thrones of conquerors who came from God knows where to conquer older kings; roads built on the bones of conquered armies; houses and palaces and subterranean passages that no man living knows the end of and few even the beginning. Dark corridors and colonnades and hollow walls; roofs that have ears and peep-holes; floors that are undermined by secret stairs; trees that have swayed with the weight of rotting human skulls and have shimmered with the silken bannerets of emperors. Such is Hanadra, half-ruined, and surrounded by a wall that was age-old in the dawn of written history.

Even its environs are mysterious; outside the walls, there are carven, gloomy palaces that once re-echoed to the tinkle of stringed instruments and the love-songs of some sultan's favorite—now fallen into ruins, or rebuilt to stable horses or shelter guns and stores and men; but eloquent in all their new-smeared whitewash, or in crumbling decay, of long-since dead intrigue. No places, those, for strong men to live alone in, where night-breezes whisper through forgotten passages and dry teak planking recreaks to the memory of dead men's footsteps.

But strong men are not the only makings of an Empire, nor yet the only sufferers. Wherever the flag of England flies above a distant outpost or droops in the stagnant moisture of an Eastern swamp, there are the graves of England's women. The bones that quarreling jackals crunch among the tombstones—the peace along the clean-kept borderline—the pride of race and conquest and the cleaner pride of work well done, these are not man's only. Man does the work, but he is held to it and cheered on by the girl who loves him.

And so, above a stone-flagged courtyard, in a room that once had echoed to the laughter of a sultan's favorite, it happened that an English girl of twenty-one was pacing back and forth. Through the open curtained window she had seen her husband lead his command out through the echoing archway to the plain beyond; she had heard his boyish voice bark out the command and had listened to the rumble of the gun-wheels dying in the distance—for the last time possibly. She knew, as many an English girl has known, that she was alone, one white woman amid a swarm of sullen Aryans, and that she must follow along the road the guns had taken, served and protected by nothing more than low-caste natives.

And yet she was dry-eyed, and her chin was high; for they are a strange breed, these Anglo-Saxon women who follow the men they love to the lonely danger-zone. Ruth Bellairs could have felt no joy in her position; she had heard her husband growling his complaint at being forced to leave her, and she guessed what her danger was. Fear must have shrunk her heartbeats and loneliness have tried her courage. But there was an ayah in the room with her, a low-caste woman of the conquered race; and pride of country came to her assistance. She was firm-lipped and, to outward seeming, brave as she was beautiful.

Even when the door resounded twice to the sharp blow of a saber-hilt, and the ayah's pock-marked ebony took on a shade of gray, she stood like a queen with an army at her back and neither blanched nor trembled.

"Who is that, ayah?" she demanded.

The ayah shrank into herself and showed the whites of her eyes and grinned, as a pariah dog might show its teeth—afraid, but scenting carrion.

"Go and see!"

The ayah shuddered and collapsed, babbling incoherencies and calling on a horde of long-neglected gods to witness she was innocent. She clutched strangely at her breast and used only one hand to drag her shawl around her face. While she babbled she glanced wild-eyed around the long, low-ceilinged room. Ruth Bellairs looked down at her pityingly and went to the door herself and opened it.

"Salaam, memsahib!" boomed a deep voice from the darkness.

Ruth Bellairs started and the ayah screamed.

"Who are you? Enter—let me see you!"

A black beard and a turban and the figure of a man—and then white teeth and a saber-hilt and eyes that gleamed moved forward from the darkness.

"It is I, Mahommed Khan!" boomed the voice again, and the Risaldar stepped out into the lamplight and closed the door behind him. Then, with a courtly, long-discarded sweep of his right arm, he saluted.

"At the heavenborn's service!"

"Mahommed Khan! Thank God!"

The old man's shabbiness was very obvious as he faced her, with his back against the iron-studded door; but he stood erect as a man of thirty, and his medals and his sword-hilt and his silver scabbard-tip were bright.

"Tell me, Mahommed Khan, you have seen my husband?"

He bowed.

"You have spoken to him?"

The old man bowed again.

"He left you in my keeping, heavenborn. I am to bring you safe to Jundhra!"

She held her hand out and he took it like a cavalier, bending until he could touch her fingers with his lips.

"What is the meaning of this hurrying of the guns to Jundhra, Risaldar?"

"Who knows, memsahib! The orders of the Sirkar come, and we of the service must obey. I am thy servant and the Sirkar's!"

"You, old friend—that were servant, as you choose to call it, to my husband's father! I am a proud woman to have such friends at call!" She pointed to the ayah, recovering sulkily and rearranging the shawl about her shoulders. "That I call service, Risaldar. She cowers when a knock comes at the door! I need you, and you answer a hardly spoken prayer; what is friendship, if yours is not?"

The Risaldar bowed low again.

"I would speak with that ayah, heavenborn!" he muttered, almost into his beard. She could hardly catch the words.

"I can't get her to speak to me at all to-night, Mahommed Khan. She's terrified almost out of her life at something. But perhaps you can do better. Try. Do you want to question her alone?"

"By the heavenborn's favor, yes."

Ruth walked down the room toward the window, drew the curtain back and leaned her head out where whatever breeze there was might fan her cheek. The Risaldar strode over to where the ayah cowered by an inner doorway.

"She-Hindu-dog!" he growled at her. "Mother of whelps! Louse-ridden scavenger of sweepings! What part hast thou in all this treachery? Speak!"

The ayah shrank away from him and tried to scream, but he gripped her by the throat and shook her.

"Speak!" he growled again.

But his ten iron fingers held her in a vise-like grip and she could not have answered him if she had tried to.

"O Risaldar!" called Ruth suddenly, with her head still out of the window. He released the ayah and let her tumble as she pleased into a heap.

"Heavenborn?"

"What is that red glow on the sky-line over yonder?"

"A burning, heavenborn!"

"A burning? What burning? Funeral pyres? It's very big for funeral pyres!"

"Nay, heavenborn!"

"What, then?"

She was still unfrightened, unsuspicious of the untoward. The Risaldar's arrival on the scene had quite restored her confidence and she felt content to ride with him to Jundhra on the morrow.

"Barracks, heavenborn!"

"Barracks? What barracks?"

"There is but one barracks between here and Jundhra."

"Then—then—then—what has happened, Mahommed Khan?"

"The worst has happened, heavenborn!"

He stood between her and the ayah, so that she could not see the woman huddled on the floor.

"The worst? You mean then—my—my—husband—you don't mean that my husband—"

"I mean, heavenborn that there is insurrection! All India is ablaze from end to end. These dogs here in Hanadra wait to rise because they think the section will return here in an hour or two; then they propose to burn it, men, guns and horses, like snakes in the summer grass. It is well that the section will not return! We will ride out safely before morning!"

"And, my husband—he knew—all this—before he left me here?"

"Nay! That he did not! Had I told him, he had disobeyed his orders and shamed his service; he is young yet, and a hothead! He will be far along the road to Jundhra before he knows what burns. And then he will remember that he trusts me and obey orders and press on!"

"And you knew and did not tell him!"

"Of a truth I knew!"

She stood in silence for a moment, gazing at the red glow on the sky-line, and then turned to read, if she could, what was on the grim, grizzled face of Mahommed Khan.

"The ayah!" he growled. "I have yet to ask questions of the ayah. Have I permission to take her to the other room?"

She was leaning through the window again and did not answer him.

"Who's that moving in the shadow down below?" she asked him suddenly.

He leaned out beside her and gazed into the shadow. Then he called softly in a tongue she did not know and some one rose up from the shadow and answered him.

"Are we spied on, Risaldar?"

"Nay. Guarded, heavenborn! That man is my half-brother. May I take the ayah through that doorway?"

"Why not question her in here?"

The mystery and sense of danger were getting the better of her; she was thoroughly afraid now—afraid to be left alone in the room for a minute even.

"There are things she would not answer in thy presence!"

"Very well. Only, please be quick!"

He bowed. Swinging the door open, he pushed the ayah through it to the room beyond. Ruth was left alone, to watch the red glow on the skyline and try to see the outline of the watcher in the gloom below. No sound came through the heavy teak door that the Risaldar had slammed behind him, and no sound came from him who watched; but from the silence of the night outside and from dark corners of the room that she was in and from the roof and walls and floor here came little eerie noises that made her flesh creep, as though she were being stared at by eyes she could not see. She felt that she must scream, or die, unless she moved; and she was too afraid to move, and by far too proud to scream! At last she tore herself away from the window and ran to a low divan and lay on it, smothering her face among the cushions. It seemed an hour before the Risaldar came out again, and then he took her by surprise.

"Heavenborn!" he said. She looked up with a start, to find him standing close beside her.

"Mahommed Khan! You're panting! What ails you?"

"The heat, heavenborn—and I am old."

His left hand was on his saber-hilt, thrusting it toward her respectfully; she noticed that it trembled.

"Have I the heavenborn's leave to lock the ayah in that inner room?"

"Why, Risaldar?"

"The fiend had this in her possession!" He showed her a thin-bladed dagger with an ivory handle; his own hand shook as he held it out to her, and she saw that there were beads of perspiration on his wrist. "She would have killed thee!"

"Oh, nonsense! Why, she wouldn't dare!"

"She confessed before she—she confessed! Have I the heavenborn's leave?"

"If you wish it."

"And to keep the key?"

"I suppose so, if you think it wise."

He strode to the inner door and locked it and hid the key in an inside pocket of his tunic.

"And now, heavenborn," he said, "I crave your leave to bring my half-brother to the presence!"

He scarcely waited for an answer, but walked to the window, leaned out of it and whistled. A minute later he was answered by the sound of fingernails scrabbling on the outer door. He turned the key and opened it.

"Enter!" he ordered.

Barefooted and ragged, but as clean as a soldier on parade and with huge knots of muscles bulging underneath his copper skin, a Rajput entered, bowing his six feet of splendid manhood almost to the floor.

"This, heavenborn, is my half-brother, son of a low-born border-woman, whom my father chose to honor thus far! The dog is loyal!"

"Salaam!" said Ruth, with little interest.

"Salaam, memsahib!" muttered the shabby Rajput. "Does any watch?" demanded the Risaldar in Hindustanee. "Aye, one."

"And he?"

"Is he of whom I spoke."

"Where watches he?"

"There is a hidden passage leading from the archway; he peeps out through a crack, having rolled back so far the stone that seals it." He held his horny fingers about an inch apart to show the distance.

"Couldst thou approach unseen?"

The Rajput nodded.

"And there are no others there?"

"No others."

"Has thy strength left thee, or thy cunning?"

"Nay!"

"Then bring him!"

Without a word in answer the giant turned and went, and the Risaldar made fast the door behind him. Ruth sat with her face between her hands, trying not to cry or shudder, but obsessed and overpowered by a sense of terror. The mystery that surrounded her was bad enough; but this mysterious ordering and coming to and fro among her friends was worse than horrible. She knew, though, that it would be useless to question Mahommed Khan before he chose to speak. They waited there in the dimly lighted room for what seemed tike an age again; she, pale and tortured by weird imaginings; he, grim and bolt-upright like a statue of a warrior. Then sounds came from the stairs again and the Risaldar hurried to the door and opened it.

In burst the Risaldar's half-brother, breathing heavily and bearing a load nearly as big as he was.

"The pig caught my wrist within the opening!" he growled, tossing his gagged and pinioned burden on the floor. "See where he all but broke it!"

"What is thy wrist to the service of the Raj? Is he the right one?"

"Aye!" He stooped and tore a twisted loin-cloth from his victim's face, and the Risaldar walked to the lamp and brought it, to hold it above the prostrate form. Ruth left the divan and stood between the men, terrified by she knew not what fear, but drawn into the lamplight by insuperable curiosity.

"This, heavenborn," said the Risaldar, prodding at the man with his scabbard-point, "is none other than the High Priest of Kharvani's temple here, the arch-ringleader in all the treachery afoot—now hostage for thy safety!"

He turned to his half-brother. "Unbind the thing he lies with!" he commanded, and the giant unwrapped a twisted piece of linen from the High Priest's mouth.

"So the big fox peeped through the trapdoor, because he feared to trust the other foxes; and the big fox fell into the trap!" grinned the Risaldar. "Bring me that table over yonder, thou!"

The half-brother did as he was told.

"Lay it here, legs upward, on the floor.

"Now, bind him to it—an arm to a leg and a leg to a leg.

"Remove his shoes.

"Put charcoal in yon brazier. Light it. Bring it hither!"

He seized a brass tongs, chose a glowing coal and held it six inches from the High Priest's naked foot.

Ruth screamed.

"Courage, heavenborn! Have courage! This is naught to what he would have done to thee! . . . Now, speak, thou priest of infidels! What plans are laid and who will rise and when?"

III

S ergeant!"
"Sir!"

The close-cropped, pipe-clayed non-commissioned officer spurred his horse into a canter until his scabbard clattered at young Bellairs' boot. Nothing but the rattling and the jolting of the guns and ammunition-wagon was audible, except just on ahead of them the click-clack, click-click-clack of the advance-guard. To the right and left of them the shadowy forms of giant banian-trees loomed and slid past them as they had done for the past four hours, and for ten paces ahead they could see the faintly outlined shape of the trunk road that they followed. The rest was silence and a pall of blackness obscuring everything. They had ridden along a valley, but they had emerged on rising ground and there was one spot of color in the pall now, or else a hole in it.

"What d'you suppose that is burning over there?"

"I couldn't say, sir."

"How far away is it?"

"Very hard to tell on a night like this, sir. It might be ten miles away and might be twenty. By my reckoning it's on our road, though, and somewhere between here and Jundhra."

"So it seems to me; our road swings round to the right presently, doesn't it? That'll lead us right to it. That would make it Doonha more or less. D'you suppose it's at Doonha?"

"I was thinking it might be, sir. If it's Doonha, it means that the sepoy barracks and all the stores are burning—there's nothing else there that would make all that flame!"

"There are two companies of the Thirty-third there, too."

"Yes, sir, but they're under canvas; tents would blaze up, but they'd die down again in a minute. That fire's steady and growing bigger!"

"It's the sepoy barracks, then!"

"Seems so to me, sir!"

"Halt!" roared Bellairs. The advance-guard kicked up a little shower of sparks, trace-chains slacked with a jingle and the jolting ceased. Bellairs rode up to the advance-guard.

"Now, Sergeant," he ordered, "it looks as though that were the Doonha barracks burning over yonder. There's no knowing, though, what it is. Send four men on, two hundred yards ahead of you, and you and the rest keep a good two hundred yards ahead of the guns. See that the men keep on the alert, and mind that they spare their horses as much as possible. If there's going to be trouble, we may just as well be ready for it!"

"Very good, sir!"

"Go ahead, then!"

At a word from the sergeant, four men clattered off and were swallowed in the darkness. A minute later the advance-guard followed them and then, after another minute's pause, young Bellairs' voice was raised into a ringing shout again.

"Section, advance! Trot, march!"

The trace-chains tightened, and the clattering, bumping, jingling procession began again, its rear brought up by the six-horse ammunition-wagon. They rode speechless for the best part of an hour, each man's eyes on the distant conflagration that had begun now to light up the whole of the sky ahead of them. They still rode in darkness, but they seemed to be approaching the red rim of the Pit. Huge, billowing clouds of smoke, red-lit on the under side, belched upward to the blackness overhead, and a something that was scarcely sound—for it was yet too distant—warned them that it was no illusion they were riding into. The conflagration grew. It seemed to be nearly white-hot down below.

Bellairs wet his finger and held it extended upward.

"There's no wind that I can feel!" he muttered. "And yet, if that were a grass-fire, there'd be game and rats and birds and things—some of 'em would bolt this way. That's the Doonha barracks burning or I'm a black man, which the Lord forbid!"

A minute later, every man in the section pricked up his ears. There was no order given; but a sensation ran the whole length of it and a movement from easy riding to tense rigidity that could be felt by some sixth sense. Every man was listening, feeling, groping with his senses for something he could neither hear as yet nor see, but that he knew was there. And then, far-distant yet—not above, but under the jolting of the gun-wheels and the rattle of the scabbards—they could hear the clickety-clickety-clickety-click of a horse hard-ridden.

They had scarcely caught that sound, they had barely tightened up their bridle-reins, when another sound, one just as unmistakable, burst out in front of them. A ragged, ill-timed volley ripped out from somewhere near the conflagration and was answered instantly by one that was close-ripped like the fire of heavy ordnance.

And then one of the advance-guard wheeled his horse and drove his spurs home rowel-deep. He came thundering back along the road with his scabbard out in the wind behind him and reined up suddenly when his horse's forefeet were abreast of the lieutenant.

"There's some one coming, sir, hard as he can gallop! He's one of our men by the sound of him. His horse is shod—and I thought I saw steel when the fire-light fell on him a minute ago!"

"Are you sure there's only one?"

"Sure, sir! You can hear him now!"

"All right! Fall in behind me!"

Bellairs felt his sword-hilt and cocked a pistol stealthily, but he gave no orders to the section. This might be a native soldier run amuck, and it might be a messenger; but in either case, friend or foe, if there was only one man he could deal with him alone.

"Halt!" roared the advance-guard suddenly. But the horse's hoof-beats never checked for a single instant.

"Halt, you! Who comes there?"

"Friend!" came the answer, in an accent that was unmistakable.

"What friend? Where are you going?"

One of the advance-guard reined his horse across the road. The others followed suit and blocked the way effectually. "Halt!" they roared in unison.

The main body of the advance came up with them.

"Who is he?" shouted the sergeant.

"We'll soon see! Here he comes!"

"Out of my way!" yelled a voice, as a foamed-flecked horse burst out of the darkness like an apparition and bore straight down on them—his head bored a little to one side, the red rims of his nostrils wide distended and his whole sense and energy, and strength concentrated on pleasing the speed-hungry Irishman who rode him. He flashed into them head-on, like a devil from the outer darkness. His head touched a man's knee—and he rose and tried to jump him! His breast crashed full into the obstruction and horse and gunner crashed down to the road.

A dozen arms reached out—twelve horses surged in a clattering mêlée—two hands gripped the reins and four arms seized the rider, and in a second the panting charger was brought up all-standing. The sergeant thrust his grim face closer and peered at their capture.

"Good ——, if it ain't an officer!" he exclaimed. "I beg your pardon, sir!"

And at that instant the section rattled, up behind them, with Bellairs in the lead.

"Halt!" roared Bellairs. "What's this?"

"Bloody murder, arson, high treason, mutiny and death! Blood and onions, man! Don't your men know an officer when they see one? Who are you? Are you Bellairs? Then why in God's name didn't you say so sooner? What have you waited for?

"How many hours is it since you got the message through from Jundhra? Couldn't you see the barracks burning? Who am I—I'm Captain O'Rourke, of the Thirty-third, sent to see what you're doing on the road, that's who I am! A full-fledged; able-bodied captain wasted in a crisis, just because you didn't choose to hurry! Poison take your confounded gunners, sir! Have they nothing better to engage them than holding up officers on the Queen's trunk road?"

"Supposing you tell me what's the matter?" suggested young Bellairs, prompt as are most of his breed to appear casual the moment there was cause to feel excited.

"Your —gunners have taken all my breath, sir. I can't speak!"

"You shouldn't take chances with a section of artillery! They're not like infantry— they don't sleep all the time—you can't ride through them as a rule!"

"Don't sleep, don't they! Then what have you been doing on the road? And what are you standing here for? Ride, man, ride! You're wanted!"

"Get out of the way, then!" suggested Bellairs, and Captain O'Rourke legged his panting charger over to the roadside.

"Advance-guard, forward, trot!" commanded the lieutenant.

"Have you brought your wife with you?" demanded O'Rourke, peering into the jingling blackness.

"No. Of course not. Why?"

"'Of course not! Why?' says the man! Hell and hot porridge! Why, the whole of India's ablaze from end to end—the sepoys have mutinied to a man, and the rest have joined them! There's bloody murder doing—they've shot their officers—Hammond's dead and Carstairs and Welfleet and heaven knows who else. They've burned their barracks and the stores and they're trying to seize the magazine. If they get that, God help every one. They're short of ammunition as it is, but two companies of the Thirty-third can't hold out for long against that horde. You'll be in the nick of time! Hurry, man! For the love of anything you like to name, get a move on!"

IV

Trot, march!
    "Canter!"

Bellairs was thinking of his wife, alone in Hanadra, unprotected except by a sixty-year-old Risaldar and a half-brother who was a civilian and an unknown quantity.

There were cold chills running down his spine and a sickening sensation in his stomach. He rode ahead of the guns, with O'Rourke keeping pace beside him. He felt that he hated O'Rourke, hated everything, hated the Service, and the country—and the guns, that could put him into such a fiendish predicament.

O'Rourke broke silence first.

"Who is with your wife?" he demanded suddenly.

"Heaven knows! I left her under the protection of Risaldar Mahommed Khan, but he was to ride off for an escort for her."

"Not your father's old Risaldar?" asked O'Rourke.

"The same."

"Then thank God! I'd sooner trust him than I would a regiment. He'll bring her in alive or slit the throats of half Asia—maybe he'll do both! Come, that's off our minds! She's safer with him than she would be here. Have you lots of ammunition?"

"I brought all I had with me at Hanadra."

"Good! What you'll need tonight is grape!"

"I've lots of it. It's nearly all grape."

"Hurrah! Then we'll treat those dirty mutineers to a dose or two of pills they won't fancy! Come on, man—set the pace a little faster!"

"Why didn't my orders say anything about a mutiny or bringing in my wife?"

"Dunno! I didn't write 'em. I can guess, though. There'd be something like nine reasons. For one thing, they'd credit you with sense enough to bring her in without being told. For another, the messenger who took the note might have got captured on the way—they wouldn't want to tell the sepoys more than they could help. Then there'd be something like a hurry. They're attacked there too—can't even send us assistance. Told us to waylay you and make use of you. Maybe they forgot your wife— maybe they didn't. It's a devil of a business anyhow!"

It was difficult to talk at the speed that they were making, with their own horses breathing heavily, O'Rourke's especially; the guns thundering along behind them and the advance-guard clattering in front, and their attention distracted every other minute by the noise of volleys on ahead and the occasional staccato rattle of independent firing. The whole sky was now alight with the reflection of the burning barracks and they could see the ragged outlines of the cracking walls silhouetted against the blazing red within. One mile or less from the burning buildings they could see, too, the occasional flash of rifles where the two companies of the Thirty-third, Honorable East India Company's Light Infantry, held out against the mutineers.

"Why did they mutiny?" asked Bellairs.

"God knows! Nobody knows! Nobody knows anything! I'm thinking—"

"Thinking *what?*"

"Forrester-Carter is commanding. We'll settle this business pretty quickly, now you've come. Then—Steady, boy! Steady! Hold up! This poor horse of mine is just about foundered, by the feel of him. He'll reach Doonha, though. Then we'll ask Carter to make a dash on Hanadra and bring Mrs. Bellairs—maybe we'll meet her and the Risaldar half-way—who knows? The sepoys wouldn't expect that, either. The move'd puzzle 'em—it'd be a good move, to my way of thinking."

"Let's hope Carter will consent!" prayed Bellairs fervently. "Now, what's the lay of things?"

"Couldn't tell you! When I left, our men were surrounded. I had to burst through the enemy to get away. Ours are all around the magazine and the sepoys are on every side of them. You'll have to use diagonal fire unless you want to hurt some of our chaps—sweep 'em cornerwise. There's high ground over to the right there, within four hundred yards of the position. Maybe they're holding it, though—there's no knowing!"

They could hear the roar of the flames now, and could see the figures of sepoys running here and there. The rattle of musketry was incessant. They could hear howls and yells and bugle-calls blown at random by the sepoys, and once, in answer as it seemed to a more than usually savage chorus from the enemy—a chorus that was punctuated by a raging din of intermittent rifle-fire—a ringing cheer.

"They must be in a tight hole!" muttered Bellairs. "Answer that, men! All together, now! Let 'em know we're coming."

The men rose in their stirrups all together, and sent roaring through the blackness the deep-throated "Hip-hip-hur-r-a-a-a-a-a!" that has gladdened more than one beleaguered British force in the course of history. It is quite different from the "Hur-o-a-o-a-u-r-rh" of a forlorn hope, or the high-pitched note of pleasure that signals the end of a review. It means "Hold on, till we get there, boys!" and it carries its meaning, clear and crisp and unmistakable, in its note.

The two beleaguered companies heard it and answered promptly with another cheer.

"By gad, they must be in a hole!" remarked Bellairs.

British soldiers do not cheer like that, all together, unless there is very good reason to feel cheerless. They fight, each man according to his temperament, swearing or laughing, sobbing or singing comic songs, until the case looks grim. Then, though, the same thrill runs through the whole of them, the same fire blazes in their eyes, and the last ditch that they line has been known to be a grave for the enemy.

"Trumpeter! Sound close-order!"

The trumpet rang. The advance-guard drew rein for the section to catch up. The guns drew abreast of one another and the mounted gunners formed in a line, two deep, in front of them. The ammunition-wagon trailed like a tail behind.

"That high ground over there, I think!" suggested O'Rourke.

"Thank you, sir. Section, right! Trot, march! Canter!"

Crash went the guns and the following wagon across the roadside ditch. The tired horses came up to the collar as service-horses always will, generous to the last ounce of strength they have in them.

"Gallop!"

The limbers bumped and jolted and the short-handled whips cracked like the sound of pistol-practise. Blind, unreconnoitered, grim—like a black thunderbolt loosed into the blackness—the two guns shot along a hollow, thundered up a ridge and burst into the fire-light up above the mutineers, in the last place where any one expected them. A howl came from the road that they had left, a hundred sepoys had rushed down to block their passage the moment that their cheer had rung above the noise of battle.

"Action—front!" roared young Bellairs, and the muzzles swung round at the gallop, jerked into position by the wheeling teams.

"With case, at four hundred!"

The orders were given and obeyed almost before the guns had lost their motion. The charges had been rammed into the greedy muzzles before the horses were away, almost—and that takes but a second—the horses vanish like blown smoke when the game begins. A howl from the mutineers told that they were seen; a volley from the British infantry announced that they were yet in time; and "boom-boom!" went both guns together.

The grapeshot whined and shrieked, and the ranks of the sepoys wilted, mown down as though a scythe had swept them. Once, and once only, they gathered for a charge on the two guns; but they were met half-way up the rise by a shrieking blast of grape that ripped through them and took the heart out of them; and the grape was followed by well-aimed volleys from behind. Then they drew off to sulk and make fresh plans at a distance, and Bellairs took his section unmolested into the Thirty-third-lined rampart round the magazine.

"What kept you, sir?" demanded Colonel Forrester-Carter, nodding to him in answer to his salute and holding out his right arm while a sergeant bandaged it.

"My wife, sir—I—"

"Where is she? Didn't you bring her?"

"No, sir—I—"

"Where is she?"

"Still at Hanadra, sir—I—"

"Let the men fall in! Call the roll at once!"

"There was nothing in my orders, sir, about—" But Colonel Carter cut him short with a motion and turned his back on him.

"Much obliged, Sergeant," he said, slipping his wounded arm into an improvised sling. "How many wagons have we here?"

"Four, sir."

"And horses?"

"All shot dead except your charger, sir."

"Oh! Ask Captain Trevor to come here."

The sergeant disappeared into the shadows, and a moment later Captain Trevor came running up and saluted.

"There are seven wounded, sir, and nineteen dead," he reported.

"Better than I had hoped, Trevor! Will you set a train to that magazine, please, and blow it up the moment we are at a safe distance?"

Trevor seemed surprised, but he saluted and said nothing.

"O'Rourke! Please see about burying the dead at once. Mr. Bellairs, let me have two horses, please, and their drivers, from each gun. Sergeant! See about putting the wounded into the lightest of the wagons and harness in four gun-horses the best way you can manage."

"Very good, sir."

"Which is your best horseman, Mr. Bellairs? Is his horse comparatively fresh? I'll need him to gallop with a message. I'll dictate it to Captain O'Rourke as soon as he is ready. Let the gunner stay here close to me."

Bellairs sought out his best man and the freshest-seeming horse in wondering silence. He felt sick with anxiety, for what could one lone veteran Risaldar do to protect Mrs. Bellairs against such a horde as was in Hanadra? He looked at the barracks, which were still blazing heavenward and illuminating the whole country-side, and shuddered as he wondered whether his quarters at Hanadra were in flames yet.

"It's a good job old Carter happened to be here!" he heard one of his men mumble to another. "He's a man, that is—I'd sooner fight under him than any I know of!"

"What d'you suppose the next move is?" asked the other man.

"I'd bet on it! I'll bet you what you like that—"

But Bellairs did not hear the rest.

A bugle rang out into the night. The gunners stood by their horses. Even the sentries, posted outside the rampart to guard against alarm, stood to attention, and

Colonel Carter, wincing from the pain in his right arm, walked out in front of where the men were lined up.

Captain O'Rourke walked up and saluted him.

"I've arranged to bury them in that trench we dug this evening, sir, when the trouble started. It's not very deep, but it holds them all. I've laid them in it."

"Are you sure they're all dead?"

"I've burnt their fingers with matches, sir. I don't know of any better way to make sure."

"Very well. Can you remember any of the burial service?"

"'Fraid not, sir."

"Um! That's a pity. And I'm afraid I can't spare the time. Take a firing-party, Captain O'Rourke, and give them the last honors, at all events."

A party marched away toward the trench, and several minutes later O'Rourke's voice was heard calling through the darkness, "All ready, sir!"

"Present arms!" ordered the colonel, and the gunners sat their horses with their hilts raised to their hips and the two long lines of infantry stood rigid at the general salute, while five volleys—bulleted—barked upward above the grave. They were, answered by sniping from the mutineers, who imagined that reprisals had commenced.

"Now, men!" said Colonel Carter, raising his voice until every officer and man along the line could hear him, "as you must have realized, things are very serious indeed. We are cut off from support, but now that the guns are here to help us, we could either hold out here until relieved or else fight our way into Jundhra, where I have no doubt we are very badly needed. But"——he spoke more slowly and distinctly now, with a distinct pause between each word—"there is an officer's lady alone, and practically unprotected at Hanadra. Our duty is clear. You are tired—I know it. You have had no supper, and will get none. It means forced marching for the rest of this night and a good part of tomorrow and more fighting, possibly on an empty stomach; it means the dust and the heat and the discomfort of the trunk road for all of us and danger of the worst kind instead of safety—for we shall have farther to go to reach Jundhra. But I would do the same, and you men all know it, for any soldier's wife in my command, or any English woman in India. We will march now on Hanadra. No! No demonstrations, please!"

His uplifted left hand was just in time to check a roar of answering approval.

"Didn't I tell you so?" exclaimed a gunner to the man beside him in an undertone. "Him leave a white woman to face this sort o' music? He'd fight all India first!"

Ten minutes later two companies of men marched out behind the guns, followed by a cart that bore their wounded. As they reached the trunk road they were saluted by a reverberating blast when the magazine that they had fought to hold blew skyward.

They turned to cheer the explosion and then settled down to march in deadly earnest and, if need be, to fight a rear-guard action all the way.

And in the opposite direction one solitary gunner rode, hell-bent-for-leather, with a note addressed to "O. C.—Jundhra." It was short and to the point. It ran:

Have blown up magazine; Mrs. Bellairs at Hanadra; have gone to rescue her.
(Signed) A. FORRESTER-CARTER (Col.)
per J. O'Rourke

V

The red glow of barracks burning—an ayah from whom a dagger has been taken locked in another room—the knowledge that there are fifty thousand Aryan brothers, itching to rebel, within a stone's throw—and two lone protectors of an alien race intent on torturing a High Priest, each and every one of these is a disturbing feature. No woman, and least of all a young woman such as Ruth Bellairs, can be blamed for being nervous under the stress of such conditions or for displaying a certain amount of feminine unreasonableness.

She stood shivering for a minute and watched spellbound while Mahommed Khan held the hot coal closer and even closer to the High Priest's naked foot. The priest writhed in anticipation of the agony and turned his eyes away, and as he turned them they met Ruth's. High priests of a religion that includes sooth-saying and prophecy and bribery of gods among its rites are students of human nature, and especially of female human nature. Knowledge of it and of how it may be gulled, and when, is the first essential of their calling. Her pale face, her blue eyes strained in terror, the parted lips and the attitude of tension, these gave him an idea. Before the charcoal touched him, he screamed—screamed like a wounded horse.

"Mahommed Khan, stop! Stop this instant! I won't have it! I won't have my life, even, on those terms! D'you hear me, sir!"

"Have courage, heavenborn! There is but one way to force a Hindu priest, unless it be by cutting off his revenues—he must be hurt! This dog is unhurt as yet—see! The fire has not yet touched his foot!"

"Don't let it, Mahommed Khan! Set that iron down! This is my room. I will not have crime committed here!"

"And how long does the heavenborn think it would be her room were this evil-living pig of a priest at large, or how long before a worse crime were committed? Heavenborn, the hour is late and the charcoal dies out rapidly when it has left the fire! See. I must choose another piece!"

He rummaged in the brazier, and she screamed again.

"I will not have it, Risaldar! You must find another way."

"Memsahib! Thy husband left thee in my care. Surely it is my right to choose the way?"

"Leave me, then! I relieve you of your trust. I will not have him tortured in my room, or anywhere!"

Mahommed Khan bowed low.

"Under favor, heavenborn," he answered, "my trust is to your husband. I can be released by him, or by death, not otherwise."

"Once, and for all, Mahommed Khan, I will not have you torture him in here!"

"Memsahib, I have yet to ride for succor! At daybreak, when these Hindus learn that the guns will not come back, they will rise to a man. Even now we must find a hiding-place or—it is not good even to think what I might find on my return!"

He leaned over the priest again, but without the charcoal this time.

"Speak, thou!" he ordered, growling in Hindustanee through his savage black mustache. "I have yet to hear what price a Hindu sets on immunity from torture!"

But the priest, it seemed, had formed a new idea. He had been looking through puckered eyes at Ruth, keen, cool calculation in his glance, and in spite of the discomfort of his strained position he contrived to nod.

"Kharvani!" he muttered, half aloud.

"Aye! Call on Kharvani!" sneered the Risaldar. "Perhaps the Bride of Sivi will appear! Call louder!"

He stirred again among the charcoal with his tongs, and Ruth and the High Priest both shuddered.

"Look!" said the High Priest in Hindustanee, nodding in Ruth's direction. It was the first word that he had addressed to them. It took them by surprise, and the Risaldar and his half-brother turned and looked. Their breath left them.

Framed in the yellow lamplight, her thin, hot-weather garments draped about her like a morning mist, Ruth stood and stared straight back at them through frightened eyes. Her blue-black hair, which had become loosened in her excitement, hung in a long plait over one shoulder and gleamed in the lamp's reflection. Her skin took on a faintly golden color from the feeble light, and her face seemed stamped with fear, anxiety, pity and suffering, all at once, that strangely enhanced her beauty, silhouetted as she was against the blackness of the wall behind, she seemed to be standing in an aura, shimmering with radiated light.

"Kharvani!" said the High Priest to himself again, and the two Rajputs stood still like men dumfounded, and stared and stared and stared. They knew Kharvani's temple. Who was there in Hanadra, Christian or Mohammedan or Hindu, who did not? The show-building of the city, the ancient, gloomy, wonderful erection where bats lived in the dome and flitted round Kharvani's image, the place where every one must go who needed favors of the priests, the central hub of treason and intrigue, where every plot was hatched and every rumor had its origin—the ultimate, mazy, greedy, undisgorging goal of every bribe and every blackmail-wrung rupee!

They knew, too, as every one must know who has ever been inside the place, the amazing, awe-inspiring picture of Kharvani painted on the inner wall; of Kharvani as she was idealized in the days when priests believed in her and artists thought the labor of a lifetime well employed in painting but one picture of her—Kharvani the sorrowful, grieving for the wickedness of earth; Kharvani, Bride of Siva, ready to intercede with Siva, the Destroyer, for the helpless, foolish, purblind sons of man.

And here, before them, stood Kharvani—to the life!

"What of Kharvani?" growled Mahommed Khan.

"'A purblind fool, a sot and a Mohammedan,'" quoted the priest maliciously, "'how many be they, three or one?'"

The Risaldar's hand went to his scabbard. His sword licked out free and trembled like a tuning-fork. He flicked with his thumb-nail at the blade and muttered: "Sharp! Sharp as death itself!"

The Hindu grinned, but the blade came down slowly until the point of it rested on the bridge of his nose. His eyes squinted inward, watching it.

"Now, make thy gentle joke again!" growled the Risaldar.

Ruth Bellairs checked a scream.

"No blood!" she exclaimed. "Don't hurt him, Risaldar! I'll not have you kill a man in here—or anywhere, in cold blood, for that matter! Return your sword, sir!"

The Risaldar swore into his beard. The High Priest grinned again. "I am not afraid to die!" he sneered. "Thrust with that toy of thine! Thrust home and make an end!"

"Memsahib!" said the Risaldar, "all this is foolishness and waste of time! The hour is past midnight and I must be going. Leave the room—leave me and my half-brother with this priest for five short minutes and we will coax from him the secret of some hiding-place where you may lie hid until I come!"

"But you'll hurt him!"

"Not if he speaks, and speaks the truth!"

"Promise me!"

"On those conditions—yes!"

"Where shall I go?"

The Risaldar's eyes glanced toward the door of the inner room, but he hesitated. "Nay! There is the ayah!" he muttered. "Is there no other room?"

"No, Risaldar, no other room except through that door. Besides, I would rather stay here! I am afraid of what you may do to that priest if I leave you alone with him!"

"Now a murrain on all women, black and white!" swore Mahommed Khan beneath his breath. Then he turned on the priest again, and placed one foot on his stomach.

"Speak!" he ordered. "What of Kharvani?"

"Listen, Mahommed Khan!" Ruth Bellairs laid one hand on his sleeve, and tried to draw him back. "Your ways are not my ways! You are a soldier and a gentleman, but please remember that you are of a different race! I can not let my life be saved by the torture of a human being—no, not even of a Hindu priest! Maybe it's all right and honorable according to your ideas; but, if you did it, I would never be able to look my husband in the face again! No, Risaldar! Let this priest go, or leave him here—I don't care which, but don't harm him! I am quite ready to ride with you, now, if you like. I suppose you have horses? But I would rather die than think that a man was put to the torture to save me! Life isn't worth that price!"

She spoke rapidly, urging him with every argument she knew; but the grim old Mohammedan shook his head.

"Better die here," he answered her, "than on the road! No, memsahib. With thirteen blades behind me, I could reach Jundhra, or at least make a bold attempt; but single-handed, and with you to guard, the feat is impossible. This dog of a Hindu here knows of some hiding-place. Let him speak!"

His hand went to his sword again, and his eyes flashed.

"Listen, heavenborn! I am no torturer of priests by trade! It is not my life that I would save!"

"I know that, Mahommed Khan! I respect your motive. It's the method that I can't tolerate."

The Risaldar drew his arm away from her and began to pace the room. The High Priest instantly began to speak to Ruth, whispering to her hurriedly in Hindustanee, but she was too little acquainted with the language to understand him.

"And I," said the Risaldar's half-brother suddenly, "am I of no further use?"

"I had forgotten thee!" exclaimed the Risaldar.

They spoke together quickly in their own language, drawing aside and muttering to each other. It was plain that the half-brother was making some suggestion and that the Risaldar was questioning him and cross-examining him about his plan, but neither Ruth nor the High Priest could understand a word that either of them said. At the end of two minutes or more, the Risaldar gave an order of some kind and the half-brother grunted and left the room without another word, closing the door noiselessly behind him. The Risaldar locked it again from the inside and drew the bolt.

"We have made another plan, heavenborn!" he announced mysteriously.

"Then—then—you won't hurt this priest?"

"Not yet," said the Risaldar. "He may be useful!"

"Won't you unbind him, then? Look! His wrists and ankles are all swollen."

"Let the dog swell!" he grunted.

But Ruth stuck to her point and made him loosen the bonds a little.

"A man lives and learns!" swore the Risaldar. "Such as he were cast into dungeons in my day, to feed on their own bellies until they had had enough of life!"

"The times have changed!" said Ruth.

The Risaldar looked out through the window toward the red glow on the sky-line.

"Ha! Changed, have they!" he muttered. "I saw one such burning, once before!"

VI

The most wonderful thing in history, pointing with the surest finger to the trail of destiny, has been the fact that in every tremendous crisis there have been leaders on the spot to meet it. It is not so wonderful that there should be such men, for the world keeps growing better, and it is more than likely that the men who have left their footprints in the sands of time would compare to their own disadvantage with their compeers of to-day. The wonderful thing is that the right men have been in the right place at the right time. Scipio met Hannibal; Philip of Spain was forced to meet Howard of Effingham and Drake; Napoleon Bonaparte, the "Man of Destiny," found Wellington and Nelson of the Nile to deal with him; and, in America, men like George Washington and Grant and Lincoln seem, in the light of history, like timed, calculated, controlling devices in an intricate machine.

It was so when the Indian Mutiny broke out. The struggle was unexpected. A handful of Europeans, commissioned and enlisted in the ordinary way, with a view to trade, not statesmanship, found themselves face to face at a minute's notice with armed and vengeful millions. Succor was a question of months, not days or weeks. India was ablaze from end to end with rebel fires that had been planned in secret through silent watchful years. The British force was scattered here and there in unconnected details, and each detail was suddenly cut off from every other one by men who had been trained to fight by the British themselves and who were not afraid to die.

The suddenness with which the outbreak came was one of the chief assets of the rebels, for they were able to seize guns and military stores and ammunition at the very start of things, before the British force could concentrate. Their hour could scarcely have been better chosen. The Crimean War was barely over. Practically the whole of England's standing army was abroad and decimated by battle and disease. At home, politics had England by the throat; the income-tax was on a Napoleonic scale and men were more bent on worsting one another than on equipping armies. They had had enough of war.

India was isolated, at the rebels' mercy, so it seemed. There were no railway trains to make swift movements of troops possible. Distances were reckoned by the hundred miles—of sun-baked, thirsty dust in the hot weather, and of mud in the rainy season. There were no telegraph-wires, and the British had to cope with the mysterious, and even yet unsolved, native means of sending news—the so-called "underground route," by which news and instructions travel faster than a pigeon flies. There was never a greater certainty or a more one-sided struggle, at the start. The only question seemed to be how many days, or possibly weeks, would pass before jackals crunched the bones of every Englishman in India.

But at the British helm was Nicholson, and under him were a hundred other men whose courage and resource had been an unknown quantity until the outbreak came. Nicholson's was the guiding spirit, but it needed only his generalship to fire all the others with that grim enthusiasm that has pulled Great Britain out of so many other scrapes. Instead of wasting time in marching and countermarching to relieve the scattered posts, a swift, sudden swoop was made on Delhi, where the eggs of the rebellion had hatched.

As many of the outposts as could be reached were told to fight their own way in, and those that could not be reached were left to defend themselves until the big blow had been struck at the heart of things. If Delhi could be taken, the rebels would be paralyzed and the rescue of beleaguered details would be easier; so, although odds of one hundred or more to one are usually considered overlarge in wartime—when the hundred hold the fort and the one must storm the gate—there was no time lost in hesitation. Delhi was the goal; and from north and south and east and west the men who could march marched, and those who could not entrenched themselves, and made ready to die in the last ditch.

Some of the natives were loyal still. There were men like Risaldar Mahommed Khan, who would have died ten deaths ten times over rather than be false in one particular to the British Government. It was these men who helped to make intercommunication possible, for they could carry messages and sometimes get through unsuspected where a British soldier would have been shot before he had ridden half a mile. Their loyalty was put to the utmost test in that hour, for they can not have believed that the British force could win. They knew the extent of what was out against them and knew, too, what their fate would be in the event of capture or defeat. There would be direr, slower vengeance wreaked on them than on the alien British. But they had eaten British salt and pledged their word, and nothing short of death could free them from it. There was not a shred of self interest to actuate them; there could not have been. Their given word was law and there it ended.

There were isolated commands, like that at Jundhra, that were too far away to strike at Delhi and too large and too efficient to be shut in by the mutineers. They were centers on their own account of isolated small detachments, and each commander was given leave to act as he saw best, provided that he acted and did it quickly. He could either march to the relief of his detachments or call them in, but under no condition was he to sit still and do nothing.

So, Colonel Carter's note addressed to O. C.—Jundhra only got two-thirds of the way from Doonha. The gunner who rode with it was brought to a sudden standstill by an advance-guard of British cavalry, and two minutes later he found himself saluting and giving up his note to the General Commanding. The rebels at Jundhra had been worsted and scattered after an eight-hour fight, and General Turner had made up his mind instantly to sweep down on Hanadra with all his force and relieve the British garrison at Doonha on his way.

Jundhra was a small town and unhealthy. Hanadra was a large city, the center of a province; and, from all accounts, Hanadra had not risen yet. By seizing Hanadra before the mutineers had time to barricade themselves inside it, he could paralyze the countryside, for in Hanadra were the money and provisions and, above all, the Hindu priests who, in that part of India at least, were the brains of the rebellion. So he burned Jundhra, to make it useless to the rebels, and started for Hanadra with every man and horse and gun and wagon and round of ammunition that he had.

Now news in India travels like the wind, first one way and then another. But, unlike the wind, it never whistles. Things happen and men know it and the information spreads—invisible, intangible, inaudible, but positive and, in nine cases out of ten, correct in detail. A government can no more censor it, or divert it, or stop it on the way, than it can stay the birthrate or tamper with the Great Monsoon.

First the priests knew it, then it filtered through the main bazaars and from them on through the smaller streets. By the time that General Turner had been two hours on the road with his command every man and woman and child in Hanadra knew that the rebels had been beaten back and that Hanadra was his objective. They knew, too, that the section had reached Doonha, had relieved it and started back again. And yet not a single rebel who had fought in either engagement was within twenty miles of Hanadra yet!

In the old, low-ceilinged room above the archway Mahommed Khan paced up and down and chewed at his black mustache, kicking his scabbard away from him each time he turned and glowering at the priest.

"That dog can solve this riddle!" he kept muttering. Then he would glare at Ruth impatiently and execrate the squeamishness of women. Ruth sat on the divan with her face between her hands, trying to force herself to realize the full extent of her predicament and beat back the feeling of hysteria that almost had her in its grip. The priest lay quiet. He was in a torture of discomfort on the upturned table, but he preferred not to give the Risaldar the satisfaction of knowing it. He eased his position quietly from time to time as much as his bandages would let him, but he made no complaint.

Suddenly, Ruth looked up. It had occurred to her that she was wasting time and that if she were to fight off the depression that had seized her she would be better occupied.

"Mahommed Khan," she said, "if I am to leave here on horseback, with you or with an escort, I had better collect some things that I would like to take with me. Let me in that room, please!"

"The horse will have all that it can carry, heavenborn, without a load of woman's trappings."

"My jewels? I can take them, I suppose?"

He bowed. "They are in there? I will bring them, heavenborn!"

"Nonsense! You don't know where to find them."

"The ayah—will—will show me!"

He fitted the key into the lock and turned it, but Ruth was at his side before he could pass in through the door.

"Nonsense, Risaldar! The ayah can't hurt me. You have taken her knife away, and that is my room. I *will* go in there alone!"

She pushed past him before he could prevent her, thrust the door back and peered in.

"Stay, heavenborn—I will explain!"

"Explain what?"

The dim light from the lamp was filtering in past them, and her eyes were slowly growing accustomed to the gloom. There was something lying on the floor, in the middle of the room, that was bulky and shapeless and unfamiliar.

"Ayah!" said Ruth. "Ayah!"

But there was no answer.

"Where is she, Risaldar?"

"She is there, heavenborn!"

"Is she asleep?"

"Aye! She sleeps deeply!"

There was, something in the Rajput's voice that was strange, that hinted at a darker meaning.

"Ayah!" she called again, afraid, though she knew not why, to enter.

"She guards the jewels, heavenborn! Wait, while I bring the lamp!"

He crossed the room, brought it and stepped with it past Ruth, straight into the room.

"See!" he said, holding the lamp up above his head. "There in her bosom are the jewels! It was there, too, that she had the knife to slay thee with! My sword is clean, yet, heavenborn! I slew her with my fingers, thus!"

He kicked the prostrate ayah, and, as the black face with the wide-open bloodshot eyes and the protruding tongue rolled sidewise and the body moved, a little heap of jewels fell upon the floor. Mahommed Khan stooped down to gather them, bending, a little painfully, on one old knee—but stopped half-way and turned. There was a thud behind him in the doorway. Ruth Bellairs had fainted, and lay as the ayah had lain when Risaldar had not yet locked her in the room.

He raised the lamp and studied her in silence for a minute, looking from her to the bound priest and back to her again.

"Now praised be Allah!" he remarked aloud, with a world of genuine relief in his voice. "Should she stay fainted for a little while, that priest—"

He stalked into the middle of the outer room. He set the lamp down on a table and looked the priest over as a butcher might survey a sheep he is about to kill.

"Now—robber of orphans—bleeder of widows' blood—dog of an idol-briber! This stands between thee and Kharvani!" He drew his sword and flicked the edges of it. "And this!" He took up the tongs again. "There is none now to plead or to forbid! Think! Show me the way out of this devil's nest, or—" He raised the tongs again.

At that minute came a quiet knock. He set the tongs down again and crossed the room and opened the door.

VII

Mahommed Khan closed the door again behind his half-brother and turned the key, but the half-brother shot the bolt home as well before he spoke, then listened intently for a minute with his ear to the keyhole.

"Where is the priest's son?" growled the Risaldar, in the Rajput tongue.

"I have him. I have the priestling in a sack. I have him trussed and bound and gagged, so that he can neither speak nor wriggle!"

"Where?"

"Hidden safely."

"I said to bring him here!"

"I could not. Listen! That ayah—where is she?"

"Dead! What has the ayah to do with it?"

"This—she was to give a sign. She was not to slay. She had leave only to take the jewels. Her orders were either to wait until she knew by questioning that the section would not return or else, when it had returned, to wait until the memsahib and Bellairs sahib slept, and then to make a sign. They grow tired of waiting now, for there is news! At Jundhra the rebels are defeated, and at Doonha likewise."

"How know you this?"

"By listening to the priests' talk while I lay in wait to snare the priestling. Nothing is known as yet as to what the guns or garrison at Doonha do, but it is known that they of Jundhra will march on Hanadra here. They search now for their High Priest, being minded to march out of here and set an ambush on the road."

"They have time. From Jundhra to here is a long march! Until tomorrow evening or the day following they have time!"

"Aye! And they have fear also! They seek their priest—listen."

There were voices plainly audible in the courtyard down below, and two more men stood at the foot of the winding stairway whispering. By listening intently they could hear almost what they said, for the stone stairway acted like a whispering-gallery, the voices echoing up it from wall to wall.

"Why do they seek him here?"

"They have sought elsewhere and not found him; and there is talk—He claimed the memsahib as his share of the plunder. They think—"

Mahommed Khan glared at the trussed-up priest and swore a savage oath beneath his breath.

"Have they touched the stables yet?" he demanded.

"No, not yet. The loot is to be divided evenly among certain of the priests, and no man may yet lay a hand on it."

"Is there a guard there?"

"No. No one would steal what the priests claim, and the priests will not trust one another. So the horses stand in their stalls unwatched."

The voices down the stairs grew louder, and the sound of footsteps began ascending, slowly and with hesitation.

"Quick!" said the Risaldar. "Light me that brazier again!"

Charcoal lights quickly, and before the steps had reached the landing Mahommed Khan had a hot coal glowing in his tongs.

"Now speak to them!" he growled at the shuddering priest. "Order them to go back to their temple and tell them that you follow!"

The priest shut his lips tight and shook his head. With rescue so near as that, he could see no reason to obey. But the hot coal touched him, and a Hindu who may be not at all afraid to die can not stand torture.

"I speak!" he answered, writhing.

"Speak, then!" said the Risaldar, choosing a larger coal.

Then, in the priest's language, which none—and least of all a Risaldar—can understand except the priests themselves, he began to shout directions, pitching his voice into a high, wailing, minor key. He was answered by another sing-song voice outside the door and he listened with a glowing coal held six inches from his eyes.

"An eye for a false move!" hissed Mahommed Khan. "Two eyes are the forfeit unless they go down the stairs again! Then my half-brother here will follow to the temple and if any watch, or stay behind, thy ears will sizzle!"

The High Priest raised his voice into a wail again, and the feet shuffled along the landing and descended.

"Put down that coal!" he pleaded. "I have done thy bidding!"

"Watch through the window!" said the Risaldar. "Then follow!"

His giant half-brother peered from behind the curtain and listened. He could hear laughter, ribald, mocking laughter, but low, and plainly not intended for the High Priest's ears.

"They go!" he growled.

"Then follow."

Once again the Risaldar was left alone with the priest and the unconscious Ruth. She was suffering from the effects of long days and nights of nerve-destroying heat, with the shock of unexpected horror super-added, and she showed no disposition to recover consciousness. The priest, though, was very far from having lost his power to think.

"You are a fool!" he sneered at the Risaldar, but the sword leaped from its scabbard at the word and he changed that line of argument. "You hold cards and know not how to play them!"

"I know along which road my honor lies! I lay no plans to murder people in their sleep."

"Honor! And what is honor? What is the interest on honor—how much percent?"

The Risaldar turned his back on him, but the High Priest laughed.

"The days of the Raj are numbered!" said the priest. "The English will be slain to the last man and then where will you be? Where will be the profit on your honor?"

The Risaldar listened, for he could not help it, but he made no answer.

"Me you hold here, a prisoner. You can slay or torture. But what good will that do? The woman that you guard will fall sooner or later into Hindu hands. You can not fight against a legion. Listen! I hold the strings of wealth. With a jerk I can unloose a fortune in your lap. I need that woman there!"

"For what?" snarled the Risaldar, whirling round on him, his eyes ablaze.

"For power! Kharvani's temple here has images and paintings and a voice that speaks—but no Kharvani!"

The Rajput turned away again and affected unconcern.

"Could Kharvani but appear, could her worshipers but see Kharvani manifest, what would a lakh, two lakhs, a crore of rupees mean to me, the High Priest of her temple? I could give thee anything! The power over all India would be in my hands! Kharvani would but appear and say thus and thus, and thus would it be done!"

The Risaldar's hand had risen to his mustache. His back was still turned on the priest, but he showed interest. His eyes wandered to where Ruth lay in a heap by the inner door and then away again.

"Who would believe it?" he growled in an undertone.

"They would all believe it! One and all! Even Mohammedans would become Hindus to worship at her shrine and beg her favors. Thou and I alone would share the secret. Listen! Loose me these bonds—my limbs ache."

Mahommed Khan turned. He stooped and cut them with his sword.

"Now I can talk," said the priest, sitting up and rubbing his ankles. "Listen. Take thou two horses and gallop off, so that the rest may think that the white woman has escaped. Then return here secretly and name thy price—and hold thy tongue!"

"And leave her in thy hands?" asked the Risaldar.

"In my keeping."

"Bah! Who would trust a Hindu priest!"

The Rajput was plainly wavering and the priest stood up, to argue with him the better.

"What need to trust me? You, sahib, will know the secret, and none other but myself will know it. Would I, think you, be fool enough to tell the rest, or, by withholding just payment from you, incite you to spread it broadcast? You and I will know it and we alone. To me the power that it will bring—to you all the wealth you ever dreamed of, and more besides!"

"No other priest would know?"

"Not one! They will think the woman escaped!"

"And she—where would you keep her?"

"In a secret place I know of, below the temple."

"Does any other know it?"

"No. Not one!"

"Listen!" said the Risaldar, stroking at his beard. "This woman never did me any wrong—but she is a woman, not a man. I owe her no fealty, and yet—I would not like to see her injured. Were I to agree to thy plan, there would needs be a third man in the secret."

"Who? Name him," said the priest, grinning his satisfaction.

"My half-brother Suliman."

"Agreed!"

"He must go with us to the hiding-place and stay there as her servant."

"Is he a silent man?"

"Silent as the dead, unless I bid him speak!"

"Then, that is agreed; he and thou and I know of this secret, and none other is to know it! Why wait? Let us remove her to the hiding-place!"

"Wait yet for Suliman. How long will I be gone, think you, on my pretended flight?"

"Nay, what think you, sahib?"

"I think many hours. There may be those that watch, or some that ride after me. I think I shall not return until long after daylight, and then there will be no suspicions. Give me a token that will admit me safely back into Hanadra—some sign that the priests will know, and a pass to show to any one that bids me halt."

The priest held out his hand. "Take off that ring of mine!" he answered. "That is the sacred ring of Kharvani—and all men know it. None will touch thee or refuse thee anything, do they have but the merest sight of it!"

The Risaldar drew off a clumsy silver ring, set with three stones—a sapphire and a ruby and an emerald, each one of which was worth a fortune by itself. He slipped it on his own finger and turned it round slowly, examining it.

"See how I trust thee," said the priest.

"More than I do thee!" muttered the Risaldar.

"I hear my brother!" growled the Risaldar after another minute. "Be ready to show the way!"

He walked across the room to Ruth, tore a covering from a divan and wrapped her in it; then he opened the outer door for his half-brother.

"Is it well?" he asked in the Rajput tongue.

"All well!" boomed the half-brother, eying the unbound priest with unconcealed surprise.

"Do any watch?"

"Not one! The priests are in the temple; all who are not priests man the walls or rush here and there making ready."

"And the priestling?"

"Is where I left him."

"Where?—I said."

"In the niche underneath the arch, where I trapped the High Priest!"

"Are the horses fed and watered?"

"Ha, sahib!"

"Good! How is the niche opened where the priestling lies?"

"There is the trunk of an elephant, carved where the largest stone of all begins to curve outward, on the side of the stone as you go outward from the courtyard."

"On which side of the archway, then?"

"On the left side, sahib. Press on the trunk downward and then pull; the stone swings outward. There are steps then—ten steps downward to the stone floor where the priestling lies."

"Good! I can find him. Now pick up the heavenborn yonder in those great arms of thine, and bear her gently! Gently, I said! So! Have a care, now, that she is not injured against the corners. My honor, aye, my honor and yours and all our duty to the Raj you bear and—and have a care of the corners?"

"Aye," answered the half-brother, stolidly, holding Ruth as though she had been a little bag of rice.

Again the Risaldar turned to the High Priest, and eyed him through eyes that glittered.

"We are ready!" he growled. "Lead on to thy hiding-place!"

VIII

The guns rode first from Doonha, for the guns take precedence. The section ground-scouts were acting scouts for the division, two hundred yards ahead of every one. Behind the guns rode Colonel Forrester-Carter, followed by the wagon with the wounded; and last of all the two companies of the Thirty-third trudged through the stifling heat.

But, though the guns were ahead of every one, they had to suit their pace to that of the men who marched. For one thing, there might be an attack at any minute, and guns that are caught at close quarters at a distance from their escort are apt to be astonishingly helpless. They can act in unison with infantry; but alone, on bad ground, in the darkness, and with their horses nearly too tired to drag them, a leash of ten puppies in a crowd would be an easier thing to hurry with.

Young Bellairs had his men dismounted and walking by their mounts. Even the drivers led their horses, for two had been taken from each gun to drag the wounded, and the guns are calculated as a load for six, not four.

As he trudged through the blood-hot dust in clumsy riding-boots and led his charger on the left flank of the guns, Harry Bellairs fumed and fretted in a way to make no man envy him. The gloomy, ghost-like trees, that had flitted past him on the road to Doonha, crawled past him now—slowly and more slowly as his tired feet blistered in his boots. He could not mount and ride, though, for very shame, while his men were marching, and he dared not let them ride, for fear the horses might give in. He could just trudge and trudge, and hate himself and every one, and wonder.

What had the Risaldar contrived to do? Why hadn't he packed up his wife's effects the moment that his orders came and ridden off with her and the section at once, instead of waiting three hours or more for an escort for her? Why hadn't he realized at once that orders that came in a hurry that way, in the night-time, were not only urgent but ominous as well? What chance had the Risaldar—an old man, however willing he might be—to ride through a swarming countryside for thirty miles or more and bring back an escort? Why, even supposing Mohammed Khan had ridden off at once, he could scarcely be back again before the section! And what would have happened in the meantime?

Supposing the Risaldar's sons and grandsons refused to obey him? Stranger things than that had been known to happen! Suppose they were disloyal? And then— blacker though than any yet!—suppose—suppose— Why had Mahommed Khan, the hard-bitten, wise old war-dog, advised him to leave his wife behind? Did that seem like honest advice, on second thought? Mohammedans had joined in this outbreak as well as Hindus. The sepoys at Doonha were Mohammedans! Why had Mahommed Khan seemed so anxious to send him on his way? As though an extra five minutes would have mattered! Why had he objected to a last good-by to Mrs. Bellairs? . . . And then—he had shown a certain knowledge of the uprising; where had he obtained it? If he were loyal, who then had told him of it? Natives who are disloyal don't brag of their plans beforehand to men who are on the other side! And if he had known of it, and was still loyal, how was it that he had not divulged his information before the outbreak came? Would a loyal man hold his tongue until the last minute? Scarcely!

He halted, pulled his horse to the middle of the road and waited for Colonel Carter to overtake him.

"Well? What is it?" asked the colonel sharply.

"Can I ride on ahead, sir? My horse is good for it and I'm in agonies of apprehension about my wife!"

"No! Certainly not! You are needed to command your section!"

"I beg your pardon, sir, but I've a sergeant who can take command. He's a first-class man and perfectly dependable."

"You could do no good, even if you did ride on," said the colonel, not unkindly.

"I'm thinking, sir, that Mahommed Khan—"

"Risaldar Mahommed Khan?"

"Yes, sir."

"Of the Rajput Horse?"

"Yes, sir. My father's Risaldar."

"You left your wife in his charge, didn't you?"

"Yes, sir, but I'm thinking that—that perhaps the Risaldar—I mean—there seem to be Mohammedans at the bottom of this business, as well as Hindus. Perhaps—"

"Bellairs! Now hear me once and for all. You thank your God that the Risaldar turned up to guard her! Thank God that your father was man enough for Mahommed Khan to love and that you are your father's son! And listen! Don't let me hear you, ever, under any circumstances, breathe a word of doubt as to that man's loyalty! D'you understand me, sir? You, a mere subaltern, a puppy just out of his 'teens, an insignificant jackanapes with two twelve-pounders in your charge, daring to impute disloyalty to Mahommed Khan!—your impudence! Remember this! That old Risaldar is the man who rode with your father through the guns at Dera! He's a pauper without a pension, for all his loyalty, but he went down the length of India to meet you, at his own expense, when you landed raw-green from England! And what d'you know of war, I'd like to know, that you didn't learn from him? Thank your God, sir, that there's some one there who'll kill your wife before she falls into the Hindus' hands!"

"But he was going to ride away, sir, to bring an escort!"

"Not before he'd made absolutely certain of her safety!" swore the colonel with conviction. "Join your section, sir!"

So Harry Bellairs joined his section and trudged along sore-footed at its side—sore-hearted, too. He wondered whether any one would ever say as much for him as Colonel Carter had chosen to say for Mahommed Khan, or whether any one would have the right to say it! He was ashamed of having left his wife behind and tortured with anxiety and smarting from the snub—a medley of sensations that were more likely to make a man of him, if he had known it, than the whole experience of a year's campaign! But in the dust and darkness, with the blisters on his heels, and fifty men, who had overheard the colonel, looking sidewise at him, his plight was pitiable.

They trudged until the dawn began to rise, bright yellow below the drooping banian trees; only Colonel Carter and the advance-guard riding. Then, when they stopped at a stream to water horses and let them graze a bit and give the men a sorely needed rest, one of the ring of outposts loosed off his rifle and shouted an alarm. They had formed square in an instant, with the guns on one side and the men on three, and the colonel and the wounded in the middle. A thousand or more of the mutineers leaned on their rifles on the shoulder of a hill and looked them over, a thousand yards away.

"Send them an invitation!" commanded Colonel Carter, and the left-hand gun barked out an overture, killing one sepoy. The rest made off in the direction of Hanadra.

"We're likely to have a hot reception when we reach there!" said Colonel Carter cheerily. "Well, we'll rest here for thirty minutes and give them a chance to get ready for us. I'm sorry there's no breakfast, men, but the sepoys will have dinner ready by the time we get there—we'll eat theirs!"

The chorus of ready laughter had scarcely died away when a horse's hoof-beats clattered in the distance from the direction of Doonha and a native cavalryman galloped into view, low-bent above his horse's neck. The foam from his horse was spattered over him and his lance swung pointing upward from the sling. On his left side the polished scabbard rose and fell in time to his horse's movement. He was urging his weary horse to put out every ounce he had in him. He drew rein, though, when he reached a turning in the road and saw the resting division in front of him, and walked his horse forward, patting his sweat-wet neck and easing him. But as he leaned to finger with the girths an ambushed sepoy fired at him, and he rammed in his spurs again and rode like a man possessed.

"This'll be another untrustworthy Mohammedan!" said Colonel Carter in a pointed undertone, and Bellairs blushed crimson underneath the tan. "He's ridden through from Jundhra, with torture waiting for him if he happened to get caught, and no possible reward beyond his pay. Look out he doesn't spike your guns!"

The trooper rode straight up to Colonel Carter and saluted. He removed a tiny package from his cheek, where he had carried it so that he might swallow it at once in case of accident, tore the oil-silk cover from it and handed it to him without a word, saluting again and leading his horse away. Colonel Carter unfolded the half-sheet of foreign notepaper and read:

DEAR COLONEL CARTER:

Your letter just received in which you say that you have blown up the magazine at Doonha and are marching to Hanadra with a view to the rescue of Mrs. Bellairs. This is in no sense intended as a criticism of your action or of your plan, but circumstances have made it seem advisable for me to transfer my own headquarters to Hanadra and I am just starting. I must ask you, please, to wait for me—at a spot as near to where this overtakes you as can be managed. If Mrs. Bellairs, or anybody else of ours, is in Hanadra, she—or they—are either dead by now or else prisoners. And if they are to be rescued by force, the larger the force employed the better. If you were to attack with your two companies before I reached you, you probably would be repulsed, and would, I think, endanger the lives of any prisoners that the enemy may hold. I am coming with my whole command as fast as possible.

Your Obedient Servant,

A. E. Turner

Genl. Officer Commanding

"Men!" said Colonel Carter, in a ringing voice that gave not the slightest indication of his feelings, "we're to wait here for a while until the whole division overtakes us. The general has vacated Jundhra. Lie down and get all the rest you can!"

The murmur from the ranks was as difficult to read as Colonel Carter's voice had been. It might have meant pleasure at the thought of rest, or anger, or contempt, or almost anything. It was undefined and indefinable.

But there was no doubt at all as to how young Bellairs felt. He was sitting on a trunnion, sobbing, with his head bent low between his hands.

IX

"Come, then!" said the High Priest.

Mahommed Khan threw open the outer door and bowed sardonically. "Precedence for priests!" he sneered, tapping at his sword-hilt. "Thou goest first! Next come I, and last Suliman with the memsahib! Thus can I reach thee with my sword, O priest, and also protect her if need be!"

"Thou art trusting as a little child!" exclaimed the priest, passing out ahead of him.

"A priest and a liar and a thief—all three are one!" hummed the Risaldar. "Bear her gently, Suliman! Have a care, now, as you turn on the winding stairs!"

"Ha, sahib!" said the half-brother, carrying Ruth as easily as though she had been a little child.

At the foot of the stairway, in the blackness that seemed alive with phantom shadows, the High Priest paused and listened, stretching out his left hand against the wall to keep the other two behind him. From somewhere beyond the courtyard came the din of hurrying sandaled feet, scudding over cobblestones in one direction. The noise was incessant and not unlike the murmur of a rapid stream. Occasionally a voice was raised in some command or other, but the stream of sound continued, hurrying, hurrying, shuffling along to the southward.

"This way and watch a while," whispered the priest.

"I have heard rats run that way!" growled the Risaldar.

They climbed up a narrow stairway leading to a sort of battlement and peered over the top, Suliman laying Ruth Bellairs down in the darkest shadow he could find. She was beginning to recover consciousness, and apparently Mahommed Khan judged it best to take no notice of her.

Down below them they could see the city gate, wide open, with a blazing torch on either side of it, and through the gate, swarming like ants before the rains, there poured an endless stream of humans that marched—and marched—and marched; four, ten, fifteen abreast; all heights and sizes, jumbled in and out among one another, anyhow, without formation, but armed, every one of them, and all intent on marching to the southward, where Jundhra and Doonha lay. Some muttered to one another and some laughed, but the greater number marched in silence.

"That for thy English!" grinned the priest. "Can the English troops overcome that horde?"

"Hey-ee! For a troop or two of Rajputs!" sighed the Risaldar. "Or English Lancers! They would ride through that as an ax does through the brush-wood!"

"Bah!" said the priest. "All soldiers boast! There will be a houghing shortly after dawn. The days of thy English are now numbered."

"By those—there?"

"Ay, by those, there! Come!"

They climbed down the steps again, the Rajput humming to himself and smiling grimly into his mustache.

"Ay! There will be a houghing shortly after dawn!" he muttered. "Would only that I were there to see! . . . Where are the sepoys?" he demanded.

"I know not. How should I know, who have been thy guest these hours past? This march is none of my ordering."

The priest pressed hard on a stone knob that seemed to be part of the carving on a wall, then he leaned his weight against the wall and a huge stone swung inward, while a fetid breath of air wafted outward in their faces.

"None know this road but I!" exclaimed the priest.

"None need to!" said the Risaldar. "Pass on, snake, into thy hole. We follow."

"Steps!" said the priest, and began descending.

"Curses!" said the Risaldar, stumbling and falling down on top of him. "Have a care, Suliman! The stone is wet and slippery."

Down, down they climbed, one behind the other, Suliman grunting beneath his burden and the Risaldar keeping up a running fire of oaths. Each time that he slipped, and that was often, he cursed the priest and cautioned Suliman. But the priest only laughed, and apparently Suliman was sure-footed, for he never stumbled once. They seemed to be diving down into the bowels of the earth. They were in pitch-black darkness, for the stone had swung to behind them of its own accord. The wall on either side of them was wet with slime and the stink of decaying ages rose and almost stifled them. But the priest kept on descending, so fast that the other two had trouble to keep up with him, and he hummed to himself as though he knew the road and liked it.

"The bottom!" he called back suddenly. "From now the going is easy, until we rise again. We pass now under the city-wall."

But they could see nothing and hear nothing except their own footfalls swishing in the ooze beneath them. Even the priest's words seemed to be lost at once, as though he spoke into a blanket, for the air they breathed was thicker than a mist and just as damp. They walked on, along a level, wet, stone passage for at least five minutes, feeling their way with one band on the wall.

"Steps, now!" said the priest. "Have a care, now, for the lower ones are slippery."

Ruth was regaining consciousness. She began to move and tried once or twice to speak.

"Here, thou!" growled the Risaldar. "Thou art a younger man than I—come back here. Help with the memsahib."

The priest came back a step or two, but Suliman declined his aid, snarling vile insults at him.

"I can manage!" he growled. "Get thou behind me, Mahommed Khan, in case I slip!"

So Mahommed Khan came last, and they slipped and grunted upward, round and round a spiral staircase that was hewn out of solid rock. No light came through from anywhere to help them, but the priest climbed on, as though he were accustomed to the stair and knew the way from constant use. After five minutes of steady climbing the stone grew gradually dry. The steps became smaller, too, and deeper, and not so hard to climb. Suddenly the priest reached out his arm and pulled at something or other that hung down in the darkness. A stone in the wall rolled open. A flood of light burst in and nearly blinded them.

"We are below Kharvani's temple!" announced the priest.

He led them through the opening into a four-square room hewn from the rock below the foundations of the temple some time in the dawn of history. The light that had blinded them when they first emerged proved to be nothing but the flicker of two small oil lamps that hung suspended by brass chains from the painted ceiling. The only furniture was mats spread on the cut-stone floor.

"By which way did we come?" asked the Risaldar, staring in amazement round the walls. There was not a door nor crack, nor any sign of one, except that a wooden ladder in one corner led to a trapdoor overhead, and they had certainly not entered by the ladder.

"Nay! That is a secret!" grinned the priest. "He who can may find the opening! Here can the woman and her servant stay until we need them."

"Here in this place?"

"Where else? No man but I knows of this crypt! The ladder there leads to another room, where there is yet another ladder, and that one leads out through a secret door I know of, straight into the temple. Art ready? There is need for haste!"

"Wait!" said the Risaldar.

"These soldiers!" sneered the priest. "It is wait—wait—wait with them, always!"

"Hast thou a son."

"Ay! But what of it?"

"I said 'hast,' not 'hadst'!"

"Ay. I have a son."

"Where?"

"In one of the temple-chambers overhead."

"Nay, priest! Thy son lies gagged and bound and trussed in a place I know of, and which thou dost not know!"

"Since when?"

"Since by my orders he was laid there."

"Thou art the devil! Thou liest, Rajput!"

"So? Go seek thy son!"

The priest's face had blanched beneath the olive of his skin, and he stared at Mahommed Khan through distended eyes.

"My son!" he muttered.

"Aye! Thy priestling! He stays where he is, as hostage, until my return! Also the heavenborn stays here! If, on my return, I find the heavenborn safe and sound, I will exchange her for thy son—and if not, I will tear thy son into little pieces before thy eyes, priest! Dost thou understand?"

"Thou liest! My son is overhead in the temple here!"

"Go seek him, then!"

The priest turned and scampered up the ladder with an agility that was astonishing in a man of his build and paunch.

"Hanuman should have been thy master!" jeered the Risaldar. "So run the bandar-log, the monkey-folk!"

But the priest had no time to answer him. He was half frantic with the sickening fear of a father for his only son. He returned ten minutes later, panting, and more scared than ever.

"Go, take thy white woman," he exclaimed, "and give me my son back!"

"Nay, priest! Shall I ride with her alone through that horde that are marching through the gate? I go now for an escort; in eight—ten—twelve—I know not how many hours, I will return for her, and then—thy son will be exchanged for her, or he dies thus in many pieces!"

He turned to Suliman. "Is she awake yet?" he demanded.

"Barely, but she recovers."

"Then tell her, when consciousness returns, that I have gone and will return for her. And stay here, thou, and guard her until I come."

"Ha, sahib!"

"Now, show the way!"

"But—" said the priest, "our bargain? The price that we agreed on—one lakh, was it not?"

"One lakh of devils take thee and tear thee into little pieces! Wouldst bribe a Rajput, a Risaldar? For that insult I will repay thee one day with interest, O priest! Now, show the way!"

"But how shall I be sure about my son?"

"Be sure that the priestling will starve to death or die of thirst or choke, unless I hurry! He is none too easy where he lies!"

"Go! Hurry, then!" swore the priest. "May all the gods there are, and thy Allah with them, afflict thee with all their curses—thee and thine! Up with you! Up that ladder! Run! But, if the gods will, I will meet thee again when the storm is over!"

"Inshallah!" growled Mahommed Khan.

Ten minutes later a crash and a clatter and a shower of sparks broke out in the sweltering courtyard where the guns had stood and waited. It was Shaitan, young Bellairs' Khaubuli charger, with his haunches under him, plunging across the flag-stones, through the black-dark archway, out on the plain beyond—in answer to the long, sharp-roweled spurs of the Risaldar Mahommed Khan.

X

Dawn broke and the roofs of old Hanadra became resplendent with the varied colors of turbans and pugrees and shawls. As though the rising sun had loosed the spell, a myriad tongues, of women chiefly, rose in a babel of clamor, and the few men who had been left in. Hanadra by the night's armed exodus came all together and growled prophetically in undertones. Now was the day of days, when that part of India, at least, should cast off the English yoke.

To the temple! The cry went up before the sun was fifteen minutes high. There are a hundred temples in Hanadra, age-old all of them and carved on the outside with strange images of heathen gods in high relief, like molds turned inside out. But there is but one temple that that cry could mean—Kharvani's; and there could be but one meaning for the cry. Man, woman and child would pray Kharvani, Bride of Siva the Destroyer, to intercede with Siva and cause him to rise and smite the English. On the sky-line, glinting like flashed signals in the early sun, bright English bayonets had appeared; and between them and Hanadra was a dense black mass, the whole of old Hanadra's able-bodied manhood, lined up to defend the city. Now was the time to pray. Fifty to one are by no means despicable odds, but the aid of the gods as well is better!

So the huge dome of Kharvani's temple began to echo to the sound of slippered feet and awe-struck whisperings, and the big, dim auditorium soon filled to overflowing. No light came in from the outer world. There was nothing to illuminate the mysteries except the chain-hung grease-lamps swinging here and there from beams, and they served only to make the darkness visible. Bats flicked in and out between them and disappeared in the echoing gloom above. Censers belched out sweet-smelling, pungent clouds of sandalwood to drown the stench of hot humanity; and the huge graven image of Kharvani—serene and smiling and indifferent—stared round-eyed from the darkness.

Then a priest's voice boomed out in a solemn incantation and the whispering hushed. He chanted age-old verses, whose very meaning was forgotten in the womb of time—forgotten as the artist who had painted the picture of idealized Kharvani on the wall. Ten priests, five on either side of the tremendous idol, emerged chanting from the gloom behind, and then a gong rang, sweetly, clearly, suddenly, and the chanting ceased. Out stepped the High Priest from a niche below the image, and his voice rose in a wailing, sing-song cadence that reechoed from the dome and sent a thrill through every one who heard.

His chant had scarcely ceased when the temple door burst open and a man rushed in.

"They have begun!" he shouted. "The battle has begun!"

As though in ready confirmation of his words, the distant reverberating boom of cannon filtered through the doorway from the world of grim realities outside.

"They have twenty cannon with them! They have more guns than we have!" wailed he who brought the news. Again began the chanting that sought the aid of Siva the Destroyer. Only, there were fewer who listened to this second chant. Those who were near the doorway slipped outside and joined the watching hundreds on the roofs.

For an hour the prayers continued in the stifling gloom, priest relieving priest and chant following on chant, until the temple was half emptied of its audience. One by one, and then by twos and threes, the worshipers succumbed to human curiosity and crept stealthily outside to watch.

Another messenger ran in and shouted: "They have charged! Their cavalry have charged! They are beaten back! Their dead lie twisted on the plain!"

At the words there was a stampede from the doorway, and half of those who had remained rushed out. There were hundreds still there, though, for that great gloomy pile of Kharvani's could hold an almost countless crowd.

Within another hour the same man rushed to the door again and shouted:

"Help comes! Horsemen are coming from the north! Rajputs, riding like leaves before the wind! Even the Mussulmans are for us!"

But the chanting never ceased. No one stopped to doubt the friendship of arrivals from the north, for to that side there were no English, and England's friends would surely follow by-roads to her aid. The city gates were wide open to admit wounded or messengers or friends—with a view, even, to a possible retreat—and whoever cared could ride through them unchallenged and unchecked.

Even when the crash of horses' hoofs rattled on the stone paving outside the temple there was no suspicion. No move was made to find out who it was who rode. But when the temple door reechoed to the thunder of a sword-hilt and a voice roared "Open!" there was something like a panic. The chanting stopped and the priests and the High Priest listened to the stamping on the stone pavement at the temple front.

"Open!" roared a voice again, and the thundering on the panels recommenced. Then some one drew the bolt and a horse's head—a huge Khaubuli stallion's—appeared, snorting and panting and wild-eyed.

"Farward!" roared the Risaldar Mahommed Khan, kneeling on young Bellairs' winded charger.

"Farm twos! Farward!"

Straight into the temple, two by two, behind the Risaldar, rode two fierce lines of Rajputs, overturning men and women—their drawn swords pointing this way and that—their dark eyes gleaming. Without a word to any one they rode up to the image, where the priests stood in an astonished herd.

"Fron-tt farm! Rear rank—'bout-face!" barked the Risaldar, and there was another clattering and stamping on the stone floor as the panting chargers pranced into the fresh formation, back to back.

"The memsahib!" growled Mahommed Khan. "Where is she?"

"My son!" said the High Priest. "Bring me my son!"

"A life for a life! Thy heavenborn first!"

"Nay! Show me my son first!"

The Risaldar leaped from his horse and tossed his reins to the man behind him. In a second his sword was at the High Priest's throat.

"Where is that secret stair?" he growled. "Lead on!"

The swordpoint pricked him. Two priests tried to interfere, but wilted and collapsed with fright as four fierce, black-bearded Rajputs spurred their horses forward. The swordpoint pricked still deeper.

"My son!" said the High Priest.

"A life for a life! Lead on!"

The High Priest surrendered, with a dark and cunning look, though, that hinted at something or other in reserve. He pulled at a piece of carving on the wail behind and pointed to a stair that showed behind the outswung door. Then he plucked another priest by the sleeve and whispered.

The priest passed on the whisper. A third priest turned and ran.

"That way!" said the High Priest, pointing.

"I? Nay! I go not down!" He raised his voice into an ululating howl. "O Suliman!" he bellowed. "Suliman! O!—Suliman! Bring up the heaven-born!"

A growl like the distant rumble from a bear-pit answered him. Then Ruth Bellairs' voice was heard calling up the stairway.

"Is that you, Mahommed Khan?"

"Ay, memsahib!"

"Good! I'm coming!"

She had recovered far enough to climb the ladder and the steep stone stair above it, and Suliman climbed up behind her, grumbling dreadful prophecies of what would happen to the priests now that Mohammed Khan had come.

"Is all well, Risaldar?" she asked him.

"Nay, heavenborn! All is not well yet! The general sahib from Jundhra and your husband's guns and others, making one division, are engaged with rebels eight or nine miles from here. We saw part of the battle as we rode!"

"Who wins?"

"It is doubtful, heavenborn! How could we tell from this distance?"

"Have you a horse for me?"

"Ay, heavenborn! Here! Bring up that horse, thou, and Suliman's! Ride him cross-saddle, heavenborn—there were no side-saddles in Siroeh! Nay, he is just a little frightened. He will stand—he will not throw thee! I did better than I thought, heavenborn. I come with four-and-twenty, making twenty-six with me and Suliman. An escort for a queen! So—sit him quietly. Leave the reins free. Suliman will lead him! Ho! Fronnnt! Rank—'bout-face!"

"My son!" wailed the High Priest. "Where is my son?"

"Tell him, Suliman!"

"Where I caught thee, thou idol-briber!" snarled the Risaldar's half-brother.

"Where? In that den of stinks. Gagged and bound all this while?"

"Ha! Gagged and bound and out of mischief where all priests and priests' sons ought to be!" laughed Mahommed Khan. "Farward! Farm twos Ter-r-r-ott!"

In went the spur, and the snorting, rattling, clanking cavalcade sidled and pranced out of the temple into the sunshine, with Ruth and Suliman in the midst of them.

"Gallop!" roared the Risaldar, the moment that the last horse was clear of the temple-doors. And in that instant he saw what the High Priest's whispering had meant.

Coming up the street toward them was a horde of silent, hurrying Hindus, armed with swords and spears, wearing all of them the caste-marks of the Brahman—well-fed, indignant relations of the priests, intent on avenging the defilement of Kharvani's temple.

"Canter! Fronnnt—farm—Gallop! Charge!"

Ruth found herself in the midst of a whirlwind of flashing sabers, astride of a lean-flanked Katiawari gelding that could streak like an antelope, knee to knee with a pair of bearded Rajputs, one of whom gripped her bridle-rein—thundering down a city street straight for a hundred swords that blocked her path. She set her eyes on the middle of Mahommed Khan's straight back, gripped the saddle with both hands, set her teeth and waited for the shock. Mahommed Khan's right arm rose and his sword flashed in the sunlight as he stood up in his stirrups. She shut her eyes. But there was no shock! There was the swish of whirling steel, the thunder of hoofs, the sound of bodies falling. There was a scream or two as well and a coarse-mouthed Rajput oath. But when she dared to open her eyes once more they were thundering still, headlong down the city street and Mahommed Khan was whirling his sword in mid-air to shake the blood from it.

Ahead lay the city gate and she could see another swarm of Hindus rushing from either side to close it. But "Charge!" yelled Mahommed Khan again, and they swept through the crowd, through the half-shut gate, out on the plain beyond, as a wind sweeps through the forest, leaving fallen tree-trunks in its wake.

"Halt!" roared the Risaldar, when they were safely out of range. "Are any hurt? No? Good for us that their rifles are all in the firing-line yonder!"

He sat for a minute peering underneath his hand at the distant, dark, serried mass of men and the steel-tipped lines beyond it, watching the belching cannon and the spurting flames of the close-range rifle-fire.

"See, heavenborn!" he said, pointing. "Those will be your husband's guns! See, over on the left, there. See! They fire! Those two! We can reach them if we make a circuit on the flank here!"

"But can we get through, Risaldar? Won't they see us and cut us off?"

"Heavenborn!" he answered, "men who dare ride into a city temple and snatch thee from the arms of priests dare and can do anything! Take this, heavenborn—take it as a keepsake, in case aught happens!"

He drew off the priest's ring, gave it to her and then, before she could reply:

"Canter!" he roared. The horses sprang forward in answer to the spurs and there was nothing for Ruth to do but watch the distant battle and listen to the deep breathing of the Rajputs on either hand.

XI

There could be no retreat that day and no thought of it. Jundhra and Doonha were in ruins. The bridges were down behind them and Hanadra lay ahead. The British had to win their way into it or perish. Tired out, breakfastless, suffering from the baking heat, the long, thin British line had got—not to hold at bay but to smash and pierce—an overwhelming force of Hindus that was stiffened up and down its length by small detachments of native soldiers who had mutinied.

Numbers were against them, and even superiority of weapons was not so overwhelmingly in their favor, for those were the days of short-range rifle-fire and smoothbore artillery, and one gun was considerably like another. The mutinous sepoys had their rifles with them; there were guns from the ramparts of Hanadra that were capable of quite efficient service at close range; and practically every man in the dense-packed rebel line had a firearm of some kind. It was only in cavalry and discipline and pluck that the British force had the advantage, and the cavalry had already charged once and had been repulsed.

General Turner rode up and down the sweltering firing-line, encouraging the men when it seemed to him they needed it and giving directions to his officers. He was hidden from view oftener than not by the rolling clouds of smoke and he popped up here and there suddenly and unexpectedly. Wherever he appeared there was an immediate stiffening among the ranks, as though he carried a supply of spare enthusiasm with him and could hand it out.

Colonel Carter, commanding the right wing, turned his head for a second at the sound of a horse's feet and found the general beside him.

"Had I better have my wounded laid in a wagon, sir?" he suggested, "in case you find it necessary to fall back?"

"There will be no retreat!" said General Turner. "Leave your wounded where they are. I never saw a cannon bleed before. How's that?"

He spurred his horse over to where one of Bellairs' guns was being run forward into place again and Colonel Carter followed him. There was blood dripping from the muzzle of it.

"We're short of water, sir!" said Colonel Carter.

And as he spoke a gunner dipped his sponge into a pool of blood and rammed it home.

Bellairs was standing between his two guns, looking like the shadow of himself, worn out with lack of sleep, disheveled, wounded. There was blood dripping from his forehead and he wore his left arm in a sling made from his shirt.

"Fire!" he ordered, and the two guns barked in unison and jumped back two yards or more.

"If you'll look," said General Turner, plucking at the colonel's sleeve, "you'll see a handful of native cavalry over yonder behind the enemy—rather to the enemy's left—there between those two clouds of smoke. D'you see them?"

"They look like Sikhs or Rajputs," said the colonel.

"Yes. Don't they? I'd like you to keep an eye on them. They've come up from the rear. I caught sight of them quite a while ago and I can't quite make them out. It's strange, but I can't believe that they belong to the enemy. D'you see?—there—they've changed direction. They're riding as though they intended to come round the enemy's left flank!"

"By gad, they are! Look! The enemy are moving to cut them off!"

"I must get back to the other wing!" said General Turner. "But that looks like the making of an opportunity! Keep both eyes lifting, Carter, and advance the moment you see any confusion in the enemy's ranks."

He rode off, and Colonel Carter stared long and steadily at the approaching horsemen. He saw a dense mass of the enemy, about a thousand strong, detach itself from the left wing and move to intercept them, and he noticed that the movement made a tremendous difference to the ranks opposed to him. He stepped up to young Bellairs and touched his sleeve. Bellairs started like a man roused from a dream.

"That's your wife over there!" said Colonel Carter. "There can't be any other white woman hereabouts riding with a Rajput escort!"

Bellairs gripped the colonel's outstretched arm.

"Where?" he almost screamed. "Where? I don't see her!"

"There, man! There, where that mass of men is moving! Look! By the Lord Harry! He's charging right through the mob! That's Mahommed Khan, I'll bet a fortune! Now's our chance Bugler!"

The bugler ran to him, and he began to puff into his instrument.

"Blow the 'attention' first!"

Out rang the clear, strident notes, and the non-commissioned officers and men took notice that a movement of some kind would shortly be required of them, but the din of firing never ceased for a single instant. Then, suddenly, an answering bugle sang out from the other flank.

"Advance in echelon!" commanded Colonel Carter, and the bugler did his best to split his cheeks in a battle-rending blast.

"You remain where you are, sir!" he ordered young Bellairs. "Keep your guns served to the utmost!"

Six-and-twenty horsemen, riding full-tilt at a thousand men, may look like a trifle, but they are disconcerting. What they hit, they kill; and if they succeed in striking home, they play old Harry with formations. And Risaldar Mahommed Khan did strike home. He changed direction suddenly and, instead of using up his horses' strength in outflanking the enemy, who had marched to intercept him, and making a running target of his small command, he did the unexpected—which is the one best thing to do in war. He led his six-and-twenty at a headlong gallop straight for the middle of the crowd—it could not be called by any military name. They fired one ragged volley at him and then had no time to load before he was in the middle of them, clashing right and left and pressing forward. They gave way, right and left, before him, and a good number of them ran. Half a hundred of them were cut down as they fled toward their firing-line. At that second, just as the Risaldar and his handful burst through the mob and the mob began rushing wildly out of his way, the British bugles blared out the command to advance in echelon.

The Indians were caught between a fire and a charge that they had good reason to fear in front of them, and a disturbance on their left flank that might mean anything. As one-half of them turned wildly to face what might be coming from this unexpected quarter, the British troops came on with a roar, and at the same moment Mahommed Khan reached the rear of their firing-line and crashed headlong into it.

In a second the whole Indian line was in confusion and in another minute it was in full retreat not knowing nor even guessing what had routed it. Retreat grew into panic and panic to stampede and, five minutes after the Risaldar's appearance on the scene, half of the Indian line was rushing wildly for Hanadra and the other half was retiring sullenly in comparatively dense and decent order.

Bellairs could not see all that happened. The smoke from his own guns obscured the view, and the necessity for giving orders to his men prevented him from watching as he would have wished. But he saw the Rajputs burst out through the Indian ranks and he saw his own charger—Shaitan the unmistakable—careering across the plain toward him riderless.

"For the love of God!" he groaned, raising both fists to heaven, "has she got this far, and then been killed! Oh, what in Hades did I entrust her to an Indian for? The pig-headed, brave old fool! Why couldn't he ride round them, instead of charging through?"

As he groaned aloud, too wretched even to think of what his duty was, a galloper rode up to him.

"Bring up your guns, sir, please!" he ordered. "You're asked to hurry! Take up position on that rising ground and warm up the enemy's retreat!"

"Limber up!" shouted Bellairs, coming to himself again. Fifteen seconds later his two guns were thundering up the rise.

As he brought them to "action front" and tried to collect his thoughts to figure out the range, a finger touched his shoulder and he turned to see another artillery officer standing by him.

"I've been lent from another section," he explained: "You're wanted."

"Where?"

"Over there, where you see Colonel Carter standing. It's your wife wants you, I think!"

Bellairs did not wait for explanations. He sent for his horse and mounted and rode across the intervening space at a breakneck gallop that he could barely stop in time to save himself from knocking the colonel over. A second later he was in Ruth's arms.

"I thought you were dead when I saw Shaitan!" he said. He was nearly sobbing.

"No, Mahommed Khan rode him," she answered, and she made no pretense about not sobbing. She was crying like a child.

"Salaam, Bellairs sahib!" said a weak voice close to him. He noticed Colonel Carter bending over a prostrate figure, lifting the head up on his knee. There were three Rajputs standing between, though, and he could not see whose the figure was.

"Come over here!" said Colonel Carter, and young Bellairs obeyed him, leaving Ruth sitting on the ground where she was.

"Wouldn't you care to thank Mohammed Khan?"

It was a little cruel of the colonel to put quite so much venom in his voice, for, when all is said and done: a man has almost a right to be forgetful when he has just had his young wife brought him out of the jaws of death. At least he has a good excuse for it. The sting of the reproof left him bereft of words and he stood looking down at the old Risaldar, saying nothing and feeling very much ashamed.

"Salaam, Bellairs sahib!" The voice was growing feebler.

"I would have done more for thy father's son! Thou art welcome. Aie! But thy charger is a good one! Good-by! Time is short, and I would talk with the colonel sahib!"

He waved Bellairs away with a motion of his hand and the lieutenant went back to his wife again.

"He sent me away just like that, too!" she told him. "He said he had no time left to talk to women!"

Colonel Carter bent down again above the Risaldar, and listened to as much as he had time to tell of what had happened.

"But couldn't you have ridden round them, Risaldar?" he asked them.

"Nay, sahib! It was touch and go! I gave the touch! I saw as I rode how close the issue was and I saw my chance and took it! Had the memsahib been slain, she had at least died in full view of the English—and there was a battle to be won. What would you? I am a soldier—I."

"Indeed you are!" swore Colonel Carter.

"Sahib! Call my sons!"

His sons were standing near him, but the colonel called up his grandsons, who had been told to stand at a little distance off. They clustered round the Risaldar in silence, and he looked them over and counted them.

"All here?" he asked.

"All here!"

"Whose sons and grandsons are ye?"

"Thine!" came the chorus.

"This sahib says that having done my bidding and delivered her ye rode to rescue, ye are no more bound to the Raj. Ye may return to your homes if ye wish."

There was no answer.

"Ye may fight for the rebels, if ye wish! There will be a safe-permit written."

Again there was no answer.

"For whom, then, fight ye?"

"For the Raj!" The deep-throated answer rang out promptly from every one of them, and they stood with their sword-hilts thrust out toward the colonel. He rose and touched each hilt in turn.

"They are now thy servants!" said the Risaldar, laying his head back. "It is good! I go now. Give my salaams to General Turner sahib!"

"Good-by, old war-dog!" growled the colonel, in an Anglo-Saxon effort to disguise emotion. He gripped at the right hand that was stretched out on the ground beside him, but it was lifeless.

Risaldar Mahommed Khan, two-medal man and pensionless gentleman-at-large, had gone to turn in his account of how he had remembered the salt which he had eaten.

LORD OF THE JACKALS

Sax Rohmer

IN THOSE DAYS, OF COURSE (SAID THE FRENCH AGENT, LOOKING OUT ACROSS
the sea of Yûssuf Effendis which billowed up against the balcony to where, in
the moonlight, the minarets of Cairo pointed the way to God), I did not occupy
the position which I occupy to-day. No, I was younger, and more ambitious; I thought
to carve in the annals of Egypt a name for myself such as that of De Lesseps.

I had a scheme—and there were those who believed in it—for extending the
borders of Egypt. Ah! my friends, Egypt after all is but a double belt of mud following
the Nile, and terminated east and west by the desert. The desert! It was the dream
of my life to exterminate that desert, that hungry gray desert; it was my plan—a
foolish plan as I know now—to link the fertile Fáyûm to the Oases! How was this to
be done? Ah!

Why should I dig up those buried skeletons? It was not done; it never could be
done; therefore, let me not bore you with how I had proposed to do it. Suffice it that
my ambitions took me far off the beaten tracks, far, even, from the caravan roads—far
into the gray heart of the desert.

But I was ambitious, and only nineteen—or scarcely twenty. At nineteen, a man
who comes from St. Rémy fears no obstacle which Fate can place in his way, and looks
upon the world as a grape-fruit to be sweetened with endeavor and sucked empty.

It was in those days, then, that I learned as your Rudyard Kipling has also
learned that "East is East"; it was in those days that I came face to face with that
"mystery of Egypt" about which so much is written, has always been written, and
always will be written, but concerning which so few people, so very few people,
know anything whatever.

Yes, I, René de Flassans, saw with my own eyes a thing that I knew to be magic,
a thing whereat my reason rebelled—a thing which my poor European intelligence
could not grapple, could not begin to explain.

It was this which you asked me to tell you, was it not? I will do so with pleasure,
because I know that I speak to men of honor, and because it is good for me, now that
I cannot count the gray hairs in my beard, to confess how poor a thing I was when I
could count every hair upon my chin—and how grand a thing I thought myself.

One evening, at the end of a dreadful day in the saddle—beneath a sky which seemed to reflect all the fires of hell, a day passed upon sands simply smoking in that merciless sun—I and my native companions came to an encampment of Arabs.

They were Bedouins—the tribe does not matter at the moment—and, as you may know, the Bedouin is the most hospitable creature whom God has yet created. The tent of the Sheikh is open to any traveller who cares to rest his weary limbs therein. Freely he may partake of all that the tribe has to offer, food and drink and entertainment; and to seek to press payment upon the host would be to insult a gentleman.

That is desert hospitality. A spear that stands thrust upright in the sand before the tent door signifies that whosoever would raise his hand against the guest has first to reckon with the Sheikh. Equally it would be an insult to erect one's own tent in the neighborhood of a Bedouin encampment.

Well, my friends, I knew this well, for I was no stranger to the nomadic life, and accordingly, without fear of the fierce-eyed throng who came forth to meet us, I made my respects to the Sheikh Saïd Mohammed, and was reckoned by him as a friend and a brother. His tent was placed at my disposal and provisions were made for the suitable entertainment of those who were with me.

You know how dusk falls in Egypt? At one moment the sky is a brilliant canvas, glorious with every color known to art, at the next the curtain—the wonderful veil of deepest violet—has fallen; the stars break through it like diamonds through the finest gauze; it is night, velvet, violet night. You see it here in this noisy modern Cairo. In the lonely desert it is ten thousand times grander, ten thousand times more impressive; it speaks to the soul with the voice of the silence. Ah, those desert nights!

So was the night of which I speak; and having partaken of the fare which the Sheikh caused to be set before me—and Bedouin fare is not for the squeamish stomach—I sipped that delicious coffee which, though an acquired taste, is the true nectar, and looked out beyond the four or five palm trees of this little oasis to where the gray carpet of the desert grew black as ebony and met the violet sweep of the sky.

Perhaps I was the first to see him; I cannot say; but certainly he was not perceived by the Bedouins, although one stood on guard at the entrance to the camp.

How can I describe him? At the time, as he approached in the moonlight with a shambling, stooping gait, I felt that I had never seen his like before. Now I know the reason of my wonder, and the reason of my doubt. I know what it was about him which inspired a kind of horror and a revulsion—a dread.

Elfin locks he had, gray and matted, falling about his angular face, shading his strange, yellow eyes. His was dressed in rags, in tatters; he was furtive, and he staggered as one who is very weak, slowly approaching out of the vastness.

Then it appeared as though every dog in the camp knew of his coming. Out from the shadows of the tents they poured, those yapping mongrels. Never have I seen such a thing. In the midst of the yellowish, snarling things, at the very entrance to the camp, the wretched old man fell, uttering a low cry.

But now, snatching up a heavy club which lay close to my hand, I rushed out of the tent. Others were thronging out too, but, first of them all, I burst in among the dogs, striking, kicking, and shouting. I stooped and raised the head of the stranger.

Mutely he thanked me, with half-closed eyes. A choking sound issued from his throat, and he clutched with his hands and pointed to his mouth.

An earthenware jar, containing cool water, stood beside a tent but a few yards away. Hurling my club at the most furious of the dogs, which, with bared fangs, still threatened to attack the recumbent man, I ran and seized the *dorak*, regained his side, and poured water between his parched lips.

The throng about me was strangely silent, until, as the poor old man staggered again to his feet, supported by my arm, a chorus arose about me—one long, vowelled word, wholly unfamiliar, although my Arabic was good. But I noted that all kept a respectful distance from myself and the man whom I had succored.

Then, pressing his way through the throng came the Sheikh Saïd Mohammed. Saluting the ragged stranger with a sort of grim respect, he asked him if he desired entertainment for the night.

The other shook his head, mumbling, pointed to the water jar, and by dint of gnashing his yellow and pointed teeth, intimated that he required food.

Food was brought to him hurriedly. He tied it up in a dirty cloth, grasped the water jar, and, with never a glance at the Arabs, turned to me. With his hand he touched his brow, his lips, and his breast in salute; then, although tottering with weakness, he made off again with that queer, loping gait.

The camp dogs began to howl, and a strange silence fell upon the Arabs about me. All stood watching the departing figure until it was lost in a dip of the desert, when the watchers began to return again to their tents.

Saïd Mohammed took my hand, and in a few direct and impressive words thanked me for having spared him and his tribe from a grave dishonor. Need I say that I was flattered? Had you met him, my friends, that fine Bedouin gentleman, polished as any noble of old France, fearless as a lion, yet gentle as a woman, you would know that I rejoiced in being able to serve him even so slightly.

Two of the dogs, unperceived by us, had followed the weird old man from the camp; for suddenly in the distance I heard their savage growls. Then, these growls were drowned in such a chorus of howling—the howling of jackals—as I had never before heard in all my desert wanderings. The howling suddenly subsided . . . but the dogs did not return.

I glanced around, meaning to address the Sheikh, but the Sheikh was gone.

Filled with wonder, then, respecting this singular incident, I entered the tent—it was at the farther end of the camp—which had been placed at my disposal, and lay down, rather to reflect than to sleep. With my mind confused in thoughts of yellow-eyed wanderers, of dogs, and of jackals, sleep came.

How long I slept I cannot say; but I was awakened as the cool fingers of dawn were touching the crests of the sand billows. A gray and dismal light filled the tent, and something was scratching at the flap.

I sat up immediately, quite wide awake, and taking my revolver, ran to the entrance and looked out.

A slinking shape melted into the shadows of the tent adjoining mine, and I concluded that a camp dog had aroused me. Then, in the early morning silence, I heard a faint call, and peering through the gloom to the east saw, in black silhouette, a solitary figure standing near the extremity of the camp.

In those days, my friends, I was a brave fellow—we are all brave at nineteen—and throwing a cloak over my shoulders I strode intrepidly towards this figure. I was within ten paces when a hand was raised to beckon me.

It was the mysterious stranger! Again he beckoned to me, and I approached yet nearer, asking him if it was he who had aroused me.

He nodded, and by means of a grotesque kind of pantomime ultimately made me understand that he had caused me to be aroused in order to communicate something to me. He turned, and indicated that we were to walk away from the camp. I accompanied him without hesitation.

Although the camp was never left unguarded, no one had challenged us; and, a hundred yards beyond the outermost tent, this strange old man stopped and turned to me.

First, he pointed back to the camp, then to myself, then out along the caravan road towards the Nile.

"Do you mean," I asked him—for I perceived that he was dumb or vowed to silence—"that I am to leave the camp?"

He nodded rapidly, his strange yellow eyes gleaming.

"Immediately?" I demanded.

Again he nodded.

"Why?"

Pantomimically he made me understand that death threatened me if I remained—that I must leave the Bedouins before sunrise.

I cannot convey to you any idea of the mad earnestness of the man. But, alas! youth regards the counsels of age with nothing but contempt; moreover, I thought this man mad, and I was unable to choke down a sort of loathing which he inspired in me.

I shook my head then, but not unkindly; and, waving my hand, prepared to leave him. At that, with a sorrow in his strange eyes which did not fail to impress me, he saluted me with gravity, turned, and passed out of sight.

Although I did not know it at the time, I had chosen of two paths the one that led through fire.

I slept little after this interview—if it was a real interview and not a dream—and feeling tired and unrefreshed, I saw the sun rise purple and angry over the distant hills.

You know what *khamsín* is like, my friends? But you cannot know what *simoom* is like—*simoom* in the heart of the desert! It came that morning—a wall of sand so high as to shut out the sunlight, so dense as to turn the day into night, so suffocating that I thought I should never live through it!

It was apparent to me that the Bedouins were prepared for the storm. The horses, the camels and the asses were tethered in an enclosure specially strengthened to exclude the choking dust, and with their cloaks about their heads the men prepared for the oncoming of this terror of the desert.

My God! it was a demon which sought to blind me, to suffocate me, and which clutched at my throat with strangling fingers of sand! This, I told myself, was the danger which I might have avoided by quitting the camp before sunrise.

Indeed, it was apparent to me that if I had taken the advice so strangely offered, I might now have been safe in the village of the Great Oasis for which I was bound. But I have since seen that the *simoom* was a minor danger, and not the real one to which this weird being had referred.

The storm passed, and every man in the encampment praised the merciful God who had spared us all. It was in the disturbance attendant upon putting the camp in order once more that I saw her.

She came out from the tent of Saïd Mohammed, to shake the sand from a carpet; the newly come sunlight twinkled upon the bracelets which clasped her smooth brown arms as she shook the gaily colored mat at the tent door. The sunlight shone upon her braided hair, upon her slight robe, upon her silver anklets, and upon her tiny feet. Transfixed I stood watching—indeed, my friends, almost holding my breath. Then the sunlight shone upon her eyes, two pools of mysterious darkness into which I found myself suddenly looking.

The face of this lovely Arab maiden flushed, and drawing the corner of her robe across those bewitching eyes, she turned and ran back into the tent.

One glance—just one glance, my friends! But never had Ulysses' bow propelled an arrow more sure, more deadly. I was nineteen, remember, and of Provence. What do you foresee! You who have been through the world, you who once were nineteen.

I feigned a sickness, a sickness brought about by the sandstorm, and taking base advantage of that desert hospitality which is unbounded, which knows no suspicion, and takes no count of cost, I remained in the tent which had been vacated for me.

In this voluntary confinement I learned little of the doings of the camp. All day I lay dreaming of two dark eyes, and at night when the jackals howled I thought of the wanderer who had counseled me to leave. One day, I lay so; a second; a third again; and the women of Saïd Mohammed's household tended me, closely veiled of course. But in vain I waited for that attendant whose absence was rendering my feigned fever a real one—whose eyes burned like torches in my dreams and for the coming of whose little bare feet across the sand to my tent door I listened hour by hour, day by day, in vain—always in vain.

But at nineteen there is no such thing as despair, and hope has strength to defy death itself. It was in the violet dusk of the fourth day, as I lay there with a sort of shame of my deception struggling for birth in my heart, that she came.

She came through the tent door bearing a bowl of soup, and the rays of the setting sun outlined her fairy shape through the gossamer robe as she entered.

At that my poor weak little conscience troubled me no more. How my heart leaped, leaped so that it threatened to choke me, who had come safe through a great sandstorm.

There is fire in the Southern blood at nineteen, my friends, which leaps into flame beneath the glances of bright eyes.

With her face modestly veiled, the Bedouin maid knelt beside me, placing the wooden bowl upon the ground. My eager gaze pierced the *yashmak*, but her black lashes were laid upon her cheek, her glorious eyes averted. My heart—or was it my vanity?—told me that she regarded me at least with interest, that she was not at ease in my company; and as, having spoken no word, having ventured no glance, she rose again to depart, I was emboldened to touch her hand.

Like a startled gazelle she gave me one rapid glance, and was gone!

She was gone—and my very soul gone with her! For hours I lay, not so much as thinking of the food beside me—dreaming of her eyes. What were my plans? Faith! Does one have plans at nineteen where two bright eyes are concerned?

Alas, my friends, I dare not tell you of my hopes, yet upon those hopes I lived. Oh, it is glorious to be nineteen and of Provence; it is glorious when all the world is young, when the fruit is ripe upon the trees and the plucking seems no sin. Yet, as we look back, we perceive that at nineteen we were scoundrels.

The Bedouin girl is a woman when a European woman is but a child, and Sakîna, whose eyes could search a man's soul, was but twelve years of age—twelve! Can you picture that child of twelve squeezing a lover's heart between her tiny hands, entwining his imagination in the coils of her hair?

You, my friend, may perhaps be able to conceive this thing, for you know the East, and the women of the East. At ten or eleven years of age many of them are adorable; at twenty-one most of them are *passé*; at twenty-six all of them—with rare exceptions— are shrieking hags.

But to you, my other friends, who are strangers to our Oriental ways, who know not that the peach only attains to perfect ripeness for one short hour, it may be strange, it may be horrifying, that I loved, with all the ardor which was mine, this little Arab maiden, who, had she been born in France, would not yet have escaped from the nursery. But I digress.

The Arabs were encamped, of course, in the neighborhood of a spring. It lay in a slight depression amid the tiny palm-grove. Here, at sunset, came the women with their pitchers on their heads, graceful of carriage, veiled, mysterious.

Many peaches have ripened and have rotted since those days of which I speak, but now—even now—I am still enslaved by the mystery of Egypt's veiled women. Untidy, bedraggled, dirty, she may be, but the real Egyptian woman when she bears her pitcher upon her head and glides, stately, sinuously, through the dusk to the well, is a figure to enchain the imagination.

Very soon, then, the barrier of reserve which, like the screen of the *harêm*, stands between Eastern women and love, was broken. My trivial scruples I had cast to the winds, and feigning weakness, I would sally forth to take the air in the cool of the evening; this two days later.

My steps, be assured, led me to the spring; and you who are men of the world will know that Sakîna, braving the reproaches of the Sheikh's household, neglectful of her duties, was last of all the women who came to the well for water.

I taught her to say my name—René! How sweet it sounded from her lips, as she strove in vain to roll the "R" in our Provençal fashion. Some *ginnee* most certainly presided over this enchanted fountain, for despite the nearness of the camp our rendezvous was never discovered, our meetings were never detected.

With her pitcher upon the ground beside her, she would sit with those wistful, wonderful eyes upraised to mine, and sway before the ardor of my impassioned words as a young and tender reed sways in the Nile breeze. Her budding soul was a love lute upon which I played in ecstasy; and when she raised her red lips to mine. . . . Ah! those nights in the boundless desert! God is good to youth, and harsh to old age!

Next to Saïd Mohammed, her father, Sakîna's brother was the finest horseman of the tribe, and his white mare their fleetest steed. I had cast covetous eyes upon this glorious creature, my friends, and secretly had made such overtures as were calculated to win her confidence.

Within two weeks, then, my plans were complete—up to a point. Since they were doomed to failure, like my great scheme, I shall not trouble you with their details, but an hour before dawn on a certain night I cut the camel-hair tethering of the white mare, and, undetected, led the beautiful creature over the silent sands to a cup-like depression, a thousand yards distant from the camp.

The Bedouin who was upon guard that night had with him a gourd of 'erksoos. This was customary, and I had chosen an occasion when the duty of filling the sentinel's gourd had fallen upon Sakîna; to his 'erksoos I had added four drops of dark brown fluid from my medicine chest.

It was an hour before dawn, then, when I stood beside the white mare, watching and listening; it was an hour before dawn when she for whom my great scheme was forgotten, for whom I was about to risk the anger, the just anger, of men amongst the most fierce in the known world, came running fleetly over the hillocks down into the little valley, and threw herself into my arms. . . .

When dawn burst in gloomy splendor over the desert, we were still five hours' ride from the spot where I had proposed temporarily to conceal myself, with perhaps an hour's start of the Arabs. I knew the desert ways well enough, but the ghostly and desolate place in which I now found myself nevertheless filled me with foreboding.

A seam of black volcanic rock split the sands for a great distance, forming a kind of natural wall of forbidding aspect. In places this wall was pierced by tunnel-like openings; I think they may have been prehistoric tombs. There was no scrap of verdure visible, north, south, east or west; only desolation, sand, grayness, and this place, ghostly and wan with that ancient sorrow, that odor of remote mortality which is called "the dust of Egypt."

Seated before me in the saddle, Sakîna looked up into my face with a never-changing confidence, having her little brown fingers interlocked about my neck. But her strength was failing. A short rest was imperative.

Thus far I had detected no evidence of pursuit and, descending from the saddle, I placed my weary companion upon a rock over which I had laid a rug, and poured out for her a draught of cool water.

Bread and dates were our breakfast fare; but bread and dates and water are nectar and ambrosia when they are sweetened with kisses. Oh! the glorious madness of youth! Sometimes, my friends, I am almost tempted to believe that the man who has never been wicked has never been happy!

Picture us, then, if you can, set amid that desolation, which for us was a rose-garden, eating of that unpalatable food—which for us was the food of the gods!

So we remained awhile, deliriously happy, though death might terminate our joys ere we again saw the sun, when something . . . *something* spoke to me. . . .

Understand me, I did not say that *someone* spoke, I did not say that anything *audible* spoke. But I know that, unlocking those velvet arms which clung to me, I stood up slowly—and, still slowly, turned and looked back at the frowning black rocks.

Merciful God! My heart beats wildly now when I recall that moment.

Motionless as a statue, but in a crouching attitude, as if about to leap down, he who had warned me so truly stood upon the highest point of the rocks watching us!

How long did I remain thus?

I cannot pretend to say; but when I turned to Sakîna—she lay trembling on the ground, with her face hidden in her hands.

Then, down over the piled-up rocks, this mysterious and ominous being came leaping. Old man though he was, he descended with the agility of a mountain goat—and sometimes, in the difficult places, *he went on all fours.*

Crossing the intervening strip of sand, he stood before me. You have seen the reproach in the eyes of a faithful dog whose master has struck him unjustly? Such a reproach shone out from the yellow eyes of this desert wanderer. I cannot account for it; I can say no more....

It was impossible for me to speak; I trembled violently; such a fear and such a madness of sorrow possessed me that I would have welcomed any death—to have freed me from that intolerable reproach.

He suddenly pointed towards the horizon where against the curtain of the dawn black figures appeared.

I fell upon my knees beside Sakîna. I was a poor, pitiable thing; the madness of my passion had left me, and already I was within the great Shadow; I could not even weep; I knew that I had brought Sakîna out into that desolate place—to die.

And now the man whose ways were unlike human ways began to babble insanely, gesticulating and plucking at me. I cannot hope to make you feel one little part of the emotion with which those instants were laden. Sakîna clung to me trembling in a way I can never forget—never, never forget. And the look in her eyes! even now I cannot bear to think of it, I cannot bear—

Those almost colorless lizards which dart about in the desert places with incredible swiftness were now coming forth from their nests; and all the while the black figures, unheard as yet, were approaching along the path of the sun.

My mad folly grew more apparent to me every moment. I realized that this which so rapidly was overtaking me had been inevitable from the first. The strange wild man stood watching me with that intolerable glare, so that my trembling companion shrank from him in horror.

But evidently he was seeking to convey some idea to me. He gesticulated constantly, pointing to the approaching Arabs and then over his shoulder to the frowning rock behind. Since it was too late for flight—for I knew that the white mare with a double burden could never outpace our pursuers—it occurred to me at the moment when the muffled beat of hoofs first became audible, that this hermit of the rocks was endeavoring to induce me to seek some hiding-place with which no doubt he was acquainted.

How I cursed the delay which had enabled the Arabs to come up with us! I know, now, of course, that even had I not delayed, our ultimate capture was certain. But at the moment, in my despair, I thought otherwise.

And now I cursed the stupidity which had prevented me from following this weird guide; I even thought wrathfully of the poor frightened child, whose weakness had necessitated the delay and whose fears had contributed considerably to this later misunderstanding.

The pursuing party, numbering four, and led by Saïd Mohammed, was no more than five hundred yards away when I came to my senses. The hermit now was tugging at my arm with frightful insistence; his eyes were glaring insanely, and he chattered in an almost pitiable manner.

"Quick!" I cried, throwing my arm about Sakîna, "up to the rocks. This man can hide us!"

"No, no!" she whispered, "I dare not—"

But I lifted her, and signing to the singular being to lead the way, staggered forward despairingly.

The distance was greater than it appeared, the climb incredibly difficult. My guide held out his hand to me to assist me to mount the slippery rocks; but I had much ado to proceed and also to support Sakîna.

Her terror of the man and of the place to which he was leading us momentarily increased. Indeed, it seemed that she was becoming mad with fear. When the man paused before an opening in the rocks not more than fifteen or sixteen inches in height, and wildly waving his arms in the air, his elfin locks flying about his shoulder, his eyes glassy, intimated that we were to crawl in—Sakîna writhed free of my grasp and bounded back some three or four paces down the slope.

"Not in there!" she cried, holding out her little hands to me pitifully. "I dare not! He would devour us!"

At the foot of the slope, Saïd Mohammed, who had dismounted from his horse, and who, far ahead of the others, was advancing towards us, at that moment raised his gun and fired. . . .

Can I go on?

It is more years ago than I care to count, but it is fresher in my mind than the things of yesterday. A lonely old age is before me, my friends—for I have been a solitary man since that shot was fired. For me it changed the face of the world, for me it ended youth, revealing me to myself for what I was.

Something more nearly resembling human speech than any sound he had yet uttered burst from the lips of the wild man as the report of Saïd Mohammed's shot whispered in echoes through the mysterious labyrinths beneath us.

Fate had stood at the Sheikh's elbow as he pulled the trigger.

With a little soft cry—I hear it now, gentle, but having in it a world of agony—Sakîna sank at my feet . . . and her blood began to trickle over the black rocks on which she lay.

The man who professes to describe to you his emotions at such a frightful moment is an impostor. The world grew black before my eyes; every emotion of which my being was capable became paralysed.

I heard nothing, I saw nothing but the little huddled figure, that red stream upon the black rock, and the agonized love in the blazing eyes of Sakîna. Groaning, I threw myself down beside her, and as she sighed out her life upon my breast, I knew—God help me—that what had been but a youthful amour, was now a life's tragedy; that for me the light of the world had gone out, that I should never again know the warmth of the sun and the gladness of the morning. . . .

The cave man, with a dog-like fidelity, sought now to drag me from my dead love, to drag me into that gloomy lair which she had shrunk from entering. His incoherent mutterings broke in upon my semi-coma; but I shook him off, I shrieked curses at him. . . .

Now the Bedouins were mounting the slope, not less than a hundred yards below me. In the growing light I could see the face of Saïd Mohammed. . . .

The man beside me exerted all his strength to drag me back into the gallery or cave—I know not what it was; but with my arms locked about Sakîna I lay watching the pursuers coming closer and closer.

Then, those persistent efforts suddenly ceased, and dully I told myself that this weird being, having done his best to save me, had fled in order to save himself.

I was wrong.

You have asked me for a story of the magic of Egypt, and although, as you see, it has cost me tears—oh! I am not ashamed of those tears, my friends!—I have recounted this story to you. You say, where is the magic? and I might reply: the magic was in the changing of my false love to a true. But there was another magic as well, and it grew up around me now at this moment when I lay inert, waiting for death.

From behind me, from above me, arose a cry—a cry. You may have heard of the Bedouin song, the "Mizmûne":

> "Ya men melek ana dêri waat sa jebb,
> Id el' ish hoos' a beb hatsa azât ta lebb."

You may have heard how when it is sung in a certain fashion, flowers drop from their stalks? Also, you may have doubted this, never having heard a magical cry.

I do not doubt it, my friends! For I *have* heard a magical cry—this cry which arose from behind me! It started some chord in my dulled consciousness which had never spoken before. I turned my head—and there upon the highest point of the rocks stood the cave man. He suddenly stretched forth his hands.

Again he uttered that uncanny, that indescribable cry. It was not human. It was not animal. Yet it was nearer to the cry of an animal than to any sound made by the human species. His eyes gleamed with an awful light, his spare body had assumed a strange significance; he was transfigured.

A third time he uttered the cry, and out from one of those openings in the rock which I have mentioned, crept a jackal. You know how a jackal avoids the day, how furtive, how nocturnal a creature it is? but there in the golden glory which proclaimed the coming of the sun, black silhouettes moved.

A great wonder possessed me, as the first jackal was followed by a second, by a third, by a fourth, by a fifth. Did I say a fifth? . . . By five hundred—by five thousand!

From every visible hole in the rocks, jackals poured forth in packs. Wonder left me, fear left me; I forgot my sorrow, I became a numbed intelligence amid a desert of jackals. Over a sea of moving furry backs, I saw that upstanding crag and the weird crouching figure upon it. Right and left, above and below, jackals moved . . . and all turned their heads towards the approaching Bedouins!

Again—again I heard that dreadful cry. The jackals, in a pack, thousands strong, began to advance upon the Bedouins!. . .

Not east or west, north or south, could you hope to find a braver man than was the Sheikh Saïd Mohammed; but—he fled!

I saw the four horsemen riding like furies into the morning sun. The white mare, riderless, galloped with them—and the desert behind was yellow with jackals! For the last time I heard the cry.

The jackals began to return!

Forgive me, dear friends, if I seem an emotional fool. But when I recovered from the swoon which blotted out that unnatural spectacle, the wizard—for now I knew him for nothing less—had dug a deep trench—and had left me, alone.

Not a jackal was in sight; the sun blazed cruelly upon the desert. With my own hands I laid my love to rest in the sands. No cross, no crescent marks her resting-place; but I left my youth upon her grave, as a last offering.

You may say that, since I had sinned so grievously, since I had betrayed the noble confidence of Saïd Mohammed, my host, I escaped lightly.

Ah! you do not know!

And what of the strange being whose gratitude I had done so little to merit but yet which knew no bounds? It is of him that I will tell you.

Years later—how many it does not matter, but I was a man with no illusions—my restless wanderings (I being still a desert bird-of-passage) brought me one night to a certain well but rarely visited. It lay in a depression, like another well that I am fated often to see in my dreams, and, as one approached, the crowns of the palm trees which grew there appeared above the mounds of sand.

I was alone and tired out; the next possible camping-place—for I had no water— was many miles away. Yet it was written that I should press on to that other distant well, weary though I was.

First, then, as I came up, I perceived numbers of vultures in the air; and I began to fear that someone near to his end lay at the well. But when, from the top of a mound, I obtained a closer view, I saw a sight that, after one quick glance, caused me to spur up my tired horse and to fly—fly, with panic in my heart.

The brilliant moon bathed the hollow in light and cast dense shadows of the palm stems upon the slope beyond. By the spring, his fallen face ghastly in the moonlight, in a clear space twenty feet across, lay a dead man.

Even from where I sat I knew him; but, had I doubted, other evidence was there of his identity. As I mounted the slope, thousands of fiery eyes were turned upon me.

God! that arena all about was alive with jackals—jackals, my friends, eaters of carrion—which, silent, watchful, guarded the wizard dead, who, living, had been their lord!

THE GREEN FLAG

Arthur Conan Doyle

WHEN JACK CONOLLY, OF THE IRISH SHOTGUN BRIGADE, THE RORY OF the Hills Inner Circle, and the extreme left wing of the Land League, was incontinently shot by Sergeant Murdoch of the constabulary, in a little moonlight frolic near Kanturk, his twin brother Dennis joined the British Army. The countryside had become too hot for him; and, as the seventy-five shillings were wanting which might have carried him to America, he took the only way handy of getting himself out of the way. Seldom has Her Majesty had a less promising recruit, for his hot Celtic blood seethed with hatred against Britain and all things British. The Sergeant, however, smiling complacently over his six feet of brawn and his forty-four-inch chest, whisked him off with a dozen other of the boys to the depot at Fermoy, whence in a few weeks they were sent on, with the spade-work kinks taken out of their backs, to the first battalion of the Royal Mallows, at the top of the roster for foreign service.

The Royal Mallows, at about that date, were as strange a lot of men as ever were paid by a great empire to fight its battles. It was the darkest hour of the land struggle, when the one side came out with crowbar and battering-ram by day, and the other with mask and with shot-gun by night. Men driven from their homes and potato-patches found their way even into the service of the Government, to which it seemed to them that they owed their troubles, and now and then they did wild things before they came. There were recruits in the Irish regiments who would forget to answer to their own names, so short had been their acquaintance with them. Of these the Royal Mallows had their full share; and, while they still retained their fame as being one of the smartest corps in the Army, no one knew better than their officers that they were dry-rotted with treason and with bitter hatred of the flag under which they served.

And the centre of all the disaffection was C Company, in which Dennis Conolly found himself enrolled. They were Celts, Catholics, and men of the tenant class to a man; and their whole experience of the British Government had been an inexorable landlord, and a constabulary who seemed to them to be always on the side of the rent-collector. Dennis was not the only moonlighter in the ranks, nor was he alone in having an intolerable family blood-feud to harden his heart. Savagery had begotten savagery in that veiled civil war. A landlord with an iron mortgage weighing down upon him had small bowels for his tenantry. He did but take what the law allowed; and yet, with men like Jim Holan, or Patrick McQuire, or Peter Flynn, who had seen the roofs torn from their cottages and their folk huddled among their pitiable furniture upon the roadside, it was ill to argue about abstract law. What matter that in that long and bitter struggle there was many another outrage on the part of the tenant, and many another grievance on the side of the landowner! A stricken man can only feel his own wound, and the rank and file of the C Company of the Royal Mallows were sore and savage to the soul. There were low whisperings in barrack-rooms and canteens, stealthy meetings in public-house parlours, bandying of passwords from mouth to mouth, and many other signs which made their officers right glad when the order came which sent them to foreign, and better still to active, service.

For Irish regiments have before now been disaffected, and have at a distance looked upon the foe as though he might, in truth, be the friend; but when they have been put face on to him, and when their officers have dashed to the front with a wave and a halloo, those rebel hearts have softened and their gallant Celtic blood has boiled with the mad joy of fight, until the slower Britons have marvelled that they ever could have doubted the loyalty of their Irish comrades. So it would be again, according to the officers, and so it would not be if Dennis Conolly and a few others could have their way.

It was a March morning upon the eastern fringe of the Nubian desert. The sun had not yet risen; but a tinge of pink flushed up as far as the cloudless zenith, and the long strip of sea lay like a rosy ribbon across the horizon. From the coast inland stretched dreary sand-plains, dotted over with thick clumps of mimosa scrub and mottled patches of thorny bush. No tree broke the monotony of that vast desert. The dull, dusty hue of the thickets and the yellow glare of the sand were the only colours, save at one point where, from a distance, it seemed that a landslip of snow-white stones had shot itself across a low foot-hill. But as the traveller approached he saw, with a thrill, that these were no stones, but the bleaching bones of a slaughtered army. With its dull tints, its gnarled viprous bushes, its arid, barren soil, and this death-streak trailed across it, it was indeed a nightmare country.

Some eight or ten miles inland the rolling plain curved upwards with a steeper slope until it ran into a line of red basaltic rock which zigzagged from north to south, heaping itself up at one point into a fantastic knoll. On the summit of this there stood upon that March morning three Arab chieftains—the Sheik Kadra of the Hadendowas, Moussa Wad Aburhegel, who led the Berber dervishes, and Hamid Wad Hussein, who had come northward with his fighting men from the land of the Baggaras. They had all three just risen from their praying-carpets, and were peering out, with fierce, high-nosed faces thrust forwards, at the stretch of country revealed by the spreading dawn.

The red rim of the sun was pushing itself now above the distant sea, and the whole coastline stood out brilliantly yellow against the rich deep blue beyond. At one spot lay a huddle of white-walled houses, a mere splotch in the distance; while four tiny cock-boats, which lay beyond, marked the position of three of Her Majesty's ten-thousand-ton troopers and the Admiral's flagship. But it was not upon the distant town, nor upon the great vessels, nor yet upon the sinister white litter which gleamed in the plain beneath them, that the Arab chieftains gazed. Two miles from where they stood, amid the sand-hills and the mimosa scrub, a great parallelogram had been marked by piled-up bushes. From the inside of this dozens of tiny blue smoke-reeks curled up into the still morning air; while there rose from it a confused deep murmur, the voices of men and the gruntings of camels blended into the same insect buzz.

"The unbelievers have cooked their morning food," said the Baggara chief, shading his eyes with his tawny, sinewy hand. "Truly their sleep has been but scanty; for Hamid and a hundred of his men have fired upon them since the rising of the moon."

"So it was with these others," answered the Sheik Kadra, pointing with his sheathed sword towards the old battle-field. "They also had a day of little water and a night of little rest, and the heart was gone out of them ere ever the sons of the Prophet had looked them in the eyes. This blade drank deep that day, and will again before the sun has travelled from the sea to the hill."

"And yet these are other men," remarked the Berber dervish. "Well, I know that Allah has placed them in the clutch of our fingers, yet it may be that they with the big hats will stand firmer than the cursed men of Egypt."

"Pray Allah that it may be so," cried the fierce Baggara, with a flash of his black eyes. "It was not to chase women that I brought seven hundred men from the river to the coast. See, my brother, already they are forming their array."

A fanfare of bugle-calls burst from the distant camp. At the same time the bank of bushes at one side had been thrown or trampled down, and the little army within began to move slowly out onto the plain. Once clear of the camp they halted, and the slant rays of the sun struck flashes from bayonet and from gun-barrel as the ranks closed up until the big pith helmets joined into a single long white ribbon. Two streaks of scarlet glowed on either side of the square, but elsewhere the fringe of fighting-men was of the dull yellow khaki tint which hardly shows against the desert sand. Inside their array was a dense mass of camels and mules bearing stores and ambulance needs. Outside a twinkling clump of cavalry was drawn up on each flank, and in front a thin scattered line of mounted infantry was already slowly advancing over the bush-strewn plain, halting on every eminence, and peering warily round as men might who have to pick their steps among the bones of those who have preceded them.

The three chieftains still lingered upon the knoll, looking down with hungry eyes and compressed lips at the dark steel-tipped patch.

"They are slower to start than the men of Egypt," the Sheik of the Hadendowas growled in his beard.

"Slower also to go back, perchance, my brother," murmured the dervish. "And yet they are not many—three thousand at the most."

"And we ten thousand, with the Prophet's grip upon our spear-hafts and his words upon our banner. See to their chieftain, how he rides upon the right and looks up at us with the glass that sees from afar! It may be that he sees this also." The Arab shook his sword at the small clump of horsemen who had spurred out from the square.

"Lo! he beckons," cried the dervish; "and see those others at the corner, how they bend and heave. Ha! by the Prophet, I had thought it."

As he spoke a little woolly puff of smoke spurted up at the corner of the square, and a seven-pound shell burst with a hard metallic smack just over their heads. The splinters knocked chips from the red rocks around them.

"Bismillah!" cried the Hadendowa; "if the gun can carry thus far, then ours can answer to it. Ride to the left, Moussa, and tell Ben Ali to cut the skin from the Egyptians if they cannot hit yonder mark. And you, Hamid, to the right, and see that three thousand men lie close in the wady that we have chosen. Let the others beat the drum and show the banner of the Prophet; for by the black stone their spears will have drunk deep ere they look upon the stars again."

A long, straggling, boulder-strewn plateau lay on the summit of the red hills, sloping very precipitously to the plain, save at one point, where a winding gully curved downwards, its mouth choked with sand-mounds and olive-hued scrub. Along the edge of this position lay the Arab host, a motley crew or shock-headed desert clansmen, fierce predatory slave-dealers of the interior, and wild dervishes from the Upper Nile, all blent together by their common fearlessness and fanaticism. Two races were there, as wide as the poles apart, the thin-lipped, straight-haired Arab, and the thick-lipped, curly negro; yet the faith of Islam had bound them closer than a blood tie. Squatting among the rocks, or lying thickly in the shadow, they peered out at the slow-moving square beneath them, while women with water-skins and bags of dhoora fluttered from group to group, calling out to each other those fighting texts from the Koran which in the hour of battle are maddening as wine to the true believer. A score of banners waved over the ragged, valiant crew, and among them, upon desert horses and white Bishareen camels, were the Emirs and Sheiks who were to lead them against the infidels.

As the Sheik Kadra sprang into his saddle and drew his sword there was a wild whoop and a clatter of waving spears, while the one-ended war-drums burst into a dull crash like a wave upon shingle. For a moment ten thousand men were up on the rocks with brandished arms and leaping figures; the next they were undercover, again waiting sternly and silently for their chieftain's orders. The square was less than half a mile from the ridge now, and shell after shell from the seven-pound guns were pitching over it. A deep roar on the right, and then a second one showed that the Egyptian Krupps were in action. Sheik Kadra's hawk eyes saw that the shells burst far beyond the mark, and he spurred his horse along to where a knot of mounted chiefs were gathered round the two guns, which were served by their captured crews.

"How is this, Ben Ali?" he cried. "It was not thus that the dogs fired when it was their own brothers in faith at whom they aimed!"

A chieftain reined his horse back, and thrust a blood-smeared sword into its sheath. Beside him two Egyptian artillerymen with their throats cut were sobbing out their lives upon the ground.

"Who lays the gun this time?" asked the fierce chief, glaring at the frightened gunners. "Here, thou black-browed child of Shaitan, aim, and aim for thy life."

It may have been chance, or it may have been skill, but the third and fourth shells burst over the square. Sheik Kadra smiled grimly and galloped back to the left, where his spearmen were streaming down into the gully. As he joined them a deep growling rose from the plain beneath, like the snarling of a sullen wild beast, and a little knot of tribesmen fell in a struggling heap, caught in the blast of lead from a Gardner. Their comrades pressed on over them, and sprang down into the ravine. From all along the crest burst the hard sharp crackle of Remington fire.

The square had slowly advanced, rippling over the low sandhills, and halting every few minutes to rearrange its formation. Now, having made sure that there was no force of the enemy in the scrub, it changed its direction, and began to take a line parallel to the Arab position. It was too steep to assail from the front, and if they moved far enough to the right the General hoped that he might turn it. On the top of those ruddy hills lay a baronetcy for him, and a few extra hundreds in his pension, and he meant having them both that day. The Remington fire was annoying, and so were those two Krupp guns: already there were more cacolets full than he cared to see. But on the whole he thought it better to hold his fire until he had more to aim at than a few hundred of fuzzy heads peeping over a razor-back ridge. He was a bulky, red-faced man, a fine whist-player, and a soldier who knew his work. His men believed in him, and he had good reason to believe in them, for he had excellent stuff under him that day. Being an ardent champion of the short-service system, he took particular care to work with veteran first battalions, and his little force was the compressed essence of an army corps.

The left front of the square was formed by four companies of the Royal Wessex, and the right by four of the Royal Mallows. On either side the other halves of the same regiments marched in quarter column of companies. Behind them, on the right was a battalion of Guards, and on the left one of Marines, while the rear was closed in by a Rifle battalion. Two Royal Artillery seven-pound screw-guns kept pace with the square, and a dozen white-bloused sailors, under their blue-coated, tight-waisted officers, trailed their Gardner in front, turning every now and then to spit up at the draggled banners which waved over the cragged ridge. Hussars and Lancers scouted in the scrub at each side, and within moved the clump of camels, with humorous eyes and supercilious lips, their comic faces a contrast to the blood stained men who already lay huddled in the cacolets on either side.

The square was now moving slowly on a line parallel with the rocks, stopping every few minutes to pick up wounded, and to allow the screw-guns and Gardner to make themselves felt. The men looked serious, for that spring onto the rocks of the Arab army had given them a vague glimpse of the number and ferocity of their foes; but their faces were set like stone, for they knew to a man that they must win or they must die—and die, too, in a particularly unlovely fashion. But most serious of all was the General, for he had seen that which brought a flush to his cheeks and a frown to his brow.

"I say, Stephen," said he to his galloper, "those Mallows seems a trifle jumpy. The right flank company bulged a bit when the niggers showed on the hill."

"Youngest troops in the square, sir," murmured the aide, looking at them critically through his eyeglass.

"Tell Colonel Flanagan to see to it, Stephen," said the General; and the galloper sped upon his way. The Colonel, a fine old Celtic warrior, was over at C Company in an instant.

"How are the men, Captain Foley?"

"Never better, sir," answered the senior captain in the spirit that makes a Madras officer look murder if you suggest recruiting his regiment from the Punjaub.

"Stiffen them up!" cried the Colonel. As he rode away a colour-sergeant seemed to trip, and fell forward into a mimosa bush.

He made no effort to rise, but lay in a heap among the thorns.

"Sergeant O'Rooke's gone, sorr," cried a voice.

"Never mind, lads," said Captain Foley. "He's died like a soldier, fighting for his Queen."

"To hell with the Queen!" shouted a hoarse voice from the ranks.

But the roar of the Gardner and the typewriter-like clicking of the hopper burst in at the tail of the words. Captain Foley heard them, and Subalterns Grice and Murphy heard them; but there are times when a deaf ear is a gift from the gods.

"Steady, Mallows!" cried the Captain, in a pause of the grunting machine-gun. "We have the honour of Ireland to guard this day."

"And well we know how to guard it, Captin!" cried the same ominous voice; and there was a buzz from the length of the company.

The Captain and the two subs, came together behind the marching line.

"They seem a bit out of hand," murmured the Captain.

"Bedad," said the Galway boy, "they mean to scoot like redshanks."

"They nearly broke when the blacks showed on the hill," said Grice.

"The first man that turns, my sword is through him," cried Foley, loud enough to be heard by five files on either side of him. Then, in a lower voice, "It's a bitter drop to swallow, but it's my duty to report what you think to the Chief and have a company of Jollies put behind us." He turned away with the safety of the square upon his mind, and before he had reached his goal the square had ceased to exist.

In their march in front of what looked like a face of cliff, they had come opposite to the mouth of the gully, in which, screened by scrub and boulders, three thousand chosen dervishes, under Hamid Wad Hussein of the Bagarras, were crouching. Tat, tat, tat, went the rifles of three mounted infantrymen in front of the left shoulder of the square, and an instant later they were spurring it for their lives, crouching over the manes of their horses, and pelting over the sandhills with thirty or forty galloping chieftains at their heels. Rocks and scrub and mimosa swarmed suddenly into life. Rushing black figures came and went in the gaps of the bushes. A howl that drowned the shouts of the officers, a long quavering yell, burst from the ambuscade. Two rolling volleys from the Royal Wessex, one crash from the screw-gun firing shrapnel, and then before a second cartridge could be rammed in, a living, glistening black wave tipped with steel, had rolled over the gun, the Royal Wessex had been dashed back among the camels, and a thousand fanatics were hewing and hacking in the heart of what had been the square.

The camels and mules in the centre, jammed more and more together as their leaders flinched from the rush of the tribesmen, shut out the view of the other three faces, who could only tell that the Arabs had got in by the yells upon Allah, which rose ever nearer and nearer amid the clouds of sand-dust, the struggling animals, and the dense mass of swaying, cursing men. Some of the Wessex fired back at the Arabs who had passed them, as excited Tommies will, and it is whispered among doctors that it was not always a Remington bullet which was cut from a wound that day. Some rallied in little knots, stabbing furiously with their bayonets at the rushing spearmen. Others turned at bay with their backs against the camels, and others round the General and his staff, who, revolver in hand, had flung themselves into the heart of it. But the whole square was sidling slowly away from the gorge, pushed back by the pressure at the shattered corner.

The officers and men at the other faces were glancing nervously to their rear, uncertain what was going on, and unable to take help to their comrades without breaking the formation.

"By Jove, they've got through the Wessex!" cried Grice of the Mallows.

"The divils have hurrooshed us, Ted," said his brother subaltern, cocking his revolver.

The ranks were breaking and crowding towards Private Conolly, all talking together as the officers peered back through the veil of dust. The sailors had run their Gardner out, and she was squirting death out of her five barrels into the flank of the rushing stream of savages.

"Oh, this bloody gun!" shouted a voice. "She's jammed again." The fierce metallic grunting had ceased, and her crew were straining and hauling at the breech.

"This damned vertical feed!" cried an officer. "The spanner, Wilson, the spanner! Stand to your cutlasses, boys, or they're into us."

His voice rose into a shriek as he ended, for a shovel-headed spear had been buried in his chest. A second wave of dervishes lapped over the hillocks, and burst upon the machine-gun and the right front of the line. The sailors were overborne in an instant, but the Mallows, with their fighting blood aflame, met the yell of the Moslem with an even wilder, fiercer cry, and dropped two hundred of them with a single point-blank volley. The howling, leaping crew swerved away to the right, and dashed on into the gap which had already been made for them.

But C Company had drawn no trigger to stop that fiery rush. The men leaned moodily upon their Martinis. Some had even thrown them upon the ground. Conolly was talking fiercely to those about him. Captain Foley, thrusting his way through the press, rushed up to him with a revolver in his hand.

"This is your doing, you villain!" he cried.

"If you raise your pistol, Captin, your brains will be over your coat," said a low voice at his side.

He saw that several rifles were turned on him. The two subs, had pressed forward, and were by his side.

"What is it, then?" he cried, looking round from one fierce mutinous face to another. "Are you Irishmen? Are you soldiers? What are you here for but to fight for your country?"

"England is no country of ours," cried several.

"You are not fighting for England. You are fighting for Ireland, and for the Empire of which it is part."

"A black curse on the Impire!" shouted Private McQuire, throwing down his rifle. "'Twas the Impire that backed the man that druv me onto the roadside. May me hand stiffen before I draw thrigger for it."

"What's the Impire to us, Captain Foley, and what's the Widdy to us ayther?" cried a voice.

"Let the constabulary foight for her."

"Ay, be God, they'd be better imployed than pullin' a poor man's thatch about his ears."

"Or shootin' his brother, as they did mine."

"It was the Impire laid my groanin' mother by the wayside. Her son will rot before he upholds it, and ye can put that in the charge-sheet in the next coort-martial."

In vain the three officers begged, menaced, persuaded. The square was still moving, ever moving, with the same bloody fight raging in its entrails. Even while they had been speaking they had been shuffling backwards, and the useless Gardner, with her slaughtered crew, was already a good hundred yards from them. And the pace was accelerating. The mass of men, tormented and writhing, was trying, by a common instinct, to reach some clearer ground where they could re-form. Three faces were still intact, but the fourth had been caved in, and badly mauled, without its comrades being able to help it. The Guards had met a fresh rush of the Hadendowas, and had blown back the tribesmen with a volley, and the Cavalry had ridden over another stream of them, as they welled out of the gully. A litter of hamstrung horses, and haggled men behind them, showed that a spearman on his face among the bushes can show some sport to the man who charges him. But, in spite of all, the square was still reeling swiftly backwards trying to shake itself clear of this torment which clung to its heart. Would it break, or would it re-form? The lives of five regiments and the honour of the flag hung upon the answer.

Some, at least, were breaking. The C Company of the Mallows had lost all military order and was pushing back in spite of the haggard officers, who cursed and shoved and prayed in the vain attempt to hold them. Their Captain and the subs, were elbowed and jostled, while the men crowded towards Private Conolly for their orders. The confusion had not spread, for the other companies, in the dust and smoke and turmoil, had lost touch with their mutinous comrades. Captain Foley saw that even now there might be time to avert a disaster.

"Think what you are doing, man," he yelled, rushing towards the ringleader. "There are a thousand Irish in the square, and they are dead men if we break."

The words alone might have had little effect on the old moonlighter. It is possible that, in his scheming brain, he had already planned how he was to club his Irish together and lead them to the sea. But at that moment the Arabs broke through the screen of camels which had fended them off. There was a struggle, a screaming, a mule rolled over, a wounded man sprang up in a cacolet with a spear through him, and then through the narrow gap surged a stream of naked savages, mad with battle, drunk with slaughter, spotted and splashed with blood—blood dripping from their spears, their arms, their faces. Their yells, their bounds, their crouching, darting figures, the horrid energy of their spear-thrusts, made them look like a blast of fiends from the pit. And were these the Allies of Ireland? Were these the men who were to strike for her against her enemies? Conolly's soul rose up in loathing at the thought.

He was a man of firm purpose, and yet at the first sight of those howling fiends that purpose faltered, and at the second it was blown to the winds. He saw a huge coal-black negro seize a shrieking camel-driver and saw at his throat with a knife. He saw a shock-headed tribesman plunge his great spear through the back of their own little bugler from Millstreet. He saw a dozen deeds of blood—the murder of the wounded, the hacking of the unarmed—and caught, too, in a glance, the good wholesome faces of the faced-about rear rank of the Marines. The Mallows, too, had faced about, and in an instant Conolly had thrown himself into the heart of C Company, striving with the officers to form the men up with their comrades.

But the mischief had gone too far. The rank and file had no heart in their work. They had broken before, and this last rush of murderous savages was a hard thing for broken men to stand against. They flinched from the furious faces and dripping forearms. Why should they throw away their lives for a flag for which they cared nothing? Why should their leader urge them to break, and now shriek to them to reform? They would not re-form. They wanted to get to the sea and to safety. He flung himself among them with outstretched arms, with words of reason, with shouts, with gaspings. It was useless; the tide was beyond his control. They were shredding out into the desert with their faces set for the coast.

"Bhoys, will ye stand for this?" screamed a voice. It was so ringing, so strenuous, that the breaking Mallows glanced backwards. They were held by what they saw. Private Conolly had planted his rifle-stock downwards in a mimosa bush. From the fixed bayonet there fluttered a little green flag with the crownless harp. God knows for what black mutiny, for what signal of revolt, that flag had been treasured up within the Corporal's tunic! Now its green wisp stood amid the rush, while three proud regimental colours were reeling slowly backwards.

"What for the flag?" yelled the private.

"My heart's blood for it! and mine! and mine!" cried a score of voices. "God bless it! The flag, boys—the flag!"

C Company were rallying upon it. The stragglers clutched at each other, and pointed. "Here, McQuire, Flynn, O'Hara," ran the shoutings. "Close on the flag! Back to the flag!" The three standards reeled backwards, and the seething square strove for a clearer space where they could form their shattered ranks; but C company, grim and powder-stained, choked with enemies and falling fast, still closed in on the little rebel ensign that flapped from the mimosa bush.

It was a good half-hour before the square, having disentangled itself from its difficulties and dressed its ranks, began to slowly move forwards over the ground, across which in its labor and anguish it had been driven. The long trail of Wessex men and Arabs showed but too clearly the path they had come.

"How many got into us, Stephen?" asked the General, tapping his snuff-box.

"I should put them down at a thousand or twelve hundred, sir."

"I did not see any get out again. What the devil were the Wessex thinking about? The Guards stood well, though; so did the Mallows."

"Colonel Flanagan reports that his front flank company was cut off, sir."

"Why, that's the Company that was out of hand when we advanced!"

"Colonel Flanagan reports, sir, that the Company took the whole brunt of the attack, and gave the square time to re-form."

"Tell the Hussars to ride forward, Stephen," said the General, "and try if they can see anything of them. There's no firing, and I fear that the Mallows will want to do some recruiting. Let the square take ground by the right, and then advance!"

But the Sheik Kadra of the Hadendowas saw from his knoll that the men with the big hats had rallied, and that they were coming back in the quiet business fashion of men whose work was before them. He took counsel with Moussa the Dervish and Hussein the Bagarra, and a woestruck man was he when he learned that the third of his men were safe in the Moslem Paradise. So, having still some signs of victory to show, he gave the word, and the desert warriors flitted off unseen and unheard, even as they had come.

A red rock plateau, a few hundred spears and Remingtons, and a plain which for the second time was strewn with slaughtered men, was all that his day's fighting gave to the English General.

It was a squadron of Hussars which came first to the spot where the rebel flag had waved. A dense litter of Arab dead marked the place. Within the flag waved no longer, but the rifle still stood in the mimosa bush, and round it, with their wounds in front, lay the Fenian private and the silent ranks of his Irishry. Sentiment is not an English failing, but the Hussar Captain raised his hilt in a salute as he rode past the blood-soaked ring.

The British General sent home dispatches to his Government, and so did the Chief of the Hadendowas to his, though the style and manner differed somewhat in each. "The Sheik Kadra of the Hadendowa people to Mohammed Ahmed, the chosen of Allah, homage and greeting," began the latter. "Know by this that on the fourth day of this moon we gave battle to the Kaffirs who call themselves Inglees, having with us the Chief Hussein with ten thousand of the faithful. By the blessing of Allah we have broken them, and chased them for a mile, though indeed these infidels are different from the dogs of Egypt, and have slain very many of our men. Yet we hope to smite them again ere the new moon be come, to which end I trust that thou wilt send us a thousand Dervishes from Omdurman. In token of our victory I send you by this messenger a flag which we have taken. By the colour it might well seem to have belonged to those of the true faith, but the Kaffirs gave their blood freely to save it, and so we think that, though small, it is very dear to them."

AT SEA

A DESCENT INTO THE MAELSTRÖM

Edgar Allan Poe

The ways of God in Nature, as in Providence, are not as our ways; nor
are the models that we frame any way commensurate to the vastness,
profundity, and unsearchableness of His works, *which have a depth in them
greater than the well of Democritus.*

JOSEPH GLANVILLE

WE HAD NOW REACHED THE SUMMIT OF THE LOFTIEST CRAG. FOR SOME
minutes the old man seemed too much exhausted to speak.

"Not long ago," said he at length, "and I could have guided you
on this route as well as the youngest of my sons; but, about three years past, there
happened to me an event such as never happened before to mortal man—or at least
such as no man ever survived to tell of—and the six hours of deadly terror which I
then endured have broken me up body and soul. You suppose me a *very* old man—but
I am not. It took less than a single day to change these hairs from a jetty black to white,
to weaken my limbs, and to unstring my nerves, so that I tremble at the least exertion,
and am frightened at a shadow. Do you know I can scarcely look over this little cliff
without getting giddy?"

The "little cliff," upon whose edge he had so carelessly thrown himself down to
rest that the weightier portion of his body hung over it, while he was only kept from
falling by the tenure of his elbow on its extreme and slippery edge—this "little cliff"
arose, a sheer unobstructed precipice of black shining rock, some fifteen or sixteen
hundred feet from the world of crags beneath us. Nothing would have tempted me to
within half a dozen yards of its brink. In truth so deeply was I excited by the perilous
position of my companion, that I fell at full length upon the ground, clung to the
shrubs around me, and dared not even glance upward at the sky—while I struggled
in vain to divest myself of the idea that the very foundations of the mountain were
in danger from the fury of the winds. It was long before I could reason myself into
sufficient courage to sit up and look out into the distance.

"You must get over these fancies," said the guide, "for I have brought you here that you might have the best possible view of the scene of that event I mentioned—and to tell you the whole story with the spot just under your eye."

"We are now," he continued, in that particularizing manner which distinguished him—"we are now close upon the Norwegian coast—in the sixty-eighth degree of latitude—in the great province of Nordland—and in the dreary district of Lofoden. The mountain upon whose top we sit is Helseggen, the Cloudy. Now raise yourself up a little higher—hold on to the grass if you feel giddy—so—and look out, beyond the belt of vapor beneath us, into the sea."

I looked dizzily, and beheld a wide expanse of ocean, whose waters wore so inky a hue as to bring at once to my mind the Nubian geographer's account of the *Mare Tenebrarum*. A panorama more deplorably desolate no human imagination can conceive. To the right and left, as far as the eye could reach, there lay outstretched, like ramparts of the world, lines of horridly black and beetling cliff, whose character of gloom was but the more forcibly illustrated by the surf which reared high up against it its white and ghastly crest, howling and shrieking for ever. Just opposite the promontory upon whose apex we were placed, and at a distance of some five or six miles out at sea, there was visible a small, bleak-looking island; or, more properly, its position was discernible through the wilderness of surge in which it was enveloped. About two miles nearer the land, arose another of smaller size, hideously craggy and barren, and encompassed at various intervals by a cluster of dark rocks.

The appearance of the ocean, in the space between the more distant island and the shore, had something very unusual about it. Although, at the time, so strong a gale was blowing landward that a brig in the remote offing lay to under a double-reefed trysail, and constantly plunged her whole hull out of sight, still there was here nothing like a regular swell, but only a short, quick, angry cross dashing of water in every direction—as well in the teeth of the wind as otherwise. Of foam there was little except in the immediate vicinity of the rocks.

"The island in the distance," resumed the old man, "is called by the Norwegians Vurrgh. The one midway is Moskoe. That a mile to the northward is Ambaaren. Yonder are Islesen, Hotholm, Keildhelm, Suarven, and Buckholm. Farther off— between Moskoe and Vurrgh—are Otterholm, Flimen, Sandflesen, and Stockholm. These are the true names of the places—but why it has been thought necessary to name them at all, is more than either you or I can understand. Do you hear any thing? Do you see any change in the water?"

We had now been about ten minutes upon the top of Helseggen, to which we had ascended from the interior of Lofoden, so that we had caught no glimpse of the sea until it had burst upon us from the summit. As the old man spoke, I became aware of a loud and gradually increasing sound, like the moaning of a vast herd of buffaloes upon an American prairie; and at the same moment I perceived that what seamen term the *chopping* character of the ocean beneath us, was rapidly changing into a current which set to the eastward. Even while I gazed, this current acquired a monstrous velocity. Each moment added to its speed—to its headlong impetuosity. In five minutes the whole sea, as far as Vurrgh, was lashed into ungovernable fury; but it was between Moskoe and the coast that the main uproar held its sway. Here the vast bed of the waters, seamed and scarred into a thousand conflicting channels, burst suddenly into phrensied convulsion—heaving, boiling, hissing—gyrating in gigantic and innumerable vortices, and all whirling and plunging on to the eastward with a rapidity which water never elsewhere assumes except in precipitous descents.

In a few minutes more, there came over the scene another radical alteration. The general surface grew somewhat more smooth, and the whirlpools, one by one, disappeared, while prodigious streaks of foam became apparent where none had been seen before. These streaks, at length, spreading out to a great distance, and entering into combination, took unto themselves the gyratory motion of the subsided vortices, and seemed to form the germ of another more vast. Suddenly—very suddenly— this assumed a distinct and definite existence, in a circle of more than a half mile in diameter. The edge of the whirl was represented by a broad belt of gleaming spray; but no particle of this slipped into the mouth of the terrific funnel, whose interior, as far as the eye could fathom it, was a smooth, shining, and jet-black wall of water, inclined to the horizon at an angle of some forty-five degrees, speeding dizzily round and round with a swaying and sweltering motion, and sending forth to the winds an appalling voice, half shriek, half roar, such as not even the mighty cataract of Niagara ever lifts up in its agony to Heaven.

The mountain trembled to its very base, and the rock rocked. I threw myself upon my face, and clung to the scant herbage in an excess of nervous agitation.

"This," said I at length, to the old man—"this *can* be nothing else than the great whirlpool of the Maelström."

"So it is sometimes termed," said he. "We Norwegians call it the Moskoe-ström, from the island of Moskoe in the midway."

The ordinary accounts of this vortex had by no means prepared me for what I saw. That of Jonas Ramus, which is perhaps the most circumstantial of any, cannot impart the faintest conception either of the magnificence, or of the horror of the scene—or of the wild bewildering sense of *the novel* which confounds the beholder. I am not sure from what point of view the writer in question surveyed it, nor at what time; but it could neither have been from the summit of Helseggen, nor during a storm. There are some passages of his description, nevertheless, which may be quoted for their details, although their effect is exceedingly feeble in conveying an impression of the spectacle.

"Between Lofoden and Moskoe," he says, "the depth of the water is between thirty-six and forty fathoms; but on the other side, toward Ver (Vurrgh) this depth decreases so as not to afford a convenient passage for a vessel, without the risk of splitting on the rocks, which happens even in the calmest weather. When it is flood, the stream runs up the country between Lofoden and Moskoe with a boisterous rapidity; but the roar of its impetuous ebb to the sea is scarce equalled by the loudest and most dreadful cataracts; the noise being heard several leagues off, and the vortices or pits are of such an extent and depth, that if a ship comes within its attraction, it is inevitably absorbed and carried down to the bottom, and there beat to pieces against the rocks; and when the water relaxes, the fragments thereof are thrown up again. But these intervals of tranquility are only at the turn of the ebb and flood, and in calm weather, and last but a quarter of an hour, its violence gradually returning. When the stream is most boisterous, and its fury heightened by a storm, it is dangerous to come within a Norway mile of it. Boats, yachts, and ships have been carried away by not guarding against it before they were within its reach. It likewise happens frequently, that whales come too near the stream, and are overpowered by its violence; and then it is impossible to describe their howlings and bellowings in their fruitless struggles to disengage themselves. A bear once, attempting to swim from Lofoden to Moskoe, was caught by the stream and borne down, while he roared terribly, so as to be heard on shore. Large stocks of firs and pine trees, after being absorbed by the current, rise again broken and torn to such a degree as if bristles grew upon them. This plainly shows the bottom to consist of craggy rocks, among which they are whirled to and fro. This stream is regulated by the flux and reflux of the sea—it being constantly high and low water every six hours. In the year 1645, early in the morning of Sexagesima Sunday, it raged with such noise and impetuosity that the very stones of the houses on the coast fell to the ground."

In regard to the depth of the water, I could not see how this could have been ascertained at all in the immediate vicinity of the vortex. The "forty fathoms" must have reference only to portions of the channel close upon the shore either of Moskoe or Lofoden. The depth in the centre of the Moskoe-ström must be immeasurably greater; and no better proof of this fact is necessary than can be obtained from even the sidelong glance into the abyss of the whirl which may be had from the highest crag of Helseggen. Looking down from this pinnacle upon the howling Phlegethon below, I could not help smiling at the simplicity with which the honest Jonas Ramus records, as a matter difficult of belief, the anecdotes of the whales and the bears; for it appeared to me, in fact, a self-evident thing, that the largest ship of the line in existence, coming within the influence of that deadly attraction, could resist it as little as a feather the hurricane, and must disappear bodily and at once.

The attempts to account for the phenomenon—some of which, I remember, seemed to me sufficiently plausible in perusal—now wore a very different and unsatisfactory aspect. The idea generally received is that this, as well as three smaller vortices among the Ferroe islands, "have no other cause than the collision of waves rising and falling, at flux and reflux, against a ridge of rocks and shelves, which confines the water so that it precipitates itself like a cataract; and thus the higher the flood rises, the deeper must the fall be, and the natural result of all is a whirlpool or vortex, the prodigious suction of which is sufficiently known by lesser experiments."—These are the words of the Encyclopædia Britannica. Kircher and others imagine that in the centre of the channel of the Maelström is an abyss penetrating the globe, and issuing in some very remote part— the Gulf of Bothnia being somewhat decidedly named in one instance. This opinion, idle in itself, was the one to which, as I gazed, my imagination most readily assented; and, mentioning it to the guide, I was rather surprised to hear him say that, although it was the view almost universally entertained of the subject by the Norwegians, it nevertheless was not his own. As to the former notion he confessed his inability to comprehend it; and here I agreed with him—for, however conclusive on paper, it becomes altogether unintelligible, and even absurd, amid the thunder of the abyss.

"You have had a good look at the whirl now," said the old man, "and if you will creep round this crag, so as to get in its lee, and deaden the roar of the water, I will tell you a story that will convince you I ought to know something of the Moskoe-ström."

I placed myself as desired, and he proceeded.

"Myself and my two brothers once owned a schooner-rigged smack of about seventy tons burthen, with which we were in the habit of fishing among the islands beyond Moskoe, nearly to Vurrgh. In all violent eddies at sea there is good fishing, at proper opportunities, if one has only the courage to attempt it; but among the whole of the Lofoden coastmen, we three were the only ones who made a regular business of going out to the islands, as I tell you. The usual grounds are a great way lower down to the southward. There fish can be got at all hours, without much risk, and therefore these places are preferred. The choice spots over here among the rocks, however, not only yield the finest variety, but in far greater abundance; so that we often got in a single day, what the more timid of the craft could not scrape together in a week. In fact, we made it a matter of desperate speculation—the risk of life standing instead of labor, and courage answering for capital.

"We kept the smack in a cove about five miles higher up the coast than this; and it was our practice, in fine weather, to take advantage of the fifteen minutes' slack to push across the main channel of the Moskoe-ström, far above the pool, and then drop down upon anchorage somewhere near Otterholm, or Sandflesen, where the eddies are not so violent as elsewhere. Here we used to remain until nearly time for slack-water again, when we weighed and made for home. We never set out upon this expedition without a steady side wind for going and coming—one that we felt sure would not fail us before our return—and we seldom made a mis-calculation upon this point. Twice, during six years, we were forced to stay all night at anchor on account of a dead calm, which is a rare thing indeed just about here; and once we had to remain on the grounds nearly a week, starving to death, owing to a gale which blew up shortly after our arrival, and made the channel too boisterous to be thought of. Upon this occasion we should have been driven out to sea in spite of everything, (for the whirlpools threw us round and round so violently, that, at length, we fouled our anchor and dragged it) if it had not been that we drifted into one of the innumerable cross currents—here to-day and gone to-morrow—which drove us under the lee of Flimen, where, by good luck, we brought up.

"I could not tell you the twentieth part of the difficulties we encountered 'on the grounds'—it is a bad spot to be in, even in good weather—but we made shift always to run the gauntlet of the Moskoe-ström itself without accident; although at times my heart has been in my mouth when we happened to be a minute or so behind or before the slack. The wind sometimes was not as strong as we thought it at starting, and then we made rather less way than we could wish, while the current rendered the smack unmanageable. My eldest brother had a son eighteen years old, and I had two stout boys of my own. These would have been of great assistance at such times, in using the sweeps, as well as afterward in fishing—but, somehow, although we ran the risk ourselves, we had not the heart to let the young ones get into the danger—for, after all is said and done, it *was* a horrible danger, and that is the truth.

"It is now within a few days of three years since what I am going to tell you occurred. It was on the tenth day of July, 18—, a day which the people of this part of the world will never forget—for it was one in which blew the most terrible hurricane that ever came out of the heavens. And yet all the morning, and indeed until late in the afternoon, there was a gentle and steady breeze from the south-west, while the sun shone brightly, so that the oldest seaman among us could not have foreseen what was to follow.

"The three of us—my two brothers and myself—had crossed over to the islands about two o'clock P.M., and had soon nearly loaded the smack with fine fish, which, we all remarked, were more plenty that day than we had ever known them. It was just seven, *by my watch*, when we weighed and started for home, so as to make the worst of the Ström at slack water, which we knew would be at eight.

"We set out with a fresh wind on our starboard quarter, and for some time spanked along at a great rate, never dreaming of danger, for indeed we saw not the slightest reason to apprehend it. All at once we were taken aback by a breeze from over Helseggen. This was most unusual—something that had never happened to us before—and I began to feel a little uneasy, without exactly knowing why. We put the boat on the wind, but could make no headway at all for the eddies, and I was upon the point of proposing to return to the anchorage, when, looking astern, we saw the whole horizon covered with a singular copper-colored cloud that rose with the most amazing velocity.

"In the meantime the breeze that had headed us off fell away, and we were dead becalmed, drifting about in every direction. This state of things, however, did not last long enough to give us time to think about it. In less than a minute the storm was upon us—in less than two the sky was entirely overcast—and what with this and the driving spray, it became suddenly so dark that we could not see each other in the smack.

"Such a hurricane as then blew it is folly to attempt describing. The oldest seaman in Norway never experienced any thing like it. We had let our sails go by the run before it cleverly took us; but, at the first puff, both our masts went by the board as if they had been sawed off—the mainmast taking with it my youngest brother, who had lashed himself to it for safety.

"Our boat was the lightest feather of a thing that ever sat upon water. It had a complete flush deck, with only a small hatch near the bow, and this hatch it had always been our custom to batten down when about to cross the Ström, by way of precaution against the chopping seas. But for this circumstance we should have foundered at once—for we lay entirely buried for some moments. How my elder brother escaped destruction I cannot say, for I never had an opportunity of ascertaining. For my part, as soon as I had let the foresail run, I threw myself flat on deck, with my feet against the narrow gunwale of the bow, and with my hands grasping a ring-bolt near the foot of the fore-mast. It was mere instinct that prompted me to do this—which was undoubtedly the very best thing I could have done—for I was too much flurried to think.

"For some moments we were completely deluged, as I say, and all this time I held my breath, and clung to the bolt. When I could stand it no longer I raised myself upon my knees, still keeping hold with my hands, and thus got my head clear. Presently our little boat gave herself a shake, just as a dog does in coming out of the water, and thus rid herself, in some measure, of the seas. I was now trying to get the better of the stupor that had come over me, and to collect my senses so as to see what was to be done, when I felt somebody grasp my arm. It was my elder brother, and my heart leaped for joy, for I had made sure that he was overboard—but the next moment all this joy was turned into horror—for he put his mouth close to my ear, and screamed out the word '*Moskoe-ström!*'

"No one ever will know what my feelings were at that moment. I shook from head to foot as if I had had the most violent fit of the ague. I knew what he meant by that one word well enough—I knew what he wished to make me understand. With the wind that now drove us on, we were bound for the whirl of the Ström, and nothing could save us!

"You perceive that in crossing the Ström *channel*, we always went a long way up above the whirl, even in the calmest weather, and then had to wait and watch carefully for the slack—but now we were driving right upon the pool itself, and in such a hurricane as this! 'To be sure,' I thought, 'we shall get there just about the slack—there is some little hope in that'—but in the next moment I cursed myself for being so great a fool as to dream of hope at all. I knew very well that we were doomed, had we been ten times a ninety-gun ship.

"By this time the first fury of the tempest had spent itself, or perhaps we did not feel it so much, as we scudded before it, but at all events the seas, which at first had been kept down by the wind, and lay flat and frothing, now got up into absolute mountains. A singular change, too, had come over the heavens. Around in every direction it was still as black as pitch, but nearly overhead there burst out, all at once, a circular rift of clear sky—as clear as I ever saw—and of a deep bright blue—and through it there blazed forth the full moon with a lustre that I never before knew her to wear. She lit up every thing about us with the greatest distinctness—but, oh God, what a scene it was to light up!

"I now made one or two attempts to speak to my brother—but, in some manner which I could not understand, the din had so increased that I could not make him hear a single word, although I screamed at the top of my voice in his ear. Presently he shook his head, looking as pale as death, and held up one of his finger, as if to say '*listen!*'

"At first I could not make out what he meant—but soon a hideous thought flashed upon me. I dragged my watch from its fob. It was not going. I glanced at its face by the moonlight, and then burst into tears as I flung it far away into the ocean. *It had run down at seven o'clock! We were behind the time of the slack, and the whirl of the Ström was in full fury!*

"When a boat is well built, properly trimmed, and not deep laden, the waves in a strong gale, when she is going large, seem always to slip from beneath her—

which appears very strange to a landsman—and this is what is called *riding*, in sea phrase. Well, so far we had ridden the swells very cleverly; but presently a gigantic sea happened to take us right under the counter, and bore us with it as it rose—up—up— as if into the sky. I would not have believed that any wave could rise so high. And then down we came with a sweep, a slide, and a plunge, that made me feel sick and dizzy, as if I was falling from some lofty mountain-top in a dream. But while we were up I had thrown a quick glance around—and that one glance was all sufficient. I saw our exact position in an instant. The Moskoe-ström whirlpool was about a quarter of a mile dead ahead—but no more like the every-day Moskoe-ström, than the whirl as you now see it is like a mill-race. If I had not known where we were, and what we had to expect, I should not have recognised the place at all. As it was, I involuntarily closed my eyes in horror. The lids clenched themselves together as if in a spasm.

"It could not have been more than two minutes afterward until we suddenly felt the waves subside, and were enveloped in foam. The boat made a sharp half turn to larboard, and then shot off in its new direction like a thunderbolt. At the same moment the roaring noise of the water was completely drowned in a kind of shrill shriek—such a sound as you might imagine given out by the waste-pipes of many thousand steam-vessels, letting off their steam all together. We were now in the belt of surf that always surrounds the whirl; and I thought, of course, that another moment would plunge us into the abyss—down which we could only see indistinctly on account of the amazing velocity with which we were borne along. The boat did not seem to sink into the water at all, but to skim like an air-bubble upon the surface of the surge. Her starboard side was next the whirl, and on the larboard arose the world of ocean we had left. It stood like a huge writhing wall between us and the horizon.

"It may appear strange, but now, when we were in the very jaws of the gulf, I felt more composed than when we were only approaching it. Having made up my mind to hope no more, I got rid of a great deal of that terror which unmanned me at first. I suppose it was despair that strung my nerves.

"It may look like boasting—but what I tell you is truth—I began to reflect how magnificent a thing it was to die in such a manner, and how foolish it was in me to think of so paltry a consideration as my own individual life, in view of so wonderful a manifestation of God's power. I do believe that I blushed with shame when this idea crossed my mind. After a little while I became possessed with the keenest curiosity about the whirl itself. I positively felt a *wish* to explore its depths, even at the sacrifice I was going to make; and my principal grief was that I should never be able to tell my old companions on shore about the mysteries I should see. These, no doubt, were singular fancies to occupy a man's mind in such extremity—and I have often thought since, that the revolutions of the boat around the pool might have rendered me a little light-headed.

"There was another circumstance which tended to restore my self-possession; and this was the cessation of the wind, which could not reach us in our present situation—for, as you saw yourself, the belt of surf is considerably lower than the general bed of the ocean, and this latter now towered above us, a high, black, mountainous ridge. If you have never been at sea in a heavy gale, you can form no idea of the confusion of mind occasioned by the wind and spray together. They blind, deafen, and strangle you, and take away all power of action or reflection. But we were now, in a great measure, rid of these annoyances—just us death-condemned felons in prison are allowed petty indulgences, forbidden them while their doom is yet uncertain.

"How often we made the circuit of the belt it is impossible to say. We careered round and round for perhaps an hour, flying rather than floating, getting gradually more and more into the middle of the surge, and then nearer and nearer to its horrible inner edge. All this time I had never let go of the ring-bolt. My brother was at the stern, holding on to a large empty water-cask which had been securely lashed under the coop of the counter, and was the only thing on deck that had not been swept overboard when the gale first took us. As we approached the brink of the pit he let go his hold upon this, and made for the ring, from which, in the agony of his terror, he endeavored to force my hands, as it was not large enough to afford us both a secure grasp. I never felt deeper grief than when I saw him attempt this act—although I thought he was a madman when he did it—a raving maniac through sheer fright. I did not care, however, to contest the point with him. I thought it could make no difference whether either of us held on at all; so I let him have the bolt, and went astern to the cask. This there was no great difficulty in doing; for the smack flew round steadily enough, and upon an even keel—only swaying to and fro, with the immense sweeps and swelters of the whirl. Scarcely had I secured myself in my new position, when we gave a wild lurch to starboard, and rushed headlong into the abyss. I muttered a hurried prayer to God, and thought all was over.

"As I felt the sickening sweep of the descent, I had instinctively tightened my hold upon the barrel, and closed my eyes. For some seconds I dared not open them—while I expected instant destruction, and wondered that I was not already in my death-struggles with the water. But moment after moment elapsed. I still lived. The sense of falling had ceased; and the motion of the vessel seemed much as it had been before while in the belt of foam, with the exception that she now lay more along. I took courage, and looked once again upon the scene.

"Never shall I forget the sensations of awe, horror, and admiration with which I gazed about me. The boat appeared to be hanging, as if by magic, midway down, upon the interior surface of a funnel vast in circumference, prodigious in depth, and whose perfectly smooth sides might have been mistaken for ebony, but for the bewildering rapidity with which they spun around, and for the gleaming and ghastly radiance they shot forth, as the rays of the full moon, from that circular rift amid the clouds which I have already described, streamed in a flood of golden glory along the black walls, and far away down into the inmost recesses of the abyss.

"At first I was too much confused to observe anything accurately. The general burst of terrific grandeur was all that I beheld. When I recovered myself a little, however, my gaze fell instinctively downward. In this direction I was able to obtain an unobstructed view, from the manner in which the smack hung on the inclined surface of the pool. She was quite upon an even keel—that is to say, her deck lay in a plane parallel with that of the water—but this latter sloped at an angle of more than forty-five degrees, so that we seemed to be lying upon our beam-ends. I could not help observing, nevertheless, that I had scarcely more difficulty in maintaining my hold and footing in this situation, than if we had been upon a dead level; and this, I suppose, was owing to the speed at which we revolved.

"The rays of the moon seemed to search the very bottom of the profound gulf; but still I could make out nothing distinctly, on account of a thick mist in which everything there was enveloped, and over which there hung a magnificent rainbow, like that narrow and tottering bridge which Mussulmen say is the only pathway between Time and Eternity. This mist, or spray, was no doubt occasioned by the clashing of the great walls of the funnel, as they all met together at the bottom—but the yell that went up to the Heavens from out of that mist, I dare not attempt to describe.

"Our first slide into the abyss itself, from the belt of foam above, had carried us a great distance down the slope; but our farther descent was by no means proportionate. Round and round we swept—not with any uniform movement—but in dizzying swings and jerks, that sent us sometimes only a few hundred feet—sometimes nearly the complete circuit of the whirl. Our progress downward, at each revolution, was slow, but very perceptible.

"Looking about me upon the wide waste of liquid ebony on which we were thus borne, I perceived that our boat was not the only object in the embrace of the whirl. Both above and below us were visible fragments of vessels, large masses of building timber and trunks of trees, with many smaller articles, such as pieces of house furniture, broken boxes, barrels and staves. I have already described the unnatural curiosity which had taken the place of my original terrors. It appeared to grow upon me as I drew nearer and nearer to my dreadful doom. I now began to watch, with a strange interest, the numerous things that floated in our company. I *must* have been delirious—for I even sought *amusement* in speculating upon the relative velocities of their several descents toward the foam below. 'This fir tree,' I found myself at one time saying, 'will certainly be the next thing that takes the awful plunge and disappears,'—and then I was disappointed to find that the wreck of a Dutch merchant ship overtook it and went down before. At length, after making several guesses of this nature, and being deceived in all—this fact—the fact of my invariable miscalculation—set me upon a train of reflection that made my limbs again tremble, and my heart beat heavily once more.

"It was not a new terror that thus affected me, but the dawn of a more exciting *hope*. This hope arose partly from memory, and partly from present observation. I called to mind the great variety of buoyant matter that strewed the coast of Lofoden, having been absorbed and then thrown forth by the Moskoe-ström. By far the greater number of the articles were shattered in the most extraordinary way—so chafed and roughened as to have the appearance of being stuck full of splinters—but then I distinctly recollected that there were *some* of them which were not disfigured at all. Now I could not account for this difference except by supposing that the roughened fragments were the only ones which had been *completely absorbed*—that the others had entered the whirl at so late a period of the tide, or, for some reason, had descended so slowly after entering, that they did not reach the bottom before the turn of the flood came, or of the ebb, as the case might be. I conceived it possible, in either instance, that they might thus be whirled up again to the level of the ocean, without undergoing the fate of those which had been drawn in more early, or absorbed more rapidly. I made, also, three important observations. The first was, that, as a general rule, the larger the bodies were, the more rapid their descent;—the second, that, between two masses of equal extent, the one spherical, and the other *of any other shape*, the superiority in speed of descent was with the sphere;—the third, that, between two masses of equal size, the one cylindrical, and the other of any other shape, the cylinder was absorbed the more slowly. Since my escape, I have had several conversations on this subject with an old school-master of the district; and it was from him that I learned the use of the words 'cylinder' and 'sphere.' He explained to me—although I have forgotten the explanation—how what I observed was, in fact, the natural consequence of the forms of the floating fragments—and showed me how it happened that a cylinder, swimming in a vortex, offered more resistance to its suction, and was drawn in with greater difficulty than an equally bulky body, of any form whatever.*

---

* See Archimedes, "*De Incidentibus in Fluido.*"—lib. 2

"There was one startling circumstance which went a great way in enforcing these observations, and rendering me anxious to turn them to account, and this was that, at every revolution, we passed something like a barrel, or else the broken yard or the mast of a vessel, while many of these things, which had been on our level when I first opened my eyes upon the wonders of the whirlpool, were now high up above us, and seemed to have moved but little from their original station.

"I no longer hesitated what to do. I resolved to lash myself securely to the water cask upon which I now held, to cut it loose from the counter, and to throw myself with it into the water. I attracted my brother's attention by signs, pointed to the floating barrels that came near us, and did everything in my power to make him understand what I was about to do. I thought at length that he comprehended my design—but, whether this was the case or not, he shook his head despairingly, and refused to move from his station by the ring-bolt. It was impossible to force him; the emergency admitted no delay; and so, with a bitter struggle, I resigned him to his fate, fastened myself to the cask by means of the lashings which secured it to the counter, and precipitated myself with it into the sea, without another moment's hesitation.

"The result was precisely what I had hoped it might be. As it is myself who now tell you this tale—as you see that I *did* escape—and as you are already in possession of the mode in which this escape was effected, and must therefore anticipate all that I have farther to say—I will bring my story quickly to conclusion. It might have been an hour, or thereabout, after my quitting the smack, when, having descended to a vast distance beneath me, it made three or four wild gyrations in rapid succession, and, bearing my loved brother with it, plunged headlong, at once and forever, into the chaos of foam below. The cask to which I was attached sank very little farther than half the distance between the bottom of the gulf and the spot at which I leaped overboard, before a great change took place in the character of the whirlpool. The slope of the sides of the vast funnel became momently less and less steep. The gyrations of the whirl grew, gradually, less and less violent. By degrees, the froth and the rainbow disappeared, and the bottom of the gulf seemed slowly to uprise. The sky was clear, the winds had gone down, and the full moon was setting radiantly in the west, when I found myself on the surface of the ocean, in full view of the shores of Lofoden, and above the spot where the pool of the Moskoe-ström *had been*. It was the hour of the slack—but the sea still heaved in mountainous waves from the effects of the hurricane. I was borne violently into the channel of the Ström, and in a few minutes was hurried down the coast into the 'grounds' of the fishermen. A boat picked me up—exhausted from fatigue—and (now that the danger was removed) speechless from the memory of its horror. Those who drew me on board were my old mates and daily companions—but they knew me no more than they would have known a traveller from the spirit-land. My hair which had been raven-black the day before, was as white as you see it now. They say too that the whole expression of my countenance had changed. I told them my story. They did not believe it. I now tell it to *you*—and I can scarcely expect you to put more faith in it than did the merry fishermen of Lofoden."

THE ALBATROSS

William Hope Hodgson

I

onfound that brute!" I shouted in sheer desperation. Then I sang out to the
'prentice, who was keeping "time" on the lee side of the poop, to bring me a
piece of spun-yarn and a marlinspike.

I was first mate of the *Skylark*, a full-rigged ship, and we were off the Horn on a
cold, absolutely windless night. It was the twelve to four watch in the early morning,
and four bells (two o'clock) had just gone.

All the watch there had been an enormous albatross flying round and round the
vessel; sometimes he would actually fly across the decks, which is a thing I have never
known to happen before.

When the boy brought the marlinspike and the yarn, I bent on about two fathoms
of the latter, so that I had a sort of handy little harpoon. Then I slipped quickly up the
mizzen rigging and out onto the cross-jack yard, while I waited with the spike ready in
one hand and the end of the line held fast in the other.

Presently, away forward in the still night, I heard the dismal *squark* of the great
bird, and immediately a spate of blasphemy from the man on the lookout, who was
evidently getting as much bothered as I by the actions of the creature.

Not a sound, then, for maybe ten minutes; and suddenly I saw something float
between me and the dim skyline and come inboard. I lost it for a moment; but
immediately there came the loud dismal *squark* out of the night to my left, and directly
afterward I saw vaguely that something was passing under the yard. I raised the
marlinspike and drove down at the thing with all my strength, letting the line fly out
to its full length. There was a rustle of feathers and a tugging on the line, and the
bird *squarked* twice. Then a jerk and the snap of something breaking, and the great
albatross was gone free.

I hauled in on the spun-yarn until I had the marlinspike again in my hand; as I
passed it between my fingers, I felt that there was something caught round the butt,
something that felt like a piece of rag. I loosed it from the spike. Then I went down
again on to the poop, and at once to the light of the main binnacle, to see what it was
that had got caught round the marlinspike.

I could not see the thing very plainly at first, and I took the lamp out of the holder so as to have a better light. I found then that it was a strip of red silk, such as might be torn from a girl's blouse. At one end was a piece of broken tape. For some minutes I examined the thing very carefully. It was in this way that I found presently a single long hair tangled in the knot of the tape. I picked it loose, gently, and looked at it; then I coiled it round and round my forefinger. It was a girl's hair, brown, with a glint of gold in it! What did it mean? We were off Cape Horn—one of the grim, lonely places of the ocean!

After a while I replaced the lamp I the binnacle and resumed my ordinary tramp of the weather side of the poop. All the while I was turning this matter over in my brain, and presently I went back to the light, so that I might have another look at the piece of silk. I saw then that it could not have been very long since it had been torn; for it was very little frayed at the tear and had no appearance of having been weatherworn for more than a few days. Also, the material was new and seemed to be of very fine quality. I grew more puzzled.

Of course it was possible that there was another sailing-ship within a hundred miles of us; it was also possible that such a vessel had a girl aboard, perhaps the captain's daughter; it was also possible that they had caught this particular albatross on a line and tied the silk to it and let it go again. But it was also exceedingly improbable. For sailors will always keep an albatross for the sake of the wing-bones, which make pipe-stems, and the webs, which make purses, and the breast, which makes a gorgeous fire-screen; while others prize the great bill and the beautiful wing-tips.

Moreover, even if the bird had been loosed, why had someone torn up a new silk garment when a piece of old bunting would have done just as well? You can see how my thoughts were trending. That piece of silk and that long, pretty hair coming to me suddenly out of the night and in that lonely and desolate sea had stirred me with vague wonderings. Yet I never put my wonderments actually into words, but went back to my constant pacing fore and aft. And so, presently, the second mate came up at eight bells to relieve me.

The next day, through all the eight to twelve forenoon watch, I kept a pretty keen lookout for the albatross, but the whole sea was lonely, and though there was such an absolute calm there was not even a Mother Carey's chicken in sight—only everywhere, so far as sight might reach, an everlasting gray desolation of water.

The afternoon watch I went below for a sleep. Then, in the first dog-watch, a little before three bells, I saw a great albatross swing and glide against the gray of the sky about a mile astern. I reached for my glasses and had a good look. I saw the bird plainly, a huge, boney-shouldered albatross, with a queer bulge below the breast. As I stared at him, I grew suddenly excited, for I saw that the bulge was really a packet of some kind tied on to the creature, and there was something fluttering from it.

In the second dog-watch I asked two of my 'prentices to come down with me into the sail-locker and help me root out an old seine-net that we carried for occasional sport. I told them I was going to have a try for the big albatross that night if he started flying across the decks again, and they were nearly as keen as I, though I had asked them to do this sail-tossing in their watch below.

When my watch came, from eight until midnight, I did nothing until the "Old Man" had turned in for the night; then I had my boys rig lines for the big net from the main and the mizzen masts, so that we could hoist it up at any moment and let it hang like a curtain between the masts.

The night was very quiet and dark, and though it was difficult to see anything, it would have been easy to hear the bird at a great distance. Yet, for over an hour after this, there was no sign of anything, and I began to think that we were not to have a visit.

However, just after four bells had gone (ten o'clock), there came from far away over the sea a strange, lonely *squark squark* of an albatross, and a few minutes later I had a vague glimpse of him flying silently round and round the ship, in the way common enough with his kind. Presently he gave out a loud *squark* and turned inboard to fly over the poop. The next instant there was a loud *squarking* up in the night, and a constant beating of heavy wings. I shouted to the boys at the lines to lower away, and a moment later I was shining the binnacle light on a fluster of beating wings and tangled net.

I sang out to the nearest 'prentice to hold the lamp while I disentangled the albatross and found out what the package was that was made fast to him. The parcel was done up in layer after layer of oilskin, and from the outside there was another such streamer of red silk as the one that had caught on my spike the night before. Then I had come to the last of the wrappings of oilskin and there were a couple of pages torn from a log-book and folded very tight and compact. I opened them and found that they were covered with hasty feminine handwriting. And this is what I read:

This is written aboard the *Unicorn*, derelict, on the twenty-first day of March, 1904. She was run down by an unknown steamer ten day ago. I am here alone, living in the chart-house. I have food and water sufficient to last me for about a week longer, if I am very careful. The vessel seems to be floating with her decks just a little above the water, and every time the sea is a bit rough, it just ours aboard of her.

I am sending this message tied round the neck of an albatross. The captain shot it the day before we were run down, and hurt the poor creature's wing. I told him he was an inhuman brute. I am sorry now, for he, along with every other soul, is dead, drowned. He was a brave man. The men crowded into the boats, and he stood with his revolver and tried to stop them, saying that no one should leave the ship before I was safe. He shot two of them, but the others threw him into the sea. They were mad. They took the boats and went away; and my maid went with them. But it was terribly rough, and I saw them sink just a little way from the ship.

I have been alone ever since, except for the albatross. I have nursed it, and now it seems as if it should be able to fly. I pray God that this message be found before it is too late! If any find it, come and save a girl from an awful and lonely death. The position of the ship is written down in the log-book here in the chart-house, so I will give it; then you will know where to search for me. It is Latitude 62° 7' S. and Longitude 67° 10' W.

I have sent other messages corked up in bottles; but this is the one in which I have all my hope. I shall tie a piece of something red to it, so that anyone seeing my albatross will know it is carrying something and try to catch it. Come, come, come, as quickly as ever you can!

There are enormous numbers of rats about. I suppose the water has driven them up out of the holds and places; but they make me afraid to sleep. Remember, the food I have won't last more than week, and I am here all alone. But I will be brave. Only don't give up searching for me. The wind has been blowing from the north ever since the night when the boats sank. It is quite calm now. Perhaps these things will help you to know where to look for me, as I can see that the wind must make the ship drift. Don't give me up! Remember, I am waiting, waiting, and trying to be brave.

MARY DORISWOLD

You can imagine how I felt when I finished reading this paper. Our position that day was 58° S. and 67° 30' W.; so that we were at least 250 miles to the north of the place where the derelict had been eighteen days earlier; for it was now the twenty-ninth of March. And there, somewhere away to the southward of us, a girl was dying of hunger and lonesomeness! And there was absolutely no sign of wind.

After a little while I told the boys to clear away the net and take the albatross down on the main deck and tie it to one of the ringbolts. Then I took a turn or two up and down the poop, and finally decided to go down and call the "Old Man" and set the matter before him.

When he heard what I had to tell, he slipped into his clothes and came out into the saloon, where he read the letter twice, very carefully. Then he had a look at the barometer, and afterward came up with me on to the poop and had a look at the weather; but there were certainly no immediate signs of wind.

Through all the rest of the watch he walked up and down with me, discussing the thing, and went several times to the binnacle to make fresh examinations of the letter. Once I suggested the possibility of manning one of the life-boats and trying down to the southward, letting the ship follow on as soon as the wind came. But, of course, he would not listen to this, and very rightly, too. For not only would it have been to risk the lives of all who went in the boat, but to risk the vessel also, because we should have had to leave her undermanned. And so the only thing we could do was to pray for the wind.

Down on the main deck I could hear presently the murmur of voices, and I knew that the men had got the news and were talking it over; but that was all that we could do.

At midnight, when the second mate came up to relieve me, he had already learned the story from the 'prentice who called him, and when finally I went below, he and the Skipper were still discussing it.

At four o'clock, when I was waked, my first inquiry was about the wind; but there was not a sign, and when I got on the poop, I could see that the weather still had the same dead, settled look.

All that day we kept waiting for the wind that never came; and at last a deputation of the men came after to ask to be allowed to volunteer to man one of the life-boats and make a search party. But the master sent them forward again, quietly enough, and even took the trouble to point out the hopelessness of such an attempt, as well as the tremendous risk. For if the derelict were still above water, she might have drifted sufficiently far to still be lost after weeks of searching in the great unknown seas to the southward.

All that day the wind never came, and all that day there was nothing else talked about aboard except the chances of saving the girl. And when at last night came, I do not believe half the watch below turned in, but paced the decks, whistling for wind and watching the weather.

The morning came, and still the calm; and at last I asked the captain whether he would give me permission to take the little gig, which was alight and handy boat, and make the trial alone. I said that if I failed, and the boat was lost, her value would be amply covered by the wages due to me. But the "Old Man" simply refused to listen to the idea, and told me, kindly enough, that it was madness.

I saw that it was no use arguing with him, for he was perfectly right in what he said; but at the same time I was determined to try, if the wind did not come by the evening. For I could not get the thought of that lonely girl out of my mind, and I kept remembering what she had said about the rats.

II

That night, when the captain had gone below, I had a talk with the steward, and afterward I gave orders to get the little gig quietly into the water. I provisioned her thoroughly and added a bottle of brandy and a bottle of rum. The second mate fitted her with a boat's compass and binnacle from one of the lifeboats, and also attend to the filling of the water-breakers and saw that all the gear was in place. Then I added my oilskins, some rugs and canvas, and my sextant and chronometer and charts and so forth. At the last I remembered my shotgun, and ran down for this and plenty of cartridges; for there was no saying how useful it might be.

I shook hands with the second mate when I returned, and went down into the boat.

"We'll be after you as soon as the wind comes," he said quietly. "Good luck!"

I nodded, and afterward mentioned one or two details of ship's work that would need attention. Then I pulled in the painter and pushed off. As I cleared the side of the vessel, there came a hushed cheering, and hoarse whispers of "Good luck, sir! Good luck, sir!"

The lamp in the little binnacle was lit, and I turned the hood round so that I could watch the compass as I pulled. Then I settled down to my work at the oars, and presently the vessel had faded away from me into the night, though for along while there would come over the sea to me the odd rustle and flap of a sail, as the ship lifted to the occasional glassy swell. But afterward I rowed on through an everlasting silence toward the south.

Twice in the night I ceased work and ate and drank; then onward again, keeping to an easy, regular pull that I knew I could keep up hour after hour.

In the morning I had a good look round, but the *Skylark* was lost below the horizon astern and the whole world seemed empty. It was a most extraordinary and depressing sensation. I had an early breakfast and rowed on. Later, I got my longitude; at midday I took my altitude and found that I had done nearly fifty miles to the south.

All that day I pulled steadily, stopping only to eat and drink at regular intervals. That night I slept for six hours, from twelve until six, and when I waked, there was still the everlasting calm.

Four more days and nights I went onward in this fashion. All the fourth day I pulled steadily, stopping every half-hour to take a look round; but there was always and only the gray emptiness of the sea. All that night I drifted; for I had passed over and was now to the southward of the position of the d relict given by the girl, and I dared not row in the darkness, for fear of passing the wreck.

Part of the night I used in making calculations, and afterward had a good long sleep. I was wakened in the dawn by the lapping of water against the boat, and found that alight breeze had sprung up from the west. This cheered me immensely, for I knew now that the *Skylark* would be able to follow, provided that the wind was not merely a local breeze. And, in any case, there was no longer need to use the oars, for I had a mast and sail in the boat.

I stepped the mast and hoisted the lug-sail; then I slipped the rudder and sat down to rest and steer. And it is impossible to express my gratitude, for my hands were raw with broken blisters and I ached in all my body with the constant and weary labor at the oars.

All that day I ran to the southward, keeping a lookout; but never a sign was there of anything, so that an utter dismay began to come down on me. Yet I did not give up hoping. That night I made fresh calculations, with the result that next morning, as soon as I had hoisted the sail (for I had let the boat drift during the darkness), I altered my course a few degrees to the eastward. At noon I found that I was a hundred and twenty-seven miles to the south and forty-six miles to the east of the last known position of the *Unicorn*. If I sighted nothing by evening, I would make a long tack next day to the north, a few miles eastward of my downward run.

I ran on until the dusk came; and then, after a final long look round, I dropped my sail for the night and set the boat to ride by the painter to a couple of oars, as I had done on the previous nights of drifting.

I felt desperately disheartened, and began to realize more thoroughly my own position, over four hundred miles from the *Skylark* and in a latitude of hopeless and weary storms and utterly unfrequented by ships. Yet I fought this down and finally settled myself to sleep, well wrapped up in my rugs, for it was bitterly cold, though so fine.

It was some time after midnight that something waked me, and I sat up in the darkness and looked about and listened. I could not imagine what had roused me, but I felt that I had heard something, though there was no sound in all the night except the low blowing of the wind and the rippling of the water against the boat.

And then, suddenly, as I sat there harking, there came over the sea from the southward the desolate mournful blowing of a foghorn. I stood up abruptly and threw all my rugs from me into the bottom of the boat.

I ran down in the direction of the foghorn, and in ten minutes or so I saw against the sky the spars of a big four-masted vessel. I dropped the sail and shipped the oars. As I pulled toward her, the sound of the horn broke out into the night in a dull roar, coming from the after-part of the vessel. I backed the boat aft, noticing as I did so that the vessel stood no more than three or four feet above the level of the sea.

Then, as I came opposite of the place where the horn seemed to be, I saw dimly the deck rose here, and that I was opposite to the poop. I rested on my oars.

"Miss Doriswold!" I shouted. "Miss Doriswold!"

The foghorn gave a short, impotent blare, and immediately a girl's voice called: "Who is that? Who is that?" in a frightened, breathless way.

"It's all right!" I shouted back. "We got your message! I'm the mate of the *Skylark*, the ship that got the message. I'm coming aboard."

The answer astonished me. "Don't come on to the ship!" the voice called back to me, shrill and anxious. "Keep the boat away! Keep the boat away! There are thousands of rats—"

It broke off abruptly and there was the sound of a pistol-shot in the darkness. At that, I had the painter fast in a moment and, catching up my gun, vaulted aboard. In an instant the girl's voice came again:

"I'm all right. Don't come aboard, whatever you do! It's the rats! Wait for the daylight!"

Even before she spoke, I was aware of a sound along the poop like the harsh noise of several saws at work. I walked aft a few steps, groping, and knew suddenly there was a faint, curious smell everywhere about me in the night. I paused and stared through the darkness.

"Where are you?" I shouted, and then I saw the black bulk of the charthouse vaguely through the darkness. I went forward a pace, and stumbled clumsily over a deck ring-bolt. "Where are you?" I shouted again. "I've come aboard."

"Go back! Go back! Go back!" called the girl's voice shrilly, with a note of utter fear and horror in it. "Get into the boat, *quick*! I'll explain. Go back! Go back!"

III

There came to me in the same moment a strange sense of restlessness all about the decks, and then suddenly, all the air seemed to be full of an odd whining noise, that rose into a horrible shrill, twittering keening of sound. I heard amassed sound, as of thousands of small, scuttering bodies coming toward me at a run through the darkness. The voice of the girl came in the same instant, crying out something in a frightened voice. But I never heard what she said, for something plucked my trousers, and immediately hundreds of creatures sprang upon me and swarmed over me, biting and tearing. My gun was utterly useless, and in an instant I knew that if I wanted to save my life I must go overboard. I made a mad, staggering run to the side of the derelict, the rats flocking about me. With my free hand I was tearing their great bodies from me and keeping them from my face. The hideous little brutes were so thick upon me that I was loaded with them. I reached the rail and got over somehow, and fell souse down into the icy water.

I stayed under water deliberately as long as I could; and the rats left me and went to the surface to breathe. I swam hard until my head felt as if it would burst; then I came up, and found that I was clear of the rats. I discovered that I still had my gun in my left hand, and I was careful not to lose it. I swam forward until I was opposite the boat. I heard the girl's voice calling something to me, but the water in my ears prevented me from hearing what it was.

"Are you safe? Are you safe? Where are you?" the girl was calling.

"I'm all right, thanks!" I shouted back. "I'm in the boat. I'll wait till daylight, if you're sure you are safe."

She assured me that she was all right, now that I had come, and could easily hold out until the morning. In the meanwhile I had stripped off my wet things and got into the spares I had brought with me and for which I was very thankful now, as you can imagine. All the time, as I changed, the girl and I kept up a conversation. I asked her about food; she told me she had eaten nothing for three days and nights, but still had some water, and I was not to try to reach her until daylight came to show me the position of everything.

This, however, would not satisfy me, and as I completed my dressing, a sudden thought came to me. I struck a match and lit the binnacle lamp and also the boat's lantern, which was in the midship locker. Then I hooked the ring of the lantern over the spike of the boat-hook and reached the lantern up on to the poop of the derelict, where I set it on the deck. I could see the chart-house plainly now, and a pale but very beautiful face was looking at me through the glass of one of the ports. It was Miss Doriswold, and I waved to her with the boat-hook. She opened the port about an inch and called out to know what I was going to do. I told her she would see very quickly. Then I stuck the boat-hook into the handle of the binnacle lamp and ran to the other end of the boat, where I was able to set it inboard on the poop deck, some way farther aft than the boat-lamp.

I got the bottom boards of the boat now and set them across from gunnel to gunnel of the boat, and then taking my gun and a pocket full of cartridges, I stood on this temporary erection and looked aboard.

I saw a most extraordinary sight and really a very horrible one; for in the light of the lamps, the *decks were literally black and moving with rats*, and the shining of their eyes in the lights made a constant, myriad twinkling from a thousand places at once, as the rats shifted this way and that. All about the base of the house there seemed to be rats, and I could see dimly that they had been at the woodwork of the house, but as there was a steel combing in at the back of the teak, very few had been able to get in, and then only by the door, as I learned afterward.

I glanced at the port, but Miss Doriswold was not there, and as I looked, there came the flare of a match and immediately the sharp report of a pistol-shot. In a minute she had returned to the port and cast out a big rat, which was instantly set upon by hundreds of others in a great black scramble. Then I raised my gun so that it was just a little above the level of the poop-deck and fired both barrels into that struggling little crowd of monsters. Several rolled over and died, and over a dozen ran about wounded and squealing, but in a moment both the wounded and the dead were covered with the living rats and literally torn to pieces.

I reloaded quickly and began to fire shot after shot among the hideous little brutes, and with every thud of the gun, they lay dying and dead over the deck, and every time the living rats would leap on the dead and wounded and destroy them, devouring them practically alive.

In ten minutes I had killed hundreds, and within the next half hour I must have destroyed a thousand, to make a rough guess. The gun was almost red-hot in my hands. The dead began now to lie about the decks; for most of the rats were destroyed and the living rats had begun to run into hiding. I waved to Miss Doriswold, and we began to talk while the gun was cooling.

She told me she had been fighting the brutes off for the last four days, but that she had burned all her candles and had been forced to stay in the dark, only striking a match now and again (of which she had several boxes left) when the sounds at the door told her that a rat had nearly gnawed his way through. Then she would fire the captain's revolver at the brute, block the hole up with coal and sit quiet in the dark, waiting for the next. Sometimes the rats got through in other places, above the steel combing. In this way she had been badly bitten several times, but had always managed to kill the rats and block the holes.

Presently, when the gun was cool again, I began to shoot systematically at every rat in sight, so that soon I had killed and driven the little monsters clear off the visible parts of the poop-deck. I jumped aboard then and walked round the house with the boat-lantern and my gun. In this way I surprised and shot a score of rats that were hiding in the shadows, and after that there was not a rat to be seen anywhere.

"They're gone!" I shouted to Miss Doriswold, and in the same moment I heard her unlocking the chart-house door, and she came out on the deck. She looked dreadfully haggard and seemed a little uncertain on her feet, but even thus I could see how pretty she was.

"Oh!" she said, and staggered and gripped the corner of the chart-house. She tried to say something further, but I thought she was going to fall and caught her arm to lead her back into the house.

"No!" she whispered breathlessly. "Not in there!" And I helped her to the seat on the side of the skylight. Then I ran to the boat for brandy, water and food, and presently I saw the life begin to come back into her. She told me later that she had not slept for four nights. And once she tried to thank me, but she was dumb that way— only her eyes said all the rest.

Afterward, I got her to the boat, and when I had seen her safe and comfortable, I left her there and walked the poop of the derelict until daylight. And she, now that she felt safe, slept through the whole night and far into the daylight.

When she waked I helped her aboard again and she insisted upon preparing our breakfast. There was a fireplace in the chart-house, and coal, and I broke up the front of one of the hen-coops for kindling-wood. Son we were drinking hot coffee and eating sea-biscuit and tinned meat. Then we went out on deck to walk up and down and talk. In this way she learned my side of the story, and questioned me closely on every point.

"Oh," she said at last, holding out both hands to me, "may God bless you!" I took her hands and looked at her with the strangest mixture of awkwardness and happiness. Then she slipped her hands from me and we went again tour constant pacing. Presently I had to send her to rest, though she would not at first, because she felt too happy to sit still; but afterward she was glad to be quiet.

Through four days and nights we waited for the *Skylark*. The days we had entirely together; the nights she slept in the chart-house, and I in the little alleyway, with just a few feet between me and the roll and gurgle of the water going through the waterlogged cabins of the half-sunk vessel. Odd whiles I would rise and see that the lamp was burning brightly in the rigging, so that the *Skylark* would not pass us in the darkness.

On the morning of the fourth day, after we had made our breakfast happily together, we went for our usual walk of the poop. The wind still continued light, but there were heavy clouds to the northward, which made me anxious. Then, suddenly, Miss Doriswold cried out that she saw the ship, and in the same moment I saw her, too. We turned and looked at each other. Yet it was not all happiness that was in us. There was a half-questioning in the girl's eyes, and abruptly I held out my arms, and she came into them with a glad little crying.

Two hours later we were safely aboard the *Skylark*, under only the main lower-topsail, and the wind coming down out of the north like thunder. To leeward the lonesome derelict was lost in huge clouds of spray and Miss Doriswold and I looked out in silence.

THE BRUTE

Joseph Conrad

DODGING IN FROM THE RAIN-SWEPT STREET, I EXCHANGED A SMILE AND A glance with Miss Blank in the bar of the Three Crows. This exchange was effected with extreme propriety. It is a shock to think that, if still alive, Miss Blank must be something over sixty now. How time passes!

Noticing my gaze directed inquiringly at the partition of glass and varnished wood, Miss Blank was good enough to say, encouragingly:

"Only Mr. Jermyn and Mr. Stonor in the parlour with another gentleman I've never seen before."

I moved towards the parlour door. A voice discoursing on the other side (it was but a matchboard partition), rose so loudly that the concluding words became quite plain in all their atrocity.

"That fellow Wilmot fairly dashed her brains out, and a good job, too!"

This inhuman sentiment, since there was nothing profane or improper in it, failed to do as much as to check the slight yawn Miss Blank was achieving behind her hand. And she remained gazing fixedly at the window-panes, which streamed with rain.

As I opened the parlour door the same voice went on in the same cruel strain:

"I was glad when I heard she got the knock from somebody at last. Sorry enough for poor Wilmot, though. That man and I used to be chums at one time. Of course that was the end of him. A clear case if there ever was one. No way out of it. None at all."

The voice belonged to the gentleman Miss Blank had never seen before. He straddled his long legs on the hearthrug. Jermyn, leaning forward, held his pocket-handkerchief spread out before the grate. He looked back dismally over his shoulder, and as I slipped behind one of the little wooden tables, I nodded to him. On the other side of the fire, imposingly calm and large, sat Mr. Stonor, jammed tight into a capacious Windsor armchair. There was nothing small about him but his short, white side-whiskers. Yards and yards of extra superfine blue cloth (made up into an overcoat) reposed on a chair by his side. And he must just have brought some liner from sea, because another chair was smothered under his black waterproof, ample as a pall, and made of three-fold oiled silk, double-stitched throughout. A man's hand-bag of the usual size looked like a child's toy on the floor near his feet.

I did not nod to him. He was too big to be nodded to in that parlour. He was a senior Trinity pilot and condescended to take his turn in the cutter only during the summer months. He had been many times in charge of royal yachts in and out of Port Victoria. Besides, it's no use nodding to a monument. And he was like one. He didn't speak, he didn't budge. He just sat there, holding his handsome old head up, immovable, and almost bigger than life. It was extremely fine. Mr. Stonor's presence reduced poor old Jermyn to a mere shabby wisp of a man, and made the talkative stranger in tweeds on the hearthrug look absurdly boyish. The latter must have been a few years over thirty, and was certainly not the sort of individual that gets abashed at the sound of his own voice, because gathering me in, as it were, by a friendly glance, he kept it going without a check.

"I was glad of it," he repeated, emphatically. "You may be surprised at it, but then you haven't gone through the experience I've had of her. I can tell you, it was something to remember. Of course, I got off scot free myself—as you can see. She did her best to break up my pluck for me though. She jolly near drove as fine a fellow as ever lived into a madhouse. What do you say to that—eh?"

Not an eyelid twitched in Mr. Stonor's enormous face. Monumental! The speaker looked straight into my eyes.

"It used to make me sick to think of her going about the world murdering people."

Jermyn approached the handkerchief a little nearer to the grate and groaned. It was simply a habit he had.

"I've seen her once," he declared, with mournful indifference. "She had a house—"

The stranger in tweeds turned to stare down at him, surprised.

"She had three houses," he corrected, authoritatively. But Jermyn was not to be contradicted.

"She had a house, I say," he repeated, with dismal obstinacy. "A great, big, ugly, white thing. You could see it from miles away—sticking up."

"So you could," assented the other readily. "It was old Colchester's notion, though he was always threatening to give her up. He couldn't stand her racket any more, he declared; it was too much of a good thing for him; he would wash his hands of her, if he never got hold of another—and so on. I daresay he would have chucked her, only—it may surprise you—his missus wouldn't hear of it. Funny, eh? But with women, you never know how they will take a thing, and Mrs. Colchester, with her moustaches and big eyebrows, set up for being as strong-minded as they make them. She used to walk about in a brown silk dress, with a great gold cable flopping about her bosom. You should have heard her snapping out: 'Rubbish!' or 'Stuff and nonsense!' I daresay she knew when she was well off. They had no children, and had never set up a home anywhere. When in England she just made shift to hang out anyhow in some cheap hotel or boarding-house. I daresay she liked to get back to the comforts she was used to. She knew very well she couldn't gain by any change. And, moreover, Colchester, though a first-rate man, was not what you may call in his first youth, and, perhaps, she may have thought that he wouldn't be able to get hold of another (as he used to say) so easily. Anyhow, for one reason or another, it was 'Rubbish' and 'Stuff and nonsense' for the good lady. I overheard once young Mr. Apse himself say to her confidentially: 'I assure you, Mrs. Colchester, I am beginning to feel quite unhappy about the name she's getting for herself.' 'Oh,' says she, with her deep little hoarse laugh, 'if one took notice of all the silly talk,' and she showed Apse all her ugly false teeth at once. 'It would take more than that to make me lose my confidence in her, I assure you,' says she."

At this point, without any change of facial expression, Mr. Stonor emitted a short, sardonic laugh. It was very impressive, but I didn't see the fun. I looked from one to another. The stranger on the hearthrug had an ugly smile.

"And Mr. Apse shook both Mrs. Colchester's hands, he was so pleased to hear a good word said for their favourite. All these Apses, young and old you know, were perfectly infatuated with that abominable, dangerous—"

"I beg your pardon," I interrupted, exasperated, for he seemed to be addressing himself exclusively to me, "but who on earth are you talking about?"

"I am talking of the Apse family," he answered, courteously.

I nearly let out a damn at this. But just then the respected Miss Blank put her head in, and said that the cab was at the door, if Mr. Stonor wanted to catch the eleven-three up.

At once the senior pilot arose in his mighty bulk and began to struggle into his coat, with awe-inspiring upheavals. The stranger and I hurried impulsively to his assistance, and directly we laid our hands on him he became perfectly quiescent. We had to raise our arms very high, and to make efforts. It was like caparisoning a docile elephant. With a "Thanks, gentlemen," he dived under and squeezed himself through the door in a great hurry.

We smiled at each other in a friendly way.

"I wonder how he manages to hoist himself up a ship's side-ladder," said the man in tweeds; and poor Jermyn, who was a mere North Sea pilot, without official status or recognition of any sort, pilot only by courtesy, groaned.

"He makes eight hundred a year."

"Are you a sailor?" I asked the stranger, who had gone back to his position on the rug.

"I used to be till a couple of years ago, when I got married," answered this communicative individual. "I even went to sea first in that very ship we were speaking of when you came in."

"What ship?" I asked, puzzled. "I never heard you mention a ship."

"I've just told you her name, my dear sir," he replied. "The *Apse Family*. Surely you've heard of the great firm of Apse & Sons, shipowners. They had a pretty big fleet. There was the *Lucy Apse*, and the *Harold Apse*, and *Anne, John, Malcolm, Clara, Juliet*, and so on—no end of *Apses*. Every brother, sister, aunt, cousin, wife—and grandmother, too, for all I know—of the firm had a ship named after them. Good, solid, old-fashioned craft they were, too, built to carry and to last. None of your new-fangled, labour-saving appliances in them, but plenty of men and plenty of good salt beef and hard tack put aboard—and off you go to fight your way out and home again."

The miserable Jermyn made a sound of approval, which sounded like a groan of pain. Those were the ships for him. He pointed out in doleful tones that you couldn't say to labour-saving appliances: "Jump lively now, my hearties." No labour-saving appliance would go aloft on a dirty night with the sands under your lee.

"No," assented the stranger, with a wink at me. "The Apses didn't believe in them either, apparently. They treated their people well—as people don't get treated nowadays, and they were awfully proud of their ships. Nothing ever happened to them. This last one, the *Apse Family*, was to be like the others, only she was to be still stronger, still safer, still more roomy and comfortable. I believe they meant her to last for ever. They had her built composite—iron, teak-wood, and greenheart, and her scantling was something fabulous. If ever an order was given for a ship in a spirit of pride this one was. Everything of the best. The commodore captain of the employ was to command her, and they planned the accommodation for him like a house on shore under a big, tall poop that went nearly to the mainmast. No wonder Mrs. Colchester wouldn't let the old man give her up. Why, it was the best home she ever had in all her married days. She had a nerve, that woman.

"The fuss that was made while that ship was building! Let's have this a little stronger, and that a little heavier; and hadn't that other thing better be changed for something a little thicker. The builders entered into the spirit of the game, and there she was, growing into the clumsiest, heaviest ship of her size right before all their eyes, without anybody becoming aware of it somehow. She was to be 2,000 tons register, or a little over; no less on any account. But see what happens. When they came to measure her she turned out 1,999 tons and a fraction. General consternation! And they say old Mr. Apse was so annoyed when they told him that he took to his bed and died. The old gentleman had retired from the firm twenty-five years before, and was ninety-six years old if a day, so his death wasn't, perhaps, so surprising. Still Mr. Lucian Apse was convinced that his father would have lived to a hundred. So we may put him at the head of the list. Next comes the poor devil of a shipwright that brute caught and squashed as she went off the ways. They called it the launch of a ship, but I've heard people say that, from the wailing and yelling and scrambling out of the way, it was more like letting a devil loose upon the river. She snapped all her checks like pack-thread, and went for the tugs in attendance like a fury. Before anybody could see what she was up to she sent one of them to the bottom, and laid up another for three months' repairs. One of her cables parted, and then, suddenly—you couldn't tell why—she let herself be brought up with the other as quiet as a lamb.

"That's how she was. You could never be sure what she would be up to next. There are ships difficult to handle, but generally you can depend on them behaving rationally. With *that* ship, whatever you did with her you never knew how it would end. She was a wicked beast. Or, perhaps, she was only just insane."

He uttered this supposition in so earnest a tone that I could not refrain from smiling. He left off biting his lower lip to apostrophize me.

"Eh! Why not? Why couldn't there be something in her build, in her lines corresponding to—what's madness? Only something just a tiny bit wrong in the make of your brain. Why shouldn't there be a mad ship—I mean mad in a ship-like way, so that under no circumstances could you be sure she would do what any other sensible ship would naturally do for you. There are ships that steer wildly, and ships that can't be quite trusted always to stay; others want careful watching when running in a gale; and, again, there may be a ship that will make heavy weather of it in every little blow. But then you expect her to be always so. You take it as part of her character, as a ship, just as you take account of a man's peculiarities of temper when you deal with him. But with her you couldn't. She was unaccountable. If she wasn't mad, then she was the most evil-minded, underhand, savage brute that ever went afloat. I've seen her run in a heavy gale beautifully for two days, and on the third broach to twice in the same afternoon. The first time she flung the helmsman clean over the wheel, but as she didn't quite manage to kill him she had another try about three hours afterwards. She swamped herself fore and aft, burst all the canvas we had set, scared all hands into a panic, and even frightened Mrs. Colchester down there in these beautiful stern cabins that she was so proud of. When we mustered the crew there was one man missing. Swept overboard, of course, without being either seen or heard, poor devil! and I only wonder more of us didn't go.

"Always something like that. Always. I heard an old mate tell Captain Colchester once that it had come to this with him, that he was afraid to open his mouth to give any sort of order. She was as much of a terror in harbour as at sea. You could never be certain what would hold her. On the slightest provocation she would start snapping ropes, cables, wire hawsers, like carrots. She was heavy, clumsy, unhandy—but that does not quite explain that power for mischief she had. You know, somehow, when I think of her I can't help remembering what we hear of incurable lunatics breaking loose now and then."

He looked at me inquisitively. But, of course, I couldn't admit that a ship could be mad.

"In the ports where she was known," he went on, "they dreaded the sight of her. She thought nothing of knocking away twenty feet or so of solid stone facing off a quay or wiping off the end of a wooden wharf. She must have lost miles of chain and hundreds of tons of anchors in her time. When she fell aboard some poor unoffending ship it was the very devil of a job to haul her off again. And she never got hurt herself—just a few scratches or so, perhaps. They had wanted to have her strong. And so she was. Strong enough to ram Polar ice with. And as she began so she went on. From the day she was launched she never let a year pass without murdering somebody. I think the owners got very worried about it. But they were a stiff-necked generation all these Apses; they wouldn't admit there could be anything wrong with the *Apse Family*. They wouldn't even change her name. 'Stuff and nonsense,' as Mrs. Colchester used to say. They ought at least to have shut her up for life in some dry dock or other, away up the river, and never let her smell salt water again. I assure you, my dear sir, that she invariably did kill someone every voyage she made. It was perfectly well-known. She got a name for it, far and wide."

I expressed my surprise that a ship with such a deadly reputation could ever get a crew.

"Then, you don't know what sailors are, my dear sir. Let me just show you by an instance. One day in dock at home, while loafing on the forecastle head, I noticed two respectable salts come along, one a middle-aged, competent, steady man, evidently, the other a smart, youngish chap. They read the name on the bows and stopped to look at her. Says the elder man: '*Apse Family*. That's the sanguinary female dog' (I'm putting it in that way) 'of a ship, Jack, that kills a man every voyage. I wouldn't sign in her—not for Joe, I wouldn't.' And the other says: 'If she were mine, I'd have her towed on the mud and set on fire, blame if I wouldn't.' Then the first man chimes in: 'Much do they care! Men are cheap, God knows.' The younger one spat in the water alongside. 'They won't have me—not for double wages.'

"They hung about for some time and then walked up the dock. Half an hour later I saw them both on our deck looking about for the mate, and apparently very anxious to be taken on. And they were."

"How do you account for this?" I asked.

"What would you say?" he retorted. "Recklessness! The vanity of boasting in the evening to all their chums: 'We've just shipped in that there *Apse Family*. Blow her. She ain't going to scare us.' Sheer sailorlike perversity! A sort of curiosity. Well—a little of all that, no doubt. I put the question to them in the course of the voyage. The answer of the elderly chap was:

"'A man can die but once.' The younger assured me in a mocking tone that he wanted to see 'how she would do it this time.' But I tell you what; there was a sort of fascination about the brute."

Jermyn, who seemed to have seen every ship in the world, broke in sulkily:

"I saw her once out of this very window towing up the river; a great black ugly thing, going along like a big hearse."

"Something sinister about her looks, wasn't there?" said the man in tweeds, looking down at old Jermyn with a friendly eye. "I always had a sort of horror of her. She gave me a beastly shock when I was no more than fourteen, the very first day—nay, hour—I joined her. Father came up to see me off, and was to go down to Gravesend with us. I was his second boy to go to sea. My big brother was already an officer then. We got on board about eleven in the morning, and found the ship ready to drop out of the basin, stern first. She had not moved three times her own length when, at a little pluck the tug gave her to enter the dock gates, she made one of her rampaging starts, and put such a weight on the check rope—a new six-inch hawser—that forward there they had no chance to ease it round in time, and it parted. I saw the broken end fly up high in the air, and the next moment that brute brought her quarter against the pier-head with a jar that staggered everybody about her decks. She didn't hurt herself. Not she! But one of the boys the mate had sent aloft on the mizzen to do something, came down on the poop-deck—thump—right in front of me. He was not much older than myself. We had been grinning at each other only a few minutes before. He must have been handling himself carelessly, not expecting to get such a jerk. I heard his startled cry—Oh!—in a high treble as he felt himself going, and looked up in time to see him go limp all over as he fell. Ough! Poor father was remarkably white about the gills when we shook hands in Gravesend. 'Are you all right?' he says, looking hard at me. 'Yes, father.' 'Quite sure?' 'Yes, father.' 'Well, then good-bye, my boy.' He told me afterwards that for half a word he would have carried me off home with him there and then. I am the baby of the family—you know," added the man in tweeds, stroking his moustache with an ingenuous smile.

I acknowledged this interesting communication by a sympathetic murmur. He waved his hand carelessly.

"This might have utterly spoiled a chap's nerve for going aloft, you know—utterly. He fell within two feet of me, cracking his head on a mooring-bitt. Never moved. Stone dead. Nice looking little fellow, he was. I had just been thinking we would be great chums. However, that wasn't yet the worst that brute of a ship could do. I served in her three years of my time, and then I got transferred to the *Lucy Apse*, for a year. The sailmaker we had in the *Apse Family* turned up there, too, and I remember him saying to me one evening, after we had been a week at sea: 'Isn't she a meek little ship?' No wonder we thought the *Lucy Apse* a dear, meek, little ship after getting clear of that big, rampaging savage brute. It was like heaven. Her officers seemed to me the restfullest lot of men on earth. To me who had known no ship but the *Apse Family*, the *Lucy* was like a sort of magic craft that did what you wanted her to do of her own accord. One evening we got caught aback pretty sharply from right ahead. In about ten minutes we had her full again, sheets aft, tacks down, decks cleared, and the officer of the watch leaning against the weather rail peacefully. It seemed simply marvellous to me. The other would have stuck for half-an-hour in irons, rolling her decks full of water, knocking the men about—spars cracking, braces snapping, yards taking charge, and a confounded scare going on aft because of her beastly rudder, which she had a way of flapping about fit to raise your hair on end. I couldn't get over my wonder for days.

"Well, I finished my last year of apprenticeship in that jolly little ship—she wasn't so little either, but after that other heavy devil she seemed but a plaything to handle. I finished my time and passed; and then just as I was thinking of having three weeks of real good time on shore I got at breakfast a letter asking me the earliest day I could be ready to join the *Apse Family* as third mate. I gave my plate a shove that shot it into the middle of the table; dad looked up over his paper; mother raised her hands in astonishment, and I went out bare-headed into our bit of garden, where I walked round and round for an hour.

"When I came in again mother was out of the dining-room, and dad had shifted berth into his big armchair. The letter was lying on the mantelpiece.

"'It's very creditable to you to get the offer, and very kind of them to make it,' he said. 'And I see also that Charles has been appointed chief mate of that ship for one voyage.'

"There was, over leaf, a P.S. to that effect in Mr. Apse's own handwriting, which I had overlooked. Charley was my big brother.

"'I don't like very much to have two of my boys together in one ship,' father goes on, in his deliberate, solemn way. 'And I may tell you that I would not mind writing Mr. Apse a letter to that effect.'

"Dear old dad! He was a wonderful father. What would you have done? The mere notion of going back (and as an officer, too), to be worried and bothered, and kept on the jump night and day by that brute, made me feel sick. But she wasn't a ship you could afford to fight shy of. Besides, the most genuine excuse could not be given without mortally offending Apse & Sons. The firm, and I believe the whole family down to the old unmarried aunts in Lancashire, had grown desperately touchy about that accursed ship's character. This was the case for answering 'Ready now' from your very death-bed if you wished to die in their good graces. And that's precisely what I did answer—by wire, to have it over and done with at once.

"The prospect of being shipmates with my big brother cheered me up considerably, though it made me a bit anxious, too. Ever since I remember myself as a little chap he had been very good to me, and I looked upon him as the finest fellow in the world. And so he was. No better officer ever walked the deck of a merchant ship. And that's a fact. He was a fine, strong, upstanding, sun-tanned, young fellow, with his brown hair curling a little, and an eye like a hawk. He was just splendid. We hadn't seen each other for many years, and even this time, though he had been in England three weeks already, he hadn't showed up at home yet, but had spent his spare time in Surrey somewhere making up to Maggie Colchester, old Captain Colchester's niece. Her father, a great friend of dad's, was in the sugar-broking business, and Charley made a sort of second home of their house. I wondered what my big brother would think of me. There was a sort of sternness about Charley's face which never left it, not even when he was larking in his rather wild fashion.

"He received me with a great shout of laughter. He seemed to think my joining as an officer the greatest joke in the world. There was a difference of ten years between us, and I suppose he remembered me best in pinafores. I was a kid of four when he first went to sea. It surprised me to find how boisterous he could be.

" 'Now we shall see what you are made of,' he cried. And he held me off by the shoulders, and punched my ribs, and hustled me into his berth. 'Sit down, Ned. I am glad of the chance of having you with me. I'll put the finishing touch to you, my young officer, providing you're worth the trouble. And, first of all, get it well into your head that we are not going to let this brute kill anybody this voyage. We'll stop her racket.'

"I perceived he was in dead earnest about it. He talked grimly of the ship, and how we must be careful and never allow this ugly beast to catch us napping with any of her damned tricks.

"He gave me a regular lecture on special seamanship for the use of the *Apse Family*; then changing his tone, he began to talk at large, rattling off the wildest, funniest nonsense, till my sides ached with laughing. I could see very well he was a bit above himself with high spirits. It couldn't be because of my coming. Not to that extent. But, of course, I wouldn't have dreamt of asking what was the matter. I had a proper respect for my big brother, I can tell you. But it was all made plain enough a day or two afterwards, when I heard that Miss Maggie Colchester was coming for the voyage. Uncle was giving her a sea-trip for the benefit of her health.

"I don't know what could have been wrong with her health. She had a beautiful colour, and a deuce of a lot of fair hair. She didn't care a rap for wind, or rain, or spray, or sun, or green seas, or anything. She was a blue-eyed, jolly girl of the very best sort, but the way she cheeked my big brother used to frighten me. I always expected it to end in an awful row. However, nothing decisive happened till after we had been in Sydney for a week. One day, in the men's dinner hour, Charley sticks his head into my cabin. I was stretched out on my back on the settee, smoking in peace.

"'Come ashore with me, Ned,' he says, in his curt way.

"I jumped up, of course, and away after him down the gangway and up George Street. He strode along like a giant, and I at his elbow, panting. It was confoundedly hot. 'Where on earth are you rushing me to, Charley?' I made bold to ask.

"'Here,' he says.

"'Here' was a jeweller's shop. I couldn't imagine what he could want there. It seemed a sort of mad freak. He thrusts under my nose three rings, which looked very tiny on his big, brown palm, growling out—

"'For Maggie! Which?'

"I got a kind of scare at this. I couldn't make a sound, but I pointed at the one that sparkled white and blue. He put it in his waistcoat pocket, paid for it with a lot of sovereigns, and bolted out. When we got on board I was quite out of breath. 'Shake hands, old chap,' I gasped out. He gave me a thump on the back. 'Give what orders you like to the boatswain when the hands turn-to,' says he; 'I am off duty this afternoon.'

"Then he vanished from the deck for a while, but presently he came out of the cabin with Maggie, and these two went over the gangway publicly, before all hands, going for a walk together on that awful, blazing hot day, with clouds of dust flying about. They came back after a few hours looking very staid, but didn't seem to have the slightest idea where they had been. Anyway, that's the answer they both made to Mrs. Colchester's question at tea-time.

"And didn't she turn on Charley, with her voice like an old night cabman's! 'Rubbish. Don't know where you've been! Stuff and nonsense. You've walked the girl off her legs. Don't do it again.'

"It's surprising how meek Charley could be with that old woman. Only on one occasion he whispered to me, 'I'm jolly glad she isn't Maggie's aunt, except by marriage. That's no sort of relationship.' But I think he let Maggie have too much of her own way. She was hopping all over that ship in her yachting skirt and a red tam o' shanter like a bright bird on a dead black tree. The old salts used to grin to themselves when they saw her coming along, and offered to teach her knots or splices. I believe she liked the men, for Charley's sake, I suppose.

"As you may imagine, the fiendish propensities of that cursed ship were never spoken of on board. Not in the cabin, at any rate. Only once on the homeward passage Charley said, incautiously, something about bringing all her crew home this time. Captain Colchester began to look uncomfortable at once, and that silly, hard-bitten old woman flew out at Charley as though he had said something indecent. I was quite confounded myself; as to Maggie, she sat completely mystified, opening her blue eyes very wide. Of course, before she was a day older she wormed it all out of me. She was a very difficult person to lie to.

" 'How awful,' she said, quite solemn. 'So many poor fellows. I am glad the voyage is nearly over. I won't have a moment's peace about Charley now.'

"I assured her Charley was all right. It took more than that ship knew to get over a seaman like Charley. And she agreed with me.

"Next day we got the tug off Dungeness; and when the tow-rope was fast Charley rubbed his hands and said to me in an undertone—

" 'We've baffled her, Ned.'

" 'Looks like it,' I said, with a grin at him. It was beautiful weather, and the sea as smooth as a millpond. We went up the river without a shadow of trouble except once, when off Hole Haven, the brute took a sudden sheer and nearly had a barge anchored just clear of the fairway. But I was aft, looking after the steering, and she did not catch me napping that time. Charley came up on the poop, looking very concerned. 'Close shave,' says he.

" 'Never mind, Charley,' I answered, cheerily. 'You've tamed her.'

"We were to tow right up to the dock. The river pilot boarded us below Gravesend, and the first words I heard him say were: 'You may just as well take your port anchor inboard at once, Mr. Mate.'

"This had been done when I went forward. I saw Maggie on the forecastle head enjoying the bustle and I begged her to go aft, but she took no notice of me, of course. Then Charley, who was very busy with the head gear, caught sight of her and shouted in his biggest voice: 'Get off the forecastle head, Maggie. You're in the way here.' For all answer she made a funny face at him, and I saw poor Charley turn away, hiding a smile. She was flushed with the excitement of getting home again, and her blue eyes seemed to snap electric sparks as she looked at the river. A collier brig had gone round just ahead of us, and our tug had to stop her engines in a hurry to avoid running slap bang into her.

"In a moment, as is usually the case, all the shipping in the reach seemed to get into a hopeless tangle. A schooner and a ketch got up a small collision all to themselves right in the middle of the river. It was exciting to watch, and, meantime, our tug remained stopped. Any other ship than that brute could have been coaxed to keep straight for a couple of minutes—but not she! Her head fell off at once, and she began to drift down, taking her tug along with her. I noticed a cluster of coasters at anchor within a quarter of a mile of us, and I thought I had better speak to the pilot. 'If you let her get amongst that lot,' I said, quietly, 'she will grind some of them to bits before we get her out again.'

"'Don't I know her!' cries he, stamping his foot in a perfect fury. And he out with his whistle to make that bothered tug get the ship's head up again as quick as possible. He blew like mad, waving his arm to port, and presently we could see that the tug's engines had been set going ahead. Her paddles churned the water, but it was as if she had been trying to tow a rock—she couldn't get an inch out of that ship. Again the pilot blew his whistle, and waved his arm to port. We could see the tug's paddles turning faster and faster away, broad on our bow.

"For a moment tug and ship hung motionless in a crowd of moving shipping, and then the terrific strain that evil, stony-hearted brute would always put on everything, tore the towing-chock clean out. The tow-rope surged over, snapping the iron stanchions of the head-rail one after another as if they had been sticks of sealing-wax. It was only then I noticed that in order to have a better view over our heads, Maggie had stepped upon the port anchor as it lay flat on the forecastle deck.

"It had been lowered properly into its hardwood beds, but there had been no time to take a turn with it. Anyway, it was quite secure as it was, for going into dock; but I could see directly that the tow-rope would sweep under the fluke in another second. My heart flew up right into my throat, but not before I had time to yell out: 'Jump clear of that anchor!'

"But I hadn't time to shriek out her name. I don't suppose she heard me at all. The first touch of the hawser against the fluke threw her down; she was up on her feet again quick as lightning, but she was up on the wrong side. I heard a horrid, scraping sound, and then that anchor, tipping over, rose up like something alive; its great, rough iron arm caught Maggie round the waist, seemed to clasp her close with a dreadful hug, and flung itself with her over and down in a terrific clang of iron, followed by heavy ringing blows that shook the ship from stem to stern—because the ring stopper held!"

"How horrible!" I exclaimed.

"I used to dream for years afterwards of anchors catching hold of girls," said the man in tweeds, a little wildly. He shuddered. "With a most pitiful howl Charley was over after her almost on the instant. But, Lord! he didn't see as much as a gleam of her red tam o' shanter in the water. Nothing! nothing whatever! In a moment there were half-a-dozen boats around us, and he got pulled into one. I, with the boatswain and the carpenter, let go the other anchor in a hurry and brought the ship up somehow. The pilot had gone silly. He walked up and down the forecastle head wringing his hands and muttering to himself: 'Killing women, now! Killing women, now!' Not another word could you get out of him.

"Dusk fell, then a night black as pitch; and peering upon the river I heard a low, mournful hail, 'Ship, ahoy!' Two Gravesend watermen came alongside. They had a lantern in their wherry, and looked up the ship's side, holding on to the ladder without a word. I saw in the patch of light a lot of loose, fair hair down there."

He shuddered again.

"After the tide turned poor Maggie's body had floated clear of one of them big mooring buoys," he explained. "I crept aft, feeling half-dead, and managed to send a rocket up—to let the other searchers know, on the river. And then I slunk away forward like a cur, and spent the night sitting on the heel of the bowsprit so as to be as far as possible out of Charley's way."

"Poor fellow!" I murmured.

"Yes. Poor fellow," he repeated, musingly. "That brute wouldn't let him—not even him—cheat her of her prey. But he made her fast in dock next morning. He did. We hadn't exchanged a word—not a single look for that matter. I didn't want to look at him. When the last rope was fast he put his hands to his head and stood gazing down at his feet as if trying to remember something. The men waited on the main deck for the words that end the voyage. Perhaps that is what he was trying to remember. I spoke for him. 'That'll do, men.'

"I never saw a crew leave a ship so quietly. They sneaked over the rail one after another, taking care not to bang their sea chests too heavily. They looked our way, but not one had the stomach to come up and offer to shake hands with the mate as is usual.

"I followed him all over the empty ship to and fro, here and there, with no living soul about but the two of us, because the old ship-keeper had locked himself up in the galley—both doors. Suddenly poor Charley mutters, in a crazy voice: 'I'm done here,' and strides down the gangway with me at his heels, up the dock, out at the gate, on towards Tower Hill. He used to take rooms with a decent old landlady in America Square, to be near his work.

"All at once he stops short, turns round, and comes back straight at me. 'Ned,' says he, I am going home.' I had the good luck to sight a four-wheeler and got him in just in time. His legs were beginning to give way. In our hall he fell down on a chair, and I'll never forget father's and mother's amazed, perfectly still faces as they stood over him. They couldn't understand what had happened to him till I blubbered out, 'Maggie got drowned, yesterday, in the river.'

"Mother let out a little cry. Father looks from him to me, and from me to him, as if comparing our faces—for, upon my soul, Charley did not resemble himself at all. Nobody moved; and the poor fellow raises his big brown hands slowly to his throat, and with one single tug rips everything open—collar, shirt, waistcoat—a perfect wreck and ruin of a man. Father and I got him upstairs somehow, and mother pretty nearly killed herself nursing him through a brain fever."

The man in tweeds nodded at me significantly.

"Ah! there was nothing that could be done with that brute. She had a devil in her."

"Where's your brother?" I asked, expecting to hear he was dead. But he was commanding a smart steamer on the China coast, and never came home now.

Jermyn fetched a heavy sigh, and the handkerchief being now sufficiently dry, put it up tenderly to his red and lamentable nose.

"She was a ravening beast," the man in tweeds started again. "Old Colchester put his foot down and resigned. And would you believe it? Apse & Sons wrote to ask whether he wouldn't reconsider his decision! Anything to save the good name of the *Apse Family*! Old Colchester went to the office then and said that he would take charge again but only to sail her out into the North Sea and scuttle her there. He was nearly off his chump. He used to be darkish iron-grey, but his hair went snow-white in a fortnight. And Mr. Lucian Apse (they had known each other as young men) pretended not to notice it. Eh? Here's infatuation if you like! Here's pride for you!

"They jumped at the first man they could get to take her, for fear of the scandal of the *Apse Family* not being able to find a skipper. He was a festive soul, I believe, but he stuck to her grim and hard. Wilmot was his second mate. A harum-scarum fellow, and pretending to a great scorn for all the girls. The fact is he was really timid. But let only one of them do as much as lift her little finger in encouragement, and there was nothing that could hold the beggar. As apprentice, once, he deserted abroad after a petticoat, and would have gone to the dogs then, if his skipper hadn't taken the trouble to find him and lug him by the ears out of some house of perdition or other.

"It was said that one of the firm had been heard once to express a hope that this brute of a ship would get lost soon. I can hardly credit the tale, unless it might have been Mr. Alfred Apse, whom the family didn't think much of. They had him in the office, but he was considered a bad egg altogether, always flying off to race meetings and coming home drunk. You would have thought that a ship so full of deadly tricks would run herself ashore some day out of sheer cussedness. But not she! She was going to last for ever. She had a nose to keep off the bottom."

Jermyn made a grunt of approval.

"A ship after a pilot's own heart, eh?" jeered the man in tweeds. "Well, Wilmot managed it. He was the man for it, but even he, perhaps, couldn't have done the trick without the green-eyed governess, or nurse, or whatever she was to the children of Mr. and Mrs. Pamphilius.

"Those people were passengers in her from Port Adelaide to the Cape. Well, the ship went out and anchored outside for the day. The skipper—hospitable soul—had a lot of guests from town to a farewell lunch—as usual with him. It was five in the evening before the last shore boat left the side, and the weather looked ugly and dark in the gulf. There was no reason for him to get under way. However, as he had told everybody he was going that day, he imagined it was proper to do so anyhow. But as he had no mind after all these festivities to tackle the straits in the dark, with a scant wind, he gave orders to keep the ship under lower topsails and foresail as close as she would lie, dodging along the land till the morning. Then he sought his virtuous couch. The mate was on deck, having his face washed very clean with hard rain squalls. Wilmot relieved him at midnight.

"The *Apse Family* had, as you observed, a house on her poop . . ."

"A big, ugly white thing, sticking up," Jermyn murmured, sadly, at the fire.

"That's it: a companion for the cabin stairs and a sort of chart-room combined. The rain drove in gusts on the sleepy Wilmot. The ship was then surging slowly to the southward, close hauled, with the coast within three miles or so to windward. There was nothing to look out for in that part of the gulf, and Wilmot went round to dodge the squalls under the lee of that chart-room, whose door on that side was open. The night was black, like a barrel of coal-tar. And then he heard a woman's voice whispering to him.

"That confounded green-eyed girl of the Pamphilius people had put the kids to bed a long time ago, of course, but it seems couldn't get to sleep herself. She heard eight bells struck, and the chief mate come below to turn in. She waited a bit, then got into her dressing-gown and stole across the empty saloon and up the stairs into the chart-room. She sat down on the settee near the open door to cool herself, I daresay.

"I suppose when she whispered to Wilmot it was as if somebody had struck a match in the fellow's brain. I don't know how it was they had got so very thick. I fancy he had met her ashore a few times before. I couldn't make it out, because, when telling the story, Wilmot would break off to swear something awful at every second word. We had met on the quay in Sydney, and he had an apron of sacking up to his chin, a big whip in his hand. A wagon-driver. Glad to do anything not to starve. That's what he had come down to.

"However, there he was, with his head inside the door, on the girl's shoulder as likely as not—officer of the watch! The helmsman, on giving his evidence afterwards, said that he shouted several times that the binnacle lamp had gone out. It didn't matter to him, because his orders were to 'sail her close.' 'I thought it funny,' he said, 'that the ship should keep on falling off in squalls, but I luffed her up every time as close as I was able. It was so dark I couldn't see my hand before my face, and the rain came in bucketfuls on my head.'

"The truth was that at every squall the wind hauled aft a little, till gradually the ship came to be heading straight for the coast, without a single soul in her being aware of it. Wilmot himself confessed that he had not been near the standard compass for an hour. He might well have confessed! The first thing he knew was the man on the look-out shouting blue murder forward there.

"He tore his neck free, he says, and yelled back at him: 'What do you say?'

"'I think I hear breakers ahead, sir,' howled the man, and came rushing aft with the rest of the watch, in the 'awfullest blinding deluge that ever fell from the sky,' Wilmot says. For a second or so he was so scared and bewildered that he could not remember on which side of the gulf the ship was. He wasn't a good officer, but he was a seaman all the same. He pulled himself together in a second, and the right orders sprang to his lips without thinking. They were to hard up with the helm and shiver the main and mizzen-topsails.

"It seems that the sails actually fluttered. He couldn't see them, but he heard them rattling and banging above his head. 'No use! She was too slow in going off,' he went on, his dirty face twitching, and the damn'd carter's whip shaking in his hand. 'She seemed to stick fast.' And then the flutter of the canvas above his head ceased. At this critical moment the wind hauled aft again with a gust, filling the sails and sending the ship with a great way upon the rocks on her lee bow. She had overreached herself in her last little game. Her time had come—the hour, the man, the black night, the treacherous gust of wind—the right woman to put an end to her. The brute deserved nothing better. Strange are the instruments of Providence. There's a sort of poetical justice—"

The man in tweeds looked hard at me.

"The first ledge she went over stripped the false keel off her. Rip! The skipper, rushing out of his berth, found a crazy woman, in a red flannel dressing-gown, flying round and round the cuddy, screeching like a cockatoo.

"The next bump knocked her clean under the cabin table. It also started the stern-post and carried away the rudder, and then that brute ran up a shelving, rocky shore, tearing her bottom out, till she stopped short, and the foremast dropped over the bows like a gangway."

"Anybody lost?" I asked.

"No one, unless that fellow, Wilmot," answered the gentleman, unknown to Miss Blank, looking round for his cap. "And his case was worse than drowning for a man. Everybody got ashore all right. Gale didn't come on till next day, dead from the West, and broke up that brute in a surprisingly short time. It was as though she had been rotten at heart." . . . He changed his tone, "Rain left off? I must get my bike and rush home to dinner. I live in Herne Bay—came out for a spin this morning."

He nodded at me in a friendly way, and went out with a swagger.

"Do you know who he is, Jermyn?" I asked.

The North Sea pilot shook his head, dismally. "Fancy losing a ship in that silly fashion! Oh, dear! oh dear!" he groaned in lugubrious tones, spreading his damp hand-kerchief again like a curtain before the glowing grate.

On going out I exchanged a glance and a smile (strictly proper) with the respectable Miss Blank, barmaid of the Three Crows.

WEST OF THE MISSISSIPPI AND SOUTH OF THE BORDER

THE CABALLERO'S WAY

O. Henry

THE CISCO KID HAD KILLED SIX MEN IN MORE OR LESS FAIR SCRIMMAGES, had murdered twice as many (mostly Mexicans), and had winged a larger number whom he modestly forbore to count. Therefore a woman loved him.

The Kid was twenty-five, looked twenty; and a careful insurance company would have estimated the probable time of his demise at, say, twenty-six. His habitat was anywhere between the Frio and the Rio Grande. He killed for the love of it—because he was quick-tempered—to avoid arrest—for his own amusement—any reason that came to his mind would suffice. He had escaped capture because he could shoot five-sixths of a second sooner than any sheriff or ranger in the service, and because he rode a speckled roan horse that knew every cow-path in the mesquite and pear thickets from San Antonio to Matamoras.

Tonia Perez, the girl who loved the Cisco Kid, was half Carmen, half Madonna, and the rest—oh, yes, a woman who is half Carmen and half Madonna can always be something more—the rest, let us say, was humming-bird. She lived in a grass-roofed *jacal* near a little Mexican settlement at the Lone Wolf Crossing of the Frio. With her lived a father or grandfather, a lineal Aztec, somewhat less than a thousand years old, who herded a hundred goats and lived in a continuous drunken dream from drinking *mescal*. Back of the *jacal* a tremendous forest of bristling pear, twenty feet high at its worst, crowded almost to its door. It was along the bewildering maze of this spinous thicket that the speckled roan would bring the Kid to see his girl. And once, clinging like a lizard to the ridge-pole, high up under the peaked grass roof, he had heard Tonia, with her Madonna face and Carmen beauty and humming-bird soul, parley with the sheriff's posse, denying knowledge of her man in her soft *mélange* of Spanish and English.

One day the adjutant-general of the State, who is, *ex officio*, commander of the ranger forces, wrote some sarcastic lines to Captain Duval of Company X, stationed at Laredo, relative to the serene and undisturbed existence led by murderers and desperadoes in the said captain's territory.

The captain turned the colour of brick dust under his tan, and forwarded the letter, after adding a few comments, per ranger Private Bill Adamson, to ranger

Lieutenant Sandridge, camped at a water hole on the Nueces with a squad of five men in preservation of law and order.

Lieutenant Sandridge turned a beautiful *couleur de rose* through his ordinary strawberry complexion, tucked the letter in his hip pocket, and chewed off the ends of his gamboge moustache.

The next morning he saddled his horse and rode alone to the Mexican settlement at the Lone Wolf Crossing of the Frio, twenty miles away.

Six feet two, blond as a Viking, quiet as a deacon, dangerous as a machine gun, Sandridge moved among the *Jacales*, patiently seeking news of the Cisco Kid.

Far more than the law, the Mexicans dreaded the cold and certain vengeance of the lone rider that the ranger sought. It had been one of the Kid's pastimes to shoot Mexicans "to see them kick": if he demanded from them moribund Terpsichorean feats, simply that he might be entertained, what terrible and extreme penalties would be certain to follow should they anger him! One and all they lounged with upturned palms and shrugging shoulders, filling the air with "*quien sabes*" and denials of the Kid's acquaintance.

But there was a man named Fink who kept a store at the Crossing—a man of many nationalities, tongues, interests, and ways of thinking.

"No use to ask them Mexicans," he said to Sandridge. "They're afraid to tell. This *hombre* they call the Kid—Goodall is his name, ain't it?—he's been in my store once or twice. I have an idea you might run across him at—but I guess I don't keer to say, myself. I'm two seconds later in pulling a gun than I used to be, and the difference is worth thinking about. But this Kid's got a half-Mexican girl at the Crossing that he comes to see. She lives in that *jacal* a hundred yards down the arroyo at the edge of the pear. Maybe she—no, I don't suppose she would, but that *jacal* would be a good place to watch, anyway."

Sandridge rode down to the *jacal* of Perez. The sun was low, and the broad shade of the great pear thicket already covered the grass-thatched hut. The goats were enclosed for the night in a brush corral near by. A few kids walked the top of it, nibbling the chaparral leaves. The old Mexican lay upon a blanket on the grass, already in a stupor from his mescal, and dreaming, perhaps, of the nights when he and Pizarro touched glasses to their New World fortunes—so old his wrinkled face seemed to proclaim him to be. And in the door of the *jacal* stood Tonia. And Lieutenant Sandridge sat in his saddle staring at her like a gannet agape at a sailorman.

The Cisco Kid was a vain person, as all eminent and successful assassins are, and his bosom would have been ruffled had he known that at a simple exchange of glances two persons, in whose minds he had been looming large, suddenly abandoned (at least for the time) all thought of him.

Never before had Tonia seen such a man as this. He seemed to be made of sunshine and blood-red tissue and clear weather. He seemed to illuminate the shadow of the pear when he smiled, as though the sun were rising again. The men she had known had been small and dark. Even the Kid, in spite of his achievements, was a stripling no larger than herself, with black, straight hair and a cold, marble face that chilled the noonday.

As for Tonia, though she sends description to the poorhouse, let her make a millionaire of your fancy. Her blue-black hair, smoothly divided in the middle and bound close to her head, and her large eyes full of the Latin melancholy, gave her the Madonna touch. Her motions and air spoke of the concealed fire and the desire to charm that she had inherited from the *gitanas* of the Basque province. As for the humming-bird part of her, that dwelt in her heart; you could not perceive it unless her bright red skirt and dark blue blouse gave you a symbolic hint of the vagarious bird.

The newly lighted sun-god asked for a drink of water. Tonia brought it from the red jar hanging under the brush shelter. Sandridge considered it necessary to dismount so as to lessen the trouble of her ministrations.

I play no spy; nor do I assume to master the thoughts of any human heart; but I assert, by the chronicler's right, that before a quarter of an hour had sped, Sandridge was teaching her how to plait a six-strand rawhide stake-rope, and Tonia had explained to him that were it not for her little English book that the peripatetic *padre* had given her and the little crippled *chivo*, that she fed from a bottle, she would be very, very lonely indeed.

Which leads to a suspicion that the Kid's fences needed repairing, and that the adjutant-general's sarcasm had fallen upon unproductive soil.

In his camp by the water hole Lieutenant Sandridge announced and reiterated his intention of either causing the Cisco Kid to nibble the black loam of the Frio country prairies or of haling him before a judge and jury. That sounded business-like. Twice a week he rode over to the Lone Wolf Crossing of the Frio, and directed Tonia's slim, slightly lemon-tinted fingers among the intricacies of the slowly growing lariata. A six-strand plait is hard to learn and easy to teach.

The ranger knew that he might find the Kid there at any visit. He kept his armament ready, and had a frequent eye for the pear thicket at the rear of the *jacal*. Thus he might bring down the kite and the humming-bird with one stone.

While the sunny-haired ornithologist was pursuing his studies the Cisco Kid was also attending to his professional duties. He moodily shot up a saloon in a small cow village on Quintana Creek, killed the town marshal (plugging him neatly in the centre of his tin badge), and then rode away, morose and unsatisfied. No true artist is uplifted by shooting an aged man carrying an old-style .38 bulldog.

On his way the Kid suddenly experienced the yearning that all men feel when wrong-doing loses its keen edge of delight. He yearned for the woman he loved to reassure him that she was his in spite of it. He wanted her to call his bloodthirstiness bravery and his cruelty devotion. He wanted Tonia to bring him water from the red jar under the brush shelter, and tell him how the *chivo* was thriving on the bottle.

The Kid turned the speckled roan's head up the ten-mile pear flat that stretches along the Arroyo Hondo until it ends at the Lone Wolf Crossing of the Frio. The roan whickered; for he had a sense of locality and direction equal to that of a belt-line street-car horse; and he knew he would soon be nibbling the rich mesquite grass at the end of a forty-foot stake-rope while Ulysses rested his head in Circe's straw-roofed hut.

More weird and lonesome than the journey of an Amazonian explorer is the ride of one through a Texas pear flat. With dismal monotony and startling variety the uncanny and multiform shapes of the cacti lift their twisted trunks, and fat, bristly hands to encumber the way. The demon plant, appearing to live without soil or rain, seems to taunt the parched traveller with its lush grey greenness. It warps itself a thousand times about what look to be open and inviting paths, only to lure the rider into blind and impassable spine-defended "bottoms of the bag," leaving him to retreat, if he can, with the points of the compass whirling in his head.

To be lost in the pear is to die almost the death of the thief on the cross, pierced by nails and with grotesque shapes of all the fiends hovering about.

But it was not so with the Kid and his mount. Winding, twisting, circling, tracing the most fantastic and bewildering trail ever picked out, the good roan lessened the distance to the Lone Wolf Crossing with every coil and turn that he made.

While they fared the Kid sang. He knew but one tune and sang it, as he knew but one code and lived it, and but one girl and loved her. He was a single-minded man of conventional ideas. He had a voice like a coyote with bronchitis, but whenever he chose to sing his song he sang it. It was a conventional song of the camps and trail, running at its beginning as near as may be to these words:

> "Don't you monkey with my Lulu girl
> Or I'll tell you what I'll do—"

and so on. The roan was inured to it, and did not mind.

But even the poorest singer will, after a certain time, gain his own consent to refrain from contributing to the world's noises. So the Kid, by the time he was within a mile or two of Tonia's *jacal*, had reluctantly allowed his song to die away—not because his vocal performance had become less charming to his own ears, but because his laryngeal muscles were aweary.

As though he were in a circus ring the speckled roan wheeled and danced through the labyrinth of pear until at length his rider knew by certain landmarks that the Lone Wolf Crossing was close at hand. Then, where the pear was thinner, he caught sight of the grass roof of the *jacal* and the hackberry tree on the edge of the arroyo. A few yards farther the Kid stopped the roan and gazed intently through the prickly openings. Then he dismounted, dropped the roan's reins, and proceeded on foot, stooping and silent, like an Indian. The roan, knowing his part, stood still, making no sound.

The Kid crept noiselessly to the very edge of the pear thicket and reconnoitred between the leaves of a clump of cactus.

Ten yards from his hiding-place, in the shade of the *jacal*, sat his Tonia calmly plaiting a rawhide lariat. So far she might surely escape condemnation; women have been known, from time to time, to engage in more mischievous occupations. But if all must be told, there is to be added that her head reposed against the broad and comfortable chest of a tall red-and-yellow man, and that his arm was about her, guiding her nimble fingers that required so many lessons at the intricate six-strand plait.

Sandridge glanced quickly at the dark mass of pear when he heard a slight squeaking sound that was not altogether unfamiliar. A gun-scabbard will make that sound when one grasps the handle of a six- shooter suddenly. But the sound was not repeated; and Tonia's fingers needed close attention.

And then, in the shadow of death, they began to talk of their love; and in the still July afternoon every word they uttered reached the ears of the Kid.

"Remember, then," said Tonia, "you must not come again until I send for you. Soon he will be here. A *vaquero* at the *tienda* said to-day he saw him on the Guadalupe three days ago. When he is that near he always comes. If he comes and finds you here he will kill you. So, for my sake, you must come no more until I send you the word."

"All right," said the stranger. "And then what?"

"And then," said the girl, "you must bring your men here and kill him. If not, he will kill you."

"He ain't a man to surrender, that's sure," said Sandridge. "It's kill or be killed for the officer that goes up against Mr. Cisco Kid."

"He must die," said the girl. "Otherwise there will not be any peace in the world for thee and me. He has killed many. Let him so die. Bring your men, and give him no chance to escape."

"You used to think right much of him," said Sandridge.

Tonia dropped the lariat, twisted herself around, and curved a lemon-tinted arm over the ranger's shoulder.

"But then," she murmured in liquid Spanish, "I had not beheld thee, thou great, red mountain of a man! And thou art kind and good, as well as strong. Could one choose him, knowing thee? Let him die; for then I will not be filled with fear by day and night lest he hurt thee or me."

"How can I know when he comes?" asked Sandridge.

"When he comes," said Tonia, "he remains two days, sometimes three. Gregorio, the small son of old Luisa, the *lavendera*, has a swift pony. I will write a letter to thee and send it by him, saying how it will be best to come upon him. By Gregorio will the letter come. And bring many men with thee, and have much care, oh, dear red one, for the rattlesnake is not quicker to strike than is '*El Chivato*,' as they call him, to send a ball from his *pistola*."

"The Kid's handy with his gun, sure enough," admitted Sandridge, "but when I come for him I shall come alone. I'll get him by myself or not at all. The Cap wrote one or two things to me that make me want to do the trick without any help. You let me know when Mr. Kid arrives, and I'll do the rest."

"I will send you the message by the boy Gregorio," said the girl. "I knew you were braver than that small slayer of men who never smiles. How could I ever have thought I cared for him?"

It was time for the ranger to ride back to his camp on the water hole. Before he mounted his horse he raised the slight form of Tonia with one arm high from the earth for a parting salute. The drowsy stillness of the torpid summer air still lay thick upon the dreaming afternoon. The smoke from the fire in the *jacal*, where the *frijoles* blubbered in the iron pot, rose straight as a plumb-line above the clay-daubed chimney. No sound or movement disturbed the serenity of the dense pear thicket ten yards away.

When the form of Sandridge had disappeared, loping his big dun down the steep banks of the Frio crossing, the Kid crept back to his own horse, mounted him, and rode back along the tortuous trail he had come.

But not far. He stopped and waited in the silent depths of the pear until half an hour had passed. And then Tonia heard the high, untrue notes of his unmusical singing coming nearer and nearer; and she ran to the edge of the pear to meet him.

The Kid seldom smiled; but he smiled and waved his hat when he saw her. He dismounted, and his girl sprang into his arms. The Kid looked at her fondly. His thick, black hair clung to his head like a wrinkled mat. The meeting brought a slight ripple of some undercurrent of feeling to his smooth, dark face that was usually as motionless as a clay mask.

"How's my girl?" he asked, holding her close.

"Sick of waiting so long for you, dear one," she answered. "My eyes are dim with always gazing into that devil's pincushion through which you come. And I can see into it such a little way, too. But you are here, beloved one, and I will not scold. *Que mal muchacho!* not to come to see your *alma* more often. Go in and rest, and let me water your horse and stake him with the long rope. There is cool water in the jar for you."

The Kid kissed her affectionately.

"Not if the court knows itself do I let a lady stake my horse for me," said he. "But if you'll run in, *chica*, and throw a pot of coffee together while I attend to the *caballo*, I'll be a good deal obliged."

Besides his marksmanship the Kid had another attribute for which he admired himself greatly. He was *muy caballero*, as the Mexicans express it, where the ladies were concerned. For them he had always gentle words and consideration. He could not have spoken a harsh word to a woman. He might ruthlessly slay their husbands and brothers, but he could not have laid the weight of a finger in anger upon a woman. Wherefore many of that interesting division of humanity who had come under the spell of his politeness declared their disbelief in the stories circulated about Mr. Kid. One shouldn't believe everything one heard, they said. When confronted by their indignant men folk with proof of the *caballero's* deeds of infamy, they said maybe he had been driven to it, and that he knew how to treat a lady, anyhow.

Considering this extremely courteous idiosyncrasy of the Kid and the pride he took in it, one can perceive that the solution of the problem that was presented to him by what he saw and heard from his hiding-place in the pear that afternoon (at least as to one of the actors) must have been obscured by difficulties. And yet one could not think of the Kid overlooking little matters of that kind.

At the end of the short twilight they gathered around a supper of *frijoles*, goat steaks, canned peaches, and coffee, by the light of a lantern in the *jacal*. Afterward, the ancestor, his flock corralled, smoked a cigarette and became a mummy in a grey blanket. Tonia washed the few dishes while the Kid dried them with the flour-sacking towel. Her eyes shone; she chatted volubly of the inconsequent happenings of her small world since the Kid's last visit; it was as all his other home-comings had been.

Then outside Tonia swung in a grass hammock with her guitar and sang sad *canciones de amor*.

"Do you love me just the same, old girl?" asked the Kid, hunting for his cigarette papers.

"Always the same, little one," said Tonia, her dark eyes lingering upon him.

"I must go over to Fink's," said the Kid, rising, "for some tobacco. I thought I had another sack in my coat. I'll be back in a quarter of an hour."

"Hasten," said Tonia, "and tell me—how long shall I call you my own this time? Will you be gone again to-morrow, leaving me to grieve, or will you be longer with your Tonia?"

"Oh, I might stay two or three days this trip," said the Kid, yawning. "I've been on the dodge for a month, and I'd like to rest up."

He was gone half an hour for his tobacco. When he returned Tonia was still lying in the hammock.

"It's funny," said the Kid, "how I feel. I feel like there was somebody lying behind every bush and tree waiting to shoot me. I never had mullygrubs like them before. Maybe it's one of them presumptions. I've got half a notion to light out in the morning before day. The Guadalupe country is burning up about that old Dutchman I plugged down there."

"You are not afraid—no one could make my brave little one fear."

"Well, I haven't been usually regarded as a jack-rabbit when it comes to scrapping; but I don't want a posse smoking me out when I'm in your *jacal*. Somebody might get hurt that oughtn't to."

"Remain with your Tonia; no one will find you here."

The Kid looked keenly into the shadows up and down the arroyo and toward the dim lights of the Mexican village.

"I'll see how it looks later on," was his decision.

At midnight a horseman rode into the rangers' camp, blazing his way by noisy "halloes" to indicate a pacific mission. Sandridge and one or two others turned out to investigate the row. The rider announced himself to be Domingo Sales, from the Lone Wolf Crossing. he bore a letter for Señor Sandridge. Old Luisa, the *lavendera*, had persuaded him to bring it, he said, her son Gregorio being too ill of a fever to ride.

Sandridge lighted the camp lantern and read the letter. These were its words:

Dear One: He has come. Hardly had you ridden away when he came out of the pear. When he first talked he said he would stay three days or more. Then as it grew later he was like a wolf or a fox, and walked about without rest, looking and listening. Soon he said he must leave before daylight when it is dark and stillest. And then he seemed to suspect that I be not true to him. He looked at me so strange that I am frightened. I swear to him that I love him, his own Tonia. Last of all he said I must prove to him I am true. He thinks that even now men are waiting to kill him as he rides from my house. To escape he says he will dress in my clothes, my red skirt and the blue waist I wear and the brown mantilla over the head, and thus ride away. But before that he says that I must put on his clothes, his *pantalones* and *camisa* and hat, and ride away on his horse from the *jacal* as far as the big road beyond the crossing and back again. This before he goes, so he can tell if I am true and if men are hidden to shoot him. It is a terrible thing. An hour before daybreak this is to be. Come, my dear one, and kill this man and take me for your Tonia. Do not try to take hold of him alive, but kill him quickly. Knowing all, you should do that. You must come long before the time and hide yourself in the little shed near the *jacal* where the wagon and saddles are kept. It is dark in there. He will wear my red skirt and blue waist and brown mantilla. I send you a hundred kisses. Come surely and shoot quickly and straight.

THINE OWN TONIA

Sandridge quickly explained to his men the official part of the missive. The rangers protested against his going alone.

"I'll get him easy enough," said the lieutenant. "The girl's got him trapped. And don't even think he'll get the drop on me."

Sandridge saddled his horse and rode to the Lone Wolf Crossing. He tied his big dun in a clump of brush on the arroyo, took his Winchester from its scabbard, and carefully approached the Perez *jacal*. There was only the half of a high moon drifted over by ragged, milk-white gulf clouds.

The wagon-shed was an excellent place for ambush; and the ranger got inside it safely. In the black shadow of the brush shelter in front of the *jacal* he could see a horse tied and hear him impatiently pawing the hard-trodden earth.

He waited almost an hour before two figures came out of the *jacal*. One, in man's clothes, quickly mounted the horse and galloped past the wagon-shed toward the crossing and village. And then the other figure, in skirt, waist, and mantilla over its head, stepped out into the faint moonlight, gazing after the rider. Sandridge thought he would take his chance then before Tonia rode back. He fancied she might not care to see it.

"Throw up your hands," he ordered loudly, stepping out of the wagon-shed with his Winchester at his shoulder.

There was a quick turn of the figure, but no movement to obey, so the ranger pumped in the bullets—one—two—three—and then twice more; for you never could be too sure of bringing down the Cisco Kid. There was no danger of missing at ten paces, even in that half moonlight.

The old ancestor, asleep on his blanket, was awakened by the shots. Listening further, he heard a great cry from some man in mortal distress or anguish, and rose up grumbling at the disturbing ways of moderns.

The tall, red ghost of a man burst into the *jacal*, reaching one hand, shaking like a *tule* reed, for the lantern hanging on its nail. The other spread a letter on the table.

"Look at this letter, Perez," cried the man. "Who wrote it?"

"*Ah, Dios*! it is Señor Sandridge," mumbled the old man, approaching. "*Pues, señor*, that letter was written by '*El Chivato*,' as he is called—by the man of Tonia. They say he is a bad man; I do not know. While Tonia slept he wrote the letter and sent it by this old hand of mine to Domingo Sales to be brought to you. Is there anything wrong in the letter? I am very old; and I did not know. *Valgame Dios*! it is a very foolish world; and there is nothing in the house to drink—nothing to drink."

Just then all that Sandridge could think of to do was to go outside and throw himself face downward in the dust by the side of his humming-bird, of whom not a feather fluttered. He was not a *caballero* by instinct, and he could not understand the niceties of revenge.

A mile away the rider who had ridden past the wagon-shed struck up a harsh, untuneful song, the words of which began:

> "Don't you monkey with my Lulu girl
> Or I'll tell you what I'll do—"

ONE DASH—HORSES

Stephen Crane

RICHARDSON PULLED UP HIS HORSE AND LOOKED BACK OVER THE TRAIL, where the crimson serape of his servant flamed amid the dusk of the mesquit. The hills in the west were carved into peaks, and were painted the most profound blue. Above them, the sky was of that marvelous tone of green—like still, sun-shot water—which people denounce in pictures.

José was muffled deep in his blanket, and his great toppling sombrero was drawn low over his brow. He shadowed his master along the dimming trail in the fashion of an assassin. A cold wind of the impending night swept over the wilderness of mesquit.

"Man," said Richardson, in lame Mexican, as the servant drew near, "I want eat! I want sleep! Understand no? Quickly! Understand?"

"Si, señor," said José, nodding. He stretched one arm out of his blanket, and pointed a yellow finger into the gloom. "Over there, small village! Si, señor."

They rode forward again. Once the American's horse shied and breathed quiveringly at something which he saw or imagined in the darkness, and the rider drew a steady, patient rein, and leaned over to speak tenderly, as if he were addressing a frightened woman. The sky had faded to white over the mountains, and the plain was a vast, pointless ocean of black.

Suddenly some low houses appeared squatting amid the bushes. The horsemen rode into a hollow until the houses rose against the somber, sundown sky, and then up a small hillock, causing these habitations to sink like boats in the sea of shadow.

A beam of red firelight fell across the trail. Richardson sat sleepily on his horse while the servant quarreled with somebody—a mere voice in the gloom—over the price of bed and board. The houses about him were for the most part like tombs in their whiteness and silence, but there were scudding black figures that seemed interested in his arrival.

José came at last to the horses' heads, and the American slid stiffly from his seat. He muttered a greeting as with his spurred feet be clicked into the adobe house that confronted him. The brown, stolid face of a woman shone in the light of the fire. He seated himself on the earthen floor, and blinked drowsily at the blaze. He was aware that the woman was clinking earthenware, and hieing here and everywhere in the manœuvers of the housewife. From a dark corner of the room there came the sound of two or three snores twining together.

The woman handed him a bowl of tortillas. She was a submissive creature, timid and large-eyed. She gazed at his enormous silver spurs, his large and impressive revolver, with the interest and admiration of the highly privileged cat of the adage. When he ate, she seemed transfixed off there in the gloom, her white teeth shining.

José entered, staggering under two Mexican saddles large enough for building-sites. Richardson decided to smoke a cigarette, and then changed his mind. It would be much finer to go to sleep. His blanket hung over his left shoulder, furled into a long pipe of cloth, according to a Mexican fashion. By doffing his sombrero, unfastening his spurs and his revolver-belt, he made himself ready for the slow, blissful twist into the blanket. Like a cautious man, he lay close to the wall, and all his property was very near his hand.

The mesquit brush burned long. José threw two gigantic wings of shadow as he flapped his blanket about him—first across his chest under his arms, and then around his neck and across his chest again, this time over his arms, with the end tossed on his right shoulder. A Mexican thus snugly enveloped can nevertheless free his fighting arm in a beautifully brisk way, merely shrugging his shoulder as he grabs for the weapon at his belt. They always wear their serapes in this manner.

The firelight smothered the rays which, streaming from a moon as large as a drum-head, were struggling at the open door. Richardson heard from the plain the fine, rhythmical trample of the hoofs of hurried horses. He went to sleep wondering who rode so fast and so late. And in the deep silence the pale rays of the moon must have prevailed against the red spears of the fire until the room was slowly flooded to its middle with a rectangle of silver light.

Richardson was awakened by the sound of a guitar. It was badly played—in this land of Mexico, from which the romance of the instrument ascends to us like a perfume. The guitar was groaning and whining like a badgered soul. A noise of scuffling feet accompanied the music. Sometimes laughter arose, and often the voices of men saying bitter things to each other; but always the guitar cried on, the treble sounding as if some one were beating iron, and the bass humming like bees.

"D—— it! They're having a dance," muttered Richardson, fretfully. He heard two men quarreling in short, sharp words like pistol-shots; they were calling each other worse names than common people know in other countries.

He wondered why the noise was so loud. Raising his head from his saddle pillow, he saw, with the help of the valiant moonbeams, a blanket hanging flat against the wall at the farther end of the room. Being of the opinion that it concealed a door, and remembering that Mexican drink made men very drunk, he pulled his revolver closer to him and prepared for sudden disaster.

Richardson was dreaming of his far and beloved North.

"Well, I would kill him, then!"

"No, you must not!"

"Yes, I will kill him! Listen! I will ask this American beast for his beautiful pistol and spurs and money and saddle, and if he will not give them—you will see!"

"But these Americans—they are a strange people. Look out, señor."

Then twenty voices took part in the discussion. They rose in quivering shrillness, as from men badly drunk.

Richardson felt the skin draw tight around his mouth, and his knee-joints turned to bread. He slowly came to a sitting posture, glaring at the motionless blanket at the far end of the room. This stiff and mechanical movement, accomplished entirely by the muscles of the wrist, must have looked like the rising of a corpse in the wan moonlight, which gave everything a hue of the grave.

My friend, take my advice, and never be executed by a hangman who doesn't talk the English language. It, or anything that resembles it, is the most difficult of deaths. The tumultuous emotions of Richardson's terror destroyed that slow and careful process of thought by means of which he understood Mexican. Then he used his instinctive comprehension of the first and universal language, which is tone. Still, it is disheartening not to be able to understand the detail of threats against the blood of your body.

Suddenly the clamor of voices ceased. There was a silence—a silence of decision. The blanket was flung aside, and the red light of a torch flared into the room. It was held high by a fat, round-faced Mexican, whose little snake-like mustache was as black as his eyes, and whose eyes were black as jet. He was insane with the wild rage of a man whose liquor is dully burning at his brain. Five or six of his fellows crowded after him. The guitar, which had been thrummed doggedly during the time of the high words, now suddenly stopped.

They contemplated each other. Richardson sat very straight and still, his right hand lost in the folds of his blanket. The Mexicans jostled in the light of the torch, their eyes blinking and glittering.

The fat one posed in the manner of a grandee. Presently his hand dropped to his belt, and from his lips there spun an epithet—a hideous word which often foreshadows knife-blows, a word peculiarly of Mexico, where people have to dig deep to find an insult that has not lost its savor.

The American did not move. He was staring at the fat Mexican with a strange fixedness of gaze, not fearful, not dauntless, not anything that could be interpreted; he simply stared.

The fat Mexican must have been disconcerted, for he continued to pose as a grandee, with more and more sublimity, until it would have been easy for him to have fallen over backward. His companions were swaying in a very drunken manner. They still blinked their beady eyes at Richardson. Ah, well, sirs, here was a mystery. At the approach of their menacing company, why did not this American cry out and turn pale, or run, or pray them mercy? The animal merely sat still, and stared, and waited for them to begin. Well, evidently he was a great fighter; or perhaps he was an idiot. Indeed, this was an embarrassing situation, for who was going forward to discover whether he was a great fighter or an idiot?

To Richardson, whose nerves were tingling and twitching like live wires, and whose heart jolted inside him, this pause was a long horror; and for these men who could so frighten him there began to swell in him a fierce hatred—a hatred that made him long to be capable of fighting all of them, a hatred that made him capable of fighting all of them. A 44-caliber revolver can make a hole large enough for little boys to shoot marbles through, and there was a certain fat Mexican with a mustache like a snake, who came extremely near to have eaten his last tomale merely because he frightened a man too much.

José had slept the first part of the night in his fashion, his body hunched into a heap, his legs crooked, his head touching his knees. Shadows had obscured him from the sight of the invaders. At this point he arose, and began to prowl quakingly over toward Richardson, as if he meant to hide behind him.

Of a sudden the fat Mexican gave a howl of glee. José had come within the torch's circle of light. With roars of singular ferocity the whole group of Mexicans pounced on the American's servant.

He shrank shuddering away from them, beseeching by every device of word and gesture. They pushed him this way and that. They beat him with their fists. They stung him with their curses. As he groveled on his knees, the fat Mexican took him by the throat and said: "I'm going to kill you!" And continually they turned their eyes to see if they were to succeed in causing the initial demonstration by the American.

Richardson looked on impassively. Under the blanket, however, his fingers were clinched as rigidly as iron upon the handle of his revolver.

Here suddenly two brilliant clashing chords from the guitar were heard, and a woman's voice, full of laughter and confidence, cried from without: "Hello! hello! Where are you?"

The lurching company of Mexicans instantly paused and looked at the ground. One said, as he stood with his legs wide apart in order to balance himself: "It is the girls! They have come!" He screamed in answer to the question of the woman: "Here!" And without waiting he started on a pilgrimage toward the blanket-covered door. One could now hear a number of female voices giggling and chattering.

Two other Mexicans said: "Yes; it is the girls! Yes!" They also started quietly away. Even the fat Mexican's ferocity seemed to be affected. He looked uncertainly at the still immovable American. Two of his friends grasped him gaily. "Come, the girls are here! Come!" He cast another glower at Richardson. "But this—" he began. Laughing, his comrades hustled him toward the door. On its threshold, and holding back the blanket with one hand, he turned his yellow face with a last challenging glare toward the American. José, bewailing his state in little sobs of utter despair and woe, crept to Richardson and huddled near his knee. Then the cries of the Mexicans meeting the girls were heard, and the guitar burst out in joyous humming.

The moon clouded, and but a faint square of light fell through the open main door of the house. The coals of the fire were silent save for occasional sputters. Richardson did not change his position. He remained staring at the blanket which hid the strategic door in the far end. At his knees José was arguing, in a low, aggrieved tone, with the saints. Without the Mexicans laughed and danced, and—it would appear from the sound—drank more.

In the stillness and night Richardson sat wondering if some serpent-like Mexican was sliding toward him in the darkness, and if the first thing he knew of it would be the deadly sting of the knife. "Sssh," he whispered to José. He drew his revolver from under the blanket and held it on his leg.

The blanket over the door fascinated him. It was a vague form, black and unmoving. Through the opening it shielded was to come, probably, menace, death. Sometimes he thought he saw it move.

As grim white sheets, the black and silver of coffins, all the panoply of death, affect us because of that which they hide, so this blanket, dangling before a hole in an adobe wall, was to Richardson a horrible emblem, and a horrible thing in itself. In his present mood Richardson could not have been brought to touch it with his finger.

The celebrating Mexicans occasionally howled in song. The guitarist played with speed and enthusiasm.

Richardson longed to run. But in this threatening gloom, his terror convinced him that a move on his part would be a signal for the pounce of death. José, crouching abjectly, occasionally mumbled. Slowly and ponderous as stars the minutes went.

Suddenly Richardson thrilled and started. His breath, for a moment, left him. In sleep his nerveless fingers had allowed his revolver to fall and clang upon the hard floor. He grabbed it up hastily, and his glance swept apprehensively over the room.

A chill blue light of dawn was in the place. Every outline was slowly growing; detail was following detail. The dread blanket did not move. The riotous company had gone or become silent.

Richardson felt in his blood the effect of this cold dawn. The candor of breaking day brought his nerve. He touched José. "Come," he said. His servant lifted his lined, yellow face and comprehended. Richardson buckled on his spurs and strode up; José obediently lifted the two great saddles. Richardson held two bridles and a blanket on his left arm; in his right hand he held his revolver. They sneaked toward the door.

The man who said that spurs jingled was insane. Spurs have a mellow clash— clash—clash. Walking in spurs—notably Mexican spurs—you remind yourself vaguely of a telegraphic lineman. Richardson was inexpressibly shocked when he came to walk. He sounded to himself like a pair of cymbals. He would have known of this if he had reflected; but then he was escaping, not reflecting. He made a gesture of despair, and from under the two saddles, José tried to make one of hopeless horror. Richardson stooped, and with shaking fingers unfastened the spurs. Taking them in his left hand, he picked up his revolver and they slunk on toward the door.

On the threshold Richardson looked back. In a corner he saw, watching him with large eyes, the Indian man and woman who had been his hosts. Throughout the night they had made no sign, and now they neither spoke nor moved. Yet Richardson thought be detected meek satisfaction at his departure.

The street was still and deserted. In the eastern sky there was a lemon-colored patch.

José had picketed the horses at the side of the house. As the two men came around the corner, Richardson's animal set up a whinny of welcome. The little horse had evidently heard them coming. He stood facing them, his ears cocked forward, his eyes bright with welcome.

Richardson made a frantic gesture, but the horse, in his happiness at the appearance of his friends, whinnied with enthusiasm.

The American felt at this time that he could have strangled his well-beloved steed. Upon the threshold of safety he was being betrayed by his horse, his friend. He felt the same hate for the horse that he would have felt for a dragon. And yet, as he glanced wildly about him, he could see nothing stirring in the street, nor at the doors of the tomb-like houses.

José had his own saddle-girth and both bridles buckled in a moment. He curled the picket ropes with a few sweeps of his arm. The fingers of Richardson, however, were shaking so that he could hardly buckle the girth. His hands were in invisible mittens. He was wondering, calculating, hoping about his horse. He knew the little animal's willingness and courage under all circumstances up to this time, but then— here it was different. Who could tell if some wretched instance of equine perversity was not about to develop. Maybe the little fellow would not feel like smoking over the plain at express-speed this morning, and so he would rebel and kick and be wicked. Maybe he would be without feeling of interest, and run listlessly. All men who have had to hurry in the saddle know what it is to be on a horse who does not understand the dramatic situation. Riding a lame sheep is bliss to it. Richardson, fumbling furiously at the girth, thought of these things.

Presently he had it fastened. He swung into the saddle, and as he did so his horse made a mad jump forward. The spurs of José scratched and tore the flanks of his great black animal, and side by side the two horses raced down the village street. The American heard his horse breathe a quivering sigh of excitement.

Those four feet skimmed. They were as light as fairy puff-balls. The houses of the village glided past in a moment, and the great, clear, silent plain appeared like a pale-blue sea of mist and wet bushes. Above the mountains the colors of the sunlight were like the first tones, the opening chords of the mighty hymn of the morning.

The American looked down at his horse. He felt in his heart the first thrill of confidence. The little animal, unurged and quite tranquil, moving his ears this way and that way with an air of interest in the scenery, was nevertheless bounding into the eye of the breaking day with the speed of a frightened antelope. Richardson, looking down, saw the long, fine reach of fore limb as steady as steel machinery. As the ground reeled past, the long, dried grasses hissed, and cactus-plants were dull blurs. A wind whirled the horse's mane over his rider's bridle hand.

José's profile was lined against the pale sky. It was as that of a man who swims alone in an ocean. His eyes glinted like metal fastened on some unknown point ahead of him, some mystic place of safety. Occasionally his mouth puckered in a little unheard cry; and his legs, bent back, worked spasmodically as his spurred heels sliced the flanks of his charger.

Richardson consulted the gloom in the west for signs of a hard-riding, yelling cavalcade. He knew that whereas his friends the enemy had not attacked him when he had sat still and with apparent calmness confronted them, they would certainly take furiously after him now that he had run from them—now that he had confessed to them that he was the weaker. Their valor would grow like weeds in the spring, and upon discovering his escape they would ride forth dauntless warriors.

Sometimes he was sure he saw them. Sometimes he was sure he heard them. Continually looking backward over his shoulder, he studied the purple expanses where the night was marching away. José rolled and shuddered in his saddle, persistently disturbing the stride of the black horse, fretting and worrying him until the white foam flew, and the great shoulders shone like satin from the sweat.

At last Richardson drew his horse carefully down to a walk. José wished to rush insanely on, but the American spoke to him sternly. As the two paced forward side by side, Richardson's little horse thrust over his soft nose and inquired into the black's condition.

Riding with José was like riding with a corpse. His face resembled a cast in lead. Sometimes he swung forward and almost pitched from his seat. Richardson was too frightened himself to do anything but hate this man for his fear. Finally he issued a mandate which nearly caused José's eyes to slide out of his head and fall to the ground like two silver coins.

"Ride behind me—about fifty paces."

"Señor—" stuttered the servant.

"Go!" cried the American, furiously. He glared at the other and laid his hand on his revolver. Jose' looked at his master wildly. He made a piteous gesture. Then slowly he fell back, watching the hard face of the American for a sign of mercy.

Richardson had resolved in his rage that at any rate he was going to use the eyes and ears of extreme fear to detect the approach of danger; and so he established his servant as a sort of an outpost.

As they proceeded he was obliged to watch sharply to see that the servant did not slink forward and join him. When José made beseeching circles in the air with his arm he replied by menacingly gripping his revolver.

José had a revolver, too; nevertheless it was very clear in his mind that the revolver was distinctly an American weapon. He had been educated in the Rio Grande country.

Richardson lost the trail once. He was recalled to it by the loud sobs of his servant.

Then at last José came clattering forward, gesticulating and wailing. The little horse sprang to the shoulder of the black. They were off.

Richardson, again looking backward, could see a slanting flare of dust on the whitening plain. He thought that he could detect small moving figures in it.

Jose's moans and cries amounted to a university course in theology. They broke continually from his quivering lips. His spurs were as motors. They forced the black horse over the plain in great headlong leaps.

But under Richardson there was a little insignificant rat-colored beast, who was running apparently with almost as much effort as it requires for a bronze statue to stand still. As a matter of truth, the ground seemed merely something to be touched from time to time with hoofs that were as light as blown leaves. Occasionally Richardson lay back and pulled stoutly at his bridle to keep from abandoning his servant.

José harried at his horse's mouth, flopped around in the saddle, and made his two heels beat like flails. The black ran like a horse in despair.

Crimson serapes in the distance resemble drops of blood on the great cloth of plain.

Richardson began to dream of all possible chances. Although quite a humane man, he did not once think of his servant. José being a Mexican, it was natural that he should be killed in Mexico; but for himself, a New-Yorker—

He remembered all the tales of such races for life, and he thought them badly written.

The great black horse was growing indifferent. The jabs of José's spurs no longer caused him to bound forward in wild leaps of pain. José had at last succeeded in teaching him that spurring was to be expected, speed or no speed, and now he took the pain of it dully and stolidly, as an animal who finds that doing his best gains him no respite.

José was turned into a raving maniac. He bellowed and screamed, working his arms and his heels like one in a fit. He resembled a man on a sinking ship, who appeals to the ship. Richardson, too, cried madly to the black horse.

The spirit of the horse responded to these calls, and, quivering and breathing heavily, he made a great effort, a sort of a final rush, not for himself apparently, but because he understood that his life's sacrifice, perhaps, had been invoked by these two men who cried to him in the universal tongue. Richardson had no sense of appreciation at this time—he was too frightened—but often now he remembers a certain black horse.

From the rear could be heard a yelling, and once a shot was fired—in the air evidently. Richardson moaned as he looked back. He kept his hand on his revolver. He tried to imagine the brief tumult of his capture—the flurry of dust from the hoofs of horses pulled suddenly to their haunches, the shrill biting curses of the men, the ring of the shots, his own last contortion. He wondered, too, if he could not somehow manage to pelt that fat Mexican, just to cure his abominable egotism.

It was José, the terror-stricken, who at last discovered safety. Suddenly he gave a howl of delight, and astonished his horse into a new burst of speed. They were on a little ridge at the time, and the American at the top of it saw his servant gallop down the slope and into the arms, so to speak, of a small column of horsemen in gray and silver clothes. In the dim light of the early morning they were as vague as shadows, but

Richardson knew them at once for a detachment of rurales, that crack cavalry corps of the Mexican army which polices the plain so zealously, being of themselves the law and the arm of it—a fierce and swift-moving body that knows little of prevention, but much of vengeance. They drew up suddenly, and the rows of great silver-trimmed sombreros bobbed in surprise.

Richardson saw José throw himself from his horse and begin to jabber at the leader of the party. When he arrived he found that his servant had already outlined the entire situation, and was then engaged in describing him, Richardson, as an American señior of vast wealth, who was the friend of almost every governmental potentate within two hundred miles. This seemed to profoundly impress the officer. He bowed gravely to Richardson and smiled significantly at his men, who unslung their carbines.

The little ridge hid the pursuers from view, but the rapid thud of their horses' feet could be heard. Occasionally they yelled and called to each other.

Then at last they swept over the brow of the hill, a wild mob of almost fifty drunken horsemen. When they discerned the pale-uniformed rurales they were sailing down the slope at top-speed.

If toboggans half-way down a hill should suddenly make up their minds to turn around and go back, there would be an effect somewhat like that now produced by the drunken horsemen. Richardson saw the rurales serenely swing their carbines forward, and, peculiar-minded person that he was, felt his heart leap into his throat at the prospective volley. But the officer rode forward alone.

It appeared that the man who owned the best horse in this astonished company was the fat Mexican with the snaky mustache, and, in consequence, this gentleman was quite a distance in the van. He tried to pull up, wheel his horse, and scuttle back over the hill as some of his companions had done, but the officer called to him in a voice harsh with rage.

"——!" howled the officer. "This señor is my friend, the friend of my friends. Do you dare pursue him, ——? ——! ——!——! ——!" These lines represent terrible names, all different, used by the officer.

The fat Mexican simply groveled on his horse's neck. His face was green; it could be seen that he expected death.

The officer stormed with magnificent intensity: "——! ——! ——!"

Finally he sprang from his saddle, and, running to the fat Mexican's side, yelled: "Go!" and kicked the horse in the belly with all his might. The animal gave a mighty leap into the air, and the fat Mexican, with one wretched glance at the contemplative rurales, aimed his steed for the top of the ridge. Richardson again gulped in expectation of a volley, for, it is said, this is one of the favorite methods of the rurales for disposing of objectionable people. The fat, green Mexican also evidently thought that he was to be killed while on the run, from the miserable look he cast at the troops. Nevertheless, he was allowed to vanish in a cloud of yellow dust at the ridge-top.

José was exultant, defiant, and, oh! bristling with courage. The black horse was drooping sadly, his nose to the ground. Richardson's little animal, with his ears bent forward, was staring at the horses of the rurales as if in an intense study. Richardson longed for speech, but he could only bend forward and pat the shining, silken shoulders. The little horse turned his head and looked back gravely.

THE MARK OF ZORRO

Johnston McCulley

I. Pedro, the Boaster

Again the sheet of rain beat against the roof of red Spanish tile, and the wind shrieked hke a soul in torment, and smoke puffed from the big fireplace as the sparks were showered over the hard dirt floor.

"'Tis a night for evil deeds!" declared Sergeant Pedro Gonzales, stretching his great feet in their loose boots toward the roaring fire and grasping the hilt of his sword in one hand and a mug filled with thin wine in the other. "Devils howl in the wind, and demons are in the raindrops! 'Tis an evil night, indeed—eh, *señor*?"

"It is!" The fat landlord agreed hastily; and he made haste, also, to fill the wine mug again, for Sergeant Pedro Gonzales had a temper that was terrible when aroused, as it always was when wine was not forthcoming.

"An evil night," the big sergeant repeated, and drained the mug without stopping to draw breath, a feat that had attracted considerable attention in its time and had gained the sergeant a certain amount of notoriety up and down El Camino Real, as they called the highway that connected the missions in one long chain.

Gonzales sprawled closer to the fire and cared not that other men thus were robbed of some of its warmth. Sergeant Pedro Gonzales often had expressed his belief that a man should look out for his own comfort before considering others; and being of great size and strength, and having much skill with the blade, he found few who had the courage to declare that they believed otherwise.

Outside the wind shrieked, and the rain dashed against the ground in a solid sheet. It was a typical February storm for southern California. At the missions the *frailes* had cared for the stock and had closed the buildings for the night. At every great *hacienda* big fires were burning in the houses. The timid natives kept to their little adobe huts, glad for shelter.

And here in the little *pueblo* of Reina de Los Angeles, where, in years to come, a great city would grow, the tavern on one side of the plaza housed for the time being men who would sprawl before the fire until the dawn rather than face the beating rain.

Sergeant Pedro Gonzales, by virtue of his rank and size, hogged the fireplace, and a corporal and three soldiers from the *presidio* sat at table a little in rear of him, drinking their thin wine and playing at cards. An Indian servant crouched on his heels in one corner, no neophyte who had accepted the religion of the *frailes*, but a gentile and renegade.

For this was in the day of the decadence of the missions, and there was little peace between the robed Franciscans who followed in the footsteps of the sainted Junipero Serra, who had founded the first mission at San Diego de Alcála, and thus made possible an empire, and those who followed the politicians and had high places in the army. The men who drank wine in the tavern at Reina de Los Angeles had no wish for a spying neophyte about them.

Just now conversation had died out, a fact that annoyed the fat landlord and caused him some fear; for Sergeant Pedro Gonzales in an argument was Sergeant Gonzales at peace; and unless he could talk the big soldier might feel moved to action and start a brawl.

Twice before Gonzales had done so, to the great damage of furniture and men's faces; and the landlord had appealed to the *comandante* of the *presidio*. Captain Ramón, only to be informed that the captain had an abundance of troubles of his own, and that running an inn was not one of them.

So the landlord regarded Gonzales warily and edged closer to the long table and spoke in an attempt to start a general conversation and so avert trouble.

"They are saying in the *pueblo*," he announced, "that this Señor Zorro is abroad again."

His words had an effect that was both unexpected and terrible to witness. Sergeant Pedro Gonzales hurled his half-filled wine mug to the hard dirt floor, straightened suddenly on the bench, and crashed a ponderous fist down upon the table, causing wine mugs and cards and coins to scatter in all directions.

The corporal and the three soldiers retreated a few feet in sudden fright, and the red face of the landlord blanched; the native sitting in the corner started to creep toward the door, having determined that he preferred the storm outside to the big sergeant's anger.

"Señor Zorro, eh?" Gonzales cried in a terrible voice. "Is it my fate always to hear that name? Señor Zorro, eh? Mr. Fox, in other words! He imagines, I take it, that he is as cunning as-one. By the saints, he raises as much stench!"

Gonzales gulped, turned to face them squarely, and continued his tirade.

"He runs up and down the length of El Camino Real like a goat of the high hills! He wears a mask, and he flashes a pretty blade, they tell me. He uses the point of it to carve his hated letter Z on the cheek of his foe! Ha! they are calling it! A pretty blade he has, in truth! But I cannot swear as to the blade—I never have seen it. He will not do me the honor of letting me see it! Señor Zorro's depredations never occur in the vicinity of Sergeant Pedro Gonzales! Perhaps this Señor Zorro can tell us the reason for that? Ha!"

He glared at the men before him, threw up his upper lip, and let the ends of his great black mustache bristle.

"They are calling him the Curse of Capistrano now," the fat landlord observed, stooping to pick up the wine mug and cards and hoping to filch a coin in the process.

"Curse of the entire highway and the whole mission chain!" Sergeant Gonzales roared. "A cutthroat, he is! A thief! Ha! A common fellow presuming to get him a reputation for bravery because he robs a *hacienda* or so and frightens a few women and natives! Señor Zorro, eh? Here is one fox it gives me pleasure to hunt! Curse of Capistrano, eh? I know I have led an evil life, but I only ask of the saints one thing now that they forgive me my sins long enough to grant me the boon of standing face to face with this pretty highwayman!"

"There is a reward—" the landlord began.

"You snatch the very words from my lips!" Sergeant Gonzales protested. "There is a pretty reward for the fellow's capture, offered by his excellency the governor. And what good fortune has come to my blade? I am away on duty at San Juan Capistrano, and the fellow makes his play at Santa Barbara. I am at Reina de Los Angeles, and he takes a fat purse at San Luis Reydine at San Gabriel, let us say, and he robs at San Diego de Alcála! A pest, he is! Once I met him——"

Sergeant Gonzales choked on his wrath and reached for the wine mug, which the landlord had filled again and placed at his elbow. He gulped down the contents. "Well, he never has visited us here," the landlord said with a sigh of thanksgiving.

"Good reason, fat one! Ample reason! We have a presidio here and a few soldiers. He rides far from any *presidio*, does this pretty Señor Zorro! He is like a fleeting sunbeam, I grant him that—and with about as much real courage!"

Sergeant Gonzales relaxed on the bench again, and the landlord gave him a glance that was full of relief, and began to hope that there would be no breakage of mugs and furniture and men's faces this rainy night.

"Yet this Señor Zorro must rest at times—he must eat and sleep," the landlord said. "It is certain that he must have some place for hiding and recuperation. Some fine day the soldiers will trail him to his den."

"Ha!" Gonzales replied. "Of course the man has to eat and sleep. And what is it that he claims now? He says that he is no real thief, by the saints! He is but punishing those who mistreat the men of the missions, he says. Friend of the oppressed, eh? He left a placard at Santa Barbara recently stating as much, did he not? Ha! And what may be the reply to that? The *frailes* of the missions are shielding him, hiding him, giving him his meat and drink! Shake down a robed *fray* and you'll find some trace of this pretty highwayman's whereabouts, else I am a lazy civilian!"

"I have no doubt that you speak the truth," the landlord replied. "I put it not past the *frailes* to do such a thing. But may this Señor Zorro never visit us here!"

"And why not, fat one?" Sergeant Gonzales cried in a voice of thunder. "Am I not here? Have I not a blade at my side? Are you an owl, and is this daylight that you cannot see as far as the end of your puny, crooked nose? By the saints—"

"I mean," said the landlord quickly and with some alarm, "that I have no wish to be robbed."

"To be—robbed of what, fat one? Of a jug of weak wine and a meal? Have you riches, fool? Ha! Let the fellow come! Let this bold and cunning Señor Zorro but enter that door and step before us! Let him make a bow, as they say he does, and let his eyes twinkle through his mask! Let me but face the fellow for an instant—and I claim the generous reward offered by his excellency!"

"He perhaps is afraid to venture so near the *presidio*," the landlord said.

"More wine!" Gonzales howled. "More wine, fat one, and place it to my account! When I have earned the reward, you shall be paid in full. I promise it on my word as a soldier! Ha! Were this brave and cunning Señor Zorro, this Curse of Capistrano, but to make entrance at that door now—" The door suddenly was opened!

II. On the Heels of the Storm

In came a gust of wind and rain and a man with it, and the candles flickered, and one was extinguished. This sudden entrance in the midst of the sergeant's boast startled them all; and Gonzales drew his blade halfway from its scabbard as his words died in his throat. The native was quick to close the door again to keep out the wind.

The newcomer turned and faced them; the landlord gave another sigh of relief. It was not Señor Zorro, of course. It was Don Diego Vega, a fair youth of excellent blood and twenty-four years, noted the length of El Camino Real for his small interest in the really important things of life.

"Ha!" Gonzales cried, and slammed his blade home.

"Is it that I startled you somewhat, *señores*?" Don Diego asked politely and in a thin voice, glancing around the big room and nodding to the men before him.

"If you did, *señor*, it was because you entered on the heels of the storm," the sergeant retorted. "Twould not be your own energy that would startle any man!"

"H-m!" grunted Don Diego, throwing aside his sombrero and flinging off his soaked serape. "Your remarks border on the perilous, my raucous friend."

"Can it be that you intend to take me to task?"

"It is true," continued Don Diego, "that I do not have a reputation for riding like a fool at risk of my neck, fighting like an idiot with every newcomer, and playing the guitar under every woman's window like a simpleton. Yet I do not care to have these things you deem my shortcomings flaunted in my face."

"Ha!" Gonzales cried, half in anger.

"We have an agreement. Sergeant Gonzales, that we can be friends, and I can forget the wide difference in birth and breeding that yawns between us only as long as you curb your tongue and stand my comrade. Your boasts amuse me, and I buy for you the wine that you crave—it is a pretty arrangement. But ridicule me again, *señor*, either in public or private, and the agreement is at an end. I may mention that I have some small influence—"

"Your pardon, *caballero* and my very good friend!" the alarmed Sergeant Gonzales cried now. "You are storming worse than the tempest outside, and merely because my tongue happened to slip. Hereafter, if any man ask, you are nimble of wit and quick with a blade, always ready to fight or to make love. You are a man of action, *caballero*! Ha! Does any dare doubt it?"

He glared around the room, half drawing his blade again, and then he slammed the sword home and threw back his head and roared with laughter and then clapped Don Diego between the shoulders; and the fat landlord hurried with more wine, knowing well that Don Diego Vega would stand the score.

For this peculiar friendship between Don Diego and Sergeant Gonzales was the talk of El Camino Real. Don Diego came from a family of blood that ruled over thousands of broad acres, countless herds of horses and cattle, great fields of grain. Don Diego, in his own right, had a *hacienda* that was like a small empire, and a house in the *pueblo* also, and was destined to inherit from his father more than thrice what he had now.

But Don Diego was unlike the other full-blooded youths of the times. It appeared that he disliked action. He seldom wore his blade, except as a matter of style and apparel. He was damnably polite to all women and paid court to none.

He sat in the sun and listened to the wild tales of other men—and now and then he smiled. He was the opposite of Sergeant Pedro Gonzales in all things, and yet they were together frequently. It was as Don Diego had said—he enjoyed the sergeant's boasts, and the sergeant enjoyed the free wine. What more could either ask in the way of a fair arrangement?

Now Don Diego went to stand before the fire and dry himself, holding a mug of red wine in one hand. He was only medium in size, yet he possessed health and good looks, and it was the despair of proud *dueñas* that he would not glance a second time at the pretty *señoritas* they protected, and for whom they sought desirable husbands.

Gonzales, afraid that he had angered his friend and that the free wine would be at an end, now strove to make peace.

"*Caballero*, we have been speaking of this notorious Señor Zorro," he said. "We have been regarding in conversation this fine Curse of Capistrano, as some nimble-witted fool has seen, fit to term the pest of the highway."

"What about him?" Don Diego asked, putting down his wine mug and hiding a yawn behind his hand. Those who knew Don Diego best declared he yawned ten score times a day.

"I have been remarking, *caballero*," said the sergeant, "that this fine Señor Zorro never appears in my vicinity, and that I am hoping the good saints will grant me the chance of facing him some fine day, that I may claim the reward offered by the governor. Señor Zorro, eh? Ha!"

"Let us not speak of him," Don Diego begged, turning from the fireplace and throwing out one hand as if in protest. "Shall it be that I never hear of anything except deeds of bloodshed and violence? Would it be possible in these turbulent times for a man to listen to words of wisdom regarding music or the poets?"

"Meal-mush and goat's milk!" snorted Sergeant Gonzales in huge disgust. "If this Señor Zorro wishes to risk his neck, let him. It is his own neck, by the saints! A cutthroat! A thief! Ha!"

"I have been hearing considerable concerning his work," Don Diego went on to say. "The fellow, no doubt, is sincere in his purpose. He has robbed none except officials who have stolen from the missions and the poor, and punished none except brutes who mistreat natives. He has slain no man, I understand. Let him have his little day in the public eye, my sergeant."

"I would rather have the reward!"

"Earn it!" Don Diego said. "Capture the man!"

"Ha! Dead or alive, the governor's proclamation says. I myself have read it."

"Then stand you up to him and run him through, if such a thing pleases you," Don Diego retorted. "And tell me all about it afterward—but spare me now."

"It will be a pretty story!" Gonzales cried. "And you shall have it entire, *caballero*, word by word! How I played with him, how I laughed at him as we fought, how I pressed him back after a time and ran him through—"

"Afterward—but not now!" Don Diego cried, exasperated. "Landlord, more wine! The only manner in which to stop this raucous boaster is to make his wide throat so slick with wine that the words cannot climb out of it!"

The landlord quickly filled the mugs. Don Diego sipped at his wine slowly, as a gentleman should, while Sergeant Gonzales took his in two great gulps. And then the scion of the house of Vega stepped across to the bench and reached for his sombrero and his serape.

"What?" the sergeant cried. "You are going to leave us at such an early hour, *caballero*? You are going to face the fury of that beating storm?"

"At least I am brave enough for that," Don Diego replied, smiling. "I but ran over from my house for a pot of honey. The fools feared the rain too much to fetch me some this day from the *hacienda*. Get me one, landlord."

"I shall escort you safely home through the rain!" Sergeant Gonzales cried, for he knew full well that Don Diego had excellent wine of age there.

"You shall remain here before the roaring fire!" Don Diego told him firmly. "I do not need an escort of soldiers from the *presidio* to cross the plaza. I am going over accounts with my secretary, and possibly may return to the tavern after we have finished. I wanted the pot of honey that we might eat as we worked."

"Ha! And why did you not send that secretary of yours for the honey, *caballero*? Why be wealthy and have servants, if a man cannot send them on errands on such a stormy night?"

"He is an old man and feeble," Don Diego explained. "He also is secretary to my aged father. The storm would kill him. Landlord, serve all here with wine and put it to my account. I may return when my books have been straightened."

Don Diego Vega picked up the pot of honey, wrapped his scrape around his head, opened the door, and plunged into the storm and darkness.

"There goes a man!" Gonzales cried, flourishing his arms. "He is my friend, that *caballero*, and I would have all men know it! He seldom wears a blade, and I doubt whether he can use one—but he is my friend! The flashing dark eyes of lovely *señoritas* do not disturb him, yet I swear he is a pattern of a man!

"Music and the poets, eh? Ha! Has he not the right, if such is his pleasure? Is he not Don Diego Vega? Has he not blue blood and broad acres and great storehouses filled with goods? Is he not liberal? He may stand on his head or wear petticoats, if it please him—yet I swear he is a pattern of a man!"

The soldiers echoed his sentiments since they were drinking Don Diego's wine and did not have the courage to combat the sergeant's statements anyway. The fat landlord served them with another round since Don Diego would pay. For it was beneath a Vega to look at his score in a public tavern, and the fat landlord many times had taken advantage of this fact.

"He cannot endure the thought of violence or bloodshed," Sergeant Gonzales continued. "He is as gentle as a breeze of spring. Yet he has a firm wrist and a deep eye. It merely is the *caballero*'s manner of seeing life. Did I but have his youth and good looks and riches—Ha! There would be a stream of broken hearts from San Diego de Alcála to San Francisco de Asis!"

"And broken heads!" the corporal offered.

"Ha! And broken heads, comrade! I would rule the country! No youngster should stand long in my way. Out with blade and at them! Cross Pedro Gonzales, eh? Ha! Through the shoulder—neatly! Ha! Through a lung!"

Gonzales was upon his feet now, and his blade had leaped from its scabbard. He swept it back and forth through the air, thrust, parried, lunged, advanced, and retreated, shouted his oaths, and roared his laughter as he fought with shadows.

"That is the manner of it!" he screeched at the fireplace. "What have we here? Two of you against one? So much the better, *señores*! We love brave odds! Ha! Have at you, dog! Die, hound! One side, poltroon!"

He reeled against the wall, gasping, his breath almost gone, the point of his blade resting on the floor, his great face purple with the exertion and the wine he had consumed, while the corporal and the soldiers and the fat landlord laughed long and loudly at this bloodless battle from which Sergeant Pedro Gonzales had emerged the unquestioned victor.

"Were—were this fine Señor Zorro only before me here and now!" the sergeant gasped.

And again the door was opened suddenly, and a man entered the inn on a gust of the storm!

III. Señor Zorro Pays a Visit

The native hurried forward to fasten the door against the force of the wind, and then retreated to his corner again. The newcomer had his back toward those in the long room. They could see that his sombrero was pulled far down on his head, as if to prevent die wind from whisking it away, and that his body was enveloped in a long cloak that was wringing wet.

With his back still toward them, he opened the cloak and shook the raindrops from it and then folded it across his breast again as the fat landlord hurried forward, rubbing his hands together in expectation, for he deemed that here was some *caballero* off the highway who would pay good coin for food and bed and care for his horse.

When the landlord was within a few feet of him and the door the stranger whirled around. The landlord gave a little cry of fear and retreated with speed. The corporal gurgled deep down in his throat; the soldiers gasped; Sergeant Pedro Gonzales allowed his lower jaw to drop and let his eyes bulge.

For the man who stood straight before them had a black mask over his face that effectually concealed his features, and through the two slits in it his eyes glittered ominously.

"Ha! What have we here?" Gonzales gasped finally, some presence of mind returning to him.

The man before them bowed.

"Señor Zorro, at your service," he said.

"By the saints I Señor Zorro, eh?" Gonzales cried.

"Do you doubt it, *señor?*"

"If you are indeed Señor Zorro, then have you lost your wits!" the sergeant declared.

"What is the meaning of that speech?"

"You are here, are you not? You have entered the inn, have you not? By all the saints, you have walked into a trap, my pretty highwayman!"

"Will the *señor* please explain?" Señor Zorro asked. His voice was deep and held a peculiar ring.

"Are you blind? Are you without sense?" Gonzales demanded. "Am I not here?"

"And what has that to do with it?"

"Am I not a soldier?"

"At least you wear a soldier's garb, *señor.*"

"By the saints, and cannot you see the good corporal and three of our comrades? Have you come to surrender your wicked sword, *señor?* Are you finished playing at rogue?"

Señor Zorro laughed, not unpleasantly, but he did not take his eyes from Gonzales.

"Most certainly I have not come to surrender," he said. "I am on business, *señor.*"

"Business?" Gonzales queried.

"Four days ago, *señor,* you brutally beat a native who had won your dislike. The affair happened on the road between here and the mission at San Gabriel."

"He was a surly dog and got in my way! And how does it concern you, my pretty highwayman?"

"I am the friend of the oppressed, *señor,* and I have come to punish you."

"Come to—to punish me, fool? You punish me? I shall die of laughter before I can run you through! You are as good as dead, Señor Zorro! His excellency has offered a pretty price for your carcass! If you are a religious man, say your prayers! I would not have it said that I slew a man without giving him time to repent his crimes. I give you the space of a hundred heartbeats."

"You are generous, *señor*, but there is no need for me to say my prayers."

"Then must I do my duty," said Gonzales, and lifted the point of his blade. "Corporal, you will remain by the table, and the men also. This fellow and the reward he means are mine!"

He blew out the ends of his mustache and advanced carefully, not making the mistake of underestimating his antagonist, for there had been certain tales of the man's skill with a blade. And when he was within the proper distance he recoiled suddenly, as if a snake had warned of a strike.

For Señor Zorro had allowed one hand to come from beneath his cloak, and the hand held a pistol, most damnable of weapons to Sergeant Gonzales.

"Back, *señor*!" Señor Zorro warned.

"Ha! So that is the way of it!" Gonzales cried. "You carry that devil's weapon and threaten men with it! Such things are for use only at a long distance and against inferior foes. Gentlemen prefer the trusty blade."

"Back, *señor*! There is death in this you call the devil's weapon. I shall not warn again."

"Somebody told me you were a brave man," Gonzales taunted, retreating a few feet. "It has been whispered that you would meet any man foot to foot and cross blades with him. I have believed it of you. And now I find you resorting to a weapon fit for nothing except to use against red natives. Can it be, *señor*, that you lack the courage I have heard you possess?"

Señor Zorro laughed again.

"As to that you shall see presently," he said. "The use of this pistol is necessary at the present time. I find myself pitted against large odds in this tavern, *señor*. I shall cross blades with you gladly when I have made such a proceeding safe."

"I wait anxiously," Gonzales sneered.

"The corporal and soldiers will retreat to that far corner," Señor Zorro directed. "Landlord, you will accompany them. The native will go there also. Quickly, *señores*. Thank you. I do not wish to have any of you disturbing me while I am punishing this sergeant here."

"Ha!" Gonzales screeched in fury. "We shall soon see as to the punishing, my pretty fox!"

"I shall hold the pistol in my left hand," Señor Zorro continued. "I shall engage this sergeant with my right, in the proper manner, and as I fight I shall keep an eye on the corner. The first move from any of you, *señores*, means that I fire. I am expert with this you have termed the devil's weapon, and if I fire some men shall cease to exist on this earth of ours. It is understood?"

The corporal and soldiers and landlord did not take the trouble to answer. Señor Zorro looked Gonzales straight in the eyes again, and a chuckle came from behind his mask.

"Sergeant, you will turn your back until I can draw my blade," he directed. "I give you my word as a *caballero* that I shall not make a foul attack."

"As a *caballero*?" Gonzales sneered.

"I said it, *señor*!" Zorro replied, his voice ringing a threat.

Gonzales shrugged his shoulders and turned his back. In an instant he heard the voice of the highwayman again.

"On guard, *señor*!"

IV. SWORDS CLASH—AND PEDRO EXPLAINS

Gonzales whirled at the word, and his blade came up. He saw that Señor Zorro had drawn his sword, and that he was holding the pistol in his left hand high above his head. Moreover, Señor Zorro was chuckling still, and the sergeant became infuriated. The blades clashed.

Sergeant Gonzales had been accustomed to battling with men who gave ground when they pleased and took it when they could, who went this way and that seeking an advantage, now advancing, now retreating, now swinging to left or right as their skill directed them.

But here he faced a man who fought in quite a different way. For Señor Zorro, it appeared, was as if rooted to one spot and unable to turn his face in any other direction. He did not give an inch, nor did he advance, nor step to either side.

Gonzales attacked furiously, as was his custom, and he found the point of his blade neatly parried. He used more caution then and tried what tricks he knew, but they seemed to avail him nothing. He attempted to pass around the man before him, and the other's blade drove him back. He tried a retreat, hoping to draw the other out, but Señor Zorro stood his ground and forced Gonzales to attack again. As for the highwayman, he did nought except put up a defense.

Anger got the better of Gonzales then, for he knew the corporal was jealous of him and that the tale of this fight would be told to all the *pueblo* tomorrow, and so travel up and down the length of El Camino Real.

He attacked furiously, hoping to drive Señor Zorro off his feet and make an end of it. But he found that his attack ended as if against a stone wall, his blade was turned aside, his breast crashed against that of his antagonist, and Señor Zorro merely threw out his chest and hurled him back half a dozen steps.

"Fight, *señor*!" Señor Zorro said.

"Fight yourself, cutthroat and thief!" the exasperated sergeant cried. "Don't stand like a piece of the hills, fool! Is it against your religion to take a step?"

"You cannot taunt me into doing it," the highwayman replied, chuckling again.

Sergeant Gonzales realized then that he had been angry, and he knew an angry man cannot fight with the blade as well as a man who controls his temper. So he became deadly cold now, and his eyes narrowed, and all boasting was gone from him.

He attacked again, but now he was alert, seeking an unguarded spot through which he could thrust without courting disaster himself. He fenced as he never had fenced in his life before. He cursed himself for having allowed wine and food to rob him of his wind. From the front, from either side, he attacked, only to be turned back again, all his tricks solved almost before he tried them.

He had been watching his antagonist's eyes, of course, and now he saw a change. They had seemed to be laughing through the mask, and now they had narrowed and seemed to send forth flakes of fire.

"We have had enough of playing," Señor Zorro said. "It is time for the punishment!"

And suddenly he began to press the fighting, taking step after step, slowly and methodically going forward and forcing Gonzales backward. The tip of his blade seemed to be a serpent's head with a thousand tongues. Gonzales felt himself at the other's mercy, but he gritted his teeth and tried to control himself and fought on.

Now he was with his back against the wall, but in such a position that Señor Zorro could give him battle and watch the men in the corner at the same time. He knew the highwayman was playing with him. He was ready to swallow his pride and call upon the corporal and soldiers to rush in and give him aid.

And then there came a sudden battering at the door, which the native had bolted. The heart of Gonzales gave a great leap. Somebody was there, wishing to enter. Whoever it was would think it peculiar that the door was not thrown open instantly by the fat landlord or his servant. Perhaps help was at hand.

"We are interrupted, *señor*," the highwayman said. "I regret it, for I will not have the time to give you the punishment you deserve, and will have to arrange to visit you another time. You scarcely are worth a double visit."

The pounding at the door was louder now. Gonzales raised his voice: "Ha! We have Señor Zorro here!"

"Poltroon!" the highwayman cried.

His blade seemed to take on new life. It darted in and out with a speed that was bewildering. It caught a thousand beams of light from the flickering candles and hurled them back.

And suddenly it darted in and hooked itself properly, and Sergeant Gonzales felt his sword torn from his grasp and saw it go flying through the air.

"So!" Señor Zorro cried.

Gonzales awaited the stroke. A sob came into his throat that this must be the end instead of on a field of battle where a soldier wishes it. But no steel entered his breast to bring forth his life's blood.

Instead, Señor Zorro swung his left hand down, passed the hilt of his blade to it and grasped it beside the pistol's butt, and with his right he slapped Pedro Gonzales once across the cheek.

"That for a man who mistreats helpless natives!" he cried.

Gonzales roared in rage and shame. Somebody was trying to smash the door in now. But Señor Zorro appeared to give it little thought. He sprang back, and sent his blade into its scabbard like a flash. He swept the pistol before him and thus threatened all in the long room. He darted to a window, sprang upon a bench.

"Until a later time, *señor*!" he cried.

And then he went through the window as a mountain goat jumps from a cliff, taking its covering with him. In rushed the wind and rain, and the candles went out.

"After him!" Gonzales screeched, springing across the room and grasping his blade again. "Unbar the door! Out and after him! Remember, there is a generous reward—"

The corporal reached the door first, and threw it open. In stumbled two men of the *pueblo*, eager for wine and an explanation of the fastened door. Sergeant Gonzales and his comrades drove over them, left them sprawling, and dashed into the storm.

But there was little use in it. It was so dark a man could not see a distance of a horse's length. The beating rain was enough to obliterate tracks almost instantly. Señor Zorro was gone—and no man could tell in what direction.

There was a tumult, of course, in which the men of the *pueblo* joined. Sergeant Gonzales and the soldiers returned to the inn to find it full of men they knew. And Sergeant Gonzales knew, also, that his reputation was now at stake.

"Nobody but a highwayman, nobody but a cutthroat and thief would have done it!" he cried aloud.

"How is that, brave one?" cried a man in the throng near the doorway.

"This pretty Señor Zorro knew, of course! Some days ago I broke the thumb of my sword hand while fencing at San Juan Capistrano. No doubt the word was passed to this Señor Zorro. And he visits me at such a time that he may afterward say he had vanquished me."

The corporal and soldiers and landlord stared at him, but none was brave enough to say a word.

"Those who were here can tell you, *señores*," Gonzales went on. "This Señor Zorro came in at the door and immediately drew a pistol—devil's weapon—from beneath his cloak. He presents it at us, and forces all except me to retire to that corner. I refused to retire.

" 'Then you shall fight me,' says this pretty highwayman, and I draw my blade, thinking to make an end of the pest. And what does he tell me then? 'We shall fight,' he says, 'and I will outpoint you, so that I may boast of it afterward. In my left hand I hold the pistol. If your attack is not to my liking, I shall fire, and afterward run you through, and so make an end of a certain sergeant.' "

The corporal gasped, and the fat landlord was almost ready to speak, but thought better of it when Sergeant Gonzales glared at him.

"Could anything be more devilish?" Gonzales asked. "I was to fight, and yet I would get a devil's chunk of lead in my carcass if I pressed the attack. Was there ever such a farce? It shows the stuff of which this pretty highwayman is made. Some day I shall meet him when he holds no pistol—and then—"

"But how did he get away?" someone in the crowd asked.

"He heard those at the door. He threatened me with the devil's pistol and forced me to toss my blade in yonder far corner. He threatened us all, ran to the window, and sprang through. And how could we find him in the darkness or track him through the sheets of rain? But I am determined now! In the morning I go to my Captain Ramón and ask permission to be absolved from all other duty, that I may take some comrades and run down this pretty Señor Zorro. Ha! We shall go fox hunting!"

The excited crowd about the door suddenly parted, and Don Diego Vega hurried into the tavern.

"What is this I hear?" he asked. "They are saying that Señor Zorro has paid a visit here."

" 'Tis a true word, *caballero*!" Gonzales answered. "And we were speaking of the cutthroat here this evening. Had you remained instead of going home to work with your secretary, you should have seen the entire affair."

"Were you not here? Can you not tell me?" Don Diego asked. "But I pray you make not the tale too bloody. I cannot see why men must be violent. Where is the highwayman's dead body?"

Gonzales choked; the fat landlord turned away to hide his smile; the corporal and soldiers began picking up wine mugs to keep busy at this dangerous moment.

"He—that is, there is no body," Gonzales managed to say.

"Have done with your modesty, sergeant!" Don Diego cried. "Am I not your friend? Did you not promise to tell me the story if you met this cutthroat? I know you would spare my feelings, knowing that I do not love violence, yet I am eager for the facts because you, my friend, have been engaged with this fellow. How much was the reward?"

"By the saints!" Gonzales swore.

"Come, sergeant! Out with the tale! Landlord, give all of us wine, that we may celebrate this affair! Your tale, sergeant! Shall you leave the army, now that you have earned the reward, and purchase a *hacienda* and take a wife?"

Sergeant Gonzales choked again and reached gropingly for a wine mug.

"You promised me," Don Diego continued, "that you would tell me the whole thing, word by word. Did he not say as much, landlord? You declared that you would relate how you played with him; how you laughed at him while you fought; how you pressed him back after a time and then ran him through—"

"By the saints!" Sergeant Gonzales roared, the words coming from between his lips like peals of thunder. "It is beyond the endurance of any man! You—Don Diego—my friend—"

"Your modesty ill becomes you at such a time," Don Diego said. "You promised the tale, and I would have it. What does this Señor Zorro look like? Have you peered at the dead face beneath the mask? It is, perhaps, some man that we all know? Cannot some one of you tell me the facts? You stand here like so many speechless images of men—"

"Wine—or I choke!" Gonzales howled. "Don Diego, you are my good friend, and I will cross swords with any man who belittles you! But do not try me too far this night—"

"I fail to understand," Don Diego said. "I have but asked you to tell me the story of the fight—how you mocked him as you battled; how you pressed him back at will, and presently ended it by running him through—"

"Enough! Am I to be taunted?" the big sergeant cried. He gulped down the wine and hurled the mug far from him.

"Is it possible that you did not win the battle?" Don Diego asked. "But surely this pretty highwayman could not stand up before you, my sergeant. How was the outcome?"

"He had a pistol—"

"Why did you not take it away from him, then, and crowd it down his throat? But perhaps that is what you did. Here is more wine, my sergeant. Drink!"

But Sergeant Gonzales was thrusting his way through the throng at the door.

"I must not forget my duty!" he said. "I must hurry to the *presidio* and report this occurrence to the *comandante*!"

"But, sergeant—"

"And as to this Señor Zorro, he will be meat for my blade before I am done!" Gonzales promised.

And then, cursing horribly, he rushed away through the rain, the first time in his life he ever had allowed duty to interfere with his pleasure and had run from good wine.

Don Diego Vega smiled as he turned toward the fireplace.

V. A RIDE IN THE MORNING

The following morning found the storm at an end, and there was not a single aloud to mar the perfect blue of the sky, and the sun was bright, and palm fronds glistened in it, and the air was bracing as it blew down the valleys from the sea.

At midmorning, Don Diego Vega came from his house in the *pueblo*, drawing on his sheepskin riding-mittens, and stood for a moment before it, glancing across the plaza at the little tavern. From the rear of the house an Indian servant led a horse.

Though Don Diego did not go galloping across the hills and up and down El Camino Real like an idiot, yet he owned a fairish bit of horseflesh. The animal had spirit and speed and endurance, and many a young blood would have purchased him, except that Don Diego had no use for more money and wanted to retain the beast.

The saddle was heavy and showed more silver than leather on its surface. The bridle was heavily chased with silver, too, and from its sides dangled leather globes studded with semiprecious stones that now glittered in the bright sunshine as if to advertise Don Diego's wealth and prestige to all the world.

Don Diego mounted, while half a score of men loitering around the plaza watched and made efforts to hide their grins. It was quite the thing in those days for a youngster to spring from the ground into his saddle, gather up the reins, rake the beast's flanks with his great spurs, and disappear in a cloud of dust all in one motion.

But Don Diego mounted a horse as he did everything else—without haste or spirit. The native held a stirrup, and Don Diego inserted the toe of his boot. Then he gathered the reins in one hand, and pulled himself into the saddle as if it had been quite a task.

Having done that much, the native held the other stirrup and guided Don Diego's other boot into it, and then he backed away, and Don Diego clucked to the magnificent beast and started it, at a walk, along the edge of the plaza toward the trail that ran to the north.

Having reached the trail, Don Diego allowed the animal to trot, and after having covered a mile in this fashion, he urged the beast into a slow gallop, and so rode along the highway.

Men were busy in the fields and orchards, and natives were tending the herds. Now and then Don Diego passed a lumbering *carreta*, and saluted whoever happened to be in it Once a young man he knew passed him at a gallop, going toward the *pueblo*, and Don Diego stopped his own horse to brush the dust from his garments after the man had gone his way.

Those same garments were more gorgeous than usual this bright morning. A glance at them was enough to establish the wealth and position of the wearer. Don Diego had dressed with much care, admonishing his servants because his newest serape was not pressed properly, and spending a great deal of time over the polishing of his boots.

He traveled for a distance of four miles and then turned from the highroad and started up a narrow, dusty trail that led to a group of buildings against the side of a hill in the distance. Don Diego Vega was about to pay a visit to the *hacienda* of Don Carlos Pulido.

This same Don Carlos had experienced numerous vicissitudes during the last few years. Once he had been second to none except Don Diego's father in position, wealth, and breeding. But he had made the mistake of getting on the wrong side of the fence politically, and he found himself stripped of a part of his broad acres, and tax-gatherers bothering him in the name of the governor, until there remained but a remnant of his former fortune, but all his inherited dignity of birth.

On this morning Don Carlos was sitting on the veranda of the *hacienda* meditating on the times, which were not at all to his liking. His wife, Doña Catalina, the sweetheart of his youth and age, was inside directing her servants. His only child, the Señorita Lolita, likewise was inside, plucking at the strings of a guitar and dreaming as a girl of eighteen dreams. Don Carlos raised his silvered head and peered down the long, twisting trail, and saw in the distance a small cloud of dust. The dust cloud told him that a single horseman was approaching, and Don Carlos feared another gatherer of taxes.

He shaded his eyes with a hand and watched the approaching horseman carefully. He noted the leisurely manner in which he rode his mount, and suddenly hope sang in his breast, for he saw the sun flashing from the silver on saddle and bridle, and he knew that men of the army did not have such rich harness to use while on duty.

The rider had made the last turning now and was in plain sight from the veranda of the house, and Don Carlos rubbed his eyes and looked again to verify the suspicion he had. Even at that distance the aged don could establish the identity of the horseman.

" 'Tis Don Diego Vega," he breathed. "May the saints grant that here is a turn in my fortunes for the better at last."

Don Diego, he knew, might only be stopping to pay a friendly visit, and yet that would be something, for when it was known abroad that the Vega family was on excellent terms with the Pulido establishment, even the politicians would stop to think twice before harassing Don Carlos further, for the Vegas were a power in the land.

So Don Carlos slapped his hands together, and a native hurried out from the house, and Don Carlos bade him draw die shades so that the sun would be kept from a corner of the veranda, and place a table and some chairs, and hurry with small cakes and wine.

He sent word into the house to the women, too, that Don Diego Vega was approaching. Doña Catalina felt her heart beginning to sing, and she herself began to hum a little song, and Señorita Lolita ran to a window to look out at the trail. When Don Diego stopped before the steps that led to the veranda, there was a native waiting to care for his horse, and Don Carlos himself walked halfway down the steps and stood waiting, his hand held out in welcome.

"I am glad to see you a visitor at my poor *hacienda*, Don Diego," he said, as the young man approached, drawing off his mittens.

"It is a long and dusty road," Don Diego said. "It wearies me, too, to ride a horse the distance."

Don Carlos almost forgot himself and smiled at that, for surely riding a horse a distance of four miles was not enough to tire a young man of blood. But he remembered Don Diego's lifelessness and did not smile, lest the smile cause anger.

He led the way to the shady nook on the veranda, and offered Don Diego wine and cakes, and waited for his guest to speak. As became the times, the women remained inside the house, not ready to show themselves unless the visitor asked for them, or their lord and master called.

"How are things in the *pueblo* of Reina de Los Angeles?" Don Carlos asked. "It has been a space of several score days since I visited there."

"Everything is the same," said Don Diego, "except that this Señor Zorro invaded the tavern last evening and had a duel with the big Sergeant Gonzales."

"Ha! Señor Zorro, eh? And what was the outcome of the fighting?"

"Though the sergeant has a crooked tongue while speaking of it," said Don Diego, "it has come to me through a corporal who was present that this Señor Zorro played with the sergeant and finally disarmed him and sprang through a window to make his escape in the rain. They could not find his tracks."

"A clever rogue," Don Carlos said. "At least, I have nothing to fear from him. It is generally known up and down El Camino Real, I suppose, that I have been stripped of almost everything the governor's men could carry away. I look for them to take the *hacienda* next."

"Um. Such a thing should be stopped!" Don Diego said, with more than his usual amount of spirit.

The eyes of Don Carlos brightened. If Don Diego Vega could be made to feel some sympathy, if one of the illustrious Vega family would but whisper a word in the governor's ear, the persecution would cease instantly, for the commands of a Vega were made to be obeyed by all men of whatever rank.

VI. DIEGO SEEKS A BRIDE

Don Diego sipped his wine slowly and looked out across the *mesa*, and Don Carlos looked at him in puzzled fashion, realizing that something was coming, and scarcely knowing what to expect.

"I did not ride through the damnable sun and dust to talk with you concerning this Señor Zorro, or any other bandit," Don Diego explained after a time.

"Whatever your errand, I am glad to welcome one of your family, *caballero*," Don Carlos said.

"I had a long talk with my father yesterday morning," Don Diego went on. "He informed me that I am approaching the age of twenty-five, and he is of a mind that I am not accepting my duties and responsibilities in the proper fashion."

"But surely—"

"Oh, doubtless he knows! My father is a wise man."

"And no man can dispute that, Don Diego!"

"He urged upon me that I awaken and do as I should. I have been dreaming, it appears. A man of my wealth and station—you will pardon me if I speak of it—must do certain things."

"It is the purse of position, *señor*."

"When my father dies I come into his fortune, naturally, being the only child. That part of it is all right. But what will happen when I die? That is what my father asks."

"I understand."

"A young man of my age, he told me, should have a wife, a mistress of his household, and shoulder—have offspring to inherit and preserve an illustrious name."

"Nothing could be truer than that," said Don Carlos.

"So I have decided to get me a wife."

"Ha! It is something every man should do, Don Diego. Well do I remember when I courted Doña Catalina. We were mad to get into each other's arms, but her father kept her from me for a time. I was only seventeen, though, so perhaps he did right. But you are nearly twenty-five. Get you a bride, by all means."

"And so I have come to see you about it," Don Diego said.

"To see me about it?" gasped Don Carlos, with something of fear and a great deal of hope in his breast.

"It will be rather a bore, I expect. Love and marriage, and all that sort of thing, is rather a necessary nuisance in its way. The idea of a man of sense running about a woman, playing a guitar for her, making up to her like a loon when everyone knows his intention!

"And then the ceremony! Being a man of wealth and station, I suppose the wedding must be an elaborate one, and the natives will have to be feasted, and all that, simply because a man is taking a bride to be mistress of his household."

"Most young men," Don Carlos observed, "delight to win a woman and are proud if they have a great and fashionable wedding."

"No doubt. But it is an awful nuisance. However, I will go through with it, *señor*. It is my father's wish, you see. You—if you will pardon me again—have fallen upon evil days. That is the result of politics, of course. But you are of excellent blood, *señor*, of the best blood in the land."

"I thank you for remembering that truth," said Don Carlos, rising long enough to put one hand over his heart and bow.

"Everybody knows it, *señor*. And a Vega, naturally, when he takes a mate, must seek out a woman of excellent blood."

"To be sure!" Don Carlos exclaimed.

"You have an only daughter, the Señorita Lolita."

"Ah! Yes, indeed, *señor*. Lolita is eighteen now, and a beautiful and accomplished girl, if her father is the man to say it."

"I have observed her at the mission and at the *pueblo*," Don Diego said. "She is, indeed, beautiful, and I have heard that she is accomplished. Of her birth and breeding there can be no doubt. I think she would be a fit woman to preside over my household."

"*Señor?*"

"That is the object of my visit today, señor."

"You—you are asking my permission to pay addresses to my fair daughter?"

"I am, *señor*."

Don Carlos's face beamed, and again he sprang from his chair, this time to bend forward and grasp Don Diego by the hand.

"She is a fair flower," the father said. "I would see her wed, and I have been to some anxiety about it, for I did not wish her to marry into a family that did not rank with mine. But there can be no question where a Vega is concerned. You have my permission, *señor*."

Don Carlos was delighted. An alliance between his daughter and Don Diego Vega! His fortunes were retrieved the moment that was consummated. He would be important and powerful again!

He called a native and sent for his wife, and within a few minutes the Doña Catalina appeared on the veranda to greet the visitor, her face beaming, for she had been listening.

"Don Diego has done us the honor to request permission to pay his respects to our daughter," Don Carlos explained.

"You have given consent?" Doña Catalina asked; for it would not do, of course, to jump for the man.

"I have given my consent," Don Carlos replied.

Doña Catalina held out her hand, and Don Diego gave it a languid grasp and then released it.

"Such an alliance would be a proud one," Doña Catalina said. "I hope that you may win her heart, *señor*."

"As to that," said Don Diego, "I trust there will be no undue nonsense. Either the lady wants me and will have me, or she will not. Will I change her mind if I play a guitar beneath her window, or hold her hand when I may, or put my hand over my heart and sigh? I want her for wife, else I would not have ridden here to ask her father for her."

"I—I—of course," said Don Carlos.

"Ah, *señor*, but a maid delights to be won," said the Doña Catalina. "It is her privilege, *señor*. The hours of courtship are held in memory during her lifetime. She remembers the pretty things her lover said, and the first kiss, when they stood beside the stream and looked into each other's eyes, and when he showed sudden fear for her while they were riding and her horse bolted—those things, *señor*.

"It is like a little game, and it has been played since the beginning of time. Foolish, *señor*? Perhaps when a person looks at it with cold reason. But delightful, nevertheless."

"I don't know anything about it," Don Diego protested. "I never ran around making love to women."

"The woman you marry will not be sorry because of that, *señor*."

"You think it is necessary for me to do these things?"

"Oh," said Don Carlos, afraid of losing an influential son-in-law, "a little bit would not hurt. A maid likes to be wooed, of course, even though she has made up her mind."

"I have a servant who is a wonder at the guitar," Don Diego said. "Tonight I shall order him to come out and play beneath the *señorita*'s window."

"And not come yourself?" Doña Catalina gasped.

"Ride out here again tonight, when the chill wind blows in from the sea?" gasped Don Diego. "It would kill me. And the native plays the guitar better than I."

"I never heard of such a thing!" Doña Catalina gasped, her sense of the fitness of things outraged.

"Let Don Diego do as he wills," Don Carlos urged.

"I had thought," said Don Diego, "that you would arrange everything and then let me know. I would have my house put in order, of course, and get me more servants. Perhaps I should purchase a coach and drive with my bride as far as Santa Barbara and visit a friend there. Is it not possible for you to attend to everything else? Just merely send me word when the wedding is to be."

Don Carlos Pulido was nettled a little himself now.

"*Caballero*," he said, "when I courted Doña Catalina she kept me on needles and pins. One day she would frown, and the next day smile. It added a spice to the affair. I would not have had it different. You will regret it, *señor*, if you do not do your own courting. Would you like to see the señorita now?"

"I suppose I must," Don Diego said.

Doña Catalina threw up her head and went into the house to fetch the girl; and soon she came, a dainty little thing with black eyes that snapped, and black hair that was wound around her head in a great coil, and dainty little feet that peeped from beneath skirts of bright hue.

"I am happy to see you again, Don Diego," she said. He bowed over her hand and assisted her to one of the chairs.

"You are as beautiful as you were when I saw you last," he said.

"Always tell a *señorita* that she is more beautiful than when you saw her last," groaned Don Carlos. "Ah, that I were young again and could make love anew!"

He excused himself and entered the house, and Doña Catalina moved to the other end of the veranda, so that the pair could talk without letting her hear the words, but from where she could watch, as a good dueña always must.

"*Señorita*," Don Diego said, "I have asked your father this morning for permission to seek you in marriage."

"Oh, *señor*!" the girl gasped.

"Do you think I would make a proper husband?"

"Why, I—that is—"

"Just say the word, *señorita*, and I shall tell my father, and your family will make arrangements for the ceremony. They can send word in to me by some native. It fatigues me to ride abroad when it is not at all necessary."

Now the pretty eyes of the Señorita Lolita began flashing warning signals, but Don Diego, it was evident, did not see them, and so he rushed forward to his destruction.

"Shall you agree to becoming my wife, *señorita*?" he asked, bending slightly toward her.

Señorita Lolita's face burned red, and she sprang from her chair, her tiny fists clenched at her side.

"Don Diego Vega," she replied, "you are of a noble family and have much wealth and will inherit more. But you are lifeless, *señor*! Is this your idea of courtship and romance? Can you not take the trouble to ride four miles on a smooth road to see the maid you would wed? What sort of blood is in your veins, *señor*?"

Doña Catalina heard that, and now she rushed across the veranda toward them, making signals to her daughter, which Señorita Lolita refused to see.

"The man who weds me must woo me and win my love," the girl went on. "He must touch my heart. Think you that I am some bronze native wench to give myself to the first man who asks? The man who becomes my husband must be a man with life enough in him to want me. Send your servant to play a guitar beneath my window? Oh, I heard, *señor*! Send him, *señor*, and I'll throw boiling water upon him and bleach his red skin! *Buenos dias, señor!*"

She threw up her head proudly, lifted her silken skirts aside, and so passed him to enter the house, disregarding her mother also. Doña Catalina moaned once for her lost hopes. Don Diego Vega looked after the disappearing *señorita* and scratched at his head thoughtfully and glanced toward his horse.

"I—I believe she is displeased with me," he said in his timid voice.

VII. A Different Sort of Man

Don Carlos lost no time in hurrying out to the veranda again—since he had been listening and so knew what had happened—and endeavoring to placate the embarrassed Don Diego Vega. Though there was consternation in his heart, he contrived to chuckle and make light of the occurrence.

"Women are fitful and filled with fancies, *señor*," he said. "At times they will rail at those whom they in reality adore. There is no telling the workings of a woman's mind—she cannot explain it with satisfaction herself."

"But I—scarcely understand," Don Diego gasped. "I used my words with care. Surely I said nothing to insult or anger the *señorita*."

"She would be wooed, I take it, in the regular fashion. Do not despair, *señor*. Both her mother and myself have agreed that you are a proper man for her husband. It is customary that a maid fight off a man to a certain extent, and then surrender. It appears to make surrender the sweeter. Perhaps the next time you visit us she will be more agreeable. I feel quite sure of it."

So Don Diego shook hands with Don Carlos Pulido and mounted his horse and rode slowly down the trail; and Don Carlos turned about and entered his house again and faced his wife and daughter, standing before the latter with his hands on his hips and regarding her with something akin to sorrow.

"He is the greatest catch in all the country!" Doña Catalina was wailing; and she dabbed at her eyes with a delicate square of filmy lace.

"He has wealth and position and could mend my broken fortunes if he were but my son-in-law," Don Carlos declared, not taking his eyes from his daughter's face.

"He has a magnificent house and a *hacienda* besides, and the best horses near Reina de Los Angeles, and he is sole heir to his wealthy father," Doña Catalina said.

"One whisper from his lips into the ear of his excellency, the governor, and a man is made—or unmade," added Don Carlos.

"He is handsome—"

"I grant you that!" exclaimed the Señorita Lolita, lifting her pretty head and glaring at them bravely. "That is what angers me! What a lover the man could be, if he would! Is it anything to make a girl proud to have it said that the man she married never looked at another woman, and so did not select her after dancing and talking and playing at love with others?"

"He preferred you to all others, else he would not have ridden out to-day," Don Carlos said.

"Certainly it must have fatigued him!" the girl said. "Why does he let himself be made the laughingstock of the country? He is handsome and rich and talented. He has health, and could lead all the other young men. Yet he has scarcely enough energy to dress himself, I doubt not."

"This is all beyond me," the Doña Catalina wailed. "When I was a girl, there was nothing like this. An honorable man comes seeking you as wife—"

"Were he less honorable and more of a man, I might look at him a second time," said the *señorita*.

"You must look at him more than a second time," put in Don Carlos, with some authority in his manner. "You cannot throw away such a fine chance. Think on it, my daughter. Be in a more amiable mood when Don Diego calls again."

Then he hurried to the *patio* on pretense that he wished to speak to a servant, but in reality to get away from the scene. Don Carlos had proved himself to be a courageous man in his youth, and now he was a wise man, also, and hence he knew better than to participate in an argument between women.

Soon the *siesta* hour was at hand, and the Señorita Lolita went into the *patio* and settled herself on a little bench near the fountain. Her father was dozing on the veranda, and her mother in her room, and the servants were scattered over the place, sleeping also. But Señorita Lolita could not sleep, for her mind was busy.

She knew her father's circumstances, of course, for it had been some time since he could hide them, and she wanted, naturally, to see him in excellent fortune again. She knew, too, that did she wed with Don Diego Vega, her father was made whole. For a Vega would not let the relatives of his wife be in any but the best of circumstances.

She called up before her a vision of Don Diego's handsome face, and wondered what it would be like if lighted with love and passion. 'Twere a pity the man was so lifeless, she told herself. But to wed a man who suggested sending a native servant to serenade her in his own place!

The splashing of the water in the fountain lulled her to sleep, and she curled up in one end of the bench, her cheek pillowed on one tiny hand, her black hair cascading to the ground.

And suddenly she was awakened by a touch on her arm, and sat up quickly, and then would have screamed except that a hand was crushed against her lips to prevent her.

Before her stood a man whose body was enveloped in a long cloak, and whose face was covered with a black mask so that she could see nothing of his features except his glittering eyes. She had heard Señor Zorro, the highwayman, described, and she guessed that this was he, and her heart almost ceased to beat, she was so afraid.

"Silence, and no harm comes to you, *señorita*," the man whispered hoarsely.

"You—you are—" she questioned on her breath.

He stepped back, removed his sombrero, and bowed low before her.

"You have guessed it, my charming *señorita*," he said. "I am known as Señor Zorro, the Curse of Capistrano."

"And—you are here—"

"I mean you no harm, no harm to any of this *hacienda, señorita*. I punish those who are unjust, and your father is not that. I admire him greatly. Rather would I punish those who do him evil than to touch him."

"I—I thank you, *señor*."

"I am weary, and the *hacienda* is an excellent place to rest," he said. "I knew it to be the siesta hour, also, and thought everyone would be asleep. It were a shame to awaken you, *señorita*, but I felt that I must speak. Your beauty would hinge a man's tongue in its middle so that both ends might be free to sing your praises."

Señorita Lolita had the grace to blush.

"I would that my beauty affected other men so," she said.

"And does it not? Is it that the Señorita Lolita lacks suitors? But that cannot be possible!"

"It is, nevertheless, *señor*. There are few bold enough to seek to ally themselves with the family of Pulido, since it is out of favor with the powers. There is one—suitor," she went on. "But he does not seem to put much life into his wooing."

"Ha! A laggard at loveand in your presence? What ails the man? Is he ill?"

"He is so wealthy that I suppose he thinks he has but to request it and a maiden will agree to wed him."

"What an imbecile! 'Tis the wooing gives the spice to romance."

"But you, *señor*! Somebody may come and see you here! You may be captured!"

"And do you not wish to see a highwayman captured? Perhaps it would mend your father's fortune were he to capture me. The governor is much vexed, I understand, concerning my operations."

"You—you had best go," she said.

"There speaks mercy in your heart. You know that capture would mean my death. Yet must I risk it, and tarry awhile."

He seated himself upon the bench, and Señorita Lolita moved away as far as she could, and then started to rise.

But Señor Zorro had been anticipating that. He grasped one of her hands and, before she guessed his intention, had bent forward, raised the bottom of his mask, and pressed his lips to its pink, moist palm.

"*Señor!*" she cried, and jerked her hand away.

"It were bold, yet a man must express his feelings," he said. "I have not offended beyond forgiveness, I hope."

"Go, *señor*, else I make an outcry!"

"And get me executed?"

"You are but a thief of the highroad!"

"Yet I love life as any other man."

"I shall call out, *señor*! There is a reward offered for your capture."

"Such pretty hands would not handle blood money."

"Go!"

"Ah, *señorita*, you are cruel. A sight of you sends the blood pounding through a man's veins. A man would fight a horde at the bidding of your sweet lips."

"*Señor!*"

"A man would die in your defense, *señorita*. Such grace, such fresh beauty."

"For the last time, *señor*! I shall make an outcry—and your fate be on your own head!"

"Your hand again—and I go."

"It may not be!"

"Then here I sit until they come and take me. No doubt I shall not have to wait long. That big Sergeant Gonzales is on the trail, I understand, and may have discovered track of me. He will have soldiers with him—"

"*Señor*, for the love of the saints—"

"Your hand."

She turned her back and gave it, and once more he pressed his lips to the palm. And then she felt herself being turned slowly, and her eyes looked deep into his. A thrill seemed to run through her. She realized that he retained her hand, and she pulled it away. And then she turned and ran quickly across the *patio* and into the house.

With her heart pounding at her ribs, she stood behind the curtains at a window and watched. Señor Zorro walked slowly to the fountain and stooped to drink. Then he put his sombrero on, looked once at the house, and stalked away. She heard the galloping hoofs of a horse die in the distance.

"A thief—yet a man!" she breathed. "If Don Diego had only half as much dash and courage!"

VIII. Don Carlos Plays a Game

She turned away from the window, thankful that none of the household had seen Señor Zorro or knew of his visit. The remainder of the day she spent on the veranda, half the time working on some lace she was making, and the other half gazing down the dusty trail that ran toward the highway.

And then came evening, and down by the natives' adobe huts big fires were lighted, and the natives gathered around them to cook and eat and speak of the events of the day. Inside the house the evening meal had been prepared, and the family was about to sit at table when someone knocked upon the door.

An Indian ran to open it, and Señor Zorro strode into the room. His sombrero came off, he bowed, and then he raised his head and looked at the speechless Doña Catalina and the half-terrified Don Carlos.

"I trust you will pardon this intrusion," he said. "I am the man known as Señor Zorro. But do not be frightened, for I have not come to rob."

Don Carlos got slowly upon his feet, while Señorita Lolita gasped at this display of the man's courage, and feared he would mention the visit of the afternoon, of which she had refrained from telling her mother.

"Scoundrel!" Don Carlos roared. "You dare to enter an honest house?"

"I am no enemy of yours, Don Carlos," Señor Zorro replied. "In fact, I have done some things that should appeal to a man who has been persecuted."

That was true, Don Carlos knew, but he was too wise to admit it and so speak treason. Heaven knew he was enough in the bad graces of the governor now without offending him more by treating with courtesy this man for whose carcass the governor had offered a reward.

"What do you wish here?" he asked.

"I crave your hospitality, *señor*. In other words, I would eat and drink. I am a *caballero*, hence make my claim injustice."

"Whatever good blood once flowed in your veins has been fouled by your actions," Don Carlos said. "A thief and highwayman has no claim upon the hospitality of this *hacienda*."

"I take it that you fear to feed me, since the governor may hear of it," Señor Zorro answered. "You may say that you were forced to do it. And that will be the truth."

Now one hand came from beneath the cloak, and it held a pistol. Doña Catalina shrieked and fainted, and Señorita Lolita cowered in her chair.

"Doubly a scoundrel, since you frighten women!" Don Carlos exclaimed angrily. "Since it is death to refuse, you may have meat and drink. But I ask you to be *caballero* enough to allow me to remove my wife to another room and call a native woman to care for her."

"By all means," Señor Zorro said. "But the *señorita* remains here as hostage for your good conduct and return."

Don Carlos glanced at the man, and then at the girl, and saw that the latter was not afraid. He. picked his wife up in his arms and bore her through the doorway, roaring for servants to come.

Señor Zorro walked around the end of the table, bowed to Lolita again, and sat down in a chair beside her.

"This is foolhardiness, no doubt, but I had to see your beaming face again," he said.

"*Señor!*"

"The sight of you this afternoon started a conflagration in my heart, *señorita*. The touch of your hand was new life to me."

Lolita turned away, her face flaming, and Señor Zorro moved his chair nearer and reached for her hand, but she eluded him.

"The longing to hear the music of your voice, *señorita*, may lure me here often," he said.

"*Señor*! You must never come again! I was lenient with you this afternoon, but I can not be again. The next time I shall shriek, and you will be taken."

"You could not be so cruel," he said.

"Your fate would be upon your own head, *señor*."

Then Don Carlos came back into the room, and Señor Zorro arose and bowed once more.

"I trust your wife has recovered from her swoon," he said. "I regret that the sight of my poor pistol frightened her."

"She has recovered," Don Carlos said. "I believe you said that you wished meat and drink? Now that I come to think of it, *señor*, you have indeed done some things that I have admired, and I am happy to grant you hospitality for a time. A servant shall furnish you food immediately."

Don Carlos walked to the door, called a native, and gave his orders. Don Carlos was well pleased with himself. Carrying his wife into the next room had given him his chance. For servants had answered his call, and among them had been one he trusted. And he had ordered the man to take the swiftest horse and ride like the wind the four miles to the *pueblo*, and there to spread the alarm that Señor Zorro was at the Pulido *hacienda*.

His object now was to delay this Señor Zorro as much as possible. For he knew the soldiers would come and the highwayman be killed or captured, and surely the governor would admit that Don Carlos was entitled to some consideration for what he had done.

"You must have had some stirring adventures, *señor*," Don Carlos said as he returned to the table.

"A few," the highwayman admitted.

"There was that affair at Santa Barbara, for instance. I never did hear the straight of that."

"I dislike to speak of my own work, *señor*."

"Please," the Señorita Lolita begged; and so Señor Zorro overcame his scruples for the time being.

"It really was nothing," he said. "I arrived in the vicinity of Santa Barbara at sunset. There is a fellow there who runs a store, and he had been beating natives and stealing from the *frailes*. He would demand that the *frailes* sell him goods from the mission, and then complain that the weight was short, and the governor's men would make the *frailes* deliver more. So I resolved to punish the man."

"Pray continue, *señor*," said Don Carlos, bending forward as if deeply interested.

"I dismounted at the door of his building and walked inside. He had candles burning, and there were half a dozen fellows trading with him. I covered them with my pistol and drove them into a corner and ordered this storekeeper before me. I frightened him thoroughly, and forced him to disgorge the money he had in a secret hiding-place. And then I lashed him with a whip taken from his own wall, and told him why I had done it."

"Excellent!" Don Carlos cried.

"Then I sprang on my horse and dashed away. At a native's hut I made a placard, saying that I was a friend of the oppressed. Feeling particularly bold that evening, I galloped up to the door of the *presidio*, brushed aside the sentry—who took me for a courier—and pinned the placard to the door of the *presidio* with my knife. Just then the soldiers came rushing out. I fired over their heads, and while they were bewildered I rode away toward the hills."

"And escaped!" Don Carlos exclaimed.

"I am here!—that is your answer."

"And why is the governor so particularly bitter against you, *señor?*" Don Carlos asked. "There are other highwaymen to whom he gives not a thought."

"Ha! I had a personal clash with his excellency. He was driving from San Francisco de Asis to Santa Barbara on official business, with an escort of soldiers about him. They stopped at a brook to refresh themselves, and the soldiers scattered while the governor spoke with his friends. I was hiding in the forest and suddenly dashed out and at them.

"Instantly I was at the open door of the coach. I presented my pistol at his head and ordered him to hand over his fat purse—which he did. Then I spurred through his soldiers, upsetting several as I did so—"

"And escaped!" Don Carlos cried.

"I am here," assented Señor Zorro.

The servant brought a tray of food and placed it before the highwayman, retreating as soon as possible, his eyes big with fear and his hands trembling, for many weird tales had been told of this same Señor Zorro and his brutality, none of which was true.

"I am sure that you will pardon me," Señor Zorro said, "when I ask you to sit at the far end of the room. As I take each bite, I must raise the bottom of my mask, for I have no wish to become known. I put the pistol before me on the table, so, to discourage treachery. And now, Don Carlos Pulido, I shall do justice to the meal you have so kindly furnished."

Don Carlos and his daughter sat where they had been directed, and the bandit ate with evident relish. Now and then he stopped to talk to them, and once he had Don Carlos send out for more wine, declaring it to be the best he had tasted for a year.

Don Carlos was only too glad to oblige him. He was playing to gain time. He knew the horse the native rode, and judged that he had reached the *presidio* at Reina de Los Angeles before this, and that the soldiers were on their way. If he could hold this Señor Zorro until they arrived!

"I am having some food prepared for you to carry with you, *señor*," he said. "You will pardon me while I get it? My daughter will entertain you."

Señor Zorro bowed, and Don Carlos hurried from the room. But Don Carlos had made a mistake in his eagerness. It was an unusual thing for a girl to be left alone in the company of a man in such fashion, especially with a man known to be an outlaw. Señor Zorro guessed at once that he was being delayed purposely. For, again, it was an unusual thing for a man like Don Carlos to go for the package of food himself when there were servants that could be called by a mere clapping of the hands. Don Carlos, in fact, had gone into the other room to listen at a window for sounds of galloping horses.

"*Señor!*" Lolita whispered across the room.

"What is it, *señorita*?"

"You must go—at once. I am afraid that my father has sent for the soldiers."

"And you are kind enough to warn me?"

"Do I wish to see you taken here? Do I wish to see fighting and bloodshed?" she asked.

"That is the only reason, *señorita*?"

"Will you not go, *señor*?"

"I am loath to rush away from such a charming presence, *señorita*. May I come again at the next *siesta* hour?"

"By the saints—no! This must end, Señor Zorro. Go your way—and take care. You have done some things that I admire, hence I would not see you captured. Go north as far as San Francisco de Asis and turn honest, *señor*. It is the better way."

"Little priest," he said.

"Shall you go, *señor?*'

"But your father has gone to fetch food for me. And could I depart without thanking him for this meal?"

Don Carlos came back into the room then, and Señor Zorro knew by the expression on his face that the soldiers were coming up the trail. The don put a package on the table.

"Some food to carry with you, *señor*," he said. "And we would relish more of your reminiscences before you start on your perilous journey."

"I have spoken too much of myself already, *señor*, and it ill becomes a *caballero* to do that. It were better that I thank you and leave you now."

"At least, *señor*, drink another mug of wine."

"I fear," said Señor Zorro, "that the soldiers are much too close, Don Carlos."

The face of the don went white at that, for the highwayman was picking up his pistol, and Don Carlos feared he was about to pay the price for his treacherous hospitality. But Señor Zorro made no move to fire.

"I forgive you this breach of hospitality, Don Carlos, because I am an outlaw and there has been a price put upon my head," he said. "And, also, I hold you no ill will because of it. *Buenos noches, señorita! Señor, á Dios!*"

Then a terrified servant who knew little concerning the events of the evening rushed in at the door.

"Master! The soldiers are here!" he cried. "They are surrounding the house!"

IX. The Clash of Blades

On the table, near its middle, was an imposing *candelero* in which half a score of candles burned brightly. Señor Zorro sprang toward it now, and with one sweep of his hand dashed it to the floor, extinguishing all the candles in an instant and plunging the room into darkness.

He evaded the wild rush of Don Carlos, springing across the room so lightly that his soft boots made not the slightest noise to give news of his whereabouts. For an instant the Señorita Lolita felt a man's arm around her waist, gently squeezing it, felt a man's breath on her cheek, and heard a man's whisper in her ear:

"Until later, *señorita*."

Don Carlos was bellowing like a bull to direct the soldiers to the scene; and already some of them were pounding at the front door. Señor Zorro rushed from the room and into the one adjoining, which happened to be the kitchen. The native servants fled before him as if he had been a ghost, and he quickly extinguished all the candles that burned there.

Then he ran to the door that opened into the *patio* and raised his voice and gave a call that was half moan and half shriek, a peculiar call, the like of which none at the Pulido *hacienda* had heard before.

As the soldiers rushed in at the front door, and as Don Carlos called for a brand with which to light the candles again, the sound of galloping hoofs was heard from the rear of the *patio*. Some powerful horse was getting under way there, the soldiers guessed immediately.

The sound of hoofs died away in the distance, but the soldiers had noted the direction in which the horse was traveling.

"The fiend escapes!" Sergeant Gonzales shrieked, he being in charge of the squad. "To horse and after him! I give the man who overtakes him one third of all the reward!"

The big sergeant rushed from the house, the men at his heels, and they tumbled into their saddles and rode furiously through the darkness, following the sound of the beating hoofs.

"Lights! Lights!" Don Carlos was shrieking inside the house.

A servant came with a brand, and the candles were lighted again. Don Carlos stood in the middle of the room, shaking his fists in impotent rage. Señorita Lolita crouched in a corner, her eyes wide with fear. Doña Catalina, fully recovered now from her fainting spell, came from her own room to ascertain the cause of the commotion.

"The rascal got away!" Don Carlos said. "It is to be hoped that the soldiers capture him."

"At least he is clever and brave," Señorita Lolita said.

"I grant him that, but he is a highwayman and a thief!" Don Carlos roared. "Why should he torment me by visiting my house?"

Señorita Lolita thought she knew, but she would be the last one to explain to her parents. There was a faint blush on her face yet because of the arm that had squeezed her and the words that had been whispered in her ear.

Don Carlos threw the front door open wide and stood in it, listening. To his ears came the sound of galloping hoofs once more.

"My sword!" he cried to a servant. "Someone comes—it may be the rascal returning! It is but one rider, by the saints!"

The galloping stopped; a man made his way across the veranda and hurried through the door into the room.

"Thank the good saints!" Don Carlos gasped.

It was not the highwayman returned; it was Captain Ramón, *comandante* of the *presidio* at Reina de Los Angeles.

"Where are my men?" the captain cried.

"Gone, *señor*! Gone after that pig of a highwayman!" Don Carlos informed him.

"He escaped?"

"He did, with your men surrounding the house. He dashed the candles to the floor, ran through the kitchen—"

"The men took after him?"

"They are upon his heels, *señor*."

"Ha! It is to be hoped that they catch this pretty bird. He is a thorn in the side of the soldiery. We do not catch him, and because we do not the governor sends sarcastic letters by his courier. This Señor Zorro is a clever gentleman, but he will be captured yet!"

And then Captain Ramón walked farther into the room and perceived the ladies and swept off his cap and bowed before them.

"You must pardon my bold entrance," he said. "When an officer is on duty—"

"The pardon is granted freely," said Doña Catalina. "You have met my daughter?"

"I have not had the honor."

The doña presented them, and Lolita retreated to her corner again and observed the soldier. He was not ill to look at—tall and straight and in a brilliant uniform, and with sword dangling at his side. As for the captain, he never had set eyes upon Señorita Lolita before, for he had been at the post at Reina de Los Angeles but a month, having been transferred there from Santa Barbara.

But now that he had looked at her once he looked a second time and a third. There was a sudden light in his eyes that pleased Doña Catalina. If Lolita could not look with favor upon Don Diego Vega, perhaps she would look with favor upon this Captain Ramón, and to have her wedded to an officer would mean that the Pulido family would have some protection.

"I could not find my men now in the darkness," the captain said, "and so, if it is not presuming too much, I shall remain here and await their return."

"By all means," Don Carlos said. "Be seated, *señor*, and I'll have a servant fetch wine."

"This Señor Zorro has about had his run," the captain said, after the wine had been tasted and found excellent. "Now and then a man of his sort pops up and endures for a little day, but he never lasts long. In the end he meets the fate."

"That is true," said Don Carlos. "The fellow was boasting to us tonight of his accomplishments."

"I was *comandante* at Santa Barbara when he made his famous visit there," the captain explained. "I was visiting at one of the houses at the time else there might have been a different story. And tonight, when the alarm came, I was not at the *presidio*, but at the residence of a friend. That is why I did not ride out with the soldiers. As soon as I was notified I came. It appears that this Señor Zorro has some knowledge of my whereabouts and is careful that I am not in a position to clash with him. I hope one day to do so."

"You think you could conquer him, *señor?*" Doña Catalina asked.

"Undoubtedly! I understand he really is an ordinary hand with a blade. He made a fool of my sergeant, but that is a different proposition—and I believe he held a pistol in one hand while he fenced, too. I should make short work of the fellow."

There was a closet in one corner of the room, and now its door was opened a crack.

"The fellow should die the death," Captain Ramón went on to say. "He is brutal in his dealings with men. He kills wantonly, I have heard. They say he caused a reign of terror in the north, in the vicinity of San Francisco de Asis. He slew men regardless, insulted women—"

The closet door was hurled open—and Señor Zorro stepped into the room.

"I shall take you to task for that statement, *señor*, since it is a falsehood!" the highwayman cried.

Don Carlos whirled around and gasped his surprise. Doña Catalina felt suddenly weak in the knees and collapsed on a chair. Señorita Lolita felt some pride in the man's statement, and a great deal of fear for him.

"I—I thought you had escaped," Don Carlos gasped.

"Ha! It was but a trick! My horse escaped—but I did not!"

"Then there shall be no escape for you now!" Captain Ramón cried, drawing his blade.

"Back, *señor!*" Zorro cried, exhibiting a pistol suddenly. "I shall fight you gladly, but the fight must be fair. Don Carlos, gather your wife and daughter beneath your arms and retire to the corner while I cross blades with this teller of falsehoods. I do not intend to have a warning given out that I still am here!"

"I thought—you escaped!" Don Carlos gasped again, seemingly unable to think of anything else, and doing as Señor Zorro commanded.

"A trick!" the highwayman repeated, laughing. "It is a noble horse I have. Perhaps you heard a peculiar cry from my lips? My beast is trained to act at that cry. He gallops away wildly, making considerable noise, and the soldiers follow him. And when he has gone some distance he turns aside and stops, and after the pursuit has passed he returns to await my bidding. No doubt he is behind the *patio* now. I shall punish this captain and then mount and ride away!"

"With a pistol in your hand!" Ramón cried.

"I put the pistol upon the table—so! There it remains if Don Carlos stays in the corner with the ladies. Now, captain!"

Señor Zorro extended his blade, and with a glad cry Captain Ramón crossed it with his own. Captain Ramón had some reputation as a master of fence, and Señor Zorro evidently knew it, for he was cautious at first, leaving no opening, on defense rather than attack.

The captain pressed him back, his blade flashing like streaks of lightning in a troubled sky. Now Señor Zorro was almost against the wall near the kitchen door, and in the captain's eyes the light of triumph already was beginning to burn. He fenced rapidly, giving the highwayman no rest, standing his ground and keeping his antagonist against the wall.

And then Señor Zorro chuckled. For now he had solved the other's manner of combat, and knew that all would be well. The captain gave ground a little as the defense turned into an attack that puzzled him. Señor Zorro began laughing lightly.

"'Twere a shame to kill you," he said. "You are an excellent officer, I have heard, and the army needs a few such. But you have spoken falsehood regarding me, and so must pay a price. Presently I shall run you through, but in such manner that your life will not emerge when I withdraw my blade."

"Boaster!" the captain snarled.

"As to that we shall see presently. Ha! I almost had you there, my captain. You are more clever than your big sergeant, but not half clever enough. Where do you prefer to be touched—the left side or the right?"

"If you are so certain run me through the right shoulder," the captain said.

"Guard it well, my captain, for I shall do as you say! Ha!"

The captain circled, trying to get the light of the candles in the highwayman's eyes, but Señor Zorro was too clever for that. He caused the captain to circle back, forced him to retreat, fought him to a corner.

"Now, my captain!" he cried.

And so he ran him through the right shoulder, as the captain had said, and twisted the blade a bit as he brought it out. He had struck a little low, and Captain Ramón dropped to the floor, a sudden weakness upon him.

Señor Zorro stepped back and sheathed his blade.

"I ask the pardon of the ladies for this scene," he said. "And I assure you that this time I am, indeed, going away. You will find that the captain is not badly injured, Don Carlos. He may return to his *presidio* within the day."

He removed his sombrero and bowed low before them, while Don Carlos sputtered and failed to think of anything to say that would be mean and cutting enough. His eyes, for a moment, met those of the Señorita Lolita, and he was glad to find that in hers there was no repugnance.

"*Buenos noches!*" he said and laughed again.

And then he dashed through the kitchen and into the *patio*, and found the horse awaiting him there as he had said it would be, and was quick to mount and ride away.

X. A HINT AT JEALOUSY

Within the space of half hour Captain Ramón's wounded shoulder had been cleansed of blood and bandaged, and the captain was sitting at one end of the table, sipping wine and looking very white in the face and tired.

Doña Catalina and Señorita Lolita had shown much sympathy, though the latter could scarcely refrain from smiling when she remembered the captain's boast regarding what he purposed doing to the highwayman, and compared it to what had happened. Don Carlos was outdoing himself to make the captain feel at home since it was well to seek influence with the army, and already had urged upon the officer that he remain at the *hacienda* a few days until his wound had healed.

Having looked into the eyes of the Señorita Lolita, the captain had answered that he would be glad to remain at least for a day and, despite his wound, was attempting polite and witty conversation, yet failing miserably.

Once more there could be heard the drumming of a horse's hoofs, and Don Carlos sent a servant to the door to open it so that the light would shine out, for they supposed that it was one of the soldiers returning.

The horseman came nearer and presently stopped before the house, and the servant hurried out to care for the beast.

There passed a moment during which those inside the house heard nothing at all, and then there were steps on the veranda, and Don Diego Vega hurried through the door.

"Ha!" he cried, as if in relief. "I am rejoiced that you all are alive arid well!"

"Don Diego!" the master of the house exclaimed. "You have ridden out from the pueblo a second time in one day?"

"No doubt I shall be ill because of it," Don Diego said. "Already I am feeling stiff, and my back aches. Yet I felt that I must come. There was an alarm in the *pueblo*, and it was noised abroad that this Señor Zorro, the highwayman, had paid a visit to the *hacienda*. I saw the soldiers ride furiously in this direction, and fear came into my heart. You understand, Don Carlos, I feel sure."

"I understand, *caballero*," Don Carlos replied, beaming upon him and glancing once at Señorita Lolita.

"I—er—felt it my duty to make the journey. And now I find that it has been made for nought—you all are alive and well. How does it happen?"

Lolita sniffed, but Don Carlos was quick to make reply.

"The fellow was here, but he made his escape after running Captain Ramón through the shoulder."

"Ha!" Don Diego said, collapsing into a chair. "So you have felt his steel, eh, captain? That should feed your desire for vengeance. Your soldiers are after the rogue?"

"They are," the captain replied shortly, for he did not like to have it said that he had been defeated in combat. "And they will continue to be after him until he is captured. I have a big sergeant, Gonzales—I think he is a friend of yours, Don Diego—who is eager to make the arrest and earn the governor's reward. I shall instruct him, when he returns, to take his squad and pursue this highwayman until he has been dealt with properly."

"Let me express the hope that the soldiers will be successful, *señor*. The rogue has annoyed Don Carlos and the ladies—and Don Carlos is my friend. I would have all men know it!"

Don Carlos beamed, and Doña Catalina smiled bewitchingly, but the Señorita Lolita fought to keep her pretty upper lip from curling with scorn.

"A mug of your refreshing wine, Don Carlos," Don Diego Vega continued. "I am fatigued. Twice to-day have I ridden here from Reina de Los Angeles, and it is about all a man can endure."

"'Tis not much of a journey—four miles," said the captain.

"Possibly not for a rough soldier," Don Diego replied, "but it is for a *caballero*."

"May not a soldier be a *caballero*?" Ramón asked, nettled somewhat at the other's words.

"It has happened before now, but we come across it rarely," Don Diego said. He glanced at Lolita as he spoke, intending that she should take notice of his words, for he had seen the manner in which the captain glanced at her, and jealousy was beginning to burn in his heart.

"Do you mean to insinuate, *señor*, that I am not of good blood?" Captain Ramón asked.

"I cannot reply as to that, *señor*, having seen none of it. No doubt this Señor Zorro could tell me. He saw the color of it, I understand."

"By the saints!" Captain Ramón cried. "You would taunt me?"

"Never be taunted by the truth," Don Diego observed. "He ran you through the shoulder, eh? 'Tis a mere scratch, I doubt not. Should you not be at the *presidio* instructing your soldiers?"

"I await their return here," the captain replied. "Also, it is a fatiguing journey from here to the *presidio*, according to your own ideas, *señor*."

"But a soldier is inured to hardship, *señor*."

"True, there are many pests he must encounter," the captain said, glancing at Don Diego with meaning.

"You term me a pest, *señor*?"

"Did I say as much?"

This was perilous ground, and Don Carlos had no mind to let an officer of the army and Don Diego Vega have trouble in his *hacienda*, for fear he would get into greater difficulties.

"More wine, *señores*!" he exclaimed in a loud voice, and stepping between their chairs in utter disregard of proper breeding. "Drink, my captain, for your wound has made you weak. And you, Don Diego, after your wild ride—"

"I doubt its wildness," Captain Ramón observed.

Don Diego accepted the proffered wine mug and turned his back upon the captain. He glanced across at Señorita Lolita and smiled. He got up deliberately and picked up his chair and carried it across the room to set it down beside her.

"And did the rogue frighten you, *señorita*?" he asked.

"Suppose he did, *señor*? Would you avenge the matter? Would you put blade at your side and ride abroad until you found him, and then punish him as he deserves?"

"By the saints, were it necessary, I might do as much. But I am able to employ a raft of strong fellows who would like nothing better than to run down the rogue. Why should I risk my own neck?"

"Oh!" she exclaimed, exasperated.

"Let us not talk further of this bloodthirsty Señor Zorro," he begged. "There are other things fit for conversation. Have you been thinking, *señorita*, on the object of my visit earlier in the day?"

Señorita Lolita thought of it now. She remembered again what the marriage would mean to her parents and their fortunes, and she recalled the highwayman, too, and remembered his dash and spirit, and wished that Don Diego could be such a man. And she could not say the word that would make her the betrothed of Don Diego Vega.

"I—I have scarcely had time to think of it, *caballero*," she replied.

"I trust you will make up your mind soon," he said.

"You are so eager?"

"My father was at me again this afternoon. He insists that I should take a wife as soon as possible. It is rather a nuisance, of course, but a man must please his father."

Lolita bit her lips because of her quick anger. Was ever girl so courted before? she wondered.

"I shall make up my mind as soon as possible, *señor*," she said finally.

"Does this Captain Ramón remain long at the *hacienda*?"

A little hope came into Lolita's breast. Could it be possible that Don Diego Vega was jealous? If that were true, possibly there might be stuff in the man after all. Perhaps he would awaken, and love and passion come to him, and he would be as other young men.

"My father has asked him to remain until he is able to travel to the *presidio*," she replied.

"He is able to travel now. A mere scratch!"

"You will not return tonight?" she asked.

"It probably will make me ill, but I must return. There are certain things that must engage my interest early in the morning. Business is such a nuisance!"

"Perhaps my father will offer to send you in the carriage."

"Ha! It were kindness if he does. A man may doze a bit in a carriage."

"But, if this highwayman should stop you?"

"I need not fear, *señorita*. Have I not wealth? Could I not purchase my release?"

"You would pay ransom rather than fight him, *señor*?"

"I have lots of money, but only one life, *señorita*. Would I be a wise man to risk having my blood let out?"

"It would be the manly part, would it not?" she asked.

"Any male can be manly at times, but it takes a clever man to be sagacious," he said.

Don Diego laughed lightly, as if it cost him an effort, and bent forward to speak in lower tones.

On the other side of the room, Don Carlos was doing his best to make Captain Ramón comfortable, and was glad that he and Don Diego remained apart for the time being.

"Don Carlos," the captain said, "I come from a good family, and the governor is friendly toward me, as no doubt you have heard. I am but twenty-three years of age, else I would hold a higher office. But my future is assured."

"I am rejoiced to learn it, *señor*."

"I never set eyes upon your daughter until this evening, but she has captivated me, *señor*. Never have I seen such grace and beauty, such flashing eyes! I ask your permission, *señor*, to pay my addresses to the *señorita*."

XI. THREE SUITORS

Here was a fix! Don Carlos had no wish to anger Don Diego Vega or a man who stood high in the governor's regard. And how was he to evade it? If Lolita could not force her heart to accept Don Diego, perhaps she could learn to love Captain Ramón. After Don Diego, he was the best potential son-in-law in the vicinity.

"Your answer, *señor*?" the captain was asking.

"I trust you will not misunderstand me, *señor*," Don Carlos said, in lower tones. "I must make a simple explanation."

"Proceed, *señor*."

"But this morning Don Diego Vega asked me the same question."

"Ha!"

"You know his blood and his family, *señor*. Could I refuse him? Of rights I could not. But I may tell you this—the *señorita* weds no man unless it is her wish. So Don Diego has my permission to pay his addresses, but if he fails to touch her heart—"

"Then I may try?" the captain asked.

"You have my permission, *señor*. Of course, Don Diego has great wealth, but you have a dashing way with you, and Don Diego—that is—he is rather—"

"I understand perfectly, *señor*," the captain said, laughing. "He is not exactly a brave and dashing *caballero*. Unless your daughter prefers wealth to a genuine man"

"My daughter will follow the dictates of her heart, *señor*!" Don Carlos said proudly.

"Then the affair is between Don Diego Vega and myself?"

"So long as you use discretion, *señor*. I would have nothing happen that would cause enmity between the Vega family and mine."

"Your interests shall be protected, Don Carlos," Captain Ramón declared.

As Don Diego talked, the Señorita Lolita observed her father and Captain Ramón, and guessed what was being said. It pleased her, of course, that a dashing officer should enter the lists for her hand, and yet she had felt no thrill when first she looked into his eyes.

Señor Zorro, now, had thrilled her to the tips of her tiny toes, and merely because he had talked to her, and touched the palm of her hand with his lips. If Don Diego Vega were only more like the highwayman! If some man appeared who combined Vega's wealth with the rogue's spirit and dash and courage!

There was a sudden tumult outside, and into the room strode the soldiers. Sergeant Gonzales at their head. They saluted their captain, and the big sergeant looked with wonder at his wounded shoulder.

"The rogue escaped us," Gonzales reported. "We followed him for a distance of three miles or so as he made his way into the hills, where we came upon him."

"Well?" Ramón questioned.

"He has allies."

"What is this?"

"Fully ten men were waiting for him there, my captain. They set upon us before we were aware of their presence. We fought them well, and three of them we wounded, but they made their escape and took their comrades with them. We had not been expecting a band, of course, and so rode into their ambush."

"Then we have to contend with a band of them!" Captain Ramón said. "Sergeant, you will select a score of men in the morning, and have command over them. You will take the trail of this Señor Zorro, and you will not stop until he is either captured or slain. I will add a quarter's wages to the reward of his excellency, the governor, if you are successful."

"Ha! It is what I have wished!" Sergeant Gonzales cried. "Now we shall run this coyote to earth in short order! I shall show you the color of his blood—"

"'Twould be no more than right, since he has seen the color of the captain's," Don Diego put in.

"What is this, Don Diego, my friend? Captain, you have crossed blades with the rogue?"

"I have," the captain assented. "You but followed a tricky horse, my sergeant. The fellow was here, in a closet, and came out after I had entered. So it must have been some other man you met with his companions up in the hills. This Señor Zorro treated me much as he treated you in the tavern—had a pistol handy in case I should prove too expert with the blade."

Captain and sergeant looked at each other squarely, each wondering how much the other had been lying; while Don Diego chuckled faintly and tried to press the Señorita Lolita's hand and failed.

"This thing can be settled only in blood!" Gonzales declared. "I shall pursue the rascal until he is run to earth. I have permission to select my men?"

"You may take any at the *presidio*," the captain said.

"Sergeant Gonzales, I should like to go with you," Don Diego said suddenly.

"By the saints! It would kill you, *caballero*. Day and night in the saddle, uphill and downhill, through dust and heat, and with a chance at fighting."

"Well, perhaps it were best for me to remain in the *pueblo*," Don Diego admitted. "But he has annoyed this family, of which I am a true friend. At least you will keep me informed? You will tell me how he escapes if he dodges you? I at least may know that you are on his trail, and where you are riding, so I may be with you in spirit?"

"Certainly, *caballero*—certainly," Sergeant Gonzales replied. "I shall give you the chance of looking upon the rogue's dead face. I swear it!"

"'Tis a terrible oath, my sergeant. Suppose it should come to pass—"

"I mean if I slay the rascal, *caballero*. My captain, do you return this night to the *presidio*?"

"Yes," Ramón replied. "Despite my wound, I can ride a horse."

He glanced toward Don Diego as he spoke, and there was almost a sneer upon his lips.

"What magnificent grit!" Don Diego said. "I, too, shall return to Reina de Los Angeles, if Don Carlos will be as good as to have his carriage around. I can tie my horse to the rear of it. To ride horseback the distance again this day would be the death of me."

Gonzales laughed and led the way from the house. Captain Ramón paid his respects to the ladies, glowered at Don Diego, and followed. The *caballero* faced Señorita Lolita again as her parents escorted the captain to the door.

"You will think of the matter?" he asked. "My father will be at me again within a few days, and I shall escape censure if I am able to tell him that it is all settled. If you decide to wed me, have your father send me word by a servant. Then I shall put my house in order against the wedding day."

"I shall think of it," the girl said.

"We could be married at the mission of San Gabriel, only we should have to make the confounded journey there. Fray Felipe, of the mission, has been my friend from the days of my boyhood, and I would have him say the words, unless you prefer otherwise. He could come to Reina de Los Angeles and read the ceremony in the little church on the plaza there."

"I shall think of it," the girl said again.

"Perhaps I may come out again to see you within a few days, if I survive this night. *Buenos noches, señorita*. I suppose I should—er—kiss your hand?"

"You need not take the trouble," Señorita Lolita replied, "It might fatigue you."

"Ah—thank you. You are thoughtful, I see. I am fortunate if I get me a thoughtful wife."

Don Diego sauntered to the door. Señorita Lolita rushed into her own room and beat at her breasts with her hands, and tore at her hair a bit, too angry, too enraged to weep. Kiss her hand, indeed! Señor Zorro had not suggested it—he had done it. Señor Zorro had dared death to visit her. Señor Zorro had laughed as he fought, and then had escaped by a trick! Ah, if Don Diego Vega were half the man this highwayman appeared!

She heard the soldiers gallop away, and after a little time she heard Don Diego Vega depart in her father's carriage. And then she went out into the great room again to her parents.

"My father, it is impossible that I wed with Don Diego Vega," she said.

"What has caused your decision, my daughter?"

"I scarcely can tell, except that he is not the sort of man I wish for my husband. He is lifeless; existence with him would be a continual torment."

"Captain Ramón also has asked permission to pay you his addresses," Doña Catalina said.

"And he is almost as bad. I do not like the look in his eyes," the girl replied.

"You are too particular," Don Carlos told her. "If the persecution continues another year we shall be beggars. Here is the best catch in the country seeking you, and you would refuse him. And you do not like a high army officer because you do not fancy the look in his eyes.

"Think on it, girl! An alliance with Don Diego Vega is much to be desired. Perhaps when you know him better, you will like him more. And the man may awaken. I thought I saw a flash of it this night, deemed him jealous because of the presence of the captain here. If you can arouse his jealousy—"

Señorita Lolita burst into tears, but soon the tempest of weeping passed, and she dried her eyes.

"I—I shall do my best to like him," she said. "But I cannot bring myself to say, yet, that I will be his wife."

She hurried into her room again, and called for the native woman who attended her. Soon the house was in darkness, and the grounds about it, save for the fires down by the adobe huts, where the natives told one another grim tales of the night's events, each trying to make his falsehood the greatest. A gentle snore came from the apartment of Don Carlos Pulido and his wife.

But the Señorita Lolita did not slumber. She had her head propped on one hand, and she was looking through a window at the fires in the distance, and her mind was full of thoughts of Señor Zorro.

She remembered the grace of his bow, the music of his deep voice, the touch of his lips upon her palm.

"I would he were not a rogue." She sighed. "How a woman could love such a man!"

XII. A Visit

Shortly after daybreak the following morning there was considerable tumult in the plaza at Reina de Los Angeles. Sergeant Pedro Gonzales was there with a score of troopers, almost all that were stationed at the local *presidio*, and they were preparing for the chase of Señor Zorro.

The big sergeant's voice roared out above the din as men adjusted saddles and looked to bridles and inspected the water-bottles and small supplies of provisions. For Sergeant Gonzales had ordered that his force travel light, and live off the country as much as possible. He had taken the commands of his captain seriously—he was going after Señor Zorro and did not propose to return until he had him—or had died in an effort to effect a capture.

"I shall nail the fellow's pelt to the *presidio* door, my friend," he told the fat landlord. "Then I shall collect the governors reward and pay the score I owe you."

"I pray the saints it may be true," the landlord said.

"What, fool? That I pay you? Do you fear to lose a few small coins?"

"I meant that I pray you may be successful in capturing the man," the landlord said, telling the falsehood glibly.

Captain Ramón was not up to see the start, having a small fever because of his wound, but the people of the *pueblo* crowded around Sergeant Gonzales and his men, asking a multitude of questions, and the sergeant found himself the center of interest.

"This Curse of Capistrano soon shall cease to exist!" he boasted loudly. "Pedro Gonzales is on his trail. Ha! When I stand face to face with the fellow—"

The front door of Don Diego Vega's house opened at that juncture, and Don Diego himself appeared, at which the townsmen wondered a bit, since it was so early in the morning. Sergeant Gonzales dropped a bundle he was handling, put his hands upon his hips, and looked at his friend with sudden interest.

"You have not been to bed," he charged.

"But I have!" Don Diego declared.

"And are up again so soon? Here is some devilish mystery that needs an explanation!"

"You made noise enough to awaken the dead," Don Diego said.

"It could not be helped, *caballero*, since we are acting under orders."

"Were it not possible to make your preparations at the *presidio* instead of here in the plaza, or did you think not enough persons would see your importance there?"

"Now, by the"

"Do not say it!" Don Diego commanded. "As a matter of fact, I am up early because I must make a confounded trip to my *hacienda*, a journey of some ten miles, to inspect the flocks and herds. Never become a wealthy man, Sergeant Gonzales, for wealth asks too much of a man."

"Something tells me that never shall I suffer on that account," said the sergeant, laughing. "Yon go with escort, my friend?"

"A couple of natives, that is all."

"If you should meet up with this Señor Zorro, he probably would hold you for a pretty ransom."

"Is he supposed to be between this place and my *hacienda*?" Don Diego asked.

"A native arrived a short time ago with word that he had been seen on the road running to Pala and San Luis Rey. We ride in that direction. And since your *hacienda* is the other way, no doubt you will not meet the rascal now."

"I feel somewhat relieved to hear you say it. So you ride toward Pala, my sergeant?"

"We do. We shall try to pick up his trail as soon as possible, and once we have it we shall run this fox down. Meanwhile, we also shall attempt to find his den. We start at once."

"I shall await news eagerly," Don Diego said. "Good fortune go with you!"

Gonzales and his men mounted, and the sergeant shouted an order, and they galloped across the plaza, raising great clouds of dust, and took the highway toward Pala and San Luis Rey.

Don Diego looked after them until nothing could be seen but a tiny dust cloud in the distance, then called for his own horse. He, too, mounted and rode away toward San Gabriel, and two native servants rode mules and followed a short distance behind.

But before he departed, Don Diego wrote a message and sent it by native courier to the Pulido *hacienda*. It was addressed to Don Carlos, and read:

The soldiers are starting this morning to pursue this Señor Zorro, and it has been reported that the highwayman has a band of rogues under his command and may offer battle. There is no telling, my friend, what may happen. I dislike having one in whom I am interested subjected to danger, meaning your daughter particularly, but also the Doña Catalina and yourself. Moreover, this bandit saw your daughter last evening, and certainly must have appreciated her beauty, and he may seek to see her again.

I beg of you to come at once to my house in Reina de Los Angeles, and make it as your home until matters are settled. I am leaving this morning for my *hacienda*, but have left orders with my servants that you are to give what commands you will. I shall hope to see you when I return, which will be in two or three days.

DIEGO

Don Carlos read that epistle aloud to his wife and daughter, and then looked up to see how they took it. He scoffed at the danger himself, being an old war horse, but did not wish to put his womenfolk in jeopardy.

"What think you?" he asked.

"It has been some time since we have visited the *pueblo*," Doña Catalina said. "I have some friends left among the ladies there. I think it will be an excellent thing to do."

"It certainly will not injure our fortunes to have it become known we are house guests of Don Diego Vega," Don Carlos said. "What does our daughter think?"

It was a concession to ask her, and Lolita realized that she was granted this unusual favor because of Don Diego's wooing. She hesitated some time before answering.

"I believe it will be all right," she said. "I should like to visit the *pueblo*, for we see scarcely anybody here at the *hacienda*. But people may talk concerning Don Diego and myself."

"Nonsense!" Don Carlos exploded. "Could there be anything more natural than that we should visit the Vegas, since our blood is almost as good as theirs and better than that of others?"

"But it is Don Diego's house, and not that of his father. Still—he will not be there for two or three days, he says, and we can return when he comes."

"Then it is settled!" Don Carlos declared. "I shall see my superintendent and give him instructions."

He hurried into the *patio* and rang the big bell for the superintendent, being well pleased. For when the Señorita Lolita saw the rich furnishings in the house of Don Diego Vega, she might the more readily accept Don Diego as a husband, he thought. When she saw the silks and satins, the elegant tapestries, the furniture inlaid with gold and studded with precious stones, when she realized that she could be mistress of this and much more besides—Don Carlos flattered himself that he knew the feminine heart.

Soon after the *siesta* hour, a *carreta* was brought before the door, drawn by mules and driven by a native. Doña Catalina and Lolita got into it, and Don Carlos bestrode his best horse and rode at its side. And so they went down the trail to the highway, and down the highway toward Reina de Los Angeles.

They passed folk who marveled to see the Pulido family thus going abroad, for it was well known that they had met with ill fortune and scarcely went anywhere now. It was even whispered that the ladies did not keep up with the fashions, and that the servants were poorly fed, but remained at the *hacienda* because their master was so kind.

But Doña Catalina and her daughter held their heads proudly, as did Don Carlos, and they greeted the people they knew, and so continued along the highway.

Presently they made a turning and could see the *pueblo* in the distance—the plaza and the church with its high cross on one side of it and the inn and storehouses and a few residences of the more pretentious sort, like Don Diego's, and the scattered huts of natives and poor folk.

The *carreta* stopped before Don Diego's door, and servants rushed out to make the guests welcome, spreading a carpet from the *carreta* to the doorway, that the ladies would not have to step in the dust. Don Carlos led the way into the house, after ordering that the horse and mules be cared for and the *carreta* put away, and there they rested for a time, and the servants brought out wine and food.

They went through the rich house then, and even the eyes of Doña Catalina, who had seen many rich houses, widened at what she saw here in Don Diego's home.

"To think that our daughter can be mistress of all this when she speaks the word!" she gasped.

Señorita Lolita said nothing, but she began thinking that perhaps it would not be so bad after all to become the wife of Don Diego. She was fighting a mental battle, was Señorita Lolita. On the one side was wealth and position, and the safety and good fortune of her parents—and a lifeless man for husband; and on the other side was the romance and ideal love she craved. Until the last hope was gone she could not give the latter up.

Don Carlos left the house and crossed the plaza to the inn, where he met several gentlemen of age, and renewed acquaintance with them, albeit he noticed that none was enthusiastic in his greeting. They feared, he supposed, to appear openly friendly to him. Since he was in the bad graces of the governor.

"You are in the *pueblo* on business?" one asked.

"Not so, *señor*," Don Carlos replied, and gladly, since here was a chance to set himself right in part. "This Señor Zorro is abroad, and the soldiers after him."

"We are aware of that."

"There may be a battle, or a series of raids, since it is whispered that now Señor Zorro has a band of cutthroats with him, and my *hacienda* is off by itself and would be at the mercy of the thief."

"Ah! And so you bring your family to the *pueblo* until the matter is at an end?"

"I had not thought of doing so, but this morning Don Diego Vega sent out to me a request that I bring my family here and make use of his house for the time being. Don Diego has gone to his *hacienda*, but will return within a short time."

The eyes of those who heard opened a bit at that, but Don Carlos pretended not to notice, and went on sipping his wine.

"Don Diego was out to visit me yesterday morning," he continued. "We renewed old times. And my *hacienda* had a visit from this Señor Zorro last night, as doubtless you have heard, and Don Diego, learning of it, galloped out again, fearing we had met with disaster."

"Twice in one day!" gasped one of those who heard.

"I have said it, *señor*."

"You—that is—your daughter is very beautiful, is she not, Don Carlos Pulido? And seventeen, is she not—about?"

"Eighteen, *señor*. She is called beautiful, I believe," Don Carlos admitted.

Those around him glanced at one another. They had the solution now. Don Diego Vega was seeking to wed Señorita Lolita Pulido. That meant that Pulido's fortunes would soon be at the flood again, and that he might feel called upon to remember his friends and look askance at those who had not stood by him.

So now, they crowded forward, alert to do him honor, and asked concerning crops and the increase of his herds and flocks, and whether the bees were doing as well as usual, and did he think the olives were excellent this year.

Don Carlos appeared to take it all as a matter of course. He accepted the wine they bought, and purchased himself, and the fat landlord darted about doing their bidding and trying to compute the day's profits in his head, which was a hopeless task for him.

When Don Carlos left the inn at dusk, several of them followed him to the door, and two of the more influential walked with him across the plaza to the door of Don Diego's house. One of these begged that Don Carlos and his wife visit his house that evening for music and talk, and Don Carlos graciously accepted the invitation.

Doña Catalina had been watching from a window, and her face was beaming when she met her husband at the door.

"Everything goes well," he said. "They have met me with open-arms. And I have accepted an invitation to visit to-night."

"But Lolita?" Doña Catahna protested.

"She must remain here, of course. Will it not be all right? There are half a hundred servants about. And I have accepted the invitation, my dear."

Such a chance to win favor again could not be disregarded, of course, and so Lolita was made acquainted with the arrangement. She was to remain in the great living-room, reading a volume of verse she had found there, and if she grew sleepy she was to retire to a certain chamber. The servants would guard her, and the *despensero* would look after her wishes personally.

Don Carlos and his wife went to make their evening visit, being lighted across the plaza by half a dozen natives who held torches in their hands, for the night was without a moon, and rain was threatening again.

Señorita Lolita curled up on a couch, the volume of verse in her lap, and began to read. Each verse treated of love, romance, passion. She marveled that Don Diego would read such, being so lifeless himself, but the volume showed that it had been much handled. She sprang from the couch to look at other books on a bench not far away. And her amazement increased.

Volume after volume of poets who sang of love; volumes that had to do with horsemanship; books that had been written at the dictation of masters offence; tales of great generals and warriors were there.

Surely these volumes were not for a man of Don Diego's blood, she told herself. And then she thought that perhaps he reveled in them, though not in the manner of life they preached. Don Diego was something of a puzzle, she told herself for the hundredth time; and she went back and began reading the poetry again.

Then Captain Ramón hammered at the front door.

XIII. Love Comes Swiftly

The *despensero* hurried to open it.

"I regret that Don Diego is not at home, *señor*," he said. "He has gone to his *hacienda*."

"I know as much. Don Carlos and wife and daughter are here, are they not?"

"Don Carlos and his wife are out on a visit this evening, *señor*."

"The *señorita*—"

"Is here, of course."

"In that case, I shall pay my respects to the *señorita*," Captain Ramón said.

"*Señor*! Pardon me, but the little lady is alone."

"Am I not a proper man?" the captain demanded.

"It—it is scarcely right for her to receive the visit of a gentleman when her *dueña* is not present."

"Who are you to speak to me of the proprieties?" Captain Ramón demanded. "Out of my way, scum! Cross me and you shall be punished. I know things concerning you."

The face of the *despensero* went white at that, for the captain spoke the truth and, at a word, could cause him considerable trouble and mayhap a term in carcel. Yet he knew what was right.

"But, *señor*—" he protested.

Captain Ramón thrust him aside with his left arm and stalked into the big living-room. Lolita sprang up in alarm when she saw him standing before her.

"Ah, *señorita*, I trust that I did not startle you," he said. "I regret that your parents are absent, yet I must have a few words with you. This servant would deny me entrance, but I imagine you have nought to fear from a man with one wounded arm."

"It—it is scarcely proper, is it, *señor*?" the girl asked, a bit frightened.

"I feel sure no harm can come of it," he said.

He went across the room and sat down on one end of the couch and admired her beauty frankly. The *despensero* hovered near.

"Go to your kitchen, fellow!" Captain Ramón commanded.

"No; allow him to remain," Lolita begged. "My father commanded it, and he courts trouble if he leaves."

"And if he remains. Go, fellow!"

The servant went.

Captain Ramón turned toward the girl again, and smiled upon her. He flattered himself that he knew women—they loved to see a man show mastery over other men.

"More beautiful than ever, *señorita*," he said in a purring voice. "I really am glad to find you thus alone, for there is something I would say to you."

"What can that be, *señor*?"

"Last night at your father's *hacienda* I asked his permission to pay my addresses to you. Your beauty has inflamed my heart, *señorita*, and I would have you for my wife. Your father consented, except that he said Don Diego Vega also had received permission. So it appears that it lies between Don Diego and myself."

"Should you speak of it, *señor*?" she asked.

"Certainly Don Diego Vega is not the man for you," he went on. "Has he courage, spirit? Is he not a laughing-stock because of his weakness?"

"You speak ill of him in his own house?" the *señorita* asked, her eyes flashing.

"I speak the truth, *señorita*. I would have your favor. Can you not look upon me with kindness? Can you not give me hope that I may win your heart and hand?"

"Captain Ramón, all this is unworthy," she said. "It is not the proper manner, and you know it. I beg you to leave me now."

"I await your answer, *señorita*."

Her outraged pride rose up at that. Why could she not be wooed as other, *señoritas*, in the proper fashion? Why was this man so bold in his words? Why did he disregard the conventions?

"You must leave me," she said firmly. "This is all wrong, and you are aware of it. Would you make my name a by-word, Captain Ramón? Suppose somebody was to come and find us like this—alone?"

"Nobody will come, *señorita*. Can you not give me an answer?"

"No!" she cried, starting to get to her feet. "It is not right that you should ask it. My father, I assure you, shall hear of this visit!"

"Your father," he sneered. "A man who has the ill will of the governor. A man who is being plucked because he possessed no political sense. I fear not your father. He should be proud of the fact that Captain Ramón looks at his daughter."

"*Señor!*"

"Do not run away," he said, clutching her hand. "I have done you the honor to ask you to be my wife—"

"Done *me* the honor!" she cried angrily, and almost in tears. "It is the man who is done the honor when a woman accepts him."

"I like you when you rage," he observed. "Sit down again—beside me here. And now give me your answer."

"*Señor*!"

"You will wed me, of course. I shall intercede with the governor for your father and get a part of his estate restored. I shall take you to San Francisco de Asis, to the governor's house, where you will be admired by persons of rank."

"*Señor*! Let me go!"

"My answer, *señorita*! You have held me off enough."

She wrenched away from him, confronted him with blazing eyes, her tiny hands clenched at her sides.

"Wed with you?" she cried. "Rather would I remain a maid all my life, rather would I wed with a native, rather would I die than wed with you! I wed a *caballero*, a gentleman, or no man! And I cannot say that you are such!"

"Pretty words from the daughter of a man who is about ruined."

"Ruin would not change the blood of the Pulidos, *señor*. I doubt whether you understand that, evidently having ill blood yourself. Don Diego shall hear of this. He is my father's friend—"

"And you would wed the rich Don Diego, eh, and straighten out your father's affairs? You would not wed an honorable soldier, but would sell yourself—"

"*Señor*!" she shrieked.

This was beyond endurance. She was alone, there was nobody near to resent the insult. So her blood called upon her to avenge it herself.

Like a flash of lightning her hand went forward, and came against Captain Ramón's cheek with a crack. Then she sprang backward, but he grasped her by an arm and drew her toward him.

"I shall take a kiss to pay for that," he said. "Such a tiny bit of womanhood can be handled with one arm, thank the saints."

She fought him, striking and scratching at his breast, for she could not reach his face. But he only laughed at her, and held her tighter until she was almost spent and breathless, and finally he threw back her head and looked down into her eyes.

"A kiss in payment, *señorita*," he said. "It will be a pleasure to tame such a wild one."

She tried to fight again, but could not. She called upon the saints to aid her. And Captain Ramón laughed more and bent his head, and his lips came close to hers.

But he never claimed the kiss. She started to wrench away from him again, and he was forced to strengthen his arm and pull her forward. And from a corner of the room there came a voice that was at once deep and stern.

"One moment, *señor!*" it said.

Captain Ramón released the girl and whirled on one heel. He blinked his eyes to pierce the gloom of the corner; he heard Señorita Lolita give a glad cry.

Then Captain Ramón, disregarding the presence of the lady, cursed, once and loudly, for Señor Zorro stood before him.

He did not pretend to know how the highwayman had entered the house; he did not stop to think of it. He realized that he was without a blade at his side, and that he could not use it had he one, because of his wounded shoulder. And Señor Zorro was walking toward him from the corner.

"Outlaw I may be, but I respect women," the Curse of Capistrano said. "And you, an officer of the army, do not, it appears. What are you doing here. Captain Ramón?"

"And what do you here?"

"I heard a lady's scream, which is warrant enough for *caballero* to enter any place, *señor*. It appears to me that you have broken all the conventions."

"Perhaps the lady has broken them also."

"*Señor!*" roared the highwayman. "Another thought like that and I cut you down where you stand, though you are a wounded man! How shall I punish you?"

"*Despensero!* Natives!" the captain shouted suddenly. "Here is Señor Zorro! A reward if you take him!"

The masked man laughed. "'Twill do you small good to call for help," he said. "Spend your breath in saying your prayers, rather."

"You do well to threaten a wounded man."

"You deserve death, *señor*, but I suppose I must allow you to escape that. But you will go down upon your knees and apologize to this *señorita*. And then you will go from this house, slink from it like the cur you are, and keep your mouth closed regarding what has transpired here. If you do not, I promise to soil my blade with your life's blood."

"Ha!"

"On your knees, *señor*, and instantly!" Señor Zorro commanded. "I have no time to waste in waiting."

"I am an officer—"

"On your knees!" commanded Señor Zorro again, in a terrible voice. He sprang forward and grasped Captain Ramón by his well shoulder, and threw him to the floor.

"Quickly, poltroon! Tell the *señorita* that you humbly beg her pardon—which she will not grant, of course, since you are beneath speaking to—and that you will not annoy her again. Say it, or, by the saints, you have made your last speech!"

Captain Ramón said it. And then Señor Zorro grasped him by the neck and lifted him, and propelled him to the door and hurled him into the darkness. And had his boots not been soft. Captain Ramón would have been injured more deeply, both in feelings and anatomy.

Señor Zorro closed the door as the *despensero* came running into the room, to stare in fright at the masked man.

"*Señorita*, I trust that I have been of service," the highwayman said. "That scoundrel will not bother you further, else he feels the sting of my blade again."

"Oh, thank you, *señor*—thank you!" she cried. "I shall tell my father this good deed you have done. *Despensero*, get him wine!"

There was naught for the butler to do except obey, since she had voiced the order, and he hurried from the room, pondering on the times and the manners.

Señorita Lohta stepped to the man's side.

"*Señor*," she breathed, "you saved me from insult. You saved me from the pollution of that man's lips. *Señor*, though you deem me unmaidenly, I offer you freely the kiss he would have taken."

She put up her face and closed her eyes.

"And I shall not look when you raise your mask," she said.

"It were too much, *señorita*," he said. "Your hand—but not your lips."

"You shame me, *señor*. I was bold to offer it, and you have refused."

"You shall feel no shame," he said.

He bent swiftly, raised the bottom of his mask, and touched lightly her lips with his.

"Ah, *señorita*," he said. "I would I were an honest man and could claim you openly. My heart is filled with love of you."

"And mine with love of you."

"This is madness. None must know."

"I would not fear to tell the world, *señor*."

"Your father and his fortunes! Don Diego!"

"I love you, *señor*."

"Your chance to be a great lady! Do you think I did not know Don Diego was the man you meant when we spoke in your father's *patio*? This is a whim, *señorita*."

"It is love, *señor*, whether anything comes of it or not. And a Pulido does not love twice."

"What possibly could come of it but distress?"

"We shall see. God is good."

"It is madness—"

"Sweet madness, *señor*."

He clasped her to him and bent his head again, and again she closed her eyes and took his kiss, only this time the kiss was longer. She made no effort to see his face.

"I may be ugly," he said.

"But I love you."

"Disfigured, *señorita*—"

"Still I love you."

"What hope can we have?"

"Go, *señor*, before my parents return. I shall say nothing except that you saved me from insult and then went your way again. They will think that you came to rob Don Diego. And turn honest, *señor*, for my sake. Turn honest, I say, and claim me. No man knows your face, and if you take off your mask forever, none ever will know your guilt. It is not as if you were an ordinary thief. I know why you have stolento avenge the helpless, to punish cruel politicians, to aid the oppressed. I know that you have given what you have stolen to the poor. Oh, *señor*!"

"But my task is not yet done, *señorita*, and I feel called upon to finish it."

"Then finish it, and may the saints guard you, as I feel sure they will. And when it is finished, come back to me. I shall know you in whatever garb you come."

"Nor shall I wait that long, *señorita*. I shall see you often. I could not exist else."

"Guard yourself."

"I shall in truth, now, since I have double reason. Life never was so sweet as now."

He backed away from her slowly. He turned and glanced toward a window near at hand.

"I must go," he said. "I cannot wait for the wine."

"That was but a subterfuge so that we could be alone," she confessed.

"Until the next time, *señorita*, and may it not be long."

"On guard, *señor*!"

"Always, loved one. *Señorita, á Dios*!"

Again their eyes met, and then he waved his hand at her, gathered his cloak close about his body, darted to the window, and went through it. The darkness outside swallowed him.

XIV. Captain Ramón Writes a Letter

Picking himself up out of the dust before Don Diego Vega's door. Captain Ramón darted through the darkness to the footpath that ran up the slope toward the *presidio*.

His blood was aflame with rage, his face was purple with wrath. There remained at the *presidio* no more than half a dozen soldiers, for the greater part of the garrison had gone with Sergeant Gonzales, and of these half-dozen four were on the sick list and two were necessary as guards.

So Captain Ramón could not send men down to the Vega house in an effort to effect a capture of the highwayman; moreover, he decided that Señor Zorro would not remain there more than a few minutes, but would mount his horse and ride away, for the highwayman had a name for not resting long in one place.

Besides, Captain Ramón had no wish to let it become known that this Señor Zorro had met him a second time, and had treated him much like a peon. Could he give out the information that he had insulted a *señorita*, and that Señor Zorro had punished him because of it, that Señor Zorro had caused him to get down upon his knees and apologize and then had kicked him through the front door like a dog?

The captain decided it were better to say nothing of the occurrence. He supposed that Señorita Lolita would tell her parents, and that the *despensero* would give testimony, but he doubted whether Don Carlos would do anything about it. Don Carlos would think twice before affronting an officer of the army, being the recipient already of the governor's frowns. Ramón only hoped that Don Diego would not learn much of the happening, for if a Vega raised hand against him, the captain would have difficulty maintaining his position.

Pacing the floor of his office, Captain Ramón allowed his wrath to grow, and thought on these things and many others. He had kept abreast of the times, and he knew that the governor and the men about him were sorely in need of more funds to waste in riotous living. They had plucked those men of wealth against whom there was the faintest breath of suspicion, and they would welcome a new victim.

Might not the captain suggest one, and at the same time strengthen his own position with the governor? Would the captain dare hint that perhaps the Vega family was wavering in its loyalty to the governor?

At least he could do one thing, he decided. He could have his revenge for the flouting the daughter of Don Carlos Pulido had given him.

Captain Ramón grinned despite his wrath as the thought came to him. He called for writing-materials, and informed one of his well men that he should prepare for a journey, being about to be named for a courier's job.

Ramón paced the floor for some minutes more, thinking on the matter and trying to decide just how to word the epistle he intended writing. And finally he sat down before the long table and addressed his message to his excellency the governor, at his mansion in San Francisco de Asis.

This is what he wrote:

Your intelligences regarding this highwayman, Señor Zorro, as he is known, have come to hand. I regret that I am unable at this writing to report the rogue's capture, but I trust that you will be lenient with me in the matter, since circumstances are somewhat unusual.

I have the greater part of my force in pursuit of the fellow, with orders to get him in person or to fetch me his corpse. But this Señor Zorro does not fight alone. He is being given succor at certain places in the neighborhood, allowed to remain in hiding when necessary, given food and drink and, no doubt, fresh horses.

Within the past day he visited the *hacienda* of Don Carlos Pulido, a *caballero* known to be hostile to your excellency. I sent men there and went myself. While my soldiers took up his trail the man came from a closet in the living-room at Don Carlos's house and attacked me treacherously. He wounded me in the right shoulder, but I fought him off until he became frightened and dashed away, making his escape. I may mention that I was hindered somewhat by this Don Carlos in pursuing the man. Also, when I arrived at the *hacienda*, indications were that the man had been eating his evening meal there.

The Pulido *hacienda* is an excellent place for such a man to hide, being somewhat off the main highway. I fear that Señor Zorro makes it his headquarters when he is in this vicinity; and I await your instructions in the matter. I may add that Don Carlos scarcely treated me with respect while I was in his presence, and that his daughter, the Señorita Lolita, scarcely could keep from showing her admiration of this highwayman and from sneering at the efforts of the soldiery to capture him.

There are also indications of a famous and wealthy family of this neighborhood wavering in loyalty to your excellency, but you will appreciate the fact that I cannot write of such a thing in a missive sent you by courier.

With deep respect,

RAMÓN, Comandante and Captain, Presidio,

Reina de Los Angeles

Ramón grinned again as he finished the letter. That last paragraph, he knew, would get the governor guessing. The Vega family was about the only famous and wealthy one that would fit the description. As for the Pulidos, Captain Ramón imagined what would happen to them. The governor would not hesitate to deal out punishment, and perhaps the Señorita Lolita would find herself without protection, and in no position to reject the advances of a captain of the army.

Now Ramón addressed himself to the task of making a second copy of the letter, intending to send one by his courier and preserve the other for his files, in case something came up and he wished to refer to it.

Having finished the copy, he folded the original and sealed it, carried it to the soldiers' lounging-room, and gave it to the man he had selected as courier. The soldier saluted, hurried out to his horse, and rode furiously toward the north, toward San Fernando and Santa Barbara, and on to San Francisco de Asis, with the orders ringing in his ears that he should make all haste and get a change of horses at every mission and *pueblo* in the name of his excellency.

Ramón returned to his office and poured out a measure of wine, and began reading over the copy of the letter. He half wished that he had made it stronger, yet he knew that it were better to make it mild, for then the governor would not think he was exaggerating.

He stopped reading now and then to curse the name of Señor Zorro, and frequently he reflected on the beauty and grace of the Señorita Lolita and told himself she should be punished for the manner in which she had treated him.

He supposed that Señor Zorro was miles away by this time, and putting more miles between himself and Reina de Los Angeles; but he was mistaken in that. For the Curse of Capistrano, as the soldiers called him, had not hurried away after leaving the house of Don Diego Vega.

XV. At the *Presidio*

Señor Zorro had gone a short distance through the darkness to where he had left his horse in the rear of a native's hut, and there he had stood, thinking of the love that had come to him.

Presently he chuckled as if well pleased, then mounted and rode slowly toward the path that led to the *presidio*. He heard a horseman galloping away from the place and thought Captain Ramón had sent a man to call back Sergeant Gonzales and the troopers and put them on the fresher trail.

Señor Zorro knew how affairs stood at the *presidio*, knew to a man how many of the soldiery were there, and that four were ill with a fever, and that there was but one well man now besides the captain since one had ridden away.

He laughed again and made his horse climb the slope slowly so as to make little noise. In the rear of the *presidio* building he dismounted and allowed the reins to drag on the ground, knowing that the animal would not move from the spot.

Now he crept through the darkness to the wall of the building and made his way around it carefully until he came to a window. He raised himself on a pile of adobe bricks and peered inside.

It was Captain Ramón's office into which he looked. He saw the *comandante* sitting before a table reading a letter which, it appeared, he had just finished writing. Captain Ramón was talking to himself, as does many an evil man.

"That will cause consternation for the pretty *señorita*," he was saying. "That will teach her not to flaunt an officer of his excellency's forces. When her father is in the *cárcel* charged with high treason, and his estates have been taken away, then perhaps she will listen to what I have to say."

Señor Zorro had no difficulty in distinguishing the words. He guessed instantly that Captain Ramón had planned a revenge, that he contemplated mischief toward the Pulidos. Beneath his mask the face of Señor Zorro grew black with rage.

He got down from the pile of adobe bricks and slipped on along the wall until he came to the corner of the building. In a socket at the side of the front door a torch was burning, and the only able-bodied man left in the garrison was pacing back and forth before the doorway, a pistol in his belt and a blade at his side.

Señor Zorro noted the length of the man's pacing. He judged the distance accurately, and just as the man turned his back to resume his march the highwayman sprang.

His hands closed around the soldier's throat as his knees struck the man in the back. Instantly they were upon the ground, the surprised trooper now doing his best to put up a fight. But Señor Zorro, knowing that a bit of noise might mean disaster for him, silenced the man by striking him on the temple with the heavy butt of his pistol.

He pulled the unconscious soldier back into the shadows, gagged him with a strip torn from the end of his *serape*, and bound his hands and feet with other strips. Then he drew his cloak about him, looked to his pistol, listened a moment to be sure the short fight with the soldier had not attracted the attention of any inside the building, and slipped once more toward the door.

He was inside in an instant. Before him was the big lounging-room with its hard dirt floor. Here were some long tables and bunks and wine mugs and harness and saddles and bridles. Señor Zorro gave it but a glance to assure himself that no man was there, and walked swiftly and almost silently across to the door that opened into the office of the *comandante*.

He made sure that his pistol was ready for instant use, and then threw the door open boldly. Captain Ramón was seated with his back toward it, and now he whirled around in his chair with a snarl on his lips, thinking one of his men had entered without the preliminary of knocking, and ready to rebuke the man.

"Not a sound, *señor*!" the highwayman warned. "You die if as much as a gasp escapes your lips!"

He kept his eyes on those of the *comandante*, closed the door behind him, and advanced into the room. He walked forward slowly, without speaking, the pistol held ready in front of him. Captain Ramón had his hands on the table before him, and his face had gone white.

"This visit is necessary, *señor*, I believe," Señor Zorro said. "I have not made it because I admire the beauty of your face."

"What do you here?" the captain asked, disregarding the order to make no sound, yet speaking in a tone scarcely above a whisper.

"I happened to look in at the window, *señor*. I saw an epistle before you on the table, and I heard you speak. 'Tis a bad thing for a man to talk to himself. Had you remained silent I might have gone on about my business. As it is—"

"Well, *señor*?" the captain asked, with a bit of his old arrogance returning to him.

"I have a mind to read that letter before you."

"Does my military business interest you that much?"

"As to that, we shall say nothing, *señor*. Kindly remove your hands from the table, but do not reach toward the pistol at your side unless you wish to die the death instantly. It would not grieve me to have to send your soul into the hereafter."

The *comandante* did as he had been directed, and Señor Zorro went forward cautiously and snatched up the letter. Then he retreated a few paces again, still watching the man before him.

"I am going to read this," he said, "but I warn you that I shall watch you closely, also. Do not make a move, *señor*, unless it is your wish to visit your ancestors."

He read swiftly, and when he had finished he looked the *comandante* straight in the eyes for some time without speaking, and his own eyes were glittering malevolently through his mask. Captain Ramón began to feel more uncomfortable.

Señor Zorro stepped across to the table, still watching the other, and held the letter to the flame of a candle. It caught fire, blazed, presently dropped to the floor, a bit of ash. Señor Zorro put one foot upon it

"The letter will not be delivered," he said. "So you fight women, do you, *señor*? A brave officer and an ornament to his excellency's forces! I doubt not he would grant you promotion if he knew of this. You insult a *señorita* because her father, for the time being, is not friendly with those in power, and because she repulses you as you deserve, you set about to cause trouble for the members of her family. Truly, it is a worthy deed."

He took a step closer and bent forward, still holding the pistol ready before him.

"Let me not hear of you sending any letter similar to the one I have just destroyed," he said. "I regret at the present time that you are unable to stand before me and cross blades. It would be an insult to my sword to run you through, yet would I do it to rid the world of such a fellow."

"You speak bold words to a wounded man."

"No doubt the wound will heal, *senor*. And I shall keep myself informed regarding it. And when it has healed and you have back your strength, I shall take the trouble to hunt you up, and call you to account for what you have attempted doing this night. Let that be understood between us."

Again their eyes blazed, each man's into those of the other, and Señor Zorro stepped backward and drew his cloak closer about him. To their ears there came suddenly a jangling of harness, the tramp of horses' feet, the raucous voice of Sergeant Pedro Gonzales.

"Do not dismount!" the sergeant was crying to his men at the door. "I but make report, and then we go on after the rogue! There shall be no rest until we take him!"

Señor Zorro glanced quickly around the room, for he knew escape by the entrance was cut off now. Captain Ramón's eyes flashed with keen anticipation.

"Ho, Gonzales!" he shrieked before Zorro could warn him against it. "To the rescue, Gonzales! Señor Zorro is here!"

And then he looked at the highwayman defiantly, as if telling him to do his worst.

But Señor Zorro had no desire to fire his pistol and let out the captain's lifeblood, it appeared, preferring to save him for the blade when his shoulder should have healed.

"Remain where you are!" he commanded, and darted toward the nearest window.

The big sergeant had heard, however. He called upon his men to follow, and rushed across the large room to the door of the office and threw it open. A bellow of rage escaped him as he saw the masked man standing beside the table, and saw the *comandante* sitting before it with his hands spread out before him.

"By the saints, we have him!" Gonzales cried. "In with you, troopers! Guard the doors! Some look to the windows!"

Señor Zorro had transferred his pistol to his left hand, and had whipped out his blade. Now he swept it forward and sidewise, and the candles were struck from the table. Zorro put his foot upon the only one that remained lighted and extinguished it in that manner—and the room was in darkness.

"Lights! Bring a torch!" Gonzales shrieked.

Señor Zorro sprang aside, against the wall, and made his way around it rapidly while Gonzales and two other men sprang into the room, and one remained guarding the door; while in the other room several ran to get a torch, and managed to get in one another's way.

The man with the torch came rushing through the door finally, and he shrieked and went down with a sword blade through his breast, and the torch fell to the floor and was extinguished. And then, before the sergeant could reach the spot, Señor Zorro was back in the darkness again and could not be found.

Gonzales was roaring his curses now and searching for the man he wished to slay, and the captain was crying to him to be careful and not put his blade through a trooper by mistake. The other men were storming around; in the other room one came with a second torch.

Zorro's pistol spoke, and the torch was shot from the man's hand. The highwayman sprang forward and stamped upon it, putting it out, and again retreated to the darkness, changing his position rapidly, listening for the deep breathing that would tell him the exact location of his various foes.

"Catch the rogue!" the *comandante* was shrieking. "Can one man thus make fools of the lot of you?"

Then he ceased to speak, for Señor Zorro had grasped him from behind and shut off his wind, and now the highwayman's voice rang out above the din.

"Soldiers, I have your captain! I am going to carry him before me and back out the door. I am going to cross the other room and so reach the outside of the building. I have discharged one pistol, but I am holding its mate at the base of the captain's brain. And when one of you attacks me, I fire, and you are without a captain."

The captain could feel cold steel at the back of his head, and he shrieked for the men to use caution. And Señor Zorro carried him to the doorway and backed out with the captain held in front of him, while Gonzales and the troopers followed as closely as they dared, watching every move, hoping for a chance to catch him unaware.

He crossed the big lounging-room of the *presidio*, and so came to the outside door. He was somewhat afraid of the men outside, for he knew that some of them had run around the building to guard the windows. The torch was still burning just outside the door, and Señor Zorro put up his hand and tore it down and extinguished it. But still there would be grave danger the moment he stepped out.

Gonzales and the troopers were before him, spread out fan-fashion across the room, bending forward, waiting for a chance to get in a blow. Gonzales held a pistol in his hand—though he made out to despise the weapon and was watching for an opportunity to shoot without endangering the life of his captain.

"Back, *señores!*" the highwayman commanded now. "I would have more room in which to make my start. That is it—I thank you. Sergeant Gonzales, were not the odds so heavy, I might be tempted to play at fence with you and disarm you again."

"By the saints—"

"Some other time, my sergeant! And now, *señores*, attention! It desolates me to say it, but I had only the one pistol. What the captain has been feeling all this time at the base of his brain is naught except a bridle buckle I picked up from the floor. Is it not a pretty jest? *Señores, á Dios!*"

Suddenly he whirled the captain forward, darted into the darkness, and started toward his horse with the whole pack at his heels and pistol flashes splitting the blackness of the night and bullets whistling by his head. His laughter came back to them on the stiffening breeze that blew in from the distant sea.

XVI. The Chase That Failed

Señor Zorro charged his horse down the treacherous slope of the hill, where there was loose gravel and a misstep would spell disaster, and where the troopers were slow to follow. Sergeant Gonzales possessed courage enough, and some of the men followed him, while others galloped off to right and left, planning to intercept the fugitive when he reached the bottom and turned.

Señor Zorro, however, was before them, and took the trail toward San Gabriel at a furious gallop, while the troopers dashed along behind, calling to one another, and now and then discharging a pistol with a great waste of powder and ball and no result so far as capturing or wounding the highwayman was concerned.

Soon the moon came up. Señor Zorro had been anticipating that, and knew that it would make his escape more difficult. But his horse was fresh and strong, while those ridden by the troopers had covered many miles during the day, and so hope was not gone.

Now he could be seen plainly by those who pursued, and he could hear Sergeant Gonzales crying upon his men to urge their beasts to the utmost and effect a capture. He glanced behind him as he rode, and observed that the troopers were scattering out in a long line, the stronger and fresher horses gaining on the others.

So they rode for some five miles, the troopers holding the distance, but not making any gain, and Señor Zorro knew that soon their horses would weaken, and that the good steed he bestrode, which gave no signs of fatigue as yet, would outdistance them. Only one thing bothered him—he wanted to be traveling in the opposite direction.

Here the hills rose abruptly on either side of the highway, and it was not possible for him to turn aside and make a great circle, nor were there any trails he could follow;

THE MARK OF ZORRO

and if he attempted to have his horse climb, he would have to make slow progress, and the troopers would come near enough to fire their pistols, and mayhap wound him.

So he rode straight ahead, gaining a bit now, knowing that two miles farther up the valley there was a trail that swung off to the right, and that by following it he would come to higher ground and so could double back on his tracks.

He had covered one of the two miles before he remembered that it had been noised abroad that a landslide had been caused by the recent torrential rain and had blocked this higher trail. So he could not use that even when he reached it; and now a bold thought came to his mind.

As he topped a slight rise in the terrain, he glanced behind once more and saw that no two of the troopers were riding side by side. They were well scattered, and there was some distance between each two of them. It would help his plan.

He dashed around a bend in the highway and pulled up his horse. He turned the animal's head back toward whence he had come, and bent forward in the saddle to listen. When he could hear the hoof-beats of his nearest pursuer's horse, he drew his blade, took a turn of the reins around his left wrist, and suddenly struck his beast in the flanks cruelly with his sharp rowels.

The animal he rode was not used to such treatment, never having felt the spurs except when in a gallop and his master wished greater speed. Now he sprang forward like a thunderbolt, dashed around die curve like a wild stallion, and bore down upon the nearest of Señor Zorro's foes.

"Make way," Señor Zorro cried.

The first man gave ground readily, not sure that this was the highwayman coming back, and when he was sure of it he shrieked the intelligence to those behind, but they could not understand because of the clatter of hoofs on the hard road.

Señor Zorro bore down upon the second man, clashed swords with him, and rode on. He dashed around another curve, and his horse struck another fairly, and hurled him from the roadway. Zorro swung at the fourth man, and missed him, and was glad that the fellow's counterstroke missed as well.

And now there was naught but the straight ribbon of road before him, and his galloping foes dotting it. Like a maniac he rode them through, cutting and slashing at them as he passed. Sergeant Gonzales, far in the rear because of his jaded mount, realized what was taking place and screeched at his men, and even as he screeched a thunderbolt seemed to strike his horse, unseating him.

And then Señor Zorro was through them and gone, and they were following him again, a cursing sergeant at their head, but at a distance slightly greater than before.

He allowed his horse to go somewhat slower now, since he could keep his distance, and rode to the first cross trail, into which he turned. He took to higher ground and looked back to see the pursuit streaming out over the hill, losing itself in the distance, but still determined.

"It was an excellent trick!" Señor Zorro said to his horse. "But we cannot try it often!"

He passed the *hacienda* of a man friendly to the governor, and a thought came to him—Gonzales might stop there and obtain fresh horses for himself and his men.

Nor was he mistaken in that. The troopers dashed up the driveway, and dogs howled a welcome. The master-of the *hacienda* came to the door, holding a *candelero* high above his head.

"We chase Señor Zorro!" Gonzales cried. "We require fresh steeds, in the name of the governor!"

The servants were called, and Gonzales and his men hurried to the corral. Magnificent horses were there, horses almost as good as the one the highwayman rode, and all were fresh. The troopers quickly stripped saddles and bridles from their jaded mounts and put them on the fresh steeds, and then dashed for the trail again and took up the pursuit. Señor Zorro had gained quite a lead, but there was only one trail he could follow, and they might overtake him.

Three miles away, on the crest of a small hill, there was a *hacienda* that had been presented to the mission of San Gabriel by a *caballero* who had died without leaving heirs. The governor had threatened to take it for the state, but so far had not done so, the Franciscans of San Gabriel having a name for protecting their property with determination.

In charge of this *hacienda* was one Fray Felipe, a member of the order who was along in years, and under his direction the neophytes made the estate a profitable one, raising much livestock and sending to the storehouses great amounts of hides and tallow and honey and fruit, as well as wine.

Gonzales knew the trail they were following led to this *hacienda*, and that just beyond it there was another trail that split, one part going to San Gabriel and the other returning to Reina de Los Angeles by a longer route.

If Señor Zorro passed the *hacienda*, it stood to reason that he would take the trail that ran toward the *pueblo*, since, had he wished to go to San Gabriel, he would have continued along the highway in the first place, instead of turning and riding back through the troopers at some risk to himself.

But he doubted whether Zorro would pass. For it was well known that the highwayman dealt harshly with those who prosecuted the *frailes*, and it was to be believed that every Franciscan held a friendly feeling for him and would give him aid.

The troopers came within sight of the *hacienda*, and could see no light. Gonzales stopped them where the driveway started, and listened in vain for sounds of the man they pursued. He dismounted and inspected the dusty road, but could not tell whether a horseman had ridden toward the house recently.

He issued quick orders, and the troop separated, half of the men remaining with their sergeant and the others scattering in such manner that they could surround the house, search the huts of the natives, and look at the great barns.

Then Sergeant Gonzales rode straight up the driveway with half his men at his back, forced his horse up the steps to the veranda as a sign that he held this place in little respect, and knocked on the door with the hilt of his sword.

XVII. Sergeant Gonzales Meets a Friend

Presently light showed through the windows, and after a time the door was thrown open. Fray Felipe stood framed in it, shading a candle with his hand—a giant of a man now past sixty, but one who had been a power in his time.

"What is all this noise?" he demanded in his deep voice. "And why do you, son of evil, ride your horse on my veranda?"

"We are chasing this pretty Señor Zorro, *fray*—this man they call the Curse of Capistrano," Gonzales said.

"And you expect to find him in this poor house?"

"Stranger things have happened. Answer me, *fray*! Have you heard a horseman gallop past within a short time?"

"I have not."

"And has this Señor Zorro paid you a visit recently?"

"I do not know the man you mean."

"You have heard of him, doubtless?"

"I have heard that he seeks to aid the oppressed, that he has punished those who have committed sacrilege, and that he has whipped those brutes who have beaten Indians."

"You are bold in your words, *fray*!"

"It is my nature to speak the truth, soldier!"

"You will be getting yourself into difficulties with the powers, my robed Franciscan."

"I fear no politician, soldier!"

"I do not like the tone of your words, *fray*. I have half a mind to dismount and give you a taste of my whip!"

"Señor!" Fray Felipe cried. "Take ten years off my shoulders and I can drag you in the dirt!"

"That is a question for dispute! However, let us get to the subject of this visit. You have not seen a masked fiend who goes by the name of Señor Zorro?"

"I have not, soldier!"

"I shall have my men search your house."

"You accuse me of falsehood?" Fray Felipe cried.

"My men must do something to pass the time, and they may as well search the house. You have nothing you wish to hide?"

"Recognizing the identity of my guests, it might be well to hide the wine-jugs," Fray Felipe said.

Sergeant Gonzales allowed an oath to escape him, and got down from his horse. The others dismounted, too, and the sergeant's mount was taken off the veranda and left with the horse-holder.

Then Gonzales drew off his gloves, sheathed his sword, and stamped through the door with the others at his heels, as Fray Felipe fell back before him, protesting against the intrusion.

From a couch in a far corner of the room there arose a man, who stepped into the circle of light cast by the *candelero*.

"As I have eyes, it is my raucous friend!" he cried.

"Don Diego! You here?" Gonzales gasped.

"I have been at my *hacienda* looking over business affairs, and I rode over to spend the night with Fray Felipe, who has known me from babyhood. These turbulent times! I thought that here, at least, in this *hacienda* that is a bit out of the way and has a *fray* in charge of it, I could for a time rest in peace without hearing of violence and bloodshed. But it appears that I cannot. Is there no place in this country where a man may meditate and consult musicians and the poets?"

"Meal mush and goat's milk!" Gonzales cried.

"Don Diego, you are my good friend and a true *caballero*. Tell me—have you seen this Señor Zorro tonight?"

"I have not, my sergeant."

"You did not hear him ride past the *hacienda*?"

"I did not. But a man could ride past and not be heard here in the house. Fray Felipe and I have been talking together, and were just about to retire when you came."

"Then the rogue has ridden on and taken the trail toward the *pueblo*!" the sergeant declared.

"You had him in view?" Don Diego asked.

"Ha! We were upon his heels, *caballero*! But at a turn in the highroad he made connection with some twenty men of his band. They rode at us and attempted to scatter us, but we drove them aside and kept on after Señor Zorro. We managed to separate him from his fellows and give chase."

"You say he has a score of men?"

"Fully a score, as my men will testify. He is a thorn in the flesh of the soldiery, but I have sworn to get him! And when once we stand face to face!"

"You will tell me of it afterward?" Don Diego asked, rubbing his hands together. "You will relate how you mocked him as he fought, how you played with him, pressed him back, and ran him through—"

"By the saints! You make mock of me, *caballero*?"

"'Tis but a jest, my sergeant. Now that we understand each other, perhaps Fray Felipe will give wine to you and your men. After such a chase, you must be fatigued."

"Wine would taste good," the sergeant said.

His corporal came in then to report that the huts and barns had been searched, and the corral also, and that no trace had been found of Señor Zorro or his horse.

Fray Felipe served the wine, though he appeared to do it with some reluctance, and it was plain that he was but answering Don Diego's request.

"And what shall you do now, my sergeant?" Don Diego asked, after the wine had been brought to the table. "Are you always to go chasing around the country and creating a tumult?"

"The rogue evidently has turned back toward Reina de Los Angeles, *caballero*," the sergeant replied. "He thinks he is clever, no doubt, but I can understand his plan."

"Ha! And what is it?"

"He will ride around Reina de Los Angeles and take the trail to San Luis Rey. He will rest for a time, no doubt, to throw off all pursuit, and then will continue to the vicinity of San Juan Capistrano. That is where he began this wild life of his, and for that reason the Curse of Capistrano he is called. Yes, he will go to Capistrano."

"And the soldiers?" Don Diego asked.

"We shall follow him leisurely. We shall work toward the place, and when the news of his next outrage is made known, we shall be within a short distance of him instead of in the *presidio* at the *pueblo*. We can find the fresh trail, and so take up the chase. There shall be no rest for us until the rogue is either slain or taken prisoner."

"And you have the reward," Don Diego added.

"You speak true words, *caballero*. The reward will come in handy. But I seek revenge, also. The rogue disarmed me once."

"Ah! That was the time he held a pistol in your face and forced you to fight not too well?"

"That was the time, my good friend. Oh, I have a score to settle with him."

"These turbulent times." Don Diego sighed. "I would they were at an end. A man has no chance for meditation. There are moments when I think I shall ride far out in the hills, where there can be found no life except rattlesnakes and coyotes, and there spend a number of days. Only in that manner may a man meditate."

"Why meditate?" Gonzales cried. "Why not cease thought and take to action? What a man you would make, *caballero*, if you let your eye flash now and then, and quarreled a bit, and showed your teeth once in a while. What you need is a few bitter enemies."

"May the saints preserve us!" Don Diego cried.

"It is the truth, *caballero*! Fight a bit—make love to some *señorita*—get drunk! Wake up and be a man!"

"Upon my soul! You almost persuade me, my sergeant. But no. I never could endure the exertion."

Gonzales growled something into his great mustache, and got up from the table.

"I have no special liking for you, *fray*, but I thank you for the wine, which was excellent," he said. "We must continue our journey. A soldier's duty never is at an end while he lives."

"Do not speak of journeys!" Don Diego cried. "I must take one myself on the morrow. My business at the *hacienda* is done, and I go back to the *pueblo*."

"Let me express the hope, my good friend, that you survive the hardship," Sergeant Gonzales said.

XVIII. Don Diego Returns

Señorita Lolita had to tell her parents, of course, what had happened during their absence, for the *despensero* knew and would tell Don Diego when he returned, and the *señorita* was wise enough to realize that it would be better to make the first explanation.

The *despensero*, having been sent for wine, knew nothing of the love scene that had been enacted, and had been told merely that Señor Zorro had hurried away. That seemed reasonable, since the *señor* was pursued by the soldiers.

So the girl told her father and mother that Captain Ramón had called while they were absent, and that he had forced his way into the big living-room to speak to her, despite the entreaties of the servant. Perhaps he had been drinking too much wine, else was not himself because of his wound, the girl explained, but he grew too bold, and pressed his suit with ardor that was repugnant, and finally insisted that he should have a kiss.

Whereupon, said the *señorita*, this Señor Zorro had stepped from the corner of the room—and how he came to be there, she did not know—and had forced Captain

Ramón to apologize, and then had thrown him out of the house. After which—and here she neglected to tell the entire truth—Señor Zorro made a courteous bow and hurried away.

Don Carlos was for getting a blade and going at once to the *presidio* and challenging Captain Ramón to mortal combat; but Doña Catalina was more calm, and showed him that to do that would be to let the world know that their daughter had been affronted, and also it would not aid their fortunes any if Don Carlos quarreled with an officer of the army; and yet again the don was of an age, and the captain probably would run him through in two passes and leave Doña Catalina a weeping widow, which she did not wish to be.

So the don paced the floor of the great living-room and fumed and fussed and wished he were ten years the younger, or that he had political power again, and he promised that when his daughter should have wedded Don Diego, and he was once more in good standing, he would see that Captain Ramón was disgraced and his uniform torn from his shoulders.

Sitting in the chamber that had been assigned to her, Señorita Lolita listened to her father's ravings, and found herself confronted with a situation. Of course, she could not wed Don Diego now. She had given her lips and her love to another, a man whose face she never had seen, a rogue pursued by soldiery—and she had spoken truly when she had said that a Pulido loved but once.

She tried to explain it all to herself, saying that it was a generous impulse that had forced her to give her lips to the man; and she told herself that it was not the truth, that her heart had been stirred when first he spoke to her at her father's *hacienda* during the *siesta* hour.

She was not prepared yet to tell her parents of the love that had come into her life, for it was sweet to keep it a secret; and, moreover, she dreaded the shock to them, and half feared that her father might cause her to be sent away to some place where she never would see Señor Zorro again.

She crossed to a window and gazed out at the plaza—and she saw Don Diego approaching in the distance. He rode slowly, as if greatly fatigued, and his two native servants rode a short distance behind him.

Men called to him as he neared the house, and he waved his hand at them languidly in response to their greeting. He dismounted slowly, one of the natives holding the stirrup and assisting him, brushed the dust from his clothes, and started toward the door.

Don Carlos and his wife were upon their feet to greet him, their faces beaming, for they had been accepted anew into society the evening before, and knew it was because they were Don Diego's house guests.

"I regret that I was not here when you arrived," Don Diego said, "but I trust that you have been made comfortable in my poor house."

"More than comfortable in this gorgeous palace!" Don Carlos exclaimed.

"Then you have been fortunate, for the saints know I have been uncomfortable enough."

"How is that, Don Diego?" Doña Catalina asked.

"My work at the *hacienda* done, I rode as far as the place of Fray Felipe, there to spend the night in quiet. But as we were about to retire, there came a thundering noise at the door, and this Sergeant Gonzales and a troop of soldiers entered. It appears that they had been chasing the highwayman called Señor Zorro, and had lost him in the darkness!"

In the other room, a dainty *señorita* gave thanks for that.

"These are turbulent times," Don Diego continued, sighing and mopping the perspiration from his forehead. "The noisy fellows were with us an hour or more, and then continued the chase. And because of what they had said of violence, I endured a horrible nightmare, so got very little rest. And this morning I was forced to continue to Reina de Los Angeles."

"You have a difficult time," Don Carlos said. "Señor Zorro was here, *caballero*, in your house, before the soldiers chased him."

"What is this intelligence?" Don Diego cried, sitting up straight in his chair and betraying sudden interest.

"Undoubtedly he came to steal, else to abduct you and hold you for ransom," Doña Catalina observed. "But I scarcely think that he stole. Don Carlos and myself were visiting friends, and Señorita Lolita remained here alone. There—there is a distressing affair to report to you—"

"I beg of you to proceed," Don Diego said.

"While we were gone. Captain Ramón, of the *presidio*, called. He was informed we were absent, but he forced his way into the house and made himself obnoxious to the señorita. This Señor Zorro came in and forced the captain to apologize and then drove him away."

"Well, that is what I call a pretty bandit!" Don Diego exclaimed. "The *señorita* suffers from the experience?"

"Indeed, no," said Doña Catalina. "She was of the opinion that Captain Ramón had taken too much wine. I shall call her."

Doña Catalina went to the door of the chamber and called her daughter, and Lolita came into the room and greeted Don Diego as became a proper maiden.

"It makes me desolate to know that you received an insult in my house," Don Diego said. "I shall consider the affair."

Doña Catalina made a motion to her husband, and they went to a far corner to sit, that the young folk might be somewhat alone, which seemed to please Don Diego, but not the *señorita*.

XIX. Captain Ramón Apologizes

"Captain Ramón is a beast!" the girl said in a voice not too loud.

"He is a worthless fellow," Don Diego agreed.

"He—that is—he wished to kiss me," she said.

"And you did not let him, of course."

"*Señor!*"

"I—confound it, I did not mean that. Certainly you did not let him. I trust that you slapped his face."

"I did," said the *señorita*. "And then he struggled with me, and he told me that I should not be so particular, since I was daughter of a man who stood in the bad graces of the governor."

"Why, the infernal brute!" Don Diego exclaimed.

"Is that all you have to say about it, *caballero?*"

"I cannot use oaths in your presence, of course."

"Do you do not understand, *señor?* This man came into your house, and insulted the girl you have asked to be your wife!"

"Confound the rascal! When next I see his excellency, I shall ask him to remove the officer to some other post."

"Oh!" the girl cried. "Have you no spirit at all? Have him removed? Were you a proper man, Don Diego, you would go to the *presidio*, you would call this Captain Ramón to account, you would pass your sword through his body and call upon all to witness that a man could not insult the *señorita* you admired and escape the consequences."

"It is such an exertion to fight," he said. "Let us not speak of violence. Perhaps I shall see the fellow and rebuke him."

"Rebuke him!" the girl cried.

"Let us talk of something else, *señorita*. Let us speak of the matter regarding which I talked the other day. My father will be after me again soon to know when I am going to take a wife. Cannot we get the matter settled in some manner? Have you decided upon the day?"

"I have not said that I would marry you," she replied.

"Why hold off?" he questioned. "Have you looked at my house? I shall make it satisfactory to you I am sure. You shall refurnish it to suit your taste, though I pray you do not disturb it too much, for I dislike to have things in a mess. You shall have a new carriage and anything you may desire."

"Is this your manner of wooing?" she asked, glancing at him from the corners of her eyes.

"What a nuisance to woo," he said. "Must I play a guitar, and make pretty speeches? Can you not give me your answer without all that foolishness?"

She was comparing this man beside her with Señor Zorro, and Don Diego did not compare to him favorably. She wanted to be done with this farce, to have Don Diego out of her vision, and none but Señor Zorro in it.

"I must speak frankly to you, *caballero*," she said. "I have searched my heart, and in it I find no love for you. I am sorry, for I know what our marriage would mean to my parents, and to myself in a financial way. But I cannot wed you, Don Diego, and it is useless for you to ask."

"Well, by the saints! I had thought it was about all settled," he said. "Do you hear that, Don Carlos? Your daughter says she cannot wed with me—that it is not in her heart to do so."

"Lolita, retire to your chamber!" Doña Catalina exclaimed.

The girl did so gladly. Don Carlos and his wife hurried across the room and sat down beside Don Diego.

"I fear you do not understand women, my friend," Don Carlos said. "Never must you take a woman's answer for the last. She always may change her mind. A woman likes to keep a man dangling, likes to make him blow cold with fear and hot with anticipation. Let her have her moods, my friend. In the end, I am sure, you shall have your way."

"It is beyond me!" Don Diego cried. "What shall I do now? I told her I would give her all her heart desired."

"Her heart desires love, I suppose," Doña Catalina said, out of the wealth of her woman's wisdom.

"But certainly I shall love and cherish her. Does not a man promise that in the ceremony? Would a Vega break his word regarding such a thing?"

"Just a little courtship," Don Carlos urged.

"But it is such a nuisance."

"A few soft words, a pressure of the hand now and then, a sigh or two, a languishing look from the eyes—"

"Nonsense!"

"It is what a maiden expects. Speak not of marriage for some time. Let the idea grow on her—"

"But my august father is liable to come to the *pueblo* any day and ask when I am to take a wife. He has rather ordered me to do it."

"No doubt your father will understand," said Don Carlos. "Tell him that her mother and myself are on your side and that you are enjoying the pleasure of winning the girl."

"I believe we should return to the *hacienda* tomorrow," Doña Catalina put in. "Lolita has seen this splendid house, and she will contrast it with ours. She will realize what it means to marry you. And there is an ancient saying that when a man and a maid are apart they grow fonder of each other."

"I do not wish to have you hurry away."

"I think it would be best under the circumstances. And do you ride out, say in three days *caballero*, and I doubt not you will find her more willing to listen to your suit."

"I presume you know best," Dom Diego said. "But you must remain at least until tomorrow. And now I think I shall got to the *presidio* and see this Captain Ramón. Possibly that will please the *señorita*. She appears to think I should call him to account."

Don Carlos thought that such a course would prove disastrous for a man who did not practice with the blade and knew little of fighting, but he refrained from saying so. A gentleman never intruded his own thoughts at such a time. Even if a *caballero* went to his death, it was all right so long as he believed he was doing the proper thing, and died as a *caballero* should.

So Don Diego went from the house and walked slowly up thought of coming to combat with such a man.

But he was cold courtesy itself when Don Diego was ushered into the *comandante*'s office.

Don Diego bowed in answer, and the chair Ramón indicated. The captain marveled that Don Diego had no blade at his side.

"I was forced to climb your confounded hill to speak to you on a certain matter," Don Diego said. "I have been informed that you visited my house during my absence, and insulted a young lady who is my guest."

"Indeed?" the captain said.

"Were you deep in wine?"

"*Señor*?"

"That would excuse the offense in part, of course. And then you were wounded, and probably in a fever. Were you in a fever, captain?"

"Undoubtedly," Ramón said.

"A fever is an awful thing—I had a siege of it once. But you should not have intruded upon the *señorita*. Not only did you affront her, but you affronted me. I have asked the *señorita* to become my wife. The matter—er—is not settled as yet, but I have some rights in this case."

"I entered your house seeking news of this Señor Zorro," the captain lied.

"You—er—found him?" Don Diego asked.

The face of the *comandante* flushed red.

"The fellow was there and he attacked me," he replied. "I was wounded, of course, and wore no weapon, and so he could work his will with me."

"It is a most remarkable thing," observed Don Diego, "that none of you soldiers can meet this Curse of Capistrano when you can be on equal terms. Always he descends upon you when you are helpless, or threatens you with a pistol while he fights you with a blade, or has his score of men about him.

"I met Sergeant Gonzales and his men at the *hacienda* of Fray Felipe last night, and the big sergeant told some harrowing tale of the highwayman and his score of men scattering his troopers."

"We shall get him yet," the captain promised. "And I might call your attention to certain significant things, *caballero*. Don Carlos Pulido, as we know, does not stand high with those in authority. This Señor Zorro was at the Pulido *hacienda*, you will remember, and attacked me there, emerging from a closet to do it."

"Ha! What mean you?"

"Again, on last night, he was in your house while you were abroad and the Pulidos were your guests. It begins to look as if Don Carlos has a hand in the work of the Señor Zorro. I am almost convinced that Don Carlos is a traitor and is aiding the rogue. You had better think twice, or half a score of times, before seeking a matrimonial alliance with the daughter of such a man."

"By the saints, what a speech!" Don Diego exclaimed, as if in admiration. "You have made my poor head ring with it. You really believe all this?"

"I do, *caballero*."

"Well, the Pulidos are returning to their own place tomorrow, I believe. I but asked them to be my guests so they could be away from the scenes of this Señor Zorro's deeds."

"And Señor Zorro followed them to the *pueblo*. You see?"

"Can it be possible?" Don Diego gasped. "I must consider the matter. Oh, these turbulent times! But they are returning to their *hacienda* tomorrow. Of course I would not have his excellency think that I harbored a traitor."

He got to his feet, bowed courteously, and then stepped slowly toward the door. And there he seemed to remember something suddenly and turned to face the captain again.

"Ha! I am at the point of forgetting all about the insult!" he exclaimed. "What have you to say, my captain, regarding the events of last night?"

"Of course, *caballero*, I apologize to you most humbly," Captain Ramón replied.

"I suppose that I must accept your apology. But please do not let such a thing happen again. You frightened my *despensero* badly, and he is an excellent servant."

Then Don Diego Vega bowed again and left the presidio, and Captain Ramón laughed long and loudly, until the sick men in the hospital room feared that their *comandante* must have lost his wits.

"What a man!" the captain exclaimed. "I have turned him away from that Pulido *señorita*, I think. And I was a fool to hint to the governor that he could be capable of treason. I must rectify that matter in some way. The man has not enough spirit to be a traitor!"

XX. DON DIEGO SHOWS INTEREST

The threatened rain did not come that day nor that night, and the following morning found the sun shining brightly and the sky blue and the scent of blossoms in the air.

Soon after the morning meal, the Pulido *carreta* was driven to the front of the house by Don Diego's servants, and Don Carlos and his wife and daughter prepared to depart for their own *hacienda*.

"It desolates me," Don Diego said at the door, "that there can be no match between the *señorita* and myself. What shall I say to my father?"

"Do not give up hope, *caballero*," Don Carlos advised him. "Perhaps when we are home again, and Lolita contrasts our humble abode with your magnificence here, she will change her mind. A woman changes her mind, *caballero*, as often as she does the method of doing her hair."

"I had thought all would be arranged before now," Don Diego said. "You think there is still hope?"

"I trust so," Don Carlos said, but he doubted it, remembering the look that had been in the *señorita*'s face. However, he intended having a serious talk with her once they were home, and possibly might decide to insist on obedience even in this matter of taking a mate.

So the usual courtesies were paid, and then the lumbering *carreta* was driven away, and Don Diego Vega turned back into his house with his head hanging upon his breast, as it always hung when he did himself the trouble to think.

Presently he decided that he needed companionship for the moment, and left the house to cross the plaza and enter the tavern. The fat landlord rushed to greet him, conducted him to a choice seat near a window, and fetched wine without being commanded to do so.

Don Diego spent the greater part of an hour looking through the window at the plaza, watching men and women come and go, observing the toiling natives, and now and then glancing up the trail that ran toward the San Gabriel road.

Down this trail, presently, he observed approaching two mounted men, and between their horses walked a third man, and Don Diego could see that ropes ran from this man's waist to the saddles of the horsemen.

"What, in the name of the saints, have we here?" he exclaimed, getting up from the bench and going closer to the window.

"Ha!" said the landlord at his shoulder. "That will be the prisoner coming now."

"Prisoner?" said Don Diego, looking at him with a question in his glance.

"A native brought the news a short tune ago, *caballero*. Once more a *fray* is in the toils."

"Explain, fat one!"

"The man is to go before the *magistrado* immediately for his trial. They say that he swindled a dealer in hides, and now must pay the penalty. He wished his trial at San Gabriel, but that was not allowed, since all there are in favor of the missions and the *frailes*."

"Who is the man?" Don Diego asked.

"He is called Fray Felipe, *caballero*."

"What is this? Fray Felipe is an old man, and my good friend. I spent night before the last with him at the *hacienda* he manages."

"No doubt he has imposed upon you, *caballero*, as upon others," the landlord said.

Don Diego showed some slight interest now. He walked briskly from the tavern and went to the office of the *magistrado* in a little adobe building on the opposite side of the plaza. The horsemen were just arriving with their prisoner. They were two soldiers who had been stationed at San Gabriel, the *frailes* having been forced to give them bed and board in the governor's name.

It was Fray Felipe. He had been forced to walk the entire distance fastened to the saddles of his guards, and there were indications that the horsemen had galloped now and then to test the *fray*'s powers of endurance.

Fray Felipe's gown was almost in rags, and was covered with dust and perspiration. Those who crowded around him now gave him jeers and coarse jests, but the *fray* held his head proudly and pretended not to see or hear them.

The soldiers dismounted and forced him into the *magistrado*'s office, and the loiterers and natives crowded forward and through the door. Don Diego hesitated a moment, and then stepped toward the door. "One side, scum!" he cried; and the natives gave way before him.

He entered and pressed through the throng. The *magistrado* saw him and beckoned him to a front seat. But Don Diego did not care to sit at that time.

"What is this we have here?" he demanded. "This is Fray Felipe, a godly man and my friend."

"He is a swindler," one of the soldiers retorted.

"If he is, then we can put our trust in no man," Don Diego observed.

"All this is quite irregular, *caballero*," the *magistrado* insisted, stepping forward. "The charges have been preferred, and the man is here to be tried."

Then Don Diego sat down, and court was convened.

The man who made the complaint was an evil-looking fellow who explained that he was a dealer in tallow and hides, and had a warehouse in San Gabriel.

"I went to the *hacienda* this *fray* manages and purchased ten hides of him," he testified. "After giving him the coins in payment and taking them to my storehouse, I found that the hides had not been cured properly. In fact they were ruined. I returned to the *hacienda* and told the *fray* as much, demanding that he return the money, which he refused to do."

"The hides were good," Fray Felipe put in. "I told him I would return the money when he returned the hides."

"They were spoiled," the dealer declared. "My assistant here will testify as much. They caused a stench, and I had them burned immediately."

The assistant testified as much.

"Have you anything to say, *fray*?" the *magistrado* asked.

"It will avail me nothing," Fray Felipe said. "I already am found guilty and sentenced. Were I a follower of a licentious governor instead of a robed Franciscan, the hides would have been good."

"You speak treason?" the *magistrado* cried.

"I speak truth."

The *magistrado* puckered his lips and frowned.

"There has been entirely too much of this swindling," he said finally. "Because a man wears a robe he cannot rob with impunity. In this case, I deem it proper to make an example, that *frailes* will see they cannot take advantage of their calling.

"The *fray* must repay the man the price of the hides. And for the swindle he shall receive across his bare back ten lashes. And for the words of treason he has spoken, he shall receive five lashes additional. It is a sentence!"

XXI. THE WHIPPING

The natives jeered and applauded. Don Diego's face went white, and for an instant his eyes met those of Fray Felipe, and in the face of the latter he saw resignation.

The office was cleared, and the soldiers led the *fray* to the place of execution in the middle of the plaza. Don Diego observed that the *magistrado* was grinning, and he realized what a farce the trial had been.

"These turbulent times!" he said to a gentleman of his acquaintance who stood near.

They tore Felipe's robe from his back and started to lash him to the post. But the *fray* had been a man of great strength in his day, and some of it remained to him in his advanced years; and it came to him now what ignominy he was to suffer.

Suddenly he whirled the soldiers aside and stooped to grasp the whip from the ground.

"You have removed my robe!" he cried. "I am man now, not *fray*! One side, dogs!"

He lashed out with the whip. He cut a soldier across the face. He struck at two natives who sprang toward him. And then the throng was upon him, beating him down, kicking and striking at him, disregarding even the soldiers' orders.

Don Diego Vega felt moved to action. He could not see his friend treated in this manner despite his docile disposition. He rushed into the midst of the throng, calling upon the natives to clear the way. But he felt a hand grasp his arm, and turned to look into the eyes of the *magistrado*.

"These are no actions for a *caballero*," the judge said in a low tone. "The man has been sentenced properly. When you raise hand to give him aid, you raise hand against his excellency. Have you stopped to think of that, Don Diego Vega?"

Apparently Don Diego had not. And he realized, too, that he could do no good to his friend by interfering now. He nodded his head to the *magistrado* and turned away.

But he did not go far. The soldiers had subdued Fray Felipe by now and had lashed him to the whipping-post. This was added insult, for the post was used for none except insubordinate natives. The lash was swung through the air, and Don Diego saw blood spurt from Fray Felipe's bare back.

He turned his face away then, for he could not bear to look. But he could count the lashes by the singing of the whip through the air, and he knew that proud old Fray Felipe was making not the slightest sound of pain and would die without doing so.

He heard the natives laughing and turned back again to find that the whipping was at an end.

"The money must be repaid within two days, or you shall have fifteen lashes more," the *magistrado* was saying.

Fray Felipe was untied and dropped to the ground at the foot of the post. The crowd began to melt away. Two *frailes* who had followed from San Gabriel aided their brother to his feet and led him aside while the natives hooted. Don Diego Vega returned to his house.

"Send me Bernardo," he ordered his *despensero*.

The butler bit his lip to keep from grinning as he went to do as he was bidden. Bernardo was a deaf-and-dumb native servant for whom Don Diego had a peculiar use. Within the minute he entered the great living-room and bowed before his master.

"Bernardo, you are a gem," Don Diego said: "You cannot speak or hear, cannot write or read, and have not sense enough to make your wants known by the sign language. You are the one man in the world to whom I can speak without having my ears talked off in reply. You do not 'Ha!' me at every turn."

Bernardo bobbed his head as if he understood. He always bobbed his head in that fashion when Don Diego's lips ceased to move.

"These are turbulent times, Bernardo," Don Diego continued. "A man can find no place where he can meditate. Even at Fray Felipe's night before last there came a big sergeant pounding at the door. A man with nerves is in a sorry state. And this whipping of old Fray Felipe—Bernardo, let us hope that this Señor Zorro, who punishes those who work injustice, hears of the affair and acts accordingly."

Bernardo bobbed his head again.

"As for myself, I am in a pretty pickle," Don Diego went on. "My father has ordered that I get me a wife, and the *señorita* I selected will have none of me. I shall have my father taking me by the ear in short order.

"Bernardo, it is time for me to leave this *pueblo* for a few days. I shall go to the *hacienda* of my father, to tell him I have got no woman to wed me yet, and ask his indulgence. And there, on the wide hills behind his house, may I hope to find some spot where I may rest and consult the poets for one entire day without highwaymen and sergeants and unjust *magistrados* bothering me. And you, Bernardo, shall accompany me, of course. I can talk to you without your taking the words out of my mouth."

Bernardo bobbed his head again. He guessed what was to come. It was a habit of Don Diego's to talk to him thus for a long time, and always there was a journey afterward. Bernardo liked that, because he worshiped Don Diego, and because he liked to visit the *hacienda* of Don Diego's father, where he always was treated with kindness.

The *despensero* had been listening in the other room and had heard what was said, and now he gave orders for Don Diego's horse to be made ready and prepared a bottle of wine and water for the master to take with him.

Within a short time Don Diego set out, Bernardo riding mule a short distance behind him. They hurried along the highroad and presently caught up with a small *carreta*, beside which walked two robed Franciscans, and in which was Fray Felipe, trying to keep back moans of pain. Don Diego dismounted beside the *carreta* as it stopped. He went over to it and clasped Fray Felipe's hands in his own.

"My poor friend," he said.

"It is but another instance of injustice," Fray Felipe said. "For twenty years we of the missions have been subjected to it, and it grows. The sainted Junipero Serra invaded this land when other men feared, and at San Diego de Alcála he built the first mission of what became a chain, thus giving an empire to the world. Our mistake was that we prospered. We did the work, and others reap the advantages."

Don Diego nodded, and the other went on:

"They began taking our mission lands from us, lands we had cultivated, which had formed a wilderness and which my brothers had turned into gardens and orchards. They robbed us of worldly goods. And not content with that they now are persecuting us.

"The mission-empire is doomed, *caballero*. The time is not far distant when mission roofs will fall in and the walls crumble away. Some day people will look at the ruins and wonder how such a thing could come to pass. But we can do nought except submit. It is one of our principles. I did forget myself for a moment in the plaza at Reina de Los Angeles, when I took the whip and struck a man. It is our lot to submit."

"Sometimes," mused Don Diego, "I wish I were a man of action."

"You give sympathy, my friend, which is worth its weight in precious stones. And action expressed in a wrong channel is worse than no action at all. Where do you ride?"

"To the *hacienda* of my father, good friend. I must crave his pardon and ask his indulgence. He has ordered that I get me a wife, and I find it a difficult task."

"That should be an easy task for a Vega. Any maiden would be proud to take that name."

"I had hoped to wed with the Señorita Lolita Pulido, she having taken my fancy."

"A worthy maiden! Her father, too, has been subjected to unjust oppression. Did you join your family to his, none would dare raise hand against him."

"All that is very well, *fray*, and the absolute truth, of course. But the *señorita* will have none of me," Don Diego complained. "It appears that I have not dash and spirit enough."

"She is hard to please, perhaps. Or possibly she is but playing at being a coquette with the hope of leading you on and increasing your ardor. A maid loves to tantalize a man, *caballero*. It is her privilege."

"I showed her my house in the *pueblo* and mentioned my great wealth and agreed to purchase a new carriage for her," Don Diego told him.

"Did you show her your heart, mention your love, and agree to be a perfect husband?"

Don Diego looked at him blankly, then batted his eyes rapidly, and scratched at his chin, as he did sometimes when he was puzzled over a matter.

"What a perfectly silly idea!" he exclaimed after a time.

"Try it, *caballero*. It may have an excellent effect."

XXII. Swift Punishment

The *frailes* drove the cart onward, Fray Felipe raised his hand in blessing, and Don Diego Vega turned aside into the other trail, the deaf-and-dumb Bernardo following at his heels on the mule.

Back in the *pueblo*, the dealer in hides and tallow was the center of attraction at the tavern. The fat landlord was kept busy supplying his guest with wine, for the dealer in hides and tallow was spending a part of the money of which he had swindled Fray Felipe. The *magistrado* was spending the rest.

There was boisterous laughter as one recounted how Fray Felipe lay about him with the whip, and how the blood spurted from his old back when the lash was applied.

"Not a whimper from him!" cried the dealer in hides and tallow. "He is a courageous old coyote! Now, last month we whipped one at San Fernando, and he howled for mercy, but some men said he had been ill and was weak, and possibly that was so. A tough lot, those *frailes*! But it is great sport when we can make one howl. More wine, landlord! Fray Felipe is paying for it!"

There was a deal of raucous laughter at that, and the dealer's assistant, who had given perjured testimony, was tossed a coin and told to play a man and do his own buying. Whereupon the apprentice purchased wine for all in the inn, and howled merrily when the fat landlord gave him no change from his piece of money.

"Are you a *fray*, that you pinch coins?" the landlord asked.

Those in the tavern howled with merriment again, and the landlord, who had cheated the assistant to the limit, grinned as he went about his business. It was a great day for the fat landlord.

"Who was the *caballero* who showed some mercy toward the *fray*?" the dealer asked.

"That was Don Diego Vega," the landlord replied.

"He will be getting himself into trouble—"

"Not Don Diego," said the landlord. "You know the great Vega family, do you not, *señor*? His excellency himself curries their favor. Did the Vegas hold up as much as a little finger, there would be a political upheaval in these parts."

"Then he is a dangerous man?" the dealer asked.

A torrent of laughter answered him.

"Dangerous? Don Diego Vega?" the landlord cried, while tears ran down his fat cheeks. "You will be the death of me! Don Diego does nought but sit in the sun and dream. He scarcely ever wears a blade, except as a matter of show. He groans if he has to ride a few miles on a horse. Don Diego is about as dangerous as a lizard basking in the sun.

"But he is an excellent gentleman, for all that!" the landlord added hastily, afraid that his words would reach Don Diego's ears, and Don Diego would take his custom elsewhere.

It was almost dusk when the dealer in hides and tallow left the tavern with his assistant, and both reeled as they walked, for they had partaken of too much wine.

They made their way to the *carreta* in which they traveled, waved their farewells to the group about the door of the tavern, and started slowly up the trail toward San Gabriel.

They made their journey in a leisurely manner, continuing to drink from a jug of wine they had purchased. They went over the crest of the first hill, and the *pueblo* of Reina de Los Angeles was lost to view, and all they could see was the highway twisting before them like a great dusty serpent, and the brown hills, and a few buildings in the distance, where some main had his *hacienda*.

They made a turning and found a horseman confronting them, sitting easily in the saddle, with his horse standing across the road in such manner that they could not pass.

"Turn your horse—turn your beast!" the dealer in hides and tallow cried. "Would you have me drive over you?"

The assistant gave an exclamation that was part of fear, and the dealer looked more closely at the horseman. His jaw dropped; his eyes bulged.

"'Tis Señor Zorro!" he exclaimed. "By the saints! 'Tis the Curse of Capistrano, away down here near San Gabriel. You would not bother me, Señor Zorro? I am a poor man, and have no money. Only yesterday, a *fray* swindled me, and I have been to the Reina de Los Angeles seeking justice."

"Did you get it?" Señor Zorro asked.

"The *magistrado* was kind, *señor*. He ordered the *fray* to repay me, but I do not know when I shall get the money."

"Get out of the *carreta*, and your assistant also!" Señor Zorro commanded.

"But I have no money—" the dealer protested.

"Out of the *carreta* with you! Do I have to request it twice? Move, or lead finds a lodging-place in your carcass!"

Now the dealer saw that the highwayman held a pistol in his hand, and he squealed with sudden fright and got out of the cart as speedily as possible, his assistant tumbling out at his heels. They stood in the dusty highway before Señor Zorro, trembling with fear, the dealer begging for mercy.

"I have no money with me, kind highwayman, but I shall get it for you!" the dealer cried. "I shall carry it to where you say, whenever you wish—"

"Silence, beast!" Señor Zorro cried. "I do not want your money, perjurer! I know all about the farce of a trial at Reina de Los Angeles; I have ways of finding out about such things speedily.

"So the aged *fray* swindled you, eh? Liar and thief! 'Tis you who are the swindler. And they gave that old and godly man fifteen lashes across his bare back because of the lies you told. And you and the *magistrado* will divide the money of which you swindled him."

"I swear by the saints—"

"Do not! You have done enough false swearing already. Step forward!"

The dealer complied, trembling as if with a disease; and Señor Zorro dismounted swiftly and walked around in front of his horse. The dealer's assistant was standing beside the *carreta*, and his face was white.

"Forward!" Señor Zorro commanded again.

Again the dealer complied; but suddenly he began to beg for mercy, for Señor Zorro had taken a mule whip from beneath his long cloak, and held it ready in his right hand, while he held the pistol in his left.

"Turn your back!" he commanded now.

"Mercy, good highwayman! Am I to be beaten as well as robbed? You would whip an honest merchant because of a thieving *fray*."

The first blow fell, and the dealer shrieked with pain. His last remark appeared to have given strength to the highwayman's arm. The second blow fell, and the dealer in hides and tallow went to his knees in the dusty highroad.

Then Señor Zorro returned his pistol to his belt and stepped forward and grasped the dealer's mop of hair with his left hand, so as to hold him up, and with the right he rained heavy blows with the mule whip upon the man's back, until his tough coat and shirt were cut to ribbons, and the blood soaked through.

"That for a man who perjures himself and has an honest *fray* punished!" Señor Zorro cried.

And then he gave his attention to the assistant.

"No doubt, young man, you but carried out your master's orders when you lied before the *magistrado*," he said, "but you must be taught to be honest and fair, no matter what the circumstances."

"Mercy, *señor!*" the assistant howled.

"Did you not laugh when the *fray* was being whipped? Are you not filled with wine now because you have been celebrating the punishment that godly man received for something he did not do?"

Señor Zorro grasped the youth by the nape of his neck, whirled him around, and sent a stiff blow at his shoulders.; The boy shrieked and then began whimpering. Five lashes in all he received, for Señor Zorro apparently did not wish to render him unconscious. And finally he hurled the boy from I him, and looped his whip.

"Let us hope both of you have learned your lesson," he said. "Get into the *carreta* and drive on. And when you speak of this occurrence, tell the truth, else I hear of it and punish you again! Let me not learn that you have said some fifteen or twenty men surrounded and held you while I worked with the whip."

The apprentice sprang into the cart, and his master followed, and they whipped up and disappeared in a cloud of dust toward San Gabriel. Señor Zorro looked after them for a time, then lifted his mask and wiped the perspiration from his face, and then mounted his horse again, fastening the mule whip to the pommel of his saddle.

XXIII. More Punishment

Señor Zorro rode quickly to the crest of the hill beneath which was the *pueblo*, and there he stopped his horse and looked down at the village.

It was almost dark, but he could see quite well enough for his purpose. Candles had been lighted in the tavern; and from the building came the sounds of raucous song and loud jest. Candles were burning at the presidio, and from some of the houses came the odor of cooking food.

Señor Zorro rode on down the hill. When he reached the edge of the plaza he put spurs to his horse and dashed up to the tavern door, before which half a dozen men were congregated, the most of them under the influence of wine.

"Landlord!" he cried.

None of the men about the door gave him particular attention at first, thinking he was but some *caballero* on a journey wishing refreshment. The landlord hurried out, rubbing his fat hands together, and stepped close to the horse. And then he saw that the rider was masked, and that the muzzle of a pistol was threatening him.

"Is the *magistrado* within?" Señor Zorro asked.

"Si, *señor!*"

"Stand where you are and pass the word for him. Say there is a *caballero* here who wishes speech with him regarding a certain matter."

The terrified landlord shrieked for the *magistrado*, and the word was passed inside. Presently the judge came staggering out, crying in a loud voice to know who had summoned him from his pleasant entertainment.

He staggered up to the horse, and put one hand against it, and looked up to find two glittering eyes regarding him through a mask. He opened his mouth to shriek, but Señor Zorro warned him in time.

"Not a sound or you die!" he said. "I have come to punish you. Today you passed judgment on a godly man who was innocent. Moreover, you knew of his innocence, and his trial was but a farce. By your order he received a certain number of lashes. You shall have the same payment."

"You dare—"

"Silence!" the highwayman commanded. "You about the door there—come to my side!" he called.

They crowded forward, the most of them peons who thought that here was a *caballero* who wished something done and had gold to pay for it. In the dusk they did not see the mask and pistol until they stood beside the horse, and it was too late to retreat then.

"We are going to punish this unjust *magistrado*," Señor Zorro told them. "The five of you will seize him now and conduct him to the post in the middle of the plaza, and there you will tie him. The first man to falter receives a slug of lead from my pistol, and my blade will deal with the others. And I wish speed, also."

The frightened *magistrado* began to screech now.

"Laugh loudly, that his cries may not be heard," the highwayman ordered; and the men laughed as loudly as they could, albeit there was a peculiar quality to their laughter.

They seized the *magistrado* by the arms and conducted him to the post and bound him there with thongs.

"You will line up," Señor Zorro told them. "You will take this whip, and each of you will lash this man five times. I shall be watching, and if I see the whip fall lightly once I shall deal out punishment. Begin."

He tossed the whip to the first man, and the punishment began. Señor Zorro had no fault to find with the manner in which it was given, for there was great fear in the hearts of the *peons*, and they whipped with strength, and willingly.

"You, also, landlord," Señor Zorro said.

"He will put me in for it afterward," the landlord wailed.

"Do you prefer *carcel* or a coffin, *señor*?" the highwayman asked.

It became evident that the landlord preferred the *carcel*. He picked up the whip, and he surpassed the *peons* in the strength of his blows.

The *magistrado* was hanging heavily from the thongs now. Unconsciousness had come to him with about the fifteenth blow, more through fear than through pain and punishment.

"Unfasten the man," the highwayman ordered.

Two men sprang forward to do his bidding.

"Carry him to his house," Señor Zorro went on. "And tell the people of the *pueblo* that this is the manner in which Señor Zorro punishes those who oppress the poor and helpless, who give unjust verdicts, and who steal in the name of the law. Go your ways!"

The *magistrado* was carried away, groaning, consciousness returning to him now. Señor Zorro turned once more to the landlord.

"We shall return to the tavern," he said. "You will go inside and fetch me a mug of wine, and stand beside my horse while I drink it. It would be only a waste of breath for me to say what will happen to you if you attempt treachery on the way."

But there was fear of the *magistrado* in the landlord's heart as great as his fear of Señor Zorro. He went back to the tavern beside the highwayman's horse, and he hurried inside as if to get the wine. But he sounded the alarm.

"Señor Zorro is without," he hissed at those nearest the table. "He has just caused the *magistrado* to be whipped cruelly. He has sent me to get him a mug of wine."

Then he went on to the wine cask and began drawing the drink slowly as possible.

There was sudden activity inside the tavern. Some half-dozen *caballeros* were there, men who followed in the footsteps of the governor. Now they drew their blades and began creeping toward the door, and one of them who possessed a pistol and had it in his sash, drew it out, saw that it was prepared for work, and followed in their wake.

Señor Zorro, sitting his horse some twenty feet from the door of the tavern, suddenly beheld a throng rush out at him, saw the light flash from half a dozen blades, heard the report of a pistol, and heard a ball whistle past his head.

The landlord was standing in the doorway, praying that the highwayman would be captured, for then he would be given some credit, and perhaps the *magistrado* would not punish him for having used the lash.

Señor Zorro caused his horse to rear high in the air, and then raked the beast with the spurs. The animal sprang forward, into the midst of the *caballeros*, scattering them.

That was what Señor Zorro wanted. His blade already was out of its scabbard, and it passed through a man's sword arm, swung over and drew blood on another.

He fenced like a maniac, maneuvering his horse to keep his antagonists separated, so that only one could get at him at a time. Now the air was filled with shrieks and cries, and men came tumbling from the houses to ascertain the cause of the commotion. Señor Zorro knew that some of them would have pistols, and while he feared no blade, he realized that a man could stand some distance away and cut him down with a pistol ball.

So he caused his horse to plunge forward again, and before the fat landlord realized it, Señor Zorro was beside him and had reached down and grasped him by the arm. The horse darted away, the fat landlord dragging, shrieking for rescue and begging for mercy in the same breath. Señor Zorro rode with him to the whipping-post.

"Hand me that whip!" he commanded.

The shrieking landlord obeyed, and called upon the saints to protect him. And then Señor Zorro turned him loose, and curled the whip around his fat middle, and as the landlord tried to run he cut at him again and again. He left him once to charge down upon those who had blades and so scatter them, and then he was back with the landlord again, applying the whip.

"You tried treachery!" he cried. "Dog of a thief! You would send men about my ears, eh? I'll strip your tough hide—"

"Mercy!" the landlord shrieked, and fell to the ground.

Señor Zorro cut at him again, bringing forth a yell more than blood. He wheeled his horse and darted at the nearest of his foes. Another pistol ball whistled past his head, another man sprang at him with blade ready. Señor Zorro ran the man neatly through the shoulder and put spurs to his horse again. He galloped as far as the whipping-post, and there he stopped his horse and faced them for an instant.

"There are not enough of you to make a fight interesting, *señores*!" he cried.

He swept off his sombrero and bowed to them in nice mockery, and then he wheeled his horse again and dashed away.

XXIV. At the *Hacienda* of Don Alejandro

Behind him he left a tumult in the town. The shrieks of the fat landlord had aroused the *pueblo*. Men came running, servants hurrying at their sides and carrying torches. Women peered from the windows of the houses. Natives stood still wherever they happened to be and shivered, for it had been their dear experience that whenever there was a tumult natives paid the price.

Many young *caballeros* of hot blood were there, and for some time there had been no excitement in the *pueblo* of Reina de Los Angeles. These young men crowded into the tavern and listened to the wails of the landlord, and some hurried to the house of the *magistrado* and saw his wounds, and heard him declaim on the indignity that had been offered the law, and therefore his excellency the governor.

Captain Ramón came down from the presidio, and when he heard the cause of the tumult he swore great oaths, and sent his only well man to ride along the Pala Road, overtake Sergeant Gonzales and his troopers, and bid them return and take the trail, since at the time being they were following a false scent.

But the young *caballeros* saw in this circumstance a chance for excitement that was to their liking, and they asked permission of the *comandante* to form a posse and take after the highwayman, a permission they received immediately.

Some thirty of them mounted horses, looked to weapons, and set out, with the intention of dividing into three bands of ten each when they came to forks in the trail.

The townsmen cheered them as they started, and they galloped rapidly up the hill and toward the San Gabriel road, making a deal of noise, glad that now there was a moon to let them see the foe when they approached him.

In time they separated, ten going toward San Gabriel proper, ten taking the trail that led to the *hacienda* of Fray Felipe, and the last ten following a road that curved down the valley to the neighborhood of a series of landed estates owned by wealthy dons of the day.

Along this road, Don Diego Vega had ridden some time before, the deaf-and-dumb Bernardo behind him on the mule. Don Diego rode with leisure, and it was long after nightfall when he turned from the main road and followed a narrower one toward his father's house.

Don Alejandro Vega, the head of the family, sat alone at his table, the remains of the evening meal before him, when he heard a horseman before the door. A servant ran to open it, and Don Diego entered, Bernardo following close behind him.

"Ah, Diego, my son!" the old don cried, extending his arms.

Don Diego was clasped for an instant to his father's breast, and then he sat down beside the table and grasped a mug of wine. Having refreshed himself, he faced Don Alejandro once more.

"It has been a fatiguing journey," he remarked.

"And the cause for it, my son?"

"I felt that I should come to the *hacienda*," Don Diego said. "It is no time to be in the *pueblo*. Wherever a man turns, he finds naught but violence and bloodshed. This confounded Señor Zorro—"

"Ha! What of him?"

"Please do not 'Ha!' me, sir and father. I have been 'Ha'd!' at from morning until night these several days. These be turbulent times.

"This Señor Zorro has made a visit to the Pulido *hacienda* and frightened everyone there. I went to my *hacienda* on business, and from there I went over to see old Fray Felipe, thinking I might get a chance to meditate in his presence. And who makes an appearance but a big sergeant and his troopers seeking this Señor Zorro."

"They caught him?"

"I believe not, sir and father. I returned to the *pueblo*; and what think you happened there this day? They brought in Fray Felipe, accused of having swindled a dealer, and after mockery of a trial they lashed him to a post and gave him the whip fifteen times across his back."

"The scoundrels!" Don Alejandro cried.

"I could stand it no longer, and so I decided to pay you a visit. Wherever I turn there is turmoil. It is enough to make a man insane. You may ask Bernardo if it is not."

Don Alejandro glanced at the deaf-and-dumb native and grinned. Bernardo grinned back as a matter of course, not knowing it was no manner in which to act in the presence of a don.

"You have something else to tell me?" Don Alejandro asked his son, looking at him searchingly.

"By the saints! Now it comes. I had hoped to avoid it, father and sir."

"Let me hear about it."

"I paid a visit to the Pulido *hacienda* and spoke with Don Carlos and his wife, also the Señorita Lolita."

"You were pleased with the *señorita*?"

"She is as lovely as any girl of my acquaintance," Don Diego said. "I spoke to Don Carlos of the matter of marriage, and he appeared to be delighted."

"Ah! He would be," said Don Alejandro.

"But the marriage cannot take place, I fear."

"How is this? There is some shadow concerning the *señorita*?"

"Not to my knowledge. She appears to be a sweet and innocent maiden, father and sir. I had them come to Reina de Los Angeles and spend a couple of days at my house. I had it arranged so that she could see the furnishings, and learn of my wealth."

"That was a wise arrangement, my son."

"But she will have none of me."

"How is this? Refuses to wed with a Vega? Refuses to become allied to the most powerful family in the country, with the best blood in the land?"

"She intimated, father and sir, that I am not the sort of man for her. She is prone to foolishness, I believe. She would have me play a guitar under her window, perhaps, and make eyes, and hold hands when her *dueña* is not looking, and all that silliness."

"By the saints! Are you a Vega?" Don Alejandro cried. "Would not any worthy man want a chance like that? Would not any *caballero* delight to serenade his love on a moonlight night? The little things you term silly are the very essence of love. I doubt not the *señorita* was displeased with you."

"But I did not see that such things were necessary," Don Diego said.

"Did you go to the *señorita* in a cold-blooded manner and suggest that you wed and have it done with? Had you the idea, young sir, that you were purchasing a horse or a bull? By the saints! And so there is no chance for you to wed the girl? She has the best blood by far, next to our own."

"Don Carlos bade me have hope," Diego replied. "He took her back to the *hacienda*, and suggested that perhaps when she had been there a time and had reflected she might change her mind."

"She is yours, if you play the game," Don Alejandro said. "You are a Vega, and therefore the best catch in the country. Be but half a lover, and the *señorita* is yours. What sort of blood is in your veins? I have half a mind to slit one of them and see."

"Cannot we allow this marriage business to drop for the time being?" Don Diego asked.

"You are twenty-five. I was quite old when you were born. Soon I shall go the way of my fathers. You are the only son, the heir, and you must have a wife and offspring. Is the Vega family to die out because your blood is water? Win you a wife within the quarter-year, young sir, and a wife I can accept into the family, or I leave my wealth to the Franciscans when I pass away!"

"My father!"

"I mean it! Get life into you! I would you had half the courage and spirit this Señor Zorro, this highwayman, has! He has principles and he fights for them. He aids the helpless and avenges the oppressed.

"I salute him! I would rather have you, my son, in his place, running the risk of death or imprisonment, than to have you a lifeless dreamer of dreams that amount to nought!"

"My father! I have been a dutiful son."

"I would you had been a little wild—it would have been more natural." Don Alejandro sighed. "I could overlook a few escapades more easily than I can lifelessness. Arouse yourself, young sir! Remember that you are a Vega.

"When I was your age, I was not a laughingstock. I was ready to fight at a wink, to make love to every pair of flashing eyes, to stand up to any *caballero* in sports rough or refined. Ha!"

"I pray you, do not 'Ha!' me, sir and father. My nerves are on edge."

"You must be more of a man!"

"I shall attempt it immediately," Don Diego said, straightening himself somewhat in his chair. "I had hoped to avoid it, but it appears that I cannot. I shall woo the Señorita Lolita as other men woo maidens. You meant what you said about your fortune?"

"I did," said Don Alejandro.

"Then I must bestir myself. It would never do, of course, to let that fortune go out of the family. I shall think these matters over in peace and quiet tonight. Perhaps I can meditate here, far from the *pueblo*. By the saints!"

The last exclamation was caused by a sudden tumult outside the house. Don Alejandro and his son heard a number of horsemen stop, heard their calls to one another, heard bridles jingling and blades rattling.

"There is no peace in all the world," Don Diego said with deepened gloom.

"It sounds like half a score of men," Don Alejandro said.

It was—exactly. A servant opened the door, and into the great room there strode ten *caballeros*, with blades at their sides and pistols in their belts.

"Ha, Don Alejandro! We crave hospitality!" the foremost cried.

"You have it without asking, *caballeros*. What manner of journey is this you take?"

"We pursue Señor Zorro, the highwayman."

"By the saints!" Don Diego cried. "One cannot escape it even here! Violence and bloodshed!"

"He invaded the plaza at Reina de Los Angeles," the spokesman went on. "He had the *magistrado* whipped because he sentenced Fray Felipe to receive the lash, and he whipped the fat landlord, and he fought half a score of men while he was about it. Then he rode away, and we made up a band to pursue him. He has not been in this neighborhood?"

"Not to my knowledge," Don Alejandro said. "My son arrived off the highway but a short time ago."

"You did not see the fellow, Don Diego?"

"I did not," Don Diego said. "That is one stroke of good fortune that came my way."

Don Alejandro had sent for servants, and now wine mugs were on the long table, and heaps of small cakes, and the *caballeros* began to eat and drink. Don Diego knew well what that meant. Their pursuit of the highwayman was at an end, their enthusiasm had waned. They would sit at his father's table and drink throughout the night, gradually getting intoxicated, shout and sing and tell stories, and in the morning ride back to Reina de Los Angeles like so many heroes.

It was the custom. The chase of Señor Zorro was but a pretext for a merry time.

The servants brought great stone jugs filled with rare wine and put them on the table, and Don Alejandro ordered that meat be fetched also. The young *caballeros* had a weakness for these parties at Don Alejandro's, for the don's good wife had been dead for several years, and there were no womenfolk except servants, and so they could make what noise they pleased throughout the night.

In time they put aside pistols and blades, and began to boast and brag, and Don Alejandro had his servants put the weapons in a far corner out of the way, for he did not wish a drunken quarrel, with a dead *caballero* or two in his house.

Don Diego drank and talked with them for a time, and then sat to one side and listened, as if such foolishness bored him.

"It were well for this Señor Zorro that we did not catch up with him," one cried. "Any one of us is a match for the fellow. Were the soldiers men of merit he would have been taken long before this."

"Ha, for a chance at him!" another screeched. "How the landlord did howl when he was whipped!"

"He rode in this direction?" Don Alejandro asked.

"We are not sure as to that. He took the San Gabriel trail, and thirty of us followed. We separated into three bands, each going a different direction. It is the good fortune of one of the other bands to have him now, I suppose. But it is our excellent good fortune to be here."

Don Diego stood before the company.

"*Señores*, you will pardon me, I know, if I retire," he said. "I am fatigued with the journey."

"Retire, by all means," one of his friends cried. "And when you are rested, come out to us again and make merry."

They laughed at that; and Don Diego bowed ceremoniously, and observed that several scarcely could get to their feet to bow in return; and then the scion of the house of Vega hurried from the room with the deaf-and-dumb man at his heels.

He entered a room that always was ready for him, and in which a candle already was burning, and closed the door behind him, and Bernardo stretched his big form on the floor just outside it, to guard his master during the night.

In the great living-room, Don Diego scarcely was missed. His father was frowning and twisting his mustache, for he would have had his son like other young men. In his youth, he was remembering, he never left such a company early in the evening. And once again he sighed and wished that the saints had given him a son with red blood in his veins.

The *caballeros* were singing now, joining in the chorus of a popular love song, and their discordant voices filled the big room. Don Alejandro smiled as he listened, for it brought his own youth back to him.

They sprawled on chairs and benches on both sides of the long table, pounding it with their mugs as they sang, laughing boisterously now and then.

"Were this Señor Zorro only here now!" one of them cried.

A voice from the doorway answered him.

"*Señores*, he is here!"

XXV. A League Is Formed

The song ceased; the laughter was stilled. They bunked their eyes and looked across the room. Señor Zorro stood just inside the door, having entered from the veranda without them knowing it. He wore his long cloak and his mask, and in one hand he held his accursed pistol, and its muzzle was pointed at the table.

"So these are the manner of men who pursue Señor Zorro and hope to take him," he said. "Make not a move, else lead flies. Your weapons, I perceive, are in the corner. I could kill some of you and be gone before you could reach them."

"'Tis he! 'Tis he!" a tipsy *caballero* was crying.

"Your noise may be heard a mile away, *señores*. What a posse to go pursuing a man! Is this the way you attend to duty? Why have you stopped to make merry while Señor Zorro rides the highway?"

"Give me my blade and let me stand before him!" one cried.

"If I allowed you to have blade, you would be unable to stand," the highwayman answered. "Think you there is one in this company who could fence with me now?"

"There is one!" cried Don Alejandro, in a loud voice, springing to his feet. "I openly say that I have admired some of the things you have done, *señor*; but now you have entered my house and are abusing my guests, and I must call you to account!"

"I have no quarrel with you, Don Alejandro, and you have none with me," Señor Zorro said. "I refuse to cross blades with you. And I am but telling these men some truths."

"By the saints, I shall make you!"

"A moment, Don Alejandro! *Señores*, this aged don would fight me, and that would mean a wound or death for him. Will you allow it?"

"Don Alejandro must not fight our battles!" one of them cried.

"Then see that he sits in his place, and all honor to him."

Don Alejandro started forward, but two of the *caballeros* sprang before him and urged him to go back, saying that his honor was safe, since he offered combat. Raging, Don Alejandro complied.

"A worthy bunch of young blades," Señor Zorro sneered. "You drink wine and make merry while injustice is all about you. Take your swords in hand and attack oppression! Live up to your noble names and your blue blood, *señores*! Drive the thieving politicians from the land! Protect the *frailes* whose work gave us these broad acres! Be men, not drunken fashion plates!"

"By the saints!" one cried and sprang to his feet.

"Back, or I fire! I have not come here to fight you in Don Alejandro's house. I respect him too much for that. I have come to tell you these truths concerning yourselves.

"Your families can make or break a governor! Band yourselves together in a good cause, *caballeros*, and make some use of your lives. You would do it, were you not afraid. You seek adventure? Here is adventure a plenty, fighting injustice."

"By the saints, it would be a lark!" cried one in answer.

"Look upon it as a lark if it pleases you, yet you would be doing some good. Would the politicians dare stand against you, scions of the most powerful families? Band yourselves together and give yourselves a name. Make yourselves feared the length and breadth of the land."

"It would be treason—"

"It is not treason to down a tyrant, *caballeros*! Is it that you are afraid?"

"By the saints—no!" they cried in chorus.

"Then make your stand!"

"You would lead us?"

"*Si, señores!*"

"But stay! Are you of good blood?"

"I am a *caballero*, of blood as good as any here," Señor Zorro told them.

"Your name? Where resides your family?"

"Those things must remain secrets for the present. I have given you my word."

"Your face—"

"Must remain masked for the time being, *señores*."

They had lurched to their feet now, and were acclaiming him wildly.

"Stay!" one cried. "This is an imposition upon Don Alejandro. He may not be in sympathy, and we are planning and plotting in his house—"

"I am in sympathy, *caballeros*, and give you my support," Don Alejandro said.

Their cheers filled the great room. None could stand against them if Don Alejandro Vega was with them. Not even the governor himself would dare oppose them.

"It is a bargain!" they cried. "We shall call ourselves the Avengers! We shall ride El Camino Real and prove terrors to those who rob honest men and mistreat natives! We shall drive the thieving politicians out!"

"And then you shall be *caballeros* in truth, knights protecting the weak," Señor Zorro said. "Never shall you repent this decision, *señores*! I lead, and I give you loyalty and expect as much. Also, I expect obedience to orders."

"What shall we do?" they cried.

"Let this remain a secret. In the morning return to Reina de Los Angeles and say you did not find Señor Zorro—say rather that you did not catch him, which will be the truth. Be ready to band yourselves together and ride. I shall send word when the time arrives."

"In what manner?"

"I know you all. I shall get word to one, and he can inform the others. It is agreed?"

"Agreed!" they shouted.

"Then I will leave you here and now. You are to remain in this room, and none is to try to follow me. It is a command. *Buenos noches, caballeros!*" He bowed before them, swung the door open, and darted through it and slammed it shut behind him.

They could hear the clatter of a horse's hoofs on the driveway. And then they raised their wine mugs and drank to their new league for the suppression of swindlers and thieves and to Señor Zorro, the Curse of Capistrano, and to Don Alejandro Vega, somewhat sobered by the agreement they had made and what it meant. They sat down again and began speaking of wrongs that should be righted, each of them knowing half a dozen.

And Don Alejandro Vega sat in one corner, by himself, a grief-stricken man because his only son was asleep in the house and had not red blood enough to take a part in such an undertaking, when by all rights, he should be one of the leaders.

As if to add to his misery, Don Diego at that moment came slowly into the room, rubbing his eyes and yawning and looking as if he had been disturbed.

"It is impossible for a man to sleep in this house tonight," he said. "Give me a mug of wine, and I shall take my place with you. Why was the cheering?"

"Señor Zorro has been here—" his father began.

"The highwayman? Been here? By the saints! It is as much as a man can endure."

"Sit down, my son," Don Alejandro urged. "Certain things have come to pass. There will be a chance now for you to show what sort of blood flows in your veins."

Don Alejandro's manner was very determined.

XXVI. An Understanding

The remainder of the night spent by the *caballeros* in loud boasts of what they intended doing, and in making plans to be submitted to Señor Zorro for his approval; and, though they appeared to look upon this thing as a lark and a means to adventure, yet there was an undercurrent of seriousness in their manner. For they knew well the state of the times and realized that things were not as they should be, and in reality they were exponents of fairness to all; they had thought of these things often, but had made no move because they had not been banded together and had no leader, and each young *caballero* waited for another to start the thing. But now this Señor Zorro had struck at the psychological moment, and things could be done.

Don Diego was informed of the state of affairs, and his father informed him, likewise, that he was to play a part and prove himself a man. Don Diego fumed considerably and declared that such a thing would cause his death, yet he would do it for his father's sake.

Early in the morning the *caballeros* ate a meal that Don Alejandro caused to be prepared, and then they started back to Reina de Los Angeles, Don Diego riding with them at his father's order. Nothing was to be said about their plans. They were to get recruits from the remainder of the thirty who had set out in pursuit of Señor Zorro. Some would join them readily, they knew, while others were the governor's men pure and simple, and would have to be kept in the dark concerning the thing contemplated.

They rode leisurely, for which Don Diego remarked that he was grateful. Bernardo was still following him on the mule, and was a little chagrined because Don Diego had not remained longer at his father's house. Bernardo knew something momentous was being planned, but could not guess what, of course, and wished that he was like other men, and could hear and speak.

When they reached the plaza, they found that the other two parties already were there, saying that they had not come up with the highwayman. Some declared that they had seen him in the distance, and one that he had fired a pistol at him, at which the *caballeros* who had been at Don Alejandro's put their tongues in their cheeks and looked at one another in a peculiar manner.

Don Diego left his companions and hurried to his house, where he donned fresh clothing and refreshed himself generally. He sent Bernardo about his business, which was to sit in the kitchen and await his master's call. And then he ordered his carriage around. That carriage was one of the most gorgeous along El Camino Real, and why Don Diego had purchased it had always been a mystery. There were some who said he did it to show his wealth, while others declared a manufacturer's agent had worried him so much that Don Diego had given him the order to be rid of him.

Don Diego came from his house dressed in his best; but he did not get into the carriage. Again there was a tumult in the plaza, and into it rode Sergeant Pedro Gonzales and his troopers. The man Captain Ramón had sent after them had overtaken them easily, for they had been riding slowly and had not covered many miles.

"Ha, Don Diego, my friend!" Gonzales cried. "Still living! in this turbulent world?"

"From necessity," Don Diego replied. "Did you capture this Señor Zorro?"

"The pretty bird escaped us, *caballero*. It appears that he turned toward San Gabriel that night, while we went chasing him toward Pala. Ah, well, 'tis nothing to make a small mistake. Our revenge shall be the greater when we find him."

"What do you now, my sergeant?"

"My men refresh themselves, and then we ride toward San Gabriel. It is said the highwayman is in that vicinity, though some thirty young men of blood failed to find him last night after he had caused the *magistrado* to be whipped. No doubt he hid himself in the brush and chuckled when the *caballeros* rode by."

"May your horse have speed and your sword-arm strength," Don Diego said and got into his carriage.

Two magnificent horses were hitched to the carriage, and a native coachman in rich livery drove them. Don Diego stretched back on the cushions and half closed his eyes as the carriage started. The driver went across the plaza and turned into the highway and started toward the *hacienda* of Don Carlos Pulido.

Sitting on his veranda, Don Carlos saw the gorgeous carriage approaching, and growled low down in his throat, and then got up and hurried into the house, to face his wife and daughter.

"*Señorita*, Don Diego comes," he said. "I have spoken words regarding the young man, and I trust that you have given heed to them as a dutiful daughter should."

Then he turned and went out to the veranda again, and the *señorita* rushed into her room and threw herself upon a couch to weep. The saints knew she wished that she could feel some love for Don Diego and take him for a husband, for it would help her father's fortunes, yet she felt that she could not.

Why did not the man act the *caballero*? Why did he not exhibit a certain measure of common sense? Why did he not show that he was a young man bursting with health, instead of acting like an aged don with one foot in the grave?

Don Diego got from the carriage and waved to the driver to continue to the stable yard. He greeted Don Carlos languidly, and Don Carlos was surprised to note that Don Diego had a guitar beneath one arm. He put the guitar down on the floor, removed his sombrero, and sighed.

"I have been out to see my father," he said.

"Ha! Don Alejandro is well, I hope?"

"He is in excellent health, as usual. He has instructed me to persist in my suit for the Señorita Lolita's hand. If I do not win me a wife within a certain time, he says, he will give his fortune to the Franciscans when he passes away."

"Indeed?"

"He said it, and my father is not a man to waste his words. Don Carlos, I must win the *señorita*. I know of no other young woman who would be as acceptable to my father as a daughter-in-law."

"A little wooing, Don Diego, I beg of you. Be not so matter-of-fact, I pray."

"I have decided to woo as other men, though it no doubt will be much of a bore. How would you suggest that I start?"

"It is difficult to give advice in such a case," Don Carlos replied, trying desperately to remember how he had done it when he had courted Doña Catalina. "A man really should be experienced, else be a man to whom such things come naturally."

"I fear I am neither," Don Diego said, sighing again and raising tired eyes to Don Carlos's face.

"It might be an excellent thing to regard the *señorita* as if you adored her. Say nothing about marriage at first, but speak rather of love. Try to talk in low, rich tones, and say those meaningless nothings in which a young woman can find a world of meaning. 'Tis a gentle art—saying one thing and meaning another."

"I fear that it is beyond me," Don Diego said. "Yet I must try, of course. I may see the *señorita* now?"

Don Carlos went to the doorway and called his wife and daughter, and the former smiled upon Don Diego in encouragement, and the latter smiled also, yet with fear and trembling. For she had given her heart to the unknown Señor! Zorro, and could love no other man, and could not wed where she did not love, not even to save her father from poverty.

Don Diego conducted the *señorita* to a bench at one end of the veranda, and started to talk of things in general, plucking at the strings of his guitar as he did so, while Don Carlos and his wife removed themselves to the other end of the veranda and hoped that things would go well.

Señorita Lolita was glad that Don Diego did not speak of marriage as he had done before. Instead, he told of what had happened in the *pueblo*, of Fray Felipe's whipping, and of how Señor Zorro had punished the *magistrado*, and fought a dozen men, and made his escape. Despite his air of languor, Don Diego spoke in an interesting manner, and the *señorita* found herself liking him more than before.

He told, too, of how he had gone to his father's *hacienda*, and of how the *caballeros* had spent the night there, drinking and making merry; but he said nothing of Señor Zorro's visit and the league that had been formed, having taken his oath not to do so.

"My father threatens to disinherit me if I do not get my wife within a specified time," Don Diego said then. "Would you like to see me lose my father's estate, *señorita?*"

"Certainly not," she replied. "There are many girls who would be proud to wed you, Don Diego."

"But not you?"

"Certainly, I would be proud. But can a girl help it if her heart does not speak? Would you wish a wife who did not I love you? Think of the long years you would have to spend beside her, and no love to make them endurable."

"You do not think, then, that you ever could learn to love me, *señorita?*"

Suddenly the girl faced him and spoke in lower tones, and earnestly.

"You are a *caballero* of the blood, *señor*. I may trust you?"

"To death, *señorita*."

"Then I have something to tell you. And I ask that you let it remain your secret. It is an explanation in a way."

"Proceed, *señorita*."

"If my heart bade me do so, nothing would please me more than to become your wife, *señor*, for I know that it would mend my father's fortunes. But perhaps I am too honest to wed where I do not love. There is one great reason why I cannot love you."

"There is some other man in your heart?"

"You have guessed it, *señor*. My heart is filled with his image. You would not want me for wife in such case. My parents do not know. You must keep my secret. I swear by the saints that I have spoken the truth."

"The man is worthy?"

"I feel sure that he is, *caballero*. Did he prove to be otherwise, I should grieve my life away, yet I never could love another man. You understand now?"

"I understand fully, *señorita*. May I express the hope that you will find him worthy and in time the man of your choice?"

"I knew you would be the true *caballero*."

"And if things should go amiss, and you need a friend, command me, *señorita*."

"My father must not suspect at the present time. We must let him think that you still seek me, and I will pretend to be thinking more of you than before. And gradually you can cease your visits—"

"I understand, *señorita*. Yet that leaves me in bad case. I have asked your father for permission to woo you, and if I go to wooing another girl now, I will have him about my ears in just anger. And if I do not woo another girl, I shall have my own father upbraiding me. It is a sorry state."

"Perhaps it will not be for long, *señor*."

"Ha! I have it! What does a man do when he is disappointed in love? He mopes, he pulls a long face, he refuses to partake of the actions and excitements of the times. *Señorita*, you have saved me in a way. I shall languish because you do not return my love. Then men will think they know the reason when I dream in the sun and meditate instead of riding and fighting like a fool. I shall be allowed to go my way in peace, and there shall be a romantic glamour cast about me. An excellent thought!"

"*Señor*, you are incorrigible!" the Señorita Lolita exclaimed, laughing.

Don Carlos and Doña Catalina heard that laugh, looked around, and then exchanged quick glances. Don Diego Vega was getting along famously with the *señorita*, they thought.

Then Don Diego continued the deception by playing his guitar and singing a verse of a song that had to do with bright eyes and love. Don Carlos and his wife glanced at each other again, this time in apprehension, and wished that he would stop, for the scion of the Vegas had many superiors as musician and vocalist, and they feared that he might lose what ground he had gained in the *señorita*'s estimation.

But if Lolita thought little of the *caballero*'s singing, she said nothing to that effect, and she did not act displeased. There was some more conversation, and just before the *siesta* hour Don Diego bade them *buenos dias* and rode away in his gorgeous carriage. From the turn in the driveway, he waved back at them.

XXVII. ORDERS FOR ARREST

Captain Ramón's courier, sent north with the letter for the governor, had dreams of gay times in San Francisco de Asis before returning to his *presidio* at Reina de Los Angeles. He knew a certain *señorita* there whose beauty caused his heart to burn.

So he rode like a fiend after leaving his *comandante*'s office, changed mounts at San Fernando and at a *hacienda* along the way, and galloped into Santa Barbara a certain evening just at dusk, with the intention of changing horses again, getting meat and bread and wine at the *presidio*, and rushing on his way.

And at Santa Barbara his hopes of basking in the *señorita*'s smiles at San Francisco de Asis were cruelly shattered. For before the door of the *presidio* there was a gorgeous carriage that made Don Diego's appear like a *carreta*, and a score of horses were tethered there, and more troopers than were stationed at Santa Barbara regularly moved about the highway, laughing and jesting with one another.

The governor was in Santa Barbara.

His excellency had left San Francisco de Asis some days before on a trip of inspection, and intended to go as far south as San Diego de Alcála, strengthening his political fences, rewarding his friends, and awarding punishment to his enemies.

He had reached Santa Barbara an hour before, and was listening to the report of the *comandante* there, after which he intended remaining during the night with a friend. His troopers were to be given quarters at the *presidio*, of course, and the journey was to continue on the morrow.

Captain Ramón's courier had been told that the letter he carried was of the utmost importance, and so he hurried to the office of the *comandante* and entered it like a man of rank.

"I come from Captain Ramón, *comandante* at Reina de Los Angeles, with a letter of importance for his excellency," he reported, standing stiffly at salute.

The governor grunted and took the letter, and the *comandante* motioned for the courier to withdraw. His excellency read the letter with speed, and when he had finished there was an unholy gleam in his eyes, and he twirled his mustache with every evidence of keen satisfaction. And then he read the letter again and frowned.

He liked the thought that he could crush Don Carlos Pulido more, but he disliked to think that Señor Zorro, the man who had affronted him, was still at liberty. He got up and paced the floor for a time, and then whirled upon the *comandante*.

"I shall leave for the south at sunrise," he said. "My presence is urgently needed at Reina de Los Angeles. You will attend to things. Tell that courier he shall ride back with my escort. I go now to the house of my friend."

And so, in the morning, the governor started south, his escort of twenty picked troopers surrounding him, the courier in their midst. He traveled swiftly, and on a certain day at midmorning entered the plaza of Reina de Los Angeles unheralded. It was the same morning that Don Diego rode to the Pulido *hacienda* in his carriage, taking his guitar with him.

The cavalcade stopped before the tavern, and the fat landlord almost suffered an apoplexy because he had not been warned of the governor's coming and was afraid he would enter the inn and find it in a dirty state.

But the governor made no effort to leave his carriage and enter the tavern. He was glancing around the square, observing many things. He never felt secure concerning the men of rank in this *pueblo*; he felt that he did not have the proper grip on them.

Now he watched carefully as news of his arrival was spread and certain *caballeros* hurried to the plaza to greet him and make him welcome. He noted those who appeared to be sincere, observed those who were in no particular haste to salute him, and noticed that several were absent.

Business must receive his first attention, he told them, and he must hasten up to the *presidio*. After that he would gladly be the guest of any of them. He accepted an invitation and ordered his driver to proceed. He was remembering Captain Ramón's letter, and he had not seen Don Diego Vega in the plaza.

Sergeant Gonzales and his men were away pursuing Señor Zorro, of course, and so Captain Ramón himself was awaiting his excellency at the *presidio* entrance, and saluted him gravely, and bowed low before him and ordered the commander of the escort to take charge of the place and police it, stationing guards in honor of the governor.

He led his excellency to the private office, and the governor sat down.

"What is the latest news?" he asked.

"My men are on the trail, excellency. But, as I wrote, this pest of a Señor Zorro has friends—a legion of them, I take it. My sergeant has reported that twice he found him with a band of followers."

"They must be broken up, killed off!" the governor cried. "A man of that sort always can get followers, and yet more followers, until he will be so strong that he can cause us serious trouble. Has he committed any further atrocities?"

"He has, excellency. Yesterday a *fray* from San Gabriel was whipped for swindling. Señor Zorro caught the witnesses against him on the highroad, and whipped them almost to death. And then he rode into the *pueblo* just at dusk and had the *magistrado* whipped.

"My soldiers were away looking for him at the time. It appears that this Señor Zorro knows the movements of my force and always strikes where the troopers are not."

"Then spies are giving him warnings?"

"It appears so, excellency. Last night some thirty young *caballeros* rode after him but did not find track of the scoundrel. They returned this morning."

"Was Don Diego Vega with them?"

"He did not ride out with them, but he returned with them. It seems that they picked him up at his father's *hacienda*. You perhaps guessed that I meant the Vegas in my letter. I am convinced now, your excellency, that my suspicions in that quarter were unjust. This Señor Zorro even invaded Don Diego's house one night while Don Diego was away."

"How is this?"

"But Don Carlos Pulido and his family were there."

"Ha! In Don Diego's house? What is the meaning of that?"

"It is amusing," said Captain Ramón, laughing lightly. "I have heard that Don Alejandro ordered Don Diego to get him a wife. The young man is not the sort to woo women. He is lifeless."

"I know the man. Proceed."

"So he rides straightway to the *hacienda* of Don Carlos and asks permission to pay his addresses to Don Carlos's only daughter. Señor Zorro was abroad, and Don Diego, going to his own *hacienda* on business, asked Don Carlos to come to the *pueblo* with his family, where it would be safer, and occupy his house until he returned. The Pulidos could not refuse, of course. And Señor Zorro, it appears, followed them."

"Ha! Go on."

"It is laughable that Don Diego fetched them here to escape Señor Zorro's wrath, when, in reality, they are hand in glove with the highwayman. Remember, this Señor Zorro had been at the Pulido *hacienda*. We got word from a native, and almost caught him there. He had been eating a meal. He was hiding in a closet, and while I was alone there and my men searching the trails, he came from the closet, ran me through the shoulder from behind, and escaped."

"The low scoundrel!" the governor exclaimed. "But do you think there will be a marriage between Don Diego and the Señorita Pulido?"

"I imagine there need be no worry in that regard, excellency. I am of the opinion that Don Diego's father put a flea in his ear. He probably called Don Diego's attention to the fact that Don Carlos does not stand very high with your excellency, and that there are daughters of other men who do.

"At any rate, the Pulidos returned to their *hacienda* after Don Diego's return. Don Diego called upon me here at the *presidio* and appeared to be anxious that I would not think him a man of treason."

"I am glad to hear it! The Vegas are powerful. They never have been my warm friends, yet never have they raised hands against me, so I cannot complain. It is good sense to keep them friendly, if that be possible. But these Pulidos—"

"Even the *señorita* appears to be giving aid to this highwayman," Captain Ramón said. "She boasted to me of what she called his courage. She sneered at the soldiers. Don Carlos Pulido and some of the *frailes* are protecting the man, giving him food and drink, hiding him, sending him news of the troopers' whereabouts. The Pulidos are hindering our efforts to capture the rogue. I would have taken steps, but I thought it best to inform you and await your decision."

"There can be but one decision in such a case," said the governor loftily. "No matter how good a man's blood may be, or what his rank, he cannot be allowed to commit treason without suffering the consequences. I had thought that Don Carlos had learned his lesson, but it appears that he has not. Are any of your men in the *presidio*?"

"Some who are ill, excellency."

"That courier of yours returned with my escort. Does he know the country well hereabouts?"

"Certainly, excellency. He has been stationed here for some little time."

"Then he can act as guide. Send half my escort at once to the *hacienda* of Don Carlos Pulido. Have them arrest the don and fetch him to carcel and incarcerate him there. That will be a blow to his high blood. I have had quite enough of these Pulidos."

"And the haughty *doña*, who sneered at me, and the proud *señorita* who scorned the troopers?"

"Ha! It is a good thought. It will teach a lesson to all in this locality. Have them fetched to *carcel* and incarcerated also," the governor said.

XXVIII. The Outrage

Don Diego's carriage had just pulled up before his house when a squad of troopers went by it in a cloud of dust. He did not recognize any of them for men he had seen about the tavern.

"Ha! There are new soldiers on the trail of Señor Zorro?" he asked a man standing near.

"They are a part of the escort of the governor, *caballero*."

"The governor is here?"

"He arrived but a short time ago, *caballero*, and has gone to the presidio."

"I suppose they must have fresh news of this highwayman to send them riding furiously through dust and sun like that. He appears to be an elusive rascal. By the saints! Had I been here when the governor arrived, no doubt he would have put up at my house. Now some other *caballero* will have the honor of entertaining him. It is much to be regretted."

And then Don Diego went into the house, and the man who had heard him speak did not know whether to doubt the sincerity of that last remark.

Led by the courier, who knew the way, the squad of troopers galloped swiftly along the highroad, and presently turned up the trail toward Don Carlos's house. They went at this business as they would have gone about capturing a desperado. As they struck the driveway, they scattered to left and right, tearing up Doña Catalina's flower-beds and sending chickens squawking out of the way, and so surrounded the house in almost an instant of time.

Don Carlos had been sitting on the veranda in his accustomed place, half in a doze, and he did not notice the advance of the troopers until he heard the beating of their horses' hoofs. He got to his feet in alarm, wondering whether Señor Zorro was in the vicinity again and the soldiers after him.

Three dismounted in a cloud of dust before the steps, and the sergeant who commanded them made his way forward, slapping the dust-from his. uniform.

"You are Don Carlos Pulido?" he asked in a loud voice.

"I have that honor, *señor.*"

"I have orders to place you under military arrest."

"Arrest!" Don Carlos cried. "Who gave you such orders?"

"His excellency, the governor. He now is in Reina de Los Angeles, *señor.*"

"And the charge?"

"Treason and aiding the enemies of the state!"

"Preposterous!" Don Carlos cried. "I am accused of treason when, though the victim of oppression, I have withheld my hand against those in power? What are the particulars of the charges?"

"You will have to ask the *magistrado* that, *señor.* I know nothing of the matter except that I am to arrest you."

"You wish me to accompany you?"

"I demand it, *señor.*"

"I am a man of blood, a *caballero*—"

"I have my orders!"

"So I cannot be trusted to appear at my place of trial? But perhaps the hearing is to be held immediately. So much the better, for all the. quicker can I clear myself. We go to the *presidio?*"

"I go to the *presidio* when this work is done. You go to *carcel,*" the sergeant said.

"To *carcel?*" Don Carlos screeched. "You would dare? You would throw a *caballero* into the filthy jail? You would place him where they keep insubordinate natives and common felons?"

"I have my orders, *señor.* You will prepare to accompany us at once."

"I must give my superintendent instructions regarding the management of the *hacienda.*"

"I'll go along with you, *señor.*"

Don Carlos's face flamed purple. His hands clenched as he regarded the sergeant.

"Am I to be insulted with every word?" he cried. "Do you think I would run away like a criminal?"

"I have my orders, *señor,*" the sergeant said.

"At least I may break this news to my wife and daughter without an outsider being at my shoulder?"

"Your wife is Doña Catalina Pulido?"

"Certainly."

"I am ordered to arrest her also, *señor*."

"Scum!" Don Carlos cried. "You would put hands on a lady? You would remove her from her house?"

"It is my orders. She, too, is charged with treason and with aiding the enemies of the state."

"By the saints! It is too much! I shall fight against you and your men as long as there is breath in my body!"

"And that will not be for long, Don Carlos, if you attempt to give battle. I am but carrying out my orders."

"My beloved wife placed under arrest like a native wench! And on such a charge! What are you to do with her, sergeant?"

"She goes to *carcel*!"

"My wife in that foul place? Is there no justice in the land? She is a tender lady of noble blood!"

"Enough of this, *señor*. My orders are my orders, and I carry them out as instructed. I am a soldier and I obey."

Now Doña Catalina came running to the veranda, for she had been listening to the conversation just inside the door. Her face was white, but there was a look of pride in it. She feared Don Carlos might make an attack on the soldier, and she feared he would be wounded or slain if he did, and knew that at least it could only double the charge held against him.

"You have heard?" Don Carlos asked.

"I have heard, my husband. It is but more persecution. I am too proud to argue the point with these common soldiers, who are but doing as they have been commanded. A Pulido can be a Pulido, my husband, even in a foul *carcel*."

"But the shame of it!" Don Carlos cried. "What does it all mean? Where will it end? And our daughter will be here alone with the servants. We have no relatives, no friends—"

"Your daughter is Señorita Lolita Pulido?" the sergeant asked. "Then do not grieve, *señor*, for you will not be separated. I have an order for the arrest of your daughter, also."

"The charge?"

"The same, *señor*."

"And you would take her—"

"To *carcel*."

"An innocent, high-born, gentle girl?"

"My orders, *señor*," said the sergeant.

"May the saints blast the man who issued them!" Don Carlos cried. "They have taken my wealth and lands. They have heaped shame upon me and mine. But, thank the saints, they cannot break our pride!"

And then Don Carlos's head went erect, and his eyes flashed, and he took his wife by the arm and turned about to enter the house, with the sergeant at his heels. He broke the news to the Señorita Lolita, who stood as if stricken dumb for an instant, and then burst into a torrent of tears. And then the pride of the Pulidos came to her, and she dried her eyes, and curled her pretty lips with scorn at the big sergeant, and pulled aside her skirts when he stepped near.

Servants brought the *carreta* before the door, and Don Carlos and his wife and daughter got into it, and the journey of shame to the *pueblo* began.

Their hearts might be bursting with grief, but not one of the Pulidos showed it. Their heads were held high, they looked straight ahead, they pretended not to hear the low taunts of the soldiers.

They passed others, who were crowded off the road by the troopers, and who looked with wonder at those in the *carreta*, but they did not speak. Some watched in sorrow, and some grinned at their plight, according to whether those who passed were of the governor's party or of the honest folk who abhorred injustice.

And so, finally, they came to the edge of Reina de Los Angeles, and there they met fresh insult. For his excellency had determined that the Pulidos should be humbled to the dust; and he had sent some of his troopers to spread news of what was being done, and to give coins to natives and peons if they would jeer the prisoners when they arrived. For the governor wished to teach a lesson that would prevent other noble families from turning against him, and wished it to appear that the Pulidos were hated by all classes alike.

At the edge of the plaza they were met by the mob. There were cruel jeers and jests, some of which no innocent *señorita* should have heard. Don Carlos's face was red with wrath, and there were tears in Doña Catalina's eyes, and Señorita Lolita's lips were trembling, but they gave no other sign that they heard.

The drive around the plaza to the *carcel* was made slow purposely. At the door of the inn there was a throng of rascals who had been drinking wine at the expense of the governor, and these added to the din.

One man threw mud, and it splashed on Don Carlos's breast, but he refused to notice it. He had one arm around his wife, the other around his daughter, as if to give them what protection he could, and he was looking straight ahead.

There were some men of blood who witnessed the scene, yet took no part in the tumult. Some of them were as old as Don Carlos, and this thing brought to their hearts fresh, yet passive, hatred of the governor.

And some were young, with the blood running hot in their veins, and they looked upon the suffering face of Doña Catalina and imagined her their own mother, and upon the lovely face of the *señorita* and imagined her their sister or betrothed.

And some of these men glanced at one another furtively, and though they did not speak they were wondering the same thing—whether Señor Zorro would hear of this, and whether he would send word around for the members of the new league to gather.

The *carreta* stopped before the carcel finally, the mob of jeering natives and peons surrounding it. The soldiers made some pretense of holding them back, and the sergeant dismounted and forced Don Carlos and his wife and daughter to step to the ground.

Uncouth and intoxicated men jostled them as they walked up the steps to the door. More mud was thrown, and some of it spattered upon Doña Catalina's gown. But if the mob expected an outburst on the part of the aged *caballero*, it was disappointed. Don Carlos held his head high, ignoring those who were striving to torment him, and so led his ladies to the door.

The sergeant beat against it with the heavy hilt of his sword. An aperture was opened, and in it appeared the evil, grinning face of the jailer.

"What have we here?" he demanded.

"Three prisoners charged with treason," the sergeant replied.

The door was thrown open. There came a last burst of jeers from the mob, and then the prisoners were inside, and the door had been closed and bolted again.

The jailer led the way along an evil-smelling hall and threw open another door.

"In with you," he directed.

The three prisoners were thrust inside, and this door was closed and barred. They blinked their eyes in the semi-gloom. Gradually they made out two windows, some benches, some human derelicts sprawled against the walls.

They had not even been given the courtesy of a clean, private room. Don Carlos and his wife and daughter had been thrust in with the scum of the *pueblo*, with drunkards and thieves and dishonored women and insulting natives.

They sat down on a bench in one corner of the room, as far from the others as possible. And then Doña Catalina and her daughter gave way to tears, and tears streamed down the face of the aged don as he tried to comfort them.

"I would to the saints that Don Diego Vega were only my son-in-law now!" the don breathed.

His daughter pressed his arm.

"Perhaps—my father—a friend will come," she whispered. "Perhaps the evil man who caused this suffering will be punished."

For it seemed to the *señorita* that a vision of Señor Zorro had appeared before her; and she had great faith in the man to whom she had given her love.

XXIX. Don Pulido Feels Ill

One hour after Don Carlos Pulido and his ladies had been incarcerated in the *carcel*, Don Diego Vega, dressed most fastidiously, made his way slowly on foot up the slope to the *presidio* to make his call on his excellency, the governor.

He walked with swinging stride, gazing both to right and left as if at the hills in the distance, and once he stopped to observe a blossom that bloomed beside the path. His rapier was at his side, his most fashionable one with its jeweled hilt, and in his right hand he carried a handkerchief of flimsy lace, which he wafted this way and that like a dandy, and now and then touched it to the tip of his nose.

He bowed ceremoniously to two or three *caballeros* who passed him, but spoke to none beyond the necessary words of greeting, and they did not seek conversation with him. For, remembering that they had thought Don Diego Vega was courting the daughter of Don Carlos, they wondered how he would take the matter of her imprisonment along with her father and mother. They did not care to discuss the matter, for their own feelings were high, and they feared they might be betrayed into utterances that might be termed treasonable.

Don Diego came to the front door of the *presidio*, and the sergeant in charge called the soldiers to attention, giving Vega the salute due his station in life. Don Diego answered it with a wave of his hand and a smile, and went on to the *comandante*'s office, where the governor was receiving such *caballeros* as cared to call and express their loyalty.

He greeted his excellency with carefully chosen words, bowed over his hand, and then took the chair the governor was kind enough to indicate.

"Don Diego Vega," the governor said, "I am doubly glad that you have called upon me today, for in these times a man who holds high office would know his friends."

"I should have called sooner, but I was away from my house at the time you arrived," Don Diego said. "You contemplate remaining long in Reina de Los Angeles, excellency?"

"Until this highwayman, known as Señor Zorro, is either slain or taken," the governor said.

"By the saints! Am I never to hear the last of that rogue?" Don Diego cried. "I have heard of nothing else for these many days. I go to spend an evening with a *fray*, and in comes a crowd of soldiers chasing this Señor Zorro. I repair to the *hacienda* of my father to get me peace and quiet, and along comes a crowd of *caballeros* seeking news of Señor Zorro. These be turbulent times. A man whose nature inclines him to music and the poets has no right to exist in the present age."

"It desolates me that you have been annoyed," the governor said, laughing. "But I hope to have the fellow soon, and so put an end to that particular annoyance. Captain Ramón has sent for his big sergeant and his troopers to return. I brought an escort of twenty. And so we have ample men to run down this Curse of Capistrano when next he makes his appearance."

"Let us hope it will end as it should," said Don Diego.

"A man in high office has many things with which to contend," the governor went on. "Look at what I was forced to do this day. I am called upon to put in prison a man of good blood and his lady wife and tender daughter. But the state must be protected."

"I suppose you mean Don Carlos Pulido and his family?"

"I do, *caballero*."

"Now that it is called to my mind again, I must say a few words regarding that," Don Diego said. "I am not sure that my honor is not involved."

"Why, *caballero*, how can that be?"

"My father has ordered that I get me a wife and set up my establishment properly. Some days ago I requested of Don Carlos Pulido permission to pay my addresses to his daughter."

"Ha! I understand. But you are not the betrothed of the young lady?"

"Not yet, excellency."

"Then your honor is not involved, Don Diego, that I can see."

"But I have been paying court to her."

"You may thank the saints that it has gone no further, Don Diego. Think how it would look if you were allied with this family now! As for getting you a wife— come north with me to San Francisco de Asis, *caballero*, where the *señoritas* are far more lovely than here in your southland.

"Look over those of good blood, and let me know your preference, and I'll guarantee that the lady will listen to your suit and accept your hand and name. And I can guarantee, also, that she will be of a loyal family with which it will be no shame to make a contract. We shall get you a wife of the proper sort, *caballero*."

"If you will pardon me, is it not taking stern measures to have Don Carlos and his ladies thrown into the *carcel*?" Don Diego asked, flicking dust from his sleeve.

"I find it necessary, *señor*."

"Do you think it will add to your popularity, excellency?"

"Whether it does or not, the state must be served."

"Men of good blood hate to see such a thing, and there may be murmurings," Don Diego warned. "I should hate to lee your excellency make a wrong step at this juncture."

"What would you have me do?" the governor asked.

"Place Don Carlos and the ladies under arrest, if you will, but do not incarcerate them. It is unnecessary; they will not run away. Bring them to trial as gentle folk should be brought to trial."

"You are bold, *caballero*."

"By the saints, am I talking too much?"

"It were better to leave these matters to the few of us who are trusted with attention to them," the governor said. "I can understand, of course, how it irks a man of good blood to see a don thrown into a *carcel*, and to see his ladies treated likewise, but in such a case as this—"

"I have not heard the nature of the case," Don Diego said.

"Ha! Perhaps you may change your mind when you learn it. You have been speaking of this Señor Zorro. What if I tell you that the highwayman is being shielded and protected and fed by Don Carlos Pulido?"

"That is astonishing!"

"And that the Doña Catalina is a party to the treason? And that the lovely *señorita* has seen fit to talk treasonably and dip her pretty hands into a conspiracy against the state?"

"This is past belief!" Don Diego cried.

"Some nights ago Señor Zorro was at the Pulido *hacienda*. Warning was fetched the *comandante* by a native who is loyal. Don Carlos aided the bandit in tricking the soldiers, hid him in a closet, and when Captain Ramón was there alone, this highwayman stepped from the closet and attacked him treacherously and wounded him."

"By the saints!"

"And while you were gone and the Pulidos were your house guests, *señor*, Señor Zorro was in your house, speaking to the *señorita*, when the *comandante* walked in upon them. And the *señorita* grasped Captain Ramón by the arm and annoyed him until this Señor Zorro had made good his escape."

"It is past comprehension!" Don Diego exclaimed.

"Captain Ramón has placed before me a hundred such items of suspicion. Can you wonder now that I had them placed in *carcel*? Did I merely have them put under arrest, this Señor Zorro would combine forces with them and aid them to escape."

"And your intentions, excellency?"

"I shall keep them in *carcel* while my troopers run down this highwayman. I shall force him to confess and implicate them—and then they shall have a trial."

"These turbulent times!" Don Diego complained.

"As a loyal man—and I hope an admirer of mine—you should hope to see foes of the state confounded."

"I do! Most sincerely do I! All real foes of the state should receive punishment."

"I am joyed to hear you say that, *caballero!*" the governor cried, and he reached across the table and grasped Don Diego fervently by the hand.

There was some more talk that amounted to nothing, and then Don Diego took his leave, for there were other men waiting to see the governor. After he had left the office the governor looked across at Captain Ramón and smiled.

"You are right, *comandante*," he said. "Such a man could not be a traitor. It would tire him too much to think treasonable thoughts. What a man! He must be enough to drive that old fire-eater of a father of his insane."

Don Diego made his way slowly down the hill, greeting those he passed, and stopping again to regard the little flowers that blossomed by the wayside. At the corner of the plaza he met a young *caballero* who was glad to call him friend, one of the small band of men who had spent the night at Don Alejandro's *hacienda*.

"Ha! Don Diego, a fair day to you!" he cried. And then he lowered his voice and stepped nearer. "Has, by any chance, the man we call leader of our league of avengers, sent you a message this day?"

"By the bright blue sky—no!" Don Diego said. "Why should the man?"

"This Pulido business. It seems an outrage. Some of us have been wondering whether our leader does not intend to take a hand in it. We have been anticipating a message."

"By the saints! Oh, I trust not!" Don Diego said. "I could not endure an adventure of any sort tonight, I—er—my head aches, and I fear I am going to have a fever. I shall have to see an apothecary about it. There are shiverings up and down my spine, also. Is not that a symptom? During the siesta hour I was bothered with a pain in my left leg just above the knee. It must be the weather."

"Let us hope that it will not result seriously." His friend laughed and hurried on across the plaza.

XXX. THE SIGN OF THE FOX

An hour after dusk that night a native sought out one of the *caballeros* with the intelligence that a gentleman wished to speak to him immediately, and that this gentleman was evidently wealthy since he had given the native a coin for carrying the message, when he might just as well have given nothing more than a cuff alongside the head, also that the mysterious gentleman would be waiting along the path that ran toward the San Gabriel trail, and to be sure that the *caballero* would come he had bade the native say that there was a fox in the neighborhood.

"A fox! Zorro—fox!" the *caballero* thought, and then he ruined the native forever by giving him another coin.

He went to the rendezvous immediately, and there he found Señor Zorro sitting his big horse, his face masked, the cloak wrapped around his body.

"You will pass the word, *caballero*," Señor Zorro said. "I would have all men who are loyal and wish to do so, meet at midnight in the little valley beyond the hill. You know the place? So? I shall be waiting."

Then Señor Zorro wheeled his horse and dashed away in the darkness, and the *caballero* went back to the *pueblo* and passed the word to those men he knew could be depended upon, and urged upon them that they pass it to others of the league. One went to Don Diego's house, but was told by the *despensero* that Don Diego had complained of a fever and had retired to his chamber and had left word that he would flay alive any servant who dared enter the room unless he called.

Near the hour of midnight the *caballeros* began slipping from the *pueblo* one at a time, each upon the back of his best horse, and each armed with sword and pistol. Each man had a mask that could be put over his features instantly, for that had been decided upon at Don Alexandra's *hacienda*, among other things.

The *pueblo* was in darkness, save that there were lights in the tavern, where some of his excellency's escort made merry with the local troopers. For Sergeant Pedro Gonzales had returned with his men just before nightfall, glad to be bad from a fruitless chase and hoping that the next scent would be warmer.

Those in the tavern had gone down the hill from the *presidio*, some leaving their horses there without paddles or bridles on, and they had no thought of an encounter with Señor Zorro this night. The fat landlord was kept busy, for the soldiers from the north had coins in their purses and were willing to spend them. Sergeant Gonzales, holding the attention of the company as usual, was detailing at length what he would do to this Señor Zorro if the saints were kind enough to let them meet and grant him his blade in his hand.

There were lights in the big lounging-room of the *presidio*, too, for few of the soldiers had retired. And there were lights in the house where his excellency was a guest, but the remainder of the *pueblo* was in darkness, and the people slept.

In the *carcel* there was no light at all except one candle burning in the office, where a sleepy man was on guard. The jailer was in his bed. Prisoners moaned on the hard benches in the prison room. Don Carlos Pulido stood before a window, looking up at the stars; and his wife and daughter huddled on a bench beside him, unable to sleep in such surroundings.

The *caballeros* found Señor Zorro waiting for them as he had said he would be, but he remained aloof, speaking scarcely a word, until all were present.

"Are all here?" he asked then.

"All except Don Diego Vega," one replied. "He is ill with a fever, *señor*."

And all the *caballeros* chuckled, for they had an idea the fever was caused by cowardice.

"I take it that you know something of what is in my mind," Señor Zorro said. "We know what has happened to Don Carlos Pulido and the ladies of his family. We know they are innocent of any treason, and were they not, they should not have been taken to *carcel* and incarcerated with common felons and drunkards.

"Think of those gentle ladies in such surroundings! Think of it—because Don Carlos has the ill will of the governor! Is it the sense of the league that something be done in this matter? If it is not, then will I do something by myself!"

"Rescue them!" a *caballero* said; and others growled their approval. Here was a chance for risk and adventure and an opportunity to do a good deed.

"We must enter the *pueblo* quietly," Señor Zorro said. "There is no moon, and we will not be observed if we use caution. We shall approach the carcel from the south. Each man will have his task to do.

"Some will surround the building to give notice if any approach it. Others must be ready to beat off the soldiers, if they respond to an alarm. Others will effect an entrance to the *carcel* with me and rescue the prisoners."

"It is an excellent plan," one said.

"That is but a small part of it. Don Carlos is a proud man and, if given time for reflection, may refuse to be rescued. We cannot allow that. Certain ones will seize him and take him from the place. Others will attend to the Doña Catalina. I will undertake to care for the *señorita*. Now—we have them free. And then what?"

He heard murmurs, but no distinct reply, and so he continued to outline the plan.

"All will ride to the highway just below this place," he said. "At that point we shall scatter. Those who have the Doña Catalina in charge will hasten with her to the *hacienda* of Don Alejandro Vega, where she can be hidden if necessary, and where the governor's soldiers will hesitate before entering and seizing her.

"Those who have Don Carlos in charge will take the road to Pala, and at a certain point some ten miles from this *pueblo* they will be met by two natives of understanding, who will give the sign of the fox. The natives will take Don Carlos in charge and care for him.

"When these things are done, each *caballero* will ride to his home quietly and alone, telling what story pleases him and using great caution. I shall have conducted the *señorita* to a safe place by that time. She shall be given into the keeping of old Fray Felipe, a man we can trust, and he will hide her if he must. Then we will watch to see what the governor does."

"What can he do?" a *caballero* asked. "Have them searched for, of course."

"We must await developments," Señor Zorro said. "Are all now ready?"

They assured him that they were, and so he named the men for each task, and then they left the little valley and rode slowly and cautiously around the little town and approached it from the south.

They heard the soldiers shouting and singing in the tavern, saw the lights in the *presidio*, and crept toward the *carcel* quietly, riding two by two.

In a short time it had been surrounded by quiet, determined men, and then Señor Zorro and four others dismounted and went to the door of the building.

XXXI. The Rescue

Señor Zorro knocked upon the door with the hilt of his sword. They heard a man gasp inside, presently heard his steps on the stone flooring, and after a little time light showed through the cracks, and the aperture was opened, and the sleepy face of the guard appeared.

"What is wanted?" he asked.

Señor Zorro thrust the muzzle of his pistol through the aperture and into the man's face, and in such fashion that the little door could not be closed.

"Open, if you value your life! Open—and make not the slightest sound!" Señor Zorro commanded.

"What—what is this?"

"Señor Zorro is talking to you!"

"By the saints—"

"Open, fool, or you die instantly!"

"I—I'll open the door. Do not shoot, good Señor Zorro! I am only a poor guard and not a fighting man! I pray you do not shoot!"

"Open quickly!"

"As soon as I can fit key to lock, good Señor Zorro!"

They heard him rattling the keys; presently one was turned in the lock, and the heavy door was thrown open.

Señor Zorro and his four companions rushed inside and slammed and fastened the door again. The guard found the muzzle of a pistol pressed against the side of his head, and would have knelt before these five masked and terrible men, only one of them caught him by the hair and held him up.

"Where sleeps the keeper of this infernal hole?" Señor Zorro demanded.

"In yonder room, *señor*."

"And where have you put Don Carlos Pulido and his ladies?"

"In the common prison-room, *señor*."

Señor Zorro motioned to the others, strode across the room, and threw open the door to the jailer's chamber. The man already was sitting up in bed, having heard the sounds in the other room, and he blinked in fright when he beheld the highwayman by the light of the candle.

"Do not make a move, *señor*," Zorro warned. "One screech, and you are a dead man! Señor Zorro confronts you!"

"May the saints preserve me—"

"Where are the keys to the prison rooms?"

"On—on that table, *señor*."

Señor Zorro picked them up and then whirled upon the jailer again and rushed toward him.

"Lie down!" he commanded. "On your face, scoundrel!" Señor Zorro tore strips from a blanket and bound the jailer's hands and feet, and made a gag which he affixed.

"To escape death," he said then, "it is necessary for you to remain exactly as you are now, without making a sound, for some time after we have left the *carcel*. I shall leave it to your own judgment to decide the length of time."

Then he hurried back into the main office, beckoned the others, and led the way down the evil-smelling hall. "Which door?" he asked of the guard.

"The second one, *señor*."

They hurried to it, and Señor Zorro unlocked it and threw it open. He forced the guard to hold a candle high above his head.

A gasp of pity came from beneath the highwayman's mask He saw the aged don standing by the window, saw the two women crouched on the bench, saw the vile companions they had in this miserable place.

"Now may Heaven forgive the governor!" he cried. Señorita Lolita looked up in alarm, and then gave a glad cry. Don Carlos whirled at the highwayman's words.

"Señor Zorro!" he gasped.

"The same, Don Carlos. I have come with some friends to rescue you."

"I cannot allow it, *señor*. I shall not run away from what is in store for me. And it would avail me little to have you do the rescuing. I am accused now of harboring you, I understand. How will it look, then, if you effect my escape?"

"There is no time for argument," Señor Zorro said. "I am not alone in this, but have twenty-six men with me. And a man of your blood, and gentle ladies such as

those of your family, shall not spend an entire night in this miserable hole if we can prevent it. *Caballeros!*"

The last word was one of command. Two of the *caballeros* threw themselves upon Don Carlos, subdued him quickly, and half carried him into the hall and along it toward the office. Two others grasped the Doña Catalina by the arms, as gently as they could, and so carried her along.

Señor Zorro bowed before the *señorita* and extended a hand, which she clasped gladly.

"You must trust me, *señorita*," he said.

"To love is to trust, *señor*."

"All things have been arranged. Ask no questions, but do as I bid. Come!"

He threw an arm around her, and so led her from the prison room, leaving the door open behind him. If some of the miserable wretches there could win through and out of the building, Señor Zorro had no wish to prevent them. More than half of them, he judged, were there because of prejudice or injustice.

Don Carlos was causing an unearthly clamor, shouting that he refused to be rescued, and that he would stay and face the governor at the trial, and show the blood that was in him. Doña Catalina was whimpering a bit because of fright, but made no resistance.

They reached the office, and Señor Zorro ordered the guard to a corner of it, with instructions to remain there quietly for some time after they had gone. And then one of the *caballeros* threw open the outside door.

There was a tumult outside at that moment. Two soldiers had approached with a fellow caught stealing at the tavern, and the *caballeros* had stopped them. One glance at the masked faces had been enough to tell the troopers that here was something wrong.

A soldier fired a pistol, and a *caballero* answered the fire, neither hitting the mark. But the shooting was enough to attract the attention of those in the tavern, and also of the guards at the *presidio*.

Troopers at the *presidio* were awakened immediately and took the places of the guards, while the latter mounted and spurred down the hill to ascertain the cause of the sudden tumult at that hour of the night. Sergeant Pedro Gonzales and others hurried from the tavern. Señor Zorro and his companions found themselves facing a resistance when they least expected it.

The jailer had gathered courage enough to work himself free of gag and bonds, and he shrieked through a window of his chamber that prisoners were being rescued by Señor Zorro. His shriek was understood by Sergeant Gonzales, who screeched for his men to follow him and earn a part of his excellency's reward.

But the *caballeros* had their three rescued prisoners on horseback, and they spurred through the gathering throng and so dashed across the plaza and toward the highway.

Shots flew about them, but no man was hit. Don Carlos Pulido was still screaming that he refused to be rescued. Doña Catalina had fainted, for which the *caballero* who had her in charge was grateful, since he could give more attention to his horse and weapons.

Señor Zorro rode wildly with the Señorita Lolita in the saddle before him. He spurred his magnificent horse ahead of all the others, and so led the way to the highroad. And when he had reached it, he pulled up his mount and watched the others come galloping to the spot, to ascertain whether there I had been casualties.

"Carry out your orders, *caballeros*!" he commanded, when he saw that all had won through safely.

And so the band was broken into three detachments. One rushed along the Pala Road with Don Carlos. Another took the highway that would lead them to the *hacienda* of Don Alejandro. Señor Zorro, riding without any of his comrades at his side, galloped toward Fray Felipe's place, the *señorita*'s arms clasped tightly about his neck, and the *señorita*'s voice in his ear.

"I knew that you would come for me, *señor*," she said. "I knew you were a true man, and would not see me and my parents remain in that miserable place."

Señor Zorro did not answer her with words, for it was not a time for speech with his enemies so close at his heels, but his arm pressed the *señorita* closer to him.

He had reached the crest of the first hill, and now he stopped the horse to listen for sounds of pursuit, and to watch the flickering lights far behind.

For there was a multitude of lights in the plaza now, and in all the houses, for the *pueblo* had been aroused. The *presidio* building was ablaze with light, and he could hear a trumpet being blown, and knew that every available trooper would be sent on the chase.

The sound of galloping horses came to his ears. The troopers knew in what direction the rescuers had traveled; and the pursuit would be swift and relentless, with his excellency on the scene to offer fabulous rewards and urge on his men with promises of good posts and promotion.

But one thing pleased Señor Zorro as his horse galloped down the dusty highway and the *señorita* clung to him and the keen wind cut into his face—he knew that the pursuit would have to be divided into three parties.

He pressed the *señorita* to him again, put spurs to his horse, and rode furiously through the night.

XXXII. Close Quarters

Over the hills peeped the moon.

Señor Zorro would have had the sky heavy with clouds this night and the moon obscured, could he have had things his own way, for now he was riding along the upper trail, and his pursuers were close behind and could see him against the brightening sky.

The horses ridden, by the troopers were fresh, too, and the most of those belonging to the men of his excellency's escort were magnificent beasts, as swift as any in the country and able to endure many miles of travel at a terrific pace.

But now the highwayman thought only of getting all the speed possible out of his own mount and of making as great as he could the distance between himself and those who followed; for at the end of his journey he would need quite a little time, if he was to accomplish what he had set out to do.

He bent low over the *señorita* and felt his horse with the reins, making himself almost a part of the animal he rode, as any good horseman can. He reached the crest of another hill and glanced back before he began the descent into the valley. He could see the foremost of his pursuers.

Had Señor Zorro been alone, no doubt the situation would have caused him no uneasiness, for many times he had been in a position more difficult and had escaped. But the *señorita* was on the saddle before him now, and he wanted to get her to a place of safety, not only because she was the *señorita* and the woman he loved, but also because he was not the sort of man to let a prisoner he had rescued be recaptured. Such an event, he felt, would be a reflection on his skill and daring.

Mile after mile he rode, the *señorita* clinging to him, and neither speaking a word. Señor Zorro knew that he had gained some on those who followed, but not enough to suit his purpose.

Now he urged his horse to greater effort, and they flew along the dusty highway, past *haciendas* where the hounds barked in sudden alarm, past the huts of natives where the clamor of beating hoofs on the hard road caused bronze men and women to tumble from their bunks and rush to their doors.

Once he charged through a flock of sheep that were being driven to Reina de Los Angeles and the market there, and scattered them to either side of the road, leaving cursing herders behind him. The herders gathered the flock again, just in time to have the pursuing soldiers scatter it once more.

On and on he rode, until he could see, far ahead, the mission buildings at San Gabriel glistening in the moonlight. He came to a fork in the road and took the trail that ran to the right, toward the *hacienda* of Fray Felipe.

Señor Zorro was a reader of men, and he was trusting to his judgment tonight. He had known that the Señorita Lolita would have to be left either where there were women or else where there was a robed Franciscan to stand guard over her, for Señor Zorro was determined to protect his lady's good name. And so he was pinning his faith to old Fray Felipe.

Now the horse was galloping over softer ground, and was not making such good speed. Señor Zorro had little hope that the troopers would turn into the San Gabriel Road when they arrived at the fork, as they might have done had it not been moonlight and they had been unable to catch sight now and then of the man they pursued. He was within a mile of Fray Felipe's *hacienda* now, and once more he gave his horse the spurs in an effort to obtain greater speed.

"I shall have scant time, *señorita*," he said, bending over her and speaking into her ear. "Everything may depend upon whether I have been able to judge a man correctly. I ask only that you trust me."

"You know that I do that, *señor*."

"And you must trust the man to whom I am carrying you, *señorita*, and listen well to his advice upon all matters concerned with this adventure. The man is a *fray*."

"Then everything will be well, *señor*," she replied, clinging to him closely.

"If the saints are kind, we shall meet again soon, *señorita*. I shall count the hours and deem each one of them an age. I believe there are happier days ahead for us."

"May Heaven grant it," the girl breathed.

"Where there is love, there may be hope, *señorita*."

"Then my hope is great, *señor*."

"And mine," he said.

He turned his horse into Fray Felipe's driveway now and dashed toward the house. His intention was to stop only long enough to leave the girl, hoping that Fray Felipe would afford her protection, and then ride on, making considerable noise and drawing the troopers after him. He wanted them to think that he was merely taking a short cut across Fray Felipe's land to the other road, and that he had not stopped at the house.

He reined in his horse before the veranda steps, sprang to the ground, and lifted the *señorita* from the saddle, hurrying with her to the door. He beat against it with his fist, praying that Fray Felipe was a light sleeper and easily aroused. From the far distance there came a low drumming sound that he knew was made by the hoofs of his pursuers' horses.

It seemed to Señor Zorro that it was an age before the old *fray* threw open the door and stood framed in it, holding a candle in one hand. The highwayman stepped in swiftly and closed the door behind him, so no light would show outside. Fray Felipe had taken a step backward in astonishment when he had beheld the masked man and the *señorita* he escorted.

"I am Señor Zorro, *fray*" the highwayman said, speaking swiftly and in low tones. "Perhaps you may feel that you owe me a small debt for certain things?"

"For punishing those who oppressed and mistreated me, I owe you a large debt, *caballero*, though it is against my principles to countenance violence of any sort," Fray Felipe replied.

"I was sure that I had made no mistake in reading your character," Señor Zorro went on. "This señorita is Lolita, the only daughter of Don Carlos Pulido."

"Ha!"

"Don Carlos is a friend of the *frailes*, as you well know, and has known oppression and persecution the same as they. Today the governor came to Reina de Los Angeles and had Don Carlos arrested and thrown into the *carcel* on a charge that has no true worth, as I happen to know. He also had the Doña Catalina and this young lady put in *carcel*, in the same prison-room with drunkards and dissolute women. With the aid of some good friends, I rescued them."

"May the saints bless you, señor, for that kind action!" Fray Felipe cried.

"Troopers are pursuing us, *fray*. It is not seemly, of course, that the señorita ride farther with me alone. Do you take her and hide her, *fray* unless you fear that such a course may cause you grave trouble."

"*Señor!*" Fray Felipe thundered.

"If the soldiers take her, they will put her in *carcel* again, and probably she will be mistreated. Care for her, then, protect her, and you will more than discharge any obligation you may feel that you owe me."

"And you, *señor?*"

"I shall ride on, that the troopers may pursue me and not stop here at your house. I shall communicate with you later, *fray*. It is agreed between us?"

"It is agreed," Fray Felipe replied solemnly. "And I would clasp you by the hand, *señor*."

That handclasp was short, yet full of expression for all that. Señor Zorro then whirled toward the door.

"Blow out your candle," he directed. "They must see no light when I open the door."

In an instant Fray Felipe had complied, and they were in darkness. Señorita Lolita felt Señor Zorro's lips press against her own for an instant, and knew that he had raised the bottom of his mask to give her this caress. And then she felt one of Fray Felipe's strong arms around her.

"Be of good courage, daughter," the *fray* said. "Señor Zorro, it appears, has as many lives as a cat, and something tells me he was not born to be slain by troopers of his excellency."

The highwayman laughed lightly at that, opened the door, and darted through, closed it softly behind him, and so was gone.

Great eucalyptus-trees shrouded the front of the house in shadows, and in the midst of these shadows was Señor Zorro's horse. He noticed, as he ran toward the beast, that the soldiers were galloping down the driveway, that they were much nearer than he had expected to find them when he emerged from the house.

He ran quickly toward his mount, tripped on a stone, and fell, and frightened the animal so that it reared and darted half a dozen paces away, and into the full moonlight.

The foremost of his pursuers shouted when he saw the horse, and dashed toward it. Señor Zorro picked himself up, gave a quick spring, caught the reins from the ground, and vaulted into the saddle.

But they were upon him now, surrounding him, their blades flashing in the moonlight. He heard the raucous voice of Sergeant Gonzales ordering the men.

"Alive, if you can, soldiers! His excellency would see the rogue suffer for his crimes. At him, troopers! By the saints!"

Señor Zorro parried a stroke with difficulty and found himself unhorsed. On foot he fought his way back into the shadows, and the troopers charged after him. With his back to the bole of a tree, Señor Zorro fought them off.

Three sprang from their saddles to rush in at him. He darted from the tree to another, but could not reach his horse. But one belonging to a dismounted trooper was near him, and he vaulted into the saddle and dashed down the slope toward the barns and corral.

"After the rogue!" he heard Sergeant Gonzales shouting. "His excellency will have us flayed alive if this pretty highwayman escapes us now!"

They charged after him, eager to win promotion and the reward. But Señor Zorro had some sort of a start of them, enough to enable him to play a trick. As he came into the shadow cast by a big barn, he slipped from the saddle, at the same time giving the horse he rode a cut with his rowels. The animal plunged ahead, snorting with pain and fright, running swiftly through the darkness toward the corral below. The soldiers dashed by in pursuit.

Señor Zorro waited until they were past and then he ran rapidly up the hill again. But he saw that some of the troopers had remained behind to guard the house, evidently with the intention of searching it later, and so he found he could not reach his horse.

And once more there rang out that peculiar cry, half shriek and half moan, with which Señor Zorro had startled those at the *hacienda* of Don Carlos Pulido. His horse raised its head, whinnied once in answer to his call, and galloped toward him.

Señor Zorro was in the saddle in an instant, spurring across a field directly in front of him. His horse went over a stone fence as if it had not been in the way. And after him speedily came a part of the troopers.

They had discovered the trick he had used. They charged at him from both sides, met behind him, followed, and strained to cut down his lead. He could hear Sergeant Pedro Gonzales shouting lustily for them to make a capture in the name of the governor.

He hoped that he had drawn them all away from Fray Felipe's house but he was not sure, and the thing that demanded his attention the most now was the matter of his own escape.

He urged his horse cruelly, knowing that this journey across plowed ground was taking the animal's strength. He longed for a hard trail, the broad highway.

And finally he reached the latter. Now he turned his horse's head toward Reina de Los Angeles, for he had work to do there. There was no *señorita* before him on the saddle now, and the horse felt the difference.

Señor Zorro glanced behind and exulted to find that he was running away from the soldiers. Over the next hill and he would be able to elude them!

But he had to be on guard, of course, for there might be troopers in front of him, too. His excellency might have sent reënforcements to Sergeant Gonzales, or might have men watching from the tops of the hills.

He glanced at the sky and saw that the moon was about to disappear behind a bank of clouds. He would have to make use of the short period of darkness, he knew.

Down into the little valley he rode, and looked back to find that his pursuers were only at the crest of the hill. Then came the darkness, and at the proper time. Señor Zorro had a lead of half a mile on the pursuing soldiers now, but it was not his intention to allow them to chase him into the *pueblo*.

He had friends in this locality. Beside the highway was an adobe hut, where there lived a native Señor Zorro had saved from a beating. Now he dismounted before the hut and kicked against the door. The frightened native opened it.

"I am pursued," Señor Zorro said.

That appeared to be all that was necessary, for the native immediately threw the door of the hut open wider. Señor Zorro led his horse inside, almost filling the crude building, and the door was hastily shut again.

Behind it, the highwayman and the native stood listening, the former with pistol in one hand and his naked blade in the other.

XXXIII. FLIGHT AND PURSUIT

That the determined pursuit of Señor Zorro and his band of *caballeros* from the *carcel* had been taken up so quickly was due to Sergeant Pedro Gonzales.

Sergeant Gonzales had heard the shots and had rushed from the tavern with the other troopers at his heels, glad of an excuse to escape without paying for the wine he had ordered. He had heard the shout of the jailer and had understood it, and immediately had grasped the situation.

"Señor Zorro is rescuing the prisoners!" he screeched. "The highwayman is in our midst again! To horse, troopers, and after him! There is a reward—"

They knew all about the reward, especially the members of the governor's body-guard, who had heard his excellency rave at mention of the highwayman's name and declare he would make a captain of the trooper who captured him or brought in his carcass.

They rushed for their horses, swung themselves into their saddles, and dashed across the plaza toward the *carcel* with Sergeant Gonzales at their head.

They saw the masked *caballeros* galloping across the plaza, and Sergeant Gonzales rubbed his eyes with the back of one hand and swore softly that he had been taking too much wine. He had lied so often about Señor Zorro having a band of men at his back, that here was the band materialized out of his falsehoods.

When the *caballeros* split into three detachments, Sergeant Gonzales and his troopers were so near them that they observed the maneuver. Gonzales quickly made three troops of the men who followed him, and sent a troop after each band.

He saw the leader of the *caballeros* turn toward San Gabriel, he recognized the leap of the great horse the highwayman rode, and he took after Señor Zorro with an exultant heart, being of a mind to capture or slay the highwayman rather than to retake any of the rescued prisoners. For Sergeant Pedro Gonzales had not forgotten the time Señor Zorro had played with him in the tavern at Reina de Los Angeles, nor had he given up the idea of taking his vengeance for it.

He had seen Señor Zorro's horse run before, and he wondered a bit now because the highwayman was not putting greater distance between himself and his pursuers. And Sergeant Gonzales guessed the reason—that Señor Zorro had Señorita Lolita Pulido on the saddle before him and was carrying her away.

Gonzales was in the lead, and now and then he turned his head and shouted orders and encouragement to his troopers. The miles flew beneath them, and Gonzales was glad because he was keeping Señor Zorro in sight.

"To Fray Felipe's—that is where he is riding!" Gonzales told himself. "I knew that old *fray* was in league with the bandit! In some manner he tricked me when I sought this Señor Zorro at his *hacienda* before. Perhaps this highwayman has a clever hiding-place there. Ha! By the saints, I shall not be tricked again!"

On they rode, now and then catching glimpses of the man they pursued, and always in the minds of Gonzales and his troopers were thoughts of the reward and promotion a capture would mean. Their horses were beginning to show some fatigue already, but they did not spare the animals.

They saw Señor Zorro turn into the driveway that led to Fray Felipe's house; and Sergeant Gonzales chuckled low down in his throat because he felt that he had guessed correctly.

He had the highwayman now! If Señor Zorro continued to ride, he could be seen and followed because of the bright moonlight; if he stopped, Señor Zorro could not hope to cope successfully with half a score of troopers with Gonzales at their head.

They dashed up to the front of the house and started to surround it. They saw Señor Zorro's horse. And then they saw the highwayman himself, and Gonzales cursed because half a dozen troopers were between him and his prey, and were at him with their swords, threatening to end the business before Gonzales could reach the scene.

He tried to force his horse into the fight. He saw Señor Zorro spring into a saddle and dash away, and the troopers after him. Gonzales, not being close, gave his attention to the other half of his duty—he bade some of his soldiers surround the house so that none could leave it.

Then he saw Señor Zorro take the stone fence, and started in pursuit, all except the guards around the house joining him. But Sergeant Gonzales went only as far as the crest of the first hill. He noticed how the highwayman's horse was running, and realized that he could not be overtaken. Perhaps the sergeant could gain some glory if he returned to Fray Felipe's house and recaptured the *señorita*.

The house was still being guarded when he dismounted before it, and his men reported that none had attempted to leave the building. He called two of his men to his side and knocked on the door. Almost instantly it was opened by Fray Felipe.

"Are you just from bed, *fray*?" Gonzales asked.

"Is it not a time of night for honest men to be abed?" Fray Felipe asked in turn.

"It is *fray*—yet we find you out of it. How does it happen that you have not come from the house before? Did we not make enough noise to awaken you?"

"I heard sounds of combat—"

"And you may hear more *fray*, else feel the sting of a whip again, unless you answer questions swiftly and to the point. Do you deny that Señor Zorro has been here?"

"I do not."

"Ha! Now we have it. You admit, then, that you are in league with this pretty highwayman, that you shield him upon occasion? You admit that, *fray?*"

"I admit nothing of the sort," Fray Felipe replied. "I never set my eyes on this Señor Zorro, to my knowledge, until a very few minutes ago."

"That is a likely story. Tell it to the stupid natives, but do not try to tell it to a wise trooper, *fray*. What did this Señor Zorro wish?"

"You were so close upon the man's heels, señor, that he scarce had time to wish for anything," Fray Felipe said.

"Yet you had some speech with him?"

"I opened the door at his knock, *señor*, the same as I opened it at yours."

"What said he?"

"That soldiers were pursuing him."

"And he asked that you hide him, so he could escape capture at our hands?"

"He did not."

"Wanted a fresh horse, did he?"

"He did not say as much, *señor*. If he is such a thief as he is painted, undoubtedly he would merely have taken a horse without asking, had he wanted it."

"Ha! What business had he with you, then? It would be well for you to answer openly, *fray*."

"Did I say that he had business with me?"

"Ha! By the saints—"

"The saints are better off your lips, *señor*—boaster and drunkard!"

"Do you wish to receive another beating, *fray?* I am riding on his excellency's business. Do not you delay me further! What said this pretty highwayman?"

"Nothing that I am at liberty to repeat to you, *señor*," Fray Felipe said.

Sergeant Gonzales pushed him aside roughly and entered the living-room, and his two troopers followed at his heels.

"Light the *candelero*," Gonzales commanded his men. "Take candles, if you can find any. We search the house."

"You search my poor house?" Fray Felipe cried. "And what do you expect to find?" Fray Felipe asked.

"I expect to find the piece of merchandise this pretty Señor Zorro left here, *fray*."

"What do you imagine he left?"

"Ha! A package of clothing, I suppose! A bundle of loot! A bottle of wine! A saddle to be mended! What would the fellow leave, *fray?* One thing impresses me— Señor Zorro's horse carried double when he arrived at your house, and was carrying none but Señor Zorro when he departed."

"And you expect to find—"

"The other half of the horse's load," replied Gonzales. "Failing to find it, we may try a twist or two of your arm to see whether you can be made to speak."

"You would dare? You would so affront a *fray*? You would descend to torture?"

"Meal mush and goat's milk!" quoth Sergeant Gonzales. "You fooled me once in some manner, but you will not so fool me again. Search the house, troopers, and be sure that you search it well. I shall remain in this room and keep this entertaining *fray* company. I shall endeavor to discover what his sensations were while he was being whipped for swindling."

"Coward and brute!" Fray Felipe thundered. "There may come a day when persecution shall cease."

"Meal mush and goat's milk!"

"When this disorder ends and honest men be given their just dues!" Fray Felipe cried. "When those who have founded a rich empire here shall receive the true fruits of their labor and daring instead of having them stolen by dishonest politicians and men who stand in their favor!"

"Goat's milk and meal mush, *fray*!"

"When there shall be a thousand Señor Zorros, and more if necessary, to ride up and down El Camino Real and punish those who do wrong! Sometimes I would that I were not a *fray*, that I might play such a game myself!"

"We'd run you down in short order and stretch a rope with your weight," Sergeant Gonzales told him. "Did you help his excellency's soldiers more, perhaps his excellency would treat you with more consideration."

"I give aid to no spawn of the devil," Fray Felipe said.

"Ha! Now you grow angry, and that is against your principles. Is it not the part of a robed *fray* to receive what comes his way and give thanks for it, no matter how much it chokes him? Answer me that, angry one."

"You have about as much knowledge of a Franciscan's principles and duties as has the horse you ride."

"I ride a wise horse, a noble animal. He comes when I call and gallops when I command. Do not deride him until you ride him. Ha! An excellent jest!"

"Imbecile!"

"Meal mush and goat's milk!" said Sergeant Gonzales.

XXXIV. The Blood of the Pulidos

The Two troopers came back into the room. They had searched the house well, they reported, invading every corner of it, and no trace had been found of any person other than Fray Felipe's native servants, all of whom were too terrified to utter a falsehood, and had said they had seen nobody around the place who did not belong there.

"Ha! Hidden away well, no doubt!" Gonzales said. "*Fray*, what is that in the corner of the room?"

"Bales of hides," Fray Felipe replied. "I have been noticing it from time to time. The dealer from San Gabriel must have been right when he said the hides he purchased of you were not properly cured. Are those?"

"I think you will find them so."

"Then why did they move?" Sergeant Gonzales asked. "Three times I saw the corner of a bale move. Soldiers, search there."

Fray Felipe sprang to his feet.

"Enough of this nonsense," he cried. "You have searched and found nothing. Search the barns next and then go! At least let me be master in my own house. You have disturbed my rest enough as it is."

"You will take a solemn oath, *fray*, that there is nothing alive behind those bales of hides?" Fray Felipe hesitated, and Sergeant Gonzales grinned. "Not ready to forswear yourself, eh?" the sergeant asked. "I had a thought you would hesitate at that, my robed Franciscan. Soldiers, search the bales."

The two men started toward the corner. But they had not covered one half the distance when Señorita Lolita Pulido stood up behind the bales of hides and faced them.

"Ha! Unearthed at last!" Gonzales cried. "Here is the package Señor Zorro left in the *fray*'s keeping! And a pretty package it is! Back to *carcel* she goes, and this escape will but make her final sentence the greater!"

But there was Pulido blood in the *señorita*'s veins, and Gonzales had not taken that into account. Now the *señorita* stepped to the end of the pile of hides, so that light from the *candelero* struck full upon her.

"One moment, *señores*," she said.

One hand came from behind her back, and in it she held a long, keen knife such as sheep skinners used. She put the point of the knife against her breast, and regarded them bravely.

"Señorita Lolita Pulido does not return to the foul *carcel* now or at any time, *señores*," she said. "Rather would she plunge this knife into her heart, and so die as a woman of good blood should. If his excellency wishes for a dead prisoner, he may have one."

Sergeant Gonzales uttered an exclamation of annoyance. He did not doubt that the *señorita* would do as she had threatened, if the men made an attempt to seize her.

And while he might have ordered the attempt in the case of an ordinary prisoner, he did not feel sure that the governor would say he had done right if he ordered it now. After all, Señorita Pulido was the daughter of a don, and her self-inflicted death might cause trouble for his excellency. It might prove the spark to the powder magazine.

"*Señorita*, the person who takes his or her own life risks eternal damnation," the sergeant said. "Ask this *fray* if it is not so. You are only under arrest, not convicted and sentenced. If you are innocent, no doubt you soon will be set at liberty."

"It is no time for lying speeches, *señor*," the girl replied. "I realize the circumstances only too well, I have said that I will not return to *carcel*, and I meant it—and mean it now. One step toward me, and I take my own life."

"*Señorita*—" Fray Felipe began.

"It is useless for you to attempt to prevent me, good *fray*," she interrupted. "I have pride left me, thank the saints. His excellency gets only my dead body, if he gets me at all."

"Here is a pretty mess," Sergeant Gonzales exclaimed. "I suppose there is nothing for us to do except retire and leave the *señorita* to her freedom."

"Ah, no, *señor*!" she cried quickly. "You are clever, but not clever enough by far. You would retire and continue to have your men surround the house? You would watch for an opportunity, and then seize me?"

Gonzales growled low in his throat, for that had been his intention, and the girl had read it.

"I shall be the one to leave," she said. "Walk backward, and stand against the wall, *señores*. Do it immediately, or I plunge this knife into my bosom."

They could do nothing except obey. The soldiers looked to the sergeant for instructions, and the sergeant was afraid to risk the *señorita*'s death, knowing it would call down upon his head the wrath of the governor, who would say that he had bungled.

Perhaps, after all, it would be better to let the girl leave the house. She might be captured afterward, for surely a girl could not escape the troopers.

She watched them closely as she darted across the room to the door. The knife was still held at her breast.

"Fray Felipe, you wash to go with me?" she asked. "You may be punished if you remain."

"Yet I must remain, *señorita*. I could not run away. May the saints protect you!"

She faced Gonzales and the soldiers once more.

"I am going through this door," she said. "You will remain in this room. There are troopers outside, of course, and they will try to stop me. I shall tell them that I have your permission to leave. If they call and ask you, you are to say that it is so."

"And if I do not?"

"Then I use the knife, *señor*."

She opened the door, turned her head for an instant and glanced out.

"I trust that your horse is an excellent one, *señor*, for I intend to use it," she told the sergeant.

She darted suddenly through the door, and slammed it shut behind her.

"After her!" Gonzales cried. "I looked into her eyes! She will not use the knife— she fears it!"

He hurled himself across the room, the two soldiers with him. But Fray Felipe had been passive long enough. He went into action now. He did not stop to consider the consequences. He threw out one leg, and tripped Sergeant Gonzales. The two troopers crashed into him, and all went to the floor in a tangle.

Fray Felipe had gained some time for her, and it had been enough. For the *señorita* had rushed to the horse and had jumped into the saddle. She could ride like a native. Her tiny feet did not reach halfway to the sergeant's stirrups, but she thought nothing of that.

She wheeled the horse's head, kicked at his sides as a trooper rushed around the corner of the house. A pistol ball whistled past her head. She bent lower over the horse's neck and rode.

Now a cursing Sergeant Gonzales was on the veranda, shouting for his men to get to horse and follow her. The moon was behind a bank of clouds again. They could not tell the direction the *señorita* was taking except by listening for the sounds of the horse's hoofs. And they had to stop to do that and if they stopped they lost time and distance.

XXXV. The Clash of Blades Again

Señor Zorro stood like a statue in the native's hut, one hand grasping his horse's muzzle. The native crouched at his side.

Down the highway came the drumming of horses' hoofs. Then the pursuit swept by, the men calling to one another and cursing the darkness, and rushed down the valley.

Señor Zorro opened the door and glanced out, listened for a moment, and then led out his horse. He tendered the native a coin.

"Not from you, *señor*," the native said.

"Take it. You have need of it, and I have not," the highwayman said.

He vaulted into the saddle and turned his horse up the steep slope of the hill behind the hut. The animal made little noise as it climbed to the summit. Señor Zorro descended into the depression on the other side, and came to a narrow trail, and along this he rode at a slow gallop, stopping his mount now and then to listen for sounds of other horsemen who might be abroad.

He rode toward Reina de Los Angeles, but he appeared to be in no hurry about arriving at the *pueblo*. Señor Zorro had another adventure planned for this night, and it had to be accomplished at a certain time and under certain conditions.

It was two hours later when he came to the crest of the hill above the town. He sat quietly in the saddle for some time, regarding the scene. The moonlight was fitful now, but now and then he could make out the plaza.

He saw no troopers, heard nothing of them, decided that they had ridden back in pursuit of him, and that those who had been sent in pursuit of Don Carlos and the Doña Catalina had not yet returned. In the tavern there were lights, and in the *presidio*, and in the house where his excellency was a guest.

Señor Zorro waited until it was dark and then urged his horse forward slowly, but off the main highway. He circled the *pueblo*, and in time approached the *presidio* from the rear.

He dismounted now and led his horse, going forward slowly, often stopping to listen, for this was a very ticklish business and might end in disaster if a mistake were made.

He stopped the horse behind the presidio where the wall of the building would cast a shadow if the moon came from behind the clouds again, and went forward cautiously, following the wall as he had done on that other night.

When he came to the office window, he peered inside. Captain Ramón was there alone, looking over some reports spread on the table before him, evidently awaiting the return of his men.

Señor Zorro crept to the corner of the building and found there was no guard. He had guessed and hoped that the *comandante* had sent every available man to die chase, but he knew that he would have to act quickly, for some of the troopers might return.

He slipped through the door and crossed the big lounging-room, and so came to the door of the office. His pistol was in his hand, and could a man have seen behind the mask, he would have observed that Señor Zorro's lips were crushed in a thin, straight line of determination.

As upon that other night. Captain Ramón whirled around in his chair when he heard the door open behind him, and once more he saw the eyes of Señor Zorro glittering through his mask, saw the muzzle of the pistol menacing him.

"Not a move. Not a sound. It would give me pleasure to fill your body with hot lead," Señor Zorro said. "You are alone—your silly troopers are chasing me where I am not."

"By the saints—" Captain Ramón breathed. "Not so much as a whisper, *señor*, if you hope to live. Turn your back to me."

"You would murder me?"

"I am not that sort, *comandante*. And I said for you to make not a sound. Put your hands behind your back, for I am going to bind your wrists."

Captain Ramón complied. Señor Zorro stepped forward swiftly, and bound the wrists with his own sash, which he tore from his waist. Then he whirled Captain Ramón around so that he faced him.

"Where is his excellency?" he asked. "At Don Juan Estados's house."

"I knew as much, but wanted to see whether you prefer to speak the truth tonight. It is well if you do so. We are going to call upon the governor."

"To call—"

"Upon his excellency, I said. And do not speak again. Come with me."

He grasped Captain Ramón by the arm and hurried him from the office, across the lounging-room, out of the door. He piloted him around the building to where the horse was waiting.

"Mount!" he commanded. "I shall sit behind you, with the muzzle of this pistol at the base of your brain. Make no mistake, *comandante*, unless you are tired of life. I am a determined man this night." Captain Ramón had observed it. He mounted as he was directed, and the highwayman mounted behind him, and held the reins with one hand and the pistol with the other.

Captain Ramón could feel the touch of cold steel at the back of his head.

Señor Zorro guided his horse with his knees instead of with the reins. He urged the beast down the slope and circled the town once more, keeping away from the beaten trails, and so approached the rear of the house where his excellency was a guest.

Here was the difficult part of the adventure. He wanted to get Captain Ramón before the governor, to talk to both of them, and to do it without having anybody else interfere. He forced the captain to dismount, and led him to the rear wall of the house. There was a *patio* there, and they entered it.

It appeared that Señor Zorro knew the interior of the house well. He entered it through a servant's room, taking Captain Ramón with him, and passed through into a hall without awakening the sleeping native. They went along the hall slowly. From one room came the sound of snoring. From beneath the door of another light streamed.

Señor Zorro stopped before that door and applied an eye to a crack at the side of it. If Captain Ramón harbored thoughts of voicing an alarm, or of offering battle, the touch of the pistol at the back of his head caused him to forget them.

And he had scant time to think of a way out of this predicament, for suddenly Señor Zorro threw open the door, hurled Captain Ramón through it, followed himself, and shut the door quickly behind him. In the room there were his excellency and his host.

"Silence, and do not move," Señor Zorro said. "The slightest alarm, and I put a pistol ball through the governor's head. That is understood? Very well, *señores!*"

"Señor Zorro!" the governor gasped.

"The same, your excellency. I ask your host to be not frightened, for I mean him no harm if he sits quietly until I am done. Captain Ram6n, kindly sit across the table from the governor. I am delighted to find the head of the state awake and awaiting news from those who are chasing me. His brain will be clear, and he can understand better what is said."

"What means this outrage?" the governor exclaimed.

"Captain Ramón, how comes this? Seize this man! You are an officer—"

"Do not blame the *comandante*," Señor Zorro said. "He knows it is death to make a move. There is a little matter that needs explanation, and since I cannot come to you in broad day as a man should, I am forced to adopt this method. Make yourselves comfortable, *señores*. This may take some little time."

His excellency fidgeted in his chair.

"You have this day insulted a family of good blood, your excellency," Señor Zorro went on. "You have forgotten the proprieties to such an extent that you have ordered thrown into your miserable *carcel* a *hidalgo* and his gentle wife and innocent daughter. You have taken such means to gratify a spite"

"They are traitors," his excellency said.

"What have they done of treason?"

"You are an outlaw with a price put upon your head. They have been guilty of harboring you, giving you aid."

"Where got you this information?"

"Captain Ramón has an abundance of evidence."

"Ha! The *comandante*, eh? We shall see about that! Captain Ramón is present, and we can get at the truth. May I ask the nature of your evidence?"

"You were at the Pulido *hacienda*," the governor said.

"I admit it."

"A native saw you and carried word to the presidio. The soldiers hurried out to effect your capture."

"A moment. Who said a native sounded the alarm?"

"Captain Ramón assured me so."

"Here is the first chance for the captain to speak the truth. As a matter of fact, *comandante*, was it not Don Carlos Pulido himself who sent the native? The truth!"

"It was a native brought word."

"And he did not tell your sergeant that Don Carlos had sent him? Did he not say that Don Carlos had slipped him the information in whispers while he was carrying his fainting wife to her room? Is it not true that Don Carlos did his best to hold me at his *hacienda* until the soldiers arrived, that might be captured? Did not Don Carlos thus try to show his loyalty to the governor?"

"By the saints, Ramón, you never told me as much!" his excellency cried.

"They are traitors," the captain declared stubbornly.

"What other evidence?" Señor Zorro asked.

"Why, when the soldiers arrived, you concealed yourself by some trick," the governor said. "And presently Captain Ramón himself reached the scene, and while he was there you crept from a closet, ran him through treacherously from behind, and made your escape. It is an evident fact that Don Carlos had hidden you in the closet."

"By the saints!" Señor Zorro swore. "I had thought. Captain Ramón, that you were man enough to admit defeat, though I knew you for a scoundrel in other things. Tell the truth!"

"That is—the truth."

"Tell the truth!" Señor Zorro commanded, stepping closer to him and bringing up the pistol. "I came from that closet and spoke to you. I gave you time to draw blade and get on guard. We fenced for fully ten minutes, did we not?

"I admit freely that for a moment you puzzled me, and then I solved your method of giving battle and knew you were at my mercy. And then, when I could have slain you easily, I but scratched your shoulder. Is not that the truth? Answer, as you hope to live!"

Captain Ramón licked his dry lips, and could not meet the governor's eyes.

"Answer!" Señor Zorro thundered.

"It is—the truth," the captain acknowledged.

"Ha! So I ran you through from behind, eh? It is an insult to my blade to have it enter your body. You see, your excellency, what manner of man you have for *comandante* here. Is there more evidence?"

"There is!" the governor said. "When the Pulidos were guests at the house of Don Diego Vega, and Don Diego was away. Captain Ramón went to pay his respects and found you there alone with the *señorita*."

"And that shows what?"

"That you are in league with the Pulidos! That they harbored you even in the house of Don Diego, a loyal man. And when the captain discovered you there, the *señorita* flung herself upon him and held him—delayed him, rather—until you made your escape through a window. Is not that enough?"

Señor Zorro bent forward, and his eyes seemed to burn through the mask and into those of Captain Ramón.

"So that is the tale he told, eh?" the highwayman said. "As a matter of fact, Captain Ramón is enamored of the *señorita*. He went to the house, found her alone, forced his attentions upon her, even told her that she should not object, since her father was in the bad graces of the governor! He attempted to caress her, and she called for help. I responded."

"How did you happen to be there?"

"I do not care to answer that, but I take my oath the *señorita* did not know of my presence. She called for aid, and I responded.

"I made this thing you call a *comandante* kneel before her and apologize. And then I took him to the door and kicked him out into the dust! And afterward I visited him at the *presidio* and told him that he had given insult to a noble *señorita*—"

"It appears that you hold some love for her yourself," the governor said.

"I do, your excellency, and am proud to admit it!"

"Ha! You condemn her and her parents by that statement! You deny now they are in league with you?"

"I do. Her parents do not know of our love!"

"This *señorita* is scarcely conventional!"

"*Señor*! Governor or no, another thought like that and I spill your blood," Señor Zorro cried. "I have told you what happened that night at the house of Don Diego Vega. Captain Ramón will testify that what I have said is the exact truth. Is it not, *comandante*? Answer!"

"It—it is the truth." The captain gulped, looking at the muzzle of the highwayman's pistol.

"Then you have told me falsehood, and can no longer be an officer of mine!" the governor cried. "It appears that this highwayman can do as he pleases with you! Ha! But I still believe that Don Carlos Pulido is a traitor, and the members of his family, and it has availed you nothing, Señor Zorro, to play this little scene.

"My soldiers shall continue to pursue them—and you! And before they are done, I'll have the Pulidos dragged in the dirt, and I'll have you stretching a rope with your carcass!"

"Quite a bold speech," observed Señor Zorro. "You set your soldiers a pretty task, your excellency. I rescued your three prisoners tonight, and they have escaped."

"They shall be retaken."

"Time alone will tell that. And now I have another duty to perform here. Your excellency, you will take your chair to that far corner and sit there, and your host will sit beside you. And there you shall remain until I have finished."

"What do you mean to do?"

"Obey me!" Señor Zorro cried. "I have scant time for argument, even with a governor."

He watched while the two chairs were placed and the governor and his host had seated themselves. And then he stepped nearer Captain Ramón.

"You insulted a pure and innocent girl, *comandante*," he said. "For that, you shall fight. Your scratched shoulder is healed now, and you wear your blade by your side. Such a man as you is not fit to breathe God's pure air! The country is better for your absence. On your feet, *señor*, and on guard!"

Captain Ramón was white with rage. He knew that he was ruined. He had been forced to confess that he had lied. He had heard the governor remove his rank. And this man before him had been the cause of all of it!

Perhaps in his anger he could kill this Señor Zorro, stretch this Curse of Capistrano on the floor with his life blood flowing away. Perhaps, if he did that, his excellency would relent.

He sprang from his chair and backward to the side of the governor.

"Unfasten my wrists!" he cried. "Let me at this dog!"

"You were as good as dead before—you certainly are dead after using that word," Señor Zorro said calmly.

The *comandante*'s wrists were untied. He whipped out his blade, sprang forward with a cry, and launched himself in a furious attack upon the highwayman.

Señor Zorro gave ground before this onslaught, and so obtained a position where the light from the *candelero* did not bother his eyes. He was skilled with a blade, and had fenced for life many times, and he knew the danger in the attack of an angered man who did not fence according to the code.

And he knew, too, that such anger is spent quickly unless a fortunate thrust makes the possessor of it victor almost at once. And so he retreated step by step, guarding well, parrying vicious strokes, alert for an unexpected move.

The governor and his host were sitting in their corner, but bending forward and watching the combat.

"Run him through, Ramón, and I reinstate and promote you!" his excellency cried.

The *comandante* thus was urged to do it. Señor Zorro found his opponent fighting much better than he had before in Don Carlos Pulido's house at the *hacienda*. He found himself forced to fight out of a dangerous corner, and the pistol he held in his left hand to intimidate the governor and his host bothered him.

And suddenly he tossed it to the table, and then swung around so that neither of the two men could dart from a corner and get it without running the chance of receiving a blade between the ribs. And there he stood his ground and fought.

Captain Ramón could not force him to give way now. His blade seemed to be a score. It darted in and out, trying to find a resting place in the captain's body; for Señor Zorro was eager to have an end of this and be gone. He knew that the dawn was not far away, and he feared that some trooper might come to the house with a report for the governor.

"Fight, insulter of girls!" he cried. "Fight, man who tells a falsehood to injure a noble family! Fight, coward and poltroon! Now death stares you in the face, and soon you'll be claimed! Ha! I almost had you then! Fight, cur!"

Captain Ramón cursed and charged, but Señor Zorro received him and drove him back, and so held his position. The perspiration was standing out on the captain's forehead in great globules. His breath was coming heavily from between his parted lips. His eyes were bright and bulging.

"Fight, weakling!" The highwayman taunted him. "This time I am not attacking from behind. If you have prayers to say, say them—for your time grows short."

The ringing blades, the shifting feet on the floor, the heavy breathing of the combatants and of the two spectators of this life-and-death struggle were the only sounds in the room. His excellency sat far forward on his chair, his hands gripping the edges of it so that his knuckles were white,

"Kill me this highwayman!" he shrieked. "Use your good skill, Ramón! At him!"

Captain Ramón rushed again, calling into play his last bit of strength, fencing with what skill he could command. His arms were as lead; his breath was fast. He thrust, he lunged—and made a mistake of a fraction of an inch.

Like the tongue of a serpent, Señor Zorro's blade shot in. Thrice it darted forward, and upon the fair brow of Ramón, just between the eyes, there flamed suddenly a red, bloody letter Z.

"The Mark of Zorro!" the highwayman cried. "You wear it forever now, *comandante*!"

Señor Zorro's face became more stern. His blade shot in again and came out dripping red. The *comandante* gasped and slipped to the floor.

"You have slain him!" the governor cried. "You have taken his life, wretch!"

"Ha! I trust so. The thrust was through the heart, excellency. He never will insult a *señorita* again."

Señor Zorro looked down at his fallen foe, regarded the governor a moment, then wiped his blade on the sash that had bound the comandante's wrists. He returned the blade to its scabbard and picked up his pistol from the table.

"My night's work is done," he said.

"And you shall hang for it!" his excellency cried.

"Perhaps—when you catch me," replied the Curse of Capistrano, bowing ceremoniously.

Then, without glancing again at the twitching body of him who had been Captain Ramón, he whirled through the door and was in the hall, and rushed through it to the *patio* and to his horse.

XXXVI. ALL AGAINST THEM

And he rushed into danger!

The dawn had come; the first pink streaks had appeared in the eastern sky, and then the sun had risen quickly above the heights to the east, and now the plaza was bathed in brilliance. There was no mist, no high fog even, and objects on the hillsides far away stood out in relief. It was no morning in which to ride for life and freedom.

Señor Zorro had delayed too long with the governor and *comandante*, else had misjudged the hour. He swung into his saddle and urged his beast out of the *patio*—and then a full realization of his imminent peril came to him.

Down the trail from San Gabriel came Sergeant Pedro Gonzales and his troopers. Down the Pala road came another detachment of soldiers that had been trailing the *caballeros* and Don Carlos and had given up in disgust. Over the hill toward the *presidio* came the third body of men, who had been in chase of those who had rescued the Doña Catalina. Señor Zorro found himself hemmed in by his foes.

The Curse of Capistrano deliberately stopped his horse and for a moment contemplated the outlook. He glanced at the three bodies of troopers, estimated the distance. And in that instant one with Sergeant Gonzales's detachment saw him and raised the alarm.

They knew that magnificent horse, that long purple cloak, that black mask and wide sombrero. They saw before them the man they had been pursuing throughout the night, the man who had made fools of them and played with them, about the hills and valleys. They feared the rage of his excellency and their superior officers, and in their hearts and minds was determination to capture or slay this Curse of Capistrano now as this last chance was offered them.

Señor Zorro put spurs to his horse and dashed across the plaza, in full view of some score of citizens. Just as he did that, the governor and his host rushed from the house, shrieking that Señor Zorro was a murderer and should be taken. Natives scurried like so many rats for shelter; men of rank stood still and gaped in astonishment.

Señor Zorro, having crossed the plaza, drove his horse at highest speed straight toward the highway. Sergeant Gonzales and his troopers rushed to cut him off and turn him back, shrieking at one another, pistols in their hands, blades loosened in their scabbards. Reward and promotion and satisfaction were to be their lot if they made an end of the highwayman here and now.

Señor Zorro was forced to swerve from his first course, for he saw that he could not win through. He had not taken his pistol from his belt, but he had drawn his blade, and it dangled from his right wrist in such fashion that he could grip the hilt of it instantly and put it into play.

He cut across the plaza again, almost running down several men of rank who were in the way. He passed within a few paces of the infuriated governor and his host, darted between two houses, and rushed toward the hills in that direction.

It appeared that he had some small chance of escaping the cordon of his foes now. He scorned paths and trails, and cut across the open ground. From both sides the troopers galloped to meet him, flying toward the angle of the wedge, hoping to reach it in time and turn him back once more.

Gonzales was shouting orders in his great voice, and he was sending a part of his men down into the *pueblo*, so they would be in proper position in case the highwayman turned back again, and could keep him from escaping to the west.

He reached the highway and started down it toward the south. It was not the direction he would have preferred, but he had no choice now. He dashed around a curve in the road, where some natives' huts cut off the view—and suddenly he pulled up his horse, almost unseating himself.

For here a new menace presented itself. Straight at him along the highway flew a horse and rider, and close behind came half a dozen troopers in pursuit!

Señor Zorro whirled his horse. He could not turn to the right because of a stone fence. His horse could have jumped it, but on the other side was soft plowed ground, and he knew he could make no progress across it, and that the troopers might cut him down with a pistol bullet.

Nor could he turn to the left, for there was a sheer precipice down which he could not hope to ride with safety. He had to turn back toward Sergeant Gonzales and the men who rode with him, hoping to get a distance of a couple of hundred yards, where he could make a descent, before Gonzales and his men arrived at the spot

He gripped his sword now, and was prepared for fight, for he knew it was going to be close work. He glanced back over his shoulder—and gasped his surprise.

For it was Señorita Lolita Pulido who rode that horse and was pursued by the half-dozen troopers, and he had thought her safe at the *hacienda* of Fray Felipe. Her long black hair was down and streaming out behind her. Her tiny heels were glued to the horse's flanks. She bent forward as she rode, holding the reins low down, and Señor Zorro, even in that instant, marveled at her skill with a mount.

"*Señor!*" he heard her shout.

And then she had reached his side, and they rode together, dashing down upon Gonzales and his troopers.

"They have been chasing me—for hours!" she gasped. "I escaped them—at Fray Felipe's!"

"Ride close! Do not waste breath!" he screeched.

"My horse—is almost done—*señor!*"

Señor Zorro glanced aside at the beast, and saw that he I was suffering from fatigue. But there was scant time to consider that now. The soldiers behind had gained some; those in front presented a menace that required consideration.

Down the trail they flew, side by side, straight at Gonzales and his men. Señor Zorro could see that pistols were out, and he doubted not that the governor had given orders to get him dead or alive, but to see that he did not escape again.

Now he spurred a few paces in advance of the *señorita*, and called upon her to ride his horse's tracks. He dropped the reins on his mount's neck, and held his blade ready. He had two weapons—his blade and his horse.

Then came the crash. Señor Zorro swerved his horse at the proper instant, and the señorita followed him. He cut at the trooper on his left, swung over and cut at the one on his right. His horse crashed into that of a third trooper, and hurled it against the animal the sergeant rode.

He heard shrill cries about him. He knew that the men who had been pursuing Señorita Lolita had run into the others, and that there was a certain amount of confusion, that they could not use blades for fear of cutting down one another.

And then he was through them, with the *señorita* riding at his side again. Once more he was at the edge of the plaza. His horse was showing signs of weariness, and he had gained nothing.

For the way to San Gabriel was not open, the way to Pala was closed, he could not hope to escape by cutting across soft ground, and on the opposite side of the plaza were more troopers, in saddle and waiting to cut him off, no matter in which direction he started.

"We are caught!" he shouted. "But we are not done, *señorita!*"

"My horse is stumbling!" she cried.

Señor Zorro saw that it was so. He knew that the beast could not make another hundred yards.

"To the tavern!" he cried.

They galloped straight across the plaza. At the door of the tavern the *señorita*'s horse staggered and fell. Señor Zorro caught the girl in his arms in time to save her from a hard fall and, still carrying her, darted through the tavern door.

"Out!" he cried to the landlord and the native servant. "Out!" he shrieked to half a dozen loiterers, exhibiting his pistol. They rushed through the door and into the plaza.

The highwayman threw the door shut and bolted it. He saw that every window was closed except the one that fronted on the plaza, and that the board and skin coverings were in place. He stepped to the table and then whirled to face the *señorita*.

"It may be the end," he said.

"*Señor*! Surely the saints will be kind to us."

"We are beset by foes, *señorita*. I care not, so that I die fighting as a *caballero* should. But you, *señorita*—"

"They shall never put me in the foul *carcel* again, *señor*! I swear it! Rather would I die with you."

She took the sheep skinner's knife from her bosom, and he caught a glance of it.

"Not that, *señorita*!" he cried.

"I have given you my heart, *señor*. Either we live together or we die together."

XXXVII. THE FOX AT BAY

He darted to the window and glanced out. The troopers were surrounding the building. He could see the governor stalking across the plaza, crying his orders. Down the San Gabriel trail came the proud Don Alejandro Vega, to pay his visit to the governor, and he stopped at the plaza's edge and began questioning men regarding the cause for the tumult.

"All are in at the death," Señor Zorro said, laughing. "I wonder where my brave *caballeros* are, those who rode with me?"

"You expect their aid?" she asked.

"Not so, *señorita*. They would have to stand together and face the governor, tell him their intentions. It was a lark with them, and I doubt whether they take it seriously enough to stand by me now. It is not to be expected. I fight it out alone!"

"Not alone, *señor*, when I am by your side!"

He clasped her in his arms, pressed her to him.

"I would we might have our chance," he said. "But it would be folly for you to let my disaster influence your life. You never have seen my face even, *señorita*. You could forget me. You could walk from this place and surrender, send word to Don Diego

Vega that you will become his bride, and the governor then would be forced to release you and clear your parents of all blame."

"Ah, *señor*—"

"Think, *señorita*. Think what it would mean. His excellency would not dare stand an instant against a Vega. Your parents would have their lands restored. You would be the bride of the richest young man in the country. You would have everything to make you happy—"

"Everything except love, *señor*, and without, love the rest is as naught!"

"Think, *señorita*, and decide for once and all. You have but a moment now!"

"I made my decision long ago, *señor*. A Pulido loves but once, and does not wed where she cannot love."

"*Cara!*" he cried, and pressed her close again.

Now there came a battering at the door. "Señor Zorro!" Sergeant Gonzales cried.

"Well, *señor?*" Zorro asked.

"I have an offer for you from his excellency the governor."

"I am listening, loud one."

"His excellency has no wish to cause your death or injury to the señorita you have inside with you. He asks that you open the door and come out with the lady."

"To what end?" Señor Zorro asked.

"You shall be given a fair trial, and the *señorita* also. Thus you may escape death and receive imprisonment instead."

"Ha! I have seen samples of his excellency's fair trials," Señor Zorro responded. "Think you I am an imbecile?"

"His excellency bids me say that this is the last chance, that the offer will not be renewed."

"His excellency is wise not to waste breath renewing it. He grows fat, and his breath is short."

"What can you expect to gain by resistance, save death?" Gonzales asked. "How can you hope to offstand a score and a half of us?"

"It has been done before, loud one!"

"We can batter in the door and take you."

"After a few of you have been stretched lifeless on the floor," Señor Zorro observed. "Who will be the first through the door, my sergeant?"

"For the last time—"

"Come in and drink a mug of wine with me," said the highwayman, laughing.

"Meal mush and goat's milk!" swore Sergeant Gonzales.

THE MARK OF ZORRO

There was quiet then for a time, and Señor Zorro, glancing through the window cautiously, so as not to attract a pistol shot, observed that the governor was in consultation with the sergeant and certain of the troopers.

The consultation ended, and Señor Zorro darted back from the window. Almost immediately, the attack upon the door began. They were pounding at it with heavy timbers, trying to smash it down. Señor Zorro, standing in the middle of the room, pointed his pistol at the door and fired, and as the ball tore through the wood and somebody outside gave a shriek of pain, he darted to the table and started loading the pistol again.

Then he hurried across to the door, and observed the hole where the bullet had gone through. The plank had been split, and there was quite a crack in it. Señor Zorro put the point of his blade at this crack, and waited.

Again the heavy timber crashed against the door, and some trooper threw his weight against it, also. Señor Zorro's blade darted through the crack like a streak of lightning, and came back red, and again there was a shriek outside. And now a volley of pistol balls came through the door, but Señor Zorro, laughing, had sprung back out of harm's way.

"Well done, *señor*!" Señorita Lolita cried.

"We shall stamp our mark on several of these hounds before we are done," he replied.

"I would that I could aid you, *señor*."

"You are doing it, *señorita*. It is your love that gives me my strength."

"If I could use a blade—"

"Ah, *señorita*, that is for a man to do. Do you pray that all may be well."

"And at the last, *señor*, if it is seen that there is no hope—may I then see your dear face?"

"I swear it, *señorita*, and feel my arms about you, and my lips on yours. Death will not be so bitter then."

The attack on the door was renewed. Now pistol shots were coming through it regularly, and through the one open window also, and there was nothing for Señor Zorro to do except stand in the middle of the room and wait, his blade held ready. There would be a lively few minutes, he promised, when the door was down and they rushed in at him.

It seemed to be giving way now. The *señorita* crept close to him, tears streaming down her cheeks, and grasped him by the arm.

"You will not forget?" she asked.

"I'll not forget, *señorita*!"

"Just before they break down the door, señor. Take me in your arms and let me see your dear face and kiss me! Then I can die with good grace, too."

"You must live——"

"Not to be sent to a foul *carcel*, *señor*! And what would life be without you?"

"There is Don Diego——"

"I think of nobody but you, *señor*. A Pulido will know how to die. And perhaps my death will bring home to men the perfidy of the governor. Perhaps it may be of service."

Again the heavy timber struck against the door. They could hear his excellency shouting encouragement to the troopers, could hear the natives shrieking and Sergeant Gonzales crying his orders in his loud voice.

Señor Zorro hurried to the window again, chancing a bullet, and glanced out. He saw that half a dozen troopers had their blades ready, were prepared to rush over the door the moment it was down. They would get him—but he would get some of them first! Again the ram against the door.

"It is almost the end, *señor*," the girl whispered.

"I know it, *señorita*."

"I would we had had better fortune, yet I can die gladly since this love has been in my life. Now—*señor*—your face and lips. The door—is crashing in!"

She ceased to sob, and lifted her face bravely. Señor Zorro sighed, and one hand fumbled with the bottom of his mask.

But suddenly there was a tumult outside in the plaza, and the battering at the door ceased, and they could hear loud voices that they had not heard before.

Señor Zorro let go of his mask, and darted to the window.

XXXVIII. The Man Unmasked

Twenty-three horsemen were galloping into the plaza. The beasts they rode were magnificent, their saddles and bridles were heavily chased with silver, their cloaks were of the finest materials, and they wore hats with plumes, as if this was somewhat of a dress affair and they wished the world to know it. Each man sat straight and proud in his saddle, his blade at his side, and every blade had a jeweled hilt, being at once serviceable and a rich ornament.

They galloped along the face of the tavern, between the door and the soldiers who had been battering it, between the building and the governor and assembled citizens, and there they turned and stood their horses side by side, facing his excellency.

"Wait! There is a better way!" their leader cried.

"Ha!" screeched the governor. "I understand. Here we have the young men of all the noble families in the southland. They have come to show their loyalty by taking this Curse of Capistrano. I thank you, *caballeros*. Yet it is not my wish to have any of you slain by this fellow. He is not worthy your blades, *señores*.

"Do you ride to one side and lend the strength of your presence, and let my troopers deal with the rogue. Again I thank you for this show of loyalty, for this demonstration that you stand for law and order and all it means, for constituted authority—"

"Peace!" their leader cried. "Your excellency, we represent power in this section, do we not?"

"You do, *caballeros*," the governor said.

"Our families say who shall rule, what laws shall be just, do they not?"

"They have great influence," the governor said.

"You would not care to stand alone against us?"

"Most assuredly not!" his excellency cried. "But I pray you, let the troopers get this fellow. It is not seemly that a *caballero* should suffer wound or death from his blade."

"It is to be regretted that you do not understand."

"Understand?" queried the governor, in a questioning tone, glancing up and down the line of mounted men.

"We have taken counsel with ourselves, excellency. We know our strength and power, and we have decided upon certain things. There have been things done that we cannot countenance.

"The *frailes* of the missions have been despoiled by officials. Natives have been treated worse than dogs. Even men of noble blood have been robbed because they have not been friendly to the ruling powers."

"*Caballero*—"

"Peace, excellency, until I have done! This thing came to a crisis when a *hidalgo* and his wife and daughter were thrown into a *carcel* by your orders. Such a thing cannot be countenanced, excellency.

"And so we have banded ourselves together, and here we take a hand. Be it known that we ourselves rode with this Señor Zorro when he invaded the *carcel* and rescued the prisoners, that we carried Don Carlos and the Doña Catalina to places of safety, and that we have pledged our words and honors and blades that they shall not be persecuted more."

"I would say—"

"Silence, until I have done! We stand together, and the strength of our united families is behind us. Call upon your soldiers to attack us, if you dare! Every man of noble blood up and down the length of El Camino Real would flock to our defense, would unseat you from your office, would see you humbled. We await your answer, excellency."

"What—what would you?" his excellency gasped.

"First, proper consideration for Don Carlos Pulido and his family. No *carcel* for them. If you have the courage to try them for treason, be sure that we will be on hand at the trial, and deal with any man who gives perjured testimony, and with any *magistrado* who does not conduct himself properly. We are determined, excellency."

"Perhaps I was hasty in the matter, but I was led to believe certain things," the governor said. "I grant you your wish. One side now, *caballeros*, while my men get at this rogue in the tavern."

"We are not done!" their leader said. "We have things to say regarding this Señor Zorro. What has he done—actually excellency? Is he guilty of any treason? He has robbed no man except those who robbed the defenseless first. He has whipped a few unjust persons. He has taken sides with the persecuted, for which we honor him. To do such a thing, he took his life in his own hands. He successfully evaded your soldiers. He resented insults, as any man has the right to do."

"What would you?"

"A complete pardon, here and now, for this man known as Señor Zorro!"

"Never!" the governor cried. "He has affronted me personally! He shall die the death!" He turned around and saw Don Alejandro Vega standing near him. "Don Alejandro, you are the most influential man in this south country," he said. "You are the one man against whom even the governor dare not stand. You are a man of justice. Tell these young *caballeros* that what they wish cannot be granted. Bid them retire to their homes, and this show of treason will be forgotten."

"I stand behind them!" Don Alejandro thundered.

"You—you stand behind them?"

"I do, your excellency! I echo every word they have spoken in your presence. Persecution must cease. Grant their requests, see that your officials do right hereafter, return to San Francisco de Asis, and I take my oath that there shall be no treason in this southland. I shall see to it myself. But oppose them, excellency, and I shall take sides against you, see you driven from office and ruined, and your foul parasites with you."

"This terrible, willful southland!" the governor cried.

"Your answer?" Don Alejandro demanded.

"I can do nothing but agree," the governor said. "But there is one thing—"

"Well?"

"I spare the man's life if he surrenders, but he must stand trial for the murder of Captain Ramón!"

"Murder?" queried the leader of the *caballeros*. "It was a duel between gentlemen, excellency. Señor Zorro resented an insult on the part of the *comandante* to the *señorita*."

"Ha! But Ramón was a *caballero*—"

"And so is this Señor Zorro. He told us as much, and we believe him, for there was no falsehood in his voice. So it was a duel, excellency, and between gentlemen, according to the code, and Captain Ramón was unfortunate that he was not a better man with a blade. That is understood? Your answer!"

"I agree," the governor said weakly. "I pardon him, and I go home to San Francisco de Asis, and persecution ceases in this locality. But I hold Don Alejandro to his promise—that there be no treason against me here if I do these things."

"I have given my word," Don Alejandro said.

The *caballeros* shrieked their happiness and dismounted. They drove the soldiers away from the door, Sergeant Gonzales growling into his mustache because here was a reward gone glimmering again.

"Within there, Señor Zorro!" one cried. "Have you heard?"

"I have heard, *caballero*!"

"Open the door and come out amongst us—a free man!"

There was a moment's hesitation, and then the battered door was unbarred and opened, and Señor Zorro stepped out with the *señorita* on his arm. He stopped just in front of the door, removed his sombrero and bowed low before them.

"A good day to you, *caballeros*!" he cried. "Sergeant, I regret that you have missed the reward, but I shall see that the amount is placed to the credit of you and your men with the landlord of the tavern."

"By the saints, he is a *caballero*!" Gonzales cried.

"Unmask, man!" cried the governor. "I would see the features of the person who has fooled my troopers, has gained *caballeros* to his banner, and has forced me to make a compromise."

"I fear that you will be disappointed when you see my poor features," Señor Zorro replied. "Do you expect me to look like Satan? Or can it be possible, on the other hand, that you believe I have an angelic countenance?"

He chuckled, glanced down at the Señorita Lolita, and then put up a hand and tore off his mask.

A chorus of gasps answered the motion, an explosive oath or two from the soldiers, cries of delight from the *caballeros*, and a screech of mingled pride and joy from one old hidalgo.

"Don Diego, my son—my son!"

And the man before them seemed to droop suddenly in the shoulders, and sighed, and spoke in a languid voice.

"These be turbulent times. Can a man never meditate on music and the poets?"

And Don Diego Vega, the Curse of Capistrano, was clasped for a moment in his father's arms.

XXXIX. "Meal Mush and Goat's Milk!"

They crowded forward—troopers, natives, *caballeros*, surrounding Don Diego Vega and the *señorita* who clutched at his arm and looked up at him from proud and glistening eyes.

"Explain! Explain!" they cried.

"It began ten years ago, when I was but a lad of fifteen," he said. "I heard tales of persecution. I saw my friends, the *frailes*, annoyed and robbed. I saw soldiers beat an old native who was my friend. And then I determined to play this game.

"It would be a difficult game to play, I knew. So I pretended to have small interest in life, so that men never would connect my name with that of the highwayman I expected to become. In secret, I practiced horsemanship and learned how to handle a blade—"

"By the saints, he did!" Sergeant Gonzales growled.

"One half of me was the languid Don Diego you all knew, and the other half was the Curse of Capistrano I hoped one day to be. And then the time came, and my work began.

"It is a peculiar thing to explain, *señores*. The moment I donned cloak and mask, the Don Diego part of me fell away. My body straightened, new blood seemed to course through my veins, my voice grew strong and firm, fire came to me! And the moment I removed cloak and mask I was the languid Don Diego again. Is it not a peculiar thing?

"I had made friends with this great Sergeant Gonzales, and for a purpose."

"Ha! I guess the purpose, *caballeros*!" Gonzales cried. "You tired whenever this Señor Zorro was mentioned, and did not wish to hear of violence and bloodshed, but always you asked me in what direction I was going with my troopers—and you went in the other direction and did your confounded work."

"You are an excellent guesser," said Don Diego, laughing, as did the others about him. "I even crossed blades with you, so you would not guess I was Señor Zorro. You remember the rainy night at the tavern? I listened to your boasts, went out and donned mask and cloak, came in and fought you, escaped, took off mask and cloak, and returned to jest with you."

"Ha!"

"I visited the Pulido *hacienda* as Don Diego and a short time later returned as Señor Zorro and held speech with the *señorita* here. You almost had me, sergeant, that night at Fray Felipe's—the first night, I mean."

"Ha! You told me there that you had not seen Señor Zorro."

"Nor had I. The *fray* does not keep a mirror, thinking that it makes for vanity. The other things were not difficult, of course. You can easily understand how, as Señor Zorro, I happened to be at my own house in town when the *comandante* insulted the *señorita*.

"And the *señorita* must forgive me the deception. I courted her as Don Diego, and she would have none of me. Then I tried it as Señor Zorro, and the saints were kind, and she gave me her love.

"Perhaps there was some method in that, also. For she turned from the wealth of Don Diego Vega to the man she loved, though she deemed him, then, an outcast and outlaw.

"She has showed me her true heart, and I am rejoiced at it. Your excellency, this *señorita* is to become my wife, and I take it you will think twice before you will annoy her family further."

His excellency threw out his hands in a gesture of resignation.

"It was difficult to fool you all, but it has been done," Don Diego continued. "Only years of practice allowed me to accomplish it. And now Señor Zorro shall ride no more, for there will be no need, and moreover a married man should take some care of his life."

"And what man do I wed?" the Señorita Lolita asked, blushing because she spoke the words where all could hear.

"What man do you love?"

"I had fancied that I loved Señor Zorro, but it comes to me now that I love the both of them," she said. "Is it not shameless? But I would rather have you Señor Zorro than the old Don Diego I knew."

"We shall endeavor to establish a golden mean," he replied, laughing again. "I shall drop the old languid ways and change gradually into the man you would have me. People will say that marriage made a man of me."

He stooped and kissed her there before them all.

"Meal mush and goat's milk!" swore Sergeant Gonzales.

THE SECRET OF MACARGER'S GULCH

Ambrose Bierce

NORTHWESTWARDLY FROM INDIAN HILL, ABOUT NINE MILES AS THE CROW flies, is Macarger's Gulch. It is not much of a gulch—a mere depression between two wooded ridges of inconsiderable height. From its mouth up to its head—for gulches, like rivers, have an anatomy of their own—the distance does not exceed two miles, and the width at bottom is at only one place more than a dozen yards; for most of the distance on either side of the little brook which drains it in winter, and goes dry in the early spring, there is no level ground at all: the steep slopes of the hills, covered with an almost impenetrable growth of manzanita and chemisal, are divided by nothing but the width of the water course. No one but an occasional enterprising hunter of the vicinity ever goes into Macarger's Gulch, and five miles away it is unknown, even by name. Within that distance in any direction are far more conspicuous topographical features without names, and one might try a long time in vain to ascertain by local inquiry the origin of the name of this one.

About midway between the head and the mouth of Macarger's Gulch, the hill on the right as you ascend is cloven by another gulch, a short dry one, and at the junction of the two is a level space of two or three acres, and there, a few years ago, stood an old board house containing one small room. How the component parts of the house, few and simple as they were, had been assembled at that almost inaccessible point is a problem, in the solution of which there would be greater satisfaction than advantage. Possibly, the creek bed is a reformed road. It is certain that the gulch was at one time pretty thoroughly prospected by miners, who must have had some means of getting in with at least pack animals carrying tools and supplies; their profits, apparently, were not such as would have justified any considerable outlay to connect Macarger's Gulch with any center of civilization enjoying the distinction of a sawmill. The house, however, was there, most of it. It lacked a door and a window frame, and the chimney of mud and stones had fallen into an unlovely heap, overgrown with rank weeds. Such humble furniture as there may once have been, and much of the lower weatherboarding, had served as fuel in the camp fires of hunters; as had also, probably, the curbing of an old well, which at the time I write of existed in the form of a rather wide but not very deep depression near by.

One afternoon in the summer of 1874, I passed up Macarger's Gulch from the narrow valley into which it opens, by following the dry bed of the brook. I was quail shooting and had made a bag of about a dozen birds by the time I had reached the house described, of whose existence I was until then unaware. After rather carelessly inspecting the ruin, I resumed my sport, and having fairly good success, prolonged it until nearly sunset, when it occurred to me that I was a long way from any human habitation—too far to reach one by nightfall. But in my game bag was food, and the old house would afford shelter, if shelter were needed on a warm and dewless night in the foothills of the Sierra Nevada, where one may sleep in comfort on the pine needles, without covering. I am fond of solitude and love the night, so my resolution to "camp out" was soon taken, and by the time that it was dark I had made my bed of boughs and grasses in a corner of the room and was roasting a quail at a fire which I had kindled on the hearth. The smoke escaped out of the ruined chimney, the light illuminated the room with a kindly glow, and as I ate my simple meal of plain bird and drank the remains of a bottle of red wine which had served me all the afternoon in place of the water, which the region did not afford, I experienced a sense of comfort which better fare and accommodations do not always give. Nevertheless, there was something lacking. I had a sense of comfort, but not of security. I detected myself staring more frequently at the open doorway and blank window than I could find warrant for doing. Outside these apertures all was black, and I was unable to repress a certain feeling of apprehension as my fancy pictured the outer world and filled it with unfriendly existences, natural and supernatural—chief among which, in their respective classes, were the grizzly bear, which I knew was occasionally still seen in that region, and the ghost, which I had reason to think was not. Unfortunately, our feelings do not always respect the law of probabilities, and to me that evening, the possible and the impossible were equally disquieting. Everyone who has had experience in the matter must have observed that one confronts the actual and imaginary perils of the night with far less apprehension in the open air than in a house with an open doorway. I felt this now as I lay on my leafy couch in a corner of the room next to the chimney and permitted my fire to die out. So strong became my sense of the presence of something malign and menacing in the place, that I found myself almost unable to withdraw my eyes from the opening, as in the deepening darkness it became more and more distinct. And when the last little flame flickered and went out I grasped the shotgun which I had laid at my side and actually turned the muzzle in the direction of the now invisible entrance, my thumb on one of the hammers, ready to cock the piece, my breath suspended, my muscles rigid and tense. A moment later I laid down the weapon with a sense of shame and mortification. What did I fear, and why—I to whom the night had been

a more familiar face
Than that of man—

I in whom that element of hereditary superstition from which none of us is altogether free had but given to solitude and darkness and silence a more alluring charm and interest. I was unable to comprehend my folly, and losing in the conjecture the thing conjectured of, I fell asleep. And, sleeping, I dreamed.

I was in a great city in a foreign land—a city whose people were of my own race, with minor differences of speech and costume; yet precisely what these were I could not say; my sense of them was indistinct. The city was dominated by a great castle upon an overlooking height whose name I knew, but could not speak. I walked through many streets, some broad and straight with high modern buildings, some narrow, gloomy, and tortuous, between the gables of quaint old houses whose overhanging stories, elaborately ornamented with carvings in wood and stone, almost met above my head. I sought someone whom I had never seen, yet knew that I should recognize when found. My quest was not aimless and fortuitous; it had a definite method. I turned from one street into another without hesitation and threaded a maze of intricate passages, devoid of the fear of losing my way.

Presently I stopped before a low door in a plain stone house which might have been the dwelling of an artisan of the better sort, and without announcing myself, entered. The room, rather sparely furnished, and lighted by a single window with small diamond-shaped panes, had but two occupants: a man and a woman. They took no notice of my intrusion, a circumstance which, in the manner of dreams, appeared entirely natural. They were not conversing; they sat apart, unoccupied and sullen.

The woman was young and rather stout, with fine large eyes and a certain grave beauty; my memory of her expression is exceedingly vivid, but in dreams one does not observe the details of faces. About her shoulders was a plaid shawl. The man was older, dark, with an evil face made more forbidding by a long scar extending from near the left temple diagonally downward into the black mustache; though in my dreams it seemed rather to haunt the face as a thing apart—I can express it no otherwise—than to belong to it. The moment that I found the man and woman I knew them to be husband and wife. What followed, I remember indistinctly; it was confused and inconsistent—made so, I think, by gleams of consciousness. It was as if two pictures, the scene of my dream, and my actual surroundings, had been blended, one overlying the other, until the former, gradually fading, disappeared, and I was broad awake in the deserted cabin, entirely and tranquilly conscious of my situation.

My foolish fear was gone and, opening my eyes, I saw that my fire, not altogether burned out, had revived by the falling of a stick and was again lighting the room. I had probably slept but a few minutes, but my commonplace dream had somehow so strongly impressed me, that I was no longer drowsy, but after a little while rose, pushed the embers of my fire together, and lighting my pipe, proceeded in a rather ludicrously methodical way to meditate upon my vision. It would have puzzled me then to say in what respect it was worth attention. In the first moment of serious thought that I gave to the matter, I recognized the city of my dream as Edinburgh, where I had never been; so if the dream was a memory, it was a memory of pictures and description. The recognition somehow deeply impressed me; it was as if something in my mind insisted rebelliously against will and reason on the importance of all this. And that faculty, whatever it was, asserted also a control of my speech. "Surely," I said aloud, quite involuntarily, "the MacGregors must have come here from Edinburgh."

At the moment, neither the substance of this remark nor the fact of my making it, surprised me in the least; it seemed entirely natural that I should know the name of my dreamfolk and something of their history. But the absurdity of it all soon dawned upon me: I laughed audibly, knocked the ashes from my pipe, and again stretched myself upon my bed of boughs and grass, where I lay staring absently into my failing fire, with no further thought of either my dream or my surroundings. Suddenly the single remaining flame crouched for a moment, then, springing upward, lifted itself clear of its embers and expired in air. The darkness seemed absolute.

At that instant—almost, it seemed, before the gleam of the blaze had faded from my eyes—there was a dull, dead sound, as of some heavy body falling upon the floor, which shook beneath me as I lay. I sprang to a sitting posture and groped at my side for my gun; my notion was that some wild beast had leaped in through the open window. While the flimsy structure was still shaking from the impact, I heard the sound of blows, the scuffling of feet upon the floor, and then—it seemed to come from almost within reach of my hand, the sharp shrieking of a woman in mortal agony. So horrible a cry I had never heard nor conceived; it utterly unnerved me; I was conscious for a moment of nothing but my own terror! Fortunately my hand now found the weapon of which it was in search, and the familiar touch somewhat restored me. I leaped to my feet, straining my eyes to pierce the darkness. The violent sounds had ceased, but more terrible than these, I heard, at what seemed long intervals, the faint intermittent gasping of some living thing!

As my eyes grew accustomed to the dim light of the coals in the fireplace, I saw first the shapes of the door and window, looking blacker than the black of the walls. Next, the distinction between wall and floor became discernible, and at last I was sensible to the form and full expanse of the latter from end to end and side to side. Nothing was visible and the silence was unbroken.

With a hand that shook a little, the other still grasping my gun, I restored my fire, and made a critical examination of the place. There was nowhere any sign that the cabin had been entered. My own tracks were visible in the dust covering the floor, but there were no others. I relit my pipe, provided fresh fuel by ripping a thin board or two from the inside of the house—I did not care to go into the darkness out of doors— and passed the rest of the night smoking and thinking, and feeding my fire; not for a hundred added years of life would I have permitted that little flame to expire again.

Some years afterward, I met in Sacramento a man named Morgan, to whom I had a note of introduction from a friend in San Francisco. Dining with him one evening at his home, I observed various "trophies" upon the wall, indicating that he was fond of shooting. It turned out that he was, and in relating some of his feats, he mentioned having been in the region of my own adventure.

"Mr. Morgan," I asked abruptly, "do you know a place up there called Macarger's Gulch?"

"I have good reason to," he replied; "it was I who gave to the newspapers, last year, the accounts of the finding of the skeleton there."

I had not heard of it; the accounts had been published, it appeared, while I was absent in the East.

"By the way," said Morgan, "the name of the gulch is a corruption; it should have been called 'MacGregor's.' My dear," he added, speaking to his wife, "Mr. Elderson has upset his wine."

That was hardly accurate—I had simply dropped it, glass and all.

"There was an old shanty once in the gulch," Morgan resumed when the ruin wrought by my awkwardness had been repaired, "but just previously to my visit it had been blown down, or rather blown away, for its *debris* was scattered all about, the very floor being parted, plank from plank. Between two of the sleepers still in position, I and my companion observed the remnant of an old plaid shawl, and examining it, found that it was wrapped about the shoulders of the body of a woman, of which but little remained beside the bones, partly covered with fragments of clothing, and brown dry skin—but we will spare Mrs. Morgan," he added, with a smile. The lady had indeed exhibited signs of disgust rather than sympathy.

"It is necessary to say, however," he went on, "that the skull was fractured in several places, as by blows of some blunt instrument; and that instrument itself—a pick handle, still stained with blood—lay under the boards near by."

Mr. Morgan turned to his wife. "Pardon me, my dear," he said with affected solemnity, "for mentioning these disagreeable particulars, the natural though regrettable incidents of a conjugal quarrel resulting, doubtless, from the wife's insubordination."

"I ought to be able to overlook it," the lady replied with composure; "you have so many times asked me to in those very words."

I thought he seemed rather glad to go on with his story.

"From these and other circumstances," he said, "the coroner's jury found that the deceased, Janet MacGregor, came to her death from blows inflicted by some person to the jury unknown; but it was added that the evidence pointed strongly to her husband, Thomas MacGregor, as the guilty person. But Thomas MacGregor has never been found nor heard of. It was learned that the couple came from Edinburgh, but not—my dear, do you not observe that Mr. Elderson's bone plate has water in it?"

I had deposited a chicken bone in my finger bowl.

"In a little cupboard I found a photograph of MacGregor, but it did not lead to his capture."

"Will you let me see it?" I said.

The picture showed a dark man with an evil face made more forbidding by a long scar extending from near the temple diagonally downward into the black mustache.

"By the way, Mr. Elderson," said my affable host, "may I know why you asked about 'Macarger's Gulch'?"

"I lost a mule near there once," I replied, "and the mischance has—has quite—upset me."

"My dear," said Mr. Morgan, with the mechanical intonation of an interpreter translating, "the loss of Mr. Elderson's mule has peppered his coffee."

A KINSMAN OF RED CLOUD

Owen Wister

I

It was thirty minutes before a June sundown at the post, and the first call had sounded for parade. Over in the barracks the two companies and the single troop lounged a moment longer, then laid their police literature down, and lifted their stocking feet from the beds to get ready. In the officers' quarters the captain rose regretfully from after-dinner digestion, and the three lieutenants sought their helmets with a sigh. Lieutenant Balwin had been dining an unconventional and impressive guest at the mess, and he now interrupted the anecdote which the guest was achieving with frontier deliberation.

"Make yourself comfortable," he said. "I'll have to hear the rest about the half-breed when I get back."

"There ain't no more—yet. He got my cash with his private poker deck that onced, and I'm fixing for to get his'n."

Second call sounded; the lines filed out and formed, the sergeant of the guard and two privates took their station by the flag, and when battalion was formed the commanding officer, towering steeple-stiff beneath his plumes, received the adjutant's salute, ordered him to his post, and began drill. At all this the unconventional guest looked on comfortably from Lieutenant Balwin's porch.

"I doubt if I could put up with that there discipline all the week," he mused. "Carry—*arms!* Present—*Arms!* I guess that's all I know of it." The winking white line of gloves stirred his approval. "Pretty good that. Gosh, see the sun on them bayonets!"

The last note of retreat merged in the sonorous gun, and the flag shining in the light of evening slid down and rested upon the earth. The blue ranks marched to a single bugle—the post was short of men and officers—and the captain, with the released lieutenants, again sought digestion and cigars. Balwin returned to his guest, and together they watched the day forsake the plain. Presently the guest rose to take his leave. He looked old enough to be the father of the young officer, but he was a civilian, and the military man proceeded to give him excellent advice.

"Now don't get into trouble, Cutler."

The slouch-shouldered scout rolled his quid gently, and smiled at his superior with indulgent regard.

"See here, Cutler, you have a highly unoccupied look about you this evening. I've been studying the customs of this population, and I've noted a fact or two."

"Let 'em loose on me, sir."

"Fact one: When any male inhabitant of Fort Laramie has a few spare moments, he hunts up a game of cards."

"Well, sir, you've called the turn on me."

"Fact two: At Fort Laramie a game of cards frequently ends in discussion."

"Fact three: Mr. Balwin, in them discussions Jarvis Cutler has the last word. You put that in your census report alongside the other two."

"Well, Cutler, if somebody's gun should happen to beat yours in an argument, I should have to hunt another wagon-master."

"I'll not forget that. When was you expecting to pull out north?"

"Whenever the other companies get here. May be three days—may be three weeks."

"Then I will have plenty time for a game to-night."

With this slight dig of his civilian independence into the lieutenant's military ribs, the scout walked away, his long, lugubrious frockcoat (worn in honor of the mess) occasionally flapping open in the breeze, and giving a view of a belt richly fluted with cartridges, and the ivory handle of a pistol looking out of its holster. He got on his horse, crossed the flat, and struck out for the cabin of his sociable friends, Loomis and Kelley, on the hill. The open door and a light inside showed the company, and Cutler gave a grunt, for sitting on the table was the half-breed, the winner of his unavenged dollars. He rode slower, in order to think, and arriving at the corral below the cabin, tied his horse to the stump of a cottonwood. A few steps towards the door, and he wheeled on a sudden thought, and under cover of the night did a crafty something which to the pony was altogether unaccountable. He unloosed both front and rear cinch of his saddle, so they hung entirely free in wide bands beneath the pony's belly. He tested their slackness with his hand several times, stopping instantly when the more and more surprised pony turned his head to see what new thing in his experience might be going on, and, seeing, gave a delicate bounce with his hind-quarters.

"Never you mind, Duster," muttered the scout. "Did you ever see a skunk-trap? Oughts is for mush-rats, and number ones is mostly used for 'coons and 'possums, and I guess they'd do for a skunk. But you and we'll call this here trap a number two, Duster, for the skunk I'm after is a big one. All you've to do is to act natural."

Cutler took the rope off the stump by which Duster had been tied securely, wound and strapped it to the tilted saddle, and instead of this former tether, made a weak knot in the reins, and tossed them over the stump. He entered the cabin with a countenance sweeter than honey.

"Good-evening, boys," he said. "Why, Toussaint, how do you do?"

The hand of Toussaint had made a slight, a very slight, movement towards his hip, but at sight of Cutler's mellow smile resumed its clasp upon his knee.

"Golly, but you're gay-like this evening," said Kelley.

"Blamed if I knowed he could look so frisky," added Loomis.

"Sporting his onced-a-year coat," Kelley pursued. "That ain't for our benefit, Joole."

"No, we're not that high in society." Both these cheerful waifs had drifted from the Atlantic coast westward.

Cutler looked from them to his costume, and then amiably surveyed the half-breed.

"Well, boys, I'm in big luck, I am. How's yourn nowadays, Toussaint?"

"Pretty good sometime. Sometime heap hell." The voice of the half-breed came as near heartiness as its singularly false quality would allow, and as he smiled he watched Cutler with the inside of his eyes.

The scout watched nobody and nothing with great care, looked about him pleasantly, inquired for the whiskey, threw aside hat and gloves, sat down, leaning the chair back against the wall, and talked with artful candor. "Them sprigs of lieutenants down there," said he, "they're a surprising lot for learning virtue to a man. You take Balwin. Why, he ain't been out of the Academy only two years, and he's been telling me how card-playing ain't good for you. And what do you suppose he's been and offered Jarvis Cutler for a job? I'm to be wagon-master." He paused, and the half-breed's attention to his next words increased. "Wagon-master, and good pay, too. Clean up to the Black Hills; and the troops'll move soon as ever them reinforcements come. Drinks on it, boys! Set 'em up, Joole Loomis. My contract's sealed with some of Uncle Sam's cash, and I'm going to play it right here. Hello! Somebody coming to join us? He's in a hurry."

There was a sound of lashing straps and hoofs beating the ground, and Cutler looked out of the door. As he had calculated, the saddle had gradually turned with Duster's movements and set the pony bucking.

"Stampeded!" said the scout, and swore the proper amount called for by such circumstances. "Some o' you boys help me stop the durned fool."

Loomis and Kelley ran. Duster had jerked the prepared reins from the cottonwood, and was lurching down a small dry gulch, with the saddle bouncing between his belly and the stones.

Cutler cast a backward eye at the cabin where Toussaint had stayed behind alone. "Head him off below, boys, and I'll head him off above," the scout sang out. He left his companions, and quickly circled round behind the cabin, stumbling once heavily, and hurrying on, anxious lest the noise had reached the lurking half-breed. But the

ivory-handled pistol, jostled from its holster, lay unheeded among the stones where
he had stumbled. He advanced over the rough ground, came close to the logs, and
craftily peered in at the small window in the back of the cabin. It was evident that he
had not been heard. The sinister figure within still sat on the table, but was crouched,
listening like an animal to the shouts that were coming from a safe distance down in
the gulch. Cutler, outside of the window, could not see the face of Toussaint, but he
saw one long brown hand sliding up and down the man's leg, and its movement put
him in mind of the tail of a cat. The hand stopped to pull out a pistol, into which fresh
cartridges were slipped. Cutler had already done this same thing after dismounting,
and he now felt confident that his weapon needed no further examination. He did not
put his hand to his holster. The figure rose from the table, and crossed the room to a
set of shelves in front of which hung a little yellow curtain. Behind it were cups, cans,
bottles, a pistol, counters, red, white, and blue, and two fresh packs of cards, blue and
pink, side by side. Seeing these, Toussaint drew a handkerchief from his pocket, and
unwrapped two further packs, both blue; and at this Cutler's intent face grew into plain
shape close to the window, but receded again into uncertain dimness. From down in
the gulch came shouts that the runaway horse was captured. Toussaint listened, ran
to the door, and quickly returning, put the blue pack from the shelf into his pocket,
leaving in exchange one of his own. He hesitated about altering the position of the
cards on the shelf, but Kelley and Loomis were unobservant young men, and the
half-breed placed the pink cards on top of his blue ones. The little yellow curtain
again hung innocently over the shelves, and Toussaint, pouring himself a drink of
whiskey, faced round, and for the first time saw the window that had been behind his
back. He was at it in an instant, wrenching its rusty pin, that did not give, but stuck
motionless in the wood. Cursing, he turned and hurried out of the door and round
the cabin. No one was there. Some hundred yards away the noiseless Cutler crawled
farther among the thickets that filled the head of the gulch. Toussaint whipped out a
match, and had it against his trousers to strike and look if there were footprints, when
second thoughts warned him this might be seen, and was not worth risking suspicion
over, since so many feet came and went by this cabin. He told himself no one could
have been there to see him, and slowly returned inside, with a mind that fell a hair's
breadth short of conviction.

The boys, coming up with the horse, met Cutler, who listened to how Duster had
stood still as soon as he had kicked free of his saddle, making no objection to being
caught. They suggested that he would not have broken loose had he been tied with
a rope; and hearing this, Cutler bit off a piece of tobacco, and told them they were
quite right: a horse should never be tied by his bridle. For a savory moment the scout

cuddled his secret, and turned it over like the tobacco lump under his tongue. Then he explained, and received serenely the amazement of Loomis and Kelley.

"When you kids have travelled this Western country awhile you'll keep your cards locked," said he. "He's going to let us win first. You'll see, he'll play a poor game with the pink deck. Then, if we don't call for fresh cards, why, he'll call for 'em himself. But, just for the fun of the thing, if any of us loses steady, why, we'll call. Then, when he gets hold of his strippers, watch out. When he makes his big play, and is stretchin' for to rake the counters in, you grab 'em, Joole; for by then I'll have my gun on him, and if he makes any trouble we'll feed him to the coyotes. I expect that must have been it, boys," he continued, in a new tone, as they came within possible ear-shot of the half-breed in the cabin. "A coyote come around him where he was tied. The fool horse has seen enough of 'em to git used to 'em, you'd think, but he don't. There; that'll hold him. I guess he'll have to pull the world along with him if he starts to run again."

The lamp was placed on the window-shelf, and the four took seats, Cutler to the left of Toussaint, with Kelley opposite. The pink cards fell harmless, and for a while the game was a dull one to see. Holding a pair of kings, Cutler won a little from Toussaint, who remarked that luck must go with the money of Uncle Sam. After a few hands, the half-breed began to bet with ostentatious folly, and, losing to one man and another, was joked upon the falling off of his game. In an hour's time his blue chips had been twice reinforced, and twice melted from the neat often-counted pile in which he arranged them; moreover, he had lost a horse from his string down on Chug Water.

"Lend me ten dollar," he said to Cutler. "You rich man now."

In the next few deals Kelley became poor. "I'm sick of this luck," said he.

"Then change it, why don't you? Let's have a new deck." And Loomis rose.

"Joole, you always are for something new," said Cutler. "Now I'm doing pretty well with these pink cards. But I'm no hog. Fetch on your fresh ones."

The eyes of the half-breed swerved to the yellow curtain. He was by a French trapper from Canada out of a Sioux squaw, one of Red Cloud's sisters, and his heart beat hot with the evil of two races, and none of their good. He was at this moment irrationally angry with the men who had won from him through his own devices, and malice undisguised shone in his lean flat face. At sight of the blue cards falling in the first deal, silence came over the company, and from the distant parade-ground the bugle sounded the melancholy strain of taps. Faint, far, solemn, melodious, the music travelled unhindered across the empty night.

"Them men are being checked off in their bunks now," said Cutler.

"What you bet this game?" demanded Toussaint.

"I've heard 'em play that same music over a soldier's grave," said Kelley.

"You goin' to bet?" Toussaint repeated.

Cutler pushed forward the two necessary white chips. No one's hand was high, and Loomis made a slight winning. The deal went its round several times, and once, when it was Toussaint's, Cutler suspected that special cards had been thrown to him by the half-breed as an experiment. He therefore played the gull to a nicety, betting gently upon his three kings; but when he stepped out boldly and bet the limit, it was not Toussaint but Kelley who held the higher hand, winning with three aces. Why the coup should be held off longer puzzled the scout, unless it was that Toussaint was carefully testing the edges of his marked cards to see if he controlled them to a certainty. So Cutler played on calmly. Presently two aces came to him in Toussaint's deal, and he wondered how many more would be in his three-card draw. Very pretty! One only, and he lost to Loomis, who had drawn three, and held four kings. The hands were getting higher, they said. The game had "something to it now." But Toussaint grumbled, for his luck was bad all this year, he said. Cutler had now made sure that the aces and kings went where the half-breed wished, and could be slid undetected from the top or the middle or the bottom of the pack; but he had no test yet how far down the scale the marking went. At Toussaint's next deal Cutler judged the time had come, and at the second round of betting he knew it. The three white men played their parts, raising each other without pause, and again there was total silence in the cabin. Every face bent to the table, watching the turn repeat its circle with obstinate increase, until new chips and more new chips had been brought to keep on with, and the heap in the middle had mounted high in the hundreds, while in front of Toussaint lay his knife and a match-box—pledges of two more horses which he had staked. He had drawn three cards, while the others took two, except Cutler, who had a pair of kings again, and drawing three, picked up two more. Kelley dropped out, remarking he had bet more than his hand was worth, which was true, and Loomis followed him. Their persistence had surprised Toussaint a little. He had not given every one suspicious hands: Cutler's four kings were enough. He bet once more, was raised by the scout, called, and threw down his four aces.

"That beats me," said Cutler, quietly, and his hand moved under his frock-coat, as the half-breed, eyeing the central pile of counters in triumph, closed his fingers over it. They were dashed off by Kelley, who looked expectantly across at Cutler, and seeing the scout's face wither into sudden old age, cried out, "For God's sake, Jarvis, where's your gun?" Kelley sprang for the yellow curtain, and reeled backward at the shot of Toussaint. His arm thrashed along the window-sill as he fell, sweeping over the lamp, and flaring channels of oil ran over his body and spread on the ground. But these could no longer hurt him. The half-breed had leaped outside the cabin, enraged that

Cutler should have got out during the moment he had been dealing with Kelley. The scout was groping for his ivory-handled pistol off in the darkness. He found it, and hurried to the little window at a second shot he heard inside. Loomis, beating the rising flame away, had seized the pistol from the shelf, and aimlessly fired into the night at Toussaint. He fired again, running to the door from the scorching heat. Cutler got round the house to save him if he could, and saw the half-breed's weapon flash, and the body pitch out across the threshold. Toussaint, gaining his horse, shot three times and missed Cutler, whom he could not clearly see; and he heard the scout's bullets sing past him as his horse bore him rushing away.

II

Jarvis Cutler lifted the dead Loomis out of the cabin. He made a try for Kelley's body, but the room had become a cave of flame, and he was driven from the door. He wrung his hands, giving himself bitter blame aloud, as he covered Loomis with his saddle-blanket, and jumped bareback upon Duster to go to the post. He had not been riding a minute when several men met him. They had seen the fire from below, and on their way up the half-breed had passed them at a run.

"Here's our point," said Cutler. "Will he hide with the Sioux, or will he take to the railroad? Well, that's my business more than being wagon-master. I'll get a warrant. You tell Lieutenant Balwin—and somebody give me a fresh horse."

A short while later, as Cutler, with the warrant in his pocket, rode out of Fort Laramie, the call of the sentinels came across the night: "Number One. Twelve o'clock, and all's well." A moment, and the refrain sounded more distant, given by Number Two. When the fourth took it up, far away along the line, the words were lost, leaving something like the faint echo of a song. The half-breed had crossed the Platte, as if he were making for his kindred tribe, but the scout did not believe in this too plain trail.

"There's Chug Water lying right the other way from where he went, and I guess it's there Mr. Toussaint is aiming for." With this idea Cutler swung from north to southwest along the Laramie. He went slowly over his shortcut, not to leave the widely circling Toussaint too much in his rear. The fugitive would keep himself carefully far on the other side of the Laramie, and very likely not cross it until the forks of Chug Water. Dawn had ceased to be gray, and the doves were cooing incessantly among the river thickets, when Cutler, reaching the forks, found a bottom where the sage-brush grew seven and eight feet high, and buried himself and his horse in its cover. Here was comfort; here both rivers could be safely watched. It seemed a good leisure-time for a little fire and some breakfast. He eased his horse of the saddle, sliced some bacon, and put a match to his pile of small sticks. As the flame caught, he stood up to enjoy the cool of a breeze that was passing through the stillness, and he suddenly stamped his fire out. The smell of another fire had come across Chug Water on the wind. It was incredible that Toussaint should be there already. There was no seeing from this bottom, and if Cutler walked up out of it the other man would see too. If it were Toussaint, he would not stay long in the vast exposed plain across Chug Water, but would go on after his meal. In twenty minutes it would be the thing to swim or wade the stream, and crawl up the mud bank to take a look. Meanwhile, Cutler dipped in water some old bread that he had and sucked it down, while the little breeze from opposite shook the cottonwood leaves and brought over the smell of cooking meat. The sun grew warmer, and the doves ceased. Cutler opened his big watch, and clapped it shut as the sound of mud heavily slopping into the other river reached him. He crawled to where he could look at the Laramie from among his sage-brush, and there was Toussaint leading his horse down to the water. The half-breed gave a shrill call, and waved his hat. His call was answered, and as he crossed the Laramie, three Sioux appeared, riding to the bank. They waited till he gained their level, when all four rode up the Chug Water, and went out of sight opposite the watching Cutler. The scout threw off some of his clothes, for the water was still high, and when he had crossed, and drawn himself to a level with the plain, there were the four squatted among the sage-brush beside a fire. They sat talking and eating for some time. One of them rose at last, pointed south, and mounting his horse, dwindled to a dot, blurred, and evaporated in the heated, trembling distance. Cutler at the edge of the bank still watched the other three, who sat on the ground. A faint shot came, and they rose at once, mounted, and vanished southward. There was no following them now in this exposed country, and Cutler, feeling sure that the signal had meant something about Toussaint's horses, made his fire, watered his own horse, and letting him drag a rope where the feed was green, ate his breakfast in ease. Toussaint would get a fresh mount, and proceed to the railroad. With the comfort of certainty and tobacco, the scout lolled by the river under the cottonwood, and even slept. In the cool of the afternoon he reached the cabin of an acquaintance twenty miles south, and changed his horse. A man had passed by, he was told. Looked as if bound for Cheyenne. "No," Cutler said, "he's known there"; and he went on, watching Toussaint's tracks. Within ten miles they veered away from Cheyenne to the southeast, and Cutler struck out on a trail of his own more freely. By midnight he was on Lodge-Pole Creek, sleeping sound among the last trees that he would pass. He slept twelve hours, having gone to bed knowing he must not come into town by daylight. About nine o'clock he arrived, and went to the railroad station; there the operator knew him. The lowest haunt in the town had a tent south of the Union Pacific tracks; and Cutler, getting his irons, and a man from the saloon, went there, and stepped in, covering the room with his pistol. The fiddle stopped, the shrieking women scattered, and Toussaint, who had a glass in his hand, let it fly at Cutler's head, for he was drunk. There were two customers besides himself.

"Nobody shall get hurt here," said Cutler, above the bedlam that was now set up. "Only that man's wanted. The quieter I get him, the quieter it'll be for others."

Toussaint had dived for his pistol, but the proprietor of the dance-hall, scenting law, struck the half-breed with the butt of another, and he rolled over, and was harmless for some minutes. Then he got on his legs, and was led out of the entertainment, which resumed more gayly than ever. Feet shuffled, the fiddle whined, and truculent treble laughter sounded through the canvas walls as Toussaint walked between Cutler and the saloon-man to jail. He was duly indicted, and upon the scout's deposition committed to trial for the murder of Loomis and Kelley. Cutler, hoping still to be wagon-master, wrote to Lieutenant Balwin, hearing in reply that the reinforcements would not arrive for two months. The session of the court came in one, and Cutler was the Territory's only witness. He gave his name and age, and hesitated over his occupation.

"Call it poker-dealer," sneered Toussaint's attorney.

"I would, but I'm such a fool one," observed the witness. "Put me down as wagon-master to the military outfit that's going to White River."

"What is your residence?"

"Well, I reside in the section that lies between the Missouri River and the Pacific Ocean."

"A pleasant neighborhood," said the judge, who knew Cutler perfectly, and precisely how well he could deal poker hands.

"It's not a pleasant neighborhood for some." And Cutler looked at Toussaint.

"You think you done with me?" Toussaint inquired, upon which silence was ordered in the court.

Upon Cutler's testimony the half-breed was found guilty, and sentenced to be hanged in six weeks from that day. Hearing this, he looked at the witness. "I see you one day agin," he said.

The scout returned to Fort Laramie, and soon the expected troops arrived, and the expedition started for White River to join Captain Brent. The captain was stationed there to impress Red Cloud, and had written to headquarters that this chief did not seem impressed very deeply, and that the lives of the settlers were insecure. Reinforcements were accordingly sent to him. On the evening before these soldiers left Laramie, news came from the south. Toussaint had escaped from jail. The country was full of roving, dubious Indians, and with the authentic news went a rumor that the jailer had received various messages. These were to the effect that the Sioux nation did not desire

Toussaint to be killed by the white man, that Toussaint's mother was the sister of Red Cloud, and that many friends of Toussaint often passed the jailer's house. Perhaps he did get such messages. They are not a nice sort to receive. However all this may have been, the prisoner was gone.

III

Fort Robinson, on the White River, is backed by yellow bluffs that break out of the foot-hills in turret and toadstool shapes, with stunt pines starving between their torrid bastions. In front of the fort the land slants away into the flat unfeatured desert, and in summer the sky is a blue-steel covet that each day shuts the sun and the earth and mankind into one box together, while it lifts at night to let in the cool of the stars. The White River, which is not wide, runs in a curve, and around this curve below the fort some distance was the agency, and beyond it a stockade, inside which in those days dwelt the settlers. All this was strung out on one side of the White River, outside of the curve; and at a point near the agency a foot-bridge of two cottonwood trunks crossed to the concave of the river's bend—a bottom of some extent, filled with growing cottonwoods, and the tepees of many Sioux families. Along the river and on the plain other tepees stood.

One morning, after Lieutenant Balwin had become established at Fort Robinson, he was talking with his friend Lieutenant Powell, when Cutler knocked at the wire door. The wagon-master was a privileged character, and he sat down and commented irrelevantly upon the lieutenant's pictures, Indian curiosities, and other well-meant attempts to conceal the walls.

"What's the trouble, Cutler?"

"Don't know as there's any trouble."

"Come to your point, man; you're not a scout now."

"Toussaint's here."

"What! in camp?"

"Hiding with the Sioux. Two Knives heard about it." (Two Knives was a friendly Indian.) "He's laying for me," Cutler added.

"You've seen him?"

"No. I want to quit my job and go after him."

"Nonsense!" said Powell.

"You can't, Cutler," said Balwin. "I can't spare you."

"You'll be having to fill my place, then, I guess."

"You mean to go without permission?" said Powell, sternly.

"Lord, no! He'll shoot me. That's all."

The two lieutenants pondered.

"And it's to-day," continued Cutler, plaintively, "that he should be gettin' hanged in Cheyenne."

Still the lieutenants pondered, while the wagon-master inspected a photograph of Marie Rose as Marguerite.

"I have it!" exclaimed Powell. "Let's kill him."

"How about the commanding officer?"

"He'd back us—but we'll tell him afterwards. Cutler, can you find Toussaint?"

"If I get the time."

"Very well, you're off duty till you do. Then report to me at once."

Just after guard-mounting two days later, Cutler came in without knocking. Toussaint was found. He was down on the river now, beyond the stockade. In ten minutes the wagon-master and the two lieutenants were rattling down to the agency in an ambulance, behind four tall blue government mules. These were handily driven by a seventeen-year-old boy whom Balwin had picked up, liking his sterling American ways. He had come West to be a cow-boy, but a chance of helping to impress Red Cloud had seemed still dearer to his heart. They drew up at the agency store, and all went in, leaving the boy nearly out of his mind with curiosity, and pretending to be absorbed with the reins. Presently they came out, Balwin with field-glasses.

"Now," said he, "where?"

"You see the stockade, sir?"

"Well?" said Powell, sticking his chin on Cutler's shoulder to look along his arm as he pouted. But the scout proposed to be deliberate.

"Now the gate of the stockade is this way, ain't it?"

"Well, well?"

"You start there and follow the fence to the corner—the left corner, towards the river. Then you follow the side that's nearest the river down to the other corner. Now that corner is about a hundred yards from the bank. You take a bee-line to the bank and go down stream, maybe thirty yards. No; it'll be forty yards, I guess. There's a lone pine-tree right agin the edge." The wagon-master stopped.

"I see all that," said Lieutenant Balwin, screwing the field-glasses. "There's a buck and a squaw lying under the tree."

"Naw, sir," drawled Cutler, "that ain't no buck. That's him lying in his Injun blanket and chinnin' a squaw."

"Why, that man's an Indian, Cutler. I tell you I can see his braids."

"Oh, he's rigged up Injun fashion, fust rate, sir. But them braids of his ain't his'n. False hair."

The lieutenants passed each other the field-glasses three times, and glared at the lone pine and the two figures in blankets. The boy on the ambulance was unable to pretend any longer, and leaned off his seat till he nearly fell.

"Well," said Balwin, "I never saw anything look more like a buck Sioux. Look at his paint. Take the glasses yourself, Cutler."

But Cutler refused. "He's like an Injun," he said. "But that's just what he wants to be." The scout's conviction bore down their doubt.

They were persuaded. "You can't come with us, Cutler," said Powell. "You must wait for us here."

"I know, sir; he'd spot us, sure. But it ain't right. I started this whole business with my poker scheme at that cabin, and I ought to stay with it clear through."

The officers went into the agency store and took down two rifles hanging at the entrance, always ready for use. "We're going to kill a man," they explained, and the owner was entirely satisfied. They left the rueful Cutler inside, and proceeded to the gate of the stockade, turning there to the right, away from the river, and following the paling round the corner down to the farther right-hand corner. Looking from behind it, the lone pine-tree stood near, and plain against the sky. The striped figures lay still in their blankets, talking, with their faces to the river. Here and there across the stream the smoke-stained peak of a tepee showed among the green leaves.

"Did you ever see a more genuine Indian?" inquired Balwin.

"We must let her rip now, anyhow," said Powell, and they stepped out into the open. They walked towards the pine till it was a hundred yards from them, and the two beneath it lay talking all the while. Balwin covered the man with his rifle and called. The man turned his head, and seeing the rifle, sat up in his blanket. The squaw sat up also. Again the officer called, keeping his rifle steadily pointed, and the man dived like a frog over the bank. Like magic his blanket had left his limbs and painted body naked, except for the breech-clout. Balwin's tardy bullet threw earth over the squaw, who went flapping and screeching down the river. Balwin and Powell ran to the edge, which dropped six abrupt feet of clay to a trail, then shelved into the swift little stream. The red figure was making up the trail to the foot-bridge that led to the Indian houses, and both officers fired. The man continued his limber flight, and they jumped down and followed, firing. They heard a yell on the plain above, and an answer to it, and then confused yells above and below, gathering all the while. The figure ran on above the river trail below the bank, and their bullets whizzed after it.

"Indian!" asserted Balwin, panting.

"Ran away, though," said Powell.

"So'd you run. Think any Sioux'd stay when an army officer comes gunning for him?"

"Shoot!" said Powell. "'S getting near bridge," and they went on, running and firing. The yells all over the plain were thickening. The air seemed like a substance of solid flashing sound. The naked runner came round the river curve into view of the people at the agency store.

"Where's a rifle?" said Cutler to the agent.

"Officers got 'em," the agent explained.

"Well, I can't stand this," said the scout, and away he went.

"That man's crazy," said the agent.

"You bet he ain't!" remarked the ambulance boy.

Cutler was much nearer to the bridge than was the man in the breech-clout, and reaching the bank, he took half a minute's keen pleasure in watching the race come up the trail. When the figure was within ten yards Cutler slowly drew an ivory-handled pistol. The lieutenants below saw the man leap to the middle of the bridge, sway suddenly with arms thrown up, and topple into White River. The current swept the body down, and as it came it alternately lifted and turned and sank as the stream played with it. Sometimes it struck submerged stumps or shallows, and bounded half out of water, then drew under with nothing but the back of the head in sight, turning round and round. The din of Indians increased, and from the tepees in the cottonwoods the red Sioux began to boil, swarming on the opposite bank, but uncertain what had happened. The man rolling in the water was close to the officers.

"It's not our man," said Balwin. "Did you or I hit him?"

"We're gone, anyhow," said Powell, quietly. "Look!"

A dozen rifles were pointing at their heads on the bank above. The Indians still hesitated, for there was Two Knives telling them these officers were not enemies, and had hurt no Sioux. Suddenly Cutler pushed among the rifles, dashing up the nearest two with his arm, and their explosion rang in the ears of the lieutenants. Powell stood grinning at the general complication of matters that had passed beyond his control, and Balwin made a grab as the head of the man in the river washed by. The false braid came off in his hand!

"Quick!" shouted Cutler from the bank. "Shove him up here!"

Two Knives redoubled his harangue, and the Indians stood puzzled, while the lieutenants pulled Toussaint out, not dead, but shot through the hip. They dragged him over the clay and hoisted him, till Cutler caught hold and jerked him to the level, as a new noise of rattling descended on the crowd, and the four blue mules wheeled up and halted. The boy had done it himself. Massing the officers' need, he had pelted down among the Sioux, heedless of their yells, and keeping his gray eyes on his team. In got the three, pushing Toussaint in front, and scoured away for the post as the squaw arrived to shriek the truth to her tribe—that Red Cloud's relation had been the victim.

Cutler sat smiling as the ambulance swung along. "I told you I belonged in this here affair," he said. And when they reached the fort he was saying it still, occasionally.

Captain Brent considered it neatly done. "But that boy put the finishing touches," he said. "Let's have him in."

The boy was had in, and ate a dinner with the officers in glum embarrassment, smoking a cigar after it without joy. Toussaint was given into the doctor's hands, and his wounds carefully dressed.

"This will probably cost an Indian outbreak," said Captain Brent, looking down at the plain. Blanketed riders galloped over it, and yelling filled the air. But Toussaint was not destined to cause this further harm. An unexpected influence intervened.

All afternoon the cries and galloping went on, and next morning (worse sign) there seemed to be no Indians in the world. The horizon was empty, the air was silent, the smoking tepees were vanished from the cottonwoods, and where those in the plain had been lay the lodge-poles, and the fires were circles of white, cold ashes. By noon an interpreter came from Red Cloud. Red Cloud would like to have Toussaint. If the white man was not willing, it should be war.

Captain Brent told the story of Loomis and Kelley. "Say to Red Cloud," he ended, "that when a white man does such things among us, he is killed. Ask Red Cloud if Toussaint should live. If he thinks yes, let him come and take Toussaint."

The next day with ceremony and feathers of state, Red Cloud came, bringing his interpreter, and after listening until every word had been told him again, requested to see the half-breed. He was taken to the hospital. A sentry stood on post outside the tent, and inside lay Toussaint, with whom Cutler and the ambulance-boy were playing whiskey-poker. While the patient was waiting to be hanged, he might as well enjoy himself within reason. Such was Cutler's frontier philosophy. We should always do what we can for the sick. At sight of Red Cloud looming in the doorway, gorgeous and grim as Fate, the game was suspended. The Indian took no notice of the white men, and walked to the bed. Toussaint clutched at his relation's fringe, but Red Cloud looked at him. Then the mongrel strain of blood told, and the half-breed poured out a chattering appeal, while Red Cloud by the bedside waited till it had spent itself. Then he grunted, and left the room. He had not spoken, and his crest of long feathers as it turned the corner was the last vision of him that the card-players had.

Red Cloud came back to the officers, and in their presence formally spoke to his interpreter, who delivered the message: "Red Cloud says Toussaint heap no good. No Injun, anyhow. He not want him. White man hunt pretty hard for him. Can keep him."

Thus was Toussaint twice sentenced. He improved under treatment, played many games of whiskey-poker, and was conveyed to Cheyenne and hanged.

These things happened in the early seventies; but there are Sioux still living who remember the two lieutenants, and how they pulled the half-breed out of White River by his false hair. It makes them laugh to this day. Almost any Indian is full of talk when he chooses, and when he gets hold of a joke he never lets go.

IN THE JUNGLE

THE GOLDEN ANACONDA

Elmer Brown Mason

I

The professor cautiously raised his flaming red head above the side of the boat, reached back, picked up a felt-wrapped wire loop attached to a thick cord, and lunged over the bow.

"Got him!" he yelled, and I threw my weight on the cord. Instantly there was a terrific splashing. The jungle awoke to the chatter of monkeys, shrieks of gorgeously colored macaws, and the clear-toned clang of a bell bird's voice. From a lather of foam emerged the head of an anaconda, the great water boa of South America, lashing the river with its sides as it swam from us. The professor calmly began to row against the great snake, while I dragged at the rope, using one of the seats as a lever. The boat slid over the captive, and the prof, dropping his oars, imprisoned its tail in another felt-protected loop. Then we caught the wicked head in a steel mesh net, hauled it on board, and tied it up—it was a little one, only about ten feet long.

Easy, wasn't it? But it didn't always work out that way. Nothing on earth has a worse disposition than an anaconda, save, perhaps, an angry bee. The day before, we had hooked onto an eighteen-foot monster and not been able to gain an inch on it. Reddy finally gave me a little slack by rowing with its pull. The anaconda decided to come into the boat of its own accord, mouth wide open, looking as though it didn't need a dentist. I shot its head to pieces and a leg of the prof's pants, with a load of No. 6, and we spent some time plugging up the bullet holes in the forward part of the skiff.

Nevertheless I liked the excitement, and the whole proposition was certainly a sporting on. Professor Ritchie McKee had blown into Père Guerrin's café in New Orleans, red head and all, with three hundred dollars, orders from every zoological garden in America covering several tons of snakes, and the proposition that I help finance an expedition up the Magdalena River into Colombia. He was a little middle-aged Scotchman, with china-blue eyes, the flaming red hair I have already mentioned, and an argument that he needed the money.

Somehow he hit me just right, and we were calling one another Reddy and Wandering within the hour while quarreling over the respective merits of different brands of canned goods in a tropical climate. The upshot of the matter was that I now found myself in the upper reaches of the Magdalena River, navigating, with the assistance of three mestizos and Mose, my cook, a flat-bottomed, broad-beamed, wood-burning thing built like a house boat and loaded with snake cages.

Don't think for a moment that we got where we were without the slightest difficulty, just paddled along, fanned by tropic breezes. We didn't. And the worst of our troubles began and never ended when we picked up the orchid hunter.

There was nothing much doing until we were well up the Magdalena, past where you take the overland route for Bogotá. The river, before that point, had been alive with alligators, which made it unhealthy for anacondas, and, as anacondas were our main objective, we did not waste time on shore looking for other kinds of snakes. Once beyond the Bogotá connection, however, we anchored and put off in a skiff to explore a small tributary. There we took our first big water snake, right at the mouth, and a pretty struggle we had, too. After carrying it aboard our flatboat, we went up farther, and a mile from the main river, came upon the most incongruous craft, deserted and tied to the bank, that you can possibly in the middle of South America. It was a thirty-foot launch, decked over, brave with white paint and brass fittings, the simple engine built to burn wood, and the most perfectly appointed thing I have ever seen.

Hardly had we finished examining it and got back into our own boat when there was a wild chorus of yells from the jungle, the spat-spat-spat! Of an automatic, and a lanky white man jumped on deck, cast off the line, and, dodging into the cabin, let the launch go down with the current. The air was instantly full of that sharp whistling sound that I had learned, on a previous trip, to associate with the tiny poisoned arrows the natives shoot from their bamboo blowguns, and I promptly yanked out boat around under the protection of the bulwarks of the larger craft. For five minutes, as we were carried swiftly down the stream, we all lay low, and then the white man put his head over the side of the launch.

He had about as disagreeable a face as I have ever looked upon: very high forehead, long pointed nose, thin lips, and the longest curved white teeth I have ever seen in a human being's mouth—they were more like an animal's than a man's—and his first remark was quite in keeping with his appearance:

"Who the devil are you, pray?"

It made me mad, of course. White men are not only polite to one another in the jungle through motives of policy, but also because they generally are really glad to see a face of their own color.

"This is King Bruce, late of Scotland," I answered, "and if you include me in your polite inquiry, allow me to present myself as the Archbishop of Canterbury."

"None of your nonsense!" he snarled. "I want to know who you are," and he actually threw an automatic on us.

There was not one thing to do. I just ached to get my hands on him, but you can't rush a twelve-shoot gun from a skiff onto a launch. I swallowed my mad as best I could, and was just beginning to tell him our entire family history when there was a whistling whir in the air, the automatic clattered to the deck, and a pretty little poisoned arrow was sticking in his wrist. He grabbed up the gun with his left hand, turning it loose into the jungle, and by that time we were both on board.

In a few moments the wounded man turned a sickly green, and we certainly had one time over him! Reddy was always loaded up with the snake-bite dope and we treated him with the dissolved purple crystals of permanganate of potash and injections of strychnine, praying at the same time, that the arrow was tipped only with snake poison, and not the deadly *wourali* for which there is really no antidote. We pulled him through finally, but only after five hours' work; and meanwhile we put several long miles between ourselves and that unhealthy locality, the launch towing behind our flat-bottomed side-wheeler.

When our involuntary guest came to, he was frankly distrustful, but somewhat more polite. He volunteered the information that his name was Hiram Jones—Hiram Jones nothing! I know a John Doe when I see one, and he certainly belong to that indefinite family—that he was collecting orchids, had just discovered what he recognized as a new species—all collectors are nuts over new species—on a tree of a native graveyard, and that the natives had jumped him when he tried to get it. Also that he was rather obliged to us, hoped to make it all right, would do as much for us under the same circumstances. We were collecting reptiles, were we not? Reptiles *exclusively*, hey, what!

I disliked the man exceedingly, felt that he was lying in other ways than about his name, and piously looked forward to getting rid of him as soon as possible. At that time he was too weak to turn off, however, and during the night his launch blew up and burned to the water's edge.

The man positively had a fit! He raved of *Cattleya Mendelli, Dowiana aurea, Odoratum coranarium*—I know something of orchids, and these certainly were valuable ones if he had 'em—and beat at the fire with his one good hand. We finally had to drag him away, and all that we saved was a little ammunition, some clothes, and a bunch of English bank notes. The orchids were between decks forward, where the fire was hottest.

At first he suggested we take him back to the Bogotá connection, which, of course, was out of the question; and then, much to my disgust, made a deal with McKee to go with us and have the privilege of the extra skiff to carry on his work.

The neighborhood where we took the ten-footer I began this yarn with was a fine place for big snakes. There were many little tributaries running into the river, and each one seemed to have its pair of anacondas. Sometimes we missed them when they were stretched out along a branch over the water, their rich olive-green bodies with the two alternate rows of large oval spots along the back and small white-eyed spots on the sides blending perfectly with the lichen-decked limb of some giant tree. Mostly, however, they lay with just a fraction of their heads above water; and the prof was a wonder at picking out, from yards away, just the ripple that showed where a great snake was patiently waiting for what the current might bring. Then, with a few cautious oar strokes, we'd drift down on it, and the rest was purely mechanical.

Reddy, who was a cheerful, even-tempered little cuss, grew happier with each successive captive, and the one of which I have just spoken making our sixth sizable snake, we rowed back contentedly toward the main river. At the mouth of the tributary, a chorus of wild yells broke on our ears, and, quickening our stroke, we shot out into the river to see Hiram Jones climbing onto the steamer, the opposite shore lined with furiously gesticulating savages.

"We'll have to go from here!" I exclaimed angrily. "That imitation English boob has been monkeying around the graveyards of the simple peasantry again."

"He shouldn't have done it," complained Reddy. "Now we have lost a good hunting ground. You had better speak to him, Wandering, while I am stowing away the snake. I'm not big enough to quarrel with him, and two men shouldn't jump on one."

Very tactfully put, I call it. The hint wasn't lost on me. I rolled my sleeves up as I got on board, and prof dove down the companionway, dragging his net full of snakes.

"Look here, alias 'Iram Jones," I said, taking care to get close enough to him so he couldn't use his gun, "we've had enough of this graveyard work, and of stirring up the natives."

What I was aiming to do was obvious, and I'll give him credit for being no coward. The fight lasted several minutes. He was a better boxer than I, but hadn't been through the school of lick-'em-or-get-half-killed I had been brought up in. When he yelled, "'Nough!" I got off him rather pleased with myself and willing to listen to what he had to say. It proved to be the same story. Native cemetery—you tell 'em by rags tied to sticks—rare orchid on tree, natives popping out from every direction when he went for it. The only difference was that this time he had brought away what he was after, and it certainly was a marvelous thing! The flower, already fading, was about a foot across, olive-green, regularly blotched with black, while the stamens were pure gold color and gave off a musky odor.

"It looks for all the world like an anaconda," said the prof, who had come on deck as soon as the noise was over.

"Just the ticket! I'll call it *Oncidum anacondæ*, Barlow"—Barlow mind you!—said the so-called Hiram Jones, and, unconscious of the name he had let slip, picked up the tangle of aerial root-lets among which the strange flower bloomed. Something round, about the size of a tennis ball, fell thumping from the mass to the deck, and, making sure it was not a reptile, I picked it up while the other men crowded nearer. Pulling away a few dead leaves, I held in my hand an infinitesimal mummy head, too small to be even that of a baby, looking as though it must have belonged to the tiniest of pygmies or else a gnome. The features, absolutely perfect in every detail, though shrunken beyond belief, were those of an old, old man, and in place of eyes were two crimson crystals sunk deep beneath the parchment-covered forehead. The whole thing was hard, like a lump of rubber, without a sign of bone in it.

For several moments we gazed, astounded, at this gruesome object; and then Barlow, alias Hiram Jones, spoke:

"Look here, you blokes, do you know what this means—a fortune for every one of us! I saw hundreds of heads hanging to this one tree—thought they were weaver birds' nests. My word! *Look* at those bloody stones! They are rubies!"

The nearest I have ever come to engaging in the ghoul business was when I helped an old scientist dig up the bones—and part of the skin and fur—of gigantic antediluvian lizards and mammoths in a salt marsh of the Brazilian coast. They say that rubies affect people's brains, however, and I'll admit for a moment I was tempted. Not so the little Scotchman.

"You dirty Sassenach!" he roared. "Do you think I'm going to turn corpse robber for all the red crystals in the world? I—I have a good mind to feed you to my anacondas. Don't you dare open your mouth to make such a suggestion again!"

"No, don't you dare!" I echoed shamefacedly, and there the matter rested.

Of course I had heard of the little mummy heads. Everybody who has been south of Panama has heard the tale. But I had never seen one before, hardly believed in them. The tribes along the Magdalena are reputed to remove the skull from the heads of their own dead as well as their enemies, and shrink them to the size of small oranges by some mysterious process that keeps the features in proportion as clear cut as in life, preserving them indefinitely. Why they were hung in trees, and how they were protected from bird and beast, was still an unwritten chapter.

II

While all this was going on, there was an awful hullabaloo from the shore, yells, beating of native drums, and the ear-splitting bray from a bamboo horn. The river was at least a mile broad there, however, and we were anchored in the middle of it; so I did not fear an attack in the daytime—savages don't come out after steamers when it is light; they have learned better. We had loaded up with wood for fuel the day before; and I didn't propose to stop again until we reached the Rio de Sucuriu—native for River of the Anaconda—a fork of the Magdalena about which I had some rather vague information, and which was really our ultimate destination.

After the crew had piled enough wood under the boilers to get up steam, I left Mose to tend them, and went forward to what I could pick up from the mestizos in regard to the local burial customs. It was little enough. They knew of the mummy heads, of course, and of the substitution of bright crystals for eyes, the standing the community of the preserved deceased being indicated by the kind of stone, but they could tell me nothing of where these same stones came from—they were sacred things in possession of the priests alone.

I had only been forward about ten minutes when a yell from Reddy told me something was wrong below.

At the door of one of the cabins I found the little Scotchman hauling the unconscious Englishman out by the legs. The olive-green orchid lay on the floor, and from it emanated an odor of musk, only muskier, that caught you by the throat and simply choked you. We soused the senseless man over the side, and by the time he took in coming to he certainly must have been pretty near to cashing in. Then we fished out the deadly orchid on the end of a long pole, and should have thrown it overboard had the sick man not begged with actual tears that we save it. Later he tied it to the end of a stick and fixed it firmly over the bow. Outdoors, the odor was not so oppressive, but we came stern, nevertheless, where we could not smell it.

Steam was up by that time, but another factor upset our calculations. The wind and river began to rise, both coming straight down on us, and finally I had to steer our unwieldy craft into the backwater near the shore to avoid being rammed by the trees that came booming down the current; and just as we anchored, the black tropic night shut down like a curtain.

You can't fool with a storm in the latitude. The river lashed into foam, great sheets of water were bodily torn from the surface and whipped to shreds in the air, whole trees came whirling down, rearing and plunging as though alive, while the heavens were rent with lightning and shaken by thunder. The worst of it was over in thirty minutes, but the river rose and rose until our anchor began to drag. With full steam I could just keep head to it, but no more, and I had to feel around for hours before I could find bottom where the anchor would hold. Thankfully my crew then turned in, and I went forward to take one last look to see we were not drifting, when through the blackness I saw what appeared to be a log coming swiftly down on us. It struck the anchor chain, split, and I had only time to recognize it as a native dugout before a naked savage described a parabola over the bow into my arms.

After a brief struggle—he was slippery as an eel—I caught his wrists and escorted him to the light of the main cabin, calling to McKee and the Englishman.

Of course the naked wild man must have been scared to death, but he gave no sign of it, just stood up swaying with the pitch of the boat, and waited apparently unperturbed, for what was to come, his eyes fixed on Reddy's flaming topknot. He was only about four and a half feet tall, gracefully formed, with features so far from being negroid that they appeared as clear cut as a young girl's, and so he was not black, but a clear light chocolate. Through his elaborately arranged hair were stuck several of the tiny poisoned arrows, though he seemed to have lost his bamboo blowgun.

We all stared at him with nothing to say. As a matter of fact, he was much more at ease than were we, and then I bethought myself of asking some questions about the Rio de Sucuriu.

There are about twelve different and distinct languages spoken along the Magdalena, but there also exists a kind of *lingua franca* common to all the tribes of the river banks. I called in one of my mestizos, and through him began to interrogate my captive.

The Rio de Sucuriu was only three canoe days farther up—he had come from there himself, caught by and driven before the storm. Yes, there were many serpents there, but they harmed not man, since man was their brothers and the son of "she who was married to the golden one, queen of all serpents."

I gave him food, which he wolfed down ravenously; and then, just as the mestizo turned to leave, a strange thing happened. From a shelf where the Englishman had placed it, the tiny mummy head fell to the floor and bounced to the savage's feet. He made a quick grab for it, but Barlow was before him, snatching it to himself with a fierce: "It's mine!" The speech was unintelligible to the naked man, but the gesture was unmistakable. He flew to his feet and pointed with two quick words.

"He says 'dead stealer,'" translated my interpreter at my look of interrogation; and then, listening to a stream of passionate sibilants continued: "He has heard of the white man, and death is waiting for him as a slave who murders his master. At once he must give him the head that it may hang on the sacred tree, lest another head he dreads come to him. He wants it now."

"Give him the thing," I ordered. "We can't afford to quarrel with the natives, especially with one who comes from where we are going. He'd put us in wrong at once."

"I won't!" snarled the Englishman. "Kill him and throw him overboard. Dead men tell no tales."

And he actually meant it. Just as cold-blooded as that. I made a snatch for the mummy head, missed it, then struck it out of his hand, and the prof picked it up and gave it to the savage.

He took it into his cupped hands and made a kind of salaam, turning it face upward, and we saw that the rubies were gone from the eye sockets, gouged out.

I believe I should have killed Barlow, alias Hiram Jones, then and there had we been alone. As it was, I turned and struck him across the mouth.

"Get out of my sight, you unclean ghoul!" I shouted, and he slunk quietly away.

I presented the little naked savage with a square of red cloth—it pleased him immensely—to wrap the head in, which he did with the greatest reverence; and, while he squatted on the floor, one hand on the bundle to keep it from rolling with the pitch of the boat, I made him a regular oration.

I told him we were capturing snakes, which, strangely enough, did not seem to astonish him, and that we hoped to find many big ones in the Rio de Sucuriu. I also tried to convey to him that the Englishman was quite mad, and that in no way had we been parties to the taking of the head. He made no comment, except to ask why we didn't burn the madman to drive the wickedness out of him; and then, after a parting look of admiration at the professor's red head, tactfully terminated the interview by curling around his precious bundle and going to sleep.

Reddy and I talked till daylight, and the upshot of our conversation may be epitomized in two paragraphs.

Though we had no intention of gouging rubies out of the mummy heads of the native dead, we hadn't the slightest objection to negotiating with the priests for them.

He wished to Heaven there was some way of getting rid of our English incubus without handing him over to the vengeance of the savages.

III

The river sank as quietly as it had risen, and we skirted the current for two whole days before we came to the fork that had been dubbed the Rio de Sucuriu. Our savage pointed out the channel all the way, and we thus avoided the usual hang-ups on sand bars.

Rather strange and most self-contained person, that naked wild man! He was outwardly quite unimpressed by the boat and its contents, all of which must have been new and very wonderful to him, but he seldom took his eyes from the prof's red head. Me, he evidently considered Reddy's subordinate, despised the Englishman, and classified the mestizos as slaves. Mose, my cook, who was a very black, black man, plainly puzzled him. The orchid stuck up in the bow was familiar to him, and he looked on it with mingled feelings of fear and disgust.

At the mouth of the Rio de Sucuriu, our guest left us, taking along the mummy head in its red wrapping, and promising to return after two darknesses to show us where we might capture more snakes. I for one was glad to see him go. He would put us right with his tribe, and it would not be necessary to keep constantly on the alert for vicious little poisoned arrows. Neither did the Englishman grieve over this departure. We hadn't treated that gentleman with undue consideration these last days, had hardly spoken to him at all in spite of his attempt at an apology. He had tried to explain his eccentric behavior in regard to the mummy head on the grounds that he did not know what he was doing from the time the deadly orchid overcame him—even claimed that he did not know what had become of the rubies. All this was mixed up in with whining over the loss of his launch and orchids—at Least a thousand pounds' worth—and, after talking interminably, he ended up borrowing some clothes from me with the excuse that his own we had saved were so shrunk by the water he could not get into them. I let him have some, of course, but I'll be dog-goned if I wanted to.

Opposite where we anchored, a spit of rock, some twenty feet broad, ran out into the water, so perfectly reproducing in shape the head of an anaconda that had the idea not been ridiculous I should have called it the work of man. Also, the Rio de Sucuriu was well named. We took three anacondas the first day, one sixteen feet long, and located a pair of monsters that we simply did not dare tackle alone. Reddy was crazy to get them, and suggested wild scheme after wild scheme for their capture. Having no desire to trouble the digestion of a thirty-foot snake, I turned all his plans down, urging that we wait until the natives appeared and then enlist their assistance. In the meantime, Barlow hunted orchids by himself, and he certainly brought in a heap of them.

At sunrise of the third day, we were awakened by a most infernal din, the throbbing beat of native drums, the savage braying of bamboo horns, accompanied by the splashing of paddles. Before the mist had gone, we found ourselves surrounded by dugouts, and, as the sun rose, a state craft paddled underneath the stern of our side-wheeler. Hewn out of a single log, it was fifty feet long, with thirty paddlers, and in the bow stood the savage whom we had picked up farther down the river.

"Grab your guns!" gasped Barlow.

"Guns nothing!" I answered, and I was scared. "There are hundreds of them. We'd be torn to pieces in ten minutes. Wits alone will get us out of this."

I summoned my mestizo interpreter, and the save in the bow of the state canoe began to speak.

I can't give his exact words, but the substance was as follows: The Red God with his friend and slaves was welcome in the territory of the Sucuriu people, though not the one with him who slew from behind and respected not the dead. There would be feasting, and many serpents would be bestowed upon us that we might be honored.

Plainly the Prof was the Red God, and our best card, so I shoved him up on the bulwarks, meanwhile orating all I knew through the mestizo. I said we much appreciated the honor done us and should be tickled to death to have the snake donation—we'd make some donation on our own side—that we had only six days to linger, then the Red God and us, his servants, must return when we had come; that the wicked one among us had been driven temporarily mad by the flower of death and was not responsible for his actions, but would be punished when we returned home to our own land.

Then we permitted—indeed, I don't see how we could have hindered—the naked savages to swarm all over the boat. Not one thing on board was taken or even touched, however, and we all rowed to shore feeling as though we were part of some fantastic dream.

The feast was no worse or better than others of its kind, and liberally watered with palm wine. The entertainment following consisted of the customary savage dances. Our party and our former guest, now host, sat, or rather squatted, a little apart from the rest of the Sucuriu people, and were served by young slaves of whom there seemed to be a large number. The entire performance was something new to the prof, and he enjoyed it all hugely, also the palm wine—until I had to warn him. You see, I had been up against it before, and I knew it was not to be trusted. Like all Scotchmen, he knew best, however, and when I discovered, in the gloom, that he had his arm around an attractive but more lightly clad brown girl, the party broke up. Savages believe in love at first sight, rapid wooings, and absolute sincerity. Besides, I'm darned if the girl wasn't extremely good looking.

The Prof was cross as a bear next morning, and took occasion to insult me seventeen separate and distinct times. I took it all gracefully, though; I've had palm-wine heads myself and know what they mean. Finally, however, he accused me of being jealous of his "way with the weemen," and myself having an eye on "yon mud-colored lassie" of the night before. This was too much. I'm a respectable widower—twice—and couldn't afford to have my name scandalously coupled with a brown girl—Père Guerin might hear of it—so I soused him over the side until he told me felt good-humored again. Reddy had come on the trip with a single crash suit, so we routed out some of Barlow's shrunken clothes. They surely had shrunk, fitted the little Scotchman exactly, and he was just half the size of the orchid hunter.

By this time several dugouts were alongside, and we prepared a dozen or so of the felt-wrapped wire loops and explained their use to the natives. They caught on at once, and we started toward where Reddy and I had seen the snakes that were too large for us to tackle alone. Anacondas, in addition to their devilish bad temper, are about as

shy as you make 'em; but the savages paddled along, singing and whooping as though
the game was a deaf stone idol instead of the alertest reptile that swims. The mestizo
interpreter could not check them, and they did not seem to understand my signs for
silence—on the contrary, whooped the louder. As we pushed into the backwater,
where we had seen the monsters, the reason for this lack of caution was apparent. Far
from being alarmed, a thirty-foot anaconda undulated swiftly toward us. A native rose
in the bow of the leading canoe, and, holding a dead capybara above his head, began a
kind of a chant. I got the translation later. Here it is:

> "Brother, thy brothers come,
>   An offering bear to thee.
>   With fear the jungle is dumb,
>   Sucuriu people are we.
>   Brother, the golden one
>   Watches, where crowned with gold,
>   She sits and basks in the sun,
>   Wrapped in HIS golden fold.
>   Brother, we bind you free,
>   Bitter though be your strife,
>   Though you our brother be,
>   We pay the debt for a life."

The anaconda raised five feet of its body out of the water, and the singer cast the
capybara into the waiting jaws. Before the snake could dive, a felt-wrapped wire loop
circled it, then another. The dugouts swarmed about it, the lashing tail was imprisoned,
and in less time than I can tell, Reddy slipped the steel-mesh net over the wicked head.
The female was not so easily captured, one savage losing a large chunk of his shoulder;
but, within two hours, both reptiles were safely ensconced within our damp hold—
and they measured respectively thirty-one and a half and twenty-eight feet.

In three days we had as many big snakes as we could cram into the large cages,
while the savages were eager to catch more, and delighted with our gifts. It had been
necessary to establish a tariff, so rapidly were the serpents brought us; not only
anacondas, but the gentler, beautifully marked boas that reach a length of ten feet
and take the place of our own domestic cat as rat catchers in the native huts. We
paid so many yards of cloth, according to length, and added an alarm clock when an
especially fine specimen was taken. Reddy became jubilant and more jubilant with
every addition to our collection, forgot all about the "mud-colored lassie," and I was

pretty well pleased myself. Barlow alone of our party was not happy, and with cause. No sooner was he out of sight of our side-wheeler than ping! A little arrow would stand up, quivering on the side of his skiff. These missiles were not poisoned, but this did not prove that the next one might be harmless. The Englishman took the hint and spent his time morosely moping on board, and begging us to go farther down the river. Selfish ugly brute he was—though, I grant him, brave enough; he had fought me— and I heartily wished us well rid of him.

The professor now began to think of smaller reptiles, and was specially desirous of grabbing onto a few fer-de-lances. These are pleasant snakes, known by the Spaniards as *rabo de huesos*—bone tails—from the curiously colored and spike-like tip at the end of the body, about the deadliest things I the reptile line, and so temperamental that only one ever survived to reach the New York zoo, where it died of excitement.

We tried a hunt on dry land, equipped with wire loops and very close mesh metal nets. Only three specimens resulted from the entire day's tramp, and these did not amount to anything, were as common as savages, Reddy said. An attempt to enlist the natives in this new sport, something we had shied away from for fear of being deluged with the commoner reptiles, was entirely unsuccessful. Our former guest, who seemed to be the chief of the Sucuriu people in spite of his youth, lucidly explained that all the lesser snakes had been captured long ago and taken to the place of the dead. Requests for information as to the location of said place of the dead met with the same chilling silence that I well remember having had from a fat lady at the only ball I ever went to in my life, when I apologized for tearing a yard off the rear end of her dress.

Not only did we fail to make a single capture the next day, but, in addition, the prof got badly stung by a large blue wasp, and the savages plainly looked with disfavor on our land expeditions. Furthermore, on the boat, the Englishman exhibited three tiny arrows, distinctly tipped with poison this time, that had been shot on board during our absence. He asserted, with unnecessary profanity, that he was going wherever we did from that time on.

Oddly enough, not one of us suggested moving on, and, when you come to think of it, it wasn't so odd, after all. You see, we were fundamentally fighting men, and the fact that the savages obviously wanted us to pull out just got our dander up. Besides I was mighty curious to see that place of the dead to which all the land reptiles had been transported, and unquestionably the prof felt the same way. That little red-headed devil had something else on his mind, however, as I was to find out later.

Before I forget it, since you always hear Scotchmen spoken of as hard-headed, I should like to state right here that the man who says Scotchmen aren't at the same time sentimental is a liar—they invented sentiment.

Barlow, of course, really wanted to stay, because he was crazy for another shy at the orchids, with which the woods in that neighborhood seemed to be crammed.

Each of us kept strictly to himself that night. The Englishman took the poisonous orchid from the bow of the boat—it smelled worse during the darkness, too—and boxed it up carefully. The professor got into a skiff and went ashore. I turned in and dreamed of thirty-foot anacondas, their heads covered with flaming red hair and their mouths full of long curved teeth.

IV

Before sunrise, the mestizo interpreter woke me with the news that there was a canoe alongside with some savages who wanted to talk to me. I stacked up the pillows under McKee's head; he was breathing heavily and had a way of sleeping flat that invited heat apoplexy—and went on deck. It was getting light as I looked down into the native boat, and what I saw there came near to doubling me up with mirth at the same time that I recognized its seriousness. In the bow sat the young chief, simply trembling with rage; the paddler was an old white-wooled brown man, evidently the father of the pretty chocolate-colored girl in the stern. For her part, she had been weeping, held her head very high, and wore, by a string around her neck—and indeed she wore little else—an unmistakable red object, an ample lock of the professor's auburn—by courtesy—hair.

The young savage shot out a stream of *sssss*'s that sounded like an angry anaconda, and the interpreter elucidated. Briefly the substance was that Reddy was trying to steal his girl, that she was ready and anxious to be stolen, and that we were therewith to beat it at once, if not sooner. Through the mestizo I promptly told his nibs to forget it; we'd stay as long as we pleased.

The answering flow of sibilants was less virulent and shorter, and translated into a query as to what we would take to go away.

Then I had an inspiration. Slowly, word by word, I had my man impart to this autocratic savage a promise that we would leave the moment the Red God had secured all the land reptiles he wanted, and there must be many; that he wished to visit the place of the dead and see what crawling things he could find there, and that if both these requirements were met he would shake the girl.

For a long time the savage hesitated, and when he finally spoke I could only gather from the rendering of his words that we were to go with him that morning, prepared to stay several days , and with everything we owned that would hold reptiles. The rest of his speech was a jumble to me: The Golden One might blast us—breath of death—sacred road—

The dugout sheared off and, going below, I beat a brisk tattoo with a pair of military brushes on the side of the cabin.

"Awake, my red-haired Lothario!" I yelled. "Awake! I have good news. Jump into your clothes, and don't wait to brush your hair; you've ruined your beauty, anyhow, by that gob you cut out of your bang. Come and catch little snakelets; we're going where there are oodles of them."

Reddy sat up, somewhat blear-eyed; then, scrambling out, looked at himself in the four-inch mirror on the wall.

"I dinna see it has changed my appearance," he remarked. "I mind some palm wine— What were you saying about wee snakes?"

I told him. The serpent made Eve forget her Adam. The mere promise of venomous reptiles made Reddy forget his Eve. The little Scotchman turned into a whirlwind, and, when the dugouts arrived, had enough collecting paraphernalia piled up to lad three of them to the guards. Every one of us, except Mose, whom I left behind in charge of the boat, mestizos as well as the Englishman, went ashore at the anaconda-head-shaped outcrop, where we found the young chief awaiting us with a dozen slaves for porters.

For an hour we followed a jungle trail, single file, the chief evidently steering by a lofty peak in the distance. The trail broadened out, and we found ourselves walking upon rock the like of which I have never before seen. It was a road, or, rather causeway, thirty feet broad, built of ten-foot square blocks of stone, and winding back and forth up to the highlands. No twenty men could have lifted one of those square blocks; no, not fifty men; and there were millions of 'em. Furthermore, the middle of the stoneway was worn smooth by the footsteps of thousands exactly like the flagstone in front of the swinging doors of Père Guerrin's café.

Not one of us said a word until we had passed along the two half-mile undulations, and then the Scotchman spoke the conclusion of his thoughts:

"We-el, 'tis Aztec. I'll say no more."

"It's a bloomin' snake miles long," said Barlow; "miles, miles long, with its head in the river."

I had nothing to say. To tell the truth, it kind of made me feel religious, awed me, especially the wearing away of the solid rock by those countless feet. They must have been bare feet, too, and their owners dead for Lord knows how many tens, hundreds, even thousands of years!

We followed the great sweeping curves of this mighty road till noon, now to the right, now to the left, always rising, until finally the mountain loomed above us, and just the causeway broke off short in a chaos of tumbled blocks of stone. On either side were acre-long enclosures that looked as though they might once have been water tanks, terraced one above the other to the base of the mountain, two miles away. Above the ruins of this ancient road a way of more recent origin had been fashioned. Zigzagging from tall forest tree to tall forest tree were a pair of thick long bamboos, one above the other, the lower a path to which bare feet might cling, the upper a handrail.

Where the road broke off, the chief halted, pointing to the splintered and shattered blocks of stone below. My eyes followed his gesture, and, ten feet beneath me, a yellow serpent was stretched out in the sun; another crawling lazily from a fissure in the rocks; a third lay coiled. There were snakes large, snakes small, snakes of every hue of the rainbow. The place was alive with reptiles.

"This is heaven," stated the professor positively, picking out a wire loop and collecting box and preparing to climb down to the jumbled bowlders.

"This is the nearest thing to hell I have ever seen," I remarked, getting ready to follow him.

We could not stay among the ruins; the reptiles were too thick about us. And, after Reddy had come within a hair's bready of being struck by a fer-de-lance whose head I shot off, we climbed back again. The broad walls of the tank furnished us with a four-foot path, however, and from it we angled, trapping snakes in a loop on the end of a bamboo pole exactly as you snare suckers with a copper wire. It was unpleasant, but exciting, sport. I, for one, was perfectly willing to land my snake on the wall, perfectly unwilling from that time to have anything to do with it. Barlow limited his activities to toting the collecting boxes and swearing. He cursed the savages, the snakes, the sky, the earth, Reddy, and me, until the Scotchmen, and after a few moments' deep thought, told him such language was "fair weeked" and it would be no sin to tip him over into the reptile den.

We took fifty snakes, ten of which were the dreaded fer-de-lances, a German flag—immortalized in Kipling's tale—three species of coral snakes, a green racer, two bush masters, and others whose names I simply can't remember. Then night came.

As the light went, a strong breeze blew down from the mountain onto our camp; but, far from being laden with the scent of flowers, it brought an aroma that to me suggested ten thousand alligators. The Englishman recognized it, however, from the first whiff.

"Death orchids!" he exclaimed. "There must be a hundred burial trees near here, perhaps rubies—"

"Which you will leave alone," I interrupted, "or I'll give you a licking that will make the last one seem like love taps, and hand you over to the savages afterward."

Of course Reddy was primarily a snake collector, and that was his dominant interest, but he was all of a man besides, and, as such, was crazy to see what was at the end of the long bamboo road. It was obvious the chief did not intend that we should go farther, and so we made our plans without consulting him. The wall of the next tank was five feet higher than the one in which we had done our strange fishing, and on it grew a tree to which ran the bamboo bridge. We decided that the next morning we three—the Englishman being unwilling to leave us for a moment—would climb this tree and follow the swaying airway to the mountain. With this purpose in view, we turned in early, after sending back the mestizos and some porters with our boxes of snakes.

V

In the morning, our project was simplified by the withdrawal of the savages farther down the stone causeway. Every evidently they did not all care for that neighborhood. Immediately after breakfast, we set out, taking a few snakes first in case any one might be spying; and then scrambling up the five-foot wall, looked down into the next tank—and stood transfixed.

For a moment—as had the Englishmen—I thought the dead trees of which the enclosure was full held an enormous colony of weaver birds' nests. On every branch and twig hung a tiny mummy head, the sunlight glinting here and there on jeweled eyes, and an odor of musk floating up to us—though more faintly than during the night—from the foot-wide, olive-green flowers of the death orchids, the only living thing, save reptiles, that flourished in that gruesome place.

"Let's go back," Barlow begged, in a whisper; "not even rubies are worth it!"

"I'm afeered," simply stated the Scotchman.

"We're in for it now; let's go on," I urged; and then I added, since I saw both of my companions were scared to death, and so, indeed, was I: "*I'm* not afraid!"

"You're a le-er!" promptly responded McKee, and began to climb the tree we had selected the night before.

From the fragile bamboo bridge we looked down for a full two miles on enclosure after enclosure full of dead trees hung with shrunken heads. There were thousands; and as we progressed, they became unquestionably more ancient, had fallen to the ground—even the trees themselves had sometimes fallen—and lay heaped like the debris of blackened combs and litter beneath a century-old wild bees' hive. On one tree I counted two hundred heads; there were fifty trees in that section, thirty separate sections in all, making, at a *low* estimate, three hundred thousand of these tiny relics of what had once been human beings. It was the vast graveyard of a mighty race, a race dwindled to the few poor survivors of the present day—the Sucuriu people.

From the swaying bamboos we stepped at last onto solid rock, a continuation of the great causeway, but narrowing like the tail of an anaconda. At the very tip lay a fifty-yard, sand-bordered pool from which it seemed the twelve-mile-long stone serpent might have emerged.

Tired and breathless, we sat gazing into the clear water that back up against a sheer cliff, and then from a small cave across us, its top just above water level, came a ripple. Something split the surface of the water, and there emerged a head as red as Reddy's own, followed by a woman's face and arm, her hand resting lightly on the neck of a nine-foot anaconda, and her body swaying side to side through the water with the undulations of the swimming serpent.

"I'm going crazy!" gasped Barlow. "Do *you* see it, you blokes?"

"'Tis extraordineery," vouchsafed the prof.

The swimmers struck shallow water, and the girl stood up, and the anaconda curled about her until its head rested on her shoulder. Snake and woman, save for her flaming hair, were both a golden yellow, and it would have been hard to say which was the more beautiful.

Quite unafraid she approached us, her eyes on the prof's glowing head, and then stopped. I rose and bowed, which was ridiculous; couldn't think of anything else to do; but she never even looked at me.

One arm she raised and pointed at McKee, and in some mysterious way the gesture asked a question as plainly as though she had traced an interrogation point on the smooth white sand. For a moment she stood pointing, and then, raising both her hands, pressed two fingers across her lips. Against the gesture needed no interpretation, was as clear as though she had put it into words—the woman was dumb.

"Puir, puir lassie!" said the prof, with infinite pity. "Puir bonnie lassie!"

And I felt my own heart go out to the beautiful voiceless thing standing like some goddess of the olden days, the golden snake coiled about her golden form.

"Let me talk to her," said the little Scotchman, and beckoning her nearer, began to trace pictures on the sand.

The Englishman may have thought he was crazy, but I *knew* I was as I watched Reddy drawing the story of our voyage. According to his pictures, we came from the rising sun—"rising" indicated by a series of dashing rays—she glanced at his hair—then came up the broad river in a great canoe—

It was a fine series of drawings, and covered ten yards of sand. When it was finished, the woman put her hand up to her hair and drew out from among the thick tresses a small skin bag. This she opened, and took out a pearl-shaped stone, with which she began to make the sand, and that stone was an inch-long ruby!

Barlow made the sign of the cross and rose to his feet.

"Let's look around a bit, Wandering," he begged, "while the children draw pictures. Perhaps we'll find a ten-headed lion with a basket of diamonds in each mouth. I'm in for what there is to see before I'm locked in the drippy house."

I needed a chance to collect my thought myself, so followed him, leaving Reddy and the girl bent absorbingly over their tracings.

To the left of the stone snake's tail, rude steps were cut in the living rock, and up these we scrambled. They led to a small platform, and again in the rock was hollowed out a little house, with windows and doors, stuck there on the cliff like a swallow's nest. Inside were jars of pottery, hammers and knives fashioned from flint, and wood evidently stacked for burning that went into dust at our touch. No human could have dwelt there for years and years; everything was too quiet, too motionless, too covered with the dust of ages. We stole silently out into the sunlight again, and, by the doorstep, the Englishman picked up a ruby carved in the likeness of a coiled snake.

More steps led to another rock-hollowed house, differing in no respect from the first, and we climbed from terrace to terrace, exploring the countless long-abandoned dwellings of a dead race. The sun was well to the west when we reached a shelf broader and longer than the others with no doors or windows cut in the rock, only a long line of bathtub-shaped depressions. Each depression held the crumbling bones of a skeleton, and every skeleton was headless! Our faces turned from this row of open graves, we walked to the far end of the shelf and came to a great hole on the brink of which, scattered among flint knives, hatchets, and little round balls of clay, were small rubies, red snakes' eyes they looked like, which Barlow eagerly gathered up. Together we peered into this pit, and mixed with the clay balls were thousands upon thousands of skulls each split nearly in half, while here and there, adhering to clay balls, was a piece of parchment-like skin.

"I'm sick!" I whispered. "Let's get out of here."

"I'm dead with thirst," Barlow answered through parched lips, his face pasty white in spite of the heat.

No nightmare could be more awful than our descent from those endless silent terraces. We slipped and clung to the edge of thousand-foot precipices, slide down the rude steps, skinning our hands and knees, and our throats were full of the dead dust of long-forgotten peoples, our lips swollen, our tongues thick. Twice the Englishman abandoned his bag of rubies; twice, sobbing, he went back for it. The sweetest music I have ever heard was Reddy's voice from near below, calling and cursing by turns. And then the sun sank, leaving the world bitter cold.

It was darker than pitch down by the pool, the only sign of light a sheen from the still water that made our faces look like white blurs in a big splash of ink. By groping around rather at haphazard, we collected a few pieces of wood for a fire, and, shivering, huddled over it. As the flames rose, picking our faces out of the gloom, it became more apparent that the prof had somehow acquired a black eye. It was a beaut, covered all one side of his face, and very naturally I asked how he got it.

"'Tis nothing," Reddy answered; "a wee bump against yon stone."

"It's a right-handed swat," I insisted. "You got fresh and the lady biffed you."

"You're a le-er," he flared; "the lassie no laid hands on me; 'twas the snake."

It isn't the easiest thing in the world to get a Scotchman to tell what he doesn't want to; but I finally gathered in his story, what there was of it.

The girl had understood his drawings, but hers were quite unintelligible to him, a series of snakes, fishes, triangles, and complicated geometrical figures. More by gesture than anything else, he gathered that food was brought her over the bamboo bridge by the savages; that she dwelt in a cave rising from the other side of the pool, and that she had been there for fifteen complete sun revolutions. "'Tis then an unfortunate thing happened," he continued. "To encourage the lassie, I put me hand on her shoulder. 'Twas by no means a caress, ye'll understand; more like a pat. And then the snake struck me with his head on the side of me face. The lassie was fair angry and drove it into the water. I dinna blame her; it spoiled the pleasure of the whole day for the both of us. At sundown she became greatly agitated, pushing me toward yon bamboo bridge, and then, when I would not go, swimming back and forth from me to the cave across the pool, making signs for me to follow her. I would have humored the puir lassie had yet not been away pleasuring all the day."

"Pleasuring?" repeated Barlow. "A peach lot of pleasure we had while you were philandering, and we've brought back a fortune."

Come to think of it, so we had. The rubies simply slipped my mind. Things get kind of out of proportion in the wilderness. We had out the bag and felt and hefted it—it was too dark to look at the stones—and it weighed all of ten or twelve pounds. Quite a hunk of jewels, and yet somehow it failed to impress me. I couldn't think of the little red things in terms of money; only as eyes of horrible shrunken mummy heads. Reddy didn't show any undignified amount of joy over them, either; refused to commit himself to any undue enthusiasm until he knew exactly what the stone would bring "within a thousand dollars say," a question on which we naturally could not enlighten him. With the Englishman it was quite different. He fair lusted over the bag in the darkness. They would buy him a boat of his own, brass fittings and all, air-tight compartment that would preserve orchids forever. He'd travel to Borneo,

Brazil, India; there should be money enough to go everywhere. His thoughts took a sudden twist—

"Look here, you blokes," he whined, "at least half of what they bring belongs to me. I was the one that found them. Any court of law would uphold me."

"We-el, let's submit it to a court of law," suggested McKee.

"We'll divide these rubies into three parts when we get back to the boat," I stated positively. "Meanwhile, since you found 'em, you can carry 'em."

The moon rose and the same moment we saw the golden maiden swimming toward us, the anaconda in her wake. She came straight to Reddy and tried to lead him into the water, carrying her hands to her nostrils, pointing out into the darkness, and beckoning imploringly. Never have I seen anything more tragic than the look of agony on her face, of striving to make the Scotchman understand.

"Puir lassie!" he said pityingly. "I'll be back. She canna bear to have me leave her."

"And you're going now," I insisted; "it won't be the easiest thing in the world to travel that thread of bamboo by moonlight, and the sooner we reach our flat scow the better."

The woman followed us, the great snake coiled about her body—she must have been as strong as an ox as well as impervious to cold—and importuned Reddy with imploring gestures to return. He shook his head, however, and slipping off our shoes and tying them around our necks, we fitted our stockinged feet to the slippery bridge.

Hardly had we gone a hundred yards, with me leading, when I stopped and held up my hand.

"Nothing doing!" I shouted. "Beat it back as quick as you can, praying that the wind doesn't change!"

And I had reason! From beneath me came the indescribable odor of the death orchids, only a hundred times stronger than I had ever smelled it before, forming a deadly barrier that no breathing thing could hope to penetrate. Already I felt my head reeling as I climbed back toward the mountain, and that with the breeze blowing from us. We reached firm ground none too soon, the girl clinging to the prof's hand and striving to drag him into the pool, for at that very moment the wind changed.

"To the pool for your lives!" I yelled, plunging in and wading out until only my face was above the surface. The poisonous miasma from the death orchids was blowing down on us like mist above a marsh, and lay suspended not six inches above the water, sinking lower and lower every second.

"We're all done for," sang the Englishman. "Just as I was rich, too. I'm no coward, but I refuse to die with my sins unconfessed. Listen to me, Wandering! I intended to murder you and that fool of a snake-collecting Scotchman so I could keep all the rubies.

I shot the top of the man's head off who hired me for this trip. He knew nothing about orchids; intended to claim all the credit for what we found; and, besides, I wanted that launch. Two years ago—"

"Can your childish babble!" I screamed. "Who cares a hoot for what you were going to do or have done? Where's Reddy? Hey, Reddy! Reddy! Reddy!" I yelled.

The water swirled; I felt a hand clutch my arm, and the golden woman rose beside me.

"Where's Reddy?" I screamed in her face, and the poor dumb thing actually smiled at me, pulling my hand.

"They say drowning's easy," droned the Englishman. "I'll just take a whiff of that corpse flower and flop over into deep water."

He stuck his head out into the grayness, and I saw it drop forward just as I caught him beneath the arm. Following the pull of the girl's hand, I swam with her towing the senseless man after me. Once the lash of the anaconda's body touched my leg, and then there was darkness. I felt, rather than saw, rock above me; next was conscious of space, inky blackness, but room all about me. My feet touched bottom. Hauling Barlow with me, I staggered forward and fell face downward on smooth dry sand.

It was Reddy's voice that brought me back.

"Are ye there, Wandering?" he whispered.

"Yes. Are you all right, Reddy?"

"Yes, the lassie saved me. Feel around till ye find me; I'd like to touch something human."

Barlow's body across my knees quivered, and I raised him to an upright position. He groaned and slid down against me. My groping hand found the little Scotchman, pulled him to me, and I threw an arm over his shoulder. Once my other hand touched the smooth wet body of the anaconda, and I snatched it quickly away. And then— wonder of wonders!—I slept dreamlessly, beautifully, blissfully.

VI

The moment of waking brought with it a full consciousness of all that had taken place. The morning came filtering in through the water that blocked the entrance to the cave, lighting it with the dim gray quietness of an empty church. Pressed against my right side lay Barlow, breathing naturally, McKee's red head was pillowed on my left shoulder, and crouching near by, her fiery red hair spread on the sand, slept the girl. There was someone else, or, rather, something else, awake beside me. The golden anaconda lay curled about the golden woman, its diamond eyes fixed unflinchingly on mine.

I shook Barlow, and he sat up while slowly the meaning of his surroundings came over him.

"I say, this isn't hell, after all!" he ejaculated, getting to his feet. "Now ain't this a rum go! I say, Wandering, I was out of my head last night. You mustn't pay any attention to what I said. I'm really very fond of you and Reddy." And he smiled at me, showing all his long curved teeth.

My hand on McKee's forehead made him open his eyes, and at the same time his teeth began to chatter.

"The lassie saved us," was the first thing he said. But she was already awake, looking up at him with adoring eyes.

"The sunlight for mine!" I chortled. "Never expected to see it again. You first, prof!"

Teeth chattering, the little Scotchman waded into the water and dove under the arch of rock, the girl and snake following him.

"Now you!" I directed Barlow.

"We'd better look around and see if she hasn't some rubies hidden here," he answered, and then splashed into the water just in time to avoid a vigorous kick.

Never did sunshine seem so blessed as that shining upon us outside; never did the whole world seem more joyous or beautiful! I just gave myself up to breathing and soaking in the warmth, gazing up at the sun till my eyes blurred.

When I finally turned to my companions, Barlow was coming out of the pool with the bag of rubies he had dropped there the night before, and the look on his face as he gloated over the open sack was that of a demon.

Then Reddy claimed my attention. He was leaning against the golden woman, her arm about him, and, though his face was red as fire, he was shivering like a leaf. It didn't take a second for me to realize what was the matter. The *calentura* fever had him, and it behooved us to get back to the boat and quinine, lots of quinine, as swiftly as possible. The knowledge of his condition was in the girl's eyes as she looked anxiously at me. Indeed, she raised her hand, palm down, moving it, shaking, in front of her face; and if that is not a good symbol for fever I have never seen one.

Had Reddy been less far gone, that two miles of climbing would have been agony for him. As it was, he moved along the slippery bamboo as only a drunkard of a man spurred on by fever could have done. At times he was delirious, shouted and sang, apologized to several imaginary "weemen" for making them love him. The girl kept her hand beneath his elbow, indeed carried him the last quarter of a mile, looping the anaconda around him to ease her burden. Barlow and I kept the bamboo length to the rear. The weight of the snake and woman plus Reddy must have been considerable, and we did not dare put too severe a strain on any one section of the seemingly slender bridge. Down our tree we climbed at last on the wall to draw breath, then yours truly, and last Barlow.

From behind me came his voice:

"Great heavens, Wandering, look below you to the right!"

I glanced over the edge of the wall, and immediately beneath me lay coiled a fer-de-lance that must have been all of twelve feet long—the most absolutely venomous object I have ever seen.

"Glad Reddy doesn't want—"

My words were drowned by the bang of an automatic, and I felt a sear of fire along my side. Spinning on my heel, and at the same time ducking low, I dodged the second bullet and caught Barlow's gun arm at the wrist in both of my hands. He snapped his left hand to my throat while I strove to twist away his weapon. Deeper sank his fingers in my flesh, deeper and deeper. I felt my eyes popping from my head, my tongue protruding, and swung him in front of me in a last furious effort to break free. From the girl's lips that I had never heard before utter a sound came three distinct hisses. Dimly I saw the anaconda uncoil from her body, writhe forward, and, quicker than light, cast a coil around Barlow's neck, while I wrenched from him, falling face over the edge of the wall. There was a mighty crunch of breaking bones, and man and snake went over me inextricably mixed, straight down upon the fer-de-lance below. The poison reptile struck three times, sinking its fangs once in the body of the anaconda and twice in the Englishman's thigh.

We did not even attempt to retrieve the dead man; left him where he lay. Reddy was our first care. Turn by turn that wonderful golden woman and I half carried, half led him the mile-long undulations of that mighty causeway, until we finally reached the stone snake's head jutting out into the river. The golden anaconda joined us, apparently none the worse for the venom from its poison cousin, and wrapped itself around its mistress. Not a savage had shown the tip of his nose all the way, and at my hail Mose came ashore the skiff unmolested.

For ten days the girl and I fought off death from the little Scotchman, and at the dawn of the eleventh day the fever broke.

Reddy was a good little man, but "weemen" were his weakness. I had pieced together disconnected fragments of his ravings with rather astonishing results. Not only did he have a wife in Scotland, but also one on the Continent. The upshot of my cogitations was, again, that Reddy was a good little man, but that was no reason why he should take all the goddess of a golden woman had to give. At present his plan was to settle down in the wilderness with her and forget the world—I was to deliver his snakes. I knew, however, that sooner or later he would return to civilization—they all do—and then what would she have left?

My mind was slowly made up, and, though I hated the plan worse than death, I began to put it into execution at once. Under my direction, the mestizos got up steam, and then I went to the woman and told her by signs to go ashore and get Reddy wild grapes, a thing she had often done before. Like a child she obeyed me.

No sooner was she out of sight than up came the anchor and we steamed away. Just in time, too, for as we rounded from the Rio de Sucuriu into the main river, the girl's crimson head showed above the water, coming swiftly after us. It was impossible for any swimmer to catch our side-wheeler, however, when it was going with the current, and the last I saw of her was her beautiful golden nude body, with its crown of flaming hair raised half out of the water, her arms held out imploringly while her dumb lips worked, the head of the great snake making an arrow-shaped ripple by her side.

Reptiles and all we reached New Orleans without adventure. It was not a pleasant trip for either of us, though. Reddy refused to speak to me when he learned what I had done while he was sick and helpless. He expressed himself as absolutely certain that the "puir dumb lassie" would pine away and die for love of him. God help me, but I can never be sure that he was not right!

Back in civilization, I took the bag of rubies—Barlow had dropped it on the wall during his last fight—to a jeweler to get them valued. However well the Englishman may have known orchids, he was distinctly not up on precious stones. His fortune in rubies proved to consist of garnets—very fine ones, it is true, but nevertheless nothing more than garnets.

One last word in connection with Barlow. The day after Reddy's fever broke, the chief of the Sucuriu people paddled out to us and threw something on board. It proved to be a package done up in the identical red cloth which I had given him to wrap the mummy head. Inside were two objects. First Barlow's head, shrunken the size of a small orange, all teeth gone save two that overlapped the wrinkled mouth like the curved tusks of a peccary, while from each socket protruded the fang of a fer-de-lance; second, also a tiny mummy head, its top blown away, leaving it roughly flat, the features unmistakably those of a high-bred Englishman, rubies—garnets I now know them—for eyes, and attached to it by a slender gold chain was a monocle.

We had given back the savage his dead; he returned ours to us.

I heard indirectly, one month after our return, of Reddy's marriage, in New York, to a widow with four children. Wonder if he sent cards to his other wives? I know none came for me. Could I have foreseen this, I never should have taken him from the golden woman, but left him in the wilderness with the pious hope that the golden anaconda might make a meal of him some dark night, mistaking him for a hog.

THE CAPTURE OF TARZAN

Edgar Rice Burroughs

THE BLACK WARRIORS LABORED IN THE HUMID HEAT OF THE JUNGLE'S STIFLING shade. With war spears they loosened the thick, black loam and the deep layers of rotting vegetation. With heavy-nailed fingers they scooped away the disintegrated earth from the center of the age-old game trail. Often they ceased their labors to squat, resting and gossiping, with much laughter, at the edge of the pit they were digging.

Against the boles of near-by trees leaned their long, oval shields of thick buffalo hide, and the spears of those who were doing the scooping. Sweat glistened upon their smooth, ebon skins, beneath which rolled rounded muscles, supple in the perfection of nature's uncontaminated health.

A reed buck, stepping warily along the trail toward water, halted as a burst of laughter broke upon his startled ears. For a moment he stood statuesque but for his sensitively dilating nostrils; then he wheeled and fled noiselessly from the terrifying presence of man.

A hundred yards away, deep in the tangle of impenetrable jungle, Numa, the lion, raised his massive head. Numa had dined well until almost daybreak and it had required much noise to awaken him. Now he lifted his muzzle and sniffed the air, caught the acrid scent spoor of the reed buck and the heavy scent of man. But Numa was well filled. With a low, disgusted grunt he rose and slunk away.

Brilliantly plumaged birds with raucous voices darted from tree to tree. Little monkeys, chattering and scolding, swung through the swaying limbs above the black warriors. Yet they were alone, for the teeming jungle with all its myriad life, like the swarming streets of a great metropolis, is one of the loneliest spots in God's great universe.

But were they alone?

Above them, lightly balanced upon a leafy tree limb, a gray-eyed youth watched with eager intentness their every move. The fire of hate, restrained, smoldered beneath the lad's evident desire to know the purpose of the black men's labors. Such a one as these it was who had slain his beloved Kala. For them there could be naught but enmity, yet he liked well to watch them, avid as he was for greater knowledge of the ways of man.

He saw the pit grow in depth until a great hole yawned the width of the trail—a hole which was amply large enough to hold at one time all of the six excavators. Tarzan could not guess the purpose of so great a labor. And when they cut long stakes, sharpened at their upper ends, and set them at intervals upright in the bottom of the pit, his wonderment but increased, nor was it satisfied with the placing of the light cross-poles over the pit, or the careful arrangement of leaves and earth which completely hid from view the work the black men had performed.

When they were done they surveyed their handiwork with evident satisfaction, and Tarzan surveyed it, too. Even to his practiced eye there remained scarce a vestige of evidence that the ancient game trail had been tampered with in any way.

So absorbed was the ape-man in speculation as to the purpose of the covered pit that he permitted the blacks to depart in the direction of their village without the usual baiting which had rendered him the terror of Mbonga's people and had afforded Tarzan both a vehicle of revenge and a source of inexhaustible delight.

Puzzle as he would, however, he could not solve the mystery of the concealed pit, for the ways of the blacks were still strange ways to Tarzan. They had entered his jungle but a short time before—the first of their kind to encroach upon the age-old supremacy of the beasts which laired there. To Numa, the lion, to Tantor, the elephant, to the great apes and the lesser apes, to each and all of the myriad creatures of this savage wild, the ways of man were new. They had much to learn of these black, hairless creatures that walked erect upon their hind paws—and they were learning it slowly, and always to their sorrow.

Shortly after the blacks had departed, Tarzan swung easily to the trail. Sniffing suspiciously, he circled the edge of the pit. Squatting upon his haunches, he scraped away a little earth to expose one of the cross-bars. He sniffed at this, touched it, cocked his head upon one side, and contemplated it gravely for several minutes. Then he carefully re-covered it, arranging the earth as neatly as had the blacks. This done, he swung himself back among the branches of the trees and moved off in search of his hairy fellows, the great apes of the tribe of Kerchak.

Once he crossed the trail of Numa, the lion, pausing for a moment to hurl a soft fruit at the snarling face of his enemy, and to taunt and insult him, calling him eater of carrion and brother of Dango, the hyena. Numa, his yellow-green eyes round and burning with concentrated hate, glared up at the dancing figure above him. Low growls vibrated his heavy jowls and his great rage transmitted to his sinuous tail a sharp, whiplike motion; but realizing from past experience the futility of long distance argument with the ape-man, he turned presently and struck off into the tangled vegetation which hid him from the view of his tormentor. With a final scream of jungle invective and an apelike grimace at his departing foe, Tarzan continued along his way.

Another mile and a shifting wind brought to his keen nostrils a familiar, pungent odor close at hand, and a moment later there loomed beneath him a huge, gray-black bulk forging steadily along the jungle trail. Tarzan seized and broke a small tree limb, and at the sudden cracking sound the ponderous figure halted. Great ears were thrown forward, and a long, supple trunk rose quickly to wave to and fro in search of the scent of an enemy, while two weak, little eyes peered suspiciously and futilely about in quest of the author of the noise which had disturbed his peaceful way.

Tarzan laughed aloud and came closer above the head of the pachyderm.

"Tantor! Tantor!" he cried. "Bara, the deer, is less fearful than you—you, Tantor, the elephant, greatest of the jungle folk with the strength of as many Numas as I have toes upon my feet and fingers upon my hands. Tantor, who can uproot great trees, trembles with fear at the sound of a broken twig."

A rumbling noise, which might have been either a sign of contempt or a sigh of relief, was Tantor's only reply as the uplifted trunk and ears came down and the beast's tail dropped to normal; but his eyes still roved about in search of Tarzan. He was not long kept in suspense, however, as to the whereabouts of the ape-man, for a second later the youth dropped lightly to the broad head of his old friend. Then stretching himself at full length, he drummed with his bare toes upon the thick hide, and as his fingers scratched the more tender surfaces beneath the great ears, he talked to Tantor of the gossip of the jungle as though the great beast understood every word that he said.

Much there was which Tarzan could make Tantor understand, and though the small talk of the wild was beyond the great, gray dreadnaught of the jungle, he stood with blinking eyes and gently swaying trunk as though drinking in every word of it with keenest appreciation. As a matter of fact it was the pleasant, friendly voice and caressing hands behind his ears which he enjoyed, and the close proximity of him whom he had often borne upon his back since Tarzan, as a little child, had once fearlessly approached the great bull, assuming upon the part of the pachyderm the same friendliness which filled his own heart.

In the years of their association Tarzan had discovered that he possessed an inexplicable power to govern and direct his mighty friend. At his bidding, Tantor would come from a great distance—as far as his keen ears could detect the shrill and piercing summons of the ape-man—and when Tarzan was squatted upon his head, Tantor would lumber through the jungle in any direction which his rider bade him go. It was the power of the man-mind over that of the brute and it was just as effective as though both fully understood its origin, though neither did.

For half an hour Tarzan sprawled there upon Tantor's back. Time had no meaning for either of them. Life, as they saw it, consisted principally in keeping their stomachs filled. To Tarzan this was a less arduous labor than to Tantor, for Tarzan's stomach was smaller, and being omnivorous, food was less difficult to obtain. If one sort did not come readily to hand, there were always many others to satisfy his hunger. He was less particular as to his diet than Tantor, who would eat only the bark of certain trees, and the wood of others, while a third appealed to him only through its leaves, and these, perhaps, just at certain seasons of the year.

Tantor must needs spend the better part of his life in filling his immense stomach against the needs of his mighty thews. It is thus with all the lower orders—their lives are so occupied either with searching for food or with the processes of digestion that they have little time for other considerations. Doubtless it is this handicap which has kept them from advancing as rapidly as man, who has more time to give to thought upon other matters.

However, these questions troubled Tarzan but little, and Tantor not at all. What the former knew was that he was happy in the companionship of the elephant. He did not know why. He did not know that because he was a human being—a normal, healthy human being—he craved some living thing upon which to lavish his affection. His childhood playmates among the apes of Kerchak were now great, sullen brutes. They felt nor inspired but little affection. The younger apes Tarzan still played with occasionally. In his savage way he loved them; but they were far from satisfying or restful companions. Tantor was a great mountain of calm, of poise, of stability. It was restful and satisfying to sprawl upon his rough pate and pour one's vague hopes and aspirations into the great ears which flapped ponderously to and fro in apparent understanding. Of all the jungle folk, Tantor commanded Tarzan's greatest love since Kala had been taken from him. Sometimes Tarzan wondered if Tantor reciprocated his affection. It was difficult to know.

It was the call of the stomach—the most compelling and insistent call which the jungle knows—that took Tarzan finally back to the trees and off in search of food, while Tantor continued his interrupted journey in the opposite direction.

For an hour the ape-man foraged. A lofty nest yielded its fresh, warm harvest. Fruits, berries, and tender plantain found a place upon his menu in the order that he happened upon them, for he did not seek such foods. Meat, meat, meat! It was always meat that Tarzan of the Apes hunted; but sometimes meat eluded him, as today.

And as he roamed the jungle his active mind busied itself not alone with his hunting, but with many other subjects. He had a habit of recalling often the events of the preceding days and hours. He lived over his visit with Tantor; he cogitated upon the digging blacks and the strange, covered pit they had left behind them. He wondered again and again what its purpose might be. He compared perceptions and arrived at judgments. He compared judgments, reaching conclusions—not always correct ones, it is true, but at least he used his brain for the purpose God intended it, which was the less difficult because he was not handicapped by the second-hand, and usually erroneous, judgment of others.

And as he puzzled over the covered pit, there loomed suddenly before his mental vision a huge, gray-black bulk which lumbered ponderously along a jungle trail. Instantly Tarzan tensed to the shock of a sudden fear. Decision and action usually occurred simultaneously in the life of the ape-man, and now he was away through the leafy branches ere the realization of the pit's purpose had scarce formed in his mind.

Swinging from swaying limb to swaying limb, he raced through the middle terraces where the trees grew close together. Again he dropped to the ground and sped, silently and light of foot, over the carpet of decaying vegetation, only to leap again into the trees where the tangled undergrowth precluded rapid advance upon the surface.

In his anxiety he cast discretion to the winds. The caution of the beast was lost in the loyalty of the man, and so it came that he entered a large clearing, denuded of trees, without a thought of what might lie there or upon the farther edge to dispute the way with him.

He was half way across when directly in his path and but a few yards away there rose from a clump of tall grasses a half dozen chattering birds. Instantly Tarzan turned aside, for he knew well enough what manner of creature the presence of these little sentinels proclaimed. Simultaneously Buto, the rhinoceros, scrambled to his short legs and charged furiously. Haphazard charges Buto, the rhinoceros. With his weak eyes he sees but poorly even at short distances, and whether his erratic rushes are due to the panic of fear as he attempts to escape, or to the irascible temper with which he is generally credited, it is difficult to determine. Nor is the matter of little moment to one whom Buto charges, for if he be caught and tossed, the chances are that naught will interest him thereafter.

And today it chanced that Buto bore down straight upon Tarzan, across the few yards of knee-deep grass which separated them. Accident started him in the direction of the ape-man, and then his weak eyes discerned the enemy, and with a series of snorts he charged straight for him. The little rhino birds fluttered and circled about their giant ward. Among the branches of the trees at the edge of the clearing, a score or more monkeys chattered and scolded as the loud snorts of the angry beast sent them scurrying affrightedly to the upper terraces. Tarzan alone appeared indifferent and serene.

Directly in the path of the charge he stood. There had been no time to seek safety in the trees beyond the clearing, nor had Tarzan any mind to delay his journey because of Buto. He had met the stupid beast before and held him in fine contempt.

And now Buto was upon him, the massive head lowered and the long, heavy horn inclined for the frightful work for which nature had designed it; but as he struck upward, his weapon raked only thin air, for the ape-man had sprung lightly aloft with a catlike leap that carried him above the threatening horn to the broad back of the rhinoceros. Another spring and he was on the ground behind the brute and racing like a deer for the trees.

Buto, angered and mystified by the strange disappearance of his prey, wheeled and charged frantically in another direction, which chanced to be not the direction of Tarzan's flight, and so the ape-man came in safety to the trees and continued on his swift way through the forest.

Some distance ahead of him Tantor moved steadily along the well-worn elephant trail, and ahead of Tantor a crouching, black warrior listened intently in the middle of the path. Presently he heard the sound for which he had been hoping—the cracking, snapping sound which heralded the approach of an elephant.

To his right and left in other parts of the jungle other warriors were watching. A low signal, passed from one to another, apprised the most distant that the quarry was afoot. Rapidly they converged toward the trail, taking positions in trees down wind from the point at which Tantor must pass them. Silently they waited and presently were rewarded by the sight of a mighty tusker carrying an amount of ivory in his long tusks that set their greedy hearts to palpitating.

No sooner had he passed their positions than the warriors clambered from their perches. No longer were they silent, but instead clapped their hands and shouted as they reached the ground. For an instant Tantor, the elephant, paused with upraised trunk and tail, with great ears up-pricked, and then he swung on along the trail at a rapid, shuffling pace—straight toward the covered pit with its sharpened stakes upstanding in the ground.

Behind him came the yelling warriors, urging him on in the rapid flight which would not permit a careful examination of the ground before him. Tantor, the elephant, who could have turned and scattered his adversaries with a single charge, fled like a frightened deer—fled toward a hideous, torturing death.

And behind them all came Tarzan of the Apes, racing through the jungle forest with the speed and agility of a squirrel, for he had heard the shouts of the warriors and had interpreted them correctly. Once he uttered a piercing call that reverberated through the jungle; but Tantor, in the panic of terror, either failed to hear, or hearing, dared not pause to heed.

Now the giant pachyderm was but a few yards from the hidden death lurking in his path, and the blacks, certain of success, were screaming and dancing in his wake, waving their war spears and celebrating in advance the acquisition of the splendid ivory carried by their prey and the surfeit of elephant meat which would be theirs this night.

So intent were they upon their gratulations that they entirely failed to note the silent passage of the man-beast above their heads, nor did Tantor, either, see or hear him, even though Tarzan called to him to stop.

A few more steps would precipitate Tantor upon the sharpened stakes; Tarzan fairly flew through the trees until he had come abreast of the fleeing animal and then had passed him. At the pit's verge the ape-man dropped to the ground in the center of the trail. Tantor was almost upon him before his weak eyes permitted him to recognize his old friend.

"Stop!" cried Tarzan, and the great beast halted to the upraised hand.

Tarzan turned and kicked aside some of the brush which hid the pit. Instantly Tantor saw and understood.

"Fight!" growled Tarzan. "They are coming behind you." But Tantor, the elephant, is a huge bunch of nerves, and now he was half panic-stricken by terror.

Before him yawned the pit, how far he did not know, but to right and left lay the primeval jungle untouched by man. With a squeal the great beast turned suddenly at right angles and burst his noisy way through the solid wall of matted vegetation that would have stopped any but him.

Tarzan, standing upon the edge of the pit, smiled as he watched Tantor's undignified flight. Soon the blacks would come. It was best that Tarzan of the Apes faded from the scene. He essayed a step from the pit's edge, and as he threw the weight of his body upon his left foot, the earth crumbled away. Tarzan made a single Herculean effort to throw himself forward, but it was too late. Backward and downward he went toward the sharpened stakes in the bottom of the pit.

When, a moment later, the blacks came they saw even from a distance that Tantor had eluded them, for the size of the hole in the pit covering was too small to have accommodated the huge bulk of an elephant. At first they thought that their prey had put one great foot through the top and then, warned, drawn back; but when they had come to the pit's verge and peered over, their eyes went wide in astonishment, for, quiet and still, at the bottom lay the naked figure of a white giant.

Some of them there had glimpsed this forest god before and they drew back in terror, awed by the presence which they had for some time believed to possess the miraculous powers of a demon; but others there were who pushed forward, thinking only of the capture of an enemy, and these leaped into the pit and lifted Tarzan out.

There was no scar upon his body. None of the sharpened stakes had pierced him—only a swollen spot at the base of the brain indicated the nature of his injury. In the falling backward his head had struck upon the side of one of the stakes, rendering him unconscious. The blacks were quick to discover this, and equally quick to bind their prisoner's arms and legs before he should regain consciousness, for they had learned to harbor a wholesome respect for this strange man-beast that consorted with the hairy tree folk.

They had carried him but a short distance toward their village when the ape-man's eyelids quivered and raised. He looked about him wonderingly for a moment, and then full consciousness returned and he realized the seriousness of his predicament. Accustomed almost from birth to relying solely upon his own resources, he did not cast about for outside aid now, but devoted his mind to a consideration of the possibilities for escape which lay within himself and his own powers.

He did not dare test the strength of his bonds while the blacks were carrying him, for fear they would become apprehensive and add to them. Presently his captors discovered that he was conscious, and as they had little stomach for carrying a heavy man through the jungle heat, they set him upon his feet and forced him forward among them, pricking him now and then with their spears, yet with every manifestation of the superstitious awe in which they held him.

When they discovered that their prodding brought no outward evidence of suffering, their awe increased, so that they soon desisted, half believing that this strange white giant was a supernatural being and so was immune from pain.

As they approached their village, they shouted aloud the victorious cries of successful warriors, so that by the time they reached the gate, dancing and waving their spears, a great crowd of men, women, and children were gathered there to greet them and hear the story of their adventure.

As the eyes of the villagers fell upon the prisoner, they went wild, and heavy jaws fell open in astonishment and incredulity. For months they had lived in perpetual terror of a weird, white demon whom but few had ever glimpsed and lived to describe. Warriors had disappeared from the paths almost within sight of the village and from the midst of their companions as mysteriously and completely as though they had been swallowed by the earth, and later, at night, their dead bodies had fallen, as from the heavens, into the village street.

This fearsome creature had appeared by night in the huts of the village, killed, and disappeared, leaving behind him in the huts with his dead, strange and terrifying evidences of an uncanny sense of humor.

But now he was in their power! No longer could he terrorize them. Slowly the realization of this dawned upon them. A woman, screaming, ran forward and struck the ape-man across the face. Another and another followed her example, until Tarzan of the Apes was surrounded by a fighting, clawing, yelling mob of natives.

And then Mbonga, the chief, came, and laying his spear heavily across the shoulders of his people, drove them from their prey.

"We will save him until night," he said.

Far out in the jungle Tantor, the elephant, his first panic of fear allayed, stood with up-pricked ears and undulating trunk. What was passing through the convolutions of his savage brain? Could he be searching for Tarzan? Could he recall and measure the service the ape-man had performed for him? Of that there can be no doubt. But did he feel gratitude? Would he have risked his own life to have saved Tarzan could he have known of the danger which confronted his friend? You will doubt it. Anyone at all familiar with elephants will doubt it. Englishmen who have hunted much with elephants in India will tell you that they never have heard of an instance in which one of these animals has gone to the aid of a man in danger, even though the man had often befriended it. And so it is to be doubted that Tantor would have attempted to overcome his instinctive fear of the black men in an effort to succor Tarzan.

The screams of the infuriated villagers came faintly to his sensitive ears, and he wheeled, as though in terror, contemplating flight; but something stayed him, and again he turned about, raised his trunk, and gave voice to a shrill cry.

Then he stood listening.

In the distant village where Mbonga had restored quiet and order, the voice of Tantor was scarcely audible to the blacks, but to the keen ears of Tarzan of the Apes it bore its message.

His captors were leading him to a hut where he might be confined and guarded against the coming of the nocturnal orgy that would mark his torture-laden death. He halted as he heard the notes of Tantor's call, and raising his head, gave vent to a terrifying scream that sent cold chills through the superstitious blacks and caused the warriors who guarded him to leap back even though their prisoner's arms were securely bound behind him.

With raised spears they encircled him as for a moment longer he stood listening. Faintly from the distance came another, an answering cry, and Tarzan of the Apes, satisfied, turned and quietly pursued his way toward the hut where he was to be imprisoned.

The afternoon wore on. From the surrounding village the ape-man heard the bustle of preparation for the feast. Through the doorway of the hut he saw the women laying the cooking fires and filling their earthen caldrons with water; but above it all his ears were bent across the jungle in eager listening for the coming of Tantor.

Even Tarzan but half believed that he would come. He knew Tantor even better than Tantor knew himself. He knew the timid heart which lay in the giant body. He knew the panic of terror which the scent of the Gomangani inspired within that savage breast, and as night drew on, hope died within his heart and in the stoic calm of the wild beast which he was, he resigned himself to meet the fate which awaited him.

All afternoon he had been working, working, working with the bonds that held his wrists. Very slowly they were giving. He might free his hands before they came to lead him out to be butchered, and if he did—Tarzan licked his lips in anticipation, and smiled a cold, grim smile. He could imagine the feel of soft flesh beneath his fingers and the sinking of his white teeth into the throats of his foemen. He would let them taste his wrath before they overpowered him!

At last they came—painted, befeathered warriors—even more hideous than nature had intended them. They came and pushed him into the open, where his appearance was greeted by wild shouts from the assembled villagers.

To the stake they led him, and as they pushed him roughly against it preparatory to binding him there securely for the dance of death that would presently encircle him, Tarzan tensed his mighty thews and with a single, powerful wrench parted the loosened thongs which had secured his hands. Like thought, for quickness, he leaped forward among the warriors nearest him. A blow sent one to earth, as, growling and snarling, the beast-man leaped upon the breast of another. His fangs were buried instantly in the jugular of his adversary and then a half hundred black men had leaped upon him and borne him to earth.

Striking, clawing, and snapping, the ape-man fought—fought as his foster people had taught him to fight—fought like a wild beast cornered. His strength, his agility, his courage, and his intelligence rendered him easily a match for half a dozen black men in a hand-to-hand struggle, but not even Tarzan of the Apes could hope to successfully cope with half a hundred.

Slowly they were overpowering him, though a score of them bled from ugly wounds, and two lay very still beneath the trampling feet, and the rolling bodies of the contestants.

Overpower him they might, but could they keep him overpowered while they bound him? A half hour of desperate endeavor convinced them that they could not, and so Mbonga, who, like all good rulers, had circled in the safety of the background, called to one to work his way in and spear the victim. Gradually, through the milling, battling men, the warrior approached the object of his quest.

He stood with poised spear above his head waiting for the instant that would expose a vulnerable part of the ape-man's body and still not endanger one of the blacks. Closer and closer he edged about, following the movements of the twisting, scuffling combatants. The growls of the ape-man sent cold chills up the warrior's spine, causing him to go carefully lest he miss at the first cast and lay himself open to an attack from those merciless teeth and mighty hands.

At last he found an opening. Higher he raised his spear, tensing his muscles, rolling beneath his glistening, ebon hide, and then from the jungle just beyond the palisade came a thunderous crashing. The spear-hand paused, the black cast a quick glance in the direction of the disturbance, as did the others of the blacks who were not occupied with the subjugation of the ape-man.

In the glare of the fires they saw a huge bulk topping the barrier. They saw the palisade belly and sway inward. They saw it burst as though built of straws, and an instant later Tantor, the elephant, thundered down upon them.

To right and left the blacks fled, screaming in terror. Some who hovered upon the verge of the strife with Tarzan heard and made good their escape, but a half dozen there were so wrapt in the blood-madness of battle that they failed to note the approach of the giant tusker.

Upon these Tantor charged, trumpeting furiously. Above them he stopped, his sensitive trunk weaving among them, and there, at the bottom, he found Tarzan, bloody, but still battling.

A warrior turned his eyes upward from the melee. Above him towered the gigantic bulk of the pachyderm, the little eyes flashing with the reflected light of the fires—wicked, frightful, terrifying. The warrior screamed, and as he screamed, the sinuous trunk encircled him, lifted him high above the ground, and hurled him far after the fleeing crowd.

Another and another Tantor wrenched from the body of the ape-man, throwing them to right and to left, where they lay either moaning or very quiet, as death came slowly or at once.

At a distance Mbonga rallied his warriors. His greedy eyes had noted the great ivory tusks of the bull. The first panic of terror relieved, he urged his men forward to attack with their heavy elephant spears; but as they came, Tantor swung Tarzan to his broad head, and, wheeling, lumbered off into the jungle through the great rent he had made in the palisade.

Elephant hunters may be right when they aver that this animal would not have rendered such service to a man, but to Tantor, Tarzan was not a man—he was but a fellow jungle beast.

And so it was that Tantor, the elephant, discharged an obligation to Tarzan of the Apes, cementing even more closely the friendship that had existed between them since Tarzan as a little, brown boy rode upon Tantor's huge back through the moonlit jungle beneath the equatorial stars.

THE QUEST OF THE GOLDEN FLEECE

Sir Hugh Clifford

ALL THE WINTRY AFTERNOON WE HAD BEEN WORMING OUR WAY DOWN THE Thames, the big steamer filtering slowly through the throng of crafts like a 'bus moving ponderously amid crowded traffic. When at last we won free of the river, the Channel chop took us on its knee and rocked us roughly, while the skud of wind and rain slapped us in the face with riotous horse-play. As we came up from dinner and struggled aft, our feet slipped and slithered over the wet decks, and the shouts of the frozen Lascars at the lookout reached us through the sopping gloom, despairing as the howls of souls in torment. The ugly, hopeless melancholy of our surroundings accorded well with the mood which possessed the majority of those on board; for we were outward bound, and men who leave England for the good of their purses carry heavy hearts with them at the start. In the smoking room, therefore, with coat-collars tugged up about our ears and hands thrust deeply into our pockets, we sat smoking with mournful earnestness, glaring at our neighbours with the open animosity of the genial Briton.

Through the thickening fog of the tobacco-smoke, the figure of a man seated immediately opposite to me was dimly visible; but presently his unusual appearance claimed my closer attention and aroused my curiosity. His emaciated body was wrapped in a huge ulster, from the up-turned collar of which a head emerged that I can only describe as being like nothing so much as that of a death's-head moth. He was clean-shaven, and his cheeks were as hollow as saucers; his temples were pinched and prominent; from the bottom of deeply sunken sockets little wild eyes glared like savage things held fast in a gin. The mouth was set hard, as though its owner were enduring agony, and trying his best to repress a scream. As much of his hair as his cap and his coat-collar suffered to be seen was of a dirty yellow-white; yet in some indefinable way the man did not give the impression of being old. Rather he seemed to be one prematurely broken; one who suffered acutely and unceasingly; one who, with rigid self-control, maintained a tight grip upon himself, as though all his nerves were on edge. I had marked a somewhat similar expression of concentrated determination upon the faces of fellow-passengers engaged in fighting the demon of sea-sickness; but this man sucked at his pipe, and obviously drew a measure of comfort from it, in a fashion which showed that he was indifferent to the choppy motion. Yet though those buried eyes of his were glaring and savage—eyes that seemed to be eternally seeking some means of escape from a haunting peril—they were not restless, but rather were fixed in a venomous scowl; while the man himself, dead quiet, save for the light that glinted from them, was apparently sunken in a fathomless abstraction.

All this I noted mechanically, but it was the extraordinary condition of his face that chiefly excited my wonder. It was literally pock-marked with little purple cicatrices, small oblong lumps, smooth and shining feebly in the lamplight, that rose above the surface of the skin, and ran this way and that at every imaginable angle. I had seen more than once the faces of German duellists wonderfully and fearfully beslashed; but the scars they wore were long and clean, wholly unlike the badly healed lumps which disfigured my queer *vis-à-vis*. I fell to speculating as to what could have caused such a multiplicity of wounds: not a gunpowder explosion, certainly, for the skin showed none of the blue tattooing inseparable from injuries so inflicted; nor yet the bursting of a gun, for that always makes at least one jagged cut, not innumerable tiny scars such as those at which I was looking. I could think of no solution that would fit the case; and as I watched, suddenly the man withdrew his hands from his pockets, waggling them before his face with a nervous motion as though he were warding off some invisible assailants. Then I saw that every inch of the backs and palms, and as much of his wrists as were exposed to view, were pitted with cicatrices similar to those with which his face was bedecked.

"Evening, you folk!" said a nasal voice in the doorway, breaking discordantly upon the sulky silence which brooded over us; and I looked up to see the figure of a typical "down-easter," slim and alert, standing just within the room. He had a keen, hard face on him, like a meat-axe, and the wet rain stood upon it in drops. He jerked his head at us in collective greeting, walked through the haze of smoke with a free gait and swinging shoulders, and threw himself down in a heap on the horse-hair bench beside the man whose strange appearance had riveted my attention. Seated thus, he looked round at us with quick humorous glances, as though our British solemnity, which made each one of us grimly isolated in a crowd, struck him as at once amusing and impossible of endurance.

"Snakes!" he exclaimed genially. "This is *mighty* cheerful!" His strident twang seemed to cut wedges out of the foggy silence. "We look as though we had swallowed a peck of tenpenny nails, and the blamed things were sitting heavy on our stomachs. Come, let us be friendly. I ain't doing any trade in sore-headed bears. Wake up, sonny." And he dug his melancholy neighbour in the ribs with an aggressive and outrageous thumb.

It was for all the world as though he had touched the spring that sets in motion the clockwork of a mechanical toy. The man's cap flew from his head—disclosing a scalp ill-covered with sparse hairs and scarred like his face—as he leaped to his feet with a scream, torn suddenly, as it were, from the depths of his self-absorbed abstraction. Casting quick nervous glances over his shoulder, he backed into the nearest corner, his hands clawing at the air, his eyes hunted, defiant, yet abject. His whole figure was instinct with terror—terror seeking impotently to defend itself against unnumbered enemies. His teeth were set, his gums drawn back over them in two rigid white lines; a sort of snarling cry broke from him—a cry that seemed to be the expression of furious rage, pain, and agonisingly concentrated effort.

It all took place in a fraction of a second—as quickly as a man jumps when badly startled—and as quickly he recovered his balance, and pulled himself together. Then he cast a murderous glance at the American—who at that moment presented a picture of petrified astonishment—let fly a venomous oath at him, and slammed out of the room in a towering rage.

"Goramercy!" ejaculated the American limply. "I want a drink. Who'll join me?" But no one responded to his invitation.

That was the occasion of my first meeting with Timothy O'Hara: but as I subsequently travelled half across the world in his company, was admitted to his friendship, and heard him relate his experiences, not once but many times, I am able to supply the key to his extraordinary behaviour that evening. I regret that it is impossible to give his story in his own words, for he told it graphically, and with force; but unfortunately his very proper indignation got the better of his discretion, with the result that he frequently waxed blasphemous in the course of his narrative, and at times was rendered altogether inarticulate by rage. However, the version which I now offer to the reader is accurate in all essential details: and my own first-hand knowledge of that gentle race called Muruts, at whose hands O'Hara fared so evilly, has helped me to fill in such blanks as may have existed in the tale as it originally reached me.

A score of years ago there was a man in North Borneo, whose name does not matter— a man who had the itch of travel in him, and loved untrodden places for their own sake. He undertook to explore the interior of the no-man's-land which the Chartered Company euphemistically described as its "property." He made his way inland from the western coast, and little more was heard of him for several months. At the end of that time a haze of disquieting rumours, as impalpable as the used-up, fever-laden wind that blows eternally from the interior, reached the little squalid stations on the seashore; and shortly afterward the body of the explorer, terribly mangled and mutilated, was sluiced down-country by a freshet, and brought up on a sand-spit near the mouth of a river on the east coast. Here it was discovered by a couple of white men, who with the aid of a handful of unwilling natives buried it in becoming state, since it was the only thing with a European father and mother which had ever travelled across the centre of North Borneo, from sea to sea, since the beginning of time.

In life the explorer had been noted for his beard, a great yellow cascade of hair which fell down his breast from his lip to his waist; and when his corpse was found this ornament was missing. The Chartered Company, whose business it was to pay dividends in adverse circumstances, did not profess to be a philanthropical institution, and could not spend its hard-squeezed revenues upon putting the fear of death into people who have made too free with the lives of white folk, as is the practice in other parts of Asia. Therefore no steps were taken by the local administration to punish the Muruts of the interior who had amused themselves by putting the explorer to an ugly death; but the knowledge that the murdered man's beard had been shorn from his chin by some truculent savage, and was even then ornamenting the knife-handle of a Murut chief in the heart of the island rankled in the minds of the white men on the spot. The wise and prudent members of the community talked a great deal, said roundly that the thing was a shame and an abomination, and took care to let their discretion carry them no farther than the spoken word. The young and foolish did not say much, but the recovery of that wisp of hair became to many of them a tremendous ambition, a dream, something that made even existence in North Borneo tolerable, while it presented itself to their imaginations as a feat possible of accomplishment. With a few this dream became an *idée fixe*, an object in a life that otherwise was unendurable; and it may even have saved a few from the perpetration of more immediate follies. The quest would be the most hazardous conceivable, a fitting enterprise for men rendered desperate by the circumstances into the midst of which fate had thrust them.

Sitting at home in England, with pleasant things to distract the mind all about you, and with nothing at hand more dangerous than a taxicab, all this pother concerning the hairs off a dead man's chin may appeal to you as something absurdly sentimental and irrational; but try for the moment to place yourself in the position of an isolated white man at an outstation of North Borneo. Picture to yourself a tumble-down thatched bungalow standing on a roughly cleared hill, with four Chinese shops and a dilapidated police-station squatting on the bank of a black, creeping river. Rub in a smudge of blue-green forest, shutting you up on flanks, front, and rear. Fill that forest with scattered huts, wherein squalid natives live the lives of beasts—natives whose language you do not know, whose ideas you do not understand, who make their presence felt only by means of savage howls raised by them in their drunken orgies—natives whose hatred of you can only be kept from active expression by such fear as your armed readiness may inspire. Add to this merciless heat, faint exhausted air, an occasional bout of the black fever of the country, and not enough of work to preserve your mind from rust. Remember that the men who are doomed to live in these places get no sport, have no recreations, no companionship; and that the long, empty, suffocating days trail by, one by one, bringing no hope of change, and that the only communication with the outer world is kept up fitfully by certain dingy steam-tramps which are always behind time, and which may, or may not, arrive once a month. Can you wonder that amid such surroundings men wax melancholy; that they take to brooding over all manner of trivial things in a fashion which is not quite sane; and that the knowledge that their continued existence is dependent upon the wholesome awe in which white folks are held sometimes gets upon their nerves, and makes them feverishly anxious to vindicate the honour of their race? When you have let the full meaning of these things sink into your minds, you will begin to understand why so much excitement prevailed in North Borneo concerning the reported ownership of the deceased explorer's beard.

Timothy O'Hara and Harold Bateman had lived lives such as those which I have described for half a dozen years or more. They had had ample leisure in which to turn the matter of the explorer's beard over and over in their minds, till the thought of it had bred something like fanaticism—a kind of still, white-hot rage within them. It chanced that their leave of absence fell due upon one and the same day. It followed that they put their heads together and decided to start upon a private raid of their own into the interior of the Murut country, with a view to redeeming the trophy. It also followed that they made their preparations with the utmost secrecy, and that they enlisted a dozen villainous little Dyaks from Sarawak to act as their punitive force. The whole thing was highly improper and very illegal, but it promised adventurous experiences, and both Bateman and O'Hara were young and not overwise. Also, it must be urged in extenuation of their conduct that they had the effects of some six years' crushing monotony to work off; and that they had learned to regard the Muruts of the interior as their natural enemies; and that the ugliness and the deadly solitude of their existence had rendered them savage, just as the tamest beast becomes wild and ferocious when it finds itself held in the painful grip of a trap.

I am in nowise concerned to justify their doings: my part is to record them. O'Hara and Bateman vanished one day from the last outpost of quasi-civilisation, having given out that they were off upcountry in search of big game—which was a fact. Their little expedition slipped into the forest, and the wilderness swallowed it up. When once they had pushed out into the unknown interior they were gone past power of recall, were lost as completely as a needle in a ten-acre hay-field; and they breathed more freely because they had escaped from the narrow zone wherein the law of the white man runs, and need guide themselves for the future merely by the dictates of their own rudimentary notions of right and wrong.

They had a very hard time of it, so far as I can gather; for the current of the rivers, which crept toward them, black and oily, from the upper country, was dead against them, and the rapids soon caused them to abandon their boats. Then they tramped it, trudging with dogged perseverance up and down the hills, clambering painfully up sheer ascents, slipping down the steep pitches on the other side, splashing and labouring through the swamps betwixt hill and hill, or wading waist-deep across wildernesses of rank *lalang*-grass, from the green surface of which the refracted heat smote them under their hat-brims with the force of blows. Aching in every limb, half-blinded by the sweat that trickled into their eyes, flayed by the sun, mired to the ears in the morasses, torn by thorn-thickets, devoured by tree-leeches, stung by all manner of jungle-insects, and oppressed by the weight of self-imposed effort that pride forbade them to abandon, they struggled forward persistently, fiercely, growing more savage and more vindictive at every painful step. The golden fleece of beard, which was the object of their quest, became an oriflamme, in the wake of which they floundered eternally through the inferno of an endless fight. Their determination to recover it became a madness, a possession: it filled their minds to the exclusion of aught else, nerved them to fresh endeavour, spurred them out of their weariness, and would not suffer them to rest. But the bitterness of their travail incensed them mightily against the Murut folk, whose lack of reverence for white men had imposed so tremendous a task upon these self-appointed champions of their race; and as they sat over their unpalatable meals when the day's toil was ended, they talked together in blood-thirsty fashion of the vengeances they would wreak and the punishment they would exact from the tribe which was discovered to be in possession of the object of their search.

One feature of their march was that prudence forbade a halt. The Murut of North Borneo is a person of mean understanding, who requires time wherein to set his slow intellect in motion. He is a dipsomaniac, a homicide by training and predilection, and he has a passion for collecting other people's skulls, which is an unscrupulous and as fanatical as that of the modern philatelist. Whenever he encounters a stranger, he immediately falls to coveting that stranger's skull; but as he is a creature of poor courage it is essential to his comfort that he should win possession of it only by means that will not endanger his own skin. The question as to how such means may be contrived presents a difficult problem for his solution, and it takes his groping mind from two to three days in which to hit upon a workable plan. The explorer, as Bateman and O'Hara were aware, had lost his life because, overcome by fatigue, he had allowed himself to commit the mistake of spending more than a single night under a hospitable Murut roof-tree, and had so given time to his hosts to plot his destruction. Had he only held steadily upon his way, all might have been well with him: for in a country where every village is at enmity with its neighbours, a short march would have carried him into a stranger's land, which he should have been able to quit in its turn ere the schemes for his immolation hatched therein had had time in which to ripen. O'Hara and Bateman, therefore, no matter how worn out they might be by that everlasting, clambering tramp across that cruel huddle of hill-caps, were rowelled by necessity into pushing forward, and still forward, as surely as the day dawned.

Often the filth and squalor of the long airless huts—each one of which accommo-dated a whole village community in its dark interior, all the pigs and fowls of the place beneath its flooring, and as many blackened human skulls as could find hanging space along its roof-beams—sickened them, and drove them forth to camp in the jungle. Here there were only wild beasts—self-respecting and on the whole cleanly beasts, which compared very favourably with the less attractive animals in the village huts— but a vigilant guard had to be maintained against possible surprise; and this, after a heart-breaking tramp, was hard alike upon white men and Dyaks.

The raiders had pitched their camp in such a place one evening; and as the party lacked meat, and the pigeons could be heard cooing in the treetops close at hand, O'Hara took his fowling piece and strolled off alone into the forest, with the intention of shooting a few birds for the pot. The jungle was very dense in this part of the country— so dense, indeed, that a man was powerless to see in any direction for a distance of more than a dozen yards; but the pigeons were plentiful, and as they fluttered from tree to tree O'Hara walked after them without in the least realising how far he was straying from his starting point. At last the fast-failing light arrested his attention, and as he stooped to pick up the last pigeon, the search for which among the brambles had occupied more time than he had fancied, it suddenly struck him that he ought to be returning to the camp, while a doubt as to its exact direction assailed him. He was in the very act of straightening himself again with a view to looking about him for some indication of the path by which he had come when a slight crackle in the underwood smote upon his ear. He remained very still, stooping forward as he was, holding his breath, and listening intently. It flashed through his mind that the sound might have been made by one of the Dyaks, who perhaps had come out of the camp in search of him and he waited the repetition of the snapping noise with eagerness, hoping that it would tell him whether it were caused by man or beast. As he stood thus for an instant with bowed shoulders, the crackle came again, louder, crisper, and much clearer than before; and at the same moment, before he had time to change his attitude or to realise that danger threatened him, something smote him heavily in the back, bringing him prone to the earth with a grunt. The concussion was caused by some yielding substance, that was yet quick and warm; and the litter of dead leaves and the tangle of underwood combined to break his fall. He was not hurt, therefore, though the breath was knocked out of him, and that unseen something, which tumbled and writhed upon his back, pinned him to the ground. He skewed his head round, trying to see what had assailed him, and immediately a diabolical face peeped over his shoulder an inch or two above it. He only saw, as it were, in a flash; but the sight was one which, he was accustomed to say, he would never forget. In after years it was wont to recur to him in dreams, and as surely as it came it woke him with a scream. It was a savage face, brown yet pallid, grimed with dirt and wood ashes, with a narrow retreating forehead, a bestial prognathous snout, and a tiny twitching chin. The little black eyes, fierce and excited, were ringed about with angry sores, for the eyelashes had been plucked out. The eyebrows had been removed, but from the upper lip a few coarse wires sprouted uncleanly. The face was split in twain by a set of uneven teeth pointed like those of a wild cat, and tightly clenched, while above and below them the gums snarled rigidly, bearing witness to the physical effort which their owner was making. The scalp was divided into even halves by a broad parting, on either side of which there rose a tangle of dirty, ill-kept hair, that was drawn back into a chignon, giving to the creature a curious sexless aspect. All these things O'Hara noted in the fraction of a second; and as the horror bred of them set him heaving and fighting as well as his cramped position made possible, a sharp knee-cap was driven into the back of his neck, and his head fell with a concussion that blinded him. For a moment he lay still and inert, and in that moment he was conscious of little deft hands, that flew this way and that, over, under, and around his limbs, and of the pressure of narrow withes, drawn suddenly taut, that ate into his flesh. Up to this time the whole affair has been transacted in a dead, unnatural silence that somehow gave to it the strangeness and unreality of a nightmare; but now, as O'Hara lay prostrate with his face buried in the underwood, the even song of the forest insects, which rings through the jungle during the gloaming hour, was suddenly interrupted by an outbreak of queer sounds—by gurgling, jerky speech intermixed with shrill squeakings and whistlings, and by the clicking cackle which stands the Murut folk instead of laughter. Yet even now the voices of his captors were subdued and hushed, as though unwilling to be overheard; and O'Hara, understanding that the Muruts feared to be interrupted by their victim's friends, made shift to raise a shout, albeit the green stuff forced its way into his mouth and choked his utterance.

Immediately the little nimble hands were busy, clutching him afresh, while the tones of those inhuman voices shrilled and gurgled and clicked more excitedly than before. O'Hara was heaved and tugged, first one way, then another, until his body was rolled over on to its back, falling with a dull bump. He shouted once more, putting all the strength that was in him into the yell, and the nearest Murut promptly stamped on his mouth with his horny heel. O'Hara bit viciously at the thing, but his teeth could make no impression upon its leathery under-surface, and before he could shout again he found himself gagged with a piece of wood, which was bound in its place by a couple of withes. Despair seized him then, and for a moment or two he lay still, with the manhood knocked fairly out of him by a crushing consciousness of impotence, while the gabble of squeak and whistle and grunt, still hushed cautiously, broke out more discordantly than ever.

The withes about his limbs bound O'Hara so cripplingly that only his neck was free to move; but presently, craning it upward, he caught sight of his persecutors for the first time. They formed a squalid group of little, half-starved, wizened creatures, not much larger than most European children of fourteen, but with brutal faces that seemed to bear the weight of whole centuries of care and animal indulgence. They were naked, save for their foul loin-clouts; they were abominably dirty, and their skins were smothered in leprous-looking ringworm; they had not an eyelash or an eyebrow among them, for the hairs had been plucked out by the root; but their scalps were covered by frowsy growths, gathered into loathsome chignons on the napes of their necks. Every man was armed with one or more spears, and from the waist of each a long knife depended, sheathed in a wooden scabbard hung with tufts of hair. One of them— the man of whose face O'Hara had caught a glimpse above his shoulder—flourished his sheathed knife insistently in his captive's face with grotesque gesticulations, and O'Hara shuddered every time that the disgusting tassels that bedecked the scabbard swept his cheek. The fading daylight was very dim now, enabling O'Hara to see only the *form* of the things by which he was surrounded; *colour* had ceased to have any meaning in those gloomy forest aisles. The grinning savage prancing and gibbering around him, and brandishing that sheathed weapon with its revolting trophies, puzzled him. If he meant murder, why did he not draw his blade? In the depth of his misery the inconsequence of this war-dance furnished O'Hara with an additional torture.

Presently two of the Muruts came suddenly within his field of vision bearing a long green pole. This they proceeded to thrust between O'Hara's flesh and the withes that were entwined about him; and when this had been accomplished, the whole party set their shoulders under the extremities of the pole and lifted their prisoner clear of the ground. Then they bore him off at a sort of jog-trot.

The thongs, tightened fearfully by the pressure thus put upon them, pinched and bruised him pitilessly; and his head, lacking all support, hung down in an attitude of dislocation, waggling this way and that at every jolt; the blood surged into his brain, causing a horrible vertigo, and seeming to thrust his eyes almost out of their sockets; he thought that he could *feel* his limbs swelling above the biting grip of the withes, and an irresistible nausea seized him. Maddening cramps tied knots in his every muscle; and had his journey been of long duration, Timothy O'Hara would never have reached its end alive. Very soon, however, the decreased pace, and the shrill whistling sounds which came from the noses of his Murut bearers, told him that the party was ascending a hill—for these strange folk do not pant like ordinary human beings, and the uncanny noise was familiar to O'Hara from many a toilsome march in the company of native porters. Presently, too, between the straining legs of the leading files, O'Hara caught a flying glimpse of distant fire; and that, he knew, betokened the neighbourhood of a village.

A few minutes later, just as he thought that he was about to lose consciousness, the village was reached—a long, narrow hut, raised on piles, and with a door at either end, from the thresholds of which crazy ladder-ways led to the ground. Up the nearest of these rude staircases the Muruts struggled with their burden, banging his head roughly against each untrimmed rung, and throwing him down on the bamboo flooring with a chorus of grunts. For a moment there was silence, while the entire community gathered round the white man, staring at him eagerly with a kind of ferocious curiosity. Then with one accord all the men, women, and children present set up a diabolical chorus of whoopings and yellings. They seemed to give themselves over to a veritable insanity of noise. Some, squatting on their heels, supporting the weight of their bodies on arms thrust well behind them, tilted their chins to the roof and howled like maniacs. Others, standing erect, opened their mouths to their fullest extent, and emitted a series of shrill blood-curdling bellows. Others, again, shut their eyes, threw their arms aloft, and, concentrating every available atom of energy in the effort, screamed till their voices broke. The ear-piercing din sounded as though all the devils in hell had of a sudden broken loose. Heard from afar, the savage triumph, the diabolical delight that found in it their fitting expression, might well have made the blood run cold in the veins of the bravest; but heard close at hand by the solitary white man whose capture had evoked that hideous outcry, and who knew himself to be utterly at the mercy of these fiends, it was almost enough to unship his reason. O'Hara told me that from that moment he forgot the pains which his bonds had occasioned him, forgot even his desire to escape, and was filled with a tremendous longing to be put out of his agony—to be set free by death from this unspeakable inferno. His mind, he said, was working with surprising activity, and "as though it belonged to somebody else." In a series of flashes he began to recall all that he had ever heard of the manners and customs of the Muruts, of the strange uses to which they put their prisoners; and all the while he was possessed by a kind of restlessness that made him eager for them to do *something*—of no matter how awful a character—that would put a period to his unendurable suspense.

Meanwhile the Muruts were enjoying themselves thoroughly. Great earthenware jars, each sufficiently large to drown a baby with comfort, were already standing round the enclosed veranda which formed the common-room of the village, on to which each family cubicle opened, and to these jars the Muruts—men, women, and children— repeatedly addressed themselves, squatting by them, and sucking up the abominable liquor which filled them through long bamboo tubes. Each toper, as he quitted the jar, fell to howling with redoubled energy; and as more and more of the fiery stuff was consumed, their cries became more savage, more inarticulate, and more diabolical.

Half a dozen men, however, were apparently busy in the performance of some task on a spot just behind O'Hara's head, for though they frequently paid visits of ceremony to the liquor-jars, they always staggered back to the same part of the room when their draughts were ended, and there fell to hacking and hammering at wood with renewed energy. O'Hara was convinced that they were employed in constructing some infernal instrument of torture; and the impossibility of ascertaining its nature was maddening, and set his imagination picturing every abominable contrivance for the infliction of anguish of which he had ever heard or read. And all the while the hideous orgies, for which his capture was the pretext, were waxing fast and furious.

Suddenly the hidden group behind him set up a shrill cat-call, and at the sound every Murut in sight leaped to his or her feet, and danced frantically with hideous outcry and maniacal laughter. A moment later a rattan rope whined as it was pulled over the main beam of the roof with something heavy at its end; and as the slack of the cord was made fast to the wall-post opposite to him, O'Hara was aware of some large object suspended in mid-air, swinging out into the middle of the veranda immediately above him. This, as he craned his neck up at it, struggling to see it more clearly in the uncertain torch-light, was presently revealed as a big cage, an uneven square in shape, the bars of which were some six inches apart, saving on one side, where a wide gap was left. He had barely had time to make this discovery when a mob of Murut men and women rushed at him, cut the bonds that bound him, and mauling him mercilessly, lifted him up, and literally threw him into the opening formed by the gap. The cage rocked crazily, while the Muruts yelled their delight, and two of their number proceeded hastily to patch up the gap with cross-pieces of wood. Then the whole crowd drew away a little, though the hubbub never slackened, and O'Hara set his teeth to smother the groans which the pains of the removed bonds nearly wrung from him. For the time fear was forgotten in the acuteness of the agony which he endured; for as the blood began to flow freely once more, every inch of his body seemed to have been transformed into so many raging teeth. His extremities felt soft and flabby—cold, too, like jellies —but O'Hara was by nature a very strong man and at the time of his capture had been in the pink of condition. In an incredibly short while, therefore, the pain subsided, and he began to regain the use of his cramped limbs.

He was first made aware of his recovered activity by the alacrity with which he bounded into the centre of the cage in obedience to a sharp prick in the back. He tried to rise to his feet, and his head came into stunning contact with the roof; then, in a crouching attitude, he turned in the direction whence the attack had reached him. What he saw filled him with horror. The leader of the Muruts who had captured him, his eyes bloodshot with drink, was staggering about in front of him with grotesque posturings, waving his knife in one hand and its wooden sheath in the other. It was the former, evidently, that had administered that painful prod to O'Hara's back, but it was the latter which chained the white man's attention even in that moment of whirling emotions, for from its base depended a long shaggy wisp of sodden yellow hair—the golden fleece of which O'Hara and Bateman were in search. In a flash the savage saw that his victim had recognised the trophy to which he had already been at some pains to direct to his attention, and the assembled Muruts gave unmistakable tokens that they all grasped the picturesqueness of the situation. They yelled and howled and bayed more frantically than ever; some of them rolled upon the floor, their limbs and faces contorted by paroxysms of savage merriment, while others staggered about, smiting their fellows on their bare shoulders, squeaking like bats, and clicking like demoralised clockwork. A second prod with a sharp point made O'Hara shy across his narrow cage like a fly-bitten horse, and before he could recover his balance a score of delicately handled weapons inflicted light wounds all over his face and hands. As each knife touched him its owner put up his head and repeated some formula in a shrill sing-song, no word of which was intelligible to O'Hara save only the name of Kina-Balu—the great mountain which dominates North Borneo, and is believed by the natives to be the eternal resting-place of the spirits which have quitted the life of earth.

Then, for the first time, O'Hara understood what was happening to him. He had often heard of the ceremony known to the wild Muruts as a *bangun,* which has for its object the maintenance of communication between the living and the dead. He had even seen a pig hung up, as he was now hanging, while the tamer Muruts prodded it to death very carefully and slowly, charging it the while with messages for the spirits of the departed; and he remembered how the abominable cruelty of the proceeding had turned him sick, and had set him longing to interfere with native religious customs in defiance of the prudent government which he served. Now he was himself to be done to death by inches, just as the pig had died, and he knew that men had spoken truly when they had explained to him that the unfortunate quadruped was only substituted for a nobler victim as a concession to European prejudice, to the great discontent of the tame Muruts.

These thoughts rushed through his mind with the speed of lightning, and all the while it seemed to him that every particle of his mental forces was concentrated upon a single object—the task of defending himself against a crowd of persecutors. Crouching in the centre of the cage, snarling like a cat, with his eyes bursting from their sockets, his every limb braced for a leap in any direction, his hands scrabbling at the air to ward off the stabs, he faced from side to side, his breath coming in quick, noisy pants. Every second one or another of the points that assailed him made him turn about with a cry of rage, and immediately his exposed back was prodded by every Murut within reach. Suddenly he heard his own voice raised in awful curses and blasphemies, and the familiar tones of his mother-tongue smote him with surprise. He had little consciousness of pain as pain, only the necessity of warding off the points of his enemies' weapons presented itself to him as something that must be accomplished at all costs, and each separate failure enraged him. He bounded about his cage with an energy and an agility that astonished him, and the rocking of his prison seemed to keep time with the lilting of his thumping heart-beats. More than once he fell, and his face and scalp were prodded terribly ere he could regain his feet; often he warded off a thrust with his bare hands. But of the wounds which he thus received he was hardly conscious; his mind was in a species of delirium of rage, and all the time he was torn with a fury of indignation because he, a white man, was being treated in this dishonouring fashion by a pack of despicable Muruts. But he received no serious injury; for the Muruts, who had many messages for their dead relations, were anxious to keep the life in him as long as might be, and in spite of their intoxication, prodded him with shrewdness and caution. How long it all lasted O'Hara never knew with certainty; but it was the exhaustion caused by loss of breath and blood, and by the wild leaping of that bursting heart of his, that caused him presently to sink on the floor of his cage in a swoon.

The Muruts, finding that he did not answer to their stabs, drew off and gathered eagerly around the liquor-jars. The lulling would come soon after dawn—as soon, in fact, as their overnight orgies made it possible—when the prisoner would be set to run the gauntlet, and would be hacked to pieces after one final delicious *bangun*. It was essential, therefore, that enough strength should be left in him to show good sport; and in the meantime their villainous home-made spirits would bring that measure of happiness which comes to the Murut from being suffered, for a little space, to forget the fact of his own repulsive existence. Accordingly, with noisy hospitality, each man tried to make his neighbour drink to greater excess than himself, and all proved willing victims. With hoots and squeals of laughter, little children were torn from their mothers' breasts and given to suck at the bamboo pipes, their ensuing intoxication being watched with huge merriment by men and women alike. The shouts raised by the revellers became more and more shaky, less and less articulate; over and over again the groups around the jars broke up, while their members crawled away, to lie about in deathlike stupors, from which they aroused themselves only to vomit and drink anew.

Long after this stage of the proceedings had been reached, O'Hara had recovered his senses; but prudence bade him lie as still as a mouse. Once or twice a drunken Murut lurched onto his feet and made a pass or two at him, and now and again he was prodded painfully; but putting forth all the self-control at his command, he gave no sign of life. At last every Murut in the place was sunken in abominable torpor, excepting only the chief, from whose knife-scabbard hung the tuft of hair which had once ornamented the chin of the explorer. His little red eyes were fixed in a drunken stare upon O'Hara, and the latter watched them with a fascination of dread through his half-closed lids. Over and over again the Murut crawled to the nearest liquor-jar, and sucked up the dregs with a horrible sibilant gurgling; and at times he even staggered to his feet, muttering and mumbling over his tiny, busy chin, waving his weapon uncertainly, ere he subsided in a limp heap upon the floor. On each occasion he gave more evident signs of drowsiness and at last his blinking eyes were covered by their lashless lids.

At the same moment a gentle gnawing sound, which had been attracting O'Hara's attention for some minutes, though he had not dared to move by so much as a finger's breadth to discover its cause, ceased abruptly. Then the faintest ghost of a whisper came to his ears from below his cage, and, moving with the greatest caution, and peering down through the uncertain light, he saw that a hole had been made by sawing away two of the lathes which formed the flooring. In the black hole immediately beneath him the faces of two of his own Dyaks were framed, and even as he looked one of them hoisted himself into the hut, and began deftly to remove the bars of the cage, working as noiselessly as a shadow. The whole thing was done so silently, and O'Hara's own mind was so racked by the emotions which his recent experiences had held for him, that he was at first persuaded that what he saw, or rather fancied he saw, was merely a figment conjured up for his torture by the delirium which possessed him. He felt that if he suffered himself to believe in this mocking delusion even for an instant, the disappointment of discovering its utter unreality would drive him mad. He was already spent with misery, physical and mental; he was constantly holding himself in leash to prevent the commission of some insane extravagance; he was seized with an unreasoning desire to scream. He fought with himself—a self that was unfamiliar to him, although its identity was never in doubt—as he might have fought with a stranger. He told himself that his senses were playing cruel pranks upon him, and that nothing should induce him to be deceived by them; and all the while—hope—mad, wild hysterical hope—was surging up in his heart, shaking him like an aspen, wringing unaccustomed tears from his eyes, and tearing his breast with noiseless sobs.

As he lay inert and utterly wretched, unable to bear up manfully under this new wanton torture of the mind, the ghost of the second Dyak clambered skilfully out of the darkness below the hut, and joined his fellow, who had already made a wide gap in the side of the cage. Then the two of them seized O'Hara, and with the same strange absence of sound lifted him bodily through the prison and through the hole in the flooring on to the earth below. Their grip upon his lacerated flesh hurt him acutely; but the very pain was welcome, for did it not prove the reality of his deliverers? What he experienced of relief and gratitude O'Hara could never tell us, for all he remembers is that, gone suddenly weak and plaintive as a child, he clung to the little Dyaks, sobbing broken-heartedly, and weeping on their shoulders without restraint or decency, in utter *abandon* of self-pity. Also he recalls dimly that centuries later he found himself standing in Bateman's camp, with his people gathering about him, and that of a sudden he was aware that he was mother-naked. After that, so he avers, all is a blank.

The closing incidents of the story were related to me by Bateman one evening when I chanced to foregather with him in an up-country outpost in Borneo. We had been talking far into the night, and our *solitude à deux* and the lateness of the hour combined to thaw his usual taciturnity and to unlock his shy confidence. Therefore I was put in possession of a secret which until then, I believe, had been closely kept.

"It was an awful night," he said, "that upon which poor O'Hara was missing. The Dyaks had gone out in couples all over the place to try to pick up his trail, but I remained in the camp; for though there was a little moon, it was too dark for a white man's eyes to be of any good. What with the inactivity, and my fears for O'Hara, I was as 'jumpy' as you make 'em; and as the Dyaks began to drop in, two at a time, each couple bringing in their tale of failure, I worked myself up to such a state of depression and misery that I thought I must be going mad. Just about three o'clock in the morning the last brace of Dyaks turned up, and I was all of a shake when I saw that they had poor O'Hara with them. He broke loose from them and stumbled into the centre of the camp stark naked, and pecked almost to bits by those infernal Murut knives; but the wounds were not overdeep, and the blood was caking over most of them. He was an awful sight, and I was for tending his hurt without delay; but he pushed me roughly aside, and I saw that his eyes were blazing with madness. He stood there in the midst of us all, throwing his arms above his head, cursing in English and in the vernacular, and gesticulating wildly. The Dyaks edged away from him, and I could see that his condition funked them mortally. I tried again and again to speak to him and calm him, but he would not listen to a word I said, and for full five minutes he stood there raving and ranting, now and again pacing frenziedly from side to side, pouring out a torrent of invective mixed with muddled orders. One of the Dyaks brought him a pair of trousers, and after looking at them as though he had never seen such things before, he put them on, and stood for a second or two staring wildly around him. Then he made a bee-line for a rifle, loaded it, and slung a bandolier across his naked shoulders; and before I could stay him he was marching out of the camp with the whole crowd of Dyaks at his heels.

"I could only follow. I had no fancy for being left alone in that wilderness, more especially just then, and one of the Dyaks told me that he was leading them back to the Murut village. You see I only speak Malay, and as O'Hara had been talking Dyak I had not been able to follow his ravings. Whatever lingo he jabbered, however, it was as plain as a pikestaff that the fellow was mad as a hatter; but I had to stop explaining this to him, for he threatened to shoot me, and the Dyaks would not listen. They clearly thought that he was possessed by a devil, and they would have gone to hell at his bidding while their fear of him was upon them.

"And his madness made him cunning too, for he stalked the Murut den wonderfully neatly, and just as the dawn was breaking we found ourselves posted in the jungle within a few yards of the two doors, which were the only means of entrance or exit for the poor devils in the hut.

"Then O'Hara leaped out of his hiding place and began yelling like the maniac he was; and in an instant the whole of that long hut was humming like a disturbed beehive. Three or four squalid creatures showed themselves at the doorway nearest O'Hara, and he greeted them with half the contents of his magazine, and shrieked with laughter as they toppled onto the ground rolling over in their death-agony. There was such a wailing and crying set up by the other inhabitants of the hut as you never heard in all your life—it was just despair made vocal—the sort of outcry that a huge menagerie of wild animals might make when they saw flames lapping at their cages; and above it all I could hear O'Hara's demoniac laughter ringing with savage delight, and the war-whoops of those little devils of Dyaks, whose blood was fairly up now. The trapped wretches in the hut made a stampede for the farther door; we could hear them scuffling and fighting with one another for the foremost places. They thought that safety lay in that direction; but the Dyaks were ready for them, and the bullets from their Winchesters drove clean through three and four of the squirming creatures at a time, and in a moment that doorway, too, and the ground about the ladder foot were a shambles.

"After that for a space there was a kind of awful lull within the hut, though without O'Hara and his Dyaks capered and yelled. Then the noise which our folk were making was drowned by a series of the most heart-breaking shrieks you ever heard or dreamed of, and immediately a second rush was made simultaneously at each door. The early morning light was getting stronger now, and I remember noting how incongruously peaceful and serene it seemed. Part of the hut near our end had caught fire somehow, and there was a lot of smoke, which hung low about the doorway. Through this I saw the crowd of Muruts struggle in that final rush, and my blood went cold when I understood what they were doing. Every man had a woman or a child held tightly in his arms— held in front of him as a buckler—and it was from these poor devils that those awful screams were coming. I jumped in front of the Dyaks and yelled to them in Malay to hold their fire; but O'Hara thrust me aside, and *shooed* the Dyaks on with shouts and curses and peals of laughter, slapping his palm on his gunstock, and capering with delight and excitement. The Dyaks took no sort of heed of me, and the volleys met the Muruts like a wall of lead.

"I had slipped and fallen when O'Hara pushed me, and as I clambered on to my feet again I saw the mob of savages fall together and crumple up, for all the world as paper crumples when burned suddenly. Most of them fell back into the dark interior of the hut, writhing in convulsions above the litter of the dead; but one or two pitched forward headlong to the ground, and I saw a little brown baby, which had escaped unharmed, crawling about over the corpses, and squeaking like a wounded rabbit. I ran forward to save it, but a Dyak was too quick for me, and before I could get near it, he had thrown himself upon it, and . . . *ugh!*

"The Muruts began cutting their way through the flooring then, and trying to bolt into the jungle. One or two of them got away, I think; and this threw O'Hara into such a passion of fury that I half expected to see him kill some of the Dyaks. He tore around to the side of the hut, and I saw him brain one Murut as he made a rush from under the low floor. One end of the building was in roaring flames by this time, and half a dozen Dyaks had gone in at the other end and were bolting the wretched creatures from their hiding places, just as ferrets bolt rabbits from their burrows, while O'Hara and the other Dyaks waited for them outside. They hardly missed one of them, sparing neither age nor sex, though I ran from one to another like a madman, trying to prevent them. It was awful . . . awful! and I was fairly blubbering with the horror of it, and with the consciousness of my own impotence. I was regularly broken up by it, and I remember at the last sitting down upon a log, burying my face in my hands, and crying like a child.

"The thing seemed to be over by then: there was no more bolting, and the Dyaks were beginning to clear out of the hut as the flames gained ground and made the place too hot for them. But, at the last, there came a terrific yell from the very heart of the fire, and a single Murut leaped out of the smoke. He was stark naked, for his loin clout had been burned to tinder; he was blackened by the smoke, and his long hair was afire behind him! His mouth was wide, and the cries that came from it went through and through my head, running up and up the scale till they hit upon a note the shrillness of which agonised me. Surrounded by the flames, he looked like a devil in the heart of the pit. In one scorched arm he brandished a long knife, the blade of which was red with the glare of the flames, and in the other was the sheath, blazing at one end, and decked at the other by a great tuft of yellow hair that was smouldering damply.

"As soon as he saw him O'Hara raised a terrible cry and threw himself at him. The two men grappled and fell, the knife and scabbard escaping from the Murut's grasp and pitching straight into the fire. The struggle lasted for nearly a minute, O'Hara and his enemy rolling over and over one another, breathing heavily but making no other sound. Then something happened—I don't clearly know what; but the Murut's head dropped, and O'Hara rose up from his dead body, moving very stiffly. He stood for a moment so, looking round him in a dazed fashion, until his eyes caught mine. Then he staggered toward me, reeling like a tipsy man.

"'Mother of heaven!' he said thickly, 'what *have* I done?'

"He stared round him at the little brown corpses, doubled up in dislocated and distorted attitudes, and his eyes were troubled.

"'God forgive me!' he muttered. 'God forgive me!'

"Then he spun about on his heel, his hands outstretched above his head, his fingers clutching at the air, a thin foam forming on his lips, and before I could reach him he had toppled over in a limp heap upon the ground.

"I had an awful business getting O'Hara down-country. He was mad as a March hare for three weeks. But the Dyaks worked like bricks—though I could not bear the sight of them—and the currents of the rivers were in our favour when we reached navigable water. I know that O'Hara was mad that morning—no white man could have acted as he did unless he had been insane—and he always swears that he has no recollection of anything that occurred after the Dyaks rescued him. I hope it may be so, but I am not certain. He is a changed man anyway, as nervous and jumpy as they make 'em, and I know that he is always brooding over that up-country trip of ours."

"Yes," I assented, "and he is constantly telling the first part of the story to every chance soul he meets."

"Exactly," said Bateman. "That is what makes me sometimes doubt the completeness of his oblivion concerning what followed. What do *you* think?"

THE WOOD OF DEVILS

Edgar Wallace

Four days out of M'Sakidanga, if native report be true, there is a trickling stream that meanders down from N'Gombi country. Native report says that this is navigable even in the dry season.

The missionaries at Bonginda ridicule this report; and Arburt, the young chief of the station, with a gentle laugh in his blue eyes, listened one day to the report of Elebi about a fabulous land at the end of this river, and was kindly incredulous.

"If it be that ivory is stored in this place," he said in the vernacular, "or great wealth lies for the lifting, go to Sandi, for this ivory belongs to the Government. But do you, Elebi, fix your heart more upon God's treasures in heaven, and your thoughts upon your unworthiness to merit a place in His kingdom, and let the ivory go."

Elebi was known to Sanders as a native evangelist of the tornado type, a thunderous, voluble sub-minister of the service; he had, in his ecstatic moments, made many converts. But there were days of reaction, when Elebi sulked in his mud hut, and reviewed Christianity calmly.

It was a service, this new religion. You could not work yourself to a frenzy in it, and then have done with the thing for a week. You must needs go on, on, never tiring, never departing from the straight path, exercising irksome self-restraint, leaving undone that which you would rather do.

"Religion is prison," grumbled Elebi, after his interview, and shrugged his broad, black shoulders.

In his hut he was in the habit of discarding his European coat for the loin cloth and the blanket, for Elebi was a savage—an imitative savage—but still barbarian. Once, preaching on the River of Devils, he had worked himself up to such a pitch of enthusiastic fervour that he had smitten a scoffer, breaking his arm, and an outraged Sanders had him arrested, whipped, and fined a thousand rods. Hereafter Elebi had figured in certain English missionary circles as a Christian martyr, for he had lied magnificently, and his punishment had been represented as a form of savage persecution.

But the ivory lay buried three days' march beyond the Secret River; thus Elebi brooded over the log that smouldered in his hut day and night. Three days beyond the river, branching off at a place where there were two graves, the country was reputably full of devils, and Elebi shuddered at the thought; but, being a missionary and a lay evangelist, and, moreover, the proud possessor of a copy of the Epistle to the Romans (laboriously rendered into the native tongue), he had little to fear. He had more to fear from a certain White Devil at a far-away headquarters, who might be expected to range the lands of the Secret River, when the rains had come and gone.

It was supposed that Elebi had one wife, conforming to the custom of the white man, but the girl who came into the hut with a steaming bowl of fish in her hands was not the wife that the missionaries recognised as such.

"Sikini," he said, "Iam going a journey by canoe."

"In the blessed service?" asked Sikini, who had come under the influence of the man in his more elated periods.

"The crackling of a fire is like a woman's tongue," quoted Elebi; "and it is easier to keep the lid on a boiling pot than a secret in a woman's heart."

Elebi had the river proverbs at his finger-tips, and the girl laughed, for she was his favourite wife, and knew that in course of time the informa- tion would come to her.

"Sikini," said the man suddenly, "you know that I have kept you when the Blood Taker would have me put you away."

(Arburt had a microscope and spent his evenings searching the blood of his flock for signs of trynosomiasis.)

"You know that for your sake I lied to him who is my father and my protector, saying: 'There shall be but one wife in my house, and that Tombolo, the coast woman.' "

The girl nodded, eyeing him stolidly.

"Therefore I tell you that I am going beyond the Secret River, three days' march, leaving the canoe at a place where there are two graves."

"What do you seek? "she asked.

"There are many teeth in that country," he said; "dead ivory that the people brought with them from a distant country, and have hidden, fearing one who is a Breaker of Stones.* I shall come back rich, and buy many wives who shall wait upon you and serve you, and then I will no longer be Christian, but will worship the red fetish as my father did, and his father."

"Go," she said, nodding thoughtfully.

He told her many things that he had not revealed to Arburt—of how the ivory came, of the people who guarded it, of the means by which he intended to secure it.

Next morning before the mission *lo-koli* sounded, he had slipped away in his canoe; and Arburt, when the news came to him, sighed and called him a disappointing

---

* Bula Matidi, *i.e.*, "Stone Breaker," is the native name for the Congo Government.

beggar—for Arburt was human, Sanders, who was also human, sent swift messengers to arrest Elebi, for it is not a good thing that treasure-hunting natives should go wandering through a strange country, such excursions meaning war, and war meaning, to Sanders at any rate, solemn official correspondence, which his soul loathed.

Who would follow the fortunes of Elebi must paddle in his wake as far as Okau, where the Barina meets the Lapoi, must take the left river path, past the silent pool of the White Devil, must follow the winding stream till the elephants' playing ground be reached. Here the forest has been destroyed for the sport of the Great Ones; the shore is strewn with tree trunks, carelessly uprooted and as carelessly tossed aside by the gambolling mammoth. The ground is innocent of herbage or bush; it is a flat wallow of mud, with the marks of pads where the elephant has passed.

Elebi drew his canoe up the bank, carefully lifted his cooking-pot, full of living fire, and emptied its contents, heaping thereon fresh twigs and scraps of dead wood. Then he made himself a feast, and went to sleep.

A wandering panther came snuffling and howling in the night, and Elebi rose and replenished the fire. In the morning he sought for the creek that led to the Secret River, and found it hidden by the hippo grass.

Elebi had many friends in the N'Gombi country. They were gathered in the village of Tambango—to the infinite embarrassment of the chief of that village—for Elebi's friends laid hands upon whatsoever they desired, being strangers and well armed, and, moreover, outnumbering the men of the village three to one. One, O'Sako, did the chief hold in greatest dread, for he said little, but stalked tragically through the untidy street of Tambango, a bright, curved execution knife in the crook of his left arm. O'Sako was tall and handsome. One broad shoulder gleamed in its nakedness, and his muscular arms were devoid of ornamentation. His thick hair was plastered with clay till it was like a European woman's, and his body was smeared with ingola dust.

Once only he condescended to address his host.

"You shall find me three young men against the Lord Elebi's arrival, and they shall lead us to the land of the Secret River."

"But, master," pleaded the chief, "no man may go to the Secret River, because of the devils."

"Three men," said O'Sako softly; "three young men swift of foot, with eyes like the N'Gombi, and mouths silent as the dead."

"—— the devils," repeated the chief weakly, but O'Sako stared straight ahead and strode on.

When the sun blazed furiously on the rim of the world in a last expiring effort, and the broad river was a flood of fire, and long shadows ran through the clearings, Elebi came to the village. He came unattended from the south, and he brought with him no evidence of his temporary sojourn in the camps of civilisation. Save for his loin cloth, and his robe of panther skin thrown about his shoulders, he was naked.

There was a palaver house at the end of the village, a thatched little wattle hut perched on a tiny hill, and the Lord Elebi gathered there his captains and the chief of the village. He made a speech.

"*Cala, cala,*" he began—and it means "long ago," and is a famous opening to speeches—"before the white man came, and when the Arabi came down from the northern countries to steal women and ivory, the people of the Secret River buried their 'points' in a Place of Devils. Their women they could not bury, so they lost them. Now all the people of the Secret River are dead. The Arabi killed some, Bula Matadi killed others, but the sickness killed most of all. Where their villages were the high grass has grown, and in their gardens only the weaver bird speaks. Yet I know of this place, for there came to me a vision and a voice that said——"

The rest of the speech from the European standpoint was pure blasphemy, because Elebi had had the training of a lay preacher, and had an easy delivery.

When he had finished, the chief of the village of Tambangu spoke. It was a serious discourse on devils. There was no doubt at all that in the forest where the *caché* was there was a veritable stronghold of devildom. Some had bad faces and were as tall as the gum-trees—taller, for they used whole trees for clubs; some were small, so small that they travelled on the wings of bees, but all were very potent, very terrible, and most effective guardians of buried treasure. Their greatest accomplishment lay in leading astray the traveller: men went into the forest in search of game or copal or rubber, and never came back, because there were a thousand ways in and no way out.

Elebi listened gravely.

"Devils of course there are," he said, "including the Devil, the Old One, who is the enemy of God. I have had much to do with the casting out of devils—in my holy capacity as a servant of the Word. Of the lesser devils I know nothing, though I do not doubt they live. Therefore I think it would be better for all if we offered prayer."

On his instruction the party knelt in full view of the village, and Elebi prayed conventionally but with great earnestness that the Powers of Darkness should not prevail, but that the Great Work should go on triumphantly.

After which, to make doubly sure, the party sacrificed two fowls before a squat *bete* that stood before the chief's door, and a crazy witch-doctor anointed Elebi with human fat.

"We will go by way of Ochori," said Elebi, who was something of a strategist. "These Ochori folk will give us food and guides, being a cowardly folk and very fearful."

He took farewell of the old chief and continued his journey, with O'Sako and his warriors behind him. So two days passed. An hour's distance from the city of the Ochori he called a conference.

"Knowing the world," he said, "I am acquainted with the Ochori, who are slaves: you shall behold their chief embrace my feet. Since it is fitting that one, such as I, who know the ways of white men and their magic, should be received with honour; let us send forward a messenger to say that the Lord Elebi comes, and bid them kill so many goats against our coming."

"That is good talk," said O'Sako, his lieutenant, and a messenger was despatched. Elebi with his caravan followed slowly.

It is said that Elebi's message came to Bosambo of Monrovia, chief of the Ochori, when he was in the despondent mood peculiar to men of action who find life running too smoothly.

It was Bosambo's practice—and one of which his people stood in some awe—to reflect aloud in English in all moments of crisis, or on any occasion when it was undesirable that his thoughts should be conveyed abroad.

He listened in silence, sitting before the door of his hut and smoking a short wooden pipe, whilst the messenger described the quality of the coming visitor, and the unparalleled honour which was to fall upon the Ochori.

Said Bosambo at the conclusion of the recital, "Damn nigger."

The messenger was puzzled by the strange tongue.

"Lord Chief," he said, "my master is a great one, knowing the ways of white men."

"I also know something of white men," said Bosambo calmly, in the River dialect, "having many friends, including Sandi, who married my brother's wife's sister, and is related to me. Also," said Bosambo daringly, "I have shaken hands with the Great White King who dwells beyond the big water, and he has given me many presents."

With this story the messenger went back to the slowly advancing caravan, and Elebi was impressed and a little bewildered.

"It is strange," he said, "no man has ever known an Ochori chief who was aught but a dog and the son of a dog—let us see this Bosambo. Did you tell him to come out and meet me?"

"No," replied the messenger frankly, "he was such a great one, and was so haughty because of Sandi, who married his brother's wife's sister; and so proud that I did not dare tell him."

There is a spot on the edge of the Ochori city where at one time Sanders had caused to be erected a. warning sign, and here Elebi found the chief waiting and was flattered. There was a long and earnest conference in the little palaver house of the city, and here Elebi told as much of his story as was necessary, and Bosambo believed as much as he could.

"And what do you need of me and my people?" asked Bosambo at length.

"Lord chief," said Elebi, "I go a long journey, being fortified with the blessed spirit of which you know nothing, that being an especial mystery of the white men."

"There is no mystery which I did not know," said Bosambo loftily, "and if you speak of spirits, I will speak of certain saints, also of a Virgin who is held in high respect by white men."

"If you speak of the blessed Paul—" began Elebi, a little at sea.

"Not only of Paul but Peter, John, Luke, Matthew, Antonio, and Thomas," recited Bosambo rapidly. He had not been a scholar at the Catholic mission for nothing. Elebi was nonplussed.

"We will let these magic matters rest," said Elebi wisely; "it is evident to me that you are a learned man. Now I go to seek some wonderful treasures. All that I told you before was a lie. Let us speak as brothers. I go to the wood of devils, where no man has been for many years. I beg you, therefore, to give me food and ten men for carriers."

"Food you can have but no men," said Bosambo, "for I have pledged my word to Sandi, who is, as you know, the husband of my brother's wife's sister, that no man of mine should leave this country."

With this Elebi had to be content, for a new spirit had come to the Ochori since he had seen them last, and there was a defiance in the timid eyes of these slaves of other days, which was disturbing. Besides they seemed well armed.

Every few hundred yards the party stopped, and Elebi tied one of the strips to a branch of a tree.

"In this way," he communicated to his lieutenant, "we may be independent of gods, and fearless of devils, for if we cannot find the ivory we can at least find our way back again."

(There had been such an experiment made by the missionaries in traversing the country between Bonguidga and the Big River, but there were no devils in that country.)

In two days' marches they came upon a place of graves. There had been a village there, for Isisi palms grew luxuriously, and pushing aside the grass they came upon a rotting roof. Also there were millions of weaver birds in the nut-palms, and a choked banana grove.

The graves, covered with broken cooking pots, Elebi found, and was satisfied.

In the forest, a league beyond the dead village, they came upon an old man, so old that you might have lifted him with a finger and thumb.

"Where do the young men go in their strength?" he mumbled childishly; "into the land of small devils? Who shall guide them back to their women? None, for the devils will confuse them, opening new roads and closing the old. Oh, Ko Ko!"

He snivelled miserably.

"Father," said Elebi, dangling strips of red flannel from his hand, "this is white man's magic, we come back by the way we go."

Then the old man fell into an insane fit of cursing, and threw at them a thousand deaths, and Elebi's followers huddled back in frowning fear.

"You have lived too long," said Elebi gently, and passed his spear through the old man's neck.

They found the ivory two days' journey beyond the place of killing. It was buried under a mound, which was overgrown with rank vegetation, and there was by European calculation some £50,000 worth.

In the morning the party set forth and Bosambo, who took no risks, saw them started on their journey. He observed that part of the equipment of the little caravan were two big baskets filled to the brim with narrow strips of red cloth.

"This is my magic," said Elebi mysteriously, when he was questioned, "it is fitting that you should know its power."

Bosambo yawned in his face with great insolence.

Clear of Ochori by one day's march, the party reached the first straggling advance guard of the Big Forest. A cloud of gum-trees formed the approach to the wood, and here the magic of Elebi's basket of cloth strips became revealed.

"We will go back and find carriers," said Elebi, "taking with us as many of the teeth as we can carry."

Two hours later the party began its return journey, following the path where at intervals of every half-mile a strip of scarlet flannelette hung from a twig.

There were many paths they might have taken, paths that looked as though they had been made by the hand of man, and Elebi was glad that he had blazed the way to safety.

For eight hours the caravan moved swiftly, finding its direction with no difficulty; then the party halted for the night.

Elebi was awakened in the night by a man who was screaming, and he leapt up, stirring the fire to a blaze.

"It is the brother of Olambo of Kinshassa, he has the sickness *mongo*," said an awe-stricken voice, and Elebi called a council.

THE WOOD OF DEVILS

"There are many ways by which white men deal with this sickness," he said wisely, "by giving certain powders and by sticking needles into arms, but to give medicine for the sickness when madness comes is useless—so I have heard the fathers at the station say, because madness only comes when the man is near death."

"He was well last night," said a hushed voice. "There are many devils in the forest, let us ask him what he has seen."

So a deputation went to the screaming, writhing figure that lay trussed and tied on the ground, and spoke with him. They found some difficulty in gaining an opening, for he jabbered and mouthed and laughed and yelled incessantly.

"On the question of devils," at last Elebi said.

"Devils," screeched the madman. "Yi! I saw six devils with fire in their mouths—death to you, Elebi! Dog—"

He said other things which were not clean.

"If there were water here," mused Elebi, "we might drown him; since there is only the forest and the earth, carry him away from the camp, and I will make him silent."

So they carried the lunatic away, eight strong men swaying through the forest, and they came back, leaving Elebi alone with his patient. The cries ceased suddenly and Elebi returned, wiping his hands on his leopard skin.

"Let us sleep," said Elebi, and lay down.

Before the dawn came up the party were on the move.

They marched less than a mile from their camping ground and then faltered and stopped.

"There is no sign, lord," the leader reported, and Elebi called him a fool and went to investigate.

But there was no red flannel, not a sign of it. They went on another mile without success.

"We have taken the wrong path, let us return," said Elebi, and the party retraced its steps to the camp they had abandoned. That day was spent in exploring the country for three miles on either side, but there was no welcome blaze to show the trail.

"We are all N'Gombi men," said Elebi, "let us to-morrow go forward, keeping the sun at our back; the forest has no terrors for the N'Gombi folk—yet I cannot understand why the white man's magic failed."

"Devils!" muttered his lieutenant sullenly.

Elebi eyed him thoughtfully.

"Devils sometimes desire sacrifices," he said with significance, "the wise goat does not bleat when the priest approaches the herd."

In the morning a great discovery was made. A crumpled piece of flannel was found on the outskirts of the camp. It lay in the very centre of a path, and Elebi shouted in his joy.

Again the caravan started on the path. A mile farther along another little red patch caught his eye, half a mile beyond, another.

Yet none of these were where he had placed them, and they all bore evidence of rude handling, which puzzled the lay brother sorely. Sometimes the little rags would be missing altogether, but a search party would come upon one some distance off the track, and the march would go on.

Near sunset Elebi halted suddenly and pondered. Before him ran his long shadow; the sun was behind him when it ought to have been in front.

"We are going in the wrong direction," he said, and the men dropped their loads and stared at him.

"Beyond any doubt," said Elebi after a pause, "this is the work of devils—let us pray."

He prayed aloud earnestly for twenty minutes, and darkness had fallen before he had finished.

They camped that night on the spot where the last red guide was, and in the morning they returned the way they had come. There was plenty of provision, but water was hard to come by, and therein lay the danger. Less than a mile they had gone before the red rags had vanished completely, and they wandered helplessly in a circle.

"This is evidently a matter not for prayer, but for sacrifice," concluded Elebi, so they slew one of the guides.

Three nights later, O'Sako, the friend of Elebi, crawled stealthily to the place where Elebi was sleeping, and settled the dispute which had arisen during the day as to who was in command of the expedition.

"Master," said Bosambo of Monrovia, "all that you ordered me to do, that I did."

Sanders sat before the chief's hut in his camp chair and nodded.

"When your word came that I should find Elebi—he being an enemy of the Government and disobeying your word—I took fifty of my young men and followed on his tracks. At first the way was easy, because he had tied strips of cloth to the trees to guide him on the backward journey, but afterwards it was hard, for the *N'Kema* that live in the wood—"

"Monkeys?" Sanders raised his eyebrows.

"Monkeys, master," Bosambo nodded his head, "the little black monkeys of the forest who love bright colours—they had come down from their trees and torn away the cloths and taken them to their houses after the fashion of the monkey people. Thus Elebi lost himself and with him his men, for I found their bones, knowing the way of the forest."

"What else did you find?" asked Sanders.

"Nothing, master," said Bosambo, looking him straight in the eye.

"That is probably a lie!" said Sanders.

Bosambo thought of the ivory buried beneath the floor of his hut and did not contradict him.

TOOLS

L. Patrick Greene

GEORGETOWN BOASTED OF ONE HOTEL, THE IMPERIAL, AND IT DIFFERED IN no degree from the tin-roofed, mud-walled building which holds a prominent place in any typical South African mining establishment.

The Imperial did not cater to transients, and its guests were more less permanent. For the most part they were miners, their wives and families.

The men can best be described offhand as "diamonds in the rough," and if they owned clothing other than the khaki slacks, gray flannel shirts, and high boots of their calling, they never gave evidence of such possession. They worked hard under trying conditions, but the wages were high, and with the optimism of the Eternal Boy which is in every man they were able to look forward to the time when they could go home and live like "fighting cocks" on their savings.

As for the women, some few struggled to preserve their femininity in this little world of men, and eagerly purchased any new toilet preparation guaranteed to preserve the bloom of youth or to protect "the most delicate complexion from the fierce rays of the African sun." Most of them, however, had long since given up the apparently hopeless struggle and slumped physically and mentally.

The evening meal, "dinner" was the one event of the day at the Imperial. Indeed it was the social event of Georgetown.

All the hotel guests came together for that one meal; and the number was augmented by such tradesman as the town supported, and occasionally officials from the Portuguese territory across the river.

The meal was served in a large barn-like room, known as the Banqueting-Hall. Save for one long deal table, covered with oilcloth of a once gorgeous pattern, some nondescript chairs, and a few small round-topped tables, the room was devoid of furniture.

Evil smelling oil lamps provided the illumination and added their iota to the oppressive heat. Flies buzzed lazily about the room, and above their low drone came the sharper, vicious "ping" of mosquitoes.

A dreary place was this banqueting-hall of the Imperial Hotel; and, it must be said, the diners made no effort to rise above their environment.

Tonight was no exception.

The men folk were weary; and the women, prostrated by the intense heat of the day, spoke rarely. It would have been better perhaps if they had kept altogether silent, for when they did speak there was a bitter rasp in their voices that set all nerves on edge and precipitated more than one domestic quarrel.

Native waiters in once white uniforms moved languidly about, serving the first course—hot, greasy soup in thick, chipped plates.

And then, conjuring up memories of another clime and different surroundings, a vision projected itself into the room.

At the sight of it what idle gossip was being indulged in stopped; domestic squalls were suddenly calmed. Women whose expression had hitherto been listless looked in admiration with perhaps a flicker of regret that they had not taken more pains with their toilet. With fluttering, patting hands, they furtively essay to smooth into a semblance of order, hair which had been disarranged during the long afternoon *siesta*.

The first effect of the vision upon the men was one of silent amazement; but that was quickly followed by a contemporaneous amusement. Some even gave vent to loud hoots of derision—quickly silenced, to be sure, by the indignant looks of the women.

As for the cause of all this, he hesitated a moment in the entrance. But his hesitation was not one of indecision, rather it was as if he waited for—well, a head waiter to lead him to the table.

Yes. Even so.

At the Ritz Carlton a man in evening dress is, to say the least, inconspicuous unless his attire be faulty. But at the Imperial Hotel in Georgetown, South Africa, such a one is a freak, a monstrosity, a darn fool, or a delectable vision. Have it any way you please.

Add to the very correct attire a man well accustomed to wearing it—and a monocle—and you will understand why these women, so long divorced from the finer refinements of social amenities, called the stranger a vision.

One of the natives finally escorted the stranger to one of the small tables; the next course was brought in, and the meal resumed.

An observer would have been interested to note the sudden change in the conversation and in the general deportment of the diners; and many a man looked at his wife with blank amazement as if he were witnessing a reincarnation, or had suddenly discovered his wife to be some one else.

Later that evening the stranger came to the bar where the men had adjourned. His appearance was hailed by rude shouts of laughter, and ruder jeers.

"Here comes the dude. Watch him, boys."

"My! Ain't he the darlingest pet?"

The man paused, and with a nonchalant air gazed dispassionately around the room.

"Pardon me, old chaps," he drawled, and screwed his monocle into place, "but do you see anything funny about me?"

As by a prearranged plan each miner put a make-believe monocle up to his eye. In some cases it was a watch crystal; others had curtain rings, while the rest made shift with large silver coins.

A broad grin spread over the stranger's face; and, taking his monocle from his eye, he threw it into the air. He caught it on his cheek as it descended, and with a swift jerk of the head once more firmly fixed it in place.

"Now, old dears," he said with a chuckle, "let me see you do that."

A loud shout of laughter greeted this feat, but this time the laugh was with the stranger, not against him.

"That's much better," he continued. "Now we're a nice, jolly little party. Really, don't you know, I was feeling quite embarrassed. Won't you drink with me?"

"We like to know the name of the man we drink with," said one of the men.

He was the owner of one of the mines.

"Ah! Yes, of course. Pardon the omission. But what's in a name. Suppose you call me the Major?"

"The Major?"

They all crowded around him.

They had heard—who had not?—much of this man who had made a laughing-stock of the South African Police; whose tricks and clever evasions of the arm of the law were the talk of the Dark Continent. None doubted that he was indeed the Major. Who else had that debonair carriage, that look—to a casual observer—of helpless inanity and an almost vacuous expression which only served as a mask to hide the keen wit of the man? Who but the major would have had the nerve to appear at such a place and in such an attire?

The miners knew of the major by repute. Knew that beneath the clothing of a fop was a red-blooded man; a man whose strength was always on the side of under dog no matter how great the odds might be against him. They knew that he was, in the eyes of the law, a notorious criminal; but they also understood that his crime—that of illicit diamond-buying—was his protest against certain unjust laws protecting the diamond-mining monopoly. And their sympathies were all with him.

"But aren't you off your beat up here, Major?" asked one of the men. "We're gold-miners. You haven't got a grudge against us, have you? The Lord knows I hope not."

"You flatter me. Really. No, gold doesn't interest me. Some day perhaps I'll—But it's so beastly heavy to cart around. No. This is just a recuperating point, so to speak, before taking a trip into Mangwato's country."

At this time two Portuguese officials who were sitting at a table in a far corner of the bar looked at each other meaningly, and one of them rose quietly and left the room unobserved.

The Major returned to the barmaid, ordered drinks for the crowd and a moment later they were noisily drinking his health.

One round was quickly followed by another; and the Major entertained the miners by the story, not told boastfully, of his latest escapade.

In the midst of the laughter which marked the conclusion of the tale a young trooper of the Transvaal Mount Police entered the bar.

The miners looked at him coldly, for Gilkerson was not popular. He was very young and full of self-importance—was apt to take a high-handed attitude.

He carried a police circular in his hand and glanced from it to the Major, then back to the paper again.

"You're the Major, I believe," he said at length.

"Quite right, old dear. Charmed to meet you."

The policeman ignored the Major's outstretched hand.

"I'd like to speak to you outside."

The Major raised his eyebrows.

"But it's so beastly dark, old chap, and there are mosquitoes, stinkflies and what not."

"It is a matter of business, Major."

His hand, the Major noted, rested on the butt of his revolver.

"My word! You mystify me."

The Major turned to the others.

"You'll pardon me, won't you?" he said.

"The law insists—and who am I to go against the law?—that I offer my bloated carcass as a feast for the mosquitoes.

"Now what is it?" the Major continued as he followed Gilkerson outside.

"I arrest you," he said in pompous tones, and stopped.

"Go on, old fellow; don't mind me. Complete the sentence. You know. Warn me that what I may say may be used as evidence against me, and all that."

Gilkerson hastily completed the formula.

"It's no laughing matter, Major," he added.

"I agree with you, old thing. Deuced serious, I should say—for you. I've been arrested so many times; and—well, I think I shall write a letter to you commanding officer commending you for the gentlemanly way in which you effected the arrest. Most considerate of you, I must say.

"But of course I shall have to bring a suit against the Government for false arrest. Yes. I must do that to protect my good name, don't you know."

The Major was enjoying himself immensely. He carried nothing incriminating upon him. As a matter of fact he had not made a deal in diamonds for some considerable time; and he knew that though they might arrest him on suspicion there was no case against him that would hold in court.

"Aren't you interested in knowing what the charge is, Major?"

"Not a bit, dear boy. Probably you have heard that I'm a nefarious highwayman or something of that sort, when as a matter of fact I'm the most law-abiding man in the colony. Really now, I mean that. Still, if it will ease your mind, what is the charge?"

"Murder."

"What!"

In his astonishment the Major allowed his eyeglass to fall from his eye, and it dropped to the ground. With an expression of alarm the Major went down on his hands and knees and groped around for his monocle. But all the time he was conscious that the muzzle of Gilkerson's revolver was not six inches from his head.

"I've found it," he said finally in relieved tones; "and, thank Heavens, unbroken.

"You know," he continued, rising to his feet and adjusting his monocle, "I'd simply be blind without this. Some chappies say that it is an affectation, but 'pon my soul it's not. It helps me to see things as they are. If you know what I mean.

"Well, what do you intend to do with me? And, I say, if it's not too much trouble I wish you would put away that beastly revolver. I'm quite harmless, you know, and revolvers make me deucedly nervous."

"Oh, come along," said Gilkerson impatiently. "You're as long-winded as an old woman."

"But where, dear boy?"

"To the police camp, of course. I won't feel safe until we've got you under lock and key."

"But surely you don't expect me to go dressed like this? Let me change first."

"Is it likely? No. You'll do just as you are."

"At least let me talk to my native servant Jim."

"No. Now get a move on; and if you have any thought in your mind of trying to escape, just remember that my revolver is loaded and will be aimed right at your head. And I'm not a bad shot," he added complacently.

The Major shrugged his shoulders and walked down the dimly lighted street, closely followed by Gilkerson.

Five minutes later the heavy door of the tiny cell swung to with a bang, and the Major was imprisoned without hope of escape.

Next day the Major's arrest was the one topic of conversation in Georgetown.

The two Portuguese officials hastened to the police camp; and, having been assured by Gilkerson that the Major was really under arrest, charged with a serious crime, they hastily composed a message addressed to the Commandant of the Portuguese territory.

One passage in that message is worthy of notice.

It read:

Disregard news sent by special runner last night. The Major has been arrested for murder, and there is no reason to believe that he can in any way interfere with our plans.

For three days Gilkerson kept the Major under close confinement by virtue of—so he said—orders from headquarters.

Further enlightenment he would not, could not, give; and, knowing the Major's reputation, he would not allow his prisoner to leave his cell under any pretext whatsoever. Neither would he allow Jim, the Major's Hottentot servant, to see his *Baas*, threatening that loyal native with arrest should he continue to loiter in the vicinity of the jail.

He refused even to send to the hotel for the prisoner's baggage, so the major was still wearing the evening dress he wore at the time of his arrest.

"You'll be more conspicuous, Major," explained Gilkerson with a laugh, "should you happen to break out of here. Not that I think that's likely. Still I prefer not to take chances; and it would be easy to trace a man wearing a dressing suit."

"You think of everything; don't you, old top?" the Major had replied sarcastically.

Early on the morning of the fourth day following his arrest the Major was awakened by voices outside the door of his cell.

"That's all right," a familiar voice was saying. "You have acted wisely. Can't afford to take chances with this fellow. Now you had better be off to the mines. You understand what you are to do."

"Yes, sir," the voice of Gilkerson replied. "I'm to be on the lookout for a native answering this description: medium build, round-shouldered, and has a crescent-shaped scar on his right shoulder."

"That's right. If you get him the case against the Major will be complete. And, Gilkerson, I'm up here unofficially, you understand. I don't want anyone to know that I'm here."

"Very good, sir."

A few minutes later a key grated in the lock, and the door of the cell swung slowly open, admitting a man so like the Major in appearance that the two men might have been taken for brothers.

They looked at each other for a moment in silence, and then the newcomer burst into laughter.

"You do me a great honor, Major. Really there was no need for you to have dressed for the occasion."

"You must thank your officious trooper for that, chief. I'll give you my word that I will never want to wear a dress suit again. But what's all this about? You are not playing the game, you know."

"Having you arrested for murder, you mean?"

"Yes. What else?"

The Major was slightly peeved.

"That's just what I'm doing," retorted the chief. "I'm playing the game."

"Oh, bosh. You have me arrested on a ridiculous charge and call that playing the game. Try again, old chap."

The other—he was the chief of police—sobered instantly.

"It was very important, Major," he said, "that I should see you—secretly if possible—and I've been trying to get in touch with you for some time; but you are as slippery as an eel. Consequently when I heard that you were making for Georgetown I telegraphed to Gilkerson that you were suspected of murder, ordering him to hold you until further notice."

"But why the charge of murder? You have given me some uneasy moments, I can tell you."

"I knew you would stay and face out such a serious charge, whereas you might have been tempted to make a bolt for it had the charge been a trivial one—I.D.B., for instance."

"Fat chance I've had of getting away. Gilkerson has been treating me as though I were a second Jack the Ripper or some other beastly cutthroat, and I'm not used to it. Other Johnnies who've arrested me have always treated me like a gentleman."

"Oh, you mustn't be to hard on Gilkerson. You are his first arrest, and the responsibility sets rather hard on him."

The Major shrugged his shoulders.

"Of course I shall sue you for false arrest."

"No, I don't think you will, Major. We need your help and I hope that you will give it."

The chief's voice suddenly lowered; his face became serious; and the Major, realizing that there was something of importance afoot, dropped his pose of injured innocence and prepared to listen.

It was late that night when Gilkerson returned from his errand at the mines. He was weary and not a little dispirited, for his search had been fruitless. Though he had examined every native working at the various mines he had failed to discover the one he was after, and had come to the conclusion that his commanding officer had been misinformed.

As he came to his hut, which was in close proximity to the cell where the Major was incarcerated, he was surprised to find it in darkness.

Thinking it strange that his chief should have gone away leaving the prisoner unattended, he quickened his steps.

Entering his hut, he lighted a lamp and found on the table a letter addressed to him. He read:

Dear Gilkerson:

I am very sorry that I shall not be able to say good-by to you, so I am taking this opportunity of thanking you for the kindness you have shown me, and all that. I trust that you will return early and release the chief at once. The old boy seems to be very peeved. I know he would swear if he could, but I flatter myself that I have gagged him very effectually.

And isn't it lucky that we are so alike in appearance, and about the same build?

You will understand and why, when you see the chief.

Ta-ta, old man.

Yours,

THE MAJOR

Lamp in hand Gilkerson rushed out to the cell. The key was in the lock and, turning it, he flung open the door.

The light of the lamp shone on a man lying prostrate on the floor. For a moment Gilkerson thought that the letter he had just read must have been a figment of his imagination. The man upon the floor was surely the Major! He wore the Major's clothes and—

Then he saw that this man was gagged and bound had and foot by all the handcuffs and leg-irons with which Gilkerson was wont to adorn the walls of his hut.

With hands clumsy because of their eagerness Gilkerson took the gag out of the chief's mouth, and the anger that had been so long imprisoned at last found utterance.

"You —— fool!" he exploded.

"But how did he do it, sir?" stammered Gilkerson.

"Don't you search your prisoners, man? Didn't you know he carried a revolver?"

"I searched him, and I'll swear he had no revolver when I arrested him, sir."

"Well, he had one," growled the chief. "He held me up with it. For Heaven's sake don't stand there like a blinking idiot. Get me out of these handcuffs."

"Yes, sir. At once, sir."

But it was a long time before he could succeed in finding the keys to unlock them, and it was fully an hour before he had finally released his wrathful superior.

"I've a good mind to put you under arrest for neglect of duty," snarled the indignant man. "You're a fine specimen of policeman! Fancy letting a desperate criminal like the Major retain a revolver!"

Gilkerson was silent.

He had hoped that his prompt capture of the Major would earn him a promotion. Instead it had seemed he was to be disgraced.

"Well! What have you got to say for yourself?"

"There's nothing I can say, sir, save to ask permission to go after him."

The chief snorted.

"What good would that do, you darned fool? The blighter is no doubt safe in Portuguese territory by this time, and thumbing his nose at us."

There was an ominous silence.

"Look here, Gilkerson," said the chief at length. "You don't show up very well in this affair, do you? For that matter neither do I. If this story gets out we'll be the laughing-stock of the country."

"That's true, sir," Gilkerson assented mournfully.

"And if it does get out I'll see that your chance of promotion is ruined forever. Do you understand what I mean?"

"I think so, sir."

"Very well, then. The train leaves for the south in an hour, doesn't it?"

"Yes, sir."

"Good. You will, as soon as you have made the necessary preparations, escort me, the Major, to the station, announcing to any one who may see fit to question you that you are taking me to Johannesburg for trial.

"Have you a suit of mufti? You have? Good. Then bring it along with you. I can change as soon as we are on the train. As long as we can fool the people here into thinking that I'm actually the Major, and that you are taking me to headquarters for trial, I can manage the rest. Do you understand what I'm driving at?"

Gilkerson was busy packing his suit-case.

"Yes, sir," he said with a salute. "All ready now, sir."

The chief's voice changed to a drawl strangely reminiscent of the Major.

"That's fine, old dear," he said with a wink, and fumbled in the pocket of his coat. "Where is my bally monocle? Ah! Here it is! Now, I can see to follow you. Lead on, Macduff."

"No. After you, Major."

Gilkerson said it with a bow.

While they were waiting at the station for the arrival of the southbound train a man approached the pseudo-Major and, speaking with a foreign accent, asked him for a match.

"I'm sorry, and all that," the other replied, "but you see how it is."

He held up his hands so that the light of the station lamp fell upon his manacled wrists.

The stranger turned to Gilkerson and repeated his request. "You have a dangerous criminal there; is it not so?" he asked as he lighted a cigarette.

"Yes. He's a murderer," replied Gilkerson. "I'm taking him to Johannesburg for trial."

"So? That makes me nervous."

He moved away a little smile of triumph on his face.

About this time the Major was riding rapidly toward a camp-fire which twinkled in the darkness of the bush. It was across the river from Georgetown, and way off the beaten track.

As he neared the fire a dusky figure sprang to meet him.

"Scoff is ready, *Baas*," joyfully announced Jim, the Hottentot.

That's good. I'm deuced hungry, Jim."

He dismounted, washed, and a moment later was eating roast buck with the appetite of a man who has not a care in the world.

"It was well planned, Jim," he said in the vernacular to the Hottentot as he carved himself another slice of the sweet white meat.

"Without doubt, *Baas*. Trekking will be easy for us two. A horse I have. And wherewithal to get food."

"You mean ammunition, Jim?"

"Aye. That and gold, *Baas*. There is much gold."

"So?"

"Yah, *Baas*. But whither do we go?"

"Truly that is a matter to be thought on, Jim. Was nothing said to you?"

"Nothing, save that I should await you at this place."

"What if we go to Mangwato's country, Jim?"

"It would be wise. Mangwato would without doubt treat you with great honor. Did you not at one time preserve the life of a son that is dear to him? Aye, let us go there and dwell in pace for a time. I am growing old and like not this continual running from place to place."

"You are always free to return to your own people, Jim."

"Nay. The *Baas* knows it was not that I meant. Some little I thought that some day perchance my *Baas* would be caught I a net from which there is no escaping."

"You're a hoary old reprobate," the Major said affectionately in English. "But your words are wise. I too would know peace for a little while, so tomorrow we go to Mangwato's country."

Senhor José Alvaro, a portly little man, dressed in the gay and much bemedaled uniform of a high official in the Portuguese Colonial Service, looked up severely from his papers as a prison guard ushered two men into his office.

"Take off those handcuffs," he ordered, "and then leave the room. You may remain on guard."

In a soft voice, which somehow had a catlike purr in it, Senhor Alvaro requested the two men be seated.

They exchanged wondering glances as they seated themselves.

"I have here," continued the commandant, rustling some papers on the desk before him, "a complete, and very interesting, record of your respective careers."

"You, Senhor 'Dirty' Norton—" he turned to the taller of the two men—"were at one time, a sergeant in the Transvaal Police, but owing to certain unmentionable activities you were obliged to flee from the Transvaal and seek refuge in this territory. Since coming here you have lived up to your reputation. You are a card-sharper, a confidence man, a thief; and to complete your list of crimes you have committed a particularly cowardly and brutal murder. For that you were sentenced to be shot.

"Pray, correct me if I am wrong, Senhor 'Dirty' Norton."

The big man was silent.

The commandant turned to the other, a scrubby little man known as "Cockney Joe."

"Of you we know even more. But what need to enumerate your many and varied crimes? Let it be sufficient to state that you are wanted very badly in England; that the police of the Transvaal offer a big reward for your arrest; and finally that you aided Senhor Dirty Norton in committing the previously mentioned murder. And you too were given the death penalty."

The two men moved uneasily in their chairs.

"The gracious governor of this colony," continued the purring voice, "has seen fit to show you clemency. But of course there are conditions."

"H'I'll promise ter be 'ave, gov'nor," whined Cockney Joe. "H'i would never 'ave done nufink h'if h'it 'adn't been for Dirty 'ere."

The other man was silent. He was watching the fat, apparently good-humored face of the commandant.

"That's very nice of you—" the commandant waved his hands airily—"but perhaps you had better let me do the talking for a little while. Yes, Senhor Norton and myself will converse for a little while."

Cockney Joe lapsed into a frightened silence.

"What do you know of Mangwato's country?"

Senhor Alvaro looked intently at Norton.

"I know that he's reputed to have a big hoard of diamonds."

The commandant looked disappointed.

"Yes. You would know that," he said testily. "But is that all?"

"That's all."

"Then listen."

The commandant turned to a map which hung on the wall behind him.

"Here—" he placed a pudgy forefinger on the map, thereby obliterating some few square miles of territory—"here is Mangwato's country. You will notice—" removing his finger—"that it is tined blue on the map, indicating that it is an independent state.

"It is bounded on the east by a patch of yellow and on the west, north and south by patches of red. Is it not so?"

Norton nodded assent, and Cockney Joe grunted something about "a blinkin' geography lesson."

"It is our desire to see that patch of blue—" again the commandant's finger obliterated a big section of Mangwato's country—"marked yellow on the map."

He paused impressively.

"Well, why don't you take it, senhor?" asked Norton. "It isn't likely that a native would put up any fight."

"Ah! That's where you come in, my friends," returned the commandant.

"You see," he continued in confidential tones, "the two powers have always adopted a hands-off policy as far as Mangwato is concerned. We have mutually agreed that any white man entering Mangwato's country should do so at his own risk; that no punitive expedition—the first step, you understand, toward annexation—should be set against Mangwato should he kill any white men on his territory.

"Of course, if he crossed the border on a raiding party, that would be another matter. But he's too wily for that. He knows of this agreement and has made the most of it.

"His country is the only tract in South Africa as yet undeveloped by white men. And it is a rich country; rich in minerals, in farming-land and in labor. He has absolutely forbidden any white man to enter his country, hoping thereby to preserve the entity of his people."

The commandant paused to light a black cigar before continuing.

"But that's soon coming to an end. Mangwato's getting old. He realizes now that it is not—as he used to boast—the strength and numbers of his fighting men that keep his country free from white men. He knows that sooner or later his country will come under the rule of the powers."

The commandant flicked the ash from his cigar and looked at Norton expectantly.

"What is it that you want us to do, senhor?" Norton asked.

"Ah! You are direct, my friend," said the commandant. "You would see the end of this wandering dissertation of mine. What you are to do is this. You are to induce Mangwato to appeal to us for protection. How you will accomplish this I don't quite know."

"But why send us? Why not send a representative of your Government?"

Norton was plainly puzzled.

"Don't you see that to do so would bring us in conflict with the British lion? It would be breaking our gentleman's agreement, and we can't afford that.

"But if you two, having escaped from prison, elect to impersonate Portuguese officials that would be another matter. That you should go on hunting expedition along the frontiers of Mangwato's country might if known cause some apprehension; still, if the British happened to make pointed inquiries concerning you, we can disclaim all official connection with you, and, once given knowledge of your whereabouts, would speedily rearrest you.

"On the other hand, should you be successful in persuading Mangwato to come under our flag and without apparent coercion on our part, well and good. The British lion could snarl as much as he pleased. With clean hands we could plead our cause before the Hague Tribunal, assured of a favorable verdict.

"Yet again. Should Mangwato kill you, ostensibly Portuguese officials on an innocent hunting expedition and on our soil, we would have good cause for sending a punitive expedition against him. And please believe that you would be well-avenged."

"But what do we get out of this, senhor?"

"If you succeed and live, freedom and a large reward. If you fail—Let us not talk about failure, my friends. It is an unpleasant subject."

"But suppose we refuse?"

"In that case," said the commandant sorrowfully, "we shall be compelled, regretfully compelled, to carry out the order of the court. In other words, you will be shot."

Norton and Cockney Joe held a whispered consultation.

"Well do it, senhor," said Norton at length.

"Allow me to congratulate you on your good sense. But please do not think that we are giving you an opportunity to escape. We shall not for one moment lose sight of you.

"When you leave here we shall at once notify the British authorities that you have escaped from prison and were last seen heading for the Transvaal border. So, you see, we will be protected, especially as the natives who accompany you will be instructed by me concerning their duties. Now I would like to make a few suggestions which you may follow or not, as you see fit."

Time is no object in Africa, the "Land of Tomorrow," and fully six months had elapsed before Dirty Norton and Cockney Joe had formed a plan which would, they hoped, gain them the promised reward and freedom.

They had, as suggested by the commandant, pitched camp close to the borders of Mangwato's country, using it as headquarters from which they made hunting forays. Dressed with bright uniforms, accompanied by a large number of native carriers—also in uniform—they looked just what they purported to be; officials of the Portuguese Government on a shooting expedition.

They made no attempt to cross the border and enter the forbidden land, but had been content with the fact that their actions were being spied upon by Mangwato's warriors. That was well. It was establishing their identity.

For long months they had shirked facing the problem that was before them, unable indeed to see how they could carry the thing through. Then only the night before Fate had put the means of success into their hands.

Certain of their bearers had crossed the boundary line and had raided the crops of a near-by village. The marauders had been observed and chased back to the camp by angry warriors. One of the bearers was wounded in the thigh by an *assegai*.

The warriors all retreated, however, at the sight of the white men. All, that is, save one, and he proved to be very truculent, insisting that the raiders be given over to him for punishment.

"I am Shimba," he said proudly, "the only son of Mangwato the chief. It is not a light matter for men to raid my crops."

On hearing that he was the chief's son, Norton made many overtures of friendship, and finally appeased the warrior's wrath by offering him a drink of whisky.

A second and third drink quickly followed the first, and in a short time the man called Shimba was overcome by the stupor of drunkenness.

Norton quickly bound and gagged the drink-sodden native.

"Wot's that for, you blasted fool?" queried Cockney Joe.

Norton laughed.

"Why, Toe, that makes everything A-1 at Lloyds for us."

"H'i don't see 'ow."

"No, you wouldn't. Well, here's the lay. Tomorrow one of us with an escort goes to interview Mangwato. There'll be no trouble getting to see the old blighter when he knows we've got his son prisoner."

"Wot do you do then?"

"Tell him that if he doesn't request the Portuguese Government to form a protectorate we'll take his son to Lourenço Marques and have him shot, and will also send an expedition to punish Mangwato because he has allowed his warriors to kill our bearers."

"But suppose 'e claims that the killin' was done on 'is territory?"

"Is it likely? He knows his word won't go for anything against ours. We're two high officials of the government, remember. Besides, there's his son. That's a big hold. He'll do anything for his son, so they say."

"Sounds h'all right," admitted Cockney Joe cautiously. "But oo's going? H'it ought to be you. You speak the lingo; H'i don't."

"I'll go all right. Now let's sleep. I want to make an early start in the morning."

* * *

As he awoke the next day, another idea had come to Dirty.

"See here, Joe," he said. "I don't expect we'll get much of a reward even if we work the thing all right. What do you say if we lift old Mangwato's diamonds?"

"Lumme! You think of h'everyfink, don't yer? But 'ow?"

"It's so easy, Joe, that it's like taking candy from a baby. It'll remind you of the days you used to steal money from the kids on their way to the corner pub to buy their old man a pint of beer.

"You see," he explained slowly, so that Cockney Joe's lower intelligence might fully grasp the idea, "I'll tell Mangwato that we will be bound to shoot his son; that's the law. Then I'll let on that I hate to do it, but that I'm a poor man and the reward I get will be great.

"He's bound to think of a reward not to take his son in to be shot. If he doesn't I'll hint. If the hint's no good I'll tell him plainly that he either hands over the diamonds of his son dies. See?"

"Lumme!" exclaimed Cockney Joe admiringly. "Yer does fink of h'everyfink."

"Well, I'm off now. Keep a good watch on Shimba. If he makes a getaway the game's all U-P."

Norton turned to mount his horse, but paused at an exclamation from the Cockney.

"Look."

Following the direction of the pointing finger, Norton saw a horseman riding swiftly toward them.

"It's a white man," muttered Dirty. "A trooper of the Transvaal Mounted."

"Wot the ——'s 'edoin' 'ere?"

"I'm going to stay and find out," Norton replied grimly. "Have your revolvers ready, Joe, in case he tries any funny business. And if he talks to you let on that you don't understand the lingo. See? You're Portuguese. You don't speak English."

"Bai jove, it's Gilkkerson. What the deuce is he doing here?"

These words, almost echoing the exclamation of Cockney Joe, came from the lips of the Major.

That ubiquitous man was hidden from view in a thick clump of bush not a quarter of a mile from the camp of the two conspirators. His eyes were glued to a pair of powerful field-glasses.

"What is it, *Baas*?"

The grizzled Hottentot sense a note of annoyance in the Major's voice.

"I don't quite know yet, Jim."

Still watching through the glasses, the Major followed the movements of the approaching horseman.

"He's at their camp now," he muttered, "and he seems to be spinning them some yarn. Norton looks rather fed up about something. Gilkerson must have let the cat out of the bag, confound him.

"Ah! He dismounted. Evidently he's going to have a scoff with them before coming on. Yes. There goes a native leading away Gilkerson's and Norton's mounts. Well, that gives me some little time to think."

He sat in silent meditation for a while.

"Yes. That will be the best plan," he said to himself. "I'll try it anyway."

Then aloud—

"Jim!"

"Yah, *Baas.*"

"Go back quickly to the village and tell the warriors that I have need of them. There is need for haste."

"Yah, *Baas.*"

Jim vanished silently into the shadows of the bush, and the Major resumed his watch.

Since his arrival in Mangwato's country six months previously the Major had accomplished many things. He was the only white man who had succeeded in winning the esteem of the old chief, and there was no honor too great for Mangwato to pay to the who had been instrumental in saving his son from death.

Possessed then of Mangwato's gratitude, it had not been a difficult matter for a man of the Major's caliber to earn his esteem and confidence. As a result the Major was given a high place in the chief's councils, Mangwato deferring to the Major in all things relating to the government of his people.

The Major concentrated his keen wit, his common understanding of native psychology into presenting acceptably the English form of colonial government to the natives, and because he was well versed in native lore and rarely made an unjust decision the natives openly, and Mangwato secretly, acknowledged that the English way was a good way.

Several times Mangwato had sought to learn the reason why the Major should take such an interest in his people.

"It's the way of the English, Mangwato. We are all meddlers."

"Such meddling has much of merit in it," the chief had replied sagaciously. "Tell me, are all men of your race like you?"

"Some better, some worse. Are all the cattle in your herds of like quality?"

"It is well answered. But I can weed out the weaklings from my herds; such a thing I could not do should your people overrun my land.

"Now," Mangwato had continued, "it shall be as the Great Spirits will it. No move will I make toward bringing the white men in. I will not go to your people, nor will I go to the Portuguese. I fear to choose."

"The choice may be forced upon you. It is for no idle reason that two of their people should stay for so long, and so near, your borders."

"I have given thought to that. I think they are but hunters. If it be otherwise I pray that death will come to me ere my people are betrayed."

There was a slight rustle in the bushes, and the voice of Jim interrupted the Major's reveries. "The warriors are here, *Baas*."

"That is good, Jim."

The Major raised his voice slightly.

"Can you hear me, O warriors of Mangwato?"

"Aye, lord."

The reply came from many men, not one of whom was visible, so cunningly had they secreted themselves.

"Then listen well. There is a game to be played."

"Now if you are ready, senhor," said Norton, "we will go to pay our respects on Mangwato. You seek the—ah—Major, and I to demand punishment of the warriors who killed my bearers."

"All right," Gilkerson replied curtly.

He was not entirely prepossessed by these officials of the Portuguese Government. The one who called himself Miguel Castello seemed all right, but the other, the one who professed to have no knowledge of English, seemed vaguely familiar, and surely he had heard him curse in very fluent English when a native spilled some hot coffee on his hands!

At that moment rifle-shots and the blood curdling cries of natives on the war-path came from the thick patch of bush which marked the boundary of Mangwato's country, and a moment later a horseman emerged, and rode at a furious pace toward the camp.

A second horseman followed, and hard at his heels a party of warriors armed with *assegais*.

The watchers saw the warriors pull the second horseman from his saddle. Spears flashed in the sunlight; and the warriors, first brandishing their weapons at the fast retreating form of the first horseman, picked up their victim and carried him in triumph back into the bush, followed, as a dog will follow its master, by the riderless horse.

The shouts of the warriors died away. Only the thud of the oncoming horse broke the stillness.

"What's it all about," Gilkerson said wonderingly.

"Can't you see?" Norton—alias Senhor Miguel Castello—cried triumphantly as the rider drew nearer. "It's the Major, the man you're after. He's been after Mangwato's diamonds, and they've got wise to him and chased him out. Now he's heading this way, hoping to find protection."

"You're right, senhor," Gilkerson said excitedly. "I'm going to get under cover. If he sees me he might make a bolt for it."

Gilkerson entered the tent and waited in a fever of impatience for the Major's arrival.

"Well!" he heard his quarry exclaim a few minutes later. "This is a delightful puzzle. I never thought I should meet you two old friends here."

Gilkerson did not catch the surly reply.

"Just my luck."

The Major was speaking again.

"Another day and I would have gotten the old duffer's diamonds. As it is I had to run to save my bloomin' skin. Poor old Jim! I'm afraid they got him.

"But what are you doing here? After diamonds too? Let's join forces. I've got a bully play."

Again Gilkerson missed the muttered reply. Still he had heard enough to realize that his first impressions regarding these so-called Portuguese officials were correct. But that was not his business. He was after the Major—that was all he cared about.

"Will you chappies give me some provisions and ammunition and I'll try to make my way to the coast? No? Then I'll have to try my luck at the *kraals* on the way."

Through a rent in the tent Gilkerson saw that the Major was preparing to mount; and, leaving his tent, he said curtly:

"Hands up, Major."

The Major's hands shot above his head, a look of blank incredulity on his face.

"Gilkerson, by all that's holy!" he exclaimed. "What are you doing here?"

"Pretty evident, isn't it, Major?" replied Gilkerson as he walked up to the Major to relieve him of his rifle and ammunition.

"Now hold out your hands."

He snapped on the handcuffs.

"That's right. You can mount now, and we'll be on our way."

"But you can't arrest me here, old dear," the Major expostulated. "This is Portuguese territory. You have no authority here."

"I'll take a chance on that."

Gilkerson turned truculently on the two pseudo-Portuguese.

Norton shrugged his shoulders. It was not likely that he would interfere in the arrest of a man who many times had frustrated his carefully thought-out plans.

"Come on," Gilkerson continued impatiently. "Mount!"

With an ill grace the Major obeyed the command; and Gilkerson, holding the reins of his prisoner's horse, led the way in the direction of Georgetown.

Dirty Norton and Cockney Joe watched them until they were hidden from sight in the thick bush veldt.

"Well, that's all right," said Norton with a sign of relief. "I tell you, Joe, we can't go wrong now. Lord, what an escape I've had! Suppose the policeman hadn't turned up. I'd have been in a pretty pickle, wouldn't I? Me going to Mangwato and pretending to be Portuguese; and all the time would have been the Major to give my game away."

"H'i thought the blighter had been in clink. Whoh'ever would'ave thought h'of 'im bein' h'up 'ere!"

"Didn't you hear Gilkerson say he escaped? Well, I'm off now. Don't forget what I said about keeping a good watch on Simba."

Once out of sight of the camp the Major's horse became suddenly lame.

"I say," said the Major apologetically, "I do wish you'd let me have a look at my horse's foot. I'm afraid he's picked up a stone or run a thorn in his frog or something."

"I'll look at it myself," grunted Gilkerson. "You needn't dismount."

Swinging from his saddle Gilkerson bent down to examine the lame foot. And as he did the Major leaped upon him, and the two men rolled over and over on the ground.

The Major, being handcuffed, was at a disadvantage, and in a very little while Gilkerson was sitting triumphantly on his prisoner's chest.

"Pretty smart, Major," he panted exultantly, "but not quite smart enough."

"No?" drawled the Major quietly. "But if you'll take the trouble to look around you will see that you're in a deuce of a mess."

Without releasing his hold Gilkerson looked cautiously behind him, and was amazed to find that a party of warriors had crept unobserved from the bushes and were closing in on him. With another start he recognized that Jim the Hottentot was their new leader.

He sprang to his feet and drew his revolver.

"Don't be a fool, Gilkerson," came the curt voice of the Major. "Haven't you any imagination? You thought Jim was killed, and now you see him leading these warriors. Doesn't that convey anything to your feeble brain?"

"You thought that these warriors were after my blood. Ask them who I am. You speak the lingo, don't you?"

"Who is this man?" Gilkerson demanded.

"Our lord, the White Induna," replied the warriors.

"What does it all mean?"

Gilkerson turned wonderingly to the Major.

"That's better. Take off these bally wrist ornaments and we will talk a little while."

"First tell me," the Major continued a moment later, "why you're after me. Not officially, I'll swear."

"No. I felt such a fool since you escaped that when I was given two weeks' leave I made up my mind to spend it looking for you. I thought I'd square myself with the chief. Instead I seem to have made an even bigger fool of myself."

"There was no need surely for you to worry. You took a prisoner to Johannesburg, didn't you? And everyone thought it was me?"

"How did you know that?"

"I planned it, dear boy. Tell me, didn't you ever question the chief's explanation of my escape?"

"Yes. I couldn't understand how you managed to have a revolver and—Tell me about it, Major! That murder charge was a fake, wasn't it?"

The Major nodded.

"That was your chief's amusing way—he will have his little joke, bless his heart—of securing an interview with me. But I got even with him for that. He didn't want to be gagged and trussed up as you found him, but once I got one pair of handcuffs on him I had matters my own sweet way. And how the dear man did swear!"

The Major chuckled softly.

"You know that Mangwato's country is an independent state?" he asked suddenly. Gilkerson nodded.

"All right, then. The Secret Service Johnnies discovered that the Portuguese were conspiring to force Mangwato to ask them to form a protectorate, and your chief appealed to me to forestall them. He knew, you see, that Mangwato was friendly with me, and what could be more natural for me than to seek safety from arrest in Mangwato's country!

"The fake escape was necessary because I had told the chappies at Georgetown that I was going to Mangwato's country. Two Portuguese officials heard me, and we knew that they would be bound to be afraid that I would interfere with their plans—pardon me if I flatter myself—though as a matter of fact at that time I was ignorant that international politics were seeking to bottle up Mangwato."

"One of them told me that you were at the hotel," interrupted Gilkerson. "And in order to make sure I'd arrest you he said you were wanted for I.D.B. This, when I had a warrant against you for murder."

"Did he? Oh, that's rich! Well, to cut a long story short, I've been up here nearly six months and have succeeded, I'll flatter myself, in showing Mangwato that the British way of doing things isn't half bad. At the same time I've been keeping my eye on the antics of those two Johnnies back yonder."

"They're not really Portuguese, are they, Major?"

"Great Scott, no! One, Norton, used to be in the Transvaal Police and was kicked out. He's a real mucker. I have several scores to settle with him. Cockney Joe, the other man, has fully as many crimes to his credit as Norton."

"Norton and Cockney Joe! Why, they're both wanted! I can see that I shall have two prisoners to take back. That's something anyway."

The Major smiled at Gilkerson's outburst.

"But what are they doing here, Major?"

"Oh, they're agents for the Portuguese Government. I imagine they were to be given a free pardon on condition they carried this thing through. I'm not quite sure how they mean to do it. But last night they managed to capture Shimba, Mangwato's son, and I think they mean to use him somehow.

"Norton was just leaving camp to play his hand when you appeared on the scene and told them I'm in on the job. And that put the whole business on the blink again."

"I seem to have played the fool all around," Gilkerson said bitterly.

"Oh, cheer up, old man. It's not your fault. I told the chief to let you in on the secret."

"Why didn't he? Didn't he trust me?"

"It wasn't that he didn't trust you. He thought that you might not be able to act well enough. Well, there's no harm done. They think I'm safely out of harm's way this time, and unless I'm very much mistaken Norton's on his way to see the chief now."

"What are you going to do? Tell Mangwato he's an impostor?"

"No. That might settle this attempt; but how abut the next? Suppose the Portuguese tried again? No. I want to discredit the Portuguese in Mangwato's eyes, not two men masquerading as Portuguese.

"Personally, I don't care a tinker's curse whether the British get Mangwato's country or not; I'd rather see the old dear run it himself. But if it's to be a choice between British and Portuguese rule then I'm going to do all I can to help Mangwato choose right.

"Will you put yourself under my orders, old fellow?"

"Do you really mean that I can help?" Gilkerson asked.

"Yes. I take it that you will? Splendid! Then I want you to stay here until dark— say an hour after sundown—and then make your way back to the camp. Take Cockney Joe prisoner—never mind about the bearers; they're harmless—and bring him to Mangwato's *kraal*. I'm going to leave Jim and these warriors with you. I don't fancy there'll be any fighting—Cockney Joe's too much of a cur for that—still you'd better be prepared for anything. Oh, yes. And be sure to bring Shimba along with you. Cockney Joe's holding him prisoner, you know."

"Very good, Major," Gilkerson said with a salute.

"Fine!"

The Major's hand went up in acknowledgment of the salute; and mounting his horse he rode swiftly away.

"His horse isn't lame now," Gilkerson mused aloud. "I wonder if I've done the right thing, or—"

"And what if I give an order to my warriors to slay you?"

Dirty Norton looked around apprehensively at the grim-faced, huge-muscled warriors who lined the large enclosure. Each one held a broad-bladed stabbing-*assegai* in his hand, and it seemed to Norton that they threatened him.

He shuddered involuntarily, and, turning, faced Mangwato again.

He saw that the old chief despite his fierce words was greatly troubled; he seemed to have aged suddenly; his portly form slumped and there was an air of utter dejection about the man.

So, assuming a bold front, Norton replied:

"What would you gain if you killed me, Mangwato? My death would not save your son; and—rest assured of this—the vengeance of my people would be great. All your young men they would put to death, and your women folk they would sell as slaves."

Mangwato was silent; but from the warriors came the ominous cry of:

"Death to the white man! Let us kill him, O Mangwato!"

Mangwato raised his hands and the cries ceased.

"It may not be, my children," he said, "lest we bring down a greater evil upon us. I have for long years known that sooner or later this choice would be forced upon me."

Turning to Norton, he asked—

"What are your conditions for the release of my son?"

"First, O Mangwato," replied Norton with a new courage, "that you give me the diamonds. So shall your son be freed from arrest and the surety of death. Secondly you must send a messenger to the *kraal* of the white men, my people, at Lourenço Marques, praying them to come into your country and aid you to rule it."

"If I do these things will you promise to release my son and to deal gently with my people?"

"Aye. That I promise."

"You will swear it?"

"Aye. I swear it."

Norton's tone was exultant. He had hardly believed that victory would be so easily won.

Again he turned to look at Mangwato's warriors.

At that moment the moon emerged from a cloud and flooded the council-place with her soft light. The broad blades of the *assegais* reflected the light, and it seemed then to Norton that they were so many scintillating diamonds.

"White man," said Mangwato, "this is a deep matter; not one to be settled in the winking of an eye. I would think it over for a little while."

"Are not all things clear? If you do not do thus and so, all things will happen as I have said. Yet to show you that I am just in all things I will grant you until the moon shines directly overhead. That much time, and no more, will I allow."

"That is but a short hour, white man, and I would hold speech with the White Induna—the rod upon whom I lean."

"Who is this White Induna? Much talk this night I have heard of him."

"Do you not know him? He is a white man even as you are, yet not as you are. He has an eye which he can take out and hold in the palm of his hand. When he talks it is as if sleep were still upon him; yet it is in my mind that that man never sleeps. Ah, he is a man among men, and wise in all things."

"He must mean the blasted Major," thought Norton. "If so, what was the Major running away for? Was that a fake? It would be just like him."

Norton was panic-stricken. It seemed that he had after all walked into a trap.

Then came the comforting remembrance of the Major, handcuffed, being escorted back to Georgetown by Gilkerson. He was sure there was no fake about that arrest. Gilkerson was quite evidently in earnest.

"Your wait will be in vain, Mangwato," he said confidently. "That one will never come here again."

But even as he spoke he was conscious of a stir among the warriors behind him. Turning, he saw that they had opened up their ranks, leaving a narrow passageway opening in the stockade.

Down the passage, dressed in a suit of immaculate white duck, swinging his monocle nonchalantly by a silken cord, came the Major.

Now and again he would pause before a warrior, and putting the monocle up to his eye, scrutinize him carefully from head to foot.

It was for all the world like an inspection of a regiment by the commanding officer.

Norton, speechless with amazement, could only watch with mouth agape.

Not until he had completed his inspection and had come out into the clearing beyond the warriors, did the Major affect to notice Norton.

"Ah! There you are again, dear old chap," he said in tones of well-simulated surprise. "'Pon my soul, we do meet in queer places. Where did you leave Cockney Joe? And where, where did you get that opera bouffe uniform? It is simply priceless."

Norton scowled.

"But you don't understand English, do you? Of course not. How stupid of me! French? No? Well, we'll use Mangwato's language. Who knows? We may set the fashion, and it may be the diplomatic language of the world."

The Major turned to the chief.

"Word came that you had need of me, Mangwato."

"Aye. A deep need, O friend of my people."

"This one—" he indicated Norton—"says that certain of my people, led by Shimba, my son, have killed his servants. My son he holds prisoner and says he will put him to death unless I give him the diamonds, and send a message to his people asking them to come in and help me rule."

"And what do you say?"

"I am minded to obey his commands, for my son is dear to me. Further, he hath sworn that with my consent or not his people will come to govern over me."

"But what if I tell you he lies? What if I tell you that your warriors did not kill his people?

"Heed well, and listen to the true story. Certain of his warriors raided the crops of your son and, he, hearing of it, drove them off. Then your son, even Shimba, went to the camp of these white men demanding that the thieves be punished. That is all, save that Shimba they kept a prisoner, holding him by trickery."

Mangwato rose slowly to his feet. His right hand held a toy *assegai*, and the symbol of his rank.

The warriors watched him intently. The dropping of the *assegai* would be a signal for Norton's death.

"Is this a true word?" the chief asked Norton.

"It is a lie. But even so, if it be a true word, what then? Your son's life I hold in the hollow of my hand. Have a care then what you do with me."

"That is true, that is true. I had forgotten that."

Mangwato slowly resumed his seat.

"There is no way out," he said mournfully to the Major. "If I would spare my son's life I must obey this liar, this trickster in all things. Aye, I call him evil names, for I am well convinced that the tale you tell me is a true one. Ah, wo is me that I must give my people over to the rule of men who achieve their ends by evil cunning!"

"Your son is a crafty warrior, Mangwato," said the Major. "It may well be that he has escaped. Listen! Once before this night I have heard the beating of the signal-drums. Now I hear it again. Listen, warriors, and proclaim its meaning."

A deep hush spread over the assemblage.

To their ears came the high, staccato notes of the signal drum—Africa's primitive wireless.

"It is from Shimba's *kraal*!" cried one of the warriors.

"Aye, but the message?"

"Shimba journeys to the *kraal* of Mangwato. Two strangers—white men—are with him."

The Major turned smilingly to Norton.

"Gilkerson is bringing our mutual friend, Cockney Joe, here under arrest. Funny, isn't it?"

With a snarl of rage Norton leaped at the Major and hit him full on the jaw.

The Major reeled before the blow; but before Norton could follow up the bow he was seized and held securely by two massive warriors.

"I didn't think you had it in you, Dirty," said the Major, "and I'm beastly sorry and all that I can't oblige you with a mill. But it isn't done, you know. We must preserve the dignity of the well-known superior race. Some other time when we're alone I'll be glad to oblige you."

Norton's response was a string of vile curses as he struggled furiously to break from his guards.

"Be quiet, you fool."

The Major's voice cut like a whip.

"Don't you see that Mangwato's toying with his *assegai*. In another minute he'll give the signal that will mean your death. As it is I'll have the dickens of a job to save your life. Don't make it any harder."

Norton's struggles ceased instantly; and the Major turned to face Mangwato, who had been watching the two white men intently.

The shouts of joy which had hailed the news from the *kraal* of Shimba died away, and all awaited in silence for word from the chief. As they waited, the signal drum from a near-by *kraal* beat out the news that Shimba and his party were but a short trek from the *kraal* of the chief, and when its notes had died away Mangwato addressed the Major.

"Again I have to thank you, O my friend, and friend of all my people. Again you have saved my son."

"Some little part I played, Mangwato. But not alone did I accomplish this. Another white man, of my race, a man high in the council of my people, wearing the dress of a chief, merits your thanks. He saved your son."

"He shall not be forgotten in this time of rejoicing. But what shall I do with this other one?"

Mangwato looked darkly at Norton.

"Death by the spear would be showing him too great an honor. First he must know pain."

"Give me his life, Mangwato. It is but a little thing to ask."

"And is it all you ask?"

"All. And it is but a little thing."

"True. Then I give him to you. Let him be taken away and guarded closely until you have made known your wishes concerning him."

As the warriors were about to lead Norton away Mangwato ordered them to wait.

"It is well," he said, "that one should see this."

"Hear me, O my people," he cried. "Long have I known that the time would come when I must make a choice between two tribes of white men who sought to rule this land of mine, and but a little while ago it seemed that an evil choice was thrust upon me. And it would have been evil to have made our rulers a people who won that honor through lying and treachery. You know well who kept the evil from us, who restored my son to me. Long has he dwelt among us, and he has been at times the rod upon which I leaned. He has taught me many things, and through the knowledge you have gotten from him you have made the crops to flourish, the herds to put on fatness.

"Nor is this all. He has ever been at my right hand when I sat in judgment. When I would have pronounced a sentence of death upon one of you he has counseled a more merciful way; aye, a better way. It was he—

"But what need for more words concerning him. He is well known to you all. What say you?"

"Aye, chief. He is a man of single heart; there is no evil in him."

"And you find no fault in his dealing with you?"

"None, lord."

The answer came with a mighty shout.

"After you, he is first in our hearts."

"Then I go the English, for his way is their way, begging them to come and rule over us as they see fit. What say you now?"

"Your words sound good to our ears, O Mangwato. We are well content."

"It is well. Now I go to meet my son."

A few days later Mangwato, escorted by a party of picked warriors, set out on his mission to the British authorities.

Gilkerson accompanied him as far as Georgetown. He had two prisoners—Norton and Cockney Joe, both of whom preferred to face the Transvaal courts rather than face the wrath of the soft-voiced, smiling Senhor José Alvaro.

SWORD OF GIMSHAI

Joseph W. Musgrave

I

Sheena lay unmoving on the bed of fragrant grasses, her hands clasped behind her blonde head. A gentle southeast wind blowing through the open door of the tree house touched her with caressing fingers, whispered of a jungle long awake and busy.

But this morning the murmurous jungle noises held no interest for Sheena. A feeling of oppression and loneliness had gripped her from the moment of her awakening.

A dozen times since sun-up her pet ape, Chim, had left his noisy pursuits in nearby tree tops to peer worriedly in the door at a mistress who would lie abed on such a wonderful day. Similarly, in the clearing below, the great elephant, Tamba, stirred restlessly, impatient and puzzled because the girl he looked upon as his own private pet hadn't appeared for the ceremony of swimming, eating, and playing over which he regularly presided.

For the first time, though, her animal friends weren't enough. The usual joy she took in teasing, rough-housing and lecturing them was gone. Even the familiar, deep cough of the powerful, black-maned lion, Sabor, coming at intervals from across the river failed to excite Sheena. She had raised Sabor from a cub, and though he would wander away for days at a time, he always came back, as he was doing this morning after an eight-day prowl, to dog her footsteps for a time and cause trouble with the other pets through his dangerous jealousy.

The jungle girl had probed without success for some explanation of her depression. She knew that black men often were sick and for a time she wondered if that could be her trouble, though the only illness she had ever known was the stomach ache from eating loo enthusiastically of unripe fruit.

She had been laid up a few times with hurts suffered in life and death battles with jungle beasts, but her feelings on those occasions were totally different from the way she felt now.

Sheena's hair was blonde and long, her eyes a deep and startling blue, her full lips as richly red as sunstruck rubies. Her skin was tanned a soft, golden hue and she had the proud, lithe carriage of a truly beautiful woman.

And yet actually Sheena had no understanding of beauty in the terms a civilized woman thinks of it. Her body was pleasing to her, yes, because in its firm, supple sleekness and sculptored lines, she recognized the same qualities she admired in the great cats and the arrow-swift antelope.

But as to whether she was attractive to men never entered her mind. That basic feminine criterion of looks, the response of the male, was a yardstick as yet unknown to her, for up to now Sheena had never known a man of her own kind.

When she was younger the indistinct faces of a white man and woman sometimes had come to her in her dreams, faces that were familiar and yet somehow beyond the reach of her memory. Her earliest memories were of the Abamas, over whom the old witch woman of the tribe, N'bid Ela, had predicted that Sheena would one day rule. To prepare her for that task, N'bid Ela had taken her into the jungle and brought her up apart from the black children as though she were a high priestess in training. But for many moons now, N'bid Ela had been dead and a great, lost loneliness grew in Sheena.

Formerly; there had been no blacks in Sheena's section of the jungle, for the Abamas lived five suns to the south and they continued to obey the dead witch-woman's taboo against invading Sheena's privacy. "She will come to you when she is ready," N'bid Ela had said.

But five moons ago the warlike Bambala had come suddenly from the north and settled near her. In her first encounter with them, Sheena had barely escaped capture. Since then, the blacks had made sporadic attempts to hunt her down. Not wanting to cause a tribal war, Sheena hadn't told the Abamas of her trouble, and more recently now, the Bambala had left her alone and she had noticed that on one of those infrequent occasions when she encountered a hunter, it was the black who turned and fled.

But Sheena did not think of these things now as she lay despondently on her bed of grasses. She thought of little except that life was no longer good and exciting.

In the clearing below the treehouse, the elephant, Tamba, trumpeted impatiently for her. Hardly had the ear-splitting noises of his summons died away when her pet ape, Chim, landed with a loud thump in the door of the house, scampered across the floor and thrust his wizened, old-man's face close to hers.

Chim chattered softly, sympathetically to her at first. Then getting no response, he fell silent, peered more intently with his little button eyes. He turned away heartbrokenly, making sad sounds in his throat as he plodded toward the door.

"Oh, all right," Sheena muttered wearily, "I'll get up if it will calm you wild dingos down. By the red eyes of Gimshai, why can't you and Tamba tend to your own business for one day and leave me alone?"

The jungle girl spoke the rapid, musical speech of the Abamas. At the sound of her voice, Chim whirled, an almost human look of delight wreathing his black little face. He began to bound up and down like a rubber ball, chattering with wild animation.

Sheena stood up, smoothing and straightening her leopard skin shorts and halter. She took her sheathed knife from a wall peg, belted it on. Then she picked up a full quiver of arrows, fastened it and a bow so they rested comfortably between her shoulderblades. She scowled at the ape, and then with sudden animal quickness, she mimicked him exactly, even to the sound of his voice.

The ape froze, his mouth open, his head inclined forward so that he peered at her like an old man looking over the top of his glasses. Then shrieking with pleasure, he turned and whipped through the door, as if meaning to tell Tamba, the elephant, of the wonderful joke.

Sheena came out on the small platform which served as a porch for the treehouse. Two purple and gold virini birds whirred upward from a nearby branch to the harsh scolding of a parrot. Ten yards away in a great slanting column of sunlight, a cloud of butterflies wheeled in an endless, dizzying dance.

The jungle girl looked down through the gently swaying pattern of branches to where Tamba, with ponderous solemnity, was scratching his tough hide against a tree. At the edge of the platform lay a coiled length of liana, one end of which was tied to a heavy branch.

With a sigh, Sheena nudged the rope into space with her foot. She leaned over, caught the vine with her hands, and swung off the platform. The swift, sure agility with which she shinnied down the liana bespoke an unusual strength for a woman.

As her feet touched the ground, the elephant was waiting for her. Tamba looked down at her from his great height, shifting his ears like mammoth fans. Then he snaked his trunk about her, and lifting her, swung toward the river twenty yards away. "No, no, Tamba," she protested irritably. "Let me down. I don't want to go swimming this morning."

The bull was at the edge of the water before he realized Sheena was in earnest. He set her down, peered at her with the remarkably intelligent eyes of his kind, seemingly trying to discover what was wrong.

His look gave Sheena a twinge of conscience, and trying to hide that fact even from herself, she turned away, stared stiffly downstream. She immediately gave an exasperated grunt. Her glance had lighted on a heavy, black-maned figure carefully working its way over the river by using a low limb as a bridge. It was Sabor, the lion, coming to make more trouble for her.

"I'm not going to pat up with it," she said fiercely. "What do these animals think I am, a slave?"

With a toss of her chin, she started across the clearing toward the jungle. She heard Tamba shift his feet, knew he was considering following her. Off to her right, Chim came somersaulting out of a tree, landed on his feet and scampered to catch her.

"Leave me alone!" she cried. And suddenly she was running, fleeing from her animal friends as though devils pursued her.

She sped into the cloaking green underbrush, careless of the branches lashing at her. She ran on and on, halting only when her breath began coming in hard gasps.

When she stopped and collected herself, she felt foolish and ashamed. She shook her blonde head, a momentary wetness in her eyes. What was wrong with her? Had she somehow caught the strange madness which sometimes came upon animals, driving them off to live in the bush alone, nursing a crazed anger against the whole jungle?

Sheena glanced around to get her bearings. She hadn't paid any heed to the course she was taking and was surprised now to find how far outside her usual hunting ground she had gone. Though there certainly never had been any agreement made between them, there was a vague line of demarcation between her own range and that of the Bambala. The blacks themselves had more or less drawn the imaginary line in the past few months and seldom penetrated beyond it.

Ordinarily, Sheena would have turned back immediately to the safety of her own lands, but in her mood today she didn't care about danger or anything else. She sat down heavily on a fallen tree and put her head in her hands.

The sun crept to nearly midway in the sky before the jungle girl finally got up. A hunger pain knifed through her, reminding her she hadn't eaten that day. She was still standing indecisively, when an errant breeze brought her the scent of ripening fruit.

In her life in the jungle, her sense of smell had become almost as keen as an animal's. She went straight to the stand of trees, heavy with large blue-skinned plums. When the taste of the plums palled, she wandered on to some nut trees and finally topped off her effortless meal with a yellow panyanox pear.

Just as she threw away the pear core, Sheena heard a distant, echoing roar like a small blast of thunder. The sound was a completely new one to her and she listened, frowning. Then twice more the muted thunder came, seeming to roll close along the ground.

Abruptly, all about her the jungle was listening. The small rustlings in the underbrush, so faint and continuous that one grew almost oblivious of them, suddenly stilled. The harsh voices of the parrots, the trilling, liquid notes of the song birds ceased in one velvet clap of silence.

The forest listened, weighing the danger in the alien sound. Then as the noise blasted thrice again and still nothing happened, like a music box slowly beginning to play, the activity of the little creatures resumed. The strange thunder was ignored and then forgotten by each animal or fowl the moment it decided it personally wasn't threatened.

But because of that odd, restless quirk in the human mind, call it a thirst for knowledge, or insatiable curiosity, or a plain contrary urge to meddle, Sheena reacted quite differently from the jungle animals. What did this new and different sound mean? What caused it? Could it be there was something in the jungle she didn't know about?

Eyes bright with interest, Sheena began running in the direction of the continuing blasts of noise. She moved with an antelope's grace, seeming to pick the quickest and easiest path by instinct. There was no resemblance between the flashing drive of her long, beautifully modeled legs and that knock-kneed, ridiculously aimless attempt of a civilized woman to run.

In a matter of minutes, she came to a broad trail burrowing like a dimly-lit tunnel through the choking growth of trees, shrubs and vines. It was one of the ancient elephant tracks which serve as the highways of Africa. The echoing blasts were very close now and coming rapidly closer to her.

She started to step out on the trail, but her ears picked up the sound of pounding feet. She drew back out of sight, and sensing for the first time that she might be running headlong into danger, she leaped high, caught a limb and drew herself up into a tree. She found a perch in the middle branches, where she commanded a clear view of the trail but would be hidden from sight herself so long as she lay flat in a nest of vines.

A dark figure sprinted around a far curve in the path. A second later, two more runners burst into view. Then a whole clot of jostling, clawing bodies was pouring around the turn.

Sheena's eyes narrowed, her body suddenly taut. As the blacks swept closer along the shadowed dimness of the trail, she realized they were strange tribesmen, not the Bambala, her enemies. They were obviously terror-stricken, each man fighting to get ahead of the others.

None of them had the look of warriors, though the three men in the lead were armed with spears and shields. Most of the natives had heavy packs strapped on their backs, and as they ran, they were tearing free of the carrying straps and letting the packs shatter on the ground. Out of sight around the turn, the explosions were sounding sharper and clearer now, each blast shocking the fleeing natives to greater speed.

Sheena couldn't imagine what horror the panting, straining natives fled from. Then, abruptly, when the stampeding blacks were no more than a short spear throw away, from both sides of the trail erupted the dread Bambala war cry, "*Bibalo Aka N'Koto!*"

That frenzied cry repeated over and over with hysterical shrillness brought back to Sheena in a rush of memory that grim morning when they first tried to capture her. swarming out of ambush, a hundred jackals against one unwarned woman. But in her they had met a raging, tearing leopard instead of a fear-stricken victim. And on that day Sheena had killed for the first time, had written in Bambala blood the first lines of the legend of the warrior-queen which month to month from that time on was to grow more fabulous.

"Blood for N'Koto!" Blood for the evil god of the Bambala! Blood for that hideous, swollen idol before which the Bambala groveled and prayed before they went out to hunt down innocent, helpless victims.

Sheena snarled like an angry cat, her lips shearing back to reveal bared teeth. Out of the underbrush along the trail, the Bambala swept in two great waves. The ambush had been perfectly planned. At point-blank range they hammered their spears into their prey, and then ripping free their swords, they charged in to complete their grisly work.

As the painted warriors fell upon the terrorized bearers, Sheena's hand darted to her bow. All thought of her own safety was gone. Rage, red and flaming, seared over her. It was but the work of a moment to tug loose the slip-knot securing the bow across her shoulders.

With the flashing speed that comes from long practice, she snapped the bow-string taut. She leaped upright on the limb, as perfectly balanced as though her feet rested on solid ground. With nerveless precision, the jungle girl began feeding arrows into the tightly packed attackers.

A Bambala warrior threw up his arms, and screaming, dropped to his knees. Another pitched forward and was trampled underfoot. Two more collapsed suddenly like puppets whose strings have been cut. The fifth bent double, an arrow hammered completely through his middle, and began to run in circles like a dog with his tail on fire.

Sheena had concentrated her fire on the Bambala nearest to her, those blocking the flight of the bearers. When she knocked those five men out of the uneven battle, it was like stabbing a knife into a water-filled bladder. The crazed bearers who had survived the initial onslaught came spurting through the opening she had created. In a blind, heedless stampede they drove out of the trap and flung off at all angles into the forest.

The mass of Bambala splintered apart, groups of three to five warriors taking out after each of the frightened human rabbits. The attackers were raging more wildly than ever, now that an easy slaughter had turned into a difficult chase.

But the warriors nearest those men dropped by Sheena's arrows didn't join the pursuit. Some of them bad seen the arrows rip into their fellows, and jabbering excitedly, they pointed out to the others that the attack had come from a new, hidden foe.

Then one of them, considering the angle at which the arrows had struck, suddenly spotted Sheena standing wide-legged high up on a swaying limb. He stabbed his finger at the slim, white figure outlined against the deep green leaves.

"Tioto Nomi!" he cried. "The Forest Woman!"

A low, hoarse, shivering sound, like the rush of wind through a deep gorge, broke from the Bambala. There was fear in that sound, and hatred, too. This was the woman they had hunted innumerable times without success. For all their numbers, all their weapons, all their wiles, she made fools of them.

Clearly, no mere woman would be able to outwit warriors. And there were other things that showed she was no ordinary flesh and blood human. For instance, hadn't she been seen talking with fierce jungle beasts, or hunting and playing with them. She had demonstrated that she was immune to the curses and spells of the witchdoctors, to the proven *juju* which would wither and kill a black man in a matter of days.

And yet at the same time, many happenings in the Bambala kraal, such as the unseasonal windstorm two moons ago which tore off the roofs of half the huts or the strange overnight invasion of snakes after the last rain, could only be attributed to the evil magic of someone like the Forest Woman. Surely, she was the spawn of demons, endowed with a powerful personal *juju*, else the jungle devils themselves would long ago have devoured her.

Fear does different things to different men. Most of the warriors were momentarily paralyzed, stunned by the knowledge that Sheena for the first time openly had invaded their lands and attacked them. But one squat, bull-chested native was galvanized into action.

"Save yourselves!" he screeched. "Strike before she kills us!"

He tugged a spear from the body of one of the murdered bearers, his eyes distended, his mouth a rubbery, gaping hole. He ran forward two steps, hefting the spear for the cast.

II

Sheena's arrow took the spearman in the throat, threw him flopping backward like a beheaded chicken. But the man's action broke the spell which held the other Bambala. They went scrambling for spears among the dead bearers.

Swift as she was, there wasn't time for Sheena to escape, and against a massed spear attack her bow couldn't save her. Too late she realized her deep-seated hatred of the Bambala had betrayed her into fatal recklessness.

Then, at that moment, as death reached for her, three men came fast around the far turn of the trail behind the warriors. Two of them were husky blacks wearing faded khaki shorts. They clutched rifles in their big hands, nearly empty cartridge belts slapping their waists as they ran.

The third man was white, a tall, broad-shouldered fellow with the driving, high-stepping gait of a football fullback. A rifle was gripped in his hands, a pistol belted about his lean middle. He was hatless, his black hair tangled and unruly. And though strain and fatigue lined his square-jawed face, giving him at first glance a deceptive look of maturity, a more searching inspection told that he was in his very early twenties.

The two blacks faltered, broke stride, when they saw the Bambala milling among the dead and dying bearers. Both of them, eyes suddenly gleaming white; cast fearful glances over their shoulders. The white man's voice lashed them, drove them on a few slowing steps further. But the same panic that had overtaken the bearers was fountaining up in the two guards.

As though invisible ropes had snared them, the guards stopped, making futile little turns and twists without ever actually stirring from their tracks. The white man's voice whipped them again, angry urgency in it.

One of them shook his head violently, saying he wouldn't charge the Bambala. The other gave no sign he even heard. For a desperate moment the white man hesitated, then his mouth twisting bitterly, he plunged forward alone, triggering his rifle from hip-level as he ran.

His shouts to the guards had jerked the Bambala warriors' attention away from Shecna. They gave cry like a dog pack when they saw the three new victims. Two of them, spears lifting high, leaped to meet the oncoming white.

Then the white man's rifle was bucking and jolting in his rigidly straining hands. At that range even unaimed shots couldn't miss. The crash of the explosions echoed and reechoed, sound piling on sound, in the cavern-like trail.

One of the charging spearmen seemed to run into a stone wall. In mid-stride he slammed against the unseen barrier, went reeling backwards in a twisting fall. By the time he hit the ground, two more men in the cluster of natives behind him were going down and a third was screaming with a shattered arm.

These were tough, hard-bitten warriors, but this was their first experience in facing gunfire. That terrible roaring firestick was as awesome as a herd of charging elephants. Fearful magic was in a weapon which in some unexplained way spat death through the air.

And the best measure of the firestick's magic was the way the lone white man ran straight at them. Only a man who knew he couldn't lose would fling himself against overwhelming odds. Aye, flesh and blood couldn't combat the magic of that firestick.

The Bambala didn't guess the colossal bluff the white man was running on them. It took iron courage to drive at those blacks, triggering the last of his rifle cartridges, realizing he was finished if they didn't break before he reached them.

It wasn't lunatic bravery that dictated his action. The jungle behind him was alive with Bambala. The main force had attacked his safari from the rear, overwhelming over half the bearers before he could bring his guns into play, stampeding the rest into this second ambush. He knew he wouldn't have a chance against the jungle-wise blacks if he turned on into the underbrush. The trail ahead offered the only avenue of flight.

He had seen in the first moments of battle that the warriors were gunshy. By fighting a fierce rearguard action, he and the two armed blacks had tried to buy time for the bearers to escape. But when their ammunition ran low, they, too, had been forced to run for it.

Thinking of their nearly empty rifles, the guards' nerves had broken when they rounded the turn and saw their retreat cut off. The white man had gritted his teeth and plowed on. He had kept his wits enough to realize that a bold front might panic the small group of natives blocking the path.

And if his bluff failed?

Well, he would only be dying a few seconds sooner than the two fear-stricken guards.

But his bluff didn't fail. Like jackals charged by a lion the Bambala suddenly took to their heels. In a trampling rush, they headed into the underbrush, leaving the path clear.

Sheena stood frozen on the limb above the trail. She was as startled by that thundering firestick as the natives, but she was even more stunned by the fact that the firestick's master was white-skinned. She didn't fear him. After all, he had saved her life. His reckless charge had turned the Bambala spears away from her in the nick of time.

It didn't occur to her that he could be anything but a friend and ally. She judged men by the only rulestick she knew, the ways of the animal world. Among the jungle creatures, like ran with like, instinctively sharing the same hatreds, hungers, and habits.

Early in life, Sheena reluctantly had concluded that she was a creature alone, doomed to spend her days without ever knowing the company of others like herself.

And now suddenly, unbelievably, she was seeing one of her own people—a male of her own kind!

That he was a male, she had no doubt. His square-jawed face, his broad shoulders, deep chest and lean hips, his deep voice and wild, fierce manner of fighting, all bespoke his maleness.

He braked to a stop almost directly beneath her, and swung about, hands busy with the firestick. The thing that had stopped the white man was the hideous upthrust of Bambala cries on the trail behind him. As he turned, fumbling in haste to jam the last of his cartridges into the rifle, he saw black warriors pouring around the turn and washing out of the jungle on both sides of the two guards who had lagged behind him.

He jerked the rifle up, slammed five deliberate shots into the swarming mass. But a score of marksmen couldn't have saved the two men. The Bambala were on them like lusting beasts, literally tearing the guards to pieces with their hands.

As the clawing, screaming mass closed over the two, the white man's finger automatically kept working the trigger. But the five shells had been his last and the hammer snapped futilely against an empty chamber. When he finally realized what he was doing, his right hand snaked for his pistol, his clean-cut face gone white with anger under his deep tan.

Then with the pistol half out of its holster, he came to his senses, realizing the uselessness of trying to challenge that overwhelming force. He spun abruptly, and still gripping the empty rifle, went pounding down the trail.

His action broke the spell which had held Sheena motionless. She had seen him feed five glittering metal tubes into the firestick, had heard it spit thunder five times and then emit only empty clicks. The five ejected cartridges lay on the trail where he had stood. Her quick mind fitted these facts together and suddenly she realized the firestick's magic was used up.

The Bambala, already starting the pursuit, soon would also realize the gun's magic was exhausted. And once the caution engendered by their fear of that gun was gone, they would make short work of the white man.

"Oh, no!" exclaimed Sheena aloud. "I can't let them get him!"

With flying fingers, she dropped the arrow she held back into the quiver, secured the bow on her back. Then with the sure agility of one of the tree people themselves, She started through the middle branches.

It was through this trick of tree travel that she had so many times mystified the Bambala, apparently vanishing into thin air just when they thought they had her cornered. As a lonesome child, she had begun imitating the monkeys and apes as strictly a matter of play, and through endless practice gradually she had become breathtakingly expert at aerial acrobatics.

In pursuing the white man, Sheena veered off to the left through the jungle, remembering that the trail made a leisurely arc. Despite his considerable lead on her, she would be able to intercept him by making the shortcut.

When she reached her destination, she saw him a hundred yards away, coming fast towards her. The Bambala weren't in sight yet, but the clearness with which their chilling cries could be heard told that they weren't far behind.

Sheena gripped a dangling length of liana, balanced to swing down onto the trail. And then, with the actual moment of meeting this strange male at hand, an overpowering shyness gripped the jungle girl. She became aware of the rapid pound of her heart, the swift rise and fail of her breast. And in her legs and the pit of her stomach, she had an odd, quaky feeling.

She hesitated, bewildered by these new and utterly unexpected sensations. Then angrily, she told herself, "You fool, don't cling in this tree like a frightened lizard while death races up on that brave man."

And with that, she leaped clear of the limb, went swinging down onto the trail. Just before her feet touched the ground, she turned loose of the vine and hit running.

As the man saw a figure hurtle out of the tree, he came to a sliding stop, tearing his pistol from its holster. His eyes flew wide as Sheena hit the trail, took three long running steps and halted, facing him. His gun arm seemed to wilt, slowly dropping back to his side.

"Good lord!" he said quite audibly. "A *white* girl!"

Sheena heard his startled exclamation, and though she didn't understand the words, the sound of his voice was pleasant to her. She saw too that her appearance had greatly confused and upset him. She couldn't know that in addition to his shock at finding a white girl in the midst of nowhere, he was suddenly frantic with the thought that the responsibility for her life was being placed in his hands when he couldn't hope to take care of himself.

His face was tragic as he stared at her fresh, young beauty. In his mental turmoil, details such as her unusual dress or the odd manner in which she had appeared didn't immediately make an impression on him. His mind was too filled with the horror of the Bambala attack for him to think logically. She was the most beautiful girl he had ever seen and it sickened him to realize he was helpless to protect her from the murderous blacks.

Then the girl was beckoning to him, dire urgency in her gestures. He dropped the pistol back into his holster. He saw by her manner that she was thoroughly aware of the pursuing blacks, but she didn't show the least sign of fear. He tried to frame what he should say to her, wondering whether to tell her right out how scant were their chances or whether to lull her with a false sense of security.

But before he could speak, she ran forward impatiently and caught him by the hand. For the merest instant, her blue eyes stared directly into his gray ones, seeming in their electric intensity to search deep within him. She turned then, and gripping his hand with surprising strength, tugged him into a run.

She kept a step ahead of him and he could no longer escape seeing the bow and quiver of arrows tied across her shoulders. He frowned, his mind struggling sluggishly with the fact that- the bow was polished by long usage, the primitive doeskin quiver worn with much handling. His glance went to the long knife riding the curve of her hip, noted that the ivory handle was shaped for a woman's grip instead of a black warrior's broad, thick fingers.

And abruptly, a host of disturbing details about her began to drop into place. He felt again the strength of her grip, watched the supple play of firm muscles beneath her velvety skin, saw the golden tan which covered her body. He noticed her leopard skin clothing, which though worked to a beautiful softness, was yet crudely cut and sewn. Her feet were bare and she wore not a single ornament.

From the first few steps he took in following her, he could sense she wasn't leading him in blind flight. There was a confidence in her movements that assured him she had a definite plan figured out. This wasn't what he had expected at all. Instead of being a frightened woman seeking protection, she had taken calm command of their escape.

She led him some fifty yards down the elephant track and then swerved to the right into what appeared to the white man an impenetrable wall of vegetation. But she wriggled with sure speed through the vine-choked bush, twisting and turning right and left as if by instinct to find clearance. Twenty paces off the main trail he already had lost all sense of direction.

He abruptly realized the going was easier and found that she had brought them to a tiny, winding game path. She turned loose of his hand and began to sprint along the narrow way like a running doe.

Branches slashed at his face, caught at his rifle as he tried to keep up with her. Bushes gripped his legs, roots snared his booted feet. He felt like a blind bull threshing through the jungle, growing angry with himself as he saw how easily she threaded through the undergrowth ahead of him.

He strained to the outermost limits of his strength to stay up with her. Sweat poured from him in a drenching flood. His legs grew unsteady and his straining lungs ached with effort. And to add to his humiliation in being unable to match the girl, he finally stumbled over the roots of a baobab tree and fell sprawling full length in the path.

With the breath knocked out of him, he was too weak for a moment even to get to his knees again. When he raised his head, he saw the blonde girl had turned back and was staring at him, a questioning look on her face,

"I'm all right," he growled sheepishly. "Blasted, clumsy boots are hard to run in."

She cocked her head at his words, but didn't say anything. He realized she hadn't spoken a single time, and suddenly wondered why. He heaved to his feet and managed a grin. He didn't want her to think him ungrateful.

His weak grin immediately brought an answering smile from her. She gestured to him to get started, and as if to reinforce her warning that he must keep running, the savage howls of their pursuers rose along their backtrail. He saw how swiftly the sound of the pack erased her smile and knew the Bambala were dangerously close.

His own features sobered. "Go on," he said, motioning her ahead. "You mustn't lag back because I'm so damnably slow. By yourself you can outrun them for sure. Forget about me and let me make out for myself."

Sheena studied him thoughtfully, puzzling out his meaning. Then setting her lips firmly, she marched forward and caught him by the arm. It was obvious she had no intention of leaving him.

"Ohhh," he said despairingly, "all right, I'll go. You'd stand here until they ran over us. But you're being plain foolish."

She started off again, this time adjusting her pace to his ability to stay up with her. It angered him to realize this, to appear a flabby weakling in her eyes, and he drove himself unmercifully in an effort to crowd her, but always she kept the same distance ahead of him, seeming to float effortlessly along the difficult path.

He did his best, but it wasn't good enough. The measure of his inadequacy was the growing speed with which the Bambala began, to overtake them. But lacking Sheena's animal-keen hearing, he didn't realize how desperately close a handful of the swifter blacks had come behind them.

Sheena knew that these warriors, the best runners of the tribe, had long since outdistanced the pack. Only the confused winding of the path concealed them from view; otherwise, they would have been in easy arrow range.

She had doubled back onto the trail she had followed in first entering the Bambala area, hoping that once she crossed the vaguely defined border between her lands and theirs that they would abandon the chase. But she had failed to take into consideration the white man's difficulty in following her through the bush.

Because of his slowness, the blacks had cut away their lead. The Bambala could tell from the white man's spoor that he was staggering with exhaustion. With their prey almost in their grasp, the frenzy of the chase submerged their hazy fears of Sheena. They plunged across the border without hesitation, confident they could make a quick and easy kill and get back to their own lands before any harm could come to them.

When the warriors failed lo turn back, a sudden chill touched Sheena's heart. The man was doomed. Despite all she could do, this black-haired, fair-skinned male of her own kind would be slain.

It would still be an easy matter for her to get away from the Bambala. But all her jungle cunning was useless to help this man. She heard him reel and clutch at a tree for support.

She stopped, turned back. His head was dropped forward on his chest, his face contorted with the struggle to breathe. He sagged against the tree for a moment, looking as though his legs were going to give under him. Then through the wetness of his shirt she saw his back and shoulder muscles tense and he shoved himself away from the tree, came weaving toward her. She sensed the effort of will behind that action.

Her blue eyes were dark with the decision she made. She put out her arms and halted him. He swayed under the suddenness of her grip.

Then slowly she stepped away from him, staring bleakly along the way the Bambala would come. He wheeled about, watching her as she reached for her bow.

Abruptly, understanding came to him. This strange, magnificent girl, rather than abandon him to his fate, was preparing to face their pursuers with no other weapon than her primitive bow.

The hoarse protest that burst from his lips was drowned by a lion's ear-splitting roar. Before his amazed eyes, a huge, black-maned lion burst from a stand of shoulder-high grass to crouch facing them in the path. The beast was a giant of his kind, a steel-thewed male in his very prime, his narrowed, yellow eyes blazing with deadliness

For the merest fraction of time, the white man was shocked into immobility. It was as though a searing electric current stabbed into him from die cat's yellow eyes. Then with a wild, warning yell to the girl, his right hand dove for his pistol.

III

Bob knew as he went for the gun how small a chance he had of stopping the lion. But his instinct was to protect the girl, and if nothing else, the shots would draw the brute's charge to him.

Suddenly, bewilderingly, then, the blonde girl plunged at him, fought his hand away from the pistol. A part of his mind dazedly registered the fact that she was screaming at him in the Abama tongue, not English. He understood the words easily for he had just come from a long stay with the Nubutus, blood cousins of the Abamas, who lived a month's trek to the west.

"No, no!" she said. "Don't harm Sabor! He's my friend! I can control him."

He thought either he had gone crazy or he was dreaming the granddaddy of all nightmares. Over the girl's shoulder he could see the cat slink forward in slow, crouching steps, the unblinking eyes riveted on his face. The realization came to him that the lion was making no effort to charge the easy target made by the girl's back, but was holding back, waiting with coiled muscles for her to move out of the way.

He was the one the lion was after, not the girl!

The girl had wrestled him back against a tree. It was suddenly all too much for the confused, bone-weary man. He quit struggling for the gun, sagged back against the rough bark. At that moment, he no longer cared whether he lived or died.

As soon as he relaxed, the girl spun around to face the black-maned cat. Keeping between the man and the slowly approaching beast, she began to talk in a calm, firm voice. The lion's ears shifted to catch her words, and after an interval, his glance flicked from the man to the girl.

When she had the cat looking at her, Sheena went up to him. The lion allowed her to stroke him, the deep-throated snarls changing in tone, becoming complaining rather thin chilling. She scratched him behind an ear, slid her arm about his neck, and with gradual pressure, turned the giant cat completely about on the trail.

Still keeping her arm around the brute's shaggy mane, she began to walk, leading him away from the man. Before she had gone five steps, the first of the pursuing blacks burst into view on the trail. The warrior rounded a turn at a terrific pace.

The native had abandoned his spear to achieve greater speed, feeling his sword and bow were weapons enough to handle the two whites. He leaned forward as he ran, arms pumping, eyes glued to the trail.

Sheena stabbed a hand toward the warrior, pygmy words spilling from her lips. The huge lion beside her stiffened, his great head lifting. Abruptly, the cat's tail lashed, a tremendous roar smashed from his throat. Then with the blinding speed of a thunderbolt, he shot down the trail toward the warrior.

The black's head jerked up as he heard the roar. His eyes seemed to triple in size, his face blanching a dirty gray. With a wild flailing of arms and legs, he managed to whip around and start back toward the turn.

But at that moment, five more warriors running in single file sprinted into view. The fleeing black hammered into the line of his fellows, screaming, "Simba, Simba!" and clawing for his sword.

His cry of "Lion, Lion!" was no warning. All he succeeded in doing wai to send the first three men sprawling over him in a confused tangle. The last two blacks did manage to keep their feet, skidding to a stop just in time to make perfect targets for the charging lion.

Sheena's savage pet shot completely over the fallen men and landed with demoniac fury on the rear two warriors. Sabor's tearing claws and fangs had ripped the blacks to shreds before he had borne them to the ground.

The great lion wasted no time on his first victims. Barely had his feet touched earth when he reared about and dove directly on the fallen mass of men. He seemed to understand that he must strike before the warriors could bring their weapons into play.

The watching white man was never to forget that awful scene. The natives' screams cut through the bloodcurdling snarls of the maddened cat. The black-maned brute was everywhere at once, leaping, twisting, spinning, striking down the terrorized warriors before they could flee.

And suddenly it was over and the bloodstained lion stood among the torn things that had once been men and cried his kingly rage to the jungle. His one loyalty was to Sheena. Baring his fangs and tossing his head, he roared defiance at all those who would harm her.

The white man rubbed a hand across his eyes, muttered, ". . . unbelievable . . . that devil obeying her . . . fighting for her. . . ." But it was only the first of the astonishing experiences in store for him.

The girl's whole being had changed. Her eyes blazed with excitement. She was no longer a person resigned to death. She ran up to him, momentarily forgetting that he had spoken in a strange tongue.

"Come!" she said exultantly in Abama. "They'll never catch us now! Tamba is bound to be close by. Nothing but jealousy would have made Sabor follow me this distance. He was afraid Tamba would get me off to himself and he'd go to any lengths to keep that from happening."

"I don't know who or what you're talking about," he answered hoarsely, "but I darn sure don't want to stay here with that lion."

She was pulling him down the path then, her darting eyes searching the jungle about them. It was a full-minute before she realized that, except for a few strange words like "darn," he had replied to her in the Abama language. She looked at him, a smile like a burst of sunlight curving her full lips.

"You do speak as I do," she said happily. "My heart sank when first I heard you speak in a strange tongue, for I thought you were different from me. But we are the same—the same skin, the same language, the same blood."

Uneasy wonder at the mystery of this strange jungle girl stirred the white man again. She had the beauty of a goddess, the ways of a wild feature. She was undoubtedly white, but spoke Abama as her native language and seemed to have no knowledge of her own race at all.

And this Tamba she spoke of, who was he? Another lion? Or was he some hulking brute of a wild man. The thought of her belonging to some man hadn't occurred to him before. He found he was oddly disturbed.

"Are you sure this Tamba person will welcome me?" he asked.

"Tamba?" she said, surprised. "He won't mind."

The white man wet his lips. "Uh—is he your husband?" He had to ask it.

She repeated the Abama word for husband under her breath as though she were unsure she had heard him aright. Then suddenly a peal of delighted laughter burst from her throat.

"Oh, no," she said, her voice husky with laughter. "The sly old lazybones has practically moved in with me and thinks he owns me, but he's hardly the type for a husband."

The white man nervously cleared his throat, his face grown more somber than ever. He failed to see any humor in the situation. It was only further proof, he told himself, of how desperately little he really knew about women.

He stared darkly at the ground, the trees, the leaf-obscured sky, anywhere so he wouldn't have to look into those dancing blue eyes. A damnable crime, he boiled silently. A young and beautiful girl like that. Looked like the picture of innocence, too. Another tragedy of environment, but probably it was far too late to do anything about it now.

Her glad cry broke into his thoughts. "There he is! There's Tamba! I knew he wouldn't be far away."

He looked grimly in the direction she pointed. For a moment, since he was prepared to see a man, his glance registered nothing but green shrubs with a huge, gray, rock-like mound vaguely visible behind them.

Then the mound moved, shoved through the undergrowth with amazing speed and quiet toward the girl, and with astonished eyes he recognized a mammoth elephant.

"That is Tamba?" he sputtered. His face reddened as he became aware of her laughing regard.

"We must hurry," she said, grown suddenly serious. "The Bambala will be slowed down by the sight of these bodies and Sabor may pick off another one or two, but so long as they have a spoor to follow, they'll stay after us."

The elephant had stopped a few paces away and was regarding her with first one keen little eye and then the other.

"Here Tamba, lift him up," she commanded. The white man retreated a step. "He won't hurt you," she said in an aside. She reached out and patted the man on the shoulder for the elephant's benefit.

"I don't feel like I can move," he said tensely, "but if it is all the same to you I'll take walking rather than this." He took another backward step away from the forest giant.

She beamed for the elephant, and said in a whisper, "Don't be foolish. He's as gentle as a baby rabbit."

"Well, why are you whispering then?" the man demanded.

"I don't want him to get the idea you're afraid," she declared. "He might not respect you."

"Oh, great!" he said. But under her serious, half-pleading look, he found himself standing stiffly while the gray giant approached, suspiciously investigated him with his trunk. The man thought of a burly cop efficiently frisking a shady character. Maybe it was imagination, but he also thought Tamba gave the girl a rather aggrieved look.

"Hurry up, Tamba," snapped Sheena. "I'll explain everything to you later."

The next thing the man knew, the elephant's trunk had snapped gently but securely about his waist and he was being swept high in the air. By the time he had scrambled to a safe perch on Tamba's back, Sheena was settling herself on the broad head, slipping her long, shapely legs down behind the beast's ears.

She drummed her heels, spoke a quick command, and the elephant turned and went at a surprisingly fast gait down the path. The girl sat the forest giant as though she were glued on, but the man jounced, slipped and slid all over the swaying back. His first experience with the ancient art of elephant riding couldn't be termed a successful one.

For what seemed an eternity, he struggled to stay on that lurching back. He was too busy trying with only two hands to hold onto his rifle, clutch the rough, loose skin and block out the branches that lashed at him with diabolical aim to pay any attention to where they were headed.

When Tamba did stop, the white man's head was whirling dizzily in one direction, his stomach in another.

The soft, little clucking sounds of sympathy Sheena made as she helped him climb down touched his masculine pride. "Isn't this a fine thing," he told himself angrily. "Here I am acting like a maiden great-aunt, and she's as fresh and strong as when this nightmare started."

She solicitously maneuvered him to where he could sit down and rest his back against the tree trunk. He felt almost as bad as he had once when he was sea-sick and he sat with his eyes closed until she suddenly was holding a gourd of cold water to his lips. He took a few cautious sips of the water and used the rest to bathe his face.

He immediately felt better. He lifted his head to thank her. A small black face with brilliant, glittering black eyes hung upside down in the air not four inches from his own startled features,

"Uuugh!" he exclaimed and slammed himself back against the tree.

"Oh, I'm sorry," apologized Sheena. "It's only Chim. He wanted to get a good look at you."

And shame-facedly, the man realized the strange apparition was nothing more than a small ape hanging from a limb by his feet.

He looked about at the pleasant, tree-shaded clearing, the tree-house high above him, the cool, clear deeps of the river.

"You live *here?*" he asked unbelievingly. "And all alone?"

She nodded enthusiastically.

Chim, apparently tiring at long last of his upside down position, loosened his grip on the limb, turned a quick flip and landed in a squatting position in the white man's lap.

"I can't imagine how you manage," he said, trying not to notice the monkey's stern, unblinking scrutiny. "How long have you lived this way?"

"Why, always," she said matter-of-factly. "Doesn't everyone live about the same way? Of course, I do live in a tree-house, whereas most natives build on the ground. There's plenty of game and plenty of water here. I don't think anyone could find a more perfect home."

He thought of the great crowded cities of America, the unnumbered kinds of stores, services and establishments, the huge manufacturing plants, the giant utilities, the layers upon layers of governing bodies. And this slim, wide-eyed, blonde girl asked him if everyone didn't live about the same way she did. An existence such as hers, let alone a happy, healthful existence, had become inconceivable to the white races of the world.

"Surely, you remember your family," he ventured.

A shadow seemed, to pass across her face. "No," she said. "They died while I was a baby. The Abamas found me, but they can tell me nothing except that my parents were of the Tribe of God." The expression was one used by natives to describe white missionaries.

Grown suddenly moody, she bit her full lower lip, stared off across the river. A wave of sympathy swept over the man. But the girl's mood swiftly passed. She turned back to him, as bright and vivacious as ever.

"You haven't told me how you are called," she said shyly.

"Great Scot," he exclaimed in English, "I really am the boy for manners."

She blinked at him. "That is your name?"

He laughed. "No, no. My name is Bob Reilly."

She pronounced it after him cautiously, like a child learning a new phrase. Then as if she had made a startling discovery, she asked, "Why do you have two names?"

Without thinking, he returned, "Why not? Most people have three."

She looked troubled. "I have only one—Sheena," she confessed in a disturbed whisper. "I guess it is bad thing to have only one name?"

It dawned on him that she wasn't joking. In her first tentative brush with civilization, he was unwittingly making her feel certain "lacks" in herself. He sought to reassure her.

"The main, reason for a name is so you'll be known and remembered," he said. "As lovely a girl as you doesn't need more than one name. There would never he a chance of your being confused with any other girl. No matter how many Sheena's there were in the world, once a man saw you, the name Sheena would never mean anyone but you." She gravely considered his words. It was the first male compliment she had ever received. It hadn't occurred to her that how she looked might have any effect on a man. She pursed her lips, trying to figure out his exact meaning.

"You mean," she picked her words slowly, "that you find it good to look upon me?"

Bob Reilly went through a considerable process of throat clearing. He should have remembered that women were quite unable to view any matter in the abstract. They dealt with everything on a purely personal basis. He noticed how she leaned her head forward and frowningly looked herself over as though wondering what there could be that was particularly pleasing about her.

"Anyone would say that you are unusually beautiful," he said with enforced calm. There, he had avoided the personal angle quite neatly.

She smiled. You could see the pleasure grow in her. "I—I feel quite different," she said, "from your saying that."

He found himself watching her apprehensively, and it was with a distinct sense of relief that he saw her turn away, walk to the river bank and lean over to study her reflection.

The monkey still squatted in his lap. He hadn't thought one of the little varmints could. stay quiet so long. Maybe the frozen-faced devil was trying to hypnotize him. Bob stole a glance at Sheena, and certain she wasn't watching him, he made the most vicious, menacing face he could at the monkey.

Chim registered absolutely no reaction. He didn't turn a hair.

Bob lifted his hands to his ears and waggled them in the universally insulting gesture of brattish children. Chim's hard little eyes didn't so much as waver. Bob bared his teeth, made ugly croaking sounds deep in his throat.

Then with insulting slowness, the monkey raised his own hands to his ears, twisted his black little features Into a leering grimace, and mimicked the man's gestures with a. brazen exactitude. When he had finished, Chim made a sound suspiciously like a horse laugh, leaped to the ground and went skittering off acres the clearing in high good humor.

IV

Bob leaned back against the tree and closed his eyes. Too much had happened to him in too short a time. "If I don't pull myself together," he told himself, "I'll be going off my trolley permanently." His conscience was hurting him because he was deliberately pushing away thoughts of the ambush and of what his next move must be. But he realized he was too confused and beat up to plan logically. The son of one of America's wealthiest men, Bob at twenty-three, with a hat full of scholastic and sports honors and an eagerness to get out and prove himself in the world, had found himself faced with even more sterile, needless years of study. His stepmother, as a means of getting him out from underfoot, had convinced his father it would be well to send him abroad for advanced schooling.

And the long submissive Bob finally rebelled. In an ugly scene with his angry, desk-pounding father and coldly scornful stepmother, he steadfastly asserted his independence, and ended by stalking out of the house in a white fury.

Imbued with a desire to get away from everything representing his old life, he recalled an expedition being organized by one of his old professors to record and study native African languages. He had demonstrated an unusual aptitude for languages in school, and that talent along with his general record of scholarship and the publicity value of his name, made it an easy task for him to get on the expedition as an assistant.

After three months in the bush, the elderly professor's health broke down and he had to return home, leaving Bob in charge. If anything, the work went better under the younger man's direction, and he began to feel he was going to show his father that be wasn't the only Reilly who could pull his own weight under difficult circumstances.

But his desire to include the more primitive and little-known tribes in his study drew him into the trackless depths of unexplored territory. He had known there was danger and had taken what he considered were adequate steps to protect his safari. But in his inexperience, he failed to realize the vast difference between the fighting qualities of his long subjugated coastal blacks and those of the fierce, marauding tribesmen of the interior.

His guards and bearers were boastful enough about their fighting prowess until trouble came. Then they fled in panic, abandoning both packs and weapons. And so Bob's attempt to stand on his own feet, to do something striking enough to impress his father, ended in utter disaster.

"I've botched the whole thing," he told himself. "I'm a failure. No expedition will give me a chance after this, and now my parents will expect me to come crawling back to them. And I'll have the blood of those murdered men on my hands the rest of my life."

It was these torturing thoughts that Bob tried to push away from Him as he sat in Sheena's clearing. At last his very weariness came to his rescue. His chin dropped forward on his chest and he slid away into deep sleep.

Night had fallen when Bob awakened. A great silver moon lay low in the sky. The moonlight washed the river with beauty, painted shifting patterns on the ground beneath the tall trees. The weird night chorus of the jungle rose all about the clearing.

Bob sat up in alarm, unable at first to identify his surroundings. A fire burned down to red coals, glowed in the center of the clearing. He smelled the savory scent of a joint of meat grilling slowly over the fire.

"Where the devil am I?" he muttered, hurriedly reassuring himself that his pistol was still in its holster.

Nothing moved in the clearing. It seemed utterly deserted. Then his glance caught on a dark bulk hunched not thirty feet from him in the shadow of a tree trunk. He caught his breath and waited. The dark bulk moved, and abruptly, two slanting yellow eyes burned wickedly at him from the shadows.

A huge cat lay crouched there, watching him!

That sight swept the cobwebs from his brain. He remembered Sheena and her savage pet. If Sheena had wandered off and left him alone with that beast, he wouldn't have a chance. He felt cold sweat trickling down his face.

What should he do? If he called out or moved, that devil might charge. He recalled the stories he had read about intrepid hunters playing dead when through some accident they had found themselves at the mercy of a lion.

But even as he thought of these storybook heroes, he saw Sabor flatten himself on the ground, creep forward a good two feet on his belly. He didn't feel the least bit intrepid at that moment.

"SHEENA!" he called loudly. "SHEENA!"

"Here I am." Her voice came from the direction of the river. "What's wrong?"

"Get this blasted lion of yours away from me! He's ready to spring."

"Oh, is that all," she said, obviously relieved. "Don't worry about Sabor. He wouldn't hurt you now for the world."

At the sound of his mistress' voice, Sabor stood up and looked toward the river. The instant those yellow eyes were off of him, Bob was up and around behind the tree against which he had been leaning. Once out of sight of the cat, he streaked for another tree, further away. When he reached it safely, he began to work his way toward the water with all the care of an infantryman under heavy fire.

He reached the bank muttering. A hasty glance over the moon-swept water failed to reveal any sign of her. He looked over his shoulder. Sabor was moving toward him with slow steps, pausing every few feet to sniff the night air.

Bob turned back toward the river just in time to see Sheena's head break the surface of the water. Of all the cold-blooded women, he thought. She amuses herself by swimming around under water while her man-killing pet stalks me.

She saw him in the moonlight. "I was beginning lo think you never would wake up," she said. "Come on in the water. It feels wonderful. The meal won't be ready for awhile yet anyway."

With Sabor stalking him, there was no room in Bob's mind for the proprieties. In nothing flat, he had tugged off his boots and stripped to his shorts. Cats, even big cats, didn't like water. He would be safe in the river.

Bob took two running steps and drove out over the water in a racing dive. He drove out toward mid-stream with a smooth powerful stroke, leaving a frothing wake.

"How swiftly you go," she exclaimed as he swam up to her. "Like the finny ones themselves! Oh, if only I could swim that way! I've studied every animal I could, trying to learn better ways of swimming, but none of them can match you."

He had meant to lecture to her about Sabor. But he found himself saying almost moderately, "You've got to do something about that lion. Didn't you realize he was creeping up to kill me?"

"Faugh," she said mildly. "On the trail—yes—he would have killed you. But now he understands you're my friend. He's been lying there looking at you since long before dark. After all, he never saw a white man before and he's kind of interested."

"I tell you he even came creeping after mc down to the river," insisted Bob. "I don't like him and he doesn't like me."

Sheena laughed. On the shore the black-maned lion coughed irritably. Both the man and the girl glanced toward him. He was standing with his head high, staring out at them over the water.

"Well, Sabor probably thinks we would be better off without you," she confessed, "but I told him you belonged to me and to leave you alone. And he'll do it!"

Bob's mind had stopped dead on the words, "I told him you belonged to me." He was suddenly puzzled. What was going on in the head of this wild, young, pagan girl?

The next thing he knew she was swimming so close to him that he could feel the touch of her bare leg against his as she treaded water.

"I've been thinking about what you said to me this afternoon," she suddenly declared.

Her eyes were disturbingly large and luminous in the moonlight.

"What was that?" he asked.

"About you finding me good to look upon," she explained. "That made me very happy. I couldn't really understand what you meant at first," Sheena went on. "I've never been around any men of my own kind, so it hadn't occurred to me that—well— that they might like me or not like me."

"Yes. Quite so," Bob said uneasily. "Don't you think you should look at the food?"

Sheena's face was instantly sympathetic. "Oh, I forgot," she said. "I'm not used to having visitors. You must be starving."

Before he could move, she had thrust her feet against the river floor and stood up. He realized for the first time that she swam unclad and her suddenly revealed beauty made his breath catch in his throat. Her bare body was a picture of Aphrodite rising from the sea.

Sheena waded to the bank. With a child's innocence, she stood there smoothing the glistening drops of water from her body with her hands. After leisurely donning her halter and shorts, she walked across to the fire, inspected the joint of meat cooking over the crossbars.

When Sheena called him to eat, Bob dressed hurriedly in the shadow of a tree and joined her near the fire. The food was delicious and he ate huge quantities of it, but actually he hardly tasted it or knew what he was eating.

Never in his life had Bob felt such conflicting emotions about anyone as he did about the jungle girl. He kept stealing glances at Sheena as she moved back and forth from the fire, waiting on him, or while she sat cross-legged beside him, eating with unconcealed enjoyment. She shone with happiness.

And suddenly he realized that he was happy too. By all rights, he felt he should have been wallowing in the depths of despair. He was lost in the depths of an untracked jungle, hunted by murderous tribesmen, left without any adequate means of protecting himself. Yet never had he felt so vibrantly alive as he did now.

V

The raucous argument of parrots on a limb above him awakened Bob in the morning. He had slept near the fire, using a zebra skin thrown over freshly-cut grasses for his bed. The moment he sat up, his eyes went to the tree house high above him.

He realized that his first thoughts were of the blonde-haired girl. "This won't do," he warned himself. "I'm supposed to be a serious, intelligent adult." He got up and began to pace the clearing, forcing everything out of his mind but his wrecked expedition. He had to decide what to do.

He could be a quitter, write off the expedition as a total loss and concentrate on trying to get out of this scrape with his own skin whole. Under the circumstances, that didn't seem too illogical.

But Bob kept remembering that a good part of the records of the expedition were in those packs abandoned by the bearers. The Bambala were certain to gather up the packs, cart them back to their village as loot. Until he knew those records were definitely destroyed, he felt bound to try to recover them.

Then, even though the cowardice of his blacks was the real reason for the debacle, he considered it his duty to go to the help of any who had survived the attack. The Bambala wouldn't have slaughtered them all. Once certain their victims were too terrorized to fight back, they would have begun taking prisoners.

And after an hour of pacing and fretting, he made up his mind. He wouldn't be able to live with himself if he didn't make a sincere attempt to free the surviving bearers and retake the records he had so painstakingly gathered. Yet even as the resolve was formed, he felt himself doomed to failure.

How could he, with a handful of pistol cartridges and an abysmal ignorance of the jungle, hope to strike any kind of a blow against the savage Bambala?

Bob was surprised to see Sheena suddenly stride from the jungle. He had thought her still asleep in the tree house. She leaned her spear against a tree, walked over and stirred the fire to life.

"I left early," she said. "I thought it wise to check on the Bambala." She knelt, placed four fresh sticks of wood in the flames.

"The Bambala didn't turn back as I had hoped," she said abruptly. "They are searching for us now."

She loosened a leather pouch belted about her slim waist, laid it on a clean rock beside the fire. Then, after selecting a long, pointed stick from a collection held in a large gourd, she reached in the pouch and drew out a freshly cleaned and dressed bird. She held it up for him to see before she spitted it on the stick for cooking.

"I thought these birds might please you for the morning meal," she said. And so he would understand they were something special, she added, "I hunted for them quite awhile."

The girl utterly baffled Bob. She seemed to have dismissed the black warriors from her mind. After learning those murderous devils were searching them out, how could she calmly go hunting and then come back to enjoy a leisurely meal.

"The birds look wonderful," he said without enthusiasm. "But frankly, Sheena, shouldn't we be getting out of here instead of thinking of eating?"

"Leave?" she said, surprised. "This is my home!"

"You can't fight off a whole tribe," he told her.

Her eyes flashed. "I can cause them enough trouble to make them wish they hadn't come. I've done it before."

"But they'll come back, Sheena," he said gravely. "And they'll keep coming back until one day they'll catch you."

She fitted the spitted birds onto the forked supports which held them over the fire. She stood up, brushed her hands The merest shadow crossed her face.

"Death must come to every living creative," declared the girl. "I will not be afraid when my time comes." She spoke with the fatalism of those to whom danger is a constant companion.

"Is there a way, Sheena," he asked suddenly, "for me to circle around these warriors and reach their village? I'd guess that most of the able-bodied men are hunting for us. This might be my best chance to slip into their village and try to free any of the bearers who were captured. If there are enough of them and they'll help me, maybe I can even recover my records."

Sheena turned in alarm. Though she had talked calmly enough of death in regard to herself, she now exclaimed, "Are you trying to kill yourself? You must be mad to speak of such a thing!"

He blinked at her, taken aback by her reaction. She paced rapidly back and forth in front of him.

"I haven't the least desire to get anywhere near that village," he admitted honestly, "but it is my duty to do it."

"Duty? I do not know this word!" She was like an aroused leopard, lithe and quick, with a wildness in her eyes. "I will not have you put yourself in danger. I will not have it, you understand!"

Bob scratched his head and frowned. He hadn't anticipated anything like this.

"It's all right for you to play dangerous games with the Bambala, but not me. Is that it?"

She gave her long blonde hair a savage toss. "I am different," she snapped. "I am Sheena!"

She reached him with quick steps, shook a finger in his face. "Put this notion from your head. You are not to go anywhere near that kraal of dangos."

"You saved my life, Sheena," he answered gently, "and I'm deeply grateful, but I'm not a new pet who will meekly do your bidding. There are some things a man must do if he is to live with himself."

And he tried to explain to her then why he had to make a stab at helping the bearers and recovering the work of many months.

"You owe those men nothing," she told him with harsh, feminine logic. "They did not value their freedom enough to fight for it. As to this work you talk of, I do not understand about it too much, but it can't be important enough to lose your life over."

"Nevertheless, I must go," he said firmly.

She was very close to him. The changeful blue depths of her eyes softened, losing the storminess of a moment before. The warm, girl scent of her came up to Bob.

He watched the curve of her full, red lips. Her teeth were small and fine and white. He had never known any woman who stirred him as she did.

Suddenly the tight control he had exerted over himself snapped. Before he knew what he did, he reached his arms about her and pressed his mouth to hers.

The startled girl's eyes flew wide. She stiffened as though either to fight or run. But she let him draw her into his embrace, made no attempt to take her mouth from his.

Abruptly he released her, but he could not move away because she held him with the rigidness of her arms about his neck.

"I'm sorry, Sheena," he mumbled. "I shouldn't have done that. I—I didn't mean to do it." He was embarrassed and angry with himself. "I only meant to tell you that though I wish I never had to see another Bambala, I have to go to their village."

Sheena slid her arms from his neck and stepped back. The strange, startled expression was still on her face. Her right hand came up to touch her mouth.

"Why did—what did you do?" she faltered.

Bob frowned, momentarily puzzled. Then he was more embarrassed than ever. Sheena had no idea what a kiss was.

"I kissed you," he said. And then he didn't know what to say next.

"But why?" she demanded.

"Uh—well, I just couldn't help myself." His face reddened. "Among our people, when a man . . ." That didn't sound right. "It's a custom. It—it means—no, that's not what I want to say." He bumbled on in a growing confusion of unfinished sentences.

"You mean," Sheena asked, "that among people with white skin it is like when a native man rubs noses with a girl?"

"Yes," he granted uncomfortably. He considered how swiftly feminine instinct had taken her to the heart of the matter.

"I have seen them," she said thoughtfully. She touched her lips with her fingers. "This is a strange thing, this 'kiss,' very strange." Then slowly, she smiled and nodded her head. "But it is far better than the natives' custom. I think our people must be very wise. First, there was the firestick which kills at a distance, then the superior way of swimming, and now this matter."

"Then you aren't angry with me?" ventured Bob.

She contemplated him gravely. "No," she said softly. "I should like you to do it again, now when I wouldn't be so surprised."

Bob swallowed heavily. "Not now," he declared. His breath came very fast. "No, not now." He might have proved himself a sorry kind of man by making a mess of his expedition, he told himself, but he'd be damned if he was sorry enough to take advantage of Sheena's innocence. She had saved his life. The least he could do was to behave himself.

Sheena sighed, tapped a forefinger against her teeth for a few moments.

"Do not worry, Bob. If you must go through with this Bambala foolishness," she said in unexpected capitulation, "Sheena will make you a plan. You sit here and rest. Fretting is not good for you."

He was relieved to know she wasn't going to continue her opposition, though he didn't take seriously her easy assurance that she would provide a plan. She was an unusual girl, but a foray such as he contemplated was rather out of a woman's line. He was amused by her swift shift from the role of a naive, young maiden to that of a wise elder mothering a child.

But later, after they had eaten, when he still hadn't laid hold of the vaguest notion of how to carry through his project, she calmly and confidently told him how the job could be done.

She said, "This will work—if anything will. I know the Bambala, how they think. And fortunately for us, only women and old men will be in the kraal."

Bob listened in amazement. Never in a thousand years would so unorthodox a scheme have occurred to him. But, by George, it might work. It was bold and dangerous, yet properly executed it could so stun and frighten the tribesmen that he would have time to free his bearers and gather up his records before a hand was raised against him.

Then his face suddenly fell. Tamba was the keystone of the whole plan, which he realized on second thought meant that Sheena was counting herself in on the raid.

"Oh, no," he cried. "You're taking no part in this. The plan won't do. I'm not risking your life on business that just concerns me."

Sheena regarded the determined set of his jaw and smiled.

"You're mistaken," she said mildly. "The fight is entirely yours. I mean only to help you get ready for it and guide you to the village. If I order it, Tamba will do your bidding well enough to get you through."

Bob subsided. "Well, that's different," he said. "I won't have you running any more risks on my account. Look at the trouble I've already caused you."

Throughout the day, Bob kept worrying that they should leave the camp, but Sheena refused to be hurried. After several trips into the jungle to gather a strange assortment of bulbs, roots, and dank, yeasty growths, she had settled down to mixing a white, glue-like substance.

"Chim and Sabor are keeping an eye on the Bambala," she told him. "They'll let us know when the dangos get too close."

Bob didn't share her confidence in the two pets. And the fact that Chim would get bored about every two hours and return to camp to see what Sheena was doing didn't help his nerves. After the jungle girl had chased the grumbling ape back to his post for the third time, she made a further concession to ease Bob's tension.

"I laid enough false trails this morning to keep the Bambala busy until nightfall, unless they should get very lucky," she explained. "And scattered along each trail are unpleasant little surprises to discourage them from hurrying."

She didn't go into detail about the surprises and he didn't ask her to, for her grim tone brought crowding into his mind, the variety of murderous traps he had seen black men use in hunting: camouflaged pits, drawn bows released when a vine in the path was touched, tiny, poisoned bamboo splinters set in the earth, snares that would jerk a grown bushbuck eight-feet in the air and break its neck, bent saplings that would hammer a lion into pulp.

But the revelation of how she had occupied the early morning shook him as badly as had the realization that Sabor, far more than a pet, was a deadly weapon she employed against her enemies.

When he looked at her now, he saw a young, mild, soft-voiced girl, anxious to please, quick to laugh. He felt at ease with this girl. In truth, he felt pleasantly superior. Then abruptly, she would shatter this mould into which he had fitted her, revealing by some action that she was more a sister to a tawny, dangerous lioness than the conventional being he tried to believe her to be.

How could he reconcile the shy, soft-mouthed girl he had held in his arms for a moment that morning with the Sheena who could meet and best the black warriors at their own savage game?

It made him almost afraid of the girl. You couldn't guess what really went on in that head of hers or predict how she would react in a given situation. How could he be sure she wouldn't turn on him, if he made a move that rubbed her the wrong way?

Sheena was too busy to notice any change in him. Not until late afternoon did she plug up with a stopper of wadded leaves the last of five large gourds of the thick, whitish liquid. She glanced at the low-lying sun and then came over to where Bob sat, stretched out on her side on the ground beside him.

She smiled up at him, her head cushioned on her right arm. "The night ahead may be long," she said simply. "I will rest until Chim comes. He would never forgive me for leaving him behind."

She closed her eyes, took a few slow, deep breaths and was immediately asleep. Bob blinked in amazement. "That's not human," he told himself. "She even sleeps like a cat."

He set his jaw firmly and looked away into the jungle. But in less than a minute his gaze had crept back to the sleeping form beside him. He studied the way the long, blonde hair tumbled about her face and shoulders, examined the long lashes lying heavy against her golden skin, watched with something more than scientific interest, the manner in which her red lips pouted in sleep.

The daylight was nearly gone when Bob realized with a start that Sheena's eyes were open and that for some time she had been silently watching him.

His confusion wasn't lessened when she said, "Chim grows impatient with my laziness."

As though ear plugs had been drawn from his ears, he suddenly heard a monkey chattering and grumbling in the tree above them. How long the little devil had been there he didn't know, but apparently for a considerable period. And though Chim had made enough noise to rouse Sheena from sleep, Bob hadn't even been conscious of his presence.

"It was nice to awaken and find you sitting beside me," she said, putting a hand on his arm. "But I couldn't help but wonder what you were thinking that made you frown so."

He got up quickly, avoiding her gaze. "I was thinking of the raid," he lied.

"Oh," she said quietly. And he had a queer feeling that she was smiling inwardly.

• • •

While they waited for it to become full dark, they ate a light meal of fruit and nuts. Then Sheena called Tamba, tied the gourds on him so they wouldn't rattle or spill. Like the low, distant rumble of thunder, came the roar of a lion. After a brief interval, answering cries from widely separated points in the jungle could be heard.

"The Bambala are close, but they won't do much more traveling tonight," said Sheena grimly. "That first roar was Sabor's victory cry, telling the jungle he had made an easy kill. Every cat within hearing will head for that area. I think we can move safely now."

And so in the pitch blackness before the moon rose, Tamba carried them along secret trails past the Bambala patrols. Bob, who had worried about the nervous, talkative Chim going along with them, noticed that the monkey huddled in front of Sheena and never uttered a sound. He was about ready to believe that the jungle girl's pets did understand what was going on.

It was after midnight when Sheena halted the elephant in a moonlit glade. "We'll do our work here," she said. "The kraal is within arrow shot."

She unfastened the gourds, detached two of them, lowered the others carefully to the ground.

"I'll paint his head and back," she told Bob. "You take care of his legs and stomach."

A half-hour later the patient elephant had been smeared completely over with the thick, white liquid brewed by Sheena. But in the darkness, the liquid revealed a property not discernible during daylight. It glowed with an eerie, phosphorescent light.

Bob stood off and looked at Tamba. "By Harry," he exclaimed, "he's the most unearthly-looking sight I ever hope to see. And that hazy, bluish glow makes him look twice as big as he is. A creature like that looming out of the night would frighten anyone."

"The Abama witchwoman who brought me up used it in her magic," explained Sheena. "I often helped her gather the materials and mix it."

Bob looked at his hands, glowing with light from the mixture he had smeared over the elephant. "I believe it may work," he excitedly declared, "if the Bambala are as superstitious as you say."

"Let us hope so," the girl said quietly. "There will be danger enough at best."

Sheena had picked up the vine rope which had been used to tie the gourds on Tamba. As she talked, she idly toyed with it, forming loose coils on the ground with one end, twisting and gathering the other end in an odd pattern.

"Well, this finishes your part of the job, anyway," said Bob. "You've been wonderful to help me."

He tried to tell her how grateful he was, but he seemed suddenly clumsy with words and his voice took on an unnatural brusqueness.

He finished lamely by saying, "I'd better paint myself up now. And then as soon as you get me started off on Tamba, I want you to get away from here—and stay away. You've taken too many chances on my account already."

Sheena didn't look at him. She kept her head down, her fingers nervously working with the rope. "Yes, Bob," she said.

She seemed small and feminine and terribly forlorn in the moonlight. The sight of her caught Bob's heart and twisted it. He had been a rotten, miserable heel to think of her as he had that afternoon.

He couldn't leave her this way,. He had to take her in his arms, tell her how he felt about her. He took two steps towards her. "Sheena," he said hoarsely, "before I go . . ."

As though her mind had been turned inward and she hadn't heard him, she suddenly interrupted. "The paint, Bob—it must be dry before you mount Tamba. Hold out your hands and let me see if it is drying properly."

Her taut, businesslike tone, so out of harmony with the mood that had swept over him, stopped Bob in his tracks. Almost angrily, he shoved out his hands for her inspection.

As to what happened next, he was to try many times afterwards to recall exactly how it did occur. But he was never to be entirely certain about any of it.

Sheena leaned as though to inspect his hands. The next thing he knew the vine rope she had been idly fingering snapped about his wrists. "What the devil?" he exclaimed.

Before he could realize what she was about, Sheena leaped backwards, the rope running through her hands with the speed of a striking snake. Then she flipped the rope, gave a powerful tug—and Bob's feet shot from under him.

One end of the vine was lashed about his wrists, the other about his ankles. There had been careful planning behind all her nonchalant handling of the rope while they talked. The loops she had thrown on the ground with seeming carelessness were those she flicked upward to lash his ankles, send him crashing to the ground.

Despite the stunning force of the fall he took, Bob lashed out wildly, trying to break free. After darting in to snatch his pistol from its holster, Sheena stood a safe distance away, watching him struggle. He fought like a maddened beast, his sanity momentarily splintered by the terrible shock of her treachery.

But the bonds held, and at last he lay gasping, his muscles trembling from the violence of his efforts. Only then did he look at her, letting the bitter acid of his wrath spill out in words.

"And to think I believed in you, trusted you," he snarled. "I should have known you'd turn on me like an animal if it were to your advantage."

His mouth was a vicious slit, his eyes narrow pools of hate. His gun made a dull thump as she dropped it at her feet.

"You fooled me, though," continued Bob. "I swallowed all your hocus-pocus, never suspecting that you'd use me to buy your own safety. Very clever! You hand me over to the Bambala and thereby buy them off of your own trail. They were getting too close for comfort. And you got to worrying that if I did raid their kraal and did some damage, they'd never forgive you for helping me." Sheena smoothed her hands nervously over her midriff, her face expressionless except for the eyes which seemed to glow in the night. Finally, her right hand slid to the knife riding the curve of her hip. The blade gleamed coldly as she lifted it from the sheath.

VI

Bob was abruptly still as he saw the bared steel in the jungle girl's hand. Then with withering contempt, he said, "Don't lose your head, my precious. The Bambala won't pay as much for me dead as they will alive. They, too, enjoy the pleasure of killing!"

A deep, pained frown cut Sheena's forehead. She had foreseen everything in her planning except Bob's reaction. The awful bitterness of his words took her by surprise.

"Yes, I play a hard trick on you," she said evenly. "But I play it to save your life, not take it away."

She turned her back on him. The gray trunk of a dead tree stood at the edge of the clearing some thirty paces in front of her. She covered half the distance to the tree with quick steps. Then Sheena lifted the knife, sent it glittering through the air to drive point-first into the dead wood.

Bob had lifted himself with difficulty to a sitting position. He watched her fling the knife into the tree and hurry back to where Tamba waited.

"What did you mean about saving my life?" he demanded.

She picked up the remaining half-gourd of phosphorescent paint, literally poured it over her head and shoulders, saving back enough to douse the protesting Chim. Then she painted both her spear and bow.

"I meant I am going in your place!" she snapped, rapidly smearing the paint evenly over her. "Foolish One, Tamba would never take your orders, and besides, I know far more about handling the Bambala than you do."

He stared at her aghast as she signaled Tamba to lift Chim and her to his back. "You intended this from the beginning?"

"Of course," she said. "If your men and packs can be wrested from the Bambala, I will do it. If I fail, then you will still be able to save yourself."

"No!" he burst out indignantly. "I won't allow it!"

He was working clumsily with his fingers to loosen the bonds on his ankles. Since Sheena had tied his hands in front of him, he had no trouble reaching his feet.

"I tied you so you'd have to allow it," she said calmly. "And don't waste your strength trying to undo those knots. You'll need my knife to get free. By the time you work your way over to that tree and get it loose, it will be too late for you to interfere at the kraal."

Sheena lifted her pet ape, dropped him to the ground.

"However, on second thought I'll leave Chim to help take care of you. The noise he's making would work me harm, but his voice and looks should protect you from anything less than a rhino."

She tried to force a light-hearted gayety into her tone, but the attempt wasn't wholly successful. "I go now!" she said abruptly, lifting her spear in an odd, quick salute.

Then Tamba was moving past Bob, bearing Sheena into the jungle. He pleaded with her not to go, nearer in his utter helplessness to tears than at any time since his early childhood. Sheena, sitting ramrod straight, didn't look back.

As the dark, green foliage closed behind her, Bob's voice trailed away brokenly. He thought of things he had said to her in anger and was ashamed and miserable. She was going into that village for him and only because of him.

He had called her an animal, immediately attributing the basest motives to her. He remembered the hurt, surprised look on her face as she heard his accusations. Yet she hadn't even rebuked him.

In that moment, the certainty crystallized in him that he would never see. Sheena again. She was riding to her death!

In one writhing effort, Bob heaved himself to his feet. He had to get free and catch her. He reeled, his legs so tightly bound he couldn't balance himself.

To keep from falling, he started hopping forward, each clumsy hop swifter and more desperate than the preceding one. But his convulsive efforts to regain his equilibrium were doomed to failure. He got no more than five yards before he crashed heavily to the hard earth.

The fall knocked the breath from him, yet he immediately fought to his elbows and knees. He heard a weird gibberish sounding right at his shoulder. He jerked his head around and saw Chim crouched on bands and knees beside him; the ape, his eerily glowing face seemingly wreathed with diabolical delight, was trying to assume the same position as Bob. The distraught man's temper exploded. "I'll teach you to mock me," he shouted. And, he reared up on his knees, lifting his bound arms to knock the ape rolling.

But Chim divined his purpose instantly. With an alarmed screech, the ape bounded backwards and fled off across the clearing like some small, incandescent demon. Bob shook his knotted fists in futile, senseless rage.

Chim literally flew over the ground, his little head twisting right and left in search of a safe refuge. The gray outlines of the dead tree caught his attention as it had Sheena's when she looked for a place to plant the knife. The ape headed for the tree. He scrambled up the trunk in mad haste, shooting past the knife to reach the bare lower limbs.

Not until then did he pause to look back. His staccato outburst revealed surprise that the man hadn't moved. He fell silent, considering the matter. Then deciding he was quite safe, his whole manner changed and he began climbing slowly down the tree, grandly announcing his outrage at being put upon like a common fellow.

When Chim reached the knife, he suddenly stopped his tirade. He recognized the scent of his beloved mistress. He gave a delighted cry and tugged the knife free.

He beamed on the weapon. It was Sheena's. He would return it to Sheena and she would be pleased with him. She was always very proud of him when he returned some belonging of hers that he found. In fact, if the truth were known, he often stole her belongings so he might return them and have her pleased with him.

His run-in with Bob had slipped as completely out of Chim's erratic little mind as had his memory that Sheena was gone. His head didn't trouble itself very often to try to hold more than one notion at a time.

He dropped from the tree and scampered happily back toward Bob. He was within three yards of the man when he realized Sheena was nowhere in sight. Chim had been too angry about the white paint being poured on him to pay any attention to Sheena's departure, and after that, Bob's antics had so engrossed him that he still didn't realize he had been deserted.

All at once now it was borne in on him that his protector was gone and that the terrible night so feared by the tree folk kept him from finding her. Chim was suddenly frightened. He looked about at the dark trees, imagining fearful enemies staring at him.

Bob had no idea what went on in Chim's mercurial mind. The white man crouched on his knees, his breath coming in hard gasps. The ape had the knife. That was all that mattered.

From the moment Chim had pulled the knife from the tree and started back toward him, Bob had been afraid to speak or move. He had to get the weapon from the little devil. But how? After the way he had treated the monkey, a word or movement from him would probably send Chim fleeing into the forest.

He wet his lips nervously. "Here Chim! Good boy, give me the knife." He uttered the words like a prayer. "Nice boy. I won't hurt you."

Chim, who had hunkered down into a little glowing knot, lifted his head and stared mournfully at the white man. Then he ducked his face and shivered.

Bob kept talking in the gentle, wheedling tone. The monkey wouldn't budge. Bob gathered his courage and edged forward a few inches. Without even lifting his head, Chim edged backward an equal distance.

Bob groaned. He'd never get the knife, never in the world. The little fool understood and obeyed every word Sheena spoke, yet at this moment, when so much depended on it, he wouldn't heed a single thing Bob said to him.

And then abruptly, Bob realized that in his excitement, he had been speaking in English. With his voice trembling with excitement, he switched to the Bambala tongue.

Chim straightened cocking his head to listen. He seemed to feel better immediately. He began to chatter and moved cautiously in towards the man.

Bob was careful to make no sudden moves. Not until the ape had snuggled against him did he gently reach for the knife. To his relief, Chim seemed actually happy to give the weapon up. Bob's face and hands were bathed with sweat and he was shaking as he cut away his rope bonds.

He shoved the knife under his belt, ran to where Sheena had dropped his pistol. Then gun in hand, he raced toward the point where the jungle girl had left the clearing, praying that he would be able to follow her in the dark.

He was in luck for once. Tamba had left a clear trail where he had forced his way through the undergrowth, and within a distance of twenty yards, Bob hit a broad trail. From the angle at which the elephant had slanted into the trail, there was no doubting the direction Sheena had taken.

As he started to run, a hysterical jabbering broke out behind him. Chim, refusing to be abandoned, came rocketing out of the underbrush and in an amazing leap, fastened himself on Bob's back. He hugged himself against the white man so tightly, his small heart pounding with fright, that Bob couldn't bring himself to throw him off.

"All right," growled Bob. "You can't play Old Man of the Sea until we come in sight of the kraal. Then you're going back on your own!" And with that, he sprinted on down the trail with redoubled effort.

After Sheena left Bob tied in the clearing, she turned her whole mind to the task ahead of her. By the time she reached the Bambala kraal, the final details of her plan were perfected.

The walled village lay silent and sleeping in the waning moonlight. If there were sentries posted, they rested listlessly out of sight, lulled by the long, monotonous hours of early morning. The campfires had died to ash-whitened coals. Sheena had carefully selected this as the most propitious time for her raid.

The jungle girl urged Tamba straight up to the big main gate. In these first few moments, boldness would be her most valuable weapon. When the elephant slowed his pace before the gate, not yet understanding what was expected of him, Sheena drummed her heels behind his ears, drove him head-on against the massive barrier.

"Forward, O Mightiest of Elephants," she encouraged him. "Let these jackals know your strength."

There was a splintering impact. For the moment, the mammoth bull seemed to hesitate. Then the big gate tore free of crossbars and hinges, fell inward with a mighty crash.

And Tamba, exhilarated by the exploit, lifted his trunk and trumpeted an ear-splitting challenge to all comers as he carried his mistress into the kraal.

Two guards who had been dozing on a catwalk. Beside the gate, crouched frozen on their knees. Their eyes gleamed out of the darkness like great, circular bulbs as they stared at the ghostly apparition sweeping into the kraal.

"Tremble, you curs," cried Sheena, gesturing toward them with her spear, "for the curse of doom is on you! I, who am the servant of Gimshai, dread god of death, proclaim this doom on the Bambala!"

Of all the fearsome jungle deities, the all-powerful Gimshai struck the greatest terror into the hearts of black men. And as every native knew, the servants of Gimshai appeared in a thousand thousand different forms, struck at their chosen victims in unnumbered wars.

The terror of one of the guards was so great that after hearing Sheena's words he toppled forward senseless on the platform. The other man, quaking in every muscle, jerked upright on the platform. Mindless, nerve-tearing screams ripped from his throat.

He literally dove off the catwalk, hit the ground with bone-breaking force. But fear anaesthetized any physical hurt he sustained, and he was on his feet and running immediately, streaking down the main way of the kraal.

The guard's screams ripped the blanket of sleep from the village. Commands, shouts, the sound of running feet boiled up from the dark dusters of huts. Dazed men and women poured from narrow, skin-hung doorways.

And into the very middle of this suddenly aroused ant-heap rode Sheena. Straight down the principal way of the village she went, looking to neither right nor left, the one completely calm, collected person in all that howling throng.

She and the mammoth elephant seemed enveloped in a swirling, blue-white haze of light. Tamba seemed even more immense than he really was, and the din of his steady trumpeting, inspired by excitement and the scent of the Bambala, was indeed like the sound of doom.

As the blacks, crowding out to learn the cause of the disturbance, saw that white, statue-like figure that was Sheena, the loud furor died away like a fading echo. A low, frightened moan that could have been the keening of the wind over a wasteland swept back and back through the massing natives.

Then Sheena's voice, harsh and savage, was heard. "From the Black Hole of Death, from the Skull-Throne of the Terrible God himself, I bring you the curse of Gimshai.

"Look at me, O members of a jackal tribe! Look at me and tremble, for I am the Clawed Hand of Gimshai; I am the Net of the Eater of Souls; I am the Sword of the God of Death."

Her words drove into the minds of the Bambala like poisoned darts. Had she rehearsed her speech to Bob Reilly he would have thought it suicidal nonsense. But Sheena knew how to open the floodgates of fear in her audience.

The entire existence of these wild and primitive natives was a web of superstition. Any strange or unexplained phenomena they attributed to gods or demons. And their over-active imaginations seized on every untoward event and embroidered it with supernatural significance.

Even now as they gazed at the strange, chalk-white she-demon, their imaginations swiftly added a variety of details to what they thought they saw. There were some who saw in the whiteness of her face the dear outlines of a deathshead. Others saw her long hair, stiffly encrusted with the white liquid, as a mass of pale squirming snakes. Some would say afterwards her eyes were hollow black sockets, others that they were red coals of fire.

It would be said that the spear in her hand squirmed and wriggled like a living thing, that the eerie, elephant-like apparition she rode was no more than a mist through which one could see, that rivulets of cold flame ran outward along the ground where the creature's feet were placed.

Sheena's audience was especially impressionable on this night when practically the whole of its fighting strength was absent Excited by their triumph of the previous day, every warrior eagerly had sought to join the hunt for Bob Reilly and the jungle girl.

Left behind in the kraal were the untried youths, the men too old or sick for trekking, and the easily frightened mass of women and children.

Sheena had counted on the absence of the real fighting men as a major help in the carrying out of her colossal bluff.

Now as she heard the whimpering of the women, saw the crowd edge backward away from her, she boldly rode into the central clearing, abandoning any hope of retreat. She knew the crowd would mass around the open space, and if she were found out, that wall of humanity would prevent her from ever reaching the gate alive.

After the habit of the Bambala, both the prisoners and the loot gained in their attack on Bob's safari were kept on display in the clearing. The miserable bearers were crowded into a foul, make-shift pen like animals, and stacked near the enclosure were the packs they once had carried.

The great feast and the ceremony of dividing the spoils which always followed a battle triumph were being delayed until Bob and Sheena were captured.

Sheena headed the elephant toward the pen, wanting to free the prisoners and march them out of the kraal before the stunned tribesmen could collect their wits.

But suddenly two of the large cooking fires in the clearing flickered into life. Yellow tongues of flame reached along the edges of the dry wood which had been thrown hastily on the coals. Sheena understood then the purpose of the commands that had sounded in the first uproar of her entrance, for revealed in the mounting light was a hollow square of armed guards grouped about two men, the two most important men in the tribe.

One was Babuli, the immensely fat chieftain of the Bambala, a brutal, self-indulgent tyrant. The other was Nyag-Nyag, a tall, thin, one-eyed man with a hatchet face and the hunched posture of a crouching weasel.

Nyag-Nyag was the Bambala witchdoctor, and more than any other member of the tribe, he had reason to hate Sheena, for time and again the most potent magic he could make against her had proved ineffectual.

VII

Sheena instantly was disturbed when she saw the two tribal leaders with the ranks of hard-bitten guards ranged about them. She certainly hadn't counted on their presence. Improvising to meet this unexpected danger, she hastily changed her plans and halted Tamba.

Gesturing contemptuously with her spear, she cried, "Hai! So now I look upon the two chief jackals!"

The elephantine Babuli clearly was more shaken by her ghostly appearance than the witchdoctor. "Why—why—have you come here?" he asked weakly.

Sheena was silent for long, ominous moments. Then like the crack of a whip her voice lashed him. "I come to take your soul to ever-lasting torment! Even now, Gimshai wrathfully awaits your coming!"

The mammoth chieftain stumbled back a step, his great belly quivering. The harsh confidence with which she spoke turned his blood to ice.

"There is some terrible mistake," he quavered. "Never by word or deed have I shown disrespect for Gimshai! Aaiiee, he is the greatest of gods! In all the jungle, no one has sent him more souls than Babuli."

"It's too late to lie," Sheena said grimly. "You honor but one god, N'Koto, god of war, and it is he who has led you to your downfall. Two suns ago you made a cowardly attack upon the safari of one who holds the special favor of Gimshai. The Taker of Souls reached out his hand and saved this white man, saying for the destruction you had wrought you would pay with your. life. And so I have come to exact payment!"

Babuli seemed to be choking. His eyes stood out like round, red marbles. Poisoned by a lifetime of superstition, he felt that already the life-force was being sucked from his body, that the fluttering in his throat was his soul struggling to escape.

"Talk to her! Appease her!" he gasped to the witchdoctor. "You know more of gods and demons than I do. Promise anything—anything—if she will let me be."

With his one good eye, the witchdoctor had been glaring at Sheena. He was not as naive as Babuli, nor as superstitious as the other tribesmen. He had practiced too much trickery and deceit, pawned off too much humbug as magic, to be taken in easily by Sheena's tricks.

He sensed something familiar in this ghostly intruder, noted also how she sought to keep back out of the firelight. It seemed to him that every time an especially high leap of the flames lighted her mount that its eerie blue-white glow disappeared.

Yet because he was both a cunning man and a coward, Nyag-Nyag proceeded with care.

He pushed through the ranks of warriors, picked a blazing stick from the fire. He lifted the torch high as though to clearly light himself for Sheena's eyes.

"Hear me, O One Who Walks the Night," he said in a false, fawning voice. "I make no plea for my worthless, unimportant self, but I do plead for the noble Babuli."

He edged nearer to Tamba as he talked, narrowly watching the effect of the torchlight on the elephant's glowing whiteness.

"Never would Babuli knowingly offend the dread Taker of Souls," he continued. "If a wrong has been done by Babuli, he stands ready to make any gifts, offerings or sacrifices the god decrees. Intercede for us, O Great One, and the Bambala will honor you endlessly. Help us to right our unmeant wrong! You have only to speak and we will obey."

Relief surged through Sheena as she listened to Nyag-Nyag's abject beseeching. The feeling that she had triumphed lessened her wariness, so that she failed to divine the witchdoctor's purpose in coming so near.

"Gimshai is merciful, as are his servants," she said haughtily. "If you have the courage to accompany me into the Black Hole of Death to plead your case before the god himself, you may do so—remembering that if you fail, there can be no return."

Nyag-Nyag seemed to debate before muttering, "I have the courage."

Sheena stared at him. "But you must approach Gimshai with clean hands." She gestured at the imprisoned bearers and stacked loot. "You must give up the spoils of your cowardly attack. You must free the beards and give them bade their arms and you must furnish men to carry these packs to their destination."

The huge-bellied chieftain, who had been bathed in sweat as he waited for Sheena's answer, literally shouted his acceptance of her terms. He was concerned with his own safety only, and cared not a whit that he might be sending a large group of his followers to their death.

"All shall be as you say!" Babuli shouted hoarsely, not wanting to give the witchdoctor time to back out of his bargain. Then he turned to his guards in the same frenzied haste, crying, "Release the prisoners! Gather men enough to carry the packs! Quickly, you curs!"

But even as the chieftain spoke, Nyag-Nyag sprang back away from Tamba, swirling the torch about his head. "No!" he roared, "Let no man move."

Babuli was so aghast that it took him a moment to find his voice. His body quivered in outrage at this treachery. "I am chieftain here," he croaked.

"You're a fool, Babuli," snarled the witchdoctor, "as blind and stupid a fool as all these others!"

It was in Nyag-Nyag's mind that after tonight he would never again have to bend his knee to the fat chieftain. What he was about to do would make Babuli a laughingstock at the same time that it enhanced his own reputation as a wizard.

"Because I amuse myself by toying with this faker," the witchdoctor said, pointing at Sheena, "don't take my acting seriously. She is no demon, no servant or Gimshai."

"What are you saying?" squeaked the chieftain, seeing his chances of salvation being shattered before his eyes.

Nyag-Nyag laughed, thinly, baring his yellow teeth. "I'm saying this supposed demon is merely Tioto Nomi, the Forest Woman. I'm saying it takes more than children's tricks to fool the jungle's greatest wizard."

Dismay had wrenched Sheena stiffly upright. But her reaction was no different from that which shook Babuli and his tribesmen. The witchdoctor's words had exploded with the violence of a thunderbolt.

"You madman!" wailed Babuli. "You'll get us all killed. You know as well as I that our warriors are pursuing Tioto Nomi far across the jungle."

Nyag-Nyag had backed dose to the guards. He tossed away his torch, took a spear and shield from one of the blacks. Then he ran out into the open space between Sheena and the warriors.

"Watch this test, my simple Babuli," he sneered. "And you need not faint from terror, because the risk falls on me alone." His whole manner was supremely confident. "A thousand shields would not protect me from a servant of Gimshai, because such a servant would be able to kill with a glance—a sign—a thought."

The ugly laughter bubbled from his lips again. After tonight, his name would ring through the jungle.

"But one shield is protection enough against Tioto Nomi," he said, "because her only weapon is her spear. She has no magic powers. Watch while I prove it! And stand ready, guards, to strike her down when she betrays herself by trying to use her one, puny weapon."

Sheena sat stupefied, a knot of panic growing and spreading in her breast. The cunning, one-eyed dango had trapped her. She sought in futile desperation for some means of escape, knowing full well that the game was played out.

Nyag-Nyag was leaping and dancing in front of her, always careful to protect himself behind the thick, heavy shield of rhino hide. "Quickly, Tioto Nomi," he taunted, "loose your terrible magic. Kill me with a look! Kill me with a thought!"

A stifling hush gripped the kraal. In the shadows around the central clearing, black men crouched, afraid to breathe. Babuli leaned forward, his face like gray paste, his mouth hanging loosely open.

"Come, O Would-be Demon," the prancing wizard jeered, "I wait for you to strike. Why do you hesitate? You try my patience, make me weary of this farce."

Sheena's mouth was dust-dry. The death she had sought to save Bob Reilly from was to be hers. And now he was to be lost to her finally and forever.

An ominous muttering stirred the watching blacks. Nyag-Nyag's ridicule was having its effect. Already the guards were edging forward, their Wads tightening on their spears.

Sheena's own spear arm tensed. Her bluff was finished. At least, she would take a few of them with her. She gritted her teeth, prepared to send Tamba charging into the guards.

Nyag-Nyag's gloating laughter rang high. "Hear me, Tioto Nomi," he shrilled. "I spit on you and on your fathers! What greater insult can one give?"

His prancing and his high-pitched screams were too much for Tamba. The huge bull elephant lifted his trunk and trumpeted with ear-splitting violence. The very air shivered with the raging sound.

Nyag-Nyag looked up startled. Then a very strange thing happened. The hatchet-faced wizard gave a queer backward leap as though he had been struck a powerful blow. His face twisted in agony and he staggered.

He let the spear drop from his fingers, and the weight of the shield slowly drew his left arm down to his side. His stringy muscles began jerking and twitching.

His single eye bulged with terror. Then his long thin legs started to buckle. All at once his mouth strained wide and a great wash of blood rushed from his lips.

That was the end. Nyag-Nyag toppled forward on his face and lay still.

Tamba fell silent at almost that same moment. It was unbelievable that a native kraal could be so still. And in that profound hush, you could feel terror sweep like a black wind over the stunned natives,

Sheena was as shocked as the tribesmen. She stared blankly at the dead wizard. She hadn't moved a muscle to harm him, yet there lay the hated Nyag-Nyag, stiffening in death.

What miracle was this? What invisible power had reached out in her hour of need to strike down that human dango?

But the jungle girl was given no time to dwell on that mystery. Babuli's hysterical screams jolted her alert. The hog-fat chieftain had crumbled to his knees and was beseeching her not to kill-him, not to blame him for Nyag-Nyag's blasphemies. Tribesmen all about the clearing were groveling in abject terror.

They thought she had slain the wizard!

She moved swiftly to take advantage of the situation. Though so upset herself that she could barely keep her voice from trembling, Sheena sternly repeated the demands she had made before. And this time the prisoners were immediately freed and Babuli's disarmed guards hurriedly loaded themselves down with the stolen packs with no thought of opposing Sheena.

Babuli collapsed in a blubbering heap, but Sheena delegated four of the bearers to prod him to his feet with their spears. The remaining bearers she placed along both sides of the pack-laden Bambala.

"Now trek," she shouted. "And any man who causes trouble will join Nyag-Nyag in his ever-lasting torment."

Her threat sent the column through the kraal at a stumbling trot. All idea of resistance was gone from the Bambala. As she urged Tamba after the bearers, the natives pressed their faces in the dirt, afraid to look at her.

Once outside the kraal, she forged to the head of the column, leading it back along the trail toward where she had left Bob Reilly. But before she had gone very far, she heard a frantic chattering, saw an eerie, glowing little figure come skittering down the dim path toward her.

"Chim!" she cried in surprise, and with a quick command, she had the elephant swing the little ape up beside her.

Chim bounded into her arms, fairly sputtering with delight at finding his mistress again. Then Sheena's keen ears heard another sound. She looked up to see Bob advancing out of the darkness. Her initial thought was that he might still be angry at her.

But there was unutterable relief, not anger, in his voice as he exclaimed, "Thank heavens you're out of that place at last! You were crazy to take such a chance, but it was the most wonderful thing I've ever seen."

"You mean you saw what went on in the kraal?" she asked, surprised.

"I not only saw—thanks to Chim, not you," he said, "but I took a small part in the proceedings. I'll frankly admit that I could never have pulled off the bluff you did."

He told her then how when he reached the kraal the witchdoctor had just begun to taunt her. Since the natives were all concentrated in the center of the village, he was able to enter the gate unobserved. He had sneaked close to the clearing, climbed up on a pile of wood stacked beside a hut.

With his pistol, he had blasted Nyag-Nyag. The sound of the shot had been covered by Tamba's wrathful trumpeting. And the unholy fear that had struck into the Bambala when they saw their witchdoctor die, had kept them from suspecting that any hand but Gimshai's had slain Nyag-Nyag.

"So you were the one who saved me," she said wonderingly.

Bob laughed. "I believe I could say the same for you."

They were a mile further down the trail and the false dawn was graying the sky when Sheena halted the elephant.

Bob sat behind her on the forest giant's back. "What do we do now?" he asked.

She gave him a long, searching look. "You will take Babuli and his guards with you and see that they are punished. You'll have no more trouble with the Bambala, so you can easily reach white man's country with your records."

"You—you—aren't going out with me?" Bob was surprised and confused.

"This is my own land," she said, gesturing toward the dark jungle with her hand. "There are many things I can do to make it a better land. I have found myself tonight, as the old witchwoman once prophesied I would."

Her head lifted and she looked up at the brightening sky.

"But you can't stay here, a lone girl," said Bob. "I've grown very fond of you, Sheena. I want you to go with me. I thought that you and I . . ."

"Even if I wished it," she interrupted him gently, "I could not go with you. I am a priestess and more to the Abamas. They have been awaiting the day when I would be ready to lead them. And now I am ready. It would mean your certain death if you tried to take me away."

And so it was that a frowning, unhappy man a few minutes later watched Sheena ride away alone toward the Abama kraal. He stood there with the soft warmth of her good-bye kiss on his lips, vowing that Abama warriors or not, he would be back as soon as his trek to the coast was finished.

IN THE
SOUTH SEAS

THE HEATHEN

Jack London

I MET HIM FIRST IN A HURRICANE; AND THOUGH WE HAD GONE THROUGH THE hurricane on the same schooner, it was not until the schooner had gone to pieces under us that I first laid eyes on him. Without doubt I had seen him with the rest of the kanaka crew on board, but I had not consciously been aware of his existence, for the *Petite Jeanne* was rather overcrowded. In addition to her eight or ten kanaka seamen, her white captain, mate, and supercargo, and her six cabin passengers, she sailed from Rangiroa with something like eighty-five deck passengers—Paumotans and Tahitians, men, women, and children each with a trade box, to say nothing of sleeping mats, blankets, and clothes bundles.

The pearling season in the Paumotus was over, and all hands were returning to Tahiti. The six of us cabin passengers were pearl buyers. Two were Americans, one was Ah Choon (the whitest Chinese I have ever known), one was a German, one was a Polish Jew, and I completed the half dozen.

It had been a prosperous season. Not one of us had cause for complaint, nor one of the eighty-five deck passengers either. All had done well, and all were looking forward to a rest-off and a good time in Papeete.

Of course, the *Petite Jeanne* was overloaded. She was only seventy tons, and she had no right to carry a tithe of the mob she had on board. Beneath her hatches she was crammed and jammed with pearl-shell and copra. Even the trade room was packed full with shell. It was a miracle that the sailors could work her. There was no moving about the decks. They simply climbed back and forth along the rails.

In the night time they walked upon the sleepers, who carpeted the deck, I'll swear, two deep. Oh! And there were pigs and chickens on deck, and sacks of yams, while every conceivable place was festooned with strings of drinking cocoanuts and bunches of bananas. On both sides, between the fore and main shrouds, guys had been stretched, just low enough for the foreboom to swing clear; and from each of these guys at least fifty bunches of bananas were suspended.

It promised to be a messy passage, even if we did make it in the two or three days that would have been required if the southeast trades had been blowing fresh. But they weren't blowing fresh. After the first five hours the trade died away in a dozen or so gasping fans. The calm continued all that night and the next day—one of those glaring, glassy, calms, when the very thought of opening one's eyes to look at it is sufficient to cause a headache.

The second day a man died—an Easter Islander, one of the best divers that season in the lagoon. Smallpox—that is what it was; though how smallpox could come on board, when there had been no known cases ashore when we left Rangiroa, is beyond me. There it was, though—smallpox, a man dead, and three others down on their backs.

There was nothing to be done. We could not segregate the sick, nor could we care for them. We were packed like sardines. There was nothing to do but rot and die— that is, there was nothing to do after the night that followed the first death. On that night, the mate, the supercargo, the Polish Jew, and four native divers sneaked away in the large whale boat. They were never heard of again. In the morning the captain promptly scuttled the remaining boats, and there we were.

That day there were two deaths; the following day three; then it jumped to eight. It was curious to see how we took it. The natives, for instance, fell into a condition of dumb, stolid fear. The captain—Oudouse, his name was, a Frenchman—became very nervous and voluble. He actually got the twitches. He was a large fleshy man, weighing at least two hundred pounds, and he quickly became a faithful representation of a quivering jelly-mountain of fat.

The German, the two Americans, and myself bought up all the Scotch whiskey, and proceeded to stay drunk. The theory was beautiful—namely, if we kept ourselves soaked in alcohol, every smallpox germ that came into contact with us would immediately be scorched to a cinder. And the theory worked, though I must confess that neither Captain Oudouse nor Ah Choon were attacked by the disease either. The Frenchman did not drink at all, while Ah Choon restricted himself to one drink daily.

It was a pretty time. The sun, going into northern declination, was straight overhead. There was no wind, except for frequent squalls, which blew fiercely for from five minutes to half an hour, and wound up by deluging us with rain. After each squall, the awful sun would come out, drawing clouds of steam from the soaked decks.

The steam was not nice. It was the vapor of death, freighted with millions and millions of germs. We always took another drink when we saw it going up from the dead and dying, and usually we took two or three more drinks, mixing them exceptionally stiff. Also, we made it a rule to take an additional several each time they hove the dead over to the sharks that swarmed about us.

We had a week of it, and then the whiskey gave out. It is just as well, or I shouldn't be alive now. It took a sober man to pull through what followed, as you will agree when I mention the little fact that only two men did pull through. The other man was the heathen—at least, that was what I heard Captain Oudouse call him at the moment I first became aware of the heathen's existence. But to come back.

It was at the end of the week, with the whiskey gone, and the pearl buyers sober, that I happened to glance at the barometer that hung in the cabin companionway. Its normal register in the Paumotus was 29.90, and it was quite customary to see it vacillate between 29.85 and 30.00, or even 30.05; but to see it as I saw it, down to 29.62, was sufficient to sober the most drunken pearl buyer that ever incinerated smallpox microbes in Scotch whiskey.

I called Captain Oudouse's attention to it, only to be informed that he had watched it going down for several hours. There was little to do, but that little he did very well, considering the circumstances. He took off the light sails, shortened right down to storm canvas, spread life lines, and waited for the wind. His mistake lay in what he did after the wind came. He hove to on the port tack, which was the right thing to do south of the Equator, if—and there was the rub—*if* one were *not* in the direct path of the hurricane.

We were in the direct path. I could see that by the steady increase of the wind and the equally steady fall of the barometer. I wanted him to turn and run with the wind on the port quarter until the barometer ceased falling, and then to heave to. We argued till he was reduced to hysteria, but budge he would not. The worst of it was that I could not get the rest of the pearl buyers to back me up. Who was I, anyway, to know more about the sea and its ways than a properly qualified captain? was what was in their minds, I knew.

Of course, the sea rose with the wind frightfully; and I shall never forget the first three seas the *Petite Jeanne* shipped. She had fallen off, as vessels do at times when hove to, and the first sea made a clean breach. The life lines were only for the strong and well, and little good were they even for them when the women and children, the bananas and cocoanuts, the pigs and trade boxes, the sick and the dying, were swept along in a solid, screeching, groaning mass.

The second sea filled the *Petite Jeanne*'s decks flush with the rails; and, as her stern sank down and her bow tossed skyward, all the miserable dunnage of life and luggage poured aft. It was a human torrent. They came head first, feet first, sidewise, rolling over and over, twisting, squirming, writhing, and crumpling up. Now and again one caught a grip on a stanchion or a rope; but the weight of the bodies behind tore such grips loose.

One man I noticed fetch up, head on and square on, with the starboard bitt. His head cracked like an egg. I saw what was coming, sprang on top of the cabin, and from there into the mainsail itself. Ah Choon and one of the Americans tried to follow me, but I was one jump ahead of them. The American was swept away and over the stern like a piece of chaff. Ah Choon caught a spoke of the wheel, and swung in behind it. But a strapping Raratonga vahine (woman)—she must have weighed two hundred and fifty—brought up against him, and got an arm around his neck. He clutched the kanaka steersman with his other hand; and just at that moment the schooner flung down to starboard.

The rush of bodies and sea that was coming along the port runway between the cabin and the rail turned abruptly and poured to starboard. Away they went—vahine, Ah Choon, and steersman; and I swear I saw Ah Choon grin at me with philosophic resignation as he cleared the rail and went under.

The third sea—the biggest of the three—did not do so much damage. By the time it arrived nearly everybody was in the rigging. On deck perhaps a dozen gasping, half-drowned, and half-stunned wretches were rolling about or attempting to crawl into safety. They went by the board, as did the wreckage of the two remaining boats. The other pearl buyers and myself, between seas, managed to get about fifteen women and children into the cabin, and battened down. Little good it did the poor creatures in the end.

Wind? Out of all my experience I could not have believed it possible for the wind to blow as it did. There is no describing it. How can one describe a nightmare? It was the same way with that wind. It tore the clothes off our bodies. I say *tore them off*, and I mean it. I am not asking you to believe it. I am merely telling something that I saw and felt. There are times when I do not believe it myself. I went through it, and that is enough. One could not face that wind and live. It was a monstrous thing, and the most monstrous thing about it was that it increased and continued to increase.

Imagine countless millions and billions of tons of sand. Imagine this sand tearing along at ninety, a hundred, a hundred and twenty, or any other number of miles per hour. Imagine, further, this sand to be invisible, impalpable, yet to retain all the weight and density of sand. Do all this, and you may get a vague inkling of what that wind was like.

Perhaps sand is not the right comparison. Consider it mud, invisible, impalpable, but heavy as mud. Nay, it goes beyond that. Consider every molecule of air to be a mud-bank in itself. Then try to imagine the multitudinous impact of mud-banks. No; it is beyond me. Language may be adequate to express the ordinary conditions of life, but it cannot possibly express any of the conditions of so enormous a blast of wind. It would have been better had I stuck by my original intention of not attempting a description.

I will say this much: The sea, which had risen at first, was beaten down by that wind. More: it seemed as if the whole ocean had been sucked up in the maw of the hurricane, and hurled on through that portion of space which previously had been occupied by the air.

Of course, our canvas had gone long before. But Captain Oudouse had on the *Petite Jeanne* something I had never before seen on a South Sea schooner—a sea-anchor. It was a conical canvas bag, the mouth of which was kept open by a huge loop of iron. The sea-anchor was bridled something like a kite, so that it bit into the water as a kite bites into the air, but with a difference. The sea anchor remained just under the surface of the ocean in a perpendicular position. A long line, in turn, connected it with the schooner. As a result, the Petite Jeanne rode bow on to the wind and to what sea there was.

The situation really would have been favorable had we not been in the path of the storm. True, the wind itself tore our canvas out of the gaskets, jerked out our topmasts, and made a raffle of our running gear, but still we would have come through nicely had we not been square in front of the advancing storm center. That was what fixed us. I was in a state of stunned, numbed, paralyzed collapse from enduring the impact of the wind, and I think I was just about ready to give up and die when the center smote us. The blow we received was an absolute lull. There was not a breath of air. The effect on one was sickening.

Remember that for hours we had been at terrific muscular tension, withstanding the awful pressure of that wind. And then, suddenly, the pressure was removed. I know that I felt as though I was about to expand, to fly apart in all directions. It seemed as if every atom composing my body was repelling every other atom and was on the verge of rushing off irresistibly into space. But that lasted only for a moment. Destruction was upon us.

In the absence of the wind and pressure the sea rose. It jumped, it leaped, it soared straight toward the clouds. Remember, from every point of the compass that inconceivable wind was blowing in toward the center of calm. The result was that the seas sprang up from every point of the compass. There was no wind to check them. They popped up like corks released from the bottom of a pail of water. There was no system to them, no stability. They were hollow, maniacal seas. They were eighty feet high at the least. They were not seas at all. They resembled no sea a man had ever seen.

They were splashes, monstrous splashes—that is all. Splashes that were eighty feet high. Eighty! They were more than eighty. They went over our mastheads. They were spouts, explosions. They were drunken. They fell anywhere, anyhow. They jostled one another; they collided. They rushed together and collapsed upon one another, or fell apart like a thousand waterfalls all at once. It was no ocean any man had ever dreamed of, that hurricane center. It was confusion thrice confounded. It was anarchy. It was a hell pit of sea water gone mad.

The *Petite Jeanne*? I don't know. The heathen told me afterwards that he did not know. She was literally torn apart, ripped wide open, beaten into a pulp, smashed into kindling wood, annihilated. When I came to I was in the water, swimming automatically, though I was about two-thirds drowned. How I got there I had no recollection. I remembered seeing the *Petite Jeanne* fly to pieces at what must have been the instant that my own consciousness was buffeted out of me. But there I was, with nothing to do but make the best of it, and in that best there was little promise. The wind was blowing again, the sea was much smaller and more regular, and I knew that I had passed through the center. Fortunately, there were no sharks about. The hurricane had dissipated the ravenous horde that had surrounded the death ship and fed off the dead.

It was about midday when the *Petite Jeanne* went to pieces, and it must have been two hours afterwards when I picked up with one of her hatch covers. Thick rain was driving at the time; and it was the merest chance that flung me and the hatch cover together. A short length of line was trailing from the rope handle; and I knew that I was good for a day, at least, if the sharks did not return. Three hours later, possibly a little longer, sticking close to the cover, and with closed eyes, concentrating my whole soul upon the task of breathing in enough air to keep me going and at the same time of avoiding breathing in enough water to drown me, it seemed to me that I heard voices. The rain had ceased, and wind and sea were easing marvelously. Not twenty feet away from me, on another hatch cover were Captain Oudouse and the heathen. They were fighting over the possession of the cover—at least, the Frenchman was.

"Païen noir!" I heard him scream, and at the same time I saw him kick the kanaka.

Now, Captain Oudouse had lost all his clothes, except his shoes, and they were heavy brogans. It was a cruel blow, for it caught the heathen on the mouth and the point of the chin, half stunning him. I looked for him to retaliate, but he contented himself with swimming about forlornly a safe ten feet away. Whenever a fling of the sea threw him closer, the Frenchman, hanging on with his hands, kicked out at him with both feet. Also, at the moment of delivering each kick, he called the kanaka a black heathen.

"For two centimes I'd come over there and drown you, you white beast!" I yelled.

The only reason I did not go was that I felt too tired. The very thought of the effort to swim over was nauseating. So I called to the kanaka to come to me, and proceeded to share the hatch cover with him. Otoo, he told me his name was (pronounced ō-tō-ō); also, he told me that he was a native of Bora Bora, the most westerly of the Society

Group. As I learned afterward, he had got the hatch cover first, and, after some time, encountering Captain Oudouse, had offered to share it with him, and had been kicked off for his pains.

And that was how Otoo and I first came together. He was no fighter. He was all sweetness and gentleness, a love creature, though he stood nearly six feet tall and was muscled like a gladiator. He was no fighter, but he was also no coward. He had the heart of a lion; and in the years that followed I have seen him run risks that I would never dream of taking. What I mean is that while he was no fighter, and while he always avoided precipitating a row, he never ran away from trouble when it started. And it was "'Ware shoal!" when once Otoo went into action. I shall never forget what he did to Bill King. It occurred in German Samoa. Bill King was hailed the champion heavyweight of the American Navy. He was a big brute of a man, a veritable gorilla, one of those hard-hitting, rough-housing chaps, and clever with his fists as well. He picked the quarrel, and he kicked Otoo twice and struck him once before Otoo felt it to be necessary to fight. I don't think it lasted four minutes, at the end of which time Bill King was the unhappy possessor of four broken ribs, a broken forearm, and a dislocated shoulder blade. Otoo knew nothing of scientific boxing. He was merely a manhandler; and Bill King was something like three months in recovering from the bit of manhandling he received that afternoon on Apia beach.

But I am running ahead of my yarn. We shared the hatch cover between us. We took turn and turn about, one lying flat on the cover and resting, while the other, submerged to the neck, merely held on with his hands. For two days and nights, spell and spell, on the cover and in the water, we drifted over the ocean. Towards the last I was delirious most of the time; and there were times, too, when I heard Otoo babbling and raving in his native tongue. Our continuous immersion prevented us from dying of thirst, though the sea water and the sunshine gave us the prettiest imaginable combination of salt pickle and sunburn.

In the end, Otoo saved my life; for I came to lying on the beach twenty feet from the water, sheltered from the sun by a couple of cocoanut leaves. No one but Otoo could have dragged me there and stuck up the leaves for shade. He was lying beside me. I went off again; and the next time I came round, it was cool and starry night, and Otoo was pressing a drinking cocoanut to my lips.

We were the sole survivors of the *Petite Jeanne*. Captain Oudouse must have succumbed to exhaustion, for several days later his hatch cover drifted ashore without him. Otoo and I lived with the natives of the atoll for a week, when we were rescued by the French cruiser and taken to Tahiti. In the meantime, however, we had performed the ceremony of exchanging names. In the South Seas such a ceremony binds two men closer together than blood brothership. The initiative had been mine; and Otoo was rapturously delighted when I suggested it.

"It is well," he said, in Tahitian. "For we have been mates together for two days on the lips of Death."

"But Death stuttered," I smiled.

"It was a brave deed you did, master," he replied, "and Death was not vile enough to speak."

"Why do you 'master' me?" I demanded, with a show of hurt feelings. "We have exchanged names. To you I am Otoo. To me you are Charley. And between you and me, forever and forever, you shall be Charley, and I shall be Otoo. It is the way of the custom. And when we die, if it does happen that we live again somewhere beyond the stars and the sky, still shall you be Charley to me, and I Otoo to you."

"Yes, master," he answered, his eyes luminous and soft with joy.

"There you go!" I cried indignantly.

"What does it matter what my lips utter?" he argued. "They are only my lips. But I shall think Otoo always. Whenever I think of myself, I shall think of you. Whenever men call me by name, I shall think of you. And beyond the sky and beyond the stars, always and forever, you shall be Otoo to me. Is it well, master?"

I hid my smile, and answered that it was well.

We parted at Papeete. I remained ashore to recuperate; and he went on in a cutter to his own island, Bora Bora. Six weeks later he was back. I was surprised, for he had told me of his wife, and said that he was returning to her, and would give over sailing on far voyages.

"Where do you go, master?" he asked, after our first greetings.

I shrugged my shoulders. It was a hard question.

"All the world," was my answer—"all the world, all the sea, and all the islands that are in the sea."

"I will go with you," he said simply. "My wife is dead."

I never had a brother; but from what I have seen of other men's brothers, I doubt if any man ever had a brother that was to him what Otoo was to me. He was brother and father and mother as well. And this I know: I lived a straighter and better man because of Otoo. I cared little for other men, but I had to live straight in Otoo's eyes. Because of him I dared not tarnish myself. He made me his ideal, compounding me, I fear, chiefly out of his own love and worship and there were times when I stood close to the steep pitch of hell, and would have taken the plunge had not the thought of Otoo restrained me. His pride in me entered into me, until it became one of the major rules in my personal code to do nothing that would diminish that pride of his.

Naturally, I did not learn right away what his feelings were toward me. He never criticized, never censured; and slowly the exalted place I held in his eyes dawned upon me, and slowly I grew to comprehend the hurt I could inflict upon him by being anything less than my best.

For seventeen years we were together; for seventeen years he was at my shoulder, watching while I slept, nursing me through fever and wounds—ay, and receiving wounds in fighting for me. He signed on the same ships with me; and together we ranged the Pacific from Hawaii to Sydney Head, and from Torres Straits to the Galapagos. We blackbirded from the New Hebrides and the Line Islands over to the westward clear through the Louisades, New Britain, New Ireland, and New Hanover. We were wrecked three times—in the Gilberts, in the Santa Cruz group, and in the Fijis. And we traded and salved wherever a dollar promised in the way of pearl and pearl shell, copra, bêche-de-mer, hawkbill turtle shell, and stranded wrecks.

It began in Papeete, immediately after his announcement that he was going with me over all the sea, and the islands in the midst thereof. There was a club in those days in Papeete, where the pearlers, traders, captains, and riffraff of South Sea adventurers forgathered. The play ran high, and the drink ran high; and I am very much afraid that I kept later hours than were becoming or proper. No matter what the hour was when I left the club, there was Otoo waiting to see me safely home.

At first I smiled; next I chided him. Then I told him flatly that I stood in need of no wet-nursing. After that I did not see him when I came out of the club. Quite by accident, a week or so later, I discovered that he still saw me home, lurking across the street among the shadows of the mango-trees. What could I do? I know what I did do.

Insensibly I began to keep better hours. On wet and stormy nights, in the thick of the folly and the fun, the thought would persist in coming to me of Otoo keeping his dreary vigil under the dripping mangoes. Truly, he made a better man of me. Yet he was not strait-laced. And he knew nothing of common Christian morality. All the people on Bora Bora were Christians; but he was a heathen, the only unbeliever on the island, a gross materialist, who believed that when he died he was dead. He believed merely in fair play and square dealing. Petty meanness, in his code, was almost as serious as wanton homicide; and I do believe that he respected a murderer more than a man given to small practices.

Concerning me, personally, he objected to my doing anything that was hurtful to me. Gambling was all right. He was an ardent gambler himself. But late hours, he explained, were bad for one's health. He had seen men who did not take care of themselves die of fever. He was no teetotaler, and welcomed a stiff nip any time when it was wet work in the boats. On the other hand, he believed in liquor in moderation. He had seen many men killed or disgraced by square-face or Scotch.

Otoo had my welfare always at heart. He thought ahead for me, weighed my plans, and took a greater interest in them than I did myself. At first, when I was unaware of this interest of his in my affairs, he had to divine my intentions, as, for instance, at Papeete, when I contemplated going partners with a knavish fellow-countryman on a guano venture. I did not know he was a knave. Nor did any white man in Papeete. Neither did Otoo know, but he saw how thick we were getting, and found out for me, and without my asking him. Native sailors from the ends of the seas knock about on the beach in Tahiti; and Otoo, suspicious merely, went among them till he had gathered sufficient data to justify his suspicions. Oh, it was a nice history, that of Randolph Waters. I couldn't believe it when Otoo first narrated it; but when I sheeted it home to Waters he gave in without a murmur, and got away on the first steamer to Aukland.

At first, I am free to confess, I couldn't help resenting Otoo's poking his nose into my business. But I knew that he was wholly unselfish; and soon I had to acknowledge his wisdom and discretion. He had his eyes open always to my main chance, and he was both keen-sighted and far-sighted. In time he became my counselor, until he knew more of my business than I did myself. He really had my interest at heart more than I did. Mine was the magnificent carelessness of youth, for I preferred romance to dollars, and adventure to a comfortable billet with all night in. So it was well that I had some one to look out for me. I know that if it had not been for Otoo, I should not be here to-day.

Of numerous instances, let me give one. I had had some experience in blackbirding before I went pearling in the Paumotus. Otoo and I were on the beach in Samoa—we really were on the beach and hard aground—when my chance came to go as recruiter on a blackbird brig. Otoo signed on before the mast; and for the next half-dozen years, in as many ships, we knocked about the wildest portions of Melanesia. Otoo saw to it that he always pulled stroke-oar in my boat. Our custom in recruiting labor was to land the recruiter on the beach. The covering boat always lay on its oars several hundred feet off shore, while the recruiter's boat, also lying on its oars, kept afloat on the edge of the beach. When I landed with my trade goods, leaving my steering sweep apeak, Otoo left his stroke position and came into the stern-sheets, where a Winchester lay ready to hand under a flap of canvas. The boat's crew was also armed, the Sniders concealed under canvas flaps that ran the length of the gunwales. While I was busy arguing and persuading the woolly-headed cannibals to come and labor on the Queensland plantations Otoo kept watch. And often and often his low voice warned me of suspicious actions and impending treachery. Sometimes it was the quick shot from his rifle, knocking a native over, that was the first warning I received. And in my rush to the boat his hand was always there to jerk me flying aboard. Once, I remember, on *Santa Anna*, the boat grounded just as the trouble began. The covering boat was dashing to our assistance, but the several score of savages would have wiped us out before it arrived. Otoo took a flying leap ashore, dug both hands into the trade-goods, and scattered tobacco, beads, tomahawks, knives, and calicoes in all directions.

This was too much for the woolly-heads. While they scrambled for the treasures, the boat was shoved clear, and we were aboard and forty feet away. And I got thirty recruits off that very beach in the next four hours.

The particular instance I have in mind was on Malaita, the most savage island in the easterly Solomons. The natives had been remarkably friendly; and how were we to know that the whole village had been taking up a collection for over two years with which to buy a white man's head? The beggars are all head-hunters, and they especially esteem a white man's head. The fellow who captured the head would receive the whole collection. As I say, they appeared very friendly; and on this day I was fully a hundred yards down the beach from the boat. Otoo had cautioned me; and, as usual when I did not heed him, I came to grief.

The first I knew, a cloud of spears sailed out of the mangrove swamp at me. At least a dozen were sticking into me. I started to run, but tripped over one that was fast in my calf, and went down. The woolly-heads made a run for me, each with a long-handled, fantail tomahawk with which to hack off my head. They were so eager for the prize that they got in one another's way. In the confusion, I avoided several hacks by throwing myself right and left on the sand.

Then Otoo arrived—Otoo the manhandler. In some way he had got hold of a heavy war club, and at close quarters it was a far more efficient weapon than a rifle. He was right in the thick of them, so that they could not spear him, while their tomahawks seemed worse than useless. He was fighting for me, and he was in a true Berserker rage. The way he handled that club was amazing. Their skulls squashed like overripe oranges. It was not until he had driven them back, picked me up in his arms, and started to run, that he received his first wounds. He arrived in the boat with four spear thrusts, got his Winchester, and with it got a man for every shot. Then we pulled aboard the schooner, and doctored up.

Seventeen years we were together. He made me. I should to-day be a supercargo, a recruiter, or a memory, if it had not been for him.

"You spend your money, and you go out and get more," he said one day. "It is easy to get money now. But when you get old, your money will be spent, and you will not be able to go out and get more. I know, master. I have studied the way of white men. On the beaches are many old men who were young once, and who could get money just like you. Now they are old, and they have nothing, and they wait about for the young men like you to come ashore and buy drinks for them.

"The black boy is a slave on the plantations. He gets twenty dollars a year. He works hard. The overseer does not work hard. He rides a horse and watches the black boy work. He gets twelve hundred dollars a year. I am a sailor on the schooner. I get fifteen dollars a month. That is because I am a good sailor. I work hard. The captain has a double awning, and drinks beer out of long bottles. I have never seen him haul a rope or pull an oar. He gets one hundred and fifty dollars a month. I am a sailor. He is a navigator. Master, I think it would be very good for you to know navigation."

Otoo spurred me on to it. He sailed with me as second mate on my first schooner, and he was far prouder of my command than I was myself. Later on it was:

"The captain is well paid, master; but the ship is in his keeping, and he is never free from the burden. It is the owner who is better paid—the owner who sits ashore with many servants and turns his money over."

"True, but a schooner costs five thousand dollars—an old schooner at that," I objected. "I should be an old man before I saved five thousand dollars."

"There be short ways for white men to make money," he went on, pointing ashore at the cocoanut-fringed beach.

We were in the Solomons at the time, picking up a cargo of ivory nuts along the east coast of Guadalcanal.

"Between this river mouth and the next it is two miles," he said. "The flat land runs far back. It is worth nothing now. Next year—who knows?—or the year after, men will pay much money for that land. The anchorage is good. Big steamers can lie close up. You can buy the land four miles deep from the old chief for ten thousand sticks of tobacco, ten bottles of square-face, and a Snider, which will cost you, maybe, one hundred dollars. Then you place the deed with the commissioner; and the next year, or the year after, you sell and become the owner of a ship."

I followed his lead, and his words came true, though in three years, instead of two. Next came the grasslands deal on Guadalcanar—twenty thousand acres, on a governmental nine hundred and ninety-nine years' lease at a nominal sum. I owned the lease for precisely ninety days, when I sold it to a company for half a fortune. Always it was Otoo who looked ahead and saw the opportunity. He was responsible for the salving of the *Doncaster*—bought in at auction for a hundred pounds, and clearing three thousand after every expense was paid. He led me into the Savaii plantation and the cocoa venture on Upolu.

We did not go seafaring so much as in the old days. I was too well off. I married, and my standard of living rose; but Otoo remained the same old-time Otoo, moving about the house or trailing through the office, his wooden pipe in his mouth, a shilling undershirt on his back, and a four-shilling lava-lava about his loins. I could not get him to spend money. There was no way of repaying him except with love, and God knows he got that in full measure from all of us. The children worshipped him; and if he had been spoilable, my wife would surely have been his undoing.

The children! He really was the one who showed them the way of their feet in the world practical. He began by teaching them to walk. He sat up with them when they were sick. One by one, when they were scarcely toddlers, he took them down to the lagoon, and made them into amphibians. He taught them more than I ever knew of the habits of fish and the ways of catching them. In the bush it was the same thing. At seven, Tom knew more woodcraft than I ever dreamed existed. At six, Mary went over the Sliding Rock without a quiver, and I have seen strong men balk at that feat. And when Frank had just turned six he could bring up shillings from the bottom in three fathoms.

"My people in Bora Bora do not like heathen—they are all Christians; and I do not like Bora Bora Christians," he said one day, when I, with the idea of getting him to spend some of the money that was rightfully his, had been trying to persuade him to make a visit to his own island in one of our schooners—a special voyage which I had hoped to make a record breaker in the matter of prodigal expense.

I say one of *our* schooners, though legally at the time they belonged to me. I struggled long with him to enter into partnership.

"We have been partners from the day the *Petite Jeanne* went down," he said at last. "But if your heart so wishes, then shall we become partners by the law. I have no work to do, yet are my expenses large. I drink and eat and smoke in plenty—it costs much, I know. I do not pay for the playing of billiards, for I play on your table; but still the money goes. Fishing on the reef is only a rich man's pleasure. It is shocking, the cost of hooks and cotton line. Yes; it is necessary that we be partners by the law. I need the money. I shall get it from the head clerk in the office."

So the papers were made out and recorded. A year later I was compelled to complain.

"Charley," said I, "you are a wicked old fraud, a miserly skinflint, a miserable land crab. Behold, your share for the year in all our partnership has been thousands of dollars. The head clerk has given me this paper. It says that in the year you have drawn just eighty-seven dollars and twenty cents."

"Is there any owing me?" he asked anxiously.

"I tell you thousands and thousands," I answered.

His face brightened, as with an immense relief.

"It is well," he said. "See that the head clerk keeps good account of it. When I want it, I shall want it, and there must not be a cent missing.

"If there is," he added fiercely, after a pause, "it must come out of the clerk's wages."

And all the time, as I afterwards learned, his will, drawn up by Carruthers, and making me sole beneficiary, lay in the American consul's safe.

But the end came, as the end must come to all human associations. It occurred in the Solomons, where our wildest work had been done in the wild young days, and where we were once more—principally on a holiday, incidentally to look after our holdings on Florida Island and to look over the pearling possibilities of the Mboli Pass. We were lying at Savo, having run in to trade for curios.

Now, Savo is alive with sharks. The custom of the woolly-heads of burying their dead in the sea did not tend to discourage the sharks from making the adjacent waters a hangout. It was my luck to be coming aboard in a tiny, overloaded, native canoe, when the thing capsized. There were four woolly-heads and myself in it, or rather, hanging to it. The schooner was a hundred yards away.

I was just hailing for a boat when one of the woolly-heads began to scream. Holding on to the end of the canoe, both he and that portion of the canoe were dragged under several times. Then he loosed his clutch and disappeared. A shark had got him.

The three remaining niggers tried to climb out of the water upon the bottom of the canoe. I yelled and cursed and struck at the nearest with my fist, but it was no use. They were in a blind funk. The canoe could barely have supported one of them. Under the three it upended and rolled sidewise, throwing them back into the water.

I abandoned the canoe and started to swim toward the schooner, expecting to be picked up by the boat before I got there. One of the niggers elected to come with me, and we swam along silently, side by side, now and again putting our faces into the water and peering about for sharks. The screams of the man who stayed by the canoe informed us that he was taken. I was peering into the water when I saw a big shark pass directly beneath me. He was fully sixteen feet in length. I saw the whole thing. He got the woolly-head by the middle, and away he went, the poor devil, head, shoulders, and arms out of the water all the time, screeching in a heart-rending way. He was carried along in this fashion for several hundred feet, when he was dragged beneath the surface.

I swam doggedly on, hoping that that was the last unattached shark. But there was another. Whether it was one that had attacked the natives earlier, or whether it was one that had made a good meal elsewhere, I do not know. At any rate, he was not in such haste as the others. I could not swim so rapidly now, for a large part of my effort was devoted to keeping track of him. I was watching him when he made his first attack. By good luck I got both hands on his nose, and, though his momentum nearly shoved me under, I managed to keep him off. He veered clear, and began circling about again. A second time I escaped him by the same manœuvre. The third rush was a miss on both sides. He sheered at the moment my hands should have landed on his nose, but his sandpaper hide (I had on a sleeveless undershirt) scraped the skin off one arm from elbow to shoulder.

By this time I was played out, and gave up hope. The schooner was still two hundred feet away. My face was in the water, and I was watching him manoeuvre for another attempt, when I saw a brown body pass between us. It was Otoo.

"Swim for the schooner, master!" he said. And he spoke gayly, as though the affair was a mere lark. "I know sharks. The shark is my brother."

I obeyed, swimming slowly on, while Otoo swam about me, keeping always between me and the shark, foiling his rushes and encouraging me.

"The davit tackle carried away, and they are rigging the falls," he explained, a minute or so later, and then went under to head off another attack.

By the time the schooner was thirty feet away I was about done for. I could scarcely move. They were heaving lines at us from on board, but they continually fell short. The shark, finding that it was receiving no hurt, had become bolder. Several times it nearly got me, but each time Otoo was there just the moment before it was too late. Of course, Otoo could have saved himself any time. But he stuck by me.

"Good-by, Charley! I'm finished!" I just managed to gasp.

I knew that the end had come, and that the next moment I should throw up my hands and go down.

But Otoo laughed in my face, saying:

"I will show you a new trick. I will make that shark feel sick!"

He dropped in behind me, where the shark was preparing to come at me.

"A little more to the left!" he next called out. "There is a line there on the water. To the left, master—to the left!"

I changed my course and struck out blindly. I was by that time barely conscious. As my hand closed on the line I heard an exclamation from on board. I turned and looked. There was no sign of Otoo. The next instant he broke surface. Both hands were off at the wrist, the stumps spouting blood.

"Otoo!" he called softly. And I could see in his gaze the love that thrilled in his voice.

Then, and then only, at the very last of all our years, he called me by that name.

"Good-by, Otoo!" he called.

Then he was dragged under, and I was hauled aboard, where I fainted in the captain's arms.

And so passed Otoo, who saved me and made me a man, and who saved me in the end. We met in the maw of a hurricane, and parted in the maw of a shark, with seventeen intervening years of comradeship, the like of which I dare to assert has never befallen two men, the one brown and the other white. If Jehovah be from His high place watching every sparrow fall, not least in His kingdom shall be Otoo, the one heathen of Bora Bora.

A GULF OF WATER

Lynn Montross

T HE MEDICAL SCIENCE HAS ITS OWN MEASURE OF A MAN. IT KNOWS ALMOST to an exact degree just how much of this and how much of that the human body can stand and still retain a beating of the heart. It knows, for instance, that there is but little variation in the amount of fever required to scorch out the life of one man and the amount that will bring to and end the mortal career of another.

But science has practically stopped at that point. It has never determined tests and experiments that were calculated to measure the spirit of a man—that abstract spark from within that almost overleaps death itself and rises triumphant from the shroud.

For there's seldom anything in a man's appearance by which you can accurately gauge his spirit. Your cursing, swashbuckling pirate may in reality be a faint sulker who is crushed at his first reverse. The hunchback cobbler who mends your shoes may be a giant.

There is a story told by seamen who are familiar with the South Seas which goes to prove that the size of a man's body, his age or his appearance has little to do with the mighty spark from within which dominates him.

Banana Island, so the story runs, is a small one even as South Sea islands go. It is quite a distance from the beaten paths of commerce but trading vessels from Papeete come to its tiny, coral-studded harbor a few times each year to put on a load of smelly copra. Outside of these visits white men are seldom seen there. The place is so utterly insignificant and out of the way that few know of its existence.

The isle has an area of perhaps ten square miles and a population of several hundred natives. It has about the usual assortment of violent odors, tangled foliage and greasy heat characteristic of the region.

As you set foot on the sandy beach of Banana Island you know immediately that you are in a spot of enchantment, a spot hidden away from the rest of the world. Banana-trees with huge, ragged leaves, are in a thicket close to the shore.

Meandering its way through them is a little path that leads to the one village on the isle.

You follow the path with the feeling that you are the first white man who ever set foot there. The air is sickly sweet with the scent of the great white flowers underfoot.

Graceful coconut-palms, mangoes and flamboyants mingle in a riot of scarlet and yellow through which the intense blue of the sky can be seen.

Banana Island resembles the places of which the poet sang in that "only man is vile." You realize this fact as you follow the path and approach the clearing. A sickening stench assails your nostrils from the countless coconuts split in two and placed in the sun by the native women. There are other odors, less powerful perhaps, but fully as nauseous.

You see a collection of thatched shacks. Lolling about in them or just outside are natives, herded together in gaping indolence. Just to the rear of the shack stands a two-room bungalow of unpainted wood almost hidden by the coconut-palms. This is the residence of Motu, the king of Banana Island.

At a glance it could be seen that Motu was of different blood from the rest of the natives. His wrinkled skin was lighter in color and his features sharper. Some say that he had a dash of Chinese blood, others aver that he was part white.

He had landed on the island from parts unknown some twenty years before. Before he'd been there a week he displayed a decided talent for government. Without any violence he induced the former king to abdicate. He took control and gave Banana Island the only peace and prosperity that the forsaken spot had ever known.

Motu didn't make much of a kingly appearance. He could not have been more than five feet tall and appeared to be at least seventy years of age. Naked except for a *pareo* of trade-cotton about his loins, his grimacing face lined with deep furrows and with one arm withered and helpless at his side, he resembled a crippled chimpanzee more than a human being.

Yet there was something regal about the result she achieved. Weak as he was physically, the old man ruled the island for a score of years without any of the natives trying to deny his authority. It remained for the white man to bring old Motu to grief.

The trading-ship had left the island on the night before on its way back to Tahiti. But two men of its motley crew stayed behind.

Morning broke bright and hot, the sticky heat of the tropics. The two men were sleeping soddenly on the beach. About them droning flies buzzed a lulling accompaniment to the lazy swish of the waves. An occasional breeze wafted the sickening smell of drying copra from the interior of the island.

Eaves, the cockney, shook the man beside him, a renegade beachcomber from the states who went by the name of Powell.

"Blime," he growled, "if you want a swig for an eye-opener, you better come to life."

The two of them finished the square black bottle to the last fiery drop.

Eaves was pretty well known in the South Seas. Dark and unsavory tales were told of him. The natives bore him a respect liberally tinged with fear. Nobody was just certain as to how he made the money that enabled him indulge his long-drawn, hideous drunks at Papeete and other ports.

Powell was his boon companion. Questions concerning a body's past are never asked among derelict white men in the South Seas, but it was whispered that Powell was a half-breed and had left the States shortly after a murder on the Dakota reservation.

"I'm—well thinkin'" said the cockney, after he had returned from throwing a dash of salt water in his face, "that we ought to gone back with the ship to Papeete."

"No," answered Powell. "No such thing. I got this straight from one of the natives in Tahiti. The old bird that runs this island has been trading in copra for fifteen or twenty years. He runs his outfit of natives and none of 'em get a cent of what he takes in. The old boy salts it down for himself. He's got a fortune in pearls, the natives tell me, hid away somewhere around here. Now if you an' me—"

"There ain't no bloomin' 'if' about it," the cockney interrupted with a crafty gleam in his little eyes. "Any pearls around here, an we'll make the ol' blighter tell where they're hid. Lots of ways to make 'em talk, myte!"

The renegades roused themselves from their bedin the sand and waded over to where the boat was. They paddled it over a few hundred feet to where a thicket crept of the water's edge and carefully concealed it with leaves.

"There, we're set," approved Powell. "All ready for a quick getaway."

The two men took the path that led to the village. At a distance they could hardly be distinguished from natives. Both were clad only in the *pareo*—a strip of trade-cotton about the loins and hanging to the knees—and between sunburn and dirt were quite brown. Their hair and bears were long and unkempt.

As they neared the collection of thatched huts, several of the natives met them. None of the blacks showed the least suspicion of the white men. They had dealt only with traders before and did not know the wiles and treachery that the beachcomber can sometimes display in the South Seas. Without any parley they took Eaves and Powell up to old Moto's dwelling. The old man was waiting in the doorway to greet them when they got there.

"He ain't no bloomin' South Sea native," whispered Eaves. "The blighter's got white or Chink blood."

Powell struck up an ogling acquaintance with one of the native women while Eaves, who was the only one of the two familiar with Motu's several dialects, entered the hut. After a few moments Eaves reappeared and the two were ceremoniously led to an empty hut by the old man and told it was theirs as long as they were the guests of Banana Island.

Old Motu beamed upon them. It was evident that he placed full trust in them and took a simple pride in his hospitality.

"What'd you find out?" Powell asked eagerly, as soon as the two were alone in the hut.

"The old blighter's goin' to be easy for the likes of me an' you," Eaves answered with a sly grin. "I tells him the ship went away and left us but that we was going to rest for a day, then hit out in our boat. He takes it all in."

Powell went to the door of the hut and sniffed.

"You can tell they're drying lots of copra here," he said, "an' there's good money in it these days. Bet the old bird's got enough money salted away to get us out of these—islands."

Powell licked a parched lip at the thought of the liquor in square-faced bottles that money would buy. He made a little hole in the thatched wall and lay down with his eye glued to the opening.

"Sooner the better," he said with an ominous twist of the lip.

Powell knew the indolent habits of the tropics. He knew that the natives were more than usually torpid from the roast-pig feast they had gorged at on the night before. By noon the heat from the overhead sun was terrific. An immense solitude brooded over the coconut-palms. All the inmates of the huts were in the shade, asleep.

Powell gave a final inspection through the peep-hole and turned away with a satisfied look.

"Now's our time!" he whispered savagely, wiping a rivulet of perspiration from his grimy forehead. "Everybody's snoozin'. We'll just step out like we're goin' for a drink."

The two renegades leisurely walked over towards Motu's shack. In the doorway sat a sentry, his head on his chest, sound asleep. Powell and Eaves noiselessly slipped past him and entered the hut.

Five minutes later they were hurrying down a little path toward the seashore carrying old Motu, who was bound hand and foot. Back in the hut the guard lay, a ragged rent in his throat. It had taken but a little while and not a soul had awakened.

"Here's the place," muttered Powell, pointing ahead to a secluded clump of banana-trees almost within reach of the lazy waves. Nothin' can be heard here. Them natives won't wake up until sundown anyway.

Old Motu, who couldn't have weighed more than ninety pounds, was unceremoniously dumped to the ground like a sack of meal. The two white men wasted little time on preliminaries. Eaves bent down and hissed in the old man's ear.

"Where's them pearls?" he demanded in a native dialect.

Old Motu's face twisted into a grimace of ferocity. His black eyes met Eaves' with a murderous gleam, but he didn't so much as open his lips. The cockney straightened up with a curse and he deliberately kicked his victim in the face.

For the next ten minutes Powell and Eaves took turns beating and kicking the tightly bound king of Banana Island. Old Motu received the blows without a groan or showing the least expression of pain on his features. He lay among the leaves so still that it seemed he had no nerves. The two men constantly drilled into his ears the same question—

"Where's them pearls?"

Motu's only answer was a look of contempt from his narrowed black eyes.

In sheer exhaustion the two renegades desisted. Powell looked at his companion in puzzled desperation.

"What if—"

"We've got to," Eaves interrupted. "Got to give him the water-cure. Know what that is? You pour water down a man till he either busts or gives in. Hate to do that even to a native, but we want them pearls."

The cockney searched around in the bushes until he found an old coconut shell. He took it to the near-by shore and brought it back brimming full of salt-water. The he picked up a hollow section of bamboo and trimmed it with his knife.

Motu lay motionless among the leaves and vines, but this eyes followed every move with a gleam of understanding. It was evident that he realized what was impending, but he showed no fear.

Eaves put his knee on old Motu's thin chest and began to insert the bamboo between the aged victim's tightly clenched teeth. It took the efforts of both men for a full five minutes before the hollow section was finally in the old man's mouth.

The cockney made a funnel out of a large leaf. Powell began slowly to pour the acrid salt-water down the king's throat, tightly gripping his nose so that he would have to swallow in order to breathe.

A picture of the terrible moments to come must have flashed through Motu's brain, but his eyes still gleamed defiance.

He even shook his head in a decided negative when, after the whole shell of water had been poured down his throat, Eaves again asked him the location of the pearls with a promise of freedom if he told.

After the refusal Powell went down to the seashore and returned with the coconut-shell filled with more salt-water. One forced gulp after another, the burning contents were poured down the old man's tortured throat. At times the victim choked and strangled as some of the fluid was involuntarily drawn into his lungs. But he firmly shook his head when Powell came to the last few drops in the shell and the cockney put the question to him again.

"Blime, he's got nerve!" Eaves exclaimed with grudging admirations, wiping the streams of sweat from his face.

More salt-water was brought. Powell gripped old Motu's nose between a horny thumb and forefinger. He poured the water into the funnel with infinite slowness so that the victim would feel the increasing pain more acutely.

Several times Powell had to stop his pouring while the writhing old man coughed and retched. But after the question had been asked and no answer obtained, the two persecutors kept on remorselessly until the last drop had disappeared from the bottom of the shell.

"He can't last much longer," said Eaves in a tone that was far from confident. "He's got to give in."

But the cockney dropped his eyes from the flaming look given him by his victim.

By this time old Motu's stomach was distended so abnormally that he appeared as a hideous, misshapen gnome. His breath came in moaning, wheezing gasps as each nerve in his abdomen shrieked a protest against the torture. The horrible enlargement of his stomach barely left room for his heart and lungs to function. But the aged victim's eyes were alive with contempt and hatred.

Powell came back with a fourth shell of sea-water and the torture was resumed.

A drop or two at a time the bitter fluid trickled down old Motu's throat until it seem that the victim must burst from the terrible pressured within. Powell's hand was beginning to tremble so that he often spilled the water on the ground. Suddenly he stopped and dropped the shell.

"My ——!" he said hoarsely. "We've got to quit—for a while anyway. I can't pour any more."

Motu lay without moving in the tangled foliage, a bloated monstrosity seemingly more dead than alive, excepting for his flaming eyes.

With a sort of awe Eaves took out his knife and cut the cords that bound the victims gnarled wrists. The old man gasped and feebly rolled over on his side.

"Aye," said the cockney, a fearful note in his voice. "It's —— well time we got out of this —— place. Let's make for the boat."

The two renegades stopped for a final look at their victim. Then happened the incident that is still told when men gather around beach-fires in the South Seas.

With a terrible groan old Motu brought his agonized form up to a sitting position. Before the spellbound gaze of the two white men the native reached over and grasped the coconut shell at their feet in which there still remained a few swallows of water.

He tremblingly brought the shell up to his bleeding lips. Then he closed his eyes and with a tremendous effort took one—two—three large gulps of salt-water.

He threw the shell away—drained empty.

Eaves and Powell gave one ghastly look into the old man's flaming eyes. They turned and ran.

THE BEACH OF FALESÁ

Robert Louis Stevenson

I. A South-Sea Bridal

I saw that island first when it was neither night nor morning. The moon was to the west, setting, but still broad and bright. To the east, and right amidships of the dawn, which was all pink, the day-star sparkled like a diamond. The land breeze blew in our faces, and smelt strong of wild lime and vanilla; other things besides, but these were the most plain; and the chill of it set me sneezing. I should say I had been for years on a low island near the line, living for the most part solitary among natives. Here was a fresh experience; even the tongue would be quite strange to me; and the look of these woods and mountains, and the rare smell of them, renewed my blood.

The captain blew out the binnacle-lamp.

"There!" said he, "there goes a bit of smoke, Mr. Wiltshire, behind the break of the reef. That's Falesá, where your station is, the last village to the east; nobody lives to windward—I don't know why. Take my glass, and you can make the houses out."

I took the glass; and the shores leaped nearer, and I saw the tangle of the woods and the breach of the surf, and the brown roofs and the black insides of houses peeped among the trees.

"Do you catch a bit of white there to the east'ard?" the captain continued. "That's your house. Coral built, stands high, veranda you could walk on three abreast; best station in the South Pacific. When old Adams saw it, he took and shook me by the hand. 'I've dropped into a soft thing here,' says he. 'So you have,' says I, 'and time too!' Poor Johnny! I never saw him again but the once, and then he had changed his tune—couldn't get on with the natives, or the whites, or something; and the next time we came round there, he was dead and buried. I took and put up a bit of a stick to him: 'John Adams, *obit* eighteen and sixty-eight. Go thou and do likewise.' I missed that man. I never could see much harm in Johnny."

"What did he die of?" I inquired.

"Some kind of sickness," says the captain. "It appears it took him sudden. Seems he got up in the night, and filled up on Pain-Killer and Kennedy's Discovery. No go—he was booked beyond Kennedy. Then he had tried to open a case of gin. No go again—not strong enough. Then he must have turned to and run out on the veranda, and capsized over the rail. When they found him, the next day, he was clean crazy—carried on all the time about somebody watering his copra. Poor John!"

"Was it thought to be the island?" I asked.

"Well, it was thought to be the island, or the trouble, or something," he replied. "I never could hear but what it was a healthy place. Our last man, Vigours, never turned a hair. He left because of the beach—said he was afraid of Black Jack and Case and Whistling Jimmie, who was still alive at the time, but got drowned soon afterward when drunk. As for old Captain Randall, he's been here any time since eighteen-forty, forty-five. I never could see much harm in Billy, nor much change. Seems as if he might live to be Old Kafoozleum. No, I guess it's healthy." "There's a boat coming now," said I. "She's right in the pass; looks to be a sixteen-foot whale; two white men in the stern-sheets."

"That's the boat that drowned Whistling Jimmie!" cried the captain; "let's see the glass. Yes, that's Case, sure enough, and the darkie. They've got a gallows bad reputation, but you know what a place the beach is for talking. My belief, that Whistling Jimmie was the worst of the trouble; and he's gone to glory, you see. What'll you bet they ain't after gin? Lay you five to two they take six cases."

When these two traders came aboard I was pleased with the looks of them at once, or, rather, with the looks of both, and the speech of one. I was sick for white neighbors after my four years at the line, which I always counted years of prison; getting tabooed, and going down to the Speak House to see and get it taken off; buying gin and going on a break, and then repenting; sitting in the house at night with the lamp for company; or walking on the beach and wondering what kind of a fool to call myself for being where I was. There were no other whites upon my island, and when I sailed to the next, rough customers made the most of the society. Now to see these two when they came aboard was a pleasure. One was a negro, to be sure; but they were both rigged out smart in striped pajamas and straw hats, and Case would have passed muster in a city. He was yellow and smallish, had a hawk's nose to his face, pale eyes, and his beard trimmed with scissors. No man knew his country, beyond he was of English speech; and it was clear he came of a good family and was splendidly educated. He was accomplished too; played the accordion first rate; and give him a piece of string or a cork or a pack of cards, and he could show you tricks equal to any professional. He could speak, when he chose, fit for a drawing-room; and when he chose he could blaspheme worse than a Yankee boatswain, and talk smart to sicken a Kanaka. The way he thought would pay best at the moment, that was Case's way, and it always seemed to come natural, and like as if he was born to it. He had the courage of a lion and the cunning of a rat; and if he's not in hell to-day, there's no such place. I know but one good point to the man—

that he was fond of his wife, and kind to her. She was a Samoa woman, and dyed her hair red—Samoa style; and when he came to die (as I have to tell of) they found one strange thing—that he had made a will, like a Christian, and the widow got the lot; all his, they said, and all Black Jack's, and the most of Billy Randall's in the bargain, for it was Case that kept the books. So she went off home in the schooner Manu'a, and does the lady to this day in her own place.

But of all this on that first morning I knew no more than a fly. Case used me like a gentleman and like a friend, made me welcome to Falesá, and put his services at my disposal, which was the more helpful from my ignorance of the natives. All the better part of the day we sat drinking better acquaintance in the cabin, and I never heard a man talk more to the point. There was no smarter trader, and none dodgier, in the islands. I thought Falesá seemed to be the right kind of a place; and the more I drank the lighter my heart. Our last trader had fled the place at half an hour's notice, taking a chance passage in a labor ship from up west. The captain, when he came, had found the station closed, the keys left with the native pastor, and a letter from the runaway, confessing he was fairly frightened of his life. Since then the firm had not been represented, and of course there was no cargo. The wind, besides, was fair, the captain hoped he could make his next island by dawn, with a good tide, and the business of landing my trade was gone about lively. There was no call for me to fool with it, Case said; nobody would touch my things, everyone was honest in Falesá, only about chickens or an odd knife or an odd stick of tobacco; and the best I could do was to sit quiet till the vessel left, then come straight to his house, see old Captain Randall, the father of the beach, take pot-luck, and go home to sleep when it got dark. So it was high noon, and the schooner was under way before I set my foot on shore at Falesá.

I had a glass or two on board; I was just off a long cruise, and the ground heaved under me like a ship's deck. The world was like all new painted; my foot went along to music; Falesá might have been Fiddler's Green, if there is such a place, and more's the pity if there isn't! It was good to foot the grass, to look aloft at the green mountains, to see the men with their green wreaths and the women in their bright dresses, red and blue. On we went, in the strong sun and the cool shadow, liking both; and all the children in the town came trotting after with their shaven heads and their brown bodies, and raising a thin kind of a cheer in our wake, like crowing poultry.

"By the bye," says Case, "we must get you a wife."

"That's so," said I; "I had forgotten."

There was a crowd of girls about us, and I pulled myself up and looked among them like a bashaw. They were all dressed out for the sake of the ship being in; and the women of Falesá are a handsome lot to see. If they have a fault, they are a trifle broad in the beam; and I was just thinking so when Case touched me.

"That's pretty," says he.

I saw one coming on the other side alone. She had been fishing; all she wore was a chemise, and it was wetted through. She was young and very slender for an island maid, with a long face, a high forehead, and a shy, strange, blindish look, between a cat's and a baby's.

"Who's she?" said I. "She'll do."

"That's Uma," said Case, and he called her up and spoke to her in the native. I didn't know what he said; but when he was in the midst she looked up at me quick and timid, like a child dodging a blow, then down again, and presently smiled. She had a wide mouth, the lips and the chin cut like any statue's; and the smile came out for a moment and was gone. Then she stood with her head bent, and heard Case to an end, spoke back in the pretty Polynesian voice, looking him full in the face, heard him again in answer, and then with an obeisance started off. I had just a share of the bow, but never another shot of her eye, and there was no more word of smiling.

"I guess it's all right," said Case. "I guess you can have her. I'll make it square with the old lady. You can have your pick of the lot for a plug of tobacco," he added, sneering.

I suppose it was the smile stuck in my memory, for I spoke back sharp. "She doesn't look that sort," I cried.

"I don't know that she is," said Case. "I believe she's as right as the mail. Keeps to herself, don't go round with the gang, and that. Oh, no, don't you misunderstand me—Uma's on the square." He spoke eager, I thought, and that surprised and pleased me. "Indeed," he went on, "I shouldn't make so sure of getting her, only she cottoned to the cut of your jib. All you have to do is to keep dark and let me work the mother my own way; and I'll bring the girl round to the captain's for the marriage."

I didn't care for the word marriage, and I said so.

"Oh, there's nothing to hurt in the marriage," says he. "Black Jack's the chaplain."

By this time we had come in view of the house of these three white men; for a negro is counted a white man, and so is a Chinese! A strange idea, but common in the islands. It was a board house with a strip of rickety veranda. The store was to the front, with a counter, scales, and the finest possible display of trade: a case or two of tinned meats; a barrel of hard bread, a few bolts of cotton stuff, not to be compared with mine; the only thing well represented being the contraband firearms and liquor. "If these are my only rivals," thinks I, "I should do well in Falesá." Indeed, there was only the one way they could touch me, and that was with the guns and drink.

In the back room was old Captain Randall, squatting on the floor native fashion, fat and pale, naked to the waist, gray as a badger, and his eyes set with drink. His body was covered with gray hair and crawled over by flies; one was in the corner of his eye—he never heeded; and the mosquitoes hummed about the man like bees. Any clean-minded man would have had the creature out at once and buried him; and to see him, and think he was seventy, and remember he had once commanded a ship, and come ashore in his smart togs, and talked big in bars and consulates, and sat in club verandas, turned me sick and sober.

He tried to get up when I came in, but that was hopeless; so he reached me a hand instead, and stumbled out some salutation.

"Papa's pretty full this morning," observed Case. "We've had an epidemic here; and Captain Randall takes gin for a prophylactic—don't you, papa?"

"Never took such a thing in my life!" cried the captain, indignantly. "Take gin for my health's sake, Mr. Wha's-ever-your-name—'s a precautionary measure."

"That's all right, papa," said Case. "But you'll have to brace up. There's going to be a marriage—Mr. Wiltshire here is going to get spliced."

The old man asked to whom.

"To Uma," said Case.

"Uma!" cried the captain. "Wha's he want Uma for? 's he come here for his health, anyway? Wha' 'n hell's he want Uma for?"

"Dry up, papa," said Case. "'Tain't you that's to marry her. I guess you're not her godfather and godmother. I guess Mr. Wiltshire's going to please himself."

With that he made an excuse to me that he must move about the marriage, and left me alone with the poor wretch that was his partner and (to speak truth) his gull. Trade and station belonged both to Randall; Case and the negro were parasites; they crawled and fed upon him like the flies, he none the wiser. Indeed, I have no harm to say of Billy Randall beyond the fact that my gorge rose at him, and the time I now passed in his company was like a nightmare.

The room was stifling hot and full of flies; for the house was dirty and low and small, and stood in a bad place, behind the village, in the borders of the bush, and sheltered from the trade. The three men's beds were on the floor, and a litter of pans and dishes. There was no standing furniture; Randall, when he was violent, tearing it to laths. There I sat and had a meal which was served us by Case's wife; and there I was entertained all day by that remains of man, his tongue stumbling among low old jokes and long old stories, and his own wheezy laughter always ready, so that he had no sense of my depression. He was nipping gin all the while. Sometimes he fell asleep, and awoke again, whimpering and shivering, and every now and again he would ask me why I wanted to marry Uma. "My friend," I was telling myself all day, "you must not come to be an old gentleman like this."

It might be four in the afternoon, perhaps, when the back door was thrust slowly open, and a strange old native woman crawled into the house almost on her belly. She was swathed in black stuff to her heels; her hair was gray in swatches; her face was tattooed, which was not the practice in that island; her eyes big and bright and crazy. These she fixed upon me with a rapt expression that I saw to be part acting. She said no plain word, but smacked and mumbled with her lips, and hummed aloud, like a child over its Christmas pudding. She came straight across the house, heading for me, and, as soon as she was alongside, caught up my hand and purred and crooned over it like a great cat. From this she slipped into a kind of song.

"Who the devil's this?" cried I, for the thing startled me.

"It's Faavao," says Randall; and I saw he had hitched along the floor into the farthest corner.

"You ain't afraid of her?" I cried.

"Me 'fraid!" cried the captain. "My dear friend, I defy her! I don't let her put her foot in here, only I suppose 's different to-day for the marriage. 's Uma's mother."

"Well, suppose it is; what's she carrying on about?" I asked, more irritated, perhaps more frightened, than I cared to show; and the captain told me she was making up a quantity of poetry in my praise because I was to marry Uma. "All right, old lady," says I, with rather a failure of a laugh, "anything to oblige. But when you're done with my hand, you might let me know."

She did as though she understood; the song rose into a cry, and stopped; the woman crouched out of the house the same way that she came in, and must have plunged straight into the bush, for when I followed her to the door she had already vanished.

"These are rum manners," said I.

"'S a rum crowd," said the captain, and, to my surprise, he made the sign of the cross on his bare bosom.

"Hillo!" says I, "are you a Papist?"

He repudiated the idea with contempt. "Hard-shell Baptis'," said he. "But, my dear friend, the Papists got some good ideas too; and th' 's one of 'em. You take my advice, and whenever you come across Uma or Faavao or Vigours, or any of that crowd, you take a leaf out o' the priests, and do what I do. Savvy?" says he, repeated the sign, and winked his dim eye at me. "No, *sir!*" he broke out again, "no Papists here!" and for a long time entertained me with his religious opinions.

I must have been taken with Uma from the first, or I should certainly have fled from that house, and got into the clean air, and the clean sea, or some convenient river—though, it's true, I was committed to Case; and, besides, I could never have held my head up in that island if I had run from a girl upon my wedding-night.

The sun was down, the sky all on fire, and the lamp had been some time lighted, when Case came back with Uma and the negro. She was dressed and scented; her kilt was of fine tapa, looking richer in the folds than any silk; her bust, which was of the color of dark honey, she wore bare, only for some half a dozen necklaces of seeds and flowers; and behind her ears and in her hair she had the scarlet flowers of the hibiscus. She showed the best bearing for a bride conceivable, serious and still; and I thought shame to stand up with her in that mean house and before that grinning negro. I thought shame, I say; for the mountebank was dressed with a big paper collar, the book he made believe to read from was an odd volume of a novel, and the words of his service not fit to be set down. My conscience smote me when we joined hands; and when she got her certificate I was tempted to throw up the bargain and confess. Here is the document. It was Case that wrote it, signatures and all, in a leaf out of the ledger:

This is to certify that Uma, daughter of Faavao of Falesá, Island of ——, is illegally married to Mr. John Wiltshire, and Mr. John Wiltshire is at liberty to send her packing when he pleases.

JOHN BLACKAMOAR,

Chaplain to the Hulks

Extracted from the Register

By William T.Randall,

　　Master Mariner

A nice paper to put in a girl's hand and see her hide away like gold. A man might easily feel cheap for less. But it was the practice in these parts, and (as I told myself) not the least the fault of us white men, but of the missionaries. If they had let the natives be, I had never needed this deception, but taken all the wives I wished, and left them when I pleased, with a clear conscience.

The more ashamed I was, the more hurry I was in to be gone ; and our desires thus jumping together, I made the less remark of a change in the traders. Case had been all eagerness to keep me; now, as though he had attained a purpose, he seemed all eagerness to have me go. Uma, he said, could show me to my house, and the three bade us farewell indoors.

The night was nearly come; the village smelt of trees and flowers and the sea and bread-fruitcooking; there came a fine roll of sea from the reef, and from a distance, among the woods and houses, many pretty sounds of men and children. It did me good to breathe free air; it did me good to be done with the captain, and see, instead, the creature at my side. I felt for all the world as though she were some girl at home in the Old Country, and forgetting myself for the minute, took her hand to walk with. Her fingers nestled into mine, I heard her breathe deep and quick, and all at once she caught my hand to her face and pressed it there. "You good!" she cried, and ran ahead of me, and stopped and looked back and smiled, and ran ahead of me again, thus guiding me through the edge of the bush, and by a quiet way to my own house.

The truth is, Case had done the courting for me in style—told her I was mad to have her, and cared nothing for the consequences; and the poor soul, knowing that which I was still ignorant of, believed it, every word, and had her head nigh turned with vanity and gratitude. Now, of all this I had no guess; I was one of those most opposed to any nonsense about native women, having seen so many whites eaten up by their wives' relatives, and made fools of into the bargain; and I told myself I must make a stand at once, and bring her to her bearings. But she looked so quaint and pretty as she ran away and then awaited me, and the thing was done so like a child or a kind dog, that the best I could do was just to follow her whenever she went on, to listen for the fall of her bare feet, and to watch in the dusk for the shining of her body. And there was another thought came in my head. She played kitten with me now when we were alone; but in the house she had carried it the way a countess might, so proud and humble. And what with her dress—for all there was so little of it, and that native enough—what with her fine tapa and fine scents, and her red flowers and seeds, that were quite as bright as jewels, only larger—it came over me she was a kind of countess really, dressed to hear great singers at a concert, and no even mate for a poor trader like myself.

She was the first in the house; and while I was still without I saw a match flash and the lamplight kindle in the windows. The station was a wonderful fine place, coral built, with quite a wide veranda, and the main room high and wide. My chests and cases had been piled in, and made rather of a mess; and there, in the thick of the confusion, stood Uma by the table, awaiting me. Her shadow went all the way up behind her into the hollow of the iron roof; she stood against it bright, the lamplight shining on her skin. I stopped in the door, and she looked at me, not speaking, with eyes that were eager and yet daunted; then she touched herself on the bosom.

"Me—your wifie," she said. It had never taken me like that before; but the want of her took and shook all through me, like the wind in the luff of a sail.

I could not speak if I had wanted; and if I could, I would not. I was ashamed to be so much moved about a native, ashamed of the marriage too, and the certificate she had treasured in her kilt; and I turned aside and made believe to rummage among my cases. The first thing I lighted on was a case of gin, the only one that I had brought; and partly for the girl's sake, and partly for horror of the recollections of old Randall, took a sudden resolve. I pried the lid off. One by one I drew the bottles with a pocket corkscrew, and sent Uma out to pour the stuff from the veranda.

She came back after the last, and looked at me puzzled like.

"No good," said I, for I was now a little better master of my tongue. "Man he drink, he no good."

She agreed with this, but kept considering. "Why you bring him?" she asked, presently. "Suppose you no want drink, you no bring him, I think."

"That's all right," said I. "One time I want drink too much; now no want. You see, I no savvy, I get one little wifie. Suppose I drink gin, my little wifie be 'fraid."

To speak to her kindly was about more than I was fit for; I had made my vow I would never let on to weakness with a native, and I had nothing for it but to stop.

She stood looking gravely down at me where I sat by the open case. "I think you good man," she said. And suddenly she had fallen before me on the floor. "I belong you all-e-same pig!" she cried.

II. The Ban

I came on the veranda just before the sun rose on the morrow. My house was the last on the east; there was a cape of woods and cliffs behind that hid the sunrise. To the west, a swift, cold river ran down, and beyond was the green of the village, dotted with cocoa-palms and bread-fruits and houses. The shutters were some of them down and some open; I saw the mosquito bars still stretched, with shadows of people new-awakened sitting up inside; and all over the green others were stalking silent, wrapped in their many-colored sleeping clothes, like Bedouins in Bible pictures. It was mortal still and solemn and chilly, and the light of the dawn on the lagoon was like the shining of a fire.

But the thing that troubled me was nearer hand. Some dozen young men and children made a piece of a half-circle, flanking my house: the river divided them, some were on the near side, some on the far, and one on a bowlder in the midst; and they all sat silent, wrapped in their sheets, and stared at me and my house as straight as pointer dogs. I thought it strange as I went out. When I had bathed and come back again, and found them all there, and two or three more along with them, I thought it stranger still. What could they see to gaze at in my house I wondered, and went in.

But the thought of these starers stuck in my mind, and presently I came out again. The sun was now up, but it was still behind the cape of woods. Say a quarter of an hour had come and gone. The crowd was greatly increased, the far bank of the river was lined for quite a way—perhaps thirty grown folk, and of children twice as many, some standing, some squatted on the ground, and all staring at my house. I have seen a house in a South-Sea village thus surrounded, but then a trader was thrashing his wife inside, and she singing out. Here was nothing—the stove was alight, the smoke going up in a Christian manner; all was shipshape and Bristol fashion. To be sure, there was a stranger come, but they had a chance to see that stranger yesterday, and took it quiet enough. What ailed them now? I leaned my arms on the rail and stared back. Devil a wink they had in them! Now and then I could see the children chatter, but they spoke so low not even the hum of their speaking came my length. The rest were like graven images: they stared at me, dumb and sorrowful, with their bright eyes; and it came upon me things would look not much different if I were ou the platform of the gallows, and these good folk had come to see me hanged.

I felt I was getting daunted, and began to be afraid I looked it, which would never do. Up I stood, made believe to stretch myself, came down the veranda stair, and strolled toward the river. There went a short buzz from one to the other, like what you hear in theatres when the curtain goes up; and some of the nearest gave back the matter of a pace. I saw a girl lay one hand on a young man and make a gesture upward with the other; at the same time she said something in the native with a gasping voice. Three little boys sat beside my path, where I must pass within three feet of them. Wrapped in their sheets, with their shaved heads and bits of topknots, and queer faces, they looked like figures on a chimney-piece. Awhile they sat their ground, solemn as judges. I came up hand over fist, doing my five knots, like a man that meant business; and I thought I saw a sort of a wink and gulp in the three faces. Then one jumped up (he was the farthest off) and ran for his mammy. The other two, trying to follow suit, got foul, came to the ground together bawling, wriggled right out of their sheets, and in a moment there were all three of them scampering for their lives, and singing out like pigs. The natives, who would never let a joke slip, even at a burial, laughed and let up, as short as a dog's bark.

They say it scares a man to be alone. No such thing. What scares him in the dark or the high bush is that he can't make sure, and there might be an army at his elbow. What scares him worst is to be right in the midst of a crowd, and have no guess of what they're driving at. When that laugh stopped, I stopped too. The boys had not yet made their offing; they were still on the full stretch going the one way, when I had already gone about ship and was sheering off the other. Like a fool I had come out, doing my five knots; like a fool I went back again again. It must have been the funniest thing to see, and what knocked me silly, this time no one laughed; only one old woman gave a kind of pious moan, the way you have heard Dissenters in their chapels at the sermon.

"I never saw such fools of Kanakas as your people here," I said once to Uma, glancing out of the window at the starers.

"Savvy nothing," says Uma, with a kind of disgusted air that she was good at.

And that was all the talk we had upon the matter, for I was put out, and Uma took the thing so much as a matter of course that I was fairly ashamed.

All day, off and on, now fewer and now more, the fools sat about the west end of my house and across the river, waiting for the show, whatever that was—fire to come down from heaven, I suppose, and consume me, bones and baggage. But by evening, like real islanders, they had wearied of the business, and got away, and had a dance instead in the big house of the village, where I heard them singing and clapping hands till, maybe, ten at night, and the next day it seemed they had forgotten I existed. If fire had come down from heaven or the earth opened and swallowed me, there would have been nobody to see the sport or take the lesson, or whatever you like to call it. But I was to find they hadn't forgot either, and kept an eye lifting for phenomena over my way.

I was hard at it both these days getting my trade in order and taking stock of what Vigours had left. This was a job that made me pretty sick, and kept me from thinking on much else. Ben had taken stock the trip before—I knew I could trust Ben—but it was plain somebody had been making free in the meantime. I found I was out by what might easily cover six months' salary and profit, and I could have kicked myself all round the village to have been such a blamed ass, sitting boozing with that Case instead of attending to my own affairs and taking stock.

However, there's no use crying over spilt milk. It was done now, and couldn't be undone. All I could do was to get what was left of it, and my new stuff (my own choice) in order, to go round and get after the rats and cockroaches, and to fix up that store regular Sydney style. A fine show I made of it; and the third morning, when I had lit my pipe and stood in the doorway and looked in, and turned and looked far up the mountain and saw the cocoa-nuts waving and posted up the tons of copra, and over the village green and saw the island dandies and reckoned up the yards of print they wanted for their kilts and dresses, I felt as if I was in the right place to make a fortune, and go home again and start a public-house. There was I, sitting in that veranda, in as handsome a piece of scenery as you could find, a splendid sun, and a fine, fresh, healthy trade that stirred up a man's blood like sea-bathing; and the whole thing was clean gone from me, and I was dreaming England, which is, after all, a nasty, cold, muddy hole, with not enough light to see to read by; and dreaming the looks of my public, by a cant of a broad high-road like an avenue and with the sign on a green tree.

So much for the morning, but the day passed and the devil anyone looked near me, and from all I knew of natives in other islands I thought this strange. People laughed a little at our firm and their fine stations, and at this station of Falesá in particular; all the copra in the district wouldn't pay for it (I had heard them say) in fifty years, which I supposed was an exaggeration. But when the day went, and no business came at all, I began to get downhearted; and, about three in the afternoon, I went out for a stroll to cheer me up. On the green I saw a white man coming with a cassock on, by which and by the face of him I knew he was a priest. He was a good-natured old soul to look at, gone a little grizzled, and so dirty you could have written with him on a piece of paper.

"Good-day, sir," said I.

He answered me eagerly in native.

"Don't you speak any English?" said I.

"French," says he.

"Well," said I, "I'm sorry, but I can't do anything there."

He tried me a while in the French, and then again in native, which he seemed to think was the best chance. I made out he was after more than passing the time of day with me, but had something to communicate, and I listened the harder. I heard the names of Adams and Case and of Randall—Randall the oftenest—and the word "poison," or something like it, and a native word that he said very often. I went home, repeating it to myself.

"What does fussy-ocky mean?" I asked of Uma, for that was as near as I could come to it.

"Make dead," said she.

"The devil it does!" says I. "Did ever you hear that Case had poisoned Johnny Adams?"

"Every man he savvy that," says Uma, scornful-like. "Give him white sand—bad sand. He got the bottle still. Suppose he give you gin, you no take him."

Now I had heard much the same sort of story in other islands, and the same white powder always to the front, which made me think the less of it. For all that, I went over to Randall's place to see what I could pick up, and found Case on the doorstep, cleaning a gun.

"Good shooting here?" says I.

"A 1," says he. "The bush is full of all kinds of birds. I wish copra was as plenty," says he—I thought, slyly—"but there don't seem anything doing."

I could see Black Jack in the store, serving a customer.

"That looks like business, though," said I.

"That's the first sale we've made in three weeks," said he.

"You don't tell me?" says I. "Three weeks? Well, well."

"If you don't believe me," he cries, a little hot, "you can go and look at the copra-house. It's half empty to this blessed hour."

"I shouldn't be much the better for that, you see," says I. "For all I can tell, it might have been whole empty yesterday."

"That's so," says he, with a bit of a laugh.

"By the by," I said, "what sort of a party is that priest? Seems rather a friendly sort."

At this Case laughed right out loud. "Ah!" says he, "I see what ails you now. Galuchet's been at you." *Father Galoshes* was the name he went by most, but Case always gave it the French quirk, which was another reason we had for thinking him above the common.

"Yes, I have seen him," I says. "I made out he didn't think much of your Captain Randall."

"That he don't!" says Case. "It was the trouble about poor Adams. The last day, when he lay dying, there was young Buncombe round. Ever met Buncombe?"

I told him no.

"He's a cure, is Buncombe!" laughs Case. "Well, Buncombe took it in his head that, as there was no other clergyman about, bar Kanaka pastors, we ought to call in Father Galuchet, and have the old man administered and take the sacrament. It was all the same to me, you may suppose; but I said I thought Adams was the fellow to consult. He was jawing away about watered copra and a sight of foolery. 'Look here,' I said, 'you're pretty sick. Would you like to see Galoshes?' He sat right up on his elbow. 'Get the priest,' says he, 'get the priest; don't let me die here like a dog!' He spoke kind of fierce and eager, but sensible enough. There was nothing to say against that, so we sent and asked Galuchet if he would come. You bet he would. He jumped in his dirty linen at the thought of it. But we had reckoned without Papa. He's a hard-shelled Baptist, is Papa; no Papists need apply. And he took and locked the door. Buncombe told him he was bigoted, and I thought he would have had a fit. 'Bigoted!' he says. 'Me bigoted? Have I lived to hear it from a jackanapes like you?' And he made for Buncombe, and I had to hold them apart; and there was Adams in the middle, gone luny again, and carrying on about copra like a born fool. It was good as the play, and I was about knocked out of time with laughing, when all of a sudden Adams sat up, clapped his hands to his chest, and went into the horrors. He died hard, did John Adams," says Case, with a kind of a sudden sternness.

"And what became of the priest?" I asked.

"The priest?" says Case. "Oh! he was hammering on the door outside, and crying on the natives to come and beat it in, and singing out it was a soul he wished to save, and that. He was in a rare taking, was the priest. But what would you have? Johnny had slipped his cable; no more Johnny in the market; and the administration racket clean played out. Next thing, word came to Randall that the priest was praying upon Johnny's grave. Papa was pretty full, and got a club, and lit out straight for the place, and there was Galoshes on his knees, and a lot of natives looking on. You wouldn't think Papa cared that much about anything, unless it was liquor; but he and the priest stuck to it two hours, slanging each other in native, and every time Galoshes tried to kneel down Papa went for him with the club. There never were such larks in Falesá. The end of it was that Captain Randall knocked over with some kind of a fit or stroke, and the priest got in his goods after all. But he was the angriest priest you ever heard of, and complained to the chiefs about the outrage, as he called it. That was no account, for our chiefs are Protestant here; and, anyway, he had been making trouble about the drum for morning school, and they were glad to give him a wipe. Now he swears old Randall gave Adams poison or something, and when the two meet they grin at each other like baboons."

He told this story as natural as could be, and like a man that enjoyed the fun; though now I come to think of it after so long, it seems rather a sickening yarn. However, Case never set up to be soft, only to be square and hearty, and a man all round; and, to tell the truth, he puzzled me entirely.

I went home and asked Uma if she were a Popey, which I had made out to be the native word for Catholics.

"*E le ai!*" says she. She always used the native when she meant "no" more than usually strong, and, indeed, there's more of it. "No good Popey," she added.

Then I asked her about Adams and the priest, and she told me much the same yarn in her own way. So that I was left not much farther on, but inclined, upon the whole, to think the bottom of the matter was the row about the sacrament, and the poisoning only talk.

The next day was a Sunday, when there was no business to be looked for. Uma asked me in the morning if I was going to " pray;" I told her she bet not, and she stopped home herself, with no more words. I thought this seemed unlike a native, and a native woman, and a woman that had new clothes to show off; however, it suited me to the ground, and I made the less of it. The queer thing was that I came next door to going to church after all, a thing I'm little likely to forget. I had turned out for a stroll, and heard the hymn tune up. You know how it is. If you hear folk singing, it seems to draw you; and pretty soon I found myself alongside the church. It was a little, long, low place, coral built, rounded off at both ends like a whale-boat, a big native roof on the top of it, windows without sashes and doorways without doors. I stuck my head into one of the windows, and the sight was so new to me—for things went quite different in the islands I was acquainted with—that I stayed and looked on. The congregation sat on the floor on mats, the women on one side, the men on the other, all rigged out to kill—the women with dresses and trade hats, the men in white jackets and shirts. The hymn was over; the pastor, a big buck Kanaka, was in the pulpit, preaching for his life; and by the way he wagged his hand, and worked his voice, and made his points, and seemed to argue with the folk, I made out he was a gun at the business. Well, he looked up suddenly and caught my eye, and I give you my word he staggered in the pulpit; his eyes bulged out of his head, his hand rose and pointed at me like as if against his will, and the sermon stopped right there.

It isn't a fine thing to say for yourself, but I ran away; and, if the same kind of a shock was given me, I should run away again to-morrow. To see that palavering Kanaka struck all of a heap at the mere sight of me gave me a feeling as if the bottom had dropped out of the world. I went right home, and stayed there, and said nothing. You might think I would tell Uma, but that was against my system. You might have thought I would have gone over and consulted Case; but the truth was I was ashamed to speak of such a thing, I thought everyone would blurt out laughing in my face. So I held my tongue, and thought all the more; and the more I thought, the less I liked the business.

By Monday night I got it clearly in my head I must be tabooed. A new store to stand open two days in a village and not a man or woman come to see the trade, was past believing.

"Uma," said I, "I think I'm tabooed."

"I think so," said she.

I thought a while whether I should ask her more, but it's a bad idea to set natives up with any notion of consulting them, so I went to Case. It was dark, and he was sitting alone, as he did mostly, smoking on the stairs.

"Case," said I, "here's a queer thing. I'm tabooed."

"Oh, fudge!" says he; "'tain't the practice in these islands."

"That maybe, or it mayn't," said I. "It's the practice where I was before. You can bet I know what it's like; and I tell it you for a fact, I'm tabooed."

"Well," said he, "what have you been doing?" "That's what I want to find out," said I.

"Oh, you can't be," said he; "it ain't possible. However, I'll tell you what I'll do. Just to put your mind at rest, I'll go round and find out for sure. Just you waltz in and talk to Papa."

"Thank you," I said, "I'd rather stay right out here on the veranda. Your house is so close."

"I'll call Papa out here, then," says he.

"My dear fellow," I says, "I wish you wouldn't. The fact is, I don't take to Mr. Randall."

Case laughed, took a lantern from the store, and set out into the village. He was gone perhaps a quarter of an hour, and he looked mighty serious when he came back.

"Well," said he, clapping down the lantern on the veranda steps, "I would never have believed it. I don't know where the impudence of these Kanakas'll go next; they seem to have lost all idea of respect for whites. What we want is a man-of-war—a German, if we could—they know how to manage Kanakas."

"I *am* tabooed, then?" I cried.

"Something of the sort," said he. "It's the worst thing of the kind I've heard of yet. But I'll stand by you, Wiltshire, man to man. You come round here to-morrow about nine, and we'll have it out with the chiefs. They're afraid of me, or they used to be; but their heads are so big by now, I don't know what to think. Understand me, Wiltshire; I don't count this your quarrel," he went on, with a great deal of resolution, "I count it all of our quarrel, I count it the White Man's Quarrel, and I'll stand to it through thick and thin, and there's my hand on it."

"Have you found out what's the reason?" I asked.

"Not yet," said Case. "But we'll fire them down to-morrow."

Altogether I was pretty well pleased with his attitude, and almost more the next day, when we met to go before the chiefs, to see him so stern and resolved. The chiefs awaited us in one of their big oval houses, which was marked out to us from a long way off by the crowd about the eaves, a hundred strong if there was one—men, women, and children. Many of the men were on their way to work and wore green wreaths, and it put me in thoughts of the first of May at home. This crowd opened and buzzed about the pair of us as we went in, with a sudden angry animation. Five chiefs were there; four mighty, stately men, the fifth old and puckered. They sat on mats in their white kilts and jackets; they had fans in their hands, like fine ladies; and two of the younger ones wore Catholic medals, which gave me matter of reflection. Our place was set, and the mats laid for us over against these grandees, on the near side of the house; the midst was empty; the crowd, close at our backs, murmured and craned and jostled to look on, and the shadows of them tossed in front of us on the clean pebbles of the floor. I was just a hair put out by the excitement of the commons, but the quiet, civil appearance of the chiefs reassured me, all the more when their spokesman began and made a long speech in a low tone of voice, sometimes waving his hand toward Case, sometimes toward me, and sometimes knocking with his knuckles on the mat. One thing was clear: there was no sign of anger in the chiefs.

"What's he been saying?" I asked, when he had done.

"Oh, just that they're glad to see you, and they understand by me you wish to make some kind of complaint, and you're to fire away, and they'll do the square thing."

"It took a precious long time to say that," said I.

"Oh, the rest was sawder and *bonjour* and that," said Case. "You know what Kanakas are."

"Well, they don't get much *bonjour* out of me," said I. "You tell them who I am. I'm a white man, and a British subject, and no end of a big chief at home; and I've come here to do them good, and bring them civilization; and no sooner have I got my trade sorted out than they go and taboo me, and no one dare come near my place! Tell them I don't mean to fly in the face of anything legal; and if what they want's a present, I'll do what's fair. I don't blame any man looking out for himself, tell them, for that's human nature; but if they think they're going to come any of their native ideas over me, they'll find themselves mistaken. And tell them plain that I demand the reason of this treatment as a white man and a British subject."

That was my speech. I knew how to deal with Kanakas: give them plain sense and fair dealing, and—I'll do them that much justice—they knuckle under every time. They haven't any real government or any real law, that's what you've got to knock into their heads; and even if they had, it would be a good joke if it was to apply to a white man. It would be a strange thing if we came all this way and couldn't do what we pleased. The mere idea has always put my monkey up, and I rapped my speech out pretty big. Then Case translated it—or made believe to, rather—and the first chief replied, and then a second, and a third, all in the same style—easy and genteel, but solemn underneath. Once a question was put to Case, and he answered it, and all hands (both chiefs and commons) laughed out aloud, and looked at me. Last of all, the puckered old fellow and the big young chief that spoke first started in to put Case through a kind of catechism. Sometimes I made out that Case was trying to fence, and they stuck to him like hounds, and the sweat ran down his face, which was no very pleasant sight to me, and at some of his answers the crowd moaned and murmured, which was a worse hearing. It's a cruel shame I knew no native, for (as I now believe) they were asking Case about my marriage, and he must have had a tough job of it to clear his feet. But leave Case alone; he had the brains to run a parliament.

"Well, is that all?" I asked, when a pause came.

"Come along," says he, mopping his face; "I'll tell you outside."

"Do you mean they won't take the taboo off?" I cried.

"It's something queer," said he. "I'll tell you outside. Better come away."

"I won't take it at their hands," cried I. "I ain't that kind of a man. You don't find me turn my back on a parcel of Kanakas."

"You'd better," said Case.

He looked at me with a signal in his eye; and the five chiefs looked at me civilly enough, but kind of pointed; and the people looked at me and craned and jostled. I remembered the folks that watched my house, and how the pastor had jumped in his pulpit at the bare sight of me; and the whole business seemed so out of the way that I rose and followed Case. The crowd opened again to let us through, but wider than before, the children on the skirts running and singing out, and as we two white men walked away they all stood and watched us.

"And now," said I, "what is all this about?"

"The truth is I can't rightly make it out myself. They have a down on you," says Case.

"Taboo a man because they have a down on him!" I cried. "I never heard the like."

"It's worse than that, you see," said Case. "You ain't tabooed—I told you that couldn't be. The people won't go near you, Wiltshire, and there's where it is."

"They won't go near me? What do you mean by that? Why won't they go near me?" I cried.

Case hesitated. "Seems they're frightened," says he, in a low voice.

I stopped dead short. "Frightened?" I repeated. "Are you gone crazy, Case? What are they frightened of?"

"I wish. I could make out," Case answered, shaking his head. "Appears like one of their tomfool superstitions. That's what I don't cotton to," he said. "It's like the business about Vigours."

"I'd like to know what you mean by that, and I'll trouble you to tell me," says I.

"Well, you know, Vigours lit out and left all standing," said he. "It was some superstition business—I never got the hang of it; but it began to look bad before the end."

"I've heard a different story about that," said I, "and I had better tell you so. I heard he ran away because of you."

"Oh! well, I suppose he was ashamed to tell the truth," says Case; "I guess he thought it silly. And it's a fact that I packed him off. 'What would you do, old man?' says he. 'Get,' says I, 'and not think twice about it.' I was the gladdest kind of man to see him clear away. It ain't my notion to turn my back on a mate when he's in a tight place, but there was that much trouble in the village that I couldn't see where it might likely end. I was a fool to be so much about with Vigours. They cast it up to me to-day. Didn't you hear Maea—that's the young chief, the big one—ripping out about 'Vika'? That was him they were after. They don't seem to forget it, somehow."

"This is all very well," said I, "but it don't tell me what's wrong; it don't tell me what they're afraid of—what their idea is."

"Well, I wish I knew," said Case. "I can't say fairer than that."

"You might have asked, I think," says I.

"And so I did," says he. "But you must have seen for yourself, unless you're blind, that the asking got the other way. I'll go as far as I dare for another white man; but when I find I'm in the scrape myself, I think first of my own bacon. The loss of me is I'm too good-natured. And I'll take the freedom of telling you you show a queer kind of gratitude to a man who's got into all this mess along of your affairs."

"There's a thing I'm thinking of," said I. "You were a fool to be so much about with Vigours. One comfort, you haven't been much about with me. I notice you've never been inside my house. Own up now; you had word of this before?"

"It's a fact I haven't been," said he. "It was an oversight, and I am sorry for it, Wiltshire. But about coming now, I'll be quite plain."

"You mean you won't?" I asked.

"Awfully sorry, old man, but that's the size of it," says Case.

"In short, you're afraid?" says I.

"In short, I'm afraid," says he.

"And I'm still to be tabooed for nothing?" I asked.

"I tell you you're not tabooed," said he. "The Kanakas won't go near you, that's all. And who's to make 'em. We traders have a lot of gall, I must say; we make these poor Kanakas take back their laws, and take up their taboos, and that, whenever it happens to suit us. But you don't mean to say you expect a law-obliging people to deal in your store whether they want to or not? You don't mean to tell me you've got the gall for that? And if you had, it would be a queer thing to propose to me. I would just like to point out to you, Witshire, that I'm a trader myself."

"I don't think I would talk of gall if I was you," said I. "Here's about what it comes to, as well as I can make out: None of the people are to trade with me, and they're all to trade with you. You're to have the copra, and I'm to go to the devil and shake myself. And I don't know any native, and you're the only man here worth mention that speaks English, and you have the gall to up and hint to me my life's in danger, and all you've got to tell me is you don't know why!"

"Well, it *is* all I have to tell you," said he. "I don't know—I wish I did."

"And so you turn your back and leave me to myself! Is that the position?" says I.

"If you like to put it nasty," says he. "I don't put it so. I say merely, 'I'm going to keep clear of you; or, if I don't I'll get in danger for myself.'"

"Well," says I, "you're a nice kind of a white man!"

"Oh, I understand; you're riled," said he. "I would be myself. I can make excuses."

"All right," I said, "go and make excuses somewhere else. Here's my way, there's yours!"

With that we parted, and I went straight home, in a hot temper, and found Uma trying on a lot of trade goods like a baby.

"Here," I said, "you quit that foolery! Here's pretty mess to have made, as if I wasn't bothered enough anyway! And I thought I told you to get dinner!"

And then I believe I gave her a bit of the rough side of my tongue, as she deserved. She stood up at once, like a sentry to his officer; for I must say she was always well brought up, and had a great respect for whites.

"And now," says I, "you belong round here, you're bound to understand this. What am I tabooed for, anyway? Or, if I ain't tabooed, what makes the folks afraid of me?"

She stood and looked at me with eyes like saucers.

"You no savvy?" she gasps at last.

"No," said I. "How would you expect me to? We don't have any such craziness where I come from."

"Ese no tell you?" she asked again.

(*Ese* was the name the natives had for Case; it may mean foreign, or extraordinary; or it might mean a mummy apple; but most like it was only his own name misheard and put in a Kanaka spelling.)

"Not much," said I.

"D——n Ese!" she cried.

You might think it funny to hear this Kanaka girl come out with a big swear. No such thing. There was no swearing in her—no, nor anger; she was beyond anger, and meant the word simple and serious. She stood there straight as she said it. I cannot justly say that I ever saw a woman look like that before or after, and it struck me mum. Then she made a kind of an obeisance, but it was the proudest kind, and threw her hands out open.

"I 'shamed," she said. "I think you savvy. Ese he tell me you savvy, he tell me you no mind, tell me you love me too much. Taboo belong me," she said, touching herself on the bosom, as she had done upon our wedding-night. "Now I go 'way, taboo he go 'way too. Then you get too much copra. You like more better, I think. Tofa, alii," says she in the native—"Farewell, chief!"

"Hold on!" I cried. "Don't be in such a hurry."

She looked at me sidelong with a smile. "You see, you get copra," she said, the same as you might offer candies to a child.

"Uma," said I, "hear reason. I didn't know, and that's a fact; and Case seems to have played it pretty mean upon the pair of us. But I do know now, and I don't mind; I love you too much. You no go 'way, you no leave me, I too much sorry."

"You no love me," she cried, "you talk me bad words!" And she threw herself in a corner of the floor, and began to cry.

Well, I'm no scholar, but I wasn't born yesterday, and I thought the worst of that trouble was over. However, there she lay—her back turned, her face to the wall—and shook with sobbing like a little child, so that her feet jumped with it. It's strange how it hits a man when he's in love; for there's no use mincing things; Kanaka and all, I was in love with her, or just as good. I tried to take her hand, but she would none of that. "Uma," I said, "there's no sense in carrying on like this. I want you stop here, I want my little wifie, I tell you true."

"No tell me true," she sobbed.

"All right," says I, "I'll wait till you're through with this." And I sat right down beside her on the floor, and set to smooth her hair with my hand. At first she wriggled away when I touched her; then she seemed to notice me no more; then her sobs grew gradually less, and presently stopped; and the next thing I knew, she raised her face to mine.

"You tell me true? You like me stop?" she asked.

"Uma," I said, "I would rather have you than all the copra in the South Seas," which was a very big expression, and the strangest thing was that I meant it.

She threw her arms about me, sprang close up, and pressed her face to mine in the island way of kissing, so that I was all wetted with her tears, and my heart went out to her wholly. I never had anything so near me as this little brown bit of a girl. Many things went together, and all helped to turn my head. She was pretty enough to eat; it seemed she was my only friend in that queer place; I was ashamed that I had spoken rough to her: and she was a woman, and my wife, and a kind of a baby besides that I was sorry for; and the salt of her tears was in my mouth. And I forgot Case and the natives; and I forgot that I knew nothing of the story, or only remembered it to banish the remembrance; and I forgot that I was to get no copra, and so could make no livelihood; and I forgot my employers, and the strange kind of service I was doing them, when I preferred my fancy to their business; and I forgot even that Uma was no true wife of mine, but just a maid beguiled, and that in a pretty shabby style. But that is to look too far on. I will come to that part of it next.

It was late before we thought of getting dinner. The stove was out, and gone stone-cold; but we fired up after awhile, and cooked each a dish, helping and hindering each other, and making a play of it like children. I was so greedy of her nearness that I sat down to dinner with my lass upon my knee, made sure of her with one hand, and ate with the other. Ay, and more than that. She was the worst cook I suppose God made; the things she set her hand to it would have sickened an honest horse to eat of; yet I made my meal that day on Uma's cookery, and can never call to mind to have been better pleased.

I didn't pretend to myself, and I didn't pretend to her. I saw I was clean gone; and if she' was to make a fool of me, she must. And I suppose it was this that set her talking, for now she made sure that we were friends. A lot she fold me, sitting in my lap and eating my dish, as I ate hers, from foolery—a lot about herself and her mother and Case, all which would be very tedious, and fill sheets if I set it down in Beach de Mar, but which I must give a hint of in plain English, and one thing about myself, which had a very big effect on my concerns, as you are soon to hear. It seems she was born in one of the Line Islands; had been only two or three years in these parts, where she had come with a white man, who was married to her mother and then died; and only the one year in Falesá. Before that they had been a good deal on the move, trekking about after the white man, who was one of those rolling stones that keep going round after a soft job. They talk about looking for gold at the end of a rainbow; but if a man wants an employment that'll last him till he dies, let him start out on the soft-job hunt. There's meat and drink in it too, and beer and skittles, for you never hear of them starving, and rarely see them sober; and as for steady sport, cock fighting isn't in the same county with it. Anyway, this beach-comber carried the woman and her daughter all over the shop, but mostly to out-of-the-way islands, where there were no police, and he thought, perhaps, the soft job hung out. I've my own view of this old party; but I was just as glad he had kept Uma clear of Apia and Papeete and these flash towns. At last he struck Falealii on this island, got some trade—the Lord knows how!—muddled it all away in the usual style, and died worth next to nothing, bar a bit of land at Falesá that he had got for a bad debt, which was what put it in the minds of the mother and daughter to come there and live. It seems Case encouraged them all he could, and helped to get their house built. He was very kind those days, and gave Uma trade, and there is no doubt he had his eye on her from the beginning. However, they had scarce settled, when up turned a young man, a native, and wanted to marry her. He was a small chief, and had some fine mats and old songs in his family, and was "very pretty," Uma said; and, altogether, it was an extraordinary match for a penniless girl and an out-islander.

At the first word of this I got downright sick with jealousy.

"And you mean to say you would have married him?" I cried.

"Ioe, yes," said she. "I like too much!"

"Well!" I said. "And suppose I had come round after?"

"I like you more better now," said she. "But suppose I marry Ioane, I one good wife. I no common Kanaka. Good girl!" says she.

Well, I had to be pleased with that; but I promise you I didn't care about the business one little bit. And I liked the end of that yarn no better than the beginning. For it seems this proposal of marriage was the start of all the trouble. It seems, before that, Uma and her mother had been looked down upon, of course, for kinless folk and out-islanders, but nothing to hurt; and, even when Ioane came forward, there was less trouble at first than might have been looked for. And then, all of a sudden, about six months before my coming, Ioane backed out and left that part of the island, and from that day to this Uma and her mother had found themselves alone. None called at their house—none spoke to them on the roads. If they went to church, the other women drew their mats away and left them in a clear place by themselves. It was a regular excommunication, like what you read of in the Middle Ages; and the cause or sense of it beyond guessing. It was some *talo pepelo*, Uma said, some lie, some calumny; and all she knew of it was that the girls who had been jealous of her luck with Ioane used to twit her with his desertion, and cry out, when they met her alone in the woods, that she would never be married. "They tell me no man he marry me. He too much 'fraid," she said.

The only soul that came about them after this desertion was Master Case. Even he was chary of showing himself, and turned up mostly by night; and pretty soon he began to table his cards and make up to Uma. I was still sore about Ioane, and when Case turned up in the same line of business I cut up downright rough.

"Well," I said, sneering, "and I suppose you thought Case 'very pretty' and 'liked too much'?"

"Now you talk silly," said she. "White man, he come here, I marry him all-a-same Kanaka; very well then, he marry me all-e-same white woman. Suppose he no marry, he go 'way, woman he stop. All-e-same thief, empty hand, Tonga-heart—no can love! Now you come marry me. You big heart—you no 'shamed island-girl. That thing I love you far too much. I proud."

I don't know that ever I felt sicker all the days of my life. I laid down my fork, and I put away "the island-girl"; I didn't seem somehow to have any use for either, and I went and walked up and down in the house, and Uma followed me with her eyes, for she was troubled, and small wonder! But troubled was no word for it with me. I so wanted, and so feared, to make a clean breast of the sweep that I had been.

And just then there came a sound of singing out of the sea; it sprang up suddenly clear and near, as the boat turned the headland, and Uma, running to the window, cried out it was "Misi" come upon his rounds.

I thought it was a strange thing I should be glad to have a missionary; but, if it was strange, it was still true.

"Uma," said I, "you stop here in this room, and don't budge a foot out of it till I come back."

III. The Missionary

A s I came out on the veranda, the mission-boat was shooting for the mouth of the river. She was a long whale-boat painted white; a bit of an awning astern; a native pastor crouched on the wedge of poop, steering; some four-and-twenty paddles flashing and dipping, true to the boat-song; and the missionary under the awning, in his white clothes, reading in a book; and set him up! It was pretty to see and hear; there's no smarter sight in the islands than a missionary boat with a good crew and a good pipe to them; and I considered it for half a minute, with a bit of envy perhaps, and then strolled down toward the river.

From the opposite side there was another man aiming for the same place, but he ran and got there first. It was Case; doubtless his idea was to keep me apart from the missionary, who might serve me as interpreter; but my mind was upon other things. I was thinking how he had jockeyed us about the marriage, and tried his hand on Uma before; and at the sight of him rage flew into my nostrils.

"Get out of that, you low, swindling thief!" I cried.

"What's that you say?" says he.

I gave him the word again, and rammed it down with a good oath. "And if ever I catch you within six fathoms of my house," I cried, "I'll clap a bullet in your measly carcass."

"You must do as you like about your house," said he, "where I told you I have no thought of going; but this is a public place."

"It's a place where I have private business," said I. "I have no idea of a hound like you eavesdropping, and I give you notice to clear out."

"I don't take it, though," says Case.

"I'll show you, then," said I.

"We'll have to see about that," said he.

He was quick with his hands, but he had neither the height nor the weight, being a flimsy creature alongside a man like me, and, besides, I was blazing to that height of wrath that I could have bit into a chisel. I gave him first the one and then the other, so that I could hear his head rattle and crack, and he went down straight.

"Have you had enough?" cries I. But he only looked up white and blank, and the blood spread upon his face like wine upon a napkin. "Have you had enough?" I cried again. "Speak up, and don't lie malingering there, or I'll take my feet to you."

He sat up at that, and held his head—by the look of him you could see it was spinning—and the blood poured on his pajamas.

"I've had enough for this time," says he, and he got up staggering, and went off by the way that he had come.

The boat was close in; I saw the missionary had laid his book to one side, and I smiled to myself. "He'll know I'm a man, anyway," thinks I.

This was the first time, in all my years in the Pacific, I had ever exchanged two words with any missionary, let alone asked one for a favor. I didn't like the lot, no trader does; they look down upon us, and make no concealment; and, besides, they're partly Kanakaized, and suck up with natives instead of with other white men like themselves. I had on a rig of clean, striped pajamas—for, of course, I had dressed decent to go before the chiefs; but when I saw the missionary step out of this boat in the regular uniform, white duck clothes, pith helmet, white shirt and tie, and yellow boots to his feet, I could have bunged stones at him. As he came nearer, queering me pretty curious (because of the fight, I suppose), I saw he looked mortal sick, for the truth was he had a fever on, and had just had a chill in the boat.

"Mr. Tarleton, I believe?" says I, for I had got his name.

"And you, I suppose, are the new trader?" says he.

"I want to tell you first that I don't hold with missions," I went on, "and that I think you and the likes of you do a sight of harm, filling up the natives with old wives' tales and bumptiousness."

"You are perfectly entitled to your opinions," says he, looking a bit ugly, "but I have no call to hear them."

"It so happens that you've got to hear them," I said. "I'm no missionary, nor missionary lover; I'm no Kanaka, nor favorer of Kanakas—I'm just a trader; I'm just a common low God-damned white man and British subject, the sort you would like to wipe your boots on. I hope that's plain!"

"Yes, my man," said he. "It's more plain than creditable. When you are sober, you'll be sorry for this."

He tried to pass on, but I stopped him with my hand. The Kanakas were beginning to growl. Guess they didn't like my tone, for I spoke to that man as free as I would to you.

"Now, you can't say I've deceived you," said I, "and I can go on. I want a service—I want two services, in fact; and, if you care to give me them, I'll perhaps take more stock in what you call your Christianity."

He was silent for a moment. Then he smiled. "You are rather a strange sort of man," says he.

"I'm the sort of man God made me," says I. "I don't set up to be a gentleman," I said.

"I am not quite so sure," said he. "And what can I do for you, Mr.?"

"Wiltshire," I says, "though I'm mostly called Welsher; but Wiltshire is the way it's spelt, if the people on the beach could only get their tongues about it. And what do I want? Well, I'll tell you the first thing. I'm what you call a sinner—what I call a sweep—and I want you to help me make it up to a person I've deceived."

He turned and spoke to his crew in the native. "And now I am at your service," said he, "but only for the time my crew are dining. I must be much farther down the coast before night. I was delayed at Papa-Malulu till this morning, and I have an engagement in Fale-alii to-morrow night."

I led the way to my house in silence, and rather pleased with myself for the way I had managed the talk, for I like a man to keep his self-respect.

"I was sorry to see you fighting," says he.

"Oh, that's part of the yarn I want to tell you," I said. "That's service number two. After you've heard it you'll let me know whether you're sorry or not."

We walked right in through the store, and I was surprised to find Uma had cleared away the dinner things. This was so unlike her ways that I saw she had done it out of gratitude, and liked her the better. She and Mr. Tarleton called each other by name, and he was very civil to her seemingly. But I thought little of that; they can always find civility for a Kanaka, it's us white men they lord it over. Besides, I didn't want much Tarleton just then. I was going to do my pitch.

"Uma," said I, "give us your marriage certificate." She looked put out. "Come," said I, "you can trust me. Hand it up."

She had it about her person, as usual; I believe she thought it was a pass to heaven, and if she died without having it handy she would go to hell. I couldn't see where she put it the first time, I couldn't see now where she took it from; it seemed to jump into her hand like that Blavatsky business in the papers. But it's the same way with all island women, and I guess they're taught it when young.

"Now," said I, with the certificate in my hand, "I was married to this girl by Black Jack, the negro. The certificate was wrote by Case, and it's a dandy piece of literature, I promise you. Since then I've found that there's a kind of cry in the place against this wife of mine, and so long as I keep her I cannot trade. Now, what would any man do in my place, if he was a man?" I said. "The first thing he would do is this, I guess." And I took and tore up the certificate and bunged the pieces on the floor.

"Aue!" cried Uma, and began to clap her hands; but I caught one of them in mine.

"And the second thing that he would do," said I, "if he was what I would call a man and you would call a man, Mr. Tarleton, is to bring the girl right before you or any other missionary, and to up and say: 'I was wrong married to this wife of mine, but I think a heap of her, and now I want to be married to her right.' Fire away, Mr. Tarleton. And I guess you'd better do it in native; it'll please the old lady," I said, giving her the proper name of a man's wife upon the spot.

So we had in two of the crew for to witness, and were spliced in our own house; and the parson prayed a good bit, I must say—but not so long as some—and shook hands with the pair of us.

"Mr. Wiltshire," he says, when he had made out the lines and packed off the witnesses, "I have to thank you for a very lively pleasure. I have rarely performed the marriage ceremony with more grateful emotions."

That was what you would call talking. He was going on, besides, with more of it, and I was ready for as much taffy as he had in stock, for I felt good. But Uma had been taken up with something half through the marriage, and cut straight in.

"How your hand he get hurt?" she asked.

"You ask Case's head, old lady," says I.

She jumped with joy, and sang out.

"You haven't made much of a Christian of this one," says I to Mr. Tarleton.

"We didn't think her one of our worst," says he, "when she was at Fale-alii; and if Uma bears malice I shall be tempted to fancy she has good cause."

"Well, there we are at service number two," said I. "I want to tell yon our yarn, and see if you can let a little daylight in."

"Is it long?" he asked.

"Yes," I cried; "it's a goodish bit of a yarn!"

"Well, I'll give you all the time I can spare," says he, looking at his watch. "But I must tell you fairly, I haven't eaten since five this morning, and, unless you can let me have something, I am not likely to eat again before seven or eight to-night."

"By God, we'll give you dinner!" I cried.

I was a little caught up at my swearing, just when all was going straight; and so was the missionary, I suppose, but he made believe to look out of the window, and thanked us.

So we ran him up a bit of a meal. I was bound to let the old lady have a hand in it, to show off, so I deputized her to brew the tea. I don't think I ever met such tea as she turned out. But that was not the worst, for she got round with the salt-box, which she considered an extra European touch, and turned my stew into sea-water. Altogether, Mr. Tarleton had a devil of a dinner of it; but he had plenty of entertainment by the way, for all the while that we were cooking, and afterward, when he was making believe to eat, I kept posting him up on Master Case and the beach of Falesá, and he putting questions that showed he was following close.

"Well," said he at last, "I am afraid you have a dangerous enemy. This man Case is very clever and seems really wicked. I must tell you I have had my eye on him for nearly a year, and have rather had the worst of our encounters. About the time when the last representative of your firm ran so suddenly away, I had a letter from Namu, the native pastor, begging me to come to Falesá at my earliest convenience, as his flock were all 'adopting Catholic practices.' I had great confidence in Namu; I fear it only shows how easily we are deceived. No one could hear him preach and not be persuaded he was a man of extraordinary parts. All our islanders easily acquire a kind of eloquence, and can roll out and illustrate, with a great deal of vigor and fancy, second-hand sermons; but Namu's sermons are his own, and I cannot deny that I have found them means of grace. Moreover, he has a keen curiosity in secular things, does not fear work, is clever at carpentering, and has made himself so much respected among the neighboring pastors that we call him, in a jest which is half serious, the Bishop of the East. In short, I was proud of the man; all the more puzzled by his letter, and took an occasion to come this way. The morning before my arrival, Vigours had been sent on board the Lion, and Namu was perfectly at his ease, apparently ashamed of his letter, and quite unwilling to explain it. This, of course, I could not allow, and he ended by confessing that he had been much concerned to find his people using the sign of the cross, but since he had learned the explanation his mind was satisfied. For Vigours had the Evil Eye, a common thing in a country of Europe called Italy, where men were often struck dead by that kind of devil, and it appeared the sign of the cross was a charm against its power.

" 'And I explain it, Misi,' said Namu, 'in this way: the country in Europe is a Popey country, and the devil of the Evil Eye may be a Catholic devil, or, at least, used to Catholic ways. So then I reasoned thus: if this sign of the cross were used in a Popey manner it would be sinful, but when it is used only to protect men from a devil, which is a thing harmless in itself, the sign too must be harmless. For the sign is neither good nor bad. But if the bottle be full of gin, the gin is bad; and if the sign be made in idolatry bad, so is the idolatry.' And, very like a native pastor, he had a text apposite about the casting out of devils.

" 'And who has been telling you about the Evil Eye?' I asked.

"He admitted it was Case. Now, I am afraid you will think me very narrow, Mr. Wiltshire, but I must tell you I was displeased, and cannot think a trader at all a good man to advise or have an influence upon my pastors. And, besides, there had been some flying talk in the country of old Adams and his being poisoned, to which I had paid no great heed; but it came back to me at the moment.

"'And is this Case a man of a sanctified life?' I asked.

"He admitted he was not; for, though he did not drink, he was profligate with women, and had no religion.

"'Then,' said I, 'I think the less you have to do with him the better.'

"But it is not easy to have the last word with a man like Namu. He was ready in a moment with an illustration. 'Misi,' said he, 'you have told me there were wise men, not pastors, not even holy, who knew many things useful to be taught—about trees, for instance, and beasts, and to print books, and about the stones that are burned to make knives of. Such men teach you in your college, and you learn from them, but take care not to learn to be unholy. Misi, Case is my college.'

"I knew not what to say. Mr. Vigours had evidently been driven out of Falesá by the machinations of Case and with something not very unlike the collusion of my pastor. I called to mind it was Namu who had reassured me about Adams and traced the rumor to the ill-will of the priest. And I saw I must inform myself more thoroughly from an impartial source. There is an old rascal of a chief here, Faiaso, whom I dare say you saw to-day at the council; he has been all his life turbulent and shy, a great fomenter of rebellions, and a thorn in the side of the mission and the island. For all that he is very shrewd, and, except in politics or about his own misdemeanors, a teller of the truth. I went to his house, told him what I had heard, and besought him to be frank. I do not think I had ever a more painful interview. Perhaps you will understand me, Mr. Wiltshire, if I tell you that I am perfectly serious in these old wives' tales with which you reproached me, and as anxious to do well for these islands as you can be to please and to protect your pretty wife. And you are to remember that I thought Namu a paragon, and was proud of the man as one of the first ripe fruits of the mission. And now I was informed that he had fallen in a sort of dependence upon Case. The beginning of it was not corrupt; it began, doubtless, in fear and respect, produced by trickery and pretence; but I was shocked to find that another element had been lately added, that Namu helped himself in the store, and was believed to be deep in Case's debt. Whatever the trader said, that Namu believed with trembling. He was not alone in this; many in the village lived in a similar subjection; but Namu's case was the most influential, it was through Namu that Case had wrought most evil; and with a certain following among the chiefs, and the pastor in his pocket, the man was as good as master of the village. You know something of Vigours and Adams, but perhaps you have never heard of old Underhill, Adams's predecessor. He was a quiet, mild old fellow, I remember, and we were told he had died suddenly: white men die very suddenly in

Falesá. The truth, as I now heard it, made my blood run cold. It seems he was struck with a general palsy, all of him dead but one eye, which he continually winked. Word was started that the helpless old man was now a devil, and this vile fellow Case worked upon the natives' fears, which he professed to share, and pretended he durst not go into the house alone. At last a grave was dug, and the living body buried at the far end of the village. Nainu, my pastor, whom I had helped to educate, offered up a prayer at the hateful scene.

"I felt myself in a very difficult position. Perhaps it was my duty to have denounced Namu and had him deposed. Perhaps I think so now, but at the time it seemed less clear. He had a great influence, it might prove greater than mine. The natives are prone to superstition; perhaps by stirring them up I might but ingrain and spread these dangerous fancies. And Namu besides, apart from this novel and accursed influence, was a good pastor, an able man, and spiritually minded. Where should I look for a better? How was I to find as good? At that moment, with Namu's failure fresh in my view, the work of my life appeared a mockery; hope was dead in me. I would rather repair such tools as I had than go abroad in quest of others that must certainly prove worse; and a scandal is, at the best, a thing to be avoided when humanly possible. Right or wrong, then, I determined on a quiet course. All that night I denounced and reasoned with the erring pastor, twitted him with his ignorance and want of faith, twitted him with his wretched attitude, making clean the outside of the cup and platter, callously helping at a murder, childishly flying in excitement about a few childish, unnecessary, and inconvenient gestures; and long before day I had him on his knees and bathed in the tears of what seemed a genuine repentance. On Sunday I took the pulpit in the morning, and preached from First Kings, nineteenth, on the fire, the earthquake, and the voice, distinguishing the true spiritual power, and referring with such plainness as I dared to recent events in Falesá. The effect produced was great, and it was much increased when Namu rose in his turn and confessed that he had been wanting in faith and conduct, and was convinced of sin. So far, then, all was well; but there was one unfortunate circumstance. It was nearing the time of our 'May' in the island, when the native contributions to the missions are received; it fell in my duty to make a notification on the subject, and this gave my enemy his chance, by which he was not slow to profit.

"News of the whole proceedings must have been carried to Case as soon as church was over, and the same afternoon he made an occasion to meet me in the midst of the village. He came up with so much intentness and animosity that I felt it would be damaging to avoid him.

" 'So,' says he, in native, 'here is the holy man. He has been preaching against me, but that was not in his heart. He has been preaching upon the love of God; but that was not in his heart, it was between his teeth. Will you know what was in his heart?' cries he. 'I will show it to you!' And, making a snatch at my hand, he made believe to pluck out a dollar, and held it in the air.

"There went that rumor through the crowd with which Polynesians receive a prodigy. As for myself, I stood amazed. The thing was a common conjuring trick which I have seen performed at home a score of times; but how was I to convince the villagers of that? I wished I had learned legerdemain instead of Hebrew, that I might have paid the fellow out with his own coin. But there I was; I could not stand there silent, and the best I could find to say was weak.

" 'I will trouble you not to lay hands on me again,' said I.

" 'I have no such thought,' said he, 'nor will I deprive you of your dollar. Here it is,' he said, and flung it at my feet. I am told it lay where it fell three days.

" 'I must say it was well played,' said I.

"Oh! he is clever," said Mr. Tarleton, "and you can now see for yourself how dangerous. He was a party to the horrid death of the paralytic; he is accused of poisoning Adams; he drove Vigours out of the place by lies that might have led to murder; and there is no question but he has now made up his mind to rid himself of you. How he means to try we have no guess; only be sure, it's something new. There is no end to his readiness and invention."

"He gives himself a sight of trouble," says I. "And after all, what for?"

"Why, how many tons of copra may they make in this district?" asked the missionary.

"I dare say as much as sixty tons," says I.

"And what is the profit to the local trader?" he asked.

"You may call it three pounds," said I.

"Then you can reckon for yourself how much he does it for," said Mr. Tarleton. "But the more important thing is to defeat him. It is clear he spread some report against Uma, in order to isolate and have his wicked will of her. Failing of that, and seeing a new rival come upon the scene, he used her in a different way. Now, the first point to find out is about Namu. Uma, when people began to leave you and your mother alone, what did Namu do?"

"Stop away all-a-same," says Uma.

"I fear the dog has returned to his vomit," said Mr. Tarleton. "And now what am I to do for you? I will speak to Namu, I will warn him he is observed; it will be strange if he allow anything to go on amiss when he is put upon his guard. At the same time, this precaution may fail, and then you must turn elsewhere. You have two people at hand to whom you might apply. There is, first of all, the priest, who might protect you by the Catholic interest; they are a wretchedly small body, but they count two chiefs. And then there is old Faiaso. Ah! if it had been some years ago you would have needed no one else; but his influence is much reduced, it has gone into Maea's hands, and Maea, I fear, is one of Case's jackals. In fine, if the worst comes to the worst, you must send up or come yourself to Fale-alii, and, though I am not due at this end of the island for a month, I will just see what can be done."

So Mr. Tarleton said farewell; and half an hour later the crew were singing and the paddles flashing in the missionary-boat.

IV. DEVIL-WORK

Near a month went by without much doing. The same night of our marriage Galoshes called round, and made himself mighty civil, and got into a habit of dropping in about dark and smoking his pipe with the family. He could talk to Uma, of course, and started to teach me native and French at the same time. He was a kind old buffer, though the dirtiest you would wish to see, and he muddled me up with foreign languages worse than the Tower of Babel.

That was one employment we had, and it made me feel less lonesome; but there was no profit in the thing, for though the priest came and sat and yarned, none of his folks could be enticed into my store, and if it hadn't been for the other occupation I struck out, there wouldn't have been a pound of copra in the house. This was the idea: Fa'avao (Uma's mother) had a score of bearing-trees. Of course we could get no labor, being all as good as tabooed, and the two women and I turned to and made copra with our own hands. It was copra to make your mouth water when it was done—I never understood how much the natives cheated me till I had made that four hundred pounds of my own hand—and it weighed so light I felt inclined to take and water it myself.

When we were at the job a good many Kanakas used to put in the best of the day looking on, and once that nigger turned up. He stood back with the natives and laughed and did the big don and the funny dog, till I began to get riled.

"Here, you nigger!" says I.

"I don't address myself to you, Sah," says the nigger. "Only speak to gen'le'um."

"I know," says I, "but it happens I was addressing myself to you, Mr. Black Jack. And all I want to know is just this: did you see Case's figure-head about a week ago?"

"No, Sah," says he.

"That's all right, then," says I; "for I'll show you the own brother to it, only black, in the inside of about two minutes."

And I began to walk toward him, quite slow, and my hands down; only there was trouble in my eye, if anybody took the pains to look.

"You're a low, obstropulous fellow, Sah," says he.

"You bet!" says I.

By that time he thought I was about as near as convenient, and lit out so it would have done your heart good to see him travel. And that was all I saw of that precious gang until what I am about to tell you.

It was one of my chief employments these days to go pot-hunting in the woods, which I found (as Case had told me) very rich in game. I have spoken of the cape which shut up the village and my station from the east. A path went about the end of it, and led into the next bay. A strong wind blew here daily, and as the line of the barrier reef stopped at the end of the cape, a heavy surf ran on the shores of the bay. A little cliffy hill cut the valley in two parts, and stood close on the beach; and at high water the sea broke right on the face of it, so that all passage was stopped. Woody mountains hemmed the place all round; the barrier to the east was particularly steep arid leafy, the lower parts of it, along the sea, falling in sheer black cliffs streaked with cinnabar; the upper part lumpy with the tops of the great trees. Some of the trees were bright green, and some red, and the sand of the beach as black as your shoes. Many birds hovered round the bay, some of them snow-white; and the flying-fox (or vampire) flew there in broad daylight, gnashing its teeth.

For a long while I came as far as this shooting, and went no farther. There was no sign of any path beyond, and the cocoa-palms in the front of the foot of the valley were the last this way. For the whole "eye," of the island, as natives call the windward end, lay desert. From Falesá round about to Papa-malulu, there was neither house, nor man, nor planted fruit-tree; and the reef being mostly absent, and the shores bluff, the sea beat direct among crags, and there was scarce a landing-place.

I should tell you that after I began to go in the woods, although no one appeared to come near my store, I found people willing enough to pass the time of day with me where nobody could see them; and as I had begun to pick up native, and most of them had a word or two of English, I began to hold little odds and ends of conversation, not to much purpose, to be sure, but they took off the worst of the feeling, for it's a miserable thing to be made a leper of.

It chanced one day, toward the end of the mouth, that I was sitting in this bay in the edge of the bush, looking east, with a Kanaka. I had given him a fill of tobacco, and we were making out to talk as best we could; indeed, he had more English than most.

I asked him if there was no road going eastward.

"One time one road," said he. "Now he dead."

"Nobody he go there?" I asked.

"No good," said he. "Too much devil he stop there."

"Oho!" says I, "got-um plenty devil, that bush?"

"Man devil, woman devil; too much devil," said my friend. "Stop there all-e-time. Man he go there, no come back."

I thought if this fellow was so well posted on devils and spoke of them so free, which is not common, I had better fish for a little information about myself and Uma.

"You think me one devil?" I asked.

"No think devil," said he, soothingly. "Think all-e-same fool."

"Uma, she devil?" I asked again.

"No, no; no devil. Devil stop bush," said the young man.

I was looking in front of me across the bay, and I saw the hanging front of the woods pushed suddenly open, and Case, with a gun in his hand, step forth into the sunshine on the black beach. He was got up in light pyjamas, near white, his gun sparkled, he looked mighty conspicuous; and the land-crabs scuttled from all around him to their holes.

"Hullo, my friend!" says I, "you no talk all-e-same true. Ese he go, he come back."

"Ese no all-e-same; Ese *Tiapolo*," says my friend; and, with a "Good-by," slunk off among the trees.

I watched Case all around the beach, where the tide was low; and let him pass me on the homeward way to Falesá. He was in deep thought, and the birds seemed to know it, trotting quite near him on the sand, or wheeling and calling in his ears. When he passed me I could see by the working of his lips that he was talking to himself, and what pleased me mightily, he had still my trade-mark on his brow. I tell you the plain truth: I had a mind to give him a gunful in his ugly mug, but I thought better of it.

All this time, and all the time I was following home, I kept repeating that native word, which I remembered by "Polly, put the kettle on and make us all some tea," tea-a-pollo.

"Uma," says I, when I got back, "what does *Tiapolo* mean?"

"Devil," says she.

"I thought *aitu* was the word for that," I said.

"*Aitu* 'nother kind of devil," said she; "stop bush, eat Kanaka. Tiapolo big chief devil, stop home; all-e-same Christian devil."

"Well, then," said I, "I'm no farther forward. How can Case be Tiapolo?"

"No all-e-same," said she. "Ese belong Tiapolo. Tiapolo too much like; Ese all-e-same his son. Suppose Ese he wish something, Tiapolo he make him."

"That's mighty convenient for Ese," says I. "And what kind of things does he make for him?"

Well, out came a rigmarole of all sorts of stories, many of which (like the dollar he took from Mr. Tarleton's head) were plain enough to me, but others I could make nothing of; and the thing that most surprised the Kanakas was what surprised me least—namely, that he would go in the desert among all the *aitus*. Some of the boldest, however, had accompanied him, and had heard him speak with the dead and give them orders, and, safe in his protection, had returned unscathed. Some said he had a church there, where he worshipped Tiapolo, and Tiapolo appeared to him; others swore that there was no sorcery at all, that he performed his miracles by the power of prayer, and the church was no church, but a prison, in which he had confined a dangerous *aitu*. Namu had been in the bush with him once, and returned glorifying God for these wonders. Altogether, I began to have a glimmer of the man's position, and the means by which he had acquired it, and, though I saw he was a tough nut to crack, I was noways cast down.

"Very well," said I, "I'll have a look at Master Case's place of worship myself, and we'll see about the glorifying."

At this Uma fell in a terrible taking; if I went in the high bush I should never return; none could go there but by the protection of Tiapolo.

"I'll chance it on God's," said I. "I'm a good sort of a fellow, Uma, as fellows go, and I guess God'll con me through."

She was silent for a while. "I think," said she, mighty solemn—and then, presently—"Victoreea, he big chief?"

"You bet!" said I.

"He like you too much?" she asked again.

I told her, with a grin, I believed the old lady was rather partial to me.

"All right," said she. "Victoreea he big chief, like you too much. No can help you here in Falesá; no can do—too far off. Maea he be small chief—stop here. Suppose he like you—make you all right. All-e-same God and Tiapolo. God he big chief—got too much work. Tiapolo he small chief—he like too much make-see, work very hard."

"I'll have to hand you over to Mr. Tarleton," said I. "Your theology's out of its bearings, Uma."

However, we stuck to this business all the evening, and, with the stories she told me of the desert and its dangers, she came near frightening herself into a fit. I don't remember half a quarter of them, of course, for I paid little heed; but two come back to me kind of clear.

About six miles up the coast there is a sheltered cove they call *Fanga-anaana*— "the haven full of caves." I've seen it from the sea myself, as near as I could get my boys to venture in; and it's a little strip of yellow sand, black cliffs overhang it, full of the black mouths of caves; great trees overhang the cliffs, and dangle-down lianas; and in one place, about the middle, a big brook pours over in a cascade. Well, there was a boat going by here, with six young men of Falesá, "all very pretty," Uma said, which was the loss of them. It blew strong, there was a heavy head sea, and by the time they opened Fanga-anaana, and saw the white cascade and the shady beach, they were all tired and thirsty, and their water had run out. One proposed to land and get a drink, and, being reckless fellows, they were all of the same mind except the youngest. Lotu was his name; he was a very good young gentleman, and very wise; and he held out that they were crazy, telling them the place was given over to spirits and devils and the dead, and there were no living folk nearer than six miles the one way, and maybe twelve the other. But they laughed at his words, and, being five to one, pulled in, beached the boat, and landed. It was a wonderful pleasant place, Lotu said, and the water excellent. They walked round the beach, but could see nowhere any way to mount the cliffs, which made them easier in their mind; and at last they sat down to make a meal on the food they had brought with them. They were scarce set, when there came out of the mouth of one of the black caves six of the most beautiful ladies ever seen; they had flowers in their hair, and the most beautiful breasts, and necklaces of scarlet seeds; and began to jest with these young gentlemen, and the young gentlemen to jest back with them, all but Lotu. As for Lotu, he saw there could be no living woman in such a place, and ran, and flung himself in the bottom of the boat, and covered his face, and prayed. All the time the business lasted Lotu made one clean break of prayer, and that was all he knew of it, until his friends came back, and made him sit up, and they put to sea again out of the bay, which was now quite desert, and no word of the six ladies. But, what frightened Lotu most, not one of the five remembered anything of what had passed, but they were all like drunken men, and sang and laughed in the boat, and skylarked. The wind freshened and came squally, and the sea rose extraordinary high; it was such weather as any man in the islands would have turned his back to and fled home to Falesá; but these five were like crazy folk, and cracked on all sail and drove their boat into the seas. Lotu went to the bailing; none of the others thought to help him, but sang and skylarked and carried on, and spoke singular things beyond a man's comprehension, and laughed out loud when they said them. So the rest of the day Lotu bailed for his life in the bottom of the boat, and was all drenched with sweat and cold sea-water; and none heeded him. Against all expectation, they came safe in a dreadful tempest to Papa-malulu, where the palms were singing out, and the cocoa-nuts flying like cannon-balls about the village green; and the same night the five young gentlemen sickened, and spoke never a reasonable word until they died.

"And do you mean to tell me you can swallow a yarn like that?" I asked.

She told me the thing was well known, and with handsome young men alone it was even common; but this was the only case where five had been slain the same day and in a company by the love of the women-devils; and it had made a great stir in the island, and she would be crazy if she doubted.

"Well, anyway," says I, "you needn't be frightened about me. I've no use for the women-devils. You're all the women I want, and all the devil too, old lady."

To this she answered there were other sorts, and she had seen one with her own eyes. She had gone one day alone to the next bay, and, perhaps, got too near the margin of the bad place. The boughs of the high bush overshadowed her from the cant of the hill, but she herself was outside on a flat place, very stony and growing full of young mummy-apples four and five feet high. It was a dark day in the rainy season, and now there came squalls that tore off the leaves and sent them flying, and now it was all still as in a house. It was in one of these still times that a whole gang of birds and flying-foxes came pegging out of the bush like creatures frightened. Presently after she heard a rustle nearer hand, and saw, coming out of the margin of the trees, among the mummy-apples, the appearance of a lean gray old boar. It seemed to think as it came, like a person; and all of a sudden, as she looked at it coming, she was aware it was no boar, but a thing that was a man with a man's thoughts. At that she ran, and the pig after her, and as the pig ran it holla'd aloud, so that the place rang with it.

"I wish I had been there with my gun," said I. "I guess that pig would have holla'd so as to surprise himself."

But she told me a gun was of no use with the like of these, which were the spirits of the dead.

Well, this kind of talk put in the evening, which was the best of it; but of course it didn't change my notion, and the next day, with my gun and a good knife, I set off upon a voyage of discovery. I made, as near as I could, for the place where I had seen Case come out; for if it was true he had some kind of establishment in the bush I reckoned I should find a path. The beginning of the desert was marked off by a wall, to call it so, for it was more of a long mound of stones. They say it reaches right across the island, but how they know it is another question, for I doubt if any one has made the journey in a hundred years, the natives sticking chiefly to the sea and their little colonies along the coast, and that part being mortal high and steep and full of cliffs. Up to the west side of the wall the ground has been cleared, and there are cocoa-palms and mummy-apples and guavas, and lots of sensitive. Just across, the bush begins outright; high bush at that, trees going up like the masts of ships, and ropes of liana hanging down like a ship's rigging, and nasty orchids growing in the forks like funguses. The ground where there was no underwood looked to be a heap of boulders. I saw many green pigeons which I might have shot, only I was there with a different idea. A number of butterflies flopped up and down along the ground like dead leaves; sometimes I would hear a bird calling, sometimes the wind overhead; and always the sea along the coast.

But the queerness of the place it's more difficult to tell of, unless to one who has been alone in the high bush himself. The brightest kind of a day it is always dim down there. A' man can see to the end of nothing; whichever way he looks the wood shuts up, one bough folding with another like the fingers of your hand; and whenever he listens he hears always something new—men talking, children laughing, the strokes of an axe a far way ahead of him, and sometimes a sort of a quick, stealthy scurry near at hand that makes him jump and look to his weapons. It's all very well for him to tell himself that he's alone, bar trees and birds; he can't make out to believe it; whichever way he turns the whole place seems to be alive and looking on. Don't think it was Uma's yarns that put me out; I don't value native talk a fourpenuy-piece; it's a thing that's natural in the bush, and that's the end of it.

As I got near the top of the hill, for the ground of the wood goes up in this place steep as a ladder, the wind began to sound straight on, and the leaves to toss and switch open and let in the sun. This suited me better; it was the same noise all the time, and nothing to startle. Well, I had got to a place where there was an underwood of what they call wild cocoanut—mighty pretty with its scarlet fruit—when there came a sound of singing in the wind that I thought I had never heard the like of. It was all very fine to tell myself it was the branches; I knew better. It was all very fine to tell myself it was a bird; I knew never a bird that sang like that. It rose and swelled, and died away and swelled again; and now I thought it was like someone weeping, only prettier; and now I thought it was like harps; and there was one thing I made sure of, it was a sight too sweet to be wholesome in a place like that. You may laugh if you like; but I declare I called to mind the six young ladies that came, with their scarlet necklaces, out of the cave at Fanga-anaana, and wondered if they sang like that. We laugh at the natives and their superstitions; but see how many traders take them up, splendidly educated white men, that have been bookkeepers (some of them) and clerks in the old country. It's my belief a superstition grows up in a place like the different kind of weeds; and as I stood there and listened to that wailing I twittered in my shoes.

You may call me a coward to be frightened; I thought myself brave enough to go on ahead. But I went mighty carefully, with my gun cocked, spying all about me like a hunter, fully expecting to see a handsome young woman sitting somewhere in the bush, and fully determined (if I did) to try her with a charge of duck-shot. And sure enough, I had not gone far when I met with a queer thing. The wind came on the top of the wood in a strong puff, the leaves in front of me burst open, and I saw for a second something hanging in a tree. It was gone in a wink, the puff blowing by and the leaves closing. I tell you the truth: I had made up my mind to see an *aitu*; and if the thing had looked like a pig or a woman, it wouldn't have given me the same turn. The trouble was that it seemed kind of square, and the idea of a square thing that was alive and sang knocked me sick and silly. I must have stood quite a while; and I made pretty certain it was right out of the same tree that the singing came. Then I began to come to myself a bit.

"Well," says I, "if this is really so, if this is a place where there are square things that sing, I'm gone up anyway. Let's have my fun for my money."

But I thought I might as well take the offchance of a prayer being any good ; so I plumped on my knees and prayed out loud; and all the time I was praying the strange sounds came out of the tree, and went up and down, and changed, for all the world like music, only you could see it wasn't human—there was nothing there that you could whistle.

As soon as I had made an end in proper style, I laid down my gun, stuck my knife between my teeth, walked right up to that tree and began to climb. I tell you my heart was like ice. But presently, as I went up, I caught another glimpse of the thing, and that relieved me, for I thought it seemed like a box; and when I had got right up to it I near fell out of the tree with laughing.

A box it was, sure enough, and a candle-box at that, with the brand upon the side of it; and it had banjo-strings stretched so as to sound when the wind blew. I believe they call the thing an Æolean harp, whatever that may mean.

"Well, Mr. Case," said I, "you frightened me once, but I defy you to frighten me again," I says, and slipped down the tree, and set out again to find my enemy's head office, which I guessed would not be far away.

The undergrowth was thick in this part; I couldn't see before my nose, and must burst my way through by main force and ply the knife as I went, slicing the cords of the lianas and slashing down whole trees at a blow. I call them trees for the bigness, but in truth they were just big weeds, and sappy to cut through like carrot. From all this crowd and kind of vegetation, I was just thinking to myself, the place might have once been cleared, when I came on my nose over a pile of stones, and saw in a moment it was some kind of a work of man. The Lord knows when it was made or when deserted, for this part of the island has lain undisturbed since long before the whites came. A few steps beyond I hit into the path I had been always looking for. It was narrow, but well beaten, and I saw that Case had plenty of disciples. It seems, indeed it was, a piece of fashionable boldness to venture up here with the trader, and a young man scarce reckoned himself grown till he had got his breech tattooed, for one thing, and seen

Case's devils for another. This is mighty like Kanakas: but, if you look at it another way, it's mighty like white folks too.

A bit along the path I was brought to a clear stand, and had to rub my eyes. There was a wall in front of me, the path passing it by a gap; it was tumbledown and plainly very old, but built of big stones very well laid; and there is no native alive to-day upon that island that could dream of such a piece of building! Along all the top of it was a line of queer figures, idols or scarecrows, or what not. They had carved and painted faces ugly to view, their eyes and teeth were of shell, their hair and their bright clothes blew in the wind, and some of them worked with the tugging. There are islands up west where they make these kind of figures till to-day; but if ever they were made in this island, the practice and the very recollection of it are now long forgotten. And the singular thing was that all these bogies were as fresh as toys out of a shop.

Then it came in my mind that Case had let out to me the first day that he was a good forger of island curiosities—a thing by which so many traders turn an honest penny. And with that I saw the whole business, and how this display served the man a double purpose: first of all, to season his curiosities, and then to frighten those that came to visit him.

But I should tell you (what made the thing more curious) that all the time the Tyrolean harps were harping round me in the trees, and even while I looked, a green-and-yellow bird (that, I suppose, was building) began to tear the hair off the head of one of the figures.

A little farther on I found the best curiosity of the museum. The first I saw of it was a longish mound of earth with a twist to it. Digging off the earth with my hands, I found underneath tarpaulin stretched on boards, so that this was plainly the roof of a cellar. It stood right on the top of the hill, and the entrance was on the far side, between two rocks, like the entrance to a cave. I went as far in as the bend, and, looking round the corner, saw a shining face. It was big and ugly, like a pantomime mask, and the brightness of it waxed and dwindled, and at times it smoked.

"Oho!" says I, "luminous paint!"

And I must say I rather admired the man's ingenuity. With a box of tools and a few mighty simple contrivances he had made out to have a devil of a temple. Any poor Kanaka brought up here in the dark, with the harps whining all round him, and shown that smoking face in the bottom of a hole, would make no kind of doubt but he had seen and heard enough devils for a lifetime. It's easy to find out what Kanakas think. Just go back to yourself anyway round from ten to fifteen years old, and there's an average Kanaka. There are some pious, just as there are pious boys; and the most of them, like the boys again, are middling honest and yet think it rather larks to steal, and are easy scared, and rather like to be so. I remember a boy I was at school with at home who played the Case business. He didn't know anything, that boy; he couldn't do anything; he had no luminous paint and no Tyrolean harps; he just boldly said he was a sorcerer, and frightened us out of our boots, and we loved it. And then it came in my mind how the master had once flogged that boy, and the surprise we were all in to see the sorcerer catch it and hum like anybody else. Thinks I to myself: "I must find some way of fixing it so for Master Case." And the next moment I had my idea.

I went back by the path, which, when once you had found it, was quite plain and easy walking; and when I stepped out on the black sands, who should I see but Master Case himself. I cocked my gun and held it handy, and we marched up and passed without a word, each keeping the tail of his eye on the other; and no sooner had we passed than we each wheeled round like fellows drilling, and stood face to face. We had each taken the same notion in his head, you see, that the other fellow might give him the load of his gun in the stern.

"You've shot nothing," says Case.

"I'm not on the shoot to-day," said I.

"Well, the devil go with you for me," says he.

"The same to you," says I.

But we stuck just the way we were; no fear of either of us moving.

Case laughed. "We can't stop here all day, though," said he.

"Don't let me detain you," says I.

He laughed again. "Look here, Wiltshire, do you think me a fool?" he asked.

"More of a knave, if you want to know," says I.

"Well, do you think it would better me to shoot you here, on this open beach?" said he. "Because I don't. Folks come fishing every day. There may be a score of them up the valley now, making copra; there might be half a dozen on the hill behind you, after pigeons; they might be watching us this minute, and I shouldn't wonder. I give you my word I don't want to shoot you. Why should I? You don't hinder me any. You haven't got one pound of copra but what you made with your own hands, like a negro slave. You're vegetating—that's what I call it—and I don't care where you vegetate, nor yet how long. Give me your word you don't mean to shoot me, and I'll give you a lead and walk away."

"Well," said I, "you're frank and pleasant, ain't you? And I'll be the same. I don't mean to shoot you to-day. Why should I? This business is beginning; it ain't done yet, Mr. Case. I've given you one turn already. I can see the marks of my knuckles on your head to this blooming hour, and I've more cooking for you. I'm not a paralee, like

Underbill. My name ain't Adams, and it ain't Vigours; and I mean to show you that you've met your match."

"This is a silly way to talk," said he. "This is not the talk to make me move on with."

"All right," said I, "stay where you are. I ain't in any hurry, and you know it. I can put in a day on this beach and never mind. I ain't got any copra to bother with. I ain't got any luminous paint to see to."

I was sorry I said that last, but it whipped out before I knew. I could see it took the wind out of his sails, and he stood and stared at me with his brow drawn up. Then I suppose he made up his mind he must get to the bottom of this.

"I take you at your word," says he, and turned his back, and walked right into the devil's bush.

I let him go, of course, for I had passed my word. But I watched him as long as he was in sight, and after he was gone lit out for cover as lively as you would want to see, and went the rest of the way home under the bush, for I didn't trust him sixpence worth. One thing I saw, I had been ass enough to give him warning, and that which I meant to do I must do at once.

You would think I had had about enough excitement for one morning, but there was another turn waiting me. As soon as I got far enough round the cape to see my house I made out there were strangers there; a little farther, and no doubt about it. There was a couple of armed sentinels squatting at my door. I could only suppose the trouble about Uma must have come to a head, and the station been seized. For aught I could think, Uma was taken up already, and these armed men were waiting to do the like with me.

However, as I came nearer, which I did at top speed, I saw there was a third native sitting on the veranda like a guest, and Uma was talking with him like a hostess. Nearer still I made out it was the big young chief, Maea, and that he was smiling away and smoking. And what was he smoking? None of your European cigarettes fit for a cat, not even the genuine big, knock-me-down native article that a fellow can really put in the time with if his pipe is broke—but a cigar, and one of my Mexicans at that, that I could swear to. At sight of this my heart started beating, and I took a wild hope in my head that the trouble was over, and Maea had come round.

Uma pointed me out to him as I came up, and he met me at the head of my own stairs like a thorough gentleman.

"Vilivili," said he, which was the best they could make of my name, "I pleased."

There is no doubt when an island chief wants to be civil he can do it. I saw the way things were from the word go. There was no call for Uma to say to me: "He no 'fraid

Ese now, come bring copra." I tell you I shook hands with that Kanaka like as if he was the best white man in Europe.

The fact was, Case and he had got after the same girl, or Maea suspected it, and concluded to make hay of the trader on the chance. He had dressed himself up, got a couple of his retainers cleaned and armed to kind of make the thing more public, and, just waiting till Case was clear of the village, came round to put the whole of Iris business my way. He was rich as well as powerful. I suppose that man was worth fifty thousand nuts per annum. I gave him the price of the beach and a quarter cent better, and as for credit, I would have advanced him the inside of the store and the fittings besides, I was so pleased to see him. I must say he bought like a gentleman: rice and tins and biscuits enough for a week's feast, and stuffs by the bolt. He was agreeable besides; he had plenty fun to him; and we cracked jests together, mostly through the interpreter, because he had mighty little English, and my native was still off color. One thing I made out: he could never really have thought much harm of Uma; he could never have been really frightened, and must just have made believe from dodginess, and because he thought Case had a strong pull in the village and could help him on.

This set me thinking that both he and I were in a tightish place. What he had done was to fly in the face of the whole village, and the thing might cost him his authority. More than that, after my talk with Case on the beach, I thought it might very well cost me my life. Case had as good as said he would pot me if ever I got any copra; he would come home to find the best business in the village had changed hands, and the best thing I thought I could do was to get in first with the potting.

"See here, Uma," says I, "tell him I'm sorry I made him wait, but I was up looking at Case's Tiapolo store in the bush."

"He want savvy if you no 'fraid?" translated Uma.

I laughed out. "Not much!" says I. "Tell him the place is a blooming toy-shop! Tell him in England we give these things to the kid to play with."

"He want savvy if you hear devil sing?" she asked next.

"Look here," I said, "I can't do it now, because I've got no banjo-strings in stock; but the next time the ship comes round I'll have one of these same contraptions right here in my veranda, and he can see for himself how much devil there is to it. Tell him, as soon as I can get the strings I'll make one for his picaninnies. The name of the concern is a Tyrolean harp; and you can tell him the name means in English that nobody but dam-fools give a cent for it."

This time he was so pleased he had to try his English again. "You talk true?" says he.

"Bather!" said I. "Talk all-a-same Bible. Bring out a Bible here, Uma, if you've got such a thing, and I'll kiss it. Or, I'll tell you what's better still," says I, taking a header, "ask him if he's afraid to go up there himself by day."

It appeared he wasn't; he could venture as far as that by day and in company.

"That's the ticket, then!" said I. "Tell him the man's a fraud and the place foolishness, and if he'll go up there to-morrow he'll see all that's left of it. But tell him this, Uma, and mind he understands it: If he gets talking it's bound to come to Case, and I'm a dead man! I'm playing his game, tell him, and if he says one word my blood will be at his door and be the damnation of him here and after."

She told him, and he shook hands with me up to the hilt, and, says he: "No talk. Go up tomollow. You my friend?"

"No, sir," says I, "no such foolishness. I've come here to trade, tell him, and not to make friends. But, as to Case, I'll send that man to glory!"

So off Maea went, pretty well pleased, as I could see.

V. NIGHT IN THE BUSH

Well, I was committed now; Tiapolo had to be smashed up before next day, and my hands were pretty full, not only with preparations, but with argument. My house was like a mechanics' debating society. Uma was so made up that I shouldn't go into the bush by night, or that, if I did, I was never to come back again. You know her style of arguing: you've had a specimen about Queen Victoria and the devil; and I leave you to fancy if I was tired of it before dark.

At last I had a good idea. "What was the use of casting my pearls before her?" I thought; some of her own chopped hay would be likelier to do the business.

"I'll tell you what, then," said I. "You fish out your Bible, and I'll take that up along with me. That'll make me right."

She swore a Bible was no use.

"That's just your Kanaka ignorance," said I. "Bring the Bible out."

She brought it, and I turned to the title-page, where I thought there would likely be some English, and so there was. "There!" said I. "Look at that! 'London: Printed for the British and Foreign Bible Society, Blackfriars,' and the date, which I can't read, owing to its being in these X's. There's no devil in hell can look near the Bible Society, Blackfriars. Why, you silly," I said, "how do you suppose we get along with our own *aitus* at home! All Bible Society!"

"I think you no got any," said she. "White man, he tell me you no got."

"Sounds likely, don't it?" I asked. "Why would these islands all be chock full of them and none in Europe?"

"Well, you no got bread-fruit," said she.

I could have torn my hair. "Now, look here, old lady," said I, "you dry up, for I'm tired of you. I'll take the Bible, which'll put me as straight as the mail, and that's the last word I've got to say."

The night fell extraordinary dark, clouds coming up with sundown and overspreading all; not a star showed; there was only an end of a moon, and that not due before the small hours. Round the village, what with the lights and the fires in the open houses, and the torches of many fishers moving on the reef, it kept as gay as an illumination; but the sea and the mountains and woods were all clean gone. I suppose it might be eight o'clock when I took the road, laden like a donkey. First there was that Bible, a book as big as your head, which I had let myself in for by my own tomfoolery. Then there was my gun, and knife, and lantern, and patent matches, all necessary. And then there was the real plant of the affair in hand, a mortal weight of gunpowder, a pair of dynamite fishing-bombs, and two or three pieces of slow match that I had hauled out of the tin cases and spliced together the best way I could; for the match was only trade stuff, and a man would be crazy that trusted it. Altogether, you see, I had the materials of a pretty good blow up! Expense was nothing to me; I wanted that thing done right.

As long as I was in the open, and had the lamp in my house to steer by, I did well. But when I got to the path, it fell so dark I could make no headway, walking into trees and swearing there, like a man looking for the matches in his bed-room. I knew it was risky to light up, for my lantern would be visible all the way to the point of the cape, and as no one went there after dark, it would be talked about, and come to Case's ears. But what was I to do? I had either to give the business over and lose caste with Maea, or light up, take my chance, and get through the thing the smartest I was able.

As long as I was on the path I walked hard, but when I came to the black beach I had to run. For the tide was now nearly flowed; and to get through with my powder dry between the surf and the steep hill, took all the quickness I possessed. As it was, even the wash caught me to the knees, and I came near falling on a stone. All this time the hurry I was in, and the free air and smell of the sea, kept my spirits lively; but when I was once in the bush and began to climb the path I took it easier. The fearsomeness of the wood had been a good bit rubbed off for me by Master Case's banjo-strings and graven images, yet I thought it was a dreary walk, and guessed, when the disciples went up there, they must be badly scared. The light of the lantern, striking among all these trunks and forked branches and twisted rope-ends of lianas, made the whole place, or all that you could see of it, a kind of a puzzle of turning shadows. They came to meet you, solid and quick like giants, and then spun off and vanished; they hove up over your head like clubs, and flew away into the night like birds. The floor of the bush glimmered with dead wood, the way the match-box used to shine after you had struck a lucifer. Big, cold drops fell on me from the branches overhead like sweat. There was no wind to mention; only a little icy breath of a land breeze that stirred nothing; and the harps were silent.

The first landfall I made was when I got through the bush of wild cocoanuts, and came in view of the bogies on the wall. Mighty queer they looked by the shining of the lantern, with their painted faces and shell eyes, and their clothes, and their hair hanging. One after another I pulled them all up and piled them in a bundle on the cellar roof, so as they might go to glory with the rest. Then I chose a place behind one of the big stones at the entrance, buried my powder and the two shells, and arranged my match along the passage. And then I had a look at the smoking head, just for good-by. It was doing fine.

"Cheer up," says I. "You're booked."

It was my first idea to light up and be getting homeward; for the darkness and the glimmer of the dead wood and the shadows of the lantern made me lonely. But I knew where one of the harps hung; it seemed a pity it shouldn't go with the rest; and at the same time I couldn't help letting on to myself that I was mortal tired of my employment, and would like best to be at home and have the door shut. I stepped out of the cellar and argued it fore and back. There was a sound of the sea far down below me on the coast; nearer hand not a leaf stirred; I might have been the only living creature this side of Cape Horn. Well, as I stood there thinking, it seemed the bush woke and became full of little noises. Little noises they were, and nothing to hurt; a bit of a crackle, a bit of a rush; but the breath jumped right out of me and my throat went as dry as a biscuit. It wasn't Case I was afraid of, which would have been common-sense; I never thought of Case; what took me, as sharp as the colic, was the old wives' tales—the devil-women and the man-pigs. It was the toss of a penny whether I should run; but I got a purchase on myself, and stepped out, and held up the lantern (like a fool) and looked all round.

In the direction of the village and the path there was nothing to be seen; but when I turned inland it's a wonder to me I didn't drop. There, coming right up out of the desert and the bad bush—there, sure enough, was a devil-woman, just as the way I had figured she would look. I saw the light shine on her bare arms and her bright eyes, and there went out of me a yell so big that I thought it was my death.

"Ah! No sing out!" says the devil-woman, in a kind of a high whisper. "Why you talk big voice? Put out light! Ese he come."

"My God Almighty, Uma, is that you?" says I.

"*Ioe*,"* says she. "I come quick. Ese here soon."

"You come along?" I asked. "You no 'fraid?"

"Ah, too much 'fraid!" she whispered, clutching me. "I think die."

"Well," says I, with a kind of a weak grin, "I'm not the one to laugh at you, Mrs. Wiltshire, for I'm about the worst scared man in the South Pacific myself."

She told me in two words what brought her. I was scarce gone, it seems, when Faavao came in, and the old woman had met Black Jack running as hard as he was fit from our house to Case's. Uma neither spoke nor stopped, but lit right out to come and warn me. She was so close at my heels that the lantern was her guide across the beach, and afterward, by the glimmer of it in the trees, she got her line up hill. It was only when I had got to the top or was in the cellar that she wandered—Lord knows where!—and lost a sight of precious time, afraid to call out lest Case was at the heels of her, and falling in the bush, so that she was all knocked and bruised. That must have been when she got too far to the southward, and how she came to take me in the flank at last and frighten me beyond what I've got the words to tell of.

Well, anything was better than a devil-woman, but I thought her yarn serious enough. Black Jack had no call to be about my house, unless he was set there to watch; and it looked to me as if my tomfool word about the paint, and perhaps some chatter of Maea's, had got us all in a clove hitch. One thing was clear: Uma and I were here for the night; we daren't try to go home before day, and even then it would be safer to strike round up the mountain and come in by the back of the village, or we might walk into an ambuscade. It was plain, too, that the mine should be sprung immediately, or Case might be in time to stop it.

I marched into the tunnel, Uma keeping tight hold of me, opened my lantern and lit the match. The first length of it burned like a spill of paper, and I stood stupid, watching it burn, and thinking we were going aloft with Tiapolo, which was none of my views. The second took to a better rate, though faster than I cared about; and at that I got my wits again, hauled Uma clear of the passage, blew out and dropped the lantern, and the pair of us groped our way into the bush until I thought it might be safe, and lay down together by a tree.

"Old lady," I said, "I won't forget this night. You're a trump, and that's what's wrong with you."

She bumped herself close up to me. She had run out the way she was, with nothing on her but her kilt; and she was all wet with the dews and the sea on the black beach, and shook straight on with cold and the terror of the dark and the devils.

---

* Yes.

"Too much 'fraid," was all she said.

The far side of Case's hill goes down near as steep as a precipice into the next valley. We were on the very edge of it, and I could see the dead wood shine and hear the sea sound far below. I didn't care about the position, which left me no retreat, but I was afraid to change.

Then I saw I had made a worse mistake about the lantern, which I should have left lighted, so that I could have had a crack at Case when he stepped into the shine of it. And since I hadn't had the wit to do that, it seemed a senseless thing to leave the good lantern to blow up with the graven images. The thing belonged to me, after all, and was worth money, and might come in handy. If I could have trusted the match, I might have run in still and rescued it. But who was going to trust to the match? You know what trade is. The stuff was good enough for Kanakas to go fishing with, where they've got to look lively anyway, and the most they risk is only to have their hand blown off. But for anyone that wanted to fool around a blow-up like mine that match was rubbish.

Altogether the best I could do was to lie still, see my shot-gun handy, and wait for the explosion. But it was a solemn kind of a business. The blackness of the night was like solid; the only thing you could see was the nasty bogy glimmer of the dead wood, and that showed you nothing but itself; and as for sounds, I stretched my ears till I thought I could have heard the match burn in the tunnel, and that bush was as silent as a coffin. Now and then there was a bit of a crack; but whether it was near or far, whether it was Case stubbing his toes within a few yards of me, or a tree breaking miles away, I knew no more than the babe unborn.

And then, all of a sudden, Vesuvius went off. It was a long time coming; but when it came (though I say it that shouldn't) no man could ask to see a better. At first it was just a son of a gun of a row, and a spout of fire, and the wood lighted up so that you could see to read. And then the trouble began. Uma and I were half buried under a wagonful of earth, and glad it was no worse, for one of the rocks at the entrance of the tunnel was fired clean into the air, fell within a couple of fathoms of where we lay, and bounded over the edge of the hill, and went pounding down into the next valley. I saw I had rather under-calculated our distance, or over-done the dynamite and powder, which you please.

And presently I saw I had made another slip. The noise of the thing began to die off, shaking the island; the dazzle was over; and yet the night didn't come back the way I expected. For the whole wood was scattered with red coals and brands from the explosion; they were all round me on the flat, some had fallen below in the valley, and some stuck and flared in the tree-tops. I had no fear of fire, for these forests are too wet to kindle. But the trouble was that the place was all lit up—not very bright, but good enough to get a shot by; and the way the coals were scattered, it was just as likely Case might have the advantage as myself. I looked all round for his white face, you may be sure; but there was not a sign of him. As for Uma, the life seemed to have been knocked right out of her by the bang and blaze of it.

There was one bad point in my game. One of the blessed graven images had come down all afire, hair and clothes and body, not four yards away from me. I cast a mighty noticing glance all round; there was still no Case, and I made up my mind I must get rid of that burning stick before he came, or I should be shot there like a dog.

It was my first idea to have crawled, and then I thought speed was the main thing, and stood half up to make a rush. The same moment, from somewhere between me and the sea, there came a flash and a report, and a rifle-bullet screeched in my ear. I swung straight round and up with my gun, but the brute had a Winchester, and before I could as much as see him his second shot knocked me over like a ninepin. I seemed to fly in the air, then came down by the run and lay half a minute, silly; and then I found my hands empty, and my gun had flown over my head as I fell. It makes a man mighty wide awake to be in the kind of box that I was in. I scarcely knew where I was hurt, or whether I was hurt or not, but turned right over on my face to crawl after my weapon. Unless you have tried to get about with a smashed leg you don't know what pain is, and I let out a howl like a bullock's.

This was the unluckiest noise that ever I made in my life. Up to then Uma had stuck to her tree like a sensible woman, knowing she would be only in the way; but as soon as she heard me sing out she ran forward. The Winchester cracked again, and down she went.

I had sat up, leg and all, to stop her; but when I saw her tumble I clapped down again where I was, lay still, and felt the handle of my knife. I had been scurried and put out before. No more of that for me. He had knocked over my girl, I had got to fix him for it; and I lay there and gritted my teeth, and footed up the chances. My leg was broke, my gun was gone. Case had still ten shots in his Winchester. It looked a kind of hopeless business. But I never despaired nor thought upon despairing: that man had got to go.

For a goodish bit not one of us let on. Then I heard Case begin to move nearer in the bush, but mighty careful. The image had burned out, there were only a few coals left here and there, and the wood was main dark, but had a kind of a low glow in it like a fire on its last legs. It was by this that I made out Case's head looking at me over a big tuft of ferns, and at the same time the brute saw me and shouldered his Winchester. I lay quite still, and as good as looked into the barrel: it was my last chance, but I thought my heart would have come right out of its bearings. Then he fired. Lucky for me it was no shot-gun, for the bullet struck within an inch of me and knocked the dirt in my eyes.

Just you try and see if you can lie quiet, and let a man take a sitting shot at you and miss you by a hair. But I did, and lucky, too. A while Case stood with the Winchester at the port-arms; then he gave a little laugh to himself and stepped round the ferns.

"Laugh!" thought I. "If you had the wit of a louse you would be praying!"

I was all as taut as a ship's hawser or the spring of a watch, and as soon as he came within reach of me I had him by the ankle, plucked the feet right out from under him, laid him out, and was upon the top of him, broken leg and all, before he breathed. His Winchester had gone the same road as my shot-gun; it was nothing to me—I defied him now. I'm a pretty strong man anyway, but I never knew what strength was till I got hold of Case. He was knocked out of time by the rattle he came down with, and threw up his hands together, more like a frightened woman, so that I caught both of them with my left. This wakened him up, and he fastened his teeth in my forearm like a weasel. Much I cared. My leg gave me all the pain I had any use for, and I drew my knife and got it in the place.

"Now," said I, "I've got you; and you're gone up, and a good job too! Do you feel the point of that? That's for Underhill! And there's for Adams! And now here's for Uma, and that's going to knock your blooming soul right out of you!"

With that I gave him the cold steel for all I was worth. His body kicked under me like a spring sofa; he gave a dreadful kind of a long moan, and lay still.

"I wonder if you're dead? I hope so!" I thought, for my head was swimming. But I wasn't going to take chances; I had his own example too close before me for that; and I tried to draw the knife out to give it him again. The blood came over my hands, I remember, hot as tea; and with that I fainted clean away, and fell with my head on the man's mouth.

When I came to myself it was pitch dark; the cinders had burned out; there was nothing to be seen but the shine of the dead wood, and I couldn't remember where I was nor why I was in such pain, nor what I was all wetted with. Then it came back, and the first thing I attended to was to give him the knife again a half a dozen times up to the handle. I believe he was dead already, but it did him no harm and did me good.

"I bet you're dead now," I said, and then I called to Uma.

Nothing answered, and I made a move to go and grope for her, fouled my broken leg, and fainted again.

When I came to myself the second time the clouds had all cleared away, except a few that sailed there, white as cotton. The moon was up—a tropic moon. The moon at home turns a wood black, but even this old butt-end of a one showed up that forest as green as by day. The night birds—or, rather, they're a kind of early morning bird—sang out with their long, falling notes like nightingales. And I could see the dead man, that I was still half resting on, looking right up into the sky with, his open eyes, no paler than when he was alive; and a little way off Uma tumbled on her side. I got over to her the best way I was able, and when I got there she was broad awake and crying, and sobbing to herself with no more noise than an insect. It appears she was afraid to cry out loud, because of the aitus. Altogether she was not much hurt, but scared beyond belief; she had come to her senses a long while ago, cried out to me, heard nothing in reply, made out we were both dead, and had lain there ever since, afraid to budge a finger. The ball had ploughed up her shoulder, and she had lost a main quantity of blood; but I soon had that tied up the way it ought to be with the tail of my shirt and a scarf I had on, got her head on my sound knee and my back against a trunk, and settled down to wait for morning. Uma was for neither use nor ornament, and could only clutch hold of me and shake and cry. I don't suppose there was ever anybody worse scared, and, to do her justice, she had had a lively night of it. As for me, I was in a good bit of pain and fever, but not so bad when I sat still; and every time I looked over to Case I could have sung and whistled. Talk about meat and drink! To see that man lying there dead as a herring filled me full.

The night birds stopped after a while; and then the light begun to change, the east came orange, the whole wood began to whirr with singing like a musical box, and there was the broad day.

I didn't expect Maea for a long while yet; and, indeed, I thought there was an off-chance he might go back on the whole idea and not come at all. I was the better pleased when, about an hour after daylight, I heard sticks smashing and a lot of Kanakas laughing and singing out to keep their courage up. Uma sat up quite brisk at the first word of it; and presently we saw a party come stringing out of the path, Maea in front, and behind him a white man in a pith helmet. It was Mr. Tarleton, who had turned up late last night in Falesá, having left his boat and walked the last stage with a lantern.

They buried Case upon the field of glory, right in the hole where he had kept the smoking head. I waited till the thing was done; and Mr. Tarleton prayed, which I thought tom-foolery, but I'm bound to say he gave a pretty sick view of the dear departed's prospects, and seemed to have his own ideas of hell. I had it out with him afterward, told him he had scamped his duty, and what he had ought to have done was to up like a man and tell the Kanakas plainly Case was damned, and a good riddance; but I never could get him to see it my way. Then they made me a litter of poles and carried me down to the station. Mr. Tarleton set my leg, and made a regular missionary splice of it, so that I limp to this day. That done, he took down my evidence, and Urna's, and Maea's, wrote it all out fine, and had us sign it; and then he got the chiefs and marched over to Papa Randall's to seize Case's papers.

All they found was a bit of a diary, kept for a good many years, and all about the price of copra, and chickens being stolen, and that; and the books of the business and the will I told you of in the beginning, by both of which the whole thing (stock, lock, and barrel) appeared to belong to the Samoa woman. It was I that bought her out at a mighty reasonable figure, for she was in a hurry to get home. As for Randall and the black, they had to tramp; got into some kind of a station on the Papa-malulu side; did very bad business, for the truth is neither of the pair was fit for it, and lived mostly on fish, which was the means of Randall's death. It seems there was a nice shoal in one day, and papa went after them with the dynamite; either the match burned too fast, or papa was full, or both, but the shell went off (in the usual way) before he threw it, and where was papa's hand? Well, there's nothing to hurt in that; the islands up north are all full of one-handed men, like the parties in the "Arabian Nights"; but either Randall was too old, or he drank too much, and the short and the long of it was that he died. Pretty soon after, the nigger was turned out of the island for stealing from white men, and went off to the west, where he found men of his own color, in case he liked that, and the men of his own color took and ate him at some kind of a corroborree, and I'm sure I hope he was to their fancy!

So there was I, left alone in my glory at Falesá; and when the schooner came round I filled her up, and gave her a deck cargo half as high as the house. I must say Mr. Tarleton did the right thing by us; but he took a meanish kind of a revenge.

"Now, Mr. Wiltshire," said he, "I've put you all square with everybody here. It wasn't difficult to do, Case being gone; but I have done it, and given my pledge besides that you will deal fairly with the natives. I must ask you to keep my word."

Well, so I did. I used to be bothered about my balances, but I reasoned it out this way. We all have queerish balances, and the natives all know it and water their copra in a proportion so that it's fair all round; but the truth is, it did use to bother me, and, though I did well in Falesá, I was half glad when the firm moved me on to another station, where I was under no kind of a pledge and could look my balances in the face.

As for the old lady, you know her as well as I do. She's only the one fault. If you don't keep your eye lifting she would give away the roof off the station. Well, it seems it's natural in Kanakas. She's turned a powerful big woman now, and could throw a London bobby over her shoulder. But that's natural in Kanakas too, and there's no manner of doubt that she's an A-1 wife.

Mr. Tarleton's gone home, his trick being over. He was the best missionary I ever struck, and now, it seems, he's parsonising down Somerset way. Well, that's best for him; he'll have no Kanakas there to get luny over.

My public-house? Not a bit of it, nor ever likely. I'm stuck here, I fancy. I don't like to leave the kids, you see: and—there's no use talking—they're better here than what they would be in a white man's country, though Ben took the eldest up to Auckland, where he's being schooled with the best. But what bothers me is the girls. They're only half-castes, of course; I know that as well as you do, and there's nobody thinks less of half-castes than I do; but they're mine, and about all I've got. I can't reconcile my mind to their taking up with Kanakas, and I'd like to know where I'm to find the whites?

MACKINTOSH

W. Somerset Maugham

H E SPLASHED ABOUT FOR A FEW MINUTES IN THE SEA; IT WAS TOO SHALLOW to swim in and for fear of sharks he could not go out of his depth; then he got out and went into the bath-house for a shower. The coldness of the fresh water was grateful after the heavy stickiness of the salt Pacific, so warm, though it was only just after seven, that to bathe in it did not brace you but rather increased your languor; and when he had dried himself, slipping into a bath-gown, he called out to the Chinese cook that he would be ready for breakfast in five minutes. He walked barefoot across the patch of coarse grass which Walker, the administrator, proudly thought was a lawn, to his own quarters and dressed. This did not take long, for he put on nothing but a shirt and a pair of duck trousers and then went over to his chief's house on the other side of the compound. The two men had their meals together, but the Chinese cook told him that Walker had set out on horseback at five and would not be back for another hour.

Mackintosh had slept badly and he looked with distaste at the paw-paw and the eggs and bacon which were set before him. The mosquitoes had been maddening that night; they flew about the net under which he slept in such numbers that their humming, pitiless and menacing, had the effect of a note, infinitely drawn out, played on a distant organ, and whenever he dozed off he awoke with a start in the belief that one had found its way inside his curtains. It was so hot that he lay naked. He turned from side to side. And gradually the dull roar of the breakers on the reef, so unceasing and so regular that generally you did not hear it, grew distinct on his consciousness, its rhythm hammered on his tired nerves and he held himself with clenched hands in the effort to bear it. The thought that nothing could stop that sound, for it would continue to all eternity, was almost impossible to bear, and, as though his strength were a match for the ruthless forces of nature, he had an insane impulse to do some violent thing. He felt he must cling to his self-control or he would go mad. And now, looking out of the window at the lagoon and the strip of foam which marked the reef, he shuddered with hatred of the brilliant scene. The cloudless sky was like an inverted bowl that hemmed it in. He lit his pipe and turned over the pile of Auckland papers that had come over from Apia a few days before. The newest of them was three weeks old. They gave an impression of incredible dullness.

Then he went into the office. It was a large, bare room with two desks in it and a bench along one side. A number of natives were seated on this, and a couple of women. They gossiped while they waited for the administrator, and when Mackintosh came in they greeted him.

"*Talofa li.*"

He returned their greeting and sat down at his desk. He began to write, working on a report which the governor of Samoa had been clamouring for and which Walker, with his usual dilatoriness, had neglected to prepare. Mackintosh as he made his notes reflected vindictively that Walker was late with his report because he was so illiterate that he had an invincible distaste for anything to do with pens and paper; and now when it was at last ready, concise and neatly official, he would accept his subordinate's work without a word of appreciation, with a sneer rather or a gibe, and send it on to his own superior as though it were his own composition. He could not have written a word of it. Mackintosh thought with rage that if his chief pencilled in some insertion it would be childish in expression and faulty in language. If he remonstrated or sought to put his meaning into an intelligible phrase, Walker would fly into a passion and cry:

"What the hell do I care about grammar? That's what I want to say and that's how I want to say it."

At last Walker came in. The natives surrounded him as he entered, trying to get his immediate attention, but he turned on them roughly and told them to sit down and hold their tongues. He threatened that if they were not quiet he would have them all turned out and see none of them that day. He nodded to Mackintosh.

"Hulloa, Mac; up at last? I don't know how you can waste the best part of the day in bed. You ought to have been up before dawn like me. Lazy beggar."

He threw himself heavily into his chair and wiped his face with a large bandana.

"By heaven, I've got a thirst."

He turned to the policeman who stood at the door, a picturesque figure in his white jacket and *lava-lava*, the loin cloth of the Samoan, and told him to bring *kava*. The *kava* bowl stood on the floor in the corner of the room, and the policeman filled a half coconut shell and brought it to Walker. He poured a few drops on the ground, murmured the customary words to the company, and drank with relish. Then he told the policeman to serve the waiting natives, and the shell was handed to each one in order of birth or importance and emptied with the same ceremonies.

Then he set about the day's work. He was a little man, considerably less than of middle height, and enormously stout; he had a large, fleshy face, clean-shaven, with the cheeks hanging on each side in great dew-laps, and three vast chins; his small features were all dissolved in fat; and, but for a crescent of white hair at the back of his head, he was completely bald. He reminded you of Mr. Pickwick. He was grotesque, a figure of fun, and yet, strangely enough, not without dignity. His blue eyes, behind large gold-rimmed spectacles, were shrewd and vivacious, and there was a great deal of determination in his face. He was sixty, but his native vitality triumphed over advancing years. Notwithstanding his corpulence his movements were quick, and he walked with a heavy, resolute tread as though he sought to impress his weight upon the earth. He spoke in a loud, gruff voice.

It was two years now since Mackintosh had been appointed Walker's assistant. Walker, who had been for a quarter of a century administrator of Talua, one of the larger islands in the Samoan group, was a man known in person or by report through the length and breadth of the South Seas; and it was with lively curiosity that Mackintosh looked forward to his first meeting with him. For one reason or another he stayed a couple of weeks at Apia before he took up his post and both at Chaplin's hotel and at the English club he heard innumerable stories about the administrator. He thought now with irony of his interest in them. Since then he had heard them a hundred times from Walker himself. Walker knew that he was a character, and, proud of his reputation, deliberately acted up to it. He was jealous of his "legend" and anxious that you should know the exact details of any of the celebrated stories that were told of him. He was ludicrously angry with anyone who had told them to the stranger incorrectly.

There was a rough cordiality about Walker which Mackintosh at first found not unattractive, and Walker, glad to have a listener to whom all he said was fresh, gave of his best. He was good-humoured, hearty, and considerate. To Mackintosh, who had lived the sheltered life of a government official in London till at the age of thirty-four an attack of pneumonia, leaving him with the threat of tuberculosis, had forced him to seek a post in the Pacific, Walker's existence seemed extraordinarily romantic. The adventure with which he started on his conquest of circumstance was typical of the man. He ran away to sea when he was fifteen and for over a year was employed in shovelling coal on a collier. He was an undersized boy and both men and mates were kind to him, but the captain for some reason conceived a savage dislike of him. He used the lad cruelly so that, beaten and kicked, he often could not sleep for the pain that racked his limbs. He loathed the captain with all his soul. Then he was given a tip for some race and managed to borrow twenty-five pounds from a friend he had picked up in Belfast. He put it on the horse, an outsider, at long odds. He had no means of repaying the money if he lost, but it never occurred to him that he could lose. He felt himself in luck. The horse won and he found himself with something over a thousand pounds in hard cash. Now his chance had come. He found out who was the best solicitor in the town—the collier lay then somewhere on the Irish coast—went to him, and, telling him that he heard the ship was for sale, asked him to arrange the purchase for him. The solicitor was amused at his small client, he was only sixteen and did not look so old, and, moved perhaps by sympathy, promised not only to arrange the matter for him but to see that he made a good bargain. After a little while Walker found himself the owner of the ship. He went back to her and had what he described as the most glorious moment of his life when he gave the skipper notice and told him that he must get off *his* ship in half an hour. He made the mate captain and sailed on the collier for another nine months, at the end of which he sold her at a profit.

He came out to the islands at the age of twenty-six as a planter. He was one of the few white men settled in Talua at the time of the German occupation and had then already some influence with the natives. The Germans made him administrator, a position which he occupied for twenty years, and when the island was seized by the British he was confirmed in his post. He ruled the island despotically, but with complete success. The prestige of this success was another reason for the interest that Mackintosh took in him.

But the two men were not made to get on. Mackintosh was an ugly man, with ungainly gestures, a tall thin fellow, with a narrow chest and bowed shoulders. He had sallow, sunken cheeks, and his eyes were large and sombre. He was a great reader, and when his books arrived and were unpacked Walker came over to his quarters and looked at them. Then he turned to Mackintosh with a coarse laugh.

"What in Hell have you brought all this muck for?" he asked.

Mackintosh flushed darkly.

"I'm sorry you think it muck. I brought my books because I want to read them."

"When you said you'd got a lot of books coming I thought there'd be something for me to read. Haven't you got any detective stories?"

"Detective stories don't interest me."

"You're a damned fool then."

"I'm content that you should think so."

Every mail brought Walker a mass of periodical literature, papers from New Zealand and magazines from America, and it exasperated him that Mackintosh showed his contempt for these ephemeral publications. He had no patience with the books that absorbed Mackintosh's leisure and thought it only a pose that he read Gibbon's *Decline and Fall* or Burton's *Anatomy of Melancholy*. And since he had never learned to put any restraint on his tongue, he expressed his opinion of his assistant freely. Mackintosh began to see the real man, and under the boisterous good-humour he discerned a vulgar cunning which was hateful; he was vain and domineering, and it was strange that he had notwithstanding a shyness which made him dislike people who were not quite of his kidney. He judged others, naïvely, by their language, and if it was free from the oaths and the obscenity which made up the greater part of his own conversation, he looked upon them with suspicion. In the evening the two men played piquet. He played badly but vaingloriously, crowing over his opponent when he won and losing his temper when he lost. On rare occasions a couple of planters or traders would drive over to play bridge, and then Walker showed himself in what Mackintosh considered a characteristic light. He played regardless of his partner, calling up in his desire to play the hand, and argued interminably, beating down opposition by the loudness of his voice. He constantly revoked, and when he did so said with an ingratiating whine: "Oh, you wouldn't count it against an old man who can hardly see." Did he know that his opponents thought it as well to keep on the right side of him and hesitated to insist on the rigour of the game? Mackintosh watched him with an icy contempt. When the game was over, while they smoked their pipes and drank whisky, they would begin telling stories. Walker told with gusto the story of his marriage. He had got so drunk at the wedding feast that the bride had fled and he had never seen her since. He had had numberless adventures, commonplace and sordid, with the women of the island and he described them with a pride in his own prowess which was an offence to Mackintosh's fastidious ears. He was a gross, sensual old man. He thought Mackintosh a poor fellow because he would not share his promiscuous amours and remained sober when the company was drunk.

He despised him also for the orderliness with which he did his official work. Mackintosh liked to do everything just so. His desk was always tidy, his papers were always neatly docketed, he could put his hand on any document that was needed, and he had at his fingers' ends all the regulations that were required for the business of their administration.

"Fudge, fudge," said Walker. "I've run this island for twenty years without red tape, and I don't want it now."

"Does it make it any easier for you that when you want a letter you have to hunt half an hour for it?" answered Mackintosh.

"You're nothing but a damned official. But you're not a bad fellow; when you've been out here a year or two you'll be all right. What's wrong about you is that you won't drink. You wouldn't be a bad sort if you got soused once a week."

The curious thing was that Walker remained perfectly unconscious of the dislike for him which every month increased in the breast of his subordinate. Although he laughed at him, as he grew accustomed to him, he began almost to like him. He had a certain tolerance for the peculiarities of others, and he accepted Mackintosh as a queer fish. Perhaps he liked him, unconsciously, because he could chaff him. His humour consisted of coarse banter and he wanted a butt. Mackintosh's exactness, his morality, his sobriety, were all fruitful subjects; his Scot's name gave an opportunity for the usual jokes about Scotland; he enjoyed himself thoroughly when two or three men were there and he could make them all laugh at the expense of Mackintosh. He would say ridiculous things about him to the natives, and Mackintosh, his knowledge of Samoan still imperfect, would see their unrestrained mirth when Walker had made an obscene reference to him. He smiled good-humouredly.

"I'll say this for you, Mac," Walker would say in his gruff loud voice, "you can take a joke."

"Was it a joke?" smiled Mackintosh. "I didn't know."

"Scots wha hae!" shouted Walker, with a bellow of laughter. "There's only one way to make a Scotchman see a joke and that's by a surgical operation."

Walker little knew that there was nothing Mackintosh could stand less than chaff. He would wake in the night, the breathless night of the rainy season, and brood sullenly over the gibe that Walker had uttered carelessly days before. It rankled. His heart swelled with rage, and he pictured to himself ways in which he might get even with the bully. He had tried answering him, but Walker had a gift of repartee, coarse and obvious, which gave him an advantage. The dullness of his intellect made him impervious to a delicate shaft. His self-satisfaction made it impossible to wound him. His loud voice, his bellow of laughter, were weapons against which Mackintosh had nothing to counter, and he learned that the wisest thing was never to betray his irritation. He learned to control himself. But his hatred grew till it was a monomania. He watched Walker with an insane vigilance. He fed his own self-esteem by every instance of meanness on Walker's part, by every exhibition of childish vanity, of cunning and of vulgarity. Walker ate greedily, noisily, filthily, and Mackintosh watched him with satisfaction. He took note of the foolish things he said and of his mistakes in grammar. He knew that Walker held him in small esteem, and he found a bitter satisfaction in his chief's opinion of him; it increased his own contempt for the narrow, complacent old man. And it gave him a singular pleasure to know that Walker was entirely unconscious of the hatred he felt for him. He was a fool who liked popularity, and he blandly fancied that everyone admired him. Once Mackintosh had overheard Walker speaking of him.

"He'll be all right when I've licked him into shape," he said. "He's a good dog and he loves his master."

Mackintosh silently, without a movement of his long, sallow face, laughed long and heartily.

But his hatred was not blind; on the contrary, it was peculiarly clear-sighted, and he judged Walker's capabilities with precision. He ruled his small kingdom with efficiency. He was just and honest. With opportunities to make money he was a poorer man than when he was first appointed to his post, and his only support for his old age was the pension which he expected when at last he retired from official life. His pride was that with an assistant and a half-caste clerk he was able to administer the island more competently than Upolu, the island of which Apia is the chief town, was administered with its army of functionaries. He had a few native policemen to sustain his authority, but he made no use of them. He governed by bluff and his Irish humour.

"They insisted on building a jail for me," he said. "What the devil do I want a jail for? I'm not going to put the natives in prison. If they do wrong I know how to deal with them."

One of his quarrels with the higher authorities at Apia was that he claimed entire jurisdiction over the natives of his island. Whatever their crimes he would not give them up to courts competent to deal with them, and several times an angry correspondence had passed between him and the Governor at Upolu. For he looked upon the natives as his children. And that was the amazing thing about this coarse, vulgar, selfish man; he loved the island on which he had lived so long with passion, and he had for the natives a strange rough tenderness which was quite wonderful.

He loved to ride about the island on his old grey mare and he was never tired of its beauty. Sauntering along the grassy roads among the coconut trees he would stop every now and then to admire the loveliness of the scene. Now and then he would come upon a native village and stop while the head man brought him a bowl of *kava*. He would look at the little group of bell-shaped huts with their high thatched roofs, like beehives, and a smile would spread over his fat face. His eyes rested happily on the spreading green of the bread-fruit trees.

"By George, it's like the garden of Eden."

Sometimes his rides took him along the coast and through the trees he had a glimpse of the wide sea, empty, with never a sail to disturb the loneliness; sometimes he climbed a hill so that a great stretch of country, with little villages nestling among the tall trees, was spread out before him like the kingdom of the world, and he would sit there for an hour in an ecstasy of delight. But he had no words to express his feelings and to relieve them would utter an obscene jest; it was as though his emotion was so violent that he needed vulgarity to break the tension.

Mackintosh observed this sentiment with an icy disdain. Walker had always been a heavy drinker, he was proud of his capacity to see men half his age under the table when he spent a night in Apia, and he had the sentimentality of the toper. He could cry over the stories he read in his magazines and yet would refuse a loan to some trader in difficulties whom he had known for twenty years. He was close with his money. Once Mackintosh said to him:

"No one could accuse you of giving money away."

He took it as a compliment. His enthusiasm for nature was but the drivelling sensibility of the drunkard. Nor had Mackintosh any sympathy for his chief's feelings towards the natives. He loved them because they were in his power, as a selfish man loves his dog, and his mentality was on a level with theirs. Their humour was obscene and he was never at a loss for the lewd remark. He understood them and they understood him. He was proud of his influence over them. He looked upon them as his children and he mixed himself in all their affairs. But he was very jealous of his authority; if he ruled them with a rod of iron, brooking no contradiction, he would not suffer any of the white men on the island to take advantage of them. He watched the missionaries suspiciously and, if they did anything of which he disapproved, was able to make life so unendurable to them that if he could not get them removed they were glad to go of their own accord. His power over the natives was so great that on his word they would refuse labour and food to their pastor. On the other hand he showed the traders no favour. He took care that they should not cheat the natives; he saw that they got a fair reward for their work and their copra and that the traders made no extravagant profit on the wares they sold them. He was merciless to a bargain that he thought unfair. Sometimes the traders would complain at Apia that they did not get fair opportunities. They suffered for it. Walker then hesitated at no calumny, at no outrageous lie, to get even with them, and they found that if they wanted not only to live at peace, but to exist at all, they had to accept the situation on his own terms. More than once the store of a trader obnoxious to him had been burned down, and there was only the appositeness of the event to show that the administrator had instigated it. Once a Swedish half-caste, ruined by the burning, had gone to him and roundly accused him of arson. Walker laughed in his face.

"You dirty dog. Your mother was a native and you try to cheat the natives. If your rotten old store is burned down it's a judgment of Providence; that's what it is, a judgment of Providence. Get out."

And as the man was hustled out by two native policemen the administrator laughed fatly.

"A judgment of Providence."

And now Mackintosh watched him enter upon the day's work. He began with the sick, for Walker added doctoring to his other activities, and he had a small room behind the office full of drugs. An elderly man came forward, a man with a crop of curly grey hair, in a blue *lava-lava*, elaborately tatooed, with the skin of his body wrinkled like a wine-skin.

"What have you come for?" Walker asked him abruptly.

In a whining voice the man said that he could not eat without vomiting and that he had pains here and pains there.

"Go to the missionaries," said Walker. "You know that I only cure children."

"I have been to the missionaries and they do me no good."

"Then go home and prepare yourself to die. Have you lived so long and still want to go on living? You're a fool."

The man broke into querulous expostulation, but Walker, pointing to a woman with a sick child in her arms, told her to bring it to his desk. He asked her questions and looked at the child.

"I will give you medicine," he said. He turned to the half-caste clerk. "Go into the dispensary and bring me some calomel pills."

He made the child swallow one there and then and gave another to the mother.

"Take the child away and keep it warm. To-morrow it will be dead or better."

He leaned back in his chair and lit his pipe.

"Wonderful stuff, calomel. I've saved more lives with it than all the hospital doctors at Apia put together."

Walker was very proud of his skill, and with the dogmatism of ignorance had no patience with the members of the medical profession.

"The sort of case I like," he said, "is the one that all the doctors have given up as hopeless. When the doctors have said they can't cure you, I say to them, 'come to me.' Did I ever tell you about the fellow who had a cancer?"

"Frequently," said Mackintosh.

"I got him right in three months."

"You've never told me about the people you haven't cured."

He finished this part of the work and went on to the rest. It was a queer medley. There was a woman who could not get on with her husband and a man who complained that his wife had run away from him.

"Lucky dog," said Walker. "Most men wish their wives would too."

There was a long complicated quarrel about the ownership of a few yards of land. There was a dispute about the sharing out of a catch of fish. There was a complaint against a white trader because he had given short measure. Walker listened attentively to every case, made up his mind quickly, and gave his decision. Then he would listen to nothing more; if the complainant went on he was hustled out of the office by a policeman. Mackintosh listened to it all with sullen irritation. On the whole, perhaps, it might be admitted that rough justice was done, but it exasperated the assistant that his chief trusted his instinct rather than the evidence. He would not listen to reason.

He browbeat the witnesses and when they did not see what he wished them to called them thieves and liars.

He left to the last a group of men who were sitting in the corner of the room. He had deliberately ignored them. The party consisted of an old chief, a tall, dignified man with short, white hair, in a new *lava-lava*, bearing a huge fly wisp as a badge of office, his son, and half a dozen of the important men of the village. Walker had had a feud with them and had beaten them. As was characteristic of him he meant now to rub in his victory, and because he had them down to profit by their helplessness. The facts were peculiar. Walker had a passion for building roads. When he had come to Talua there were but a few tracks here and there, but in course of time he had cut roads through the country, joining the villages together, and it was to this that a great part of the island's prosperity was due. Whereas in the old days it had been impossible to get the produce of the land, copra chiefly, down to the coast where it could be put on schooners or motor launches and so taken to Apia, now transport was easy and simple. His ambition was to make a road right round the island and a great part of it was already built.

"In two years I shall have done it, and then I can die or they can fire me, I don't care."

His roads were the joy of his heart and he made excursions constantly to see that they were kept in order. They were simple enough, wide tracks, grass covered, cut through the scrub or through the plantations; but trees had to be rooted out, rocks dug up or blasted, and here and there levelling had been necessary. He was proud that he had surmounted by his own skill such difficulties as they presented. He rejoiced in his disposition of them so that they were not only convenient, but showed off the beauties of the island which his soul loved. When he spoke of his roads he was almost a poet. They meandered through those lovely scenes, and Walker had taken care that here and there they should run in a straight line, giving you a green vista through the tall trees, and here and there should turn and curve so that the heart was rested by the diversity. It was amazing that this coarse and sensual man should exercise so subtle an ingenuity to get the effects which his fancy suggested to him. He had used in making his roads all the fantastic skill of a Japanese gardener. He received a grant from headquarters for the work but took a curious pride in using but a small part of it, and the year before had spent only a hundred pounds of the thousand assigned to him.

"What do they want money for?" he boomed. "They'll only spend it on all kinds of muck they don't want; what the missionaries leave them, that is to say."

For no particular reason, except perhaps pride in the economy of his administration and the desire to contrast his efficiency with the wasteful methods of the authorities at Apia, he got the natives to do the work he wanted for wages that were almost nominal. It was owing to this that he had lately had difficulty with the village whose chief men now were come to see him. The chief's son had been in Upolu for a year and on coming back had told his people of the large sums that were paid at Apia for the public works. In long, idle talks he had inflamed their hearts with the desire for gain. He held out to them visions of vast wealth and they thought of the whisky they could buy—it was dear, since there was a law that it must not be sold to natives, and so it cost them double what the white man had to pay for it—they thought of the great sandal-wood boxes in which they kept their treasures, and the scented soap and potted salmon, the luxuries for which the Kanaka will sell his soul; so that when the administrator sent for them and told them he wanted a road made from their village to a certain point along the coast and offered them twenty pounds, they asked him a hundred. The chief's son was called Manuma. He was a tall, handsome fellow, copper-coloured, with his fuzzy hair dyed red with lime, a wreath of red berries round his neck, and behind his ear a flower like a scarlet flame against his brown face. The upper part of his body was naked, but to show that he was no longer a savage, since he had lived in Apia, he wore a pair of dungarees instead of a *lava-lava*. He told them that if they held together the administrator would be obliged to accept their terms. His heart was set on building the road and when he found they would not work for less he would give them what they asked. But they must not move; whatever he said they must not abate their claim; they had asked a hundred and that they must keep to. When they mentioned the figure, Walker burst into a shout of his long, deep-voiced laughter. He told them not to make fools of themselves, but to set about the work at once. Because he was in a good humour that day he promised to give them a feast when the road was finished. But when he found that no attempt was made to start work, he went to the village and asked the men what silly game they were playing. Manuma had coached them well. They were quite calm, they did not attempt to argue—and argument is a passion with the Kanaka—they merely shrugged their shoulders: they would do it for a hundred pounds, and if he would not give them that they would do no work. He could please himself. They did not care. Then Walker flew into a passion. He was ugly then. His short fat neck swelled ominously, his red face grew purple, he foamed at the mouth. He set upon the natives with invective. He knew well how to wound and how to humiliate. He was terrifying. The older men grew pale and uneasy. They hesitated. If it had not been for Manuma, with his knowledge of the great world, and their dread of his ridicule, they would have yielded. It was Manuma who answered Walker.

"Pay us a hundred pounds and we will work."

Walker, shaking his fist at him, called him every name he could think of. He riddled him with scorn. Manuma sat still and smiled. There may have been more bravado than confidence in his smile, but he had to make a good show before the others. He repeated his words.

"Pay us a hundred pounds and we will work."

They thought that Walker would spring on him. It would not have been the first time that he had thrashed a native with his own hands; they knew his strength, and though Walker was three times the age of the young man and six inches shorter they did not doubt that he was more than a match for Manuma. No one had ever thought of resisting the savage onslaught of the administrator. But Walker said nothing. He chuckled.

"I am not going to waste my time with a pack of fools," he said. "Talk it over again. You know what I have offered. If you do not start in a week, take care."

He turned round and walked out of the chief's hut. He untied his old mare and it was typical of the relations between him and the natives that one of the elder men hung on to the off stirrup while Walker from a convenient boulder hoisted himself heavily into the saddle.

That same night when Walker according to his habit was strolling along the road that ran past his house, he heard something whizz past him and with a thud strike a tree. Something had been thrown at him. He ducked instinctively. With a shout, "Who's that?" he ran towards the place from which the missile had come and he heard the sound of a man escaping through the bush. He knew it was hopeless to pursue in the darkness, and besides he was soon out of breath, so he stopped and made his way back to the road. He looked about for what had been thrown, but could find nothing. It was quite dark. He went quickly back to the house and called Mackintosh and the Chinese boy.

"One of those devils has thrown something at me. Come along and let's find out what it was."

He told the boy to bring a lantern and the three of them made their way back to the place. They hunted about the ground, but could not find what they sought. Suddenly the boy gave a guttural cry. They turned to look. He held up the lantern, and there, sinister in the light that cut the surrounding darkness, was a long knife sticking into the trunk of a coconut tree. It had been thrown with such force that it required quite an effort to pull it out.

"By George, if he hadn't missed me I'd have been in a nice state."

Walker handled the knife. It was one of those knives, made in imitation of the sailor knives brought to the islands a hundred years before by the first white men, used to divide the coconuts in two so that the copra might be dried. It was a murderous weapon, and the blade, twelve inches long, was very sharp. Walker chuckled softly.

"The devil, the impudent devil."

He had no doubt it was Manuma who had flung the knife. He had escaped death by three inches. He was not angry. On the contrary, he was in high spirits; the adventure exhilarated him, and when they got back to the house, calling for drinks, he rubbed his hands gleefully.

"I'll make them pay for this!"

His little eyes twinkled. He blew himself out like a turkey-cock, and for the second time within half an hour insisted on telling Mackintosh every detail of the affair. Then he asked him to play piquet, and while they played he boasted of his intentions. Mackintosh listened with tightened lips.

"But why should you grind them down like this?" he asked. "Twenty pounds is precious little for the work you want them to do."

"They ought to be precious thankful I give them anything."

"Hang it all, it's not your own money. The government allots you a reasonable sum. They won't complain if you spend it."

"They're a bunch of fools at Apia."

Mackintosh saw that Walker's motive was merely vanity. He shrugged his shoulders.

"It won't do you much good to score off the fellows at Apia at the cost of your life."

"Bless you, they wouldn't hurt me, these people. They couldn't do without me. They worship me. Manuma is a fool. He only threw that knife to frighten me."

The next day Walker rode over again to the village. It was called Matautu. He did not get off his horse. When he reached the chief's house he saw that the men were sitting round the floor in a circle, talking, and he guessed they were discussing again the question of the road. The Samoan huts are formed in this way: Trunks of slender trees are placed in a circle at intervals of perhaps five or six feet; a tall tree is set in the middle and from this downwards slopes the thatched roof. Venetian blinds of coconut leaves can be pulled down at night or when it is raining. Ordinarily the hut is open all round so that the breeze can blow through freely. Walker rode to the edge of the hut and called out to the chief.

"Oh, there, Tangatu, your son left his knife in a tree last night. I have brought it back to you."

He flung it down on the ground in the midst of the circle, and with a low burst of laughter ambled off.

On Monday he went out to see if they had started work. There was no sign of it. He rode through the village. The inhabitants were about their ordinary avocations. Some were weaving mats of the pandanus leaf, one old man was busy with a *kava* bowl, the children were playing, the women went about their household chores. Walker, a smile on his lips, came to the chief's house.

"*Talofa-li*," said the chief.

"*Talofa*," answered Walker.

Manuma was making a net. He sat with a cigarette between his lips and looked up at Walker with a smile of triumph.

"You have decided that you will not make the road?"

The chief answered.

"Not unless you pay us one hundred pounds."

"You will regret it." He turned to Manuma. "And you, my lad, I shouldn't wonder if your back was very sore before you're much older."

He rode away chuckling. He left the natives vaguely uneasy. They feared the fat sinful old man, and neither the missionaries' abuse of him nor the scorn which Manuma had learnt in Apia made them forget that he had a devilish cunning and that no man had ever braved him without in the long run suffering for it. They found out within twenty-four hours what scheme he had devised. It was characteristic. For next morning a great band of men, women, and children came into the village and the chief men said that they had made a bargain with Walker to build the road. He had offered them twenty pounds and they had accepted. Now the cunning lay in this, that the Polynesians have rules of hospitality which have all the force of laws; an etiquette of absolute rigidity made it necessary for the people of the village not only to give lodging to the strangers, but to provide them with food and drink as long as they wished to stay. The inhabitants of Matautu were outwitted. Every morning the workers went out in a joyous band, cut down trees, blasted rocks, levelled here and there and then in the evening tramped back again, and ate and drank, ate heartily, danced, sang hymns, and enjoyed life. For them it was a picnic. But soon their hosts began to wear long faces; the strangers had enormous appetites, and the plantains and the bread-fruit vanished before their rapacity; the alligator-pear trees, whose fruit sent to Apia might sell for good money, were stripped bare. Ruin stared them in the face. And then they found that the strangers were working very slowly. Had they received a hint from Walker that they might take their time? At this rate by the time the road was finished there would not be a scrap of food in the village. And worse than this, they were a laughing-stock; when one or other of them went to some distant hamlet on an errand he found that the story had got there before him, and he was met with derisive laughter. There is nothing the Kanaka can endure less than ridicule. It was not long before much angry talk passed among the sufferers. Manuma was no longer a hero; he had to put up with a good deal of plain speaking, and one day what Walker had suggested came to pass: a heated argument turned into a quarrel and half a dozen of the young men set upon the chief's son and gave him such a beating that for a week he lay bruised and sore on the pandanus mats. He turned from side to side and could find no ease. Every day or two the administrator rode over on his old mare and watched the progress of the road. He was not a man to resist the temptation of taunting the fallen foe, and he missed no opportunity to rub into the shamed inhabitants of Matautu the bitterness of their humiliation. He broke their spirit. And one morning, putting their pride in their pockets, a figure of speech, since pockets they had not, they all set out with the strangers and started working on the road. It was urgent to get it done quickly if they wanted to save any food at all, and the whole village joined in. But they worked silently, with rage and mortification in their hearts, and even the children toiled in silence. The women wept as they carried away bundles of brushwood. When Walker saw them he laughed so much that he almost rolled out of his saddle. The news spread quickly and tickled the people of the island to death. This was the greatest joke of all, the crowning triumph of that cunning old white man whom no Kanaka had ever been able to circumvent; and they came from distant villages, with their wives and children, to look at the foolish folk who had refused twenty pounds to make the road and now were forced to work for nothing. But the harder they worked the more easily went the guests. Why should they hurry, when they were getting good food for nothing and the longer they took about the job the better the joke became? At last the wretched villagers could stand it no longer, and they were come this morning to beg the administrator to send the strangers back to their own homes. If he would do this they promised to finish the road themselves for nothing. For him it was a victory complete and unqualified. They were humbled. A look of arrogant complacence spread over his large, naked face, and he seemed to swell in his chair like a great bullfrog. There was something sinister in his appearance, so that Mackintosh shivered with disgust. Then in his booming tones he began to speak.

"Is it for my good that I make the road? What benefit do you think I get out of it? It is for you, so that you can walk in comfort and carry your copra in comfort. I offered to pay you for your work, though it was for your own sake the work was done. I offered to pay you generously. Now *you* must pay. I will send the people of Manua back to their homes if you will finish the road and pay the twenty pounds that I have to pay them."

There was an outcry. They sought to reason with him. They told him they had not the money. But to everything they said he replied with brutal gibes. Then the clock struck.

"Dinner time," he said. "Turn them all out."

He raised himself heavily from his chair and walked out of the room. When Mackintosh followed him he found him already seated at table, a napkin tied round his neck, holding his knife and fork in readiness for the meal the Chinese cook was about to bring. He was in high spirits.

"I did 'em down fine," he said, as Mackintosh sat down. "I shan't have much trouble with the roads after this."

"I suppose you were joking," said Mackintosh icily.

"What do you mean by that?"

"You're not really going to make them pay twenty pounds?"

"You bet your life I am."

"I'm not sure you've got any right to."

"Ain't you? I guess I've got the right to do any damned thing I like on this island."

"I think you've bullied them quite enough."

Walker laughed fatly. He did not care what Mackintosh thought.

"When I want your opinion I'll ask for it." Mackintosh grew very white. He knew by bitter experience that he could do nothing but keep silence, and the violent effort at self-control made him sick and faint. He could not eat the food that was before him and with disgust he watched Walker shovel meat into his vast mouth. He was a dirty feeder, and to sit at table with him needed a strong stomach. Mackintosh shuddered. A tremendous desire seized him to humiliate that gross and cruel man; he would give anything in the world to see him in the dust, suffering as much as he had made others suffer. He had never loathed the bully with such loathing as now.

The day wore on. Mackintosh tried to sleep after dinner, but the passion in his heart prevented him; he tried to read, but the letters swam before his eyes. The sun beat down pitilessly, and he longed for rain; but he knew that rain would bring no coolness; it would only make it hotter and more steamy. He was a native of Aberdeen and his heart yearned suddenly for the icy winds that whistled through the granite streets of that city. Here he was a prisoner, imprisoned not only by that placid sea, but by his hatred for that horrible old man. He pressed his hands to his aching head. He would like to kill him. But he pulled himself together. He must do something to distract his mind, and since he could not read he thought he would set his private papers in order. It was a job which he had long meant to do and which he had constantly put off. He unlocked the drawer of his desk and took out a handful of letters. He caught sight of his revolver. An impulse, no sooner realised than set aside, to put a bullet through his head and so escape from the intolerable bondage of life flashed through his mind. He noticed that in the damp air the revolver was slightly rusted, and he got an oil rag and began to clean it. It was while he was thus occupied that he grew aware of someone slinking round the door. He looked up and called:

"Who is there?"

There was a moment's pause, then Manuma showed himself.

"What do you want?"

The chief's son stood for a moment, sullen and silent, and when he spoke it was with a strangled voice.

"We can't pay twenty pounds. We haven't the money."

"What am I to do?" said Mackintosh. "You heard what Mr. Walker said."

Manuma began to plead, half in Samoan and half in English. It was a sing-song whine, with the quavering intonations of a beggar, and it filled Mackintosh with disgust. It outraged him that the man should let himself be so crushed. He was a pitiful object.

"I can do nothing," said Mackintosh irritably. "You know that Mr. Walker is master here."

Manuma was silent again. He still stood in the doorway.

"I am sick," he said at last. "Give me some medicine."

"What is the matter with you?"

"I do not know. I am sick. I have pains in my body."

"Don't stand there," said Mackintosh sharply. "Come in and let me look at you."

Manuma entered the little room and stood before the desk.

"I have pains here and here."

He put his hands to his loins and his face assumed an expression of pain. Suddenly Mackintosh grew conscious that the boy's eyes were resting on the revolver which he had laid on the desk when Manuma appeared in the doorway. There was a silence between the two which to Mackintosh was endless. He seemed to read the thoughts which were in the Kanaka's mind. His heart beat violently. And then he felt as though something possessed him so that he acted under the compulsion of a foreign will. Himself did not make the movements of his body, but a power that was strange to him. His throat was suddenly dry, and he put his hand to it mechanically in order to help his speech. He was impelled to avoid Manuma's eyes.

"Just wait here," he said, his voice sounded as though someone had seized him by the windpipe, "and I'll fetch you something from the dispensary."

He got up. Was it his fancy that he staggered a little? Manuma stood silently, and though he kept his eyes averted, Mackintosh knew that he was looking dully out of the door. It was this other person that possessed him that drove him out of the room, but it was himself that took a handful of muddled papers and threw them on the revolver in order to hide it from view. He went to the dispensary. He got a pill and poured out some blue draught into a small bottle, and then came out into the compound. He did not want to go back into his own bungalow, so he called to Manuma.

"Come here."

He gave him the drugs and instructions how to take them. He did not know what it was that made it impossible for him to look at the Kanaka. While he was speaking to him he kept his eyes on his shoulder. Manuma took the medicine and slunk out of the gate.

Mackintosh went into the dining-room and turned over once more the old newspapers. But he could not read them. The house was very still. Walker was upstairs in his room asleep, the Chinese cook was busy in the kitchen, the two policemen were out fishing. The silence that seemed to brood over the house was unearthly, and there hammered in Mackintosh's head the question whether the revolver still lay where he had placed it. He could not bring himself to look. The uncertainty was horrible, but the certainty would be more horrible still. He sweated. At last he could stand the silence no longer, and he made up his mind to go down the road to the trader's, a man named Jervis, who had a store about a mile away. He was a half-caste, but even that amount of white blood made him possible to talk to. He wanted to get away from his bungalow, with the desk littered with untidy papers, and underneath them something, or nothing. He walked along the road. As he passed the fine hut of a chief a greeting was called out to him. Then he came to the store. Behind the counter sat the trader's daughter, a swarthy broad-featured girl in a pink blouse and a white drill skirt. Jervis hoped he would marry her. He had money, and he had told Mackintosh that his daughter's husband would be well-to-do. She flushed a little when she saw Mackintosh.

"Father's just unpacking some cases that have come in this morning. I'll tell him you're here."

He sat down and the girl went out behind the shop. In a moment her mother waddled in, a huge old woman, a chiefess, who owned much land in her own right; and gave him her hand. Her monstrous obesity was an offence, but she managed to convey an impression of dignity. She was cordial without obsequiousness; affable, but conscious of her station.

"You're quite a stranger, Mr. Mackintosh. Teresa was saying only this morning: 'Why, we never see Mr. Mackintosh now.'"

He shuddered a little as he thought of himself as that old native's son-in-law. It was notorious that she ruled her husband, notwithstanding his white blood, with a firm hand. Hers was the authority and hers the business head. She might be no more than Mrs. Jervis to the white people, but her father had been a chief of the blood royal, and his father and his father's father had ruled as kings. The

trader came in, small beside his imposing wife, a dark man with a black beard
going grey, in ducks, with handsome eyes and flashing teeth. He was very British,
and his conversation was slangy, but you felt he spoke English as a foreign tongue;
with his family he used the language of his native mother. He was a servile man,
cringing and obsequious.

"Ah, Mr. Mackintosh, this is a joyful surprise. Get the whisky, Teresa; Mr.
Mackintosh will have a gargle with us."

He gave all the latest news of Apia, watching his guest's eyes the while, so that he
might know the welcome thing to say.

"And how is Walker? We've not seen him just lately. Mrs. Jervis is going to send
him a sucking-pig one day this week."

"I saw him riding home this morning," said Teresa.

"Here's how," said Jervis, holding up his whisky.

Mackintosh drank. The two women sat and looked at him, Mrs. Jervis in her black
Mother Hubbard, placid and haughty, and Teresa, anxious to smile whenever she
caught his eye, while the trader gossiped insufferably.

"They were saying in Apia it was about time Walker retired. He ain't so young
as he was. Things have changed since he first come to the islands and he ain't changed
with them."

"He'll go too far," said the old chiefess. "The natives aren't satisfied."

"That was a good joke about the road," laughed the trader. "When I told them
about it in Apia they fair split their sides with laughing. Good old Walker."

Mackintosh looked at him savagely. What did he mean by talking of him in that
fashion? To a half-caste trader he was Mr. Walker. It was on his tongue to utter a harsh
rebuke for the impertinence. He did not know what held him back.

"When he goes I hope you'll take his place, Mr. Mackintosh," said Jervis. "We all
like you on the island. You understand the natives. They're educated now, they must
be treated differently to the old days. It wants an educated man to be administrator
now. Walker was only a trader same as I am."

Teresa's eyes glistened.

"When the time comes if there's anything anyone can do here, you bet your
bottom dollar we'll do it. I'd get all the chiefs to go over to Apia and make a petition."

Mackintosh felt horribly sick. It had not struck him that if anything happened to
Walker it might be he who would succeed him. It was true that no one in his official
position knew the island so well. He got up suddenly and scarcely taking his leave
walked back to the compound. And now he went straight to his room. He took a quick
look at his desk. He rummaged among the papers.

The revolver was not there.

His heart thumped violently against his ribs. He looked for the revolver every-where. He hunted in the chairs and in the drawers. He looked desperately, and all the time he knew he would not find it. Suddenly he heard Walker's gruff, hearty voice.

"What the devil are you up to, Mac?"

He started. Walker was standing in the doorway and instinctively he turned round to hide what lay upon his desk.

"Tidying up?" quizzed Walker. "I've told 'em to put the grey in the trap. I'm going down to Tafoni to bathe. You'd better come along."

"All right," said Mackintosh.

So long as he was with Walker nothing could happen. The place they were bound for was about three miles away, and there was a fresh-water pool, separated by a thin barrier of rock from the sea, which the administrator had blasted out for the natives to bathe in. He had done this at spots round the island, wherever there was a spring; and the fresh water, compared with the sticky warmth of the sea, was cool and invigorating. They drove along the silent grassy road, splashing now and then through fords, where the sea had forced its way in, past a couple of native villages, the bell-shaped huts spaced out roomily and the white chapel in the middle, and at the third village they got out of the trap, tied up the horse, and walked down to the pool. They were accompanied by four or five girls and a dozen children. Soon they were all splashing about, shouting and laughing, while Walker, in a *lava-lava*, swam to and fro like an unwieldy porpoise. He made lewd jokes with the girls, and they amused themselves by diving under him and wriggling away when he tried to catch them. When he was tired he lay down on a rock, while the girls and children surrounded him; it was a happy family; and the old man, huge, with his crescent of white hair and his shining bald crown, looked like some old sea god. Once Mackintosh caught a queer soft look in his eyes.

"They're dear children," he said. "They look upon me as their father."

And then without a pause he turned to one of the girls and made an obscene remark which sent them all into fits of laughter. Mackintosh started to dress. With his thin legs and thin arms he made a grotesque figure, a sinister Don Quixote, and Walker began to make coarse jokes about him. They were acknowledged with little smothered laughs. Mackintosh struggled with his shirt. He knew he looked absurd, but he hated being laughed at. He stood silent and glowering.

"If you want to get back in time for dinner you ought to come soon."

"You're not a bad fellow, Mac. Only you're a fool. When you're doing one thing you always want to do another. That's not the way to live."

But all the same he raised himself slowly to his feet and began to put on his clothes. They sauntered back to the village, drank a bowl of *kava* with the chief, and then, after a joyful farewell from all the lazy villagers, drove home.

After dinner, according to his habit, Walker, lighting his cigar, prepared to go for a stroll. Mackintosh was suddenly seized with fear.

"Don't you think it's rather unwise to go out at night by yourself just now?"

Walker stared at him with his round blue eyes.

"What the devil do you mean?"

"Remember the knife the other night. You've got those fellows' backs up."

"Pooh! They wouldn't dare."

"Someone dared before."

"That was only a bluff. They wouldn't hurt me. They look upon me as a father. They know that whatever I do is for their own good."

Mackintosh watched him with contempt in his heart. The man's self-complacency outraged him, and yet something, he knew not what, made him insist.

"Remember what happened this morning. It wouldn't hurt you to stay at home just to-night. I'll play piquet with you."

"I'll play piquet with you when I come back. The Kanaka isn't born yet who can make me alter my plans."

"You'd better let me come with you."

"You stay where you are."

Mackintosh shrugged his shoulders. He had given the man full warning. If he did not heed it that was his own lookout. Walker put on his hat and went out. Mackintosh began to read; but then he thought of something; perhaps it would be as well to have his own whereabouts quite clear. He crossed over to the kitchen and, inventing some pretext, talked for a few minutes with the cook. Then he got out the gramophone and put a record on it, but while it ground out its melancholy tune, some comic song of a London music-hall, his ear was strained for a sound away there in the night. At his elbow the record reeled out its loudness, the words were raucous, but notwithstanding he seemed to be surrounded by an unearthly silence. He heard the dull roar of the breakers against the reef. He heard the breeze sigh, far up, in the leaves of the coconut trees. How long would it be? It was awful.

He heard a hoarse laugh.

"Wonders will never cease. It's not often you play yourself a tune, Mac."

Walker stood at the window, red-faced, bluff and jovial.

"Well, you see I'm alive and kicking. What were you playing for?"

Walker came in.

"Nerves a bit dicky, eh? Playing a tune to keep your pecker up?"

"I was playing your requiem."

"What the devil's that?"

"'Alf o' bitter an' a pint of stout."

"A rattling good song too. I don't mind how often I hear it. Now I'm ready to take your money off you at piquet."

They played and Walker bullied his way to victory, bluffing his opponent, chaffing him, jeering at his mistakes, up to every dodge, browbeating him, exulting. Presently Mackintosh recovered his coolness, and standing outside himself, as it were, he was able to take a detached pleasure in watching the overbearing old man and in his own cold reserve. Somewhere Manuma sat quietly and awaited his opportunity.

Walker won game after game and pocketed his winnings at the end of the evening in high good humour.

"You'll have to grow a little bit older before you stand much chance against me, Mac. The fact is I have a natural gift for cards."

"I don't know that there's much gift about it when I happen to deal you fourteen aces."

"Good cards come to good players," retorted Walker. "I'd have won if I'd had your hands."

He went on to tell long stories of the various occasions on which he had played cards with notorious sharpers and to their consternation had taken all their money from them. He boasted. He praised himself. And Mackintosh listened with absorption. He wanted now to feed his hatred; and everything Walker said, every gesture, made him more detestable. At last Walker got up.

"Well, I'm going to turn in," he said with a loud yawn. "I've got a long day to-morrow."

"What are you going to do?"

"I'm driving over to the other side of the island. I'll start at five, but I don't expect I shall get back to dinner till late."

They generally dined at seven.

"We'd better make it half past seven then."

"I guess it would be as well."

Mackintosh watched him knock the ashes out of his pipe. His vitality was rude and exuberant. It was strange to think that death hung over him. A faint smile flickered in Mackintosh's cold, gloomy eyes.

"Would you like me to come with you?"

"What in God's name should I want that for? I'm using the mare and she'll have enough to do to carry me; she don't want to drag you over thirty miles of road."

"Perhaps you don't quite realise what the feeling is at Matautu. I think it would be safer if I came with you."

Walker burst into contemptuous laughter.

"You'd be a fine lot of use in a scrap. I'm not a great hand at getting the wind up."

Now the smile passed from Mackintosh's eyes to his lips. It distorted them painfully.

"*Quem deus vult perdere prius dementat.*"

"What the hell is that?" said Walker.

"Latin," answered Mackintosh as he went out.

And now he chuckled. His mood had changed. He had done all he could and the matter was in the hands of fate. He slept more soundly than he had done for weeks. When he awoke next morning he went out. After a good night he found a pleasant exhilaration in the freshness of the early air. The sea was a more vivid blue, the sky more brilliant, than on most days, the trade wind was fresh, and there was a ripple on the lagoon as the breeze brushed over it like velvet brushed the wrong way. He felt himself stronger and younger. He entered upon the day's work with zest. After luncheon he slept again, and as evening drew on he had the bay saddled and sauntered through the bush. He seemed to see it all with new eyes. He felt more normal. The extraordinary thing was that he was able to put Walker out of his mind altogether. So far as he was concerned he might never have existed.

He returned late, hot after his ride, and bathed again. Then he sat on the verandah, smoking his pipe, and looked at the day declining over the lagoon. In the sunset the lagoon, rosy and purple and green, was very beautiful. He felt at peace with the world and with himself. When the cook came out to say that dinner was ready and to ask whether he should wait, Mackintosh smiled at him with friendly eyes. He looked at his watch.

"It's half-past seven. Better not wait. One can't tell when the boss'll be back."

The boy nodded, and in a moment Mackintosh saw him carry across the yard a bowl of steaming soup. He got up lazily, went into the dining-room, and ate his dinner. Had it happened? The uncertainty was amusing and Mackintosh chuckled in the silence. The food did not seem so monotonous as usual, and even though there was Hamburger steak, the cook's invariable dish when his poor invention failed him, it tasted by some miracle succulent and spiced. After dinner he strolled over lazily to his bungalow to get a book. He liked the intense stillness, and now that the night had fallen the stars were blazing in the sky. He shouted for a lamp and in a moment the Chink pattered over on his bare feet, piercing the darkness with a ray of light. He put the lamp on the desk and noiselessly slipped out of the room. Mackintosh stood rooted to the floor, for there, half hidden by untidy papers, was his revolver. His heart throbbed painfully, and he broke into a sweat. It was done then.

He took up the revolver with a shaking hand. Four of the chambers were empty. He paused a moment and looked suspiciously out into the night, but there was no one there. He quickly slipped four cartridges into the empty chambers and locked the revolver in his drawer.

He sat down to wait.

An hour passed, a second hour passed. There was nothing. He sat at his desk as though he were writing, but he neither wrote nor read. He merely listened. He strained his ears for a sound travelling from a far distance. At last he heard hesitating footsteps and knew it was the Chinese cook.

"Ah-Sung," he called.

The boy came to the door.

"Boss velly late," he said. "Dinner no good."

Mackintosh stared at him, wondering whether he knew what had happened, and whether, when he knew, he would realise on what terms he and Walker had been. He went about his work, sleek, silent, and smiling, and who could tell his thoughts?

"I expect he's had dinner on the way, but you must keep the soup hot at all events."

The words were hardly out of his mouth when the silence was suddenly broken into by a confusion, cries, and a rapid patter of naked feet. A number of natives ran into the compound, men and women and children; they crowded round Mackintosh and they all talked at once. They were unintelligible. They were excited and frightened and some of them were crying. Mackintosh pushed his way through them and went to the gateway. Though he had scarcely understood what they said he knew quite well what had happened. And as he reached the gate the dog-cart arrived. The old mare was being led by a tall Kanaka, and in the dog-cart crouched two men, trying to hold Walker up. A little crowd of natives surrounded it.

The mare was led into the yard and the natives surged in after it. Mackintosh shouted to them to stand back and the two policemen, sprang suddenly from God knows where, pushed them violently aside. By now he had managed to understand that some lads who had been fishing, on their way back to their village had come across the cart on the home side of the ford. The mare was nuzzling about the herbage and in the darkness they could just see the great white bulk of the old man sunk between the seat and the dashboard. At first they thought he was drunk and they peered in,

grinning, but then they heard him groan, and guessed that something was amiss. They
ran to the village and called for help. It was when they returned, accompanied by half
a hundred people, that they discovered Walker had been shot.

With a sudden thrill of horror Mackintosh asked himself whether he was already
dead. The first thing at all events was to get him out of the cart, and that, owing to
Walker's corpulence, was a difficult job. It took four strong men to lift him. They
jolted him and he uttered a dull groan. He was still alive. At last they carried him
into the house, up the stairs, and placed him on his bed. Then Mackintosh was able
to see him, for in the yard, lit only by half a dozen hurricane lamps, everything had
been obscured. Walker's white ducks were stained with blood, and the men who had
carried him wiped their hands, red and sticky, on their *lava-lavas*. Mackintosh held
up the lamp. He had not expected the old man to be so pale. His eyes were closed.
He was breathing still, his pulse could be just felt, but it was obvious that he was
dying. Mackintosh had not bargained for the shock of horror that convulsed him.
He saw that the native clerk was there, and in a voice hoarse with fear told him to
go into the dispensary and get what was necessary for a hypodermic injection. One
of the policemen had brought up the whisky, and Mackintosh forced a little into the
old man's mouth. The room was crowded with natives. They sat about the floor,
speechless now and terrified, and every now and then one wailed aloud. It was very
hot, but Mackintosh felt cold, his hands and his feet were like ice, and he had to make
a violent effort not to tremble in all his limbs. He did not know what to do. He did
not know if Walker was bleeding still, and if he was, how he could stop the bleeding.

The clerk brought the hypodermic needle.

"You give it to him," said Mackintosh. "You're more used to that sort of thing
than I am."

His head ached horribly. It felt as though all sorts of little savage things were
beating inside it, trying to get out. They watched for the effect of the injection.
Presently Walker opened his eyes slowly. He did not seem to know where he was.

"Keep quiet," said Mackintosh. "You're at home. You're quite safe."

Walker's lips outlined a shadowy smile.

"They've got me," he whispered.

"I'll get Jervis to send his motor-boat to Apia at once. We'll get a doctor out by
to-morrow afternoon."

There was a long pause before the old man answered,

"I shall be dead by then."

A ghastly expression passed over Mackintosh's pale face. He forced himself
to laugh.

"What rot! You keep quiet and you'll be as right as rain."

"Give me a drink," said Walker. "A stiff one."

With shaking hand Mackintosh poured out whisky and water, half and half, and held the glass while Walker drank greedily. It seemed to restore him. He gave a long sigh and a little colour came into his great fleshy face. Mackintosh felt extraordinarily helpless. He stood and stared at the old man.

"If you'll tell me what to do I'll do it," he said.

"There's nothing to do. Just leave me alone. I'm done for."

He looked dreadfully pitiful as he lay on the great bed, a huge, bloated, old man; but so wan, so weak, it was heart-rending. As he rested, his mind seemed to grow clearer.

"You were right, Mac," he said presently. "You warned me."

"I wish to God I'd come with you."

"You're a good chap, Mac, only you don't drink."

There was another long silence, and it was clear that Walker was sinking. There was an internal hæmorrhage and even Mackintosh in his ignorance could not fail to see that his chief had but an hour or two to live. He stood by the side of the bed stock still. For half an hour perhaps Walker lay with his eyes closed, then he opened them.

"They'll give you my job," he said, slowly. "Last time I was in Apia I told them you were all right. Finish my road. I want to think that'll be done. All round the island."

"I don't want your job. You'll get all right."

Walker shook his head wearily.

"I've had my day. Treat them fairly, that's the great thing. They're children. You must always remember that. You must be firm with them, but you must be kind. And you must be just. I've never made a bob out of them. I haven't saved a hundred pounds in twenty years. The road's the great thing. Get the road finished."

Something very like a sob was wrung from Mackintosh.

"You're a good fellow, Mac. I always liked you."

He closed his eyes, and Mackintosh thought that he would never open them again. His mouth was so dry that he had to get himself something to drink. The Chinese cook silently put a chair for him. He sat down by the side of the bed and waited. He did not know how long a time passed. The night was endless. Suddenly one of the men sitting there broke into uncontrollable sobbing, loudly, like a child, and Mackintosh grew aware that the room was crowded by this time with natives. They sat all over the floor on their haunches, men and women, staring at the bed.

"What are all these people doing here?" said Mackintosh. "They've got no right. Turn them out, turn them out, all of them."

His words seemed to rouse Walker, for he opened his eyes once more, and now they were all misty. He wanted to speak, but he was so weak that Mackintosh had to strain his ears to catch what he said.

"Let them stay. They're my children. They ought to be here."

Mackintosh turned to the natives.

"Stay where you are. He wants you. But be silent."

A faint smile came over the old man's white face.

"Come nearer," he said.

Mackintosh bent over him. His eyes were closed and the words he said were like a wind sighing through the fronds of the coconut trees.

"Give me another drink. I've got something to say."

This time Mackintosh gave him his whisky neat. Walker collected his strength in a final effort of will.

"Don't make a fuss about this. In 'ninety-five when there were troubles white men were killed, and the fleet came and shelled the villages. A lot of people were killed who'd had nothing to do with it. They're damned fools at Apia. If they make a fuss they'll only punish the wrong people. I don't want anyone punished."

He paused for a while to rest.

"You must say it was an accident. No one's to blame. Promise me that."

"I'll do anything you like," whispered Mackintosh.

"Good chap. One of the best. They're children. I'm their father. A father don't let his children get into trouble if he can help it."

A ghost of a chuckle came out of his throat. It was astonishingly weird and ghastly.

"You're a religious chap, Mac. What's that about forgiving them? You know."

For a while Mackintosh did not answer. His lips trembled.

"Forgive them, for they know not what they do?"

"That's right. Forgive them. I've loved them, you know, always loved them."

He sighed. His lips faintly moved, and now Mackintosh had to put his ears quite close to them in order to hear.

"Hold my hand," he said.

Mackintosh gave a gasp. His heart seemed wrenched. He took the old man's hand, so cold and weak, a coarse, rough hand, and held it in his own. And thus he sat until he nearly started out of his seat, for the silence was suddenly broken by a long rattle. It was terrible and unearthly. Walker was dead. Then the natives broke out with loud cries. The tears ran down their faces, and they beat their breasts.

Mackintosh disengaged his hand from the dead man's, and staggering like one drunk with sleep he went out of the room. He went to the locked drawer in his writing-desk and took out the revolver. He walked down to the sea and walked into the lagoon; he waded out cautiously, so that he should not trip against a coral rock, till the water came to his arm-pits. Then he put a bullet through his head.

An hour later half a dozen slim brown sharks were splashing and struggling at the spot where he fell.

EVEN THE WORM TURNS

David Wright O'Brien

THE BURLY FELLOW'S OPEN-PALMED SLAP MADE WISP'S TEETH RATTLE. THEN he slapped him again, and blood trickled slowly from Wisp's mouth. Brand's other hand clutched tightly at the little man's dirty collar, and between every slap he shook him violently.

"Honest, Brand," Wisp was bleating in terror, "I didn't think you'd mind none. They was just cigarettes, a half a pack at that. They was lying there—"

He was interrupted by another jarring blow from the beefy trading captain's palm, and this time he slumped in Brand's grasp until his knees were almost touching the boards of the wharf. Wisp's watery gray eyes were clouded by fear.

"Take what don't belong to yuh, yuh little thief," the massive dark-jowled trader snarled, "and yuh'll get worse'n the next time!"

"Toss 'em off the wharf, Cap'n," suggested Brand's second officer, a tall cadaverous man named Slade.

"Please," the Wisp's voice was thin, piping, as he turned his eyes pleadingly from his first tormentor to the second, "I don't swim none."

"Take it easy, Brand," said a new voice behind the three.

The trader wheeled around, releasing his grasp on Wisp who collapsed in a thankful heap on the damp boards of the wharf. Slade turned around and the two of them glared at the newcomer.

He was a large man, younger and, Wisp thought gratefully, more powerful than Brand. He carried a superbly muscled two-hundred pounds gracefully on a frame several inches above six feet.

Wisp sighed in relief. It was Big Jan Harmon. Anyone in the South Seas could tell you that Brand feared and hated Harmon, who commanded a rival trading school which had been taking most of Brand's revenue away during the past two years. Gossip throughout the islands had it that Brand would kill Big Jan Harmon if the opportunity ever presented itself.

Big Jan saw Wisp then. His cleanly chiseled features hardened beneath his tan. "So you've taken to beating jelly fish like that, eh?" He looked directly at Brand, ignoring Wisp.

"Lissen," Wisp saw Brand's face darken as he spat words at Big Jan, "this lousy little beachcomber stole from me. I don't need no help from you to take care of him."

"What did he take?" Big Jan's tone was casual, too casual.

"Cigarettes," Wisp broke in hastily, "a half pack of cigarettes which I didn't think he wanted." The little beachcomber looked with dog-like appeal at the muscular young man.

Big Jan hitched his belt slightly, letting his wide hand brush his revolver holster significantly. "Beat it, Brand." His eyes shot to Slade, "You too," he added.

Wisp remained silent, watching the hateful eyes of Slade and Brand as they took in Big Jan's menacing gesture. Then the two of them turned slowly and started back up the wharf in the direction of the island saloon. Wisp heard Brand muttering something to Slade as they climbed the wooden steps at the end of the dock.

When they were out of sight, Wisp licked his thin lips and ran a skinny hand across his pinched features. He was an emaciated little fellow with an elfin appearance and a sly, darting manner of moving his eyes. His weasel-like countenance was topped by a thin thatch of pale, stringy hair. He bared his yellow teeth in a weak effort at a grin. "Thanks," he said rising from the wharf. Then he turned to leave.

"What happened, Jan?" The voice was young, soft, and feminine, and Wisp saw a dark-haired girl coming across the dock from the far side. He recognized her as Marcia Cole, daughter of the plantation manager of the island. She arrived on Tomauh Island several weeks ago to visit her father.

"Nothing much," Big Jan was saying, "sorry to have kept you waiting up there, but when I heard Brand's voice raising a fuss I had to come down here and have a look-see."

She was looking at Wisp, her pretty face curious. "Did someone have a fight with him?"

Big Jan laughed at the picture of Wisp engaging anyone in a fight. "No," he said, "he just got into trouble with Brand when he stole his cigarettes."

"Poor fellow," the girl said to Wisp. "You're on the beach here, aren't you?"

"Yes, lady," said Wisp, wishing that he would be allowed to leave.

"Here," she said, fumbling in a tiny bag she carried. "Get some cigarettes with these." She dropped a handful of coins into the little man's palm. Wisp gripped them tightly in his claw-like fist, easing away from the pair.

"Thanks, lady," he mumbled over his shoulder.

"You'll soon find out," Big Jan said as he guided the girl up the wharf steps, "that sympathy for a cowardly little rat like that is useless."

"But he seemed so weak and helpless," Wisp heard Marcia's voice float back in reply.

* * *

When Wisp woke up the following morning, he began his usual patrol of Tomauh beach. He was ferreting through some driftwood when Marcia Cole spoke. She came up silently behind him. Wisp was startled when he saw her, and amazed when he realized she was addressing him. He wasn't used to being selected for conversation.

"Do you feel better this morning?" the girl asked.

"Lots," Wisp mumbled, fixing his shifty gaze over his shoulder in embarrassment.

"Have you been on the island long?"

"Oh, awhile lady," he said vaguely.

"Why don't you try to get a job?"

The question struck Wisp as funny, and he grinned foolishly at the thought of someone hiring him. "There ain't none handy," he answered.

"I'm sure you could persuade my father to give you something to do on the plantation," she declared.

Wisp shifted uneasily. He wasn't particularly anxious to work on a plantation. Then he realized that the girl was new to the islands, felt sorry for him and was trying to make something out of him.

"We need someone around to run errands and do light work," she said by way of explanation.

Wisp knew a soft touch when he saw one. It would be easy living for a few weeks until she got disgusted with trying to reform him, and then he could return to the beach. He kept his eyes painfully riveted on her shoes. "Okay, lady," said Wisp.

As he watched her walk off down the bleached beach, continuing her morning stroll, Wisp smiled. She wanted to make a man of him. He knew his limitations.

Working for Marcia Cole was easier than Wisp imagined it would be. Aside from going to the village on foolish little errands which any native boy could run, there was little for him to do. The girl cornered him every so often, giving him books to read in the little hut they had given him on the edge of the plantation.

The books, which were all the inspiration type, comprised more reading than the little beachcomber had ever done in his life. He paged down doggedly through them, however, for Marcia Cole always questioned him on them. Some of them were even interesting, especially the one that had the poem about every man being the master of his fate, the captain of his soul. Then there was a quotation which Marcia made him memorize, "Courage is Man's bridge between Death and Immortality."

Wisp knew that fear would always dwell within him, however, for his literal mind connected the last quotation with one of his many actual fears, a rope bridge which spanned a volcanic gash that ran across the island and almost divided Tomauh into two sections. The quickest way from the plantation to the village entailed crossing that bridge, for the natural crevasse separated the two places. But Wisp never dared to venture out on the swaying structure. When he was forced to go to the village he took a long, out-of-the-way route along the beach, rather than cross the bridge.

Sometimes Wisp overheard Big Jan and Marcia talking on the veranda of the plantation house, and as he listened to their conversation he would remember the books, and pretend he was someone like Big Jan, someone without fear.

From their conversations he was also able to pick up gossip of events on the island. He learned, for example, that Brand's schooner was still anchored off the island, and that both Big Jan and Brand were staying on Tomauh to bargain with the natives for a supply of copra.

"That man hates you," Marcia said to Big Jan. "If I were you I'd watch out for him."

Big Jan laughed his deep powerful laugh. "What can he do?" he'd replied. "He doesn't dare cross me."

That made a queer lump come to Wisp's scrawny throat, and he wished that he could laugh away any fear of people like Brand. Every time he was forced to make a trip into the village, Wisp made it a point to avoid the huge, ugly trader and his dour companion Slade.

He saw Brand only once since his beating on the wharf, and then the burly trading captain gave him a look that turned Wisp's knees to water and set his hands to trembling.

It was a little over two weeks after Wisp had been working for Marcia Cole that he realized he liked it. Not because it was a soft touch so much, but because, well, it was kind of nice feeling close to human and being a part of something. The reading made him do a lot of thinking and although he realized, unlike Marcia Cole, that a bunch of high-sounding words couldn't change the way you are, he felt better for it.

At times Wisp got to wishing that he was any sort of man, even Brand, or Slade. Then he might—, but he carefully avoided thinking about Marcia Cole. It was foolish. Such thoughts were for the Big Jan Harmons who had never known fear in their lives.

On the night Marcia Cole sent Wisp down to the village for some odds and ends in the way of spices, she gave him a pocketful of change. By the time Wisp completed the long route along the beach he was hot and thirsty, which were two good reasons for his visiting the saloon in the native sector of Tomauh.

He seated himself at a little table in an alcove just off the bar and was sipping his drink thoughtfully when he heard the voices. There was no mistaking the first speaker, and as the voice floated over the thin partition which separated his booth from the adjoining one, Wisp paled.

"Sure," the voice was Brand's, "sure, it's all set. No one will ever know the difference. It's a cinch. We fake this message from one of his crew, see? It says the guy is in trouble in the village, that he needs help."

"And Big Jan will come hell-bent to help him?" Slade was the other speaker.

"Of course, there's no reason for him to suspect nothing. A native boy'll give him the message while he's sitting on the Cole veranda. Naturally he'll take the quickest way to the village. The way everybody goes."

"Which," said Slade, "is over the rope bridge."

"You catch on fast," chuckled Brand, with heavy sarcasm.

There was admiration in Slade's voice. "Then the bridge gives way when he's in the middle of it, seven hundred feet in the air. It's perfect, Cap'n," he chortled. "It can't miss!"

"It's gonna be a pleasure," said Brand's voice, and he chuckled throatily, unpleasantly.

Wisp sat there frozen by fear, scarcely daring to breathe lest his presence be discovered. His brain was a tumult of thoughts. Marcia, Big Jan, the bridge, they all swirled crazily around in his mind.

"He's stepped on my toes for the last time," Brand was saying.

"Yeah," Slade agreed, "there won't be any interference from him no more."

The conversation continued, and Wisp learned that Big Jan had beaten Brand to the copra deal with the natives, that Brand, knowing Big Jan was at Marcia Cole's tonight, was planning to carry out his scheme in the next few hours. At last Wisp heard the scraping of chairs being pushed away from a table. Then he heard them leaving through the front of the saloon.

Wisp sat there shivering violently as the full import of their words struck home. They were going to murder Big Jan tonight, this very evening, in less than two hours!

Somehow Wisp managed to leave the saloon, and he started back for the plantation in an odd, stumbling, half-running gait. He had proceeded that way for almost a mile before he realized that he was on the main route to the plantation, the route that would lead him to the dread rope bridge. Sobbing from lack of breath and instinctive fear, the little beachcomber turned, then started back in the direction of the path which would take him back along the beach.

It was almost an hour after Wisp had left the saloon, therefore, when he arrived at the big veranda of the Cole plantation. He saw that Big Jan had arrived and that, as usual, the trading captain and the girl sat talking.

"Why, what's wrong, Wisp?" Marcia had noticed the white pallor of terror that bleached the little man's face.

Wisp was about to pour forth the entire story, but a picture of Brand's cruel face flashed before him, bringing cold sweat to his forehead. Instead he muttered, "Nothin', Miss Cole. I just ain't feelin' good." "I wonder what you feel like when you're feeling good," Big Jan laughed.

Wisp forced a foolish smile in reply, backing down the steps to the veranda. Then he turned and started back in the direction of his hut. His heart was hammering wildly against his puny chest, and his knees were knocking violently when he entered the little shack. Wisp struck a match and turned the wick of the kerosene lamp high. Then he went over to a little shelf above his bed, taking down a thick volume which he began to page through with trembling hands.

There it was, on a grimy, thumb-soiled page, "I am the master of my fate. I am the captain of my soul."

Things he could never put into words were swelling inside the frail confinements of his narrow chest. Wisp felt suddenly sick inside, and his pale eyes became even more watery. It wasn't any use. He was more afraid than ever before. It came to him then that his whole life had been spent groveling beneath the gnarled fist of terror.

Leaving the book open, Wisp got up and walked back to the shelf above his bed. He reached far back behind the row of books, and when he brought his hand forth again it held something cold, steel, and flat. It was his secret.

Wisp had stolen the gun from the cabinet in the plantation house during his first week working for the Coles. It was loaded, its automatic chamber carrying seven shots.

As he stood there fondling the gun, Wisp suddenly knew that, for this brief moment, he had suppressed the terror in his soul. It was a symbol, making him as good as Big Jan, Brand, or Slade. Its cold, quiet, heavy presence in his damp palm made him the equal of any of them.

Then his dream was gone and he remembered who he was, Wisp, the jellyfish. He was afraid of the gun now, but he forced himself to release the safety catch on the side of it, and with supreme effort he dropped it into his side pocket. He left the kerosene lamp burning, and started back to the plantation.

Marcia Cole was alone on the veranda.

"Where, where is he?" Wisp stammered hoarsely.

Marcia looked puzzled at Wisp's question. "Do you mean Jan?"

"Yes," Wisp was almost incoherent, "please, Miss Cole. I gotta see him. I gotta."

"Why," Marcia replied, smiling at the little fellow's anxiety, "he just got a message of some kind. He had to go back to the village at once."

"Which way," Wisp gasped, "did he go?"

"By the regular route, of course, but—"

Marcia Cole never finished her sentence, for Wisp had darted off in the direction Big Jan had taken.

The little beachcomber wasn't used to running, and inside of a scant hundred yards his breath was wheezing in his overtaxed lungs. Then he remembered a short-cut to the bridge. It was through the heavy underbrush, but it would enable Wisp to reach the crevasse ahead of Big Jan.

It was difficult going. With every step he took, the heavy automatic banged into his thin shank, reminding him of its ominous presence. Once his feet slipped on some loose slag and he tumbled into a gully. And when the twisting lianas caught his feet and sent him sprawling again, he found himself wondering if the jungle were not conspiring against him.

Scratched and bleeding by his battle through the brush, Wisp at last arrived at the edge of the clearing which marked the start of the bridge. He looked swiftly about from his vantage point. There was no sign of Big Jan, and the bridge was still swinging above the span.

Forcing himself to keep back the wheezing of his scrawny throat, Wisp dropped to the ground, hugging the slimy earth and listening. At last he heard a muffled whisper. It came from the thick foliage which rose on either side of the bridge platform, on the lip of the deep crevasse.

Then as Wisp raised his head he could see, revealed for an instant by a patch of pale moonlight, two white-clad figures. They crouched on the foliage, and Wisp knew that Brand and Slade were waiting for Big Jan.

When he heard Big Jan approaching down the path, Wisp felt faint with horror. He tried to quell his mounting terror, tried to think only of Marcia Cole and the boon on the bed. The gun was still in his pocket and he put his hand on it, even though touching it brought cold sweat to his forehead.

"There is nothing in life for anyone to fear," Marcia Cole had told him once. As he remembered it now he knew, as he did then, that she had been wrong, all wrong. She could never understand the sickness of fear.

Big Jan stepped across the bridge platform, started out across the terrifying structure of rope mesh. Wisp tried to scream, but no words came to his throat, just a choked, inaudible gurgle. Even his muscles refused to respond. He was literally paralyzed by fear.

Then Brand stood up. Wisp saw the flash of a huge brush knife in the fellow's hand, raised above the first bridge support rope. Suddenly Wisp broke from his hiding, clutching the gun clumsily in his right hand, knowing that it had to be now, that fear had probably made him too late.

Big Jan, at the middle of the bridge, heard the shot and wheeled, his quick movement making the flimsy ropework sway sickeningly under his weight. He saw the orange flashes of flame, heard the banging, and acted on instinct. He whipped his revolver from its holster.

Wisp was squeezing the trigger, pointing blindly at the men who had risen from the bushes. At the third shot, Wisp saw Brand release the big knife and tumble awkwardly forward on his face. Then his companion broke into a mad dash directly at Wisp, pulling for a gun as he ran. Wisp's third shot brought the fellow up short, and his fourth, fifth, and sixth tore into the man's chest as he sank to the ground.

Wisp felt like shouting in fierce triumph. He wanted to scream out the news. "I did it for you, Big Jan. I got them before you knew what happened. I got them. I'm as good as you are, Big Jan, and better than they are. Do you hear? I'm better than—"

But Wisp wasn't able to put his emotions into words. He wasn't able to point triumphantly at the dead bodies of Slade and Brand which lay near the lip of the crevasse. Big Jan, even from his unsteady stance on a swaying bridge, was able to fell the man who he believed was shooting at him.

Voices floated hazily in and out of Wisp's consciousness. He seemed to be surrounded by a vast, white sea which was somehow placid and comforting. A voice, Marcia Cole's, kept returning to him above all others.

"Then you're sure?" the voices said.

The island doctor rose from the side of Wisp's bed. "Quite certain," he assured her. "Just a question of rest . . . fit as ever in a few weeks . . . flesh wounds."

Then Big Jan spoke, his voice strangely husky, "thank God that bridge made me unsteady for once. I owe him a lot . . . Men like Wisp are . . ."

The rest of the words were muffled, but the little fellow had heard enough. "Men like the Wisp," Big Jan had said that. Big Jan himself! In a feeble effort, Wisp lifted his arm above the white sheets, then through the fog he made out Big Jan's face bending over him. "I'll even it somehow, Wisp. What do you say? Is it a bargain?"

Before consciousness left him again, Wisp managed a sickly grin and his whispered reply was audible only to the trading captain. "Man to man, Big Jan, it's a bargain!"

IN TERRA INCOGNITA

KING SOLOMON'S MINES

H. Rider Haggard

INTRODUCTION

Now that this book is printed, and about to be given to the world, a sense of its shortcomings both in style and contents, weighs very heavily upon me. As regards the latter, I can only say that it does not pretend to be a full account of everything we did and saw. There are many things connected with our journey into Kukuanaland that I should have liked to dwell upon at length, which, as it is, have been scarcely alluded to. Amongst these are the curious legends which I collected about the chain armour that saved us from destruction in the great battle of Loo, and also about the "Silent Ones" or Colossi at the mouth of the stalactite cave. Again, if I had given way to my own impulses, I should have wished to go into the differences, some of which are to my mind very suggestive, between the Zulu and Kukuana dialects. Also a few pages might have been given up profitably to the consideration of the indigenous flora and fauna of Kukuanaland.* Then there remains the most interesting subject—that, as it is, has only been touched on incidentally—of the magnificent system of military organisation in force in that country, which, in my opinion, is much superior to that inaugurated by Chaka in Zululand, inasmuch as it permits of even more rapid mobilisation, and does not necessitate the employment of the pernicious system of enforced celibacy. Lastly, I have scarcely spoken of the domestic and family customs of the Kukuanas, many of which are exceedingly quaint, or of their proficiency in the art of smelting and welding metals. This science they carry to considerable perfection, of which a good example is to be seen in their "tollas," or heavy throwing knives, the backs of these weapons being made of hammered iron, and the edges of beautiful steel welded with great skill on to the iron frames. The fact of the matter is, I thought, with Sir Henry Curtis and Captain Good, that the best plan would be to tell my story in a plain, straightforward manner, and to leave these matters to be dealt with subsequently in whatever way ultimately may appear to be desirable. In the meanwhile I shall, of course, be delighted to give all information in my power to anybody interested in such things.

---

* I discovered eight varieties of antelope, with which I was previously totally unacquainted, and many new species of plants, for the most part of the bulbous tribe.—A.Q.

And now it only remains for me to offer apologies for my blunt way of writing. I can but say in excuse of it that I am more accustomed to handle a rifle than a pen, and cannot make any pretence to the grand literary flights and flourishes which I see in novels—for sometimes I like to read a novel. I suppose they—the flights and flourishes—are desirable, and I regret not being able to supply them; but at the same time I cannot help thinking that simple things are always the most impressive, and that books are easier to understand when they are written in plain language, though perhaps I have no right to set up an opinion on such a matter. "A sharp spear," runs the Kukuana saying, "needs no polish"; and on the same principle I venture to hope that a true story, however strange it may be, does not require to be decked out in fine words.

ALLAN QUATERMAIN

I. I Meet Sir Henry Curtis

It is a curious thing that at my age—fifty-five last birthday—I should find myself taking up a pen to try to write a history. I wonder what sort of a history it will be when I have finished it, if ever I come to the end of the trip! I have done a good many things in my life, which seems a long one to me, owing to my having begun work so young, perhaps. At an age when other boys are at school I was earning my living as a trader in the old Colony. I have been trading, hunting, fighting, or mining ever since. And yet it is only eight months ago that I made my pile. It is a big pile now that I have got it—I don't yet know how big—but I do not think I would go through the last fifteen or sixteen months again for it; no, not if I knew that I should come out safe at the end, pile and all. But then I am a timid man, and dislike violence; moreover, I am almost sick of adventure. I wonder why I am going to write this book: it is not in my line. I am not a literary man, though very devoted to the Old Testament and also to the "Ingoldsby Legends." Let me try to set down my reasons, just to see if I have any.

First reason: Because Sir Henry Curtis and Captain John Good asked me.

Second reason: Because I am laid up here at Durban with the pain in my left leg. Ever since that confounded lion got hold of me I have been liable to this trouble, and being rather bad just now, it makes me limp more than ever. There must be some poison in a lion's teeth, otherwise how is it that when your wounds are healed they break out again, generally, mark you, at the same time of year that you got your mauling? It is a hard thing when one has shot sixty-five lions or more, as I have in the course of my life, that the sixty-sixth should chew your leg like a quid of tobacco. It breaks the routine of the thing, and putting other considerations aside, I am an orderly man and don't like that. This is by the way.

Third reason: Because I want my boy Harry, who is over there at the hospital in London studying to become a doctor, to have something to amuse him and keep him out of mischief for a week or so. Hospital work must sometimes pall and grow rather dull, for even of cutting up dead bodies there may come satiety, and as this history will not be dull, whatever else it may be, it will put a little life into things for a day or two while Harry is reading it.

Fourth reason and last: Because I am going to tell the strangest story that I remember. It may seem a queer thing to say, especially considering that there is no woman in it—except Foulata. Stop, though! there is Gagaoola, if she was a woman, and not a fiend. But she was a hundred at least, and therefore not marriageable, so I don't count her. At any rate, I can safely say that there is not a *petticoat* in the whole history.

Well, I had better come to the yoke. It is a stiff place, and I feel as though I were bogged up to the axle. But, *"sutjes, sutjes,"* as the Boers say—I am sure I don't know how they spell it—softly does it. A strong team will come through at last, that is, if they are not too poor. You can never do anything with poor oxen. Now to make a start.

I, Allan Quatermain, of Durban, Natal, Gentleman, make oath and say—That's how I headed my deposition before the magistrate about poor Khiva's and Ventvögel's sad deaths; but somehow it doesn't seem quite the right way to begin a book. And, besides, am I a gentleman? What is a gentleman? I don't quite know, and yet I have had to do with niggers—no, I will scratch out that word "niggers," for I do not like it. I've known natives who *are*, and so you will say, Harry, my boy, before you have done with this tale, and I have known mean whites with lots of money and fresh out from home, too, who *are not*.

At any rate, I was born a gentleman, though I have been nothing but a poor travelling trader and hunter all my life. Whether I have remained so I known not, you must judge of that. Heaven knows I've tried. I have killed many men in my time, yet I have never slain wantonly or stained my hand in innocent blood, but only in self-defence. The Almighty gave us our lives, and I suppose He meant us to defend them, at least I have always acted on that, and I hope it will not be brought up against me when my clock strikes. There, there, it is a cruel and a wicked world, and for a timid man I have been mixed up in a great deal of fighting. I cannot tell the rights of it, but at any rate I have never stolen, though once I cheated a Kafir out of a herd of cattle. But then he had done me a dirty turn, and it has troubled me ever since into the bargain.

Well, it is eighteen months or so ago since first I met Sir Henry Curtis and Captain Good. It was in this way. I had been up elephant hunting beyond Bamangwato, and had met with bad luck. Everything went wrong that trip, and to top up with I got the fever badly. So soon as I was well enough I trekked down to the Diamond Fields, sold such ivory as I had, together with my wagon and oxen, discharged my hunters, and took the post-cart to the Cape. After spending a week in Cape Town, finding that they overcharged me at the hotel, and having seen everything there was to see, including the botanical gardens, which seem to me likely to confer a great benefit on the country, and the new Houses of Parliament, which I expect will do nothing of the sort, I determined to go back to Natal by the *Dunkeld*, then lying at the docks waiting for the *Edinburgh Castle* due in from England. I took my berth and went aboard, and that afternoon the Natal passengers from the *Edinburgh Castle* transhipped, and we weighed and put to sea.

Among these passengers who came on board were two who excited my curiosity. One, a gentleman of about thirty, was perhaps the biggest-chested and longest-armed man I ever saw. He had yellow hair, a thick yellow beard, clear-cut features, and large grey eyes set deep in his head. I never saw a finer-looking man, and somehow he reminded me of an ancient Dane. Not that I know much of ancient Danes, though I knew a modern Dane who did me out of ten pounds; but I remember once seeing a picture of some of those gentry, who, I take it, were a kind of white Zulus. They were drinking out of big horns, and their long hair hung down their backs. As I looked at my friend standing there by the companion-ladder, I thought that if he only let his grow a little, put one of those chain shirts on to his great shoulders, and took hold of a battle-axe and a horn mug, he might have sat as a model for that picture. And by the way it is a curious thing, and just shows how the blood will out, I discovered afterwards that Sir Henry Curtis, for that was the big man's name, is of Danish blood.* He also reminded me strongly of somebody else, but at the time I could not remember who it was.

The other man, who stood talking to Sir Henry, was stout, and dark, and of quite a different cut. I suspected at once that he was a naval officer; I don't know why, but it is difficult to mistake a navy man. I have gone shooting trips with several of them in the course of my life, and they have always proved themselves the best and bravest and nicest fellows I ever met, though sadly given, some of them, to the use of profane language. I asked a page or two back, what is a gentleman? I'll answer the question now: A Royal Naval officer is, in a general sort of way, though of course there may be a black sheep among them here and there. I fancy it is just the wide seas and the breath of God's winds that wash their hearts and blow the bitterness out of their minds and make them what men ought to be.

Well, to return, I proved right again; I ascertained that the dark man *was* a naval officer, a lieutenant of thirty-one, who, after seventeen years' service, had been turned

---

* Mr. Quatermain's ideas about ancient Danes seem to be rather confused; we have always understood that they were dark-haired people. Probably he was thinking of Saxons.—EDITOR

out of her Majesty's employ with the barren honour of a commander's rank, because it was impossible that he should be promoted. This is what people who serve the Queen have to expect: to be shot out into the cold world to find a living just when they are beginning really to understand their work, and to reach the prime of life. I suppose they don't mind it, but for my own part I had rather earn my bread as a hunter. One's halfpence are as scarce perhaps, but you do not get so many kicks.

The officer's name I found out—by referring to the passengers' lists—was Good—Captain John Good. He was broad, of medium height, dark, stout, and rather a curious man to look at. He was so very neat and so very clean-shaved, and he always wore an eye-glass in his right eye. It seemed to grow there, for it had no string, and he never took it out except to wipe it. At first I thought he used to sleep in it, but afterwards I found that this was a mistake. He put it in his trousers pocket when he went to bed, together with his false teeth, of which he had two beautiful sets that, my own being none of the best, have often caused me to break the tenth commandment. But I am anticipating.

Soon after we had got under way evening closed in, and brought with it very dirty weather. A keen breeze sprung up off land, and a kind of aggravated Scotch mist soon drove everybody from the deck. As for the *Dunkeld*, she is a flat-bottomed punt, and going up light as she was, she rolled very heavily. It almost seemed as though she would go right over, but she never did. It was quite impossible to walk about, so I stood near the engines where it was warm, and amused myself with watching the pendulum, which was fixed opposite to me, swinging slowly backwards and forwards as the vessel rolled, and marking the angle she touched at each lurch.

"That pendulum's wrong; it is not properly weighted," suddenly said a somewhat testy voice at my shoulder. Looking round I saw the naval officer whom I had noticed when the passengers came aboard.

"Indeed, now what makes you think so?" I asked.

"Think so. I don't think at all. Why there"—as she righted herself after a roll—"if the ship had really rolled to the degree that thing pointed to, then she would never have rolled again, that's all. But it is just like these merchant skippers, they are always so confoundedly careless."

Just then the dinner bell rung, and I was not sorry, for it is a dreadful thing to have to listen to an officer of the Royal Navy when he gets on to that subject. I only know one worse thing, and that is to hear a merchant skipper express his candid opinion of officers of the Royal Navy.

Captain Good and I went down to dinner together, and there we found Sir Henry Curtis already seated. He and Captain Good were placed together, and I sat opposite to them. The captain and I soon fell into talk about shooting and what not; he asking me many questions, for he is very inquisitive about all sorts of things, and I answering them as well as I could. Presently he got on to elephants.

"Ah, sir," called out somebody who was sitting near me, "you've reached the right man for that; Hunter Quatermain should be able to tell you about elephants if anybody can."

Sir Henry, who had been sitting quite quiet listening to our talk, started visibly.

"Excuse me, sir," he said, leaning forward across the table, and speaking in a low deep voice, a very suitable voice, it seemed to me, to come out of those great lungs. "Excuse me, sir, but is your name Allan Quatermain?"

I said that it was.

The big man made no further remark, but I heard him mutter "fortunate" into his beard.

Presently dinner came to an end, and as we were leaving the saloon Sir Henry strolled up and asked me if I would come into his cabin to smoke a pipe. I accepted, and he led the way to the *Dunkeld* deck cabin, and a very good cabin it is. It had been two cabins, but when Sir Garnet Wolseley or one of those big swells went down the coast in the *Dunkeld*, they knocked away the partition and have never put it up again. There was a sofa in the cabin, and a little table in front of it. Sir Henry sent the steward for a bottle of whisky, and the three of us sat down and lit our pipes.

"Mr. Quatermain," said Sir Henry Curtis, when the man had brought the whisky and lit the lamp, "the year before last about this time, you were, I believe, at a place called Bamangwato, to the north of the Transvaal."

"I was," I answered, rather surprised that this gentleman should be so well acquainted with my movements, which were not, so far as I was aware, considered of general interest.

"You were trading there, were you not?" put in Captain Good, in his quick way.

"I was. I took up a wagon-load of goods, made a camp outside the settlement, and stopped till I had sold them."

Sir Henry was sitting opposite to me in a Madeira chair, his arms leaning on the table. He now looked up, fixing his large grey eyes full upon my face. There was a curious anxiety in them, I thought.

"Did you happen to meet a man called Neville there?"

"Oh, yes; he outspanned alongside of me for a fortnight to rest his oxen before going on to the interior. I had a letter from a lawyer a few months back, asking me if I knew what had become of him, which I answered to the best of my ability at the time."

"Yes," said Sir Henry, "your letter was forwarded to me. You said in it that the gentleman called Neville left Bamangwato at the beginning of May in a wagon with a driver, a voorlooper, and a Kafir hunter called Jim, announcing his intention of trekking if possible as far as Inyati, the extreme trading post in the Matabele country, where he would sell his wagon and proceed on foot. You also said that he did sell his wagon, for six months afterwards you saw the wagon in the possession of a Portuguese trader, who told you that he had bought it at Inyati from a white man whose name he had forgotten, and that he believed the white man with the native servant had started off for the interior on a shooting trip."

"Yes."

Then came a pause.

"Mr. Quatermain," said Sir Henry suddenly, "I suppose you know or can guess nothing more of the reasons of my—of Mr. Neville's journey to the northward, or as to what point that journey was directed?"

"I heard something," I answered, and stopped. The subject was one which I did not care to discuss.

Sir Henry and Captain Good looked at each other, and Captain Good nodded.

"Mr. Quatermain," went on the former, "I am going to tell you a story, and ask your advice, and perhaps your assistance. The agent who forwarded me your letter told me that I might rely on it implicitly, as you were," he said, "well known and universally respected in Natal, and especially noted for your discretion."

I bowed and drank some whisky and water to hide my confusion, for I am a modest man—and Sir Henry went on.

"Mr. Neville was my brother."

"Oh," I said, starting, for now I knew of whom Sir Henry had reminded me when first I saw him. His brother was a much smaller man and had a dark beard, but now that I thought of it, he possessed eyes of the same shade of grey and with the same keen look in them: the features too were not unlike.

"He was," went on Sir Henry, "my only and younger brother, and till five years ago I do not suppose that we were ever a month away from each other. But just about five years ago a misfortune befell us, as sometimes does happen in families. We quarrelled bitterly, and I behaved unjustly to my brother in my anger."

Here Captain Good nodded his head vigorously to himself. The ship gave a big roll just then, so that the looking-glass, which was fixed opposite us to starboard, was for a moment nearly over our heads, and as I was sitting with my hands in my pockets and staring upwards, I could see him nodding like anything.

"As I daresay you know," went on Sir Henry, "if a man dies intestate, and has no property but land, real property it is called in England, it all descends to his eldest son. It so happened that just at the time when we quarrelled our father died intestate. He had put off making his will until it was too late. The result was that my brother, who had not been brought up to any profession, was left without a penny. Of course it would have been my duty to provide for him, but at the time the quarrel between us was so bitter that I did not—to my shame I say it (and he sighed deeply)—offer to do anything. It was not that I grudged him justice, but I waited for him to make advances, and he made none. I am sorry to trouble you with all this, Mr. Quatermain, but I must to make things clear, eh, Good?"

"Quite so, quite so," said the captain. "Mr. Quatermain will, I am sure, keep this history to himself."

"Of course," said I, for I rather pride myself on my discretion, for which, as Sir Henry had heard, I have some repute.

"Well," went on Sir Henry, "my brother had a few hundred pounds to his account at the time. Without saying anything to me he drew out this paltry sum, and, having adopted the name of Neville, started off for South Africa in the wild hope of making a fortune. This I learned afterwards. Some three years passed, and I heard nothing of my brother, though I wrote several times. Doubtless the letters never reached him. But as time went on I grew more and more troubled about him. I found out, Mr. Quatermain, that blood is thicker than water."

"That's true," said I, thinking of my boy Harry.

"I found out, Mr. Quatermain, that I would have given half my fortune to know that my brother George, the only relation I possess, was safe and well, and that I should see him again."

"But you never did, Curtis," jerked out Captain Good, glancing at the big man's face.

"Well, Mr. Quatermain, as time went on I became more and more anxious to find out if my brother was alive or dead, and if alive to get him home again. I set enquiries on foot, and your letter was one of the results. So far as it went it was satisfactory, for it showed that till lately George was alive, but it did not go far enough. So, to cut a long story short, I made up my mind to come out and look for him myself, and Captain Good was so kind as to come with me."

"Yes," said the captain; "nothing else to do, you see. Turned out by my Lords of the Admiralty to starve on half pay. And now perhaps, sir, you will tell us what you know or have heard of the gentleman called Neville."

II. THE LEGEND OF SOLOMON'S MINES

What was it that you heard about my brother's journey at Bamangwato?" asked Sir Henry, as I paused to fill my pipe before answering Captain Good.

"I heard this," I answered, "and I have never mentioned it to a soul till to-day. I heard that he was starting for Solomon's Mines."

"Solomon's Mines?" ejaculated both my hearers at once. "Where are they?"

"I don't know," I said; "I know where they are said to be. Once I saw the peaks of the mountains that border them, but there were a hundred and thirty miles of desert between me and them, and I am not aware that any white man ever got across it save one. But perhaps the best thing I can do is to tell you the legend of Solomon's Mines as I know it, you passing your word not to reveal anything I tell you without my permission. Do you agree to that? I have my reasons for asking."

Sir Henry nodded, and Captain Good replied, "Certainly, certainly."

"Well," I began, "as you may guess, generally speaking, elephant hunters are a rough set of men, who do not trouble themselves with much beyond the facts of life and the ways of Kafirs. But here and there you meet a man who takes the trouble to collect traditions from the natives, and tries to make out a little piece of the history of this dark land. It was such a man as this who first told me the legend of Solomon's Mines, now a matter of nearly thirty years ago. That was when I was on my first elephant hunt in the Matabele country. His name was Evans, and he was killed the following year, poor fellow, by a wounded buffalo, and lies buried near the Zambesi Falls. I was telling Evans one night, I remember, of some wonderful workings I had found whilst hunting koodoo and eland in what is now the Lydenburg district of the Transvaal. I see they have come across these workings again lately in prospecting for gold, but I knew of them years ago. There is a great wide wagon road cut out of the solid rock, and leading to the mouth of the working or gallery. Inside the mouth of this gallery are stacks of gold quartz piled up ready for roasting, which shows that the workers, whoever they were, must have left in a hurry. Also, about twenty paces in, the gallery is built across, and a beautiful bit of masonry it is."

" 'Ay,' said Evans, 'but I will spin you a queerer yarn than that'; and he went on to tell me how he had found in the far interior a ruined city, which he believed to be the Ophir of the Bible, and, by the way, other more learned men have said the same long since poor Evans's time. I was, I remember, listening open-eared to all these wonders, for I was young at the time, and this story of an ancient civilisation and of the treasures which those old Jewish or Phoenician adventurers used to extract from a country long since lapsed into the darkest barbarism took a great hold upon my imagination, when suddenly he said to me, 'Lad, did you ever hear of the Suliman Mountains up to the north-west of the Mashukulumbwe country?' I told him I never had. 'Ah, well,' he said, 'that is where Solomon really had his mines, his diamond mines, I mean.'

" 'How do you know that?' I asked.

" 'Know it! why, what is "Suliman" but a corruption of Solomon?* Besides, an old Isanusi or witch doctoress up in the Manica country told me all about it. She said that

---

* Suliman is the Arabic form of Solomon.—EDITOR

the people who lived across those mountains were a "branch" of the Zulus, speaking a dialect of Zulu, but finer and bigger men even; that there lived among them great wizards, who had learnt their art from white men when "all the world was dark," and who had the secret of a wonderful mine of "bright stones." '

"Well, I laughed at this story at the time, though it interested me, for the Diamond Fields were not discovered then, but poor Evans went off and was killed, and for twenty years I never thought any more of the matter. However, just twenty years afterwards—and that is a long time, gentlemen; an elephant hunter does not often live for twenty years at his business—I heard something more definite about Suliman's Mountains and the country which lies beyond them. I was up beyond the Manica country, at a place called Sitanda's Kraal, and a miserable place it was, for a man could get nothing to eat, and there was but little game about. I had an attack of fever, and was in a bad way generally, when one day a Portugee arrived with a single companion—a half-breed. Now I know your low-class Delagoa Portugee well. There is no greater devil unhung in a general way, battening as he does upon human agony and flesh in the shape of slaves. But this was quite a different type of man to the mean fellows whom I had been accustomed to meet; indeed, in appearance he reminded me more of the polite doms I have read about, for he was tall and thin, with large dark eyes and curling grey mustachios. We talked together for a while, for he could speak broken English, and I understood a little Portugee, and he told me that his name was José Silvestre, and that he had a place near Delagoa Bay. When he went on next day with his half-breed companion, he said 'Good-bye,' taking off his hat quite in the old style.

" 'Good-bye, señor,' he said; 'if ever we meet again I shall be the richest man in the world, and I will remember you.' I laughed a little—I was too weak to laugh much—and watched him strike out for the great desert to the west, wondering if he was mad, or what he thought he was going to find there.

"A week passed, and I got the better of my fever. One evening I was sitting on the ground in front of the little tent I had with me, chewing the last leg of a miserable fowl I had bought from a native for a bit of cloth worth twenty fowls, and staring at the hot red sun sinking down over the desert, when suddenly I saw a figure, apparently that of a European, for it wore a coat, on the slope of the rising ground opposite to me, about three hundred yards away. The figure crept along on its hands and knees, then it got up and staggered forward a few yards on its legs, only to fall and crawl again. Seeing that it must be somebody in distress, I sent one of my hunters to help him, and presently he arrived, and who do you suppose it turned out to be?"

"José Silvestre, of course," said Captain Good.

"Yes, José Silvestre, or rather his skeleton and a little skin. His face was a bright yellow with bilious fever, and his large dark eyes stood nearly out of his head, for all the flesh had gone. There was nothing but yellow parchment-like skin, white hair, and the gaunt bones sticking up beneath.

"'Water! for the sake of Christ, water!' he moaned, and I saw that his lips were cracked, and his tongue, which protruded between them, was swollen and blackish.

"I gave him water with a little milk in it, and he drank it in great gulps, two quarts or so, without stopping. I would not let him have any more. Then the fever took him again, and he fell down and began to rave about Suliman's Mountains, and the diamonds, and the desert. I carried him into the tent and did what I could for him, which was little enough; but I saw how it must end. About eleven o'clock he grew quieter, and I lay down for a little rest and went to sleep. At dawn I woke again, and in the half light saw Silvestre sitting up, a strange, gaunt form, and gazing out towards the desert. Presently the first ray of the sun shot right across the wide plain before us till it reached the faraway crest of one of the tallest of the Suliman Mountains more than a hundred miles away.

"'There it is!' cried the dying man in Portuguese, and pointing with his long, thin arm, 'but I shall never reach it, never. No one will ever reach it!'

"Suddenly, he paused, and seemed to take a resolution. 'Friend,' he said, turning towards me, 'are you there? My eyes grow dark.'

"'Yes,' I said; 'yes, lie down now, and rest.'

"'Ay,' he answered, 'I shall rest soon, I have time to rest—all eternity. Listen, I am dying! You have been good to me. I will give you the writing. Perhaps you will get there if you can live to pass the desert, which has killed my poor servant and me.'

"Then he groped in his shirt and brought out what I thought was a Boer tobacco pouch made of the skin of the Swart-vet-pens or sable antelope. It was fastened with a little strip of hide, what we call a rimpi, and this he tried to loose, but could not. He handed it to me. 'Untie it,' he said. I did so, and extracted a bit of torn yellow linen on which something was written in rusty letters. Inside this rag was a paper.

"Then he went on feebly, for he was growing weak: 'The paper has all that is on the linen. It took me years to read. Listen: my ancestor, a political refugee from Lisbon, and one of the first Portuguese who landed on these shores, wrote that when he was dying on those mountains which no white foot ever pressed before or since. His name was José da Silvestra, and he lived three hundred years ago. His slave, who waited for him on this side of the mountains, found him dead, and brought the writing home to Delagoa. It has been in the family ever since, but none have cared to read it, till at last I did. And I have lost my life over it, but another may succeed, and become the richest man in the world—the richest man in the world. Only give it to no one, señor; go yourself!'" Then he began to wander again, and in an hour it was all over.

"God rest him! he died very quietly, and I buried him deep, with big boulders on his breast; so I do not think that the jackals can have dug him up. And then I came away."

"Ay, but the document?" said Sir Henry, in a tone of deep interest.

"Yes, the document; what was in it?" added the captain.

"Well, gentlemen, if you like I will tell you. I have never showed it to anybody yet except to a drunken old Portuguese trader who translated it for me, and had forgotten all about it by the next morning. The original rag is at my home in Durban, together with poor Dom José's translation, but I have the English rendering in my pocket-book, and a facsimile of the map, if it can be called a map. Here it is."

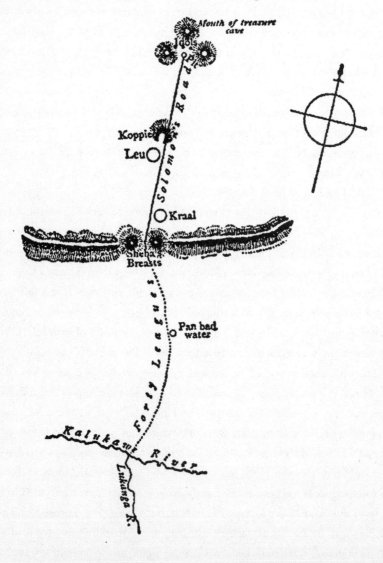

I, José da Silvestra, who am now dying of hunger in the little cave where no snow is on the north side of the nipple of the southernmost of the two mountains I have named Sheba's Breasts, write this in the year 1590 with a cleft bone upon a remnant of my raiment, my blood being the ink. If my slave should find it when he comes, and should bring it to Delagoa, let my friend (name illegible) bring the matter to the knowledge of the king, that he may send an army which, if they live through the desert and the mountains, and can overcome the brave Kukuanes and their devilish arts, to which end many priests should be brought, will make him the richest king since Solomon. With my own eyes I have seen the countless diamonds stored in Solomon's treasure chamber behind the white Death; but through the treachery of Gagool the witch-finder I might bring nought away, scarcely my life. Let him who comes follow the map, and climb the snow of Sheba's left breast till he reaches the nipple, on the north side of which is the great road Solomon made, from whence three days' journey to the King's Palace. Let him kill Gagool. Pray for my soul. Farewell.

JOSÉ DA SILVESTRA

When I had finished reading the above, and shown the copy of the map, drawn by the dying hand of the old Dom with his blood for ink, there followed a silence of astonishment.

"Well," said Captain Good, "I have been round the world twice, and put in at most ports, but may I be hung for a mutineer if ever I heard a yarn like this out of a story book, or in it either, for the matter of that."

"It's a queer tale, Mr. Quatermain," said Sir Henry. "I suppose you are not hoaxing us? It is, I know, sometimes thought allowable to take in a greenhorn."

"If you think that, Sir Henry," I said, much put out, and pocketing my paper—for I do not like to be thought one of those silly fellows who consider it witty to tell lies, and who are for ever boasting to newcomers of extraordinary hunting adventures which never happened—"if you think that, why, there is an end to the matter," and I rose to go.

Sir Henry laid his large hand upon my shoulder. "Sit down, Mr. Quatermain," he said, "I beg your pardon; I see very well you do not wish to deceive us, but the story sounded so strange that I could hardly believe it."

"You shall see the original map and writing when we reach Durban," I answered, somewhat mollified, for really when I came to consider the question it was scarcely wonderful that he should doubt my good faith. "But," I went on, "I have not told you about your brother. I knew the man Jim who was with him. He was a Bechuana by birth, a good hunter, and for a native a very clever man. That morning on which Mr. Neville was starting I saw Jim standing by my wagon and cutting up tobacco on the disselboom.

" 'Jim,' said I, 'where are you off to this trip? Is it elephants?'

" 'No, Baas,' he answered, 'we are after something worth much more than ivory.'

" 'And what might that be?' I said, for I was curious. 'Is it gold?'

" 'No, Baas, something worth more than gold,' and he grinned.

"I asked no more questions, for I did not like to lower my dignity by seeming inquisitive, but I was puzzled. Presently Jim finished cutting his tobacco.

" 'Baas,' said he.

"I took no notice.

" 'Baas,' said he again.

" 'Eh, boy, what is it?' I asked.

" 'Baas, we are going after diamonds.'

" 'Diamonds! why, then, you are steering in the wrong direction; you should head for the Fields.'

" 'Baas, have you ever heard of Suliman's Berg?'—that is, Solomon's Mountains, Sir Henry.

" 'Ay!'

" 'Have you ever heard of the diamonds there?'

" 'I have heard a foolish story, Jim.'

" 'It is no story, Baas. Once I knew a woman who came from there, and reached Natal with her child, she told me:—she is dead now.'

" 'Your master will feed the assvögels'—that is, vultures—'Jim, if he tries to reach Suliman's country, and so will you if they can get any pickings off your worthless old carcass,' said I.

"He grinned. 'Mayhap, Baas. Man must die; I'd rather like to try a new country myself; the elephants are getting worked out about here.'

" 'Ah! my boy,' I said, 'you wait till the "pale old man" gets a grip of your yellow throat, and then we shall hear what sort of a tune you sing.'

"Half an hour after that I saw Neville's wagon move off. Presently Jim came back running. 'Good-bye, Baas,' he said. 'I didn't like to start without bidding you good-bye, for I daresay you are right, and that we shall never trek south again.'

" 'Is your master really going to Suliman's Berg, Jim, or are you lying?'

" 'No,' he answered, 'he is going. He told me he was bound to make his fortune somehow, or try to; so he might as well have a fling for the diamonds.'

"'Oh!' I said; 'wait a bit, Jim; will you take a note to your master, Jim, and promise not to give it to him till you reach Inyati?' which was some hundred miles off.

"'Yes, Baas.'

"So I took a scrap of paper, and wrote on it, 'Let him who comes . . . climb the snow of Sheba's left breast, till he reaches the nipple, on the north side of which is Solomon's great road.'

"'Now, Jim,' I said, 'when you give this to your master, tell him he had better follow the advice on it implicitly. You are not to give it to him now, because I don't want him back asking me questions which I won't answer. Now be off, you idle fellow, the wagon is nearly out of sight.'

"Jim took the note and went, and that is all I know about your brother, Sir Henry; but I am much afraid—"

"Mr. Quatermain," said Sir Henry, "I am going to look for my brother; I am going to trace him to Suliman's Mountains, and over them if necessary, till I find him, or until I know that he is dead. Will you come with me?"

I am, as I think I have said, a cautious man, indeed a timid one, and this suggestion frightened me. It seemed to me that to undertake such a journey would be to go to certain death, and putting other considerations aside, as I had a son to support, I could not afford to die just then.

"No, thank you, Sir Henry, I think I had rather not," I answered. "I am too old for wild-goose chases of that sort, and we should only end up like my poor friend Silvestre. I have a son dependent on me, so I cannot afford to risk my life foolishly."

Both Sir Henry and Captain Good looked very disappointed.

"Mr. Quatermain," said the former, "I am well off, and I am bent upon this business. You may put the remuneration for your services at whatever figure you like in reason, and it shall be paid over to you before we start. Moreover, I will arrange in the event of anything untoward happening to us or to you, that your son shall be suitably provided for. You will see from this offer how necessary I think your presence. Also if by chance we should reach this place, and find diamonds, they shall belong to you and Good equally. I do not want them. But of course that promise is worth nothing at all, though the same thing would apply to any ivory we might get. You may pretty well make your own terms with me, Mr. Quatermain; and of course I shall pay all expenses."

"Sir Henry," said I, "this is the most liberal proposal I ever had, and one not to be sneezed at by a poor hunter and trader. But the job is the biggest I have come across, and I must take time to think it over. I will give you my answer before we get to Durban."

"Very good," answered Sir Henry, and then I said good-night and turned in, and dreamt about poor long-dead Silvestre and the diamonds.

III. Umbopa Enters Our Service

It takes from four to five days, according to the speed of the vessel and the state of the weather, to run up from the Cape to Durban. Sometimes, if the landing is bad at East London, where they have not yet made that wonderful harbour they talk so much of, and sink such a mint of money in, a ship is delayed for twenty-four hours before the cargo boats can get out to take off the goods. But on this occasion we had not to wait at all, for there were no breakers on the Bar to speak of, and the tugs came out at once with the long strings of ugly flat-bottomed boats behind them, into which the packages were bundled with a crash. It did not matter what they might be, over they went slap bang; whether they contained china or woollen goods they met with the same treatment. I saw one case holding four dozen of champagne smashed all to bits, and there was the champagne fizzing and boiling about in the bottom of the dirty cargo boat. It was a wicked waste, and evidently so the Kafirs in the boat thought, for they found a couple of unbroken bottles, and knocking off the necks drank the contents. But they had not allowed for the expansion caused by the fizz in the wine, and, feeling themselves swelling, rolled about in the bottom of the boat, calling out that the good liquor was "tagati"—that is, bewitched. I spoke to them from the vessel, and told them it was the white man's strongest medicine, and that they were as good as dead men. Those Kafirs went to the shore in a very great fright, and I do not think that they will touch champagne again.

Well, all the time that we were steaming up to Natal I was thinking over Sir Henry Curtis's offer. We did not speak any more on the subject for a day or two, though I told them many hunting yarns, all true ones. There is no need to tell lies about hunting, for so many curious things happen within the knowledge of a man whose business it is to hunt; but this is by the way.

At last, one beautiful evening in January, which is our hottest month, we steamed past the coast of Natal, expecting to make Durban Point by sunset. It is a lovely coast all along from East London, with its red sandhills and wide sweeps of vivid green, dotted here and there with Kafir kraals, and bordered by a ribbon of white surf, which spouts up in pillars of foam where it hits the rocks. But just before you come to Durban there is a peculiar richness about the landscape. There are the sheer kloofs cut in the hills by the rushing rains of centuries, down which the rivers sparkle; there is the deepest green of the bush, growing as God planted it, and the other greens of the mealie gardens and the sugar patches, while now and again a white house, smiling out at the placid sea, puts a finish and gives an air of homeliness to the scene. For to my mind, however beautiful a view may be, it requires the presence of man to make it complete, but perhaps that is because I have lived so much in the wilderness, and therefore know the value of civilisation, though to be sure it drives away the game. The Garden of Eden, no doubt, looked fair before man was, but I always think that it must have been fairer when Eve was walking about it.

To return, we had miscalculated a little, and the sun was well down before we dropped anchor off the Point, and heard the gun which told the good folks of Durban that the English Mail was in. It was too late to think of getting over the Bar that night, so we went comfortably to dinner, after seeing the Mails carried off in the life-boat.

When we came up again the moon was out, and shining so brightly over sea and shore that she almost paled the quick, large flashes from the lighthouse. From the shore floated sweet spicy odours that always remind me of hymns and missionaries, and in the windows of the houses on the Berea sparkled a hundred lights. From a large brig lying near also came the music of the sailors as they worked at getting the anchor up in order to be ready for the wind. Altogether it was a perfect night, such a night as you sometimes get in Southern Africa, and it threw a garment of peace over everybody as the moon threw a garment of silver over everything. Even the great bulldog, belonging to a sporting passenger, seemed to yield to its gentle influences, and forgetting his yearning to come to close quarters with the baboon in a cage on the fo'c'sle, snored happily at the door of the cabin, dreaming no doubt that he had finished him, and happy in his dream.

We three—that is, Sir Henry Curtis, Captain Good, and myself—went and sat by the wheel, and were quiet for a while.

"Well, Mr. Quatermain," said Sir Henry presently, "have you been thinking about my proposals?"

"Ay," echoed Captain Good, "what do you think of them, Mr. Quatermain? I hope that you are going to give us the pleasure of your company so far as Solomon's Mines, or wherever the gentleman you knew as Neville may have got to."

I rose and knocked out my pipe before I answered. I had not made up my mind, and wanted an additional moment to decide. Before the burning tobacco had fallen into the sea I had decided; just that little extra second did the trick. It is often the way when you have been bothering a long time over a thing.

"Yes, gentlemen," I said, sitting down again, "I will go, and by your leave I will tell you why, and on what conditions. First for the terms which I ask.

"1. You are to pay all expenses, and any ivory or other valuables we may get is to be divided between Captain Good and myself.

"2. That you give me £500 for my services on the trip before we start, I undertaking to serve you faithfully till you choose to abandon the enterprise, or till we succeed, or disaster overtakes us.

"3. That before we trek you execute a deed agreeing, in the event of my death or disablement, to pay my boy Harry, who is studying medicine over there in London, at Guy's Hospital, a sum of £200 a year for five years, by which time he ought to be able to earn a living for himself if he is worth his salt. That is all, I think, and I daresay you will say quite enough too."

"No," answered Sir Henry, "I accept them gladly. I am bent upon this project, and would pay more than that for your help, considering the peculiar and exclusive knowledge which you possess."

"Pity I did not ask it, then, but I won't go back on my word. And now that I have got my terms I will tell you my reasons for making up my mind to go. First of all, gentlemen, I have been observing you both for the last few days, and if you will not think me impertinent I may say that I like you, and believe that we shall come up well to the yoke together. That is something, let me tell you, when one has a long journey like this before one.

"And now as to the journey itself, I tell you flatly, Sir Henry and Captain Good, that I do not think it probable we can come out of it alive, that is, if we attempt to cross the Suliman Mountains. What was the fate of the old Dom da Silvestra three hundred years ago? What was the fate of his descendant twenty years ago? What has been your brother's fate? I tell you frankly, gentlemen, that as their fates were so I believe ours will be."

I paused to watch the effect of my words. Captain Good looked a little uncomfortable, but Sir Henry's face did not change. "We must take our chance," he said.

"You may perhaps wonder," I went on, "why, if I think this, I, who am, as I told you, a timid man, should undertake such a journey. It is for two reasons. First I am a fatalist, and believe that my time is appointed to come quite without reference to my own movements and will, and that if I am to go to Suliman's Mountains to be killed, I shall go there and shall be killed. God Almighty, no doubt, knows His mind about me, so I need not trouble on that point. Secondly, I am a poor man. For nearly forty years I have hunted and traded, but I have never made more than a living. Well, gentlemen, I don't know if you are aware that the average life of an elephant hunter from the time he takes to the trade is between four and five years. So you see I have lived through about seven generations of my class, and I should think that my time cannot be far off, anyway. Now, if anything were to happen to me in the ordinary course of business, by the time my debts are paid there would be nothing left to support my son Harry whilst he was getting in the way of earning a living, whereas now he will be set up for five years. There is the whole affair in a nutshell."

"Mr. Quatermain," said Sir Henry, who had been giving me his most serious attention, "your motives for undertaking an enterprise which you believe can only end in disaster reflect a great deal of credit on you. Whether or not you are right, of course time and the event alone can show. But whether you are right or wrong, I may as well tell you at once that I am going through with it to the end, sweet or bitter. If we are to be knocked on the head, all I have to say is, that I hope we get a little shooting first, eh, Good?"

"Yes, yes," put in the captain. "We have all three of us been accustomed to face danger, and to hold our lives in our hands in various ways, so it is no good turning back now. And now I vote we go down to the saloon and take an observation just for luck, you know." And we did—through the bottom of a tumbler.

Next day we went ashore, and I put up Sir Henry and Captain Good at the little shanty I have built on the Berea, and which I call my home. There are only three rooms and a kitchen in it, and it is constructed of green brick with a galvanised iron roof, but there is a good garden with the best loquot trees in it that I know, and some nice young mangoes, of which I hope great things. The curator of the botanical gardens gave them to me. It is looked after by an old hunter of mine named Jack, whose thigh was so badly broken by a buffalo cow in Sikukunis country that he will never hunt again. But he can potter about and garden, being a Griqua by birth. You will never persuade a Zulu to take much interest in gardening. It is a peaceful art, and peaceful arts are not in his line.

Sir Henry and Good slept in a tent pitched in my little grove of orange trees at the end of the garden, for there was no room for them in the house, and what with the smell of the bloom, and the sight of the green and golden fruit—in Durban you will see all three on the tree together—I daresay it is a pleasant place enough, for we have few mosquitos here on the Berea, unless there happens to come an unusually heavy rain.

Well, to get on—for if I do not, Harry, you will be tired of my story before ever we fetch up at Suliman's Mountains—having once made up my mind to go I set about making the necessary preparations. First I secured the deed from Sir Henry, providing for you, my boy, in case of accidents. There was some difficulty about its legal execution, as Sir Henry was a stranger here, and the property to be charged is over the water; but it was ultimately got over with the help of a lawyer, who charged £20 for the job—a price that I thought outrageous. Then I pocketed my cheque for £500.

Having paid this tribute to my bump of caution, I purchased a waggon and a span of oxen on Sir Henry's behalf, and beauties they were. It was a twenty-two-foot waggon with iron axles, very strong, very light, and built throughout of stink wood; not quite a new one, having been to the Diamond Fields and back, but, in my opinion, all the better for that, for I could see that the wood was well seasoned. If anything is going to give in a wagon, or if there is green wood in it, it will show out on the first trip. This particular vehicle was what we call a "half-tented" waggon, that is to say, only covered in over the after twelve feet, leaving all the front part free for the necessaries we had to carry with us. In this after part were a hide "cartle," or bed, on which two people could sleep, also racks for rifles, and many other little conveniences. I gave £125 for it, and think that it was cheap at the price.

Then I bought a beautiful team of twenty Zulu oxen, which I had kept my eye on for a year or two. Sixteen oxen is the usual number for a team, but I took four extra to allow for casualties. These Zulu cattle are small and light, not more than half the size of the Africander oxen, which are generally used for transport purposes; but they will live where the Africanders would starve, and with a moderate load can make five miles a day better going, being quicker and not so liable to become footsore. What is more, this lot were thoroughly "salted," that is, they had worked all over South Africa, and so had become proof, comparatively speaking, against red water, which so frequently destroys whole teams of oxen when they get on to strange "veldt" or grass country. As for "lung sick," which is a dreadful form of pneumonia, very prevalent in this country, they had all been inoculated against it. This is done by cutting a slit in the tail of an ox, and binding in a piece of the diseased lung of an animal which has died of the sickness. The result is that the ox sickens, takes the disease in a mild form, which causes its tail to drop off, as a rule about a foot from the root, and becomes proof against future attacks. It seems cruel to rob the animal of his tail, especially in a country where there are so many flies, but it is better to sacrifice the tail and keep the ox than to lose both tail and ox, for a tail without an ox is not much good, except to dust with. Still it does look odd to trek along behind twenty stumps, where there ought to be tails. It seems as though Nature made a trifling mistake, and stuck the stern ornaments of a lot of prize bull-dogs on to the rumps of the oxen.

Next came the question of provisioning and medicines, one which required the most careful consideration, for what we had to do was to avoid lumbering the waggon, and yet to take everything absolutely necessary. Fortunately, it turned out that Good is a bit of a doctor, having at some point in his previous career managed to pass through a course of medical and surgical instruction, which he has more or less kept up. He is not, of course, qualified, but he knows more about it than many a man who can write M.D. after his name, as we found out afterwards, and he had a splendid travelling medicine chest and a set of instruments. Whilst we were at Durban he cut off a Kafir's

big toe in a way which it was a pleasure to see. But he was quite nonplussed when the
Kafir, who had sat stolidly watching the operation, asked him to put on another, saying
that a "white one" would do at a pinch.

There remained, when these questions were satisfactorily settled, two further
important points for consideration, namely, that of arms and that of servants. As to the
arms I cannot do better than put down a list of those which we finally decided on from
among the ample store that Sir Henry had brought with him from England, and those
which I owned. I copy it from my pocket-book, where I made the entry at the time.

"Three heavy breech-loading double-eight elephant guns, weighing about fifteen
pounds each, to carry a charge of eleven drachms of black powder." Two of these were
by a well-known London firm, most excellent makers, but I do not know by whom
mine, which is not so highly finished, was made. I have used it on several trips, and
shot a good many elephants with it, and it has always proved a most superior weapon,
thoroughly to be relied on.

"Three double-500 Expresses, constructed to stand a charge of six drachms,"
sweet weapons, and admirable for medium-sized game, such as eland or sable antelope,
or for men, especially in an open country and with the semi-hollow bullet.

"One double No. 12 central-fire Keeper's shot-gun, full choke both barrels." This
gun proved of the greatest service to us afterwards in shooting game for the pot.

"Three Winchester repeating rifles (not carbines), spare guns.

"Three single-action Colt's revolvers, with the heavier, or American pattern
of cartridge."

This was our total armament, and doubtless the reader will observe that the
weapons of each class were of the same make and calibre, so that the cartridges were
interchangeable, a very important point. I make no apology for detailing it at length, as
every experienced hunter will know how vital a proper supply of guns and ammunition
is to the success of an expedition.

Now as to the men who were to go with us. After much consultation we decided
that their number should be limited to five, namely, a driver, a leader, and three servants.

The driver and leader I found without much difficulty, two Zulus, named respectively Goza and Tom; but to get the servants proved a more difficult matter. It was
necessary that they should be thoroughly trustworthy and brave men, as in a business
of this sort our lives might depend upon their conduct. At last I secured two, one a
Hottentot named Ventvögel, or "wind-bird," and one a little Zulu named Khiva, who
had the merit of speaking English perfectly. Ventvögel I had known before; he was
one of the most perfect "spoorers," that is, game trackers, I ever had to do with, and
tough as whipcord. He never seemed to tire. But he had one failing, so common with

his race, drink. Put him within reach of a bottle of grog and you could not trust him. However, as we were going beyond the region of grog-shops this little weakness of his did not so much matter.

Having secured these two men I looked in vain for a third to suit my purpose, so we determined to start without one, trusting to luck to find a suitable man on our way up country. But, as it happened, on the evening before the day we had fixed for our departure the Zulu Khiva informed me that a Kafir was waiting to see me. Accordingly, when we had done dinner, for we were at table at the time, I told Khiva to bring him in. Presently a tall, handsome-looking man, somewhere about thirty years of age, and very light-coloured for a Zulu, entered, and lifting his knob-stick by way of salute, squatted himself down in the corner on his haunches, and sat silent. I did not take any notice of him for a while, for it is a great mistake to do so. If you rush into conversation at once, a Zulu is apt to think you a person of little dignity or consequence. I observed, however, that he was a "Keshla" or ringed man; that is, he wore on his head the black ring, made of a species of gum polished with fat and worked up in the hair, which is usually assumed by Zulus on attaining a certain age or dignity. Also it struck me that his face was familiar to me.

"Well," I said at last, "What is your name?"

"Umbopa," answered the man in a slow, deep voice.

"I have seen your face before."

"Yes; the Inkoosi, the chief, my father, saw my face at the place of the Little Hand"—that is, Isandhlwana—"on the day before the battle."

Then I remembered. I was one of Lord Chelmsford's guides in that unlucky Zulu War, and had the good fortune to leave the camp in charge of some waggons on the day before the battle. While I was waiting for the cattle to be inspanned I fell into conversation with this man, who held some small command among the native auxiliaries, and he had expressed to me his doubts as to the safety of the camp. At the time I told him to hold his tongue, and leave such matters to wiser heads; but afterwards I thought of his words.

"I remember," I said; "what is it you want?"

"It is this, 'Macumazahn.'" That is my Kafir name, and means the man who gets up in the middle of the night, or, in vulgar English, he who keeps his eyes open. "I hear that you go on a great expedition far into the North with the white chiefs from over the water. Is it a true word?"

"It is."

"I hear that you go even to the Lukanga River, a moon's journey beyond the Manica country. Is this so also, 'Macumazahn?'"

"Why do you ask whither we go? What is it to you?" I answered suspiciously, for the objects of our journey had been kept a dead secret.

"It is this, O white men, that if indeed you travel so far I would travel with you."

There was a certain assumption of dignity in the man's mode of speech, and especially in his use of the words "O white men," instead of "O Inkosis," or chiefs, which struck me.

"You forget yourself a little," I said. "Your words run out unawares. That is not the way to speak. What is your name, and where is your kraal? Tell us, that we may know with whom we have to deal."

"My name is Umbopa. I am of the Zulu people, yet not of them. The house of my tribe is in the far North; it was left behind when the Zulus came down here a 'thousand years ago,' long before Chaka reigned in Zululand. I have no kraal. I have wandered for many years. I came from the North as a child to Zululand. I was Cetewayo's man in the Nkomabakosi Regiment, serving there under the great Captain, Umslopogaasi of the Axe, who taught my hands to fight. Afterwards I ran away from Zululand and came to Natal because I wanted to see the white man's ways. Next I fought against Cetewayo in the war. Since then I have been working in Natal. Now I am tired, and would go North again. Here is not my place. I want no money, but I am a brave man, and am worth my place and meat. I have spoken."

I was rather puzzled by this man and his way of speech. It was evident to me from his manner that in the main he was telling the truth, but somehow he seemed different from the ordinary run of Zulus, and I rather mistrusted his offer to come without pay. Being in a difficulty, I translated his words to Sir Henry and Good, and asked them their opinion.

Sir Henry told me to ask him to stand up. Umbopa did so, at the same time slipping off the long military great coat which he wore, and revealing himself naked except for the moocha round his centre and a necklace of lions' claws. Certainly he was a magnificent-looking man; I never saw a finer native. Standing about six foot three high he was broad in proportion, and very shapely. In that light, too, his skin looked scarcely more than dark, except here and there where deep black scars marked old assegai wounds. Sir Henry walked up to him and looked into his proud, handsome face.

"They make a good pair, don't they?" said Good; "one as big as the other."

"I like your looks, Mr. Umbopa, and I will take you as my servant," said Sir Henry in English.

Umbopa evidently understood him, for he answered in Zulu, "It is well"; and then added, with a glance at the white man's great stature and breadth, "We are men, thou and I."

IV. An Elephant Hunt

Now I do not propose to narrate at full length all the incidents of our long travel up to Sitanda's Kraal, near the junction of the Lukanga and Kalukwe Rivers. It was a journey of more than a thousand miles from Durban, the last three hundred or so of which we had to make on foot, owing to the frequent presence of the dreadful "tsetse" fly, whose bite is fatal to all animals except donkeys and men.

We left Durban at the end of January, and it was in the second week of May that we camped near Sitanda's Kraal. Our adventures on the way were many and various, but as they are of the sort which befall every African hunter—with one exception to be presently detailed—I shall not set them down here, lest I should render this history too wearisome.

At Inyati, the outlying trading station in the Matabele country, of which Lobengula (a great and cruel scoundrel) is king, with many regrets we parted from our comfortable waggon. Only twelve oxen remained to us out of the beautiful span of twenty which I had bought at Durban. One we lost from the bite of a cobra, three had perished from "poverty" and the want of water, one strayed, and the other three died from eating the poisonous herb called "tulip." Five more sickened from this cause, but we managed to cure them with doses of an infusion made by boiling down the tulip leaves. If administered in time this is a very effective antidote.

The waggon and the oxen we left in the immediate charge of Goza and Tom, our driver and leader, both trustworthy boys, requesting a worthy Scotch missionary who lived in this distant place to keep an eye on them. Then, accompanied by Umbopa, Khiva, Ventvögel, and half a dozen bearers whom we hired on the spot, we started off on foot upon our wild quest. I remember we were all a little silent on the occasion of this departure, and I think that each of us was wondering if we should ever see our waggon again; for my part I never expected to do so. For a while we tramped on in silence, till Umbopa, who was marching in front, broke into a Zulu chant about how some brave men, tired of life and the tameness of things, started off into a vast wilderness to find new things or die, and how, lo and behold! when they had travelled far into the wilderness they found that it was not a wilderness at all, but a beautiful place full of young wives and fat cattle, of game to hunt and enemies to kill.

Then we all laughed and took it for a good omen. Umbopa was a cheerful savage, in a dignified sort of way, when he was not suffering from one of his fits of brooding, and he had a wonderful knack of keeping up our spirits. We all grew very fond of him.

And now for the one adventure to which I am going to treat myself, for I do dearly love a hunting yarn.

About a fortnight's march from Inyati we came across a peculiarly beautiful bit of well-watered woodland country. The kloofs in the hills were covered with dense bush, "idoro" bush as the natives call it, and in some places, with the "wacht-een-beche," or "wait-a-little thorn," and there were great quantities of the lovely "machabell" tree, laden with refreshing yellow fruit having enormous stones. This tree is the elephant's favourite food, and there were not wanting signs that the great brutes had been about, for not only was their spoor frequent, but in many places the trees were broken down and even uprooted. The elephant is a destructive feeder.

One evening, after a long day's march, we came to a spot of great loveliness. At the foot of a bush-clad hill lay a dry river-bed, in which, however, were to be found pools of crystal water all trodden round with the hoof-prints of game. Facing this hill was a park-like plain, where grew clumps of flat-topped mimosa, varied with occasional glossy-leaved machabells, and all round stretched the sea of pathless, silent bush.

As we emerged into this river-bed path suddenly we started a troop of tall giraffes, who galloped, or rather sailed off, in their strange gait, their tails screwed up over their backs, and their hoofs rattling like castanets. They were about three hundred yards from us, and therefore practically out of shot, but Good, who was walking ahead, and who had an express loaded with solid ball in his hand, could not resist temptation. Lifting his gun, he let drive at the last, a young cow. By some extraordinary chance the ball struck it full on the back of the neck, shattering the spinal column, and that giraffe went rolling head over heels just like a rabbit. I never saw a more curious thing.

"Curse it!" said Good—for I am sorry to say he had a habit of using strong language when excited—contracted, no doubt, in the course of his nautical career; "curse it! I've killed him."

"*Ou*, Bougwan," ejaculated the Kafirs; "*ou! ou!*"

They called Good "Bougwan," or Glass Eye, because of his eye-glass.

"Oh, 'Bougwan!'" re-echoed Sir Henry and I, and from that day Good's reputation as a marvellous shot was established, at any rate among the Kafirs. Really he was a bad one, but whenever he missed we overlooked it for the sake of that giraffe.

Having set some of the "boys" to cut off the best of the giraffe's meat, we went to work to build a "scherm" near one of the pools and about a hundred yards to its right. This is done by cutting a quantity of thorn bushes and piling them in the shape of a circular hedge. Then the space enclosed is smoothed, and dry tambouki grass, if obtainable, is made into a bed in the centre, and a fire or fires lighted.

By the time the "scherm" was finished the moon peeped up, and our dinners of giraffe steaks and roasted marrow-bones were ready. How we enjoyed those marrow-bones, though it was rather a job to crack them! I know of no greater luxury than giraffe marrow, unless it is elephant's heart, and we had that on the morrow. We ate our simple meal by the light of the moon, pausing at times to thank Good for his wonderful shot; then we began to smoke and yarn, and a curious picture we must have made squatting there round the fire. I, with my short grizzled hair sticking up straight, and Sir Henry with his yellow locks, which were getting rather long, were rather a contrast, especially as I am thin, and short, and dark, weighing only nine stone and a half, and Sir Henry is tall, and broad, and fair, and weighs fifteen. But perhaps the most curious-looking of the three, taking all the circumstances of the case into consideration, was Captain John Good, R.N. There he sat upon a leather bag, looking just as though he had come in from a comfortable day's shooting in a civilised country, absolutely clean, tidy, and well dressed. He wore a shooting suit of brown tweed, with a hat to match, and neat gaiters. As usual, he was beautifully shaved, his eye-glass and his false teeth appeared to be in perfect order, and altogether he looked the neatest man I ever had to do with in the wilderness. He even sported a collar, of which he had a supply, made of white gutta-percha.

"You see, they weigh so little," he said to me innocently, when I expressed my astonishment at the fact; "and I always like to turn out like a gentleman." Ah! if he could have foreseen the future and the raiment prepared for him.

Well, there we three sat yarning away in the beautiful moonlight, and watching the Kafirs a few yards off sucking their intoxicating "daccha" from a pipe of which the mouthpiece was made of the horn of an eland, till one by one they rolled themselves up in their blankets and went to sleep by the fire, that is, all except Umbopa, who was a little apart, his chin resting on his hand, and thinking deeply. I noticed that he never mixed much with the other Kafirs.

Presently, from the depths of the bush behind us, came a loud "*woof, woof!*" "That's a lion," said I, and we all started up to listen. Hardly had we done so, when from the pool, about a hundred yards off, we heard the strident trumpeting of an elephant. "*Unkungunklovo! Indlovu!*" "Elephant! Elephant!" whispered the Kafirs, and a few minutes afterwards we saw a succession of vast shadowy forms moving slowly from the direction of the water towards the bush.

Up jumped Good, burning for slaughter, and thinking, perhaps, that it was as easy to kill elephant as he had found it to shoot giraffe, but I caught him by the arm and pulled him down.

"It's no good," I whispered, "let them go."

"It seems that we are in a paradise of game. I vote we stop here a day or two, and have a go at them," said Sir Henry, presently.

I was rather surprised, for hitherto Sir Henry had always been for pushing forward as fast as possible, more especially since we ascertained at Inyati that about two years ago an Englishman of the name of Neville *had* sold his waggon there, and gone on up country. But I suppose his hunter instincts got the better of him for a while.

Good jumped at the idea, for he was longing to have a shot at those elephants; and so, to speak the truth, did I, for it went against my conscience to let such a herd as that escape without a pull at them.

"All right, my hearties," said I. "I think we want a little recreation. And now let's turn in, for we ought to be off by dawn, and then perhaps we may catch them feeding before they move on."

The others agreed, and we proceeded to make our preparations. Good took off his clothes, shook them, put his eye-glass and his false teeth into his trousers pocket, and folding each article neatly, placed it out of the dew under a corner of his mackintosh sheet. Sir Henry and I contented ourselves with rougher arrangements, and soon were curled up in our blankets, and dropping off into the dreamless sleep that rewards the traveller.

Going, going, go— What was that?

Suddenly, from the direction of the water came sounds of violent scuffling, and next instant there broke upon our ears a succession of the most awful roars. There was no mistaking their origin; only a lion could make such a noise as that. We all jumped up and looked towards the water, in the direction of which we saw a confused mass, yellow and black in colour, staggering and struggling towards us. We seized our rifles, and slipping on our veldtschoons, that is shoes made of untanned hide, ran out of the scherm. By this time the mass had fallen, and was rolling over and over on the ground, and when we reached the spot it struggled no longer, but lay quite still.

Now we saw what it was. On the grass there lay a sable antelope bull—the most beautiful of all the African antelopes—quite dead, and transfixed by its great curved horns was a magnificent black-maned lion, also dead. Evidently what had happened was this: The sable antelope had come down to drink at the pool where the lion—no doubt the same which we had heard—was lying in wait. While the antelope drank, the lion had sprung upon him, only to be received upon the sharp curved horns and transfixed. Once before I saw a similar thing happen. Then the lion, unable to free himself, had torn and bitten at the back and neck of the bull, which, maddened with fear and pain, had rushed on until it dropped dead.

As soon as we had examined the beasts sufficiently we called the Kafirs, and between us managed to drag their carcases up to the scherm. After that we went in and lay down, to wake no more till dawn.

With the first light we were up and making ready for the fray. We took with us the three eight-bore rifles, a good supply of ammunition, and our large water-bottles, filled with weak cold tea, which I have always found the best stuff to shoot on. After swallowing a little breakfast we started, Umbopa, Khiva, and Ventvögel accompanying us. The other Kafirs we left with instructions to skin the lion and the sable antelope, and to cut up the latter.

We had no difficulty in finding the broad elephant trail, which Ventvögel, after examination, pronounced to have been made by between twenty and thirty elephants, most of them full-grown bulls. But the herd had moved on some way during the night, and it was nine o'clock, and already very hot, before, by the broken trees, bruised leaves and bark, and smoking droppings, we knew that we could not be far from them.

Presently we caught sight of the herd, which numbered, as Ventvögel had said, between twenty and thirty, standing in a hollow, having finished their morning meal, and flapping their great ears. It was a splendid sight, for they were only about two hundred yards from us. Taking a handful of dry grass, I threw it into the air to see how the wind was; for if once they winded us I knew they would be off before we could get a shot. Finding that, if anything, it blew from the elephants to us, we crept on stealthily, and thanks to the cover managed to get within forty yards or so of the great brutes. Just in front of us, and broadside on, stood three splendid bulls, one of them with enormous tusks. I whispered to the others that I would take the middle one; Sir Henry covering the elephant to the left, and Good the bull with the big tusks.

"Now," I whispered.

Boom! boom! boom! went the three heavy rifles, and down came Sir Henry's elephant dead as a hammer, shot right through the heart. Mine fell on to its knees and I thought that he was going to die, but in another moment he was up and off, tearing along straight past me. As he went I gave him the second barrel in the ribs, and this brought him down in good earnest. Hastily slipping in two fresh cartridges I ran close up to him, and a ball through the brain put an end to the poor brute's struggles. Then I turned to see how Good had fared with the big bull, which I had heard screaming with rage and pain as I gave mine its quietus. On reaching the captain I found him in a great state of excitement. It appeared that on receiving the bullet the bull had turned and come straight for his assailant, who had barely time to get out of his way, and then charged on blindly past him, in the direction of our encampment. Meanwhile the herd had crashed off in wild alarm in the other direction.

For a while we debated whether to go after the wounded bull or to follow the herd, and finally deciding for the latter alternative, departed, thinking that we had seen the last of those big tusks. I have often wished since that we had. It was easy work to follow the elephants, for they had left a trail like a carriage road behind them, crushing down the thick bush in their furious flight as though it were tambouki grass.

But to come up with them was another matter, and we had struggled on under the broiling sun for over two hours before we found them. With the exception of one bull, they were standing together, and I could see, from their unquiet way and the manner in which they kept lifting their trunks to test the air, that they were on the look-out for mischief. The solitary bull stood fifty yards or so to this side of the herd, over which he was evidently keeping sentry, and about sixty yards from us. Thinking that he would see or wind us, and that it would probably start them off again if we tried to get nearer, especially as the ground was rather open, we all aimed at this bull, and at my whispered word, we fired. The three shots took effect, and down he went dead. Again the herd started, but unfortunately for them about a hundred yards further on was a nullah, or dried-out water track, with steep banks, a place very much resembling the one where the Prince Imperial was killed in Zululand. Into this the elephants plunged, and when we reached the edge we found them struggling in wild confusion to get up the other bank, filling the air with their screams, and trumpeting as they pushed one another aside in their selfish panic, just like so many human beings. Now was our opportunity, and firing away as quickly as we could load, we killed five of the poor beasts, and no doubt should have bagged the whole herd, had they not suddenly given up their attempts to climb the bank and rushed headlong down the nullah. We were too tired to follow them, and perhaps also a little sick of slaughter, eight elephants being a pretty good bag for one day.

So after we were rested a little, and the Kafirs had cut out the hearts of two of the dead elephants for supper, we started homewards, very well pleased with our day's work, having made up our minds to send the bearers on the morrow to chop away the tusks.

Shortly after we re-passed the spot where Good had wounded the patriarchal bull we came across a herd of eland, but did not shoot at them, as we had plenty of meat. They trotted past us, and then stopped behind a little patch of bush about a hundred yards away, wheeling round to look at us. As Good was anxious to get a near view of them, never having seen an eland close, he handed his rifle to Umbopa, and, followed by Khiva, strolled up to the patch of bush. We sat down and waited for him, not sorry of the excuse for a little rest.

The sun was just going down in its reddest glory, and Sir Henry and I were admiring the lovely scene, when suddenly we heard an elephant scream, and saw its huge and rushing form with uplifted trunk and tail silhouetted against the great fiery globe of the sun. Next second we saw something else, and that was Good and

Khiva tearing back towards us with the wounded bull—for it was he—charging after them. For a moment we did not dare to fire—though at that distance it would have been of little use if we had done so—for fear of hitting one of them, and the next a dreadful thing happened—Good fell a victim to his passion for civilised dress. Had he consented to discard his trousers and gaiters like the rest of us, and to hunt in a flannel shirt and a pair of veldt-schoons, it would have been all right. But as it was, his trousers cumbered him in that desperate race, and presently, when he was about sixty yards from us, his boot, polished by the dry grass, slipped, and down he went on his face right in front of the elephant.

We gave a gasp, for we knew that he must die, and ran as hard as we could towards him. In three seconds it had ended, but not as we thought. Khiva, the Zulu boy, saw his master fall, and brave lad as he was, turned and flung his assegai straight into the elephant's face. It stuck in his trunk.

With a scream of pain, the brute seized the poor Zulu, hurled him to the earth, and placing one huge foot on to his body about the middle, twined its trunk round his upper part and *tore him in two.*

We rushed up mad with horror, and fired again and again, till presently the elephant fell upon the fragments of the Zulu.

As for Good, he rose and wrung his hands over the brave man who had given his life to save him, and, though I am an old hand, I felt a lump grow in my throat. Umbopa stood contemplating the huge dead elephant and the mangled remains of poor Khiva.

"Ah, well," he said presently, "he is dead, but he died like a man!"

V. Our March Into the Desert

We had killed nine elephants, and it took us two days to cut out the tusks, and having brought them into camp, to bury them carefully in the sand under a large tree, which made a conspicuous mark for miles round. It was a wonderfully fine lot of ivory. I never saw a better, averaging as it did between forty and fifty pounds a tusk. The tusks of the great bull that killed poor Khiva scaled one hundred and seventy pounds the pair, so nearly as we could judge.

As for Khiva himself, we buried what remained of him in an ant-bear hole, together with an assegai to protect himself with on his journey to a better world. On the third day we marched again, hoping that we might live to return to dig up our buried ivory, and in due course, after a long and wearisome tramp, and many adventures which I have not space to detail, we reached Sitanda's Kraal, near the Lukanga River, the real starting-point of our expedition. Very well do I recollect our arrival at that place. To the right was a scattered native settlement with a few stone cattle kraals and some cultivated lands down by the water, where these savages grew their scanty supply of grain, and beyond it stretched great tracts of waving "veldt" covered with tall grass, over which herds of the smaller game were wandering. To the left lay the vast desert. This spot appears to be the outpost of the fertile country, and it would be difficult to say to what natural causes such an abrupt change in the character of the soil is due. But so it is.

Just below our encampment flowed a little stream, on the farther side of which is a stony slope, the same down which, twenty years before, I had seen poor Silvestre creeping back after his attempt to reach Solomon's Mines, and beyond that slope begins the waterless desert, covered with a species of karoo shrub.

It was evening when we pitched our camp, and the great ball of the sun was sinking into the desert, sending glorious rays of many-coloured light flying all over its vast expanse. Leaving Good to superintend the arrangement of our little camp, I took Sir Henry with me, and walking to the top of the slope opposite, we gazed across the desert. The air was very clear, and far, far away I could distinguish the faint blue outlines, here and there capped with white, of the Suliman Berg.

"There," I said, "there is the wall round Solomon's Mines, but God knows if we shall ever climb it."

"My brother should be there, and if he is, I shall reach him somehow," said Sir Henry, in that tone of quiet confidence which marked the man.

"I hope so," I answered, and turned to go back to the camp, when I saw that we were not alone. Behind us, also gazing earnestly towards the far-off mountains, stood the great Kafir Umbopa.

The Zulu spoke when he saw that I had observed him, addressing Sir Henry, to whom he had attached himself.

"Is it to that land that thou wouldst journey, Incubu?" (a native word meaning, I believe, an elephant, and the name given to Sir Henry by the Kafirs), he said, pointing towards the mountain with his broad assegai.

I asked him sharply what he meant by addressing his master in that familiar way. It is very well for natives to have a name for one among themselves, but it is not decent that they should call a white man by their heathenish appellations to his face. The Zulu laughed a quiet little laugh which angered me.

"How dost thou know that I am not the equal of the Inkosi whom I serve?" he said. "He is of a royal house, no doubt; one can see it in his size and by his mien; so, mayhap, am I. At least, I am as great a man. Be my mouth, O Macumazahn, and say my words to the Inkoos Incubu, my master, for I would speak to him and to thee."

I was angry with the man, for I am not accustomed to be talked to in that way by Kafirs, but somehow he impressed me, and besides I was curious to know what he had to say. So I translated, expressing my opinion at the same time that he was an impudent fellow, and that his swagger was outrageous.

"Yes, Umbopa," answered Sir Henry, "I would journey there."

"The desert is wide and there is no water in it, the mountains are high and covered with snow, and man cannot say what lies beyond them behind the place where the sun sets; how shalt thou come thither, Incubu, and wherefore dost thou go?"

I translated again.

"Tell him," answered Sir Henry, "that I go because I believe that a man of my blood, my brother, has gone there before me, and I journey to seek him."

"That is so, Incubu; a Hottentot I met on the road told me that a white man went out into the desert two years ago towards those mountains with one servant, a hunter. They never came back."

"How do you know it was my brother?" asked Sir Henry.

"Nay, I know not. But the Hottentot, when I asked what the white man was like, said that he had thine eyes and a black beard. He said, too, that the name of the hunter with him was Jim; that he was a Bechuana hunter and wore clothes."

"There is no doubt about it," said I; "I knew Jim well."

Sir Henry nodded. "I was sure of it," he said. "If George set his mind upon a thing he generally did it. It was always so from his boyhood. If he meant to cross the Suliman Berg he has crossed it, unless some accident overtook him, and we must look for him on the other side."

Umbopa understood English, though he rarely spoke it.

"It is a far journey, Incubu," he put in, and I translated his remark.

"Yes," answered Sir Henry, "it is far. But there is no journey upon this earth that a man may not make if he sets his heart to it. There is nothing, Umbopa, that he cannot do, there are no mountains he may not climb, there are no deserts he cannot cross, save a mountain and a desert of which you are spared the knowledge, if love leads him and he holds his life in his hands counting it as nothing, ready to keep it or lose it as Heaven above may order."

I translated.

"Great words, my father," answered the Zulu—I always called him a Zulu, though he was not really one—"great swelling words fit to fill the mouth of a man. Thou art right, my father Incubu. Listen! what is life? It is a feather, it is the seed of the grass, blown hither and thither, sometimes multiplying itself and dying in the act, sometimes carried away into the heavens. But if that seed be good and heavy it may perchance travel a little way on the road it wills. It is well to try and journey one's road and to fight with the air. Man must die. At the worst he can but die a little sooner. I will go with thee across the desert and over the mountains, unless perchance I fall to the ground on the way, my father."

He paused a while, and then went on with one of those strange bursts of rhetorical eloquence that Zulus sometimes indulge in, which to my mind, full though they are of vain repetitions, show that the race is by no means devoid of poetic instinct and of intellectual power.

"What is life? Tell me, O white men, who are wise, who know the secrets of the world, and of the world of stars, and the world that lies above and around the stars; who flash your words from afar without a voice; tell me, white men, the secret of our life—whither it goes and whence it comes!

"You cannot answer me; you know not. Listen, I will answer. Out of the dark we came, into the dark we go. Like a storm-driven bird at night we fly out of the Nowhere; for a moment our wings are seen in the light of the fire, and, lo! we are gone again into the Nowhere. Life is nothing. Life is all. It is the Hand with which we hold off Death. It is the glow-worm that shines in the night-time and is black in the morning; it is the white breath of the oxen in winter; it is the little shadow that runs across the grass and loses itself at sunset."

"You are a strange man," said Sir Henry, when he had ceased.

Umbopa laughed. "It seems to me that we are much alike, Incubu. Perhaps I seek a brother over the mountains."

I looked at him suspiciously. "What dost thou mean?" I asked; "what dost thou know of those mountains?"

"A little; a very little. There is a strange land yonder, a land of witchcraft and beautiful things; a land of brave people, and of trees, and streams, and snowy peaks, and of a great white road. I have heard of it. But what is the good of talking? It grows dark. Those who live to see will see."

Again I looked at him doubtfully. The man knew too much.

"You need not fear me, Macumazahn," he said, interpreting my look. "I dig no holes for you to fall in. I make no plots. If ever we cross those mountains behind the sun I will tell what I know. But Death sits upon them. Be wise and turn back. Go and hunt elephants, my masters. I have spoken."

And without another word he lifted his spear in salutation, and returned towards the camp, where shortly afterwards we found him cleaning a gun like any other Kafir.

"That is an odd man," said Sir Henry.

"Yes," answered I, "too odd by half. I don't like his little ways. He knows something, and will not speak out. But I suppose it is no use quarrelling with him. We are in for a curious trip, and a mysterious Zulu won't make much difference one way or another."

Next day we made our arrangements for starting. Of course it was impossible to drag our heavy elephant rifles and other kit with us across the desert, so, dismissing our bearers, we made an arrangement with an old native who had a kraal close by to take care of them till we returned. It went to my heart to leave such things as those sweet tools to the tender mercies of an old thief of a savage whose greedy eyes I could see gloating over them. But I took some precautions.

First of all I loaded all the rifles, placing them at full cock, and informed him that if he touched them they would go off. He tried the experiment instantly with my eight-bore, and it did go off, and blew a hole right through one of his oxen, which were just then being driven up to the kraal, to say nothing of knocking him head over heels with the recoil. He got up considerably startled, and not at all pleased at the loss of the ox, which he had the impudence to ask me to pay for, and nothing would induce him to touch the guns again.

"Put the live devils out of the way up there in the thatch," he said, "or they will murder us all."

Then I told him that, when we came back, if one of those things was missing I would kill him and his people by witchcraft; and if we died and he tried to steal the rifles I would come and haunt him and turn his cattle mad and his milk sour till life was a weariness, and would make the devils in the guns come out and talk to him in a way he did not like, and generally gave him a good idea of judgment to come. After that he promised to look after them as though they were his father's spirit. He was a very superstitious old Kafir and a great villain.

Having thus disposed of our superfluous gear we arranged the kit we five—Sir Henry, Good, myself, Umbopa, and the Hottentot Ventvögel—were to take with us on our journey. It was small enough, but do what we would we could not get its weight down under about forty pounds a man. This is what it consisted of:—

The three express rifles and two hundred rounds of ammunition.

The two Winchester repeating rifles (for Umbopa and Ventvögel), with two hundred rounds of cartridge.

Three "Colt" revolvers and sixty rounds of cartridge.

Five Cochrane's water-bottles, each holding four pints.

Five blankets.

Twenty-five pounds' weight of biltong—*i.e.* sun-dried game flesh.

Ten pounds' weight of best mixed beads for gifts.

A selection of medicine, including an ounce of quinine, and one or two small surgical instruments.

Our knives, a few sundries, such as a compass, matches, a pocket filter, tobacco, a trowel, a bottle of brandy, and the clothes we stood in.

This was our total equipment, a small one indeed for such a venture, but we dared not attempt to carry more. Indeed, that load was a heavy one per man with which to travel across the burning desert, for in such places every additional ounce tells. But we could not see our way to reducing the weight. There was nothing taken but what was absolutely necessary.

With great difficulty, and by the promise of a present of a good hunting-knife each, I succeeded in persuading three wretched natives from the village to come with us for the first stage, twenty miles, and to carry a large gourd holding a gallon of water apiece. My object was to enable us to refill our water-bottles after the first night's march, for we determined to start in the cool of the evening. I gave out to these natives that we were going to shoot ostriches, with which the desert abounded. They jabbered and shrugged their shoulders, saying that we were mad and should perish of thirst, which I must say seemed probable; but being desirous of obtaining the knives, which were almost unknown treasures up there, they consented to come, having probably reflected that, after all, our subsequent extinction would be no affair of theirs.

All next day we rested and slept, and at sunset ate a hearty meal of fresh beef washed down with tea, the last, as Good remarked sadly, we were likely to drink for many a long day. Then, having made our final preparations, we lay down and waited for the moon to rise. At last, about nine o'clock, up she came in all her glory, flooding the wild country with light, and throwing a silver sheen on the expanse of rolling desert before us, which looked as solemn and quiet and as alien to man as the star-studded firmament above. We rose up, and in a few minutes were ready, and yet we hesitated a little, as human nature is prone to hesitate on the threshold of an irrevocable step. We three white men stood by ourselves. Umbopa, assegai in hand and a rifle across his shoulders, looked out fixedly across the desert a few paces ahead of us; while the hired natives, with the gourds of water, and Ventvögel, were gathered in a little knot behind.

"Gentlemen," said Sir Henry presently, in his deep voice, "we are going on about as strange a journey as men can make in this world. It is very doubtful if we can succeed in it. But we are three men who will stand together for good or for evil to the last. Now before we start let us for a moment pray to the Power who shapes the destinies of men, and who ages since has marked out our paths, that it may please Him to direct our steps in accordance with His will."

Taking off his hat, for the space of a minute or so, he covered his face with his hands, and Good and I did likewise.

I do not say that I am a first-rate praying man, few hunters are, and as for Sir Henry, I never heard him speak like that before, and only once since, though deep down in his heart I believe that he is very religious. Good too is pious, though apt to swear. Anyhow I do not remember, excepting on one single occasion, ever putting up a better prayer in my life than I did during that minute, and somehow I felt the happier for it. Our future was so completely unknown, and I think that the unknown and the awful always bring a man nearer to his Maker.

"And now," said Sir Henry, "*trek*!"

So we started.

We had nothing to guide ourselves by except the distant mountains and old José da Silvestre's chart, which, considering that it was drawn by a dying and half-distraught man on a fragment of linen three centuries ago, was not a very satisfactory sort of thing to work with. Still, our sole hope of success depended upon it, such as it was. If we failed in finding that pool of bad water which the old Dom marked as being situated in the middle of the desert, about sixty miles from our starting-point, and as far from the mountains, in all probability we must perish miserably of thirst. But to my mind the chances of our finding it in that great sea of sand and karoo scrub seemed almost infinitesimal. Even supposing that da Silvestra had marked the pool right, what was there to prevent its having been dried up by the sun generations ago, or trampled in by game, or filled with the drifting sand?

On we tramped silently as shades through the night and in the heavy sand. The karoo bushes caught our feet and retarded us, and the sand worked into our veldtschoons and Good's shooting boots, so that every few miles we had to stop and empty them; but still the night kept fairly cool, though the atmosphere was thick and heavy, giving a sort of creamy feel to the air, and we made fair progress. It was very silent and lonely there in the desert, oppressively so indeed. Good felt this, and once began to whistle the "Girl I left behind me," but the notes sounded lugubrious in that vast place, and he gave it up.

Shortly afterwards a little incident occurred which, though it startled us at the time, gave rise to a laugh. Good was leading, as the holder of the compass, which, being a sailor, of course he understood thoroughly, and we were toiling along in single file behind him, when suddenly we heard the sound of an exclamation, and he vanished. Next second there arose all around us a most extraordinary hubbub, snorts, groans, and wild sounds of rushing feet. In the faint light, too, we could descry dim galloping forms half hidden by wreaths of sand. The natives threw down their loads and prepared to bolt, but remembering that there was nowhere to run to, they cast themselves upon the ground and howled out that it was ghosts. As for Sir Henry and myself, we stood amazed; nor was our amazement lessened when we perceived the form of Good careering off in the direction of the mountains, apparently mounted on the back of a horse and halloaing wildly. In another second he threw up his arms, and we heard him come to the earth with a thud.

Then I saw what had happened; we had stumbled upon a herd of sleeping quagga, on to the back of one of which Good actually had fallen, and the brute naturally enough got up and made off with him. Calling out to the others that it was all right, I ran towards Good, much afraid lest he should be hurt, but to my great relief I found him sitting in the sand, his eye-glass still fixed firmly in his eye, rather shaken and very much frightened, but not in any way injured.

After this we travelled on without any further misadventure till about one o'clock, when we called a halt, and having drunk a little water, not much, for water was precious, and rested for half an hour, we started again.

On, on we went, till at last the east began to blush like the cheek of a girl. Then there came faint rays of primrose light, that changed presently to golden bars, through which the dawn glided out across the desert. The stars grew pale and paler still, till at last they vanished; the golden moon waxed wan, and her mountain ridges stood out against her sickly face like the bones on the cheek of a dying man. Then came spear upon spear of light flashing far away across the boundless wilderness, piercing and firing the veils of mist, till the desert was draped in a tremulous golden glow, and it was day.

Still we did not halt, though by this time we should have been glad enough to do so, for we knew that when once the sun was fully up it would be almost impossible for us to travel. At length, about an hour later, we spied a little pile of boulders rising out of the plain, and to this we dragged ourselves. As luck would have it, here we found an overhanging slab of rock carpeted beneath with smooth sand, which afforded a most grateful shelter from the heat. Underneath this we crept, and each of us having drunk some water and eaten a bit of biltong, we lay down and soon were sound asleep.

It was three o'clock in the afternoon before we woke, to find our bearers preparing to return. They had seen enough of the desert already, and no number of knives would have tempted them to come a step farther. So we took a hearty drink, and having emptied our water-bottles, filled them up again from the gourds that they had brought with them, and then watched them depart on their twenty miles' tramp home.

At half-past four we also started. It was lonely and desolate work, for with the exception of a few ostriches there was not a single living creature to be seen on all the vast expanse of sandy plain. Evidently it was too dry for game, and with the exception of a deadly-looking cobra or two we saw no reptiles. One insect, however, we found abundant, and that was the common or house fly. There they came, "not as single spies, but in battalions," as I think the Old Testament* says somewhere. He is an extraordinary animal is the house fly. Go where you will you find him, and so it must have been always. I have seen him enclosed in amber, which is, I was told, quite half a million years old, looking exactly like his descendant of to-day, and I have little doubt but that when the last man lies dying on the earth he will be buzzing round—if this event should happen to occur in summer—watching for an opportunity to settle on his nose.

At sunset we halted, waiting for the moon to rise. At last she came up, beautiful and serene as ever, and, with one halt about two o'clock in the morning, we trudged on wearily through the night, till at last the welcome sun put a period to our labours. We drank a little and flung ourselves down on the sand, thoroughly tired out, and soon were all asleep. There was no need to set a watch, for we had nothing to fear from anybody or anything in that vast untenanted plain. Our only enemies were heat, thirst, and flies, but far rather would I have faced any danger from man or beast than that awful trinity. This time we were not so lucky as to find a sheltering rock to guard us from the glare of the sun, with the result that about seven o'clock we woke up experiencing the exact sensations one would attribute to a beefsteak on a gridiron. We were literally being baked through and through. The burning sun seemed to be sucking our very blood out of us. We sat up and gasped.

"Phew," said I, grabbing at the halo of flies which buzzed cheerfully round my head. The heat did not affect *them*.

"My word!" said Sir Henry.

"It *is* hot!" echoed Good.

It was hot, indeed, and there was not a bit of shelter to be found. Look where we would there was no rock or tree, nothing but an unending glare, rendered dazzling by the heated air that danced over the surface of the desert as it dances over a red-hot stove.

"What is to be done?" asked Sir Henry; "we can't stand this for long."

We looked at each other blankly.

"I have it," said Good, "we must dig a hole, get in it, and cover ourselves with the karoo bushes."

It did not seem a very promising suggestion, but at least it was better than nothing, so we set to work, and, with the trowel we had brought with us and the help of our hands, in about an hour we succeeded in delving out a patch of ground some ten feet

---

*Readers must beware of accepting Mr. Quatermain's references as accurate, as, it has been found, some are prone to do. Although his reading evidently was limited, the impression produced by it upon his mind was mixed. Thus to him the Old Testament and Shakespeare were interchangeable authorities.—EDITOR

long by twelve wide to the depth of two feet. Then we cut a quantity of low scrub with our hunting-knives, and creeping into the hole, pulled it over us all, with the exception of Ventvögel, on whom, being a Hottentot, the heat had no particular effect. This gave us some slight shelter from the burning rays of the sun, but the atmosphere in that amateur grave can be better imagined than described. The Black Hole of Calcutta must have been a fool to it; indeed, to this moment I do not know how we lived through the day. There we lay panting, and every now and again moistening our lips from our scanty supply of water. Had we followed our inclinations we should have finished all we possessed in the first two hours, but we were forced to exercise the most rigid care, for if our water failed us we knew that very soon we must perish miserably.

But everything has an end, if only you live long enough to see it, and somehow that miserable day wore on towards evening. About three o'clock in the afternoon we determined that we could bear it no longer. It would be better to die walking that to be killed slowly by heat and thirst in this dreadful hole. So taking each of us a little drink from our fast diminishing supply of water, now warmed to about the same temperature as a man's blood, we staggered forward.

We had then covered some fifty miles of wilderness. If the reader will refer to the rough copy and translation of old da Silvestra's map, he will see that the desert is marked as measuring forty leagues across, and the "pan bad water" is set down as being about in the middle of it. Now forty leagues is one hundred and twenty miles, consequently we ought at the most to be within twelve or fifteen miles of the water if any should really exist.

Through the afternoon we crept slowly and painfully along, scarcely doing more than a mile and a half in an hour. At sunset we rested again, waiting for the moon, and after drinking a little managed to get some sleep.

Before we lay down, Umbopa pointed out to us a slight and indistinct hillock on the flat surface of the plain about eight miles away. At the distance it looked like an ant-hill, and as I was dropping off to sleep I fell to wondering what it could be.

With the moon we marched again, feeling dreadfully exhausted, and suffering tortures from thirst and prickly heat. Nobody who has not felt it can know what we went through. We walked no longer, we staggered, now and again falling from exhaustion, and being obliged to call a halt every hour or so. We had scarcely energy left in us to speak. Up to this Good had chatted and joked, for he is a merry fellow; but now he had not a joke in him.

At last, about two o'clock, utterly worn out in body and mind, we came to the foot of the queer hill, or sand koppie, which at first sight resembled a gigantic ant-heap about a hundred feet high, and covering at the base nearly two acres of ground.

Here we halted, and driven to it by our desperate thirst, sucked down our last drops of water. We had but half a pint a head, and each of us could have drunk a gallon.

Then we lay down. Just as I was dropping off to sleep I heard Umbopa remark to himself in Zulu—

"If we cannot find water we shall all be dead before the moon rises to-morrow."

I shuddered, hot as it was. The near prospect of such an awful death is not pleasant, but even the thought of it could not keep me from sleeping.

VI. WATER! WATER!

In two hours' time, that is, about four o'clock, I woke up. So soon as the first heavy demand of bodily fatigue had been satisfied, the torturing thirst from which I was suffering asserted itself. I could sleep no more. I had been dreaming that I was bathing in a running stream, with green banks and trees upon them, and I awoke to find myself in this arid wilderness, and to remember, as Umbopa had said, that if we did not find water this day we must perish miserably. No human creature could live long without water in that heat. I sat up and rubbed my grimy face with my dry and horny hands, as my lips and eyelids were stuck together, and it was only after some friction and with an effort that I was able to open them. It was not far from dawn, but there was none of the bright feel of dawn in the air, which was thick with a hot murkiness that I cannot describe. The others were still sleeping. Presently it began to grow light enough to read, so I drew out a little pocket copy of the "Ingoldsby Legends" which I had brought with me, and read "The Jackdaw of Rheims." When I got to where

> A nice little boy held a golden ewer,
> Embossed, and filled with water as pure
> As any that flows between Rheims and Namur,

literally I smacked my cracking lips, or rather tried to smack them. The mere thought of that pure water made me mad. If the Cardinal had been there with his bell, book, and candle, I would have whipped in and drunk his water up, yes, even if he had filled it already with the suds of soap worthy of washing the hands of the Pope, and I knew that the whole consecrated curse of the Catholic Church should fall upon me for so doing. I almost think that I must have been a little light-headed with thirst, weariness and the want of food; for I fell to thinking how astonished the Cardinal and his nice little boy and the jackdaw would have looked to see a burnt up, brown-eyed, grizzly-haired little elephant hunter suddenly bound between them, put his dirty face into the basin, and swallow every drop of the precious water. The idea amused me so much that I laughed or rather cackled aloud, which woke the others, and they began to rub *their* dirty faces and drag *their* gummed-up lips and eyelids apart.

As soon as we were all well awake we began to discuss the situation, which was serious enough. Not a drop of water was left. We turned the bottles upside down, and licked their tops, but it was a failure, they were dry as a bone. Good, who had charge of the bottle of brandy, got it out and looked at it longingly; but Sir Henry promptly took it away from him, for to drink raw spirit would only have been to precipitate the end.

"If we do not find water we shall die," he said.

"If we can trust to the old Dom's map there should be some about," I said; but nobody seemed to derive much satisfaction from this remark. It was so evident that no great faith could be put in the map. Now it was gradually growing light, and as we sat staring blankly at each other, I observed the Hottentot Ventvögel rise and begin to walk about with his eyes on the ground. Presently he stopped short, and uttering a guttural exclamation, pointed to the earth.

"What is it?" we exclaimed; and rising simultaneously we went to where he was standing staring at the ground.

"Well," I said, "it is fresh Springbok spoor; what of it?"

"Springbucks do not go far from water," he answered in Dutch.

"No," I answered, "I forgot; and thank God for it."

This little discovery put new life into us; for it is wonderful, when a man is in a desperate position, how he catches at the slightest hope, and feels almost happy. On a dark night a single star is better than nothing.

Meanwhile Ventvögel was lifting his snub nose, and sniffing the hot air for all the world like an old Impala ram who scents danger. Presently he spoke again.

"I *smell* water," he said.

Then we felt quite jubilant, for we knew what a wonderful instinct these wild-bred men possess.

Just at that moment the sun came up gloriously, and revealed so grand a sight to our astonished eyes that for a moment or two we even forgot our thirst.

There, not more than forty or fifty miles from us, glittering like silver in the early rays of the morning sun, soared Sheba's Breasts; and stretching away for hundreds of miles on either side of them ran the great Suliman Berg. Now that, sitting here, I attempt to describe the extraordinary grandeur and beauty of that sight, language seems to fail me. I am impotent even before its memory. Straight before us, rose two enormous mountains, the like of which are not, I believe, to be seen in Africa, if indeed there are any other such in the world, measuring each of them at least fifteen thousand feet in height, standing not more than a dozen miles apart, linked together by a precipitous cliff of rock, and towering in awful white solemnity straight into the sky. These mountains placed thus, like the pillars of a gigantic gateway, are shaped after the fashion of a woman's breasts, and at times the mists and shadows beneath them take the form of a recumbent woman, veiled mysteriously in sleep. Their bases swell gently from the plain, looking at that distance perfectly round and smooth; and upon the top of each is a vast hillock covered with snow, exactly corresponding to the nipple on the female breast. The stretch of cliff that connects them appears to be some thousands of feet in height, and perfectly precipitous, and on each flank of them, so far as the eye can reach, extent similar lines of cliff, broken only here and there by flat table-topped mountains, something like the world-famed one at Cape Town; a formation, by the way, that is very common in Africa.

To describe the comprehensive grandeur of that view is beyond my powers. There was something so inexpressibly solemn and overpowering about those huge volcanoes—for doubtless they are extinct volcanoes—that it quite awed us. For a while the morning lights played upon the snow and the brown and swelling masses beneath, and then, as though to veil the majestic sight from our curious eyes, strange mists and clouds gathered and increased around the mountains, till presently we could only trace their pure and gigantic outlines, showing ghostlike through the fleecy envelope. Indeed, as we afterwards discovered, usually they were wrapped in this gauze-like mist, which doubtless accounted for our not having seen them more clearly before.

Sheba's Breasts had scarcely vanished into cloud-clad privacy, before our thirst— literally a burning question—reasserted itself.

It was all very well for Ventvögel to say that he smelt water, but we could see no signs of it, look which way we would. So far as the eye might reach there was nothing but arid sweltering sand and karoo scrub. We walked round the hillock and gazed about anxiously on the other side, but it was the same story, not a drop of water could be found; there was no indication of a pan, a pool, or a spring.

"You are a fool," I said angrily to Ventvögel; "there is no water."

But still he lifted his ugly snub nose and sniffed.

"I smell it, Baas," he answered; "it is somewhere in the air."

"Yes," I said, "no doubt it is in the clouds, and about two months hence it will fall and wash our bones."

Sir Henry stroked his yellow beard thoughtfully. "Perhaps it is on the top of the hill," he suggested.

"Rot," said Good; "whoever heard of water being found at the top of a hill!"

"Let us go and look," I put in, and hopelessly enough we scrambled up the sandy sides of the hillock, Umbopa leading. Presently he stopped as though he was petrified.

"*Nanzia manzie!*" that is, "Here is water," he cried with a loud voice.

We rushed up to him, and there, sure enough, in a deep cut or indentation on the very top of the sand koppie, was an undoubted pool of water. How it came to be in such a strange place we did not stop to inquire, nor did we hesitate at its black and unpleasant appearance. It was water, or a good imitation of it, and that was enough for us. We gave a bound and a rush, and in another second we were all down on our stomachs sucking up the uninviting fluid as though it were nectar fit for the gods. Heavens, how we did drink! Then when we had done drinking we tore off our clothes and sat down in the pool, absorbing the moisture through our parched skins. You, Harry, my boy, who have only to turn on a couple of taps to summon "hot" and "cold" from an unseen, vasty boiler, can have little idea of the luxury of that muddy wallow in brackish tepid water.

After a while we rose from it, refreshed indeed, and fell to on our "biltong," of which we had scarcely been able to touch a mouthful for twenty-four hours, and ate our fill. Then we smoked a pipe, and lay down by the side of that blessed pool, under the overhanging shadow of its bank, and slept till mid-day.

All that day we rested there by the water, thanking our stars that we had been lucky enough to find it, bad as it was, and not forgetting to render a due share of gratitude to the shade of the long-departed da Silvestra, who had set its position down so accurately on the tail of his shirt. The wonderful thing to us was that the pan should have lasted so long, and the only way in which I can account for this is on the supposition that it is fed by some spring deep down in the sand.

Having filled both ourselves and our water-bottles as full as possible, in far better spirits we started off again with the moon. That night we covered nearly five-and-twenty miles; but, needless to say, found no more water, though we were lucky enough the following day to get a little shade behind some ant-heaps. When the sun rose, and, for awhile, cleared away the mysterious mists, Suliman's Berg with the two majestic Breasts, now only about twenty miles off, seemed to be towering right above us, and looked grander than ever. At the approach of evening we marched again, and, to cut a long story short, by daylight next morning found ourselves upon the lowest slopes of Sheba's left breast, for which we had been steadily steering. By this time our water was exhausted once more, and we were suffering severely from thirst, nor indeed could we see any chance of relieving it till we reached the snow line far, far above us. After resting an hour or two, driven to it by our torturing thirst, we went on, toiling painfully in the burning heat up the lava slopes, for we found that the huge base of the mountain was composed entirely of lava beds belched from the bowels of the earth in some far past age.

By eleven o'clock we were utterly exhausted, and, generally speaking, in a very bad state indeed. The lava clinker, over which we must drag ourselves, though smooth compared with some clinker I have heard of, such as that on the Island of Ascension, for instance, was yet rough enough to make our feet very sore, and this, together with our other miseries, had pretty well finished us. A few hundred yards above us were some large lumps of lava, and towards these we steered with the intention of lying down beneath their shade. We reached them, and to our surprise, so far as we had a capacity for surprise left in us, on a little plateau or ridge close by we saw that the clinker was covered with a dense green growth. Evidently soil formed of decomposed lava had rested there, and in due course had become the receptacle of seeds deposited by birds. But we did not take much further interest in the green growth, for one cannot live on grass like Nebuchadnezzar. That requires a special dispensation of Providence and peculiar digestive organs. So we sat down under the rocks and groaned, and for one I wished heartily that we had never started on this fool's errand. As we were sitting there I saw Umbopa get up and hobble towards the patch of green, and a few minutes afterwards, to my great astonishment, I perceived that usually very dignified individual dancing and shouting like a maniac, and waving something green. Off we all scrambled towards him as fast as our wearied limbs would carry us, hoping that he had found water.

"What is it, Umbopa, son of a fool?" I shouted in Zulu.

"It is food and water, Macumazahn," and again he waved the green thing.

Then I saw what he had found. It was a melon. We had hit upon a patch of wild melons, thousands of them, and dead ripe.

"Melons!" I yelled to Good, who was next me; and in another minute his false teeth were fixed in one of them.

I think we ate about six each before we had done, and poor fruit as they were, I doubt if I ever thought anything nicer.

But melons are not very nutritious, and when we had satisfied our thirst with their pulpy substance, and put a stock to cool by the simple process of cutting them in two and setting them end on in the hot sun to grow cold by evaporation, we began to feel exceedingly hungry. We had still some biltong left, but our stomachs turned from biltong, and besides, we were obliged to be very sparing of it, for we could not say when we should find more food. Just at this moment a lucky thing chanced. Looking across the desert I saw a flock of about ten large birds flying straight towards us.

"*Skit, Baas, skit!*" "Shoot, master, shoot!" whispered the Hottentot, throwing himself on his face, an example which we all followed.

Then I saw that the birds were a flock of *pauw* or bustards, and that they would pass within fifty yards of my head. Taking one of the repeating Winchesters, I waited till they were nearly over us, and then jumped to my feet. On seeing me the *pauw* bunched up together, as I expected that they would, and I fired two shots straight into the thick of them, and, as luck would have it, brought one down, a fine fellow, that weighed about twenty pounds. In half an hour we had a fire made of dry melon stalks, and he was toasting over it, and we made such a feed as we had not tasted for a week. We ate that *pauw*; nothing was left of him but his leg-bones and his beak, and we felt not a little the better afterwards.

That night we went on again with the moon, carrying as many melons as we could with us. As we ascended we found the air grew cooler and cooler, which was a great relief to us, and at dawn, so far as we could judge, we were not more than about a dozen miles from the snow line. Here we discovered more melons, and so had no longer any anxiety about water, for we knew that we should soon get plenty of snow. But the ascent had now become very precipitous, and we made but slow progress, not more than a mile an hour. Also that night we ate our last morsel of biltong. As yet, with the exception of the *pauw*, we had seen no living thing on the mountain, nor had we come across a single spring or stream of water, which struck us as very odd, considering the expanse of snow above us, which must, we thought, melt sometimes. But as we afterwards discovered, owing to a cause which it is quite beyond my power to explain, all the streams flowed down upon the north side of the mountains.

Now we began to grow very anxious about food. We had escaped death by thirst, but it seemed probable that it was only to die of hunger. The events of the next three miserable days are best described by copying the entries made at the time in my note-book.

"21st May.—Started 11 A.M., finding the atmosphere quite cold enough to travel by day, and carrying some water-melons with us. Struggled on all day, but found no more melons, having evidently passed out of their district. Saw no game of any sort. Halted for the night at sundown, having had no food for many hours. Suffered much during the night from cold.

"22nd.—Started at sunrise again, feeling very faint and weak. Only made about five miles all day; found some patches of snow, of which we ate, but nothing else. Camped at night under the edge of a great plateau. Cold bitter. Drank a little brandy each, and huddled ourselves together, each wrapped up in his blanket, to keep ourselves alive. Are now suffering frightfully from starvation and weariness. Thought that Ventvögel would have died during the night.

"23rd.—Struggled forward once more as soon as the sun was well up, and had thawed our limbs a little. We are now in a dreadful plight, and I fear that unless we get food this will be our last day's journey. But little brandy left. Good, Sir Henry, and Umbopa bear up wonderfully, but Ventvögel is in a very bad way. Like most

Hottentots, he cannot stand cold. Pangs of hunger not so bad, but have a sort of numb feeling about the stomach. Others say the same. We are now on a level with the precipitous chain, or wall of lava, linking the two Breasts, and the view is glorious. Behind us the glowing desert rolls away to the horizon, and before us lie mile upon mile of smooth hard snow almost level, but swelling gently upwards, out of the centre of which the nipple of the mountain, that appears to be some miles in circumference, rises about four thousand feet into the sky. Not a living thing is to be seen. God help us; I fear that our time has come."

And now I will drop the journal, partly because it is not very interesting reading; and also because what follows requires telling rather more fully.

All that day—the 23rd May—we struggled slowly up the incline of snow, lying down from time to time to rest. A strange gaunt crew we must have looked, while, laden as we were, we dragged our weary feet over the dazzling plain, glaring round us with hungry eyes. Not that there was much use in glaring, for we could see nothing to eat. We did not accomplish more than seven miles that day. Just before sunset we found ourselves exactly under the nipple of Sheba's left Breast, which towered thousands of feet into the air, a vast smooth hillock of frozen snow. Weak as we were, we could not but appreciate the wonderful scene, made even more splendid by the flying rays of light from the setting sun, which here and there stained the snow blood-red, and crowned the great dome above us with a diadem of glory.

"I say," gasped Good, presently, "we ought to be somewhere near that cave the old gentleman wrote about."

"Yes," said I, "if there is a cave."

"Come, Quatermain," groaned Sir Henry, "don't talk like that; I have every faith in the Dom; remember the water! We shall find the place soon."

"If we don't find it before dark we are dead men, that is all about it," was my consolatory reply.

For the next ten minutes we trudged in silence, when suddenly Umbopa, who was marching along beside me, wrapped in his blanket, and with a leather belt strapped so tightly round his stomach, to "make his hunger small," as he said, that his waist looked like a girl's, caught me by the arm.

"Look!" he said, pointing towards the springing slope of the nipple.

I followed his glance, and some two hundred yards from us perceived what appeared to be a hole in the snow.

"It is the cave," said Umbopa.

We made the best of our way to the spot, and found sure enough that the hole was the mouth of a cavern, no doubt the same as that of which da Silvestra wrote. We were not too soon, for just as we reached shelter the sun went down with startling rapidity, leaving the world nearly dark, for in these latitudes there is but little twilight. So we crept into the cave, which did not appear to be very big, and huddling ourselves together for warmth, swallowed what remained of our brandy—barely a mouthful each—and tried to forget our miseries in sleep. But the cold was too intense to allow us to do so, for I am convinced that at this great altitude the thermometer cannot have marked less than fourteen or fifteen degrees below freezing point. What such a temperature meant to us, enervated as we were by hardship, want of food, and the great heat of the desert, the reader may imagine better than I can describe. Suffice it to say that it was something as near death from exposure as I have ever felt. There we sat hour after hour through the still and bitter night, feeling the frost wander round and nip us now in the finger, now in the foot, now in the face. In vain did we huddle up closer and closer; there was no warmth in our miserable starved carcases. Sometimes one of us would drop into an uneasy slumber for a few minutes, but we could not sleep much, and perhaps this was fortunate, for if we had I doubt if we should have ever woke again. Indeed, I believe that it was only by force of will that we kept ourselves alive at all.

Not very long before dawn I heard the Hottentot Ventvögel, whose teeth had been chattering all night like castanets, give a deep sigh. Then his teeth stopped chattering. I did not think anything of it at the time, concluding that he had gone to sleep. His back was resting against mine, and it seemed to grow colder and colder, till at last it felt like ice.

At length the air began to grow grey with light, then golden arrows sped across the snow, and at last the glorious sun peeped above the lava wall and looked in upon our half-frozen forms. Also it looked upon Ventvögel, sitting there amongst us, *stone dead*. No wonder his back felt cold, poor fellow. He had died when I heard him sigh, and was now frozen almost stiff. Shocked beyond measure, we dragged ourselves from the corpse—how strange is that horror we mortals have of the companionship of a dead body—and left it sitting there, its arms clasped about its knees.

By this time the sunlight was pouring its cold rays, for here they were cold, straight into the mouth of the cave. Suddenly I heard an exclamation of fear from someone, and turned my head.

And this is what I saw: Sitting at the end of the cavern—it was not more than twenty feet long—was another form, of which the head rested on its chest and the long arms hung down. I stared at it, and saw that this too was a *dead man*, and, what was more, a white man.

The others saw also, and the sight proved too much for our shattered nerves. One and all we scrambled out of the cave as fast as our half-frozen limbs would allow.

VII. SOLOMON'S ROAD

Outside the cavern we halted, feeling rather foolish.

"I am going back," said Sir Henry.

"Why?" asked Good.

"Because it has struck me that—what we saw—may be my brother."

This was a new idea, and we re-entered the place to put it to the proof. After the bright light outside, our eyes, weak as they were with staring at the snow, could not pierce the gloom of the cave for a while. Presently, however, they grew accustomed to the semi-darkness, and we advanced towards the dead man.

Sir Henry knelt down and peered into his face.

"Thank God," he said, with a sigh of relief, "it is *not* my brother."

Then I drew near and looked. The body was that of a tall man in middle life with aquiline features, grizzled hair, and a long black moustache. The skin was perfectly yellow, and stretched tightly over the bones. Its clothing, with the exception of what seemed to be the remains of a woollen pair of hose, had been removed, leaving the skeleton-like frame naked. Round the neck of the corpse, which was frozen perfectly stiff, hung a yellow ivory crucifix.

"Who on earth can it be?" said I.

"Can't you guess?" asked Good.

I shook my head.

"Why, the old Dom, José da Silvestra, of course—who else?"

"Impossible," I gasped; "he died three hundred years ago."

"And what is there to prevent him from lasting for three thousand years in this atmosphere, I should like to know?" asked Good. "If only the temperature is sufficiently low, flesh and blood will keep fresh as New Zealand mutton for ever, and Heaven knows it is cold enough here. The sun never gets in here; no animal comes here to tear or destroy. No doubt his slave, of whom he speaks on the writing, took off his clothes and left him. He could not have buried him alone. Look!" he went on, stooping down to pick up a queerly-shaped bone scraped at the end into a sharp point, "here is the 'cleft bone' that Silvestra used to draw the map with."

We gazed for a moment astonished, forgetting our own miseries in this extraordinary and, as it seemed to us, semi-miraculous sight.

"Ay," said Sir Henry, "and this is where he got his ink from," and he pointed to a small wound on the Dom's left arm. "Did ever man see such a thing before?"

There was no longer any doubt about the matter, which for my own part I confess perfectly appalled me. There he sat, the dead man, whose directions, written some ten generations ago, had led us to this spot. Here in my own hand was the rude pen with which he had written them, and about his neck hung the crucifix that his dying lips had kissed. Gazing at him, my imagination could reconstruct the last scene of the drama, the traveller dying of cold and starvation, yet striving to convey to the world the great secret which he had discovered:——the awful loneliness of his death, of which the evidence sat before us. It even seemed to me that I could trace in his strongly-marked features a likeness to those of my poor friend Silvestre his descendant, who had died twenty years before in my arms, but perhaps that was fancy. At any rate, there he sat, a sad memento of the fate that so often overtakes those who would penetrate into the unknown; and there doubtless he will still sit, crowned with the dread majesty of death, for centuries yet unborn, to startle the eyes of wanderers like ourselves, if ever any such should come again to invade his loneliness. The thing overpowered us, already nearly done to death as we were with cold and hunger.

"Let us go," said Sir Henry in a low voice; "stay, we will give him a companion," and lifting up the dead body of the Hottentot Ventvögel, he placed it near to that of the old Dom. Then he stooped, and with a jerk broke the rotten string of the crucifix which hung round da Silvestra's neck, for his fingers were too cold to attempt to unfasten it. I believe that he has it still. I took the bone pen, and it is before me as I write—sometimes I use it to sign my name.

Then leaving these two, the proud white man of a past age, and the poor Hottentot, to keep their eternal vigil in the midst of the eternal snows, we crept out of the cave into the welcome sunshine and resumed our path, wondering in our hearts how many hours it would be before we were even as they are.

When we had walked about half a mile we came to the edge of the plateau, for the nipple of the mountain does not rise out of its exact centre, though from the desert side it seemed to do so. What lay below us we could not see, for the landscape was wreathed in billows of morning fog. Presently, however, the higher layers of mist cleared a little, and revealed, at the end of a long slope of snow, a patch of green grass, some five hundred yards beneath us, through which a stream was running. Nor was this all. By the stream, basking in the bright sun, stood and lay a group of from ten to fifteen *large antelopes*—at that distance we could not see of what species.

The sight filled us with an unreasoning joy. If only we could get it, there was food in plenty. But the question was how to do so. The beasts were fully six hundred yards off, a very long shot, and one not to be depended on when our lives hung on the result.

Rapidly we discussed the advisability of trying to stalk the game, but in the end dismissed it reluctantly. To begin with, the wind was not favourable, and further, we must certainly be perceived, however careful we were, against the blinding background of snow, which we should be obliged to traverse.

"Well, we must have a try from where we are," said Sir Henry. "Which shall it be, Quatermain, the repeating rifles or the expresses?"

Here again was a question. The Winchester repeaters—of which we had two, Umbopa carrying poor Ventvögel's as well as his own—were sighted up to a thousand yards, whereas the expresses were only sighted to three hundred and fifty, beyond which distance shooting with them was more or less guesswork. On the other hand, if they did hit, the express bullets, being "expanding," were much more likely to bring the game down. It was a knotty point, but I made up my mind that we must risk it and use the expresses.

"Let each of us take the buck opposite to him. Aim well at the point of the shoulder and high up," said I; "and Umbopa, do you give the word, so that we may all fire together."

Then came a pause, each of us aiming his level best, as indeed a man is likely to do when he knows that life itself depends upon the shot.

"Fire," said Umbopa in Zulu, and at almost the same instant the three rifles rang out loudly; three clouds of smoke hung for a moment before us, and a hundred echoes went flying over the silent snow. Presently the smoke cleared, and revealed—oh, joy!—a great buck lying on its back and kicking furiously in its death agony. We gave a yell of triumph—we were saved—we should not starve. Weak as we were, we rushed down the intervening slope of snow, and in ten minutes from the time of shooting, that animal's heart and liver were lying before us. But now a new difficulty arose, we had no fuel, and therefore could make no fire to cook them. We gazed at each other in dismay.

"Starving men should not be fanciful," said Good; "we must eat raw meat."

There was no other way out of the dilemma, and our gnawing hunger made the proposition less distasteful than it would otherwise have been. So we took the heart and liver and buried them for a few minutes in a patch of snow to cool them. Then we washed them in the ice-cold water of the stream, and lastly ate them greedily. It sounds horrible enough, but honestly, I never tasted anything so good as that raw meat. In a quarter of an hour we were changed men. Our life and vigour came back to us, our feeble pulses grew strong again, and the blood went coursing through our veins. But mindful of the results of over-feeding on starved stomachs, we were careful not to eat too much, stopping whilst we were still hungry.

"Thank Heaven!" said Sir Henry; "that brute has saved our lives. What is it, Quatermain?"

I rose and went to look at the antelope, for I was not certain. It was about the size of a donkey, with large curved horns. I had never seen one like it before; the species was new to me. It was brown in colour, with faint red stripes, and grew a thick coat.

I afterwards discovered that the natives of that wonderful country call these bucks "*Inco*." They are very rare, and only found at a great altitude where no other game will live. This animal was fairly hit high up in the shoulder, though whose bullet brought it down we could not, of course, discover. I believe that Good, mindful of his marvellous shot at the giraffe, secretly set it down to his own prowess, and we did not contradict him.

We had been so busy satisfying our hunger that hitherto we had not found time to look about us. But now, having set Umbopa to cut off as much of the best meat as we were likely to be able to carry, we began to inspect our surroundings. The mist had cleared away, for it was eight o'clock, and the sun had sucked it up, so we were able to take in all the country before us at a glance. I know not how to describe the glorious panorama which unfolded itself to our gaze. I have never seen anything like it before, nor shall, I suppose, again.

Behind and over us towered Sheba's snowy Breasts, and below, some five thousand feet beneath where we stood, lay league on league of the most lovely champaign country. Here were dense patches of lofty forest, there a great river wound its silvery way. To the left stretched a vast expanse of rich, undulating veld or grass land, whereon we could just make out countless herds of game or cattle, at that distance we could not tell which. This expanse appeared to be ringed in by a wall of distant mountains. To the right the country was more or less mountainous; that is, solitary hills stood up from its level, with stretches of cultivated land between, amongst which we could see groups of dome-shaped huts. The landscape lay before us as a map, wherein rivers flashed like silver snakes, and Alp-like peaks crowned with wildly twisted snow wreaths rose in grandeur, whilst over all was the glad sunlight and the breath of Nature's happy life.

Two curious things struck us as we gazed. First, that the country before us must lie at least three thousand feet higher than the desert we had crossed, and secondly, that all the rivers flowed from south to north. As we had painful reason to know, there was no water upon the southern side of the vast range on which we stood, but on the northern face were many streams, most of which appeared to unite with the great river we could see winding away farther than our eyes could follow.

We sat down for a while and gazed in silence at this wonderful view. Presently Sir Henry spoke.

"Isn't there something on the map about Solomon's Great Road?" he said.

I nodded, for I was still gazing out over the far country.

"Well, look; there it is!" and he pointed a little to our right.

Good and I looked accordingly, and there, winding away towards the plain, was what appeared to be a wide turnpike road. We had not seen it at first because, on reaching the plain, it turned behind some broken country. We did not say anything, at least, not much; we were beginning to lose the sense of wonder. Somehow it did not seem particularly unnatural that we should find a sort of Roman road in this strange land. We accepted the fact, that was all.

"Well," said Good, "it must be quite near us if we cut off to the right. Hadn't we better be making a start?"

This was sound advice, and so soon as we had washed our faces and hands in the stream we acted on it. For a mile or more we made our way over boulders and across patches of snow, till suddenly, on reaching the top of the little rise, we found the road at our feet. It was a splendid road cut out of the solid rock, at least fifty feet wide, and apparently well kept; though the odd thing was that it seemed to begin there. We walked down and stood on it, but one single hundred paces behind us, in the direction of Sheba's Breasts, it vanished, the entire surface of the mountain being strewn with boulders interspersed with patches of snow.

"What do you make of this, Quatermain?" asked Sir Henry.

I shook my head, I could make nothing of it.

"I have it!" said Good; "the road no doubt ran right over the range and across the desert on the other side, but the sand there has covered it up, and above us it has been obliterated by some volcanic eruption of molten lava."

This seemed a good suggestion; at any rate, we accepted it, and proceeded down the mountain. It proved a very different business travelling along down hill on that magnificent pathway with full stomachs from what it was travelling uphill over the snow quite starved and almost frozen. Indeed, had it not been for melancholy recollections of poor Ventvögel's sad fate, and of that grim cave where he kept company with the old Dom, we should have felt positively cheerful, notwithstanding the sense of unknown dangers before us. Every mile we walked the atmosphere grew softer and balmier, and the country before us shone with a yet more luminous beauty. As for the road itself, I never saw such an engineering work, though Sir Henry said that the great road over the St. Gothard in Switzerland is very similar. No difficulty had been too great for the Old World engineer who laid it out. At one place we came to a ravine three hundred feet broad and at least a hundred feet deep. This vast gulf was actually filled in with huge blocks of dressed stone, having arches pierced through them at the bottom for a waterway, over which the road went on sublimely. At another place it was cut in zigzags out of the side of a precipice five hundred feet deep, and in a third it tunnelled through the base of an intervening ridge, a space of thirty yards or more.

Here we noticed that the sides of the tunnel were covered with quaint sculptures, mostly of mailed figures driving in chariots. One, which was exceedingly beautiful, represented a whole battle scene with a convoy of captives being marched off in the distance.

"Well," said Sir Henry, after inspecting this ancient work of art, "it is very well to call this Solomon's Road, but my humble opinion is that the Egyptians had been here before Solomon's people ever set a foot on it. If this isn't Egyptian or Phoenician handiwork, I must say that it is very like it."

By midday we had advanced sufficiently down the mountain to search the region where wood was to be met with. First we came to scattered bushes which grew more and more frequent, till at last we found the road winding through a vast grove of silver trees similar to those which are to be seen on the slopes of Table Mountain at Cape Town. I had never before met with them in all my wanderings, except at the Cape, and their appearance here astonished me greatly.

"Ah!" said Good, surveying these shining-leaved trees with evident enthusiasm, "here is lots of wood, let us stop and cook some dinner; I have about digested that raw liver."

Nobody objected to this, so leaving the road we made our way to a stream which was babbling away not far off, and soon had a goodly fire of dry boughs blazing. Cutting off some substantial hunks from the flesh of the *inco* which we had brought with us, we proceeded to toast them on the end of sharp sticks, as one sees the Kafirs do, and ate them with relish. After filling ourselves, we lit our pipes and gave ourselves up to enjoyment that, compared with the hardships we had recently undergone, seemed almost heavenly.

The brook, of which the banks were clothed with dense masses of a gigantic species of maidenhair fern interspersed with feathery tufts of wild asparagus, sung merrily at our side, the soft air murmured through the leaves of the silver trees, doves cooed around, and bright-winged birds flashed like living gems from bough to bough. It was a Paradise.

The magic of the place combined with an overwhelming sense of dangers left behind, and of the promised land reached at last, seemed to charm us into silence. Sir Henry and Umbopa sat conversing in a mixture of broken English and Kitchen Zulu in a low voice, but earnestly enough, and I lay, with my eyes half shut, upon that fragrant bed of fern and watched them.

Presently I missed Good, and I looked to see what had become of him. Soon I observed him sitting by the bank of the stream, in which he had been bathing. He had nothing on but his flannel shirt, and his natural habits of extreme neatness having reasserted themselves, he was actively employed in making a most elaborate toilet. He had washed his gutta-percha collar, had thoroughly shaken out his trousers, coat and waistcoat, and was now folding them up neatly till he was ready to put them on, shaking his head sadly as he scanned the numerous rents and tears in them, which naturally had resulted from our frightful journey. Then he took his boots, scrubbed them with a handful of fern, and finally rubbed them over with a piece of fat, which he had carefully saved from the *inco* meat, till they looked, comparatively speaking, respectable. Having inspected them judiciously through his eye-glass, he put the boots on and began a fresh operation. From a little bag that he carried he produced a pocket-comb in which was fixed a tiny looking-glass, and in this he surveyed himself. Apparently he was not satisfied, for he proceeded to do his hair with great care. Then came a pause whilst he again contemplated the effect; still it was not satisfactory. He felt his chin, on which the accumulated scrub of a ten days' beard was flourishing.

"Surely," thought I, "he is not going to try to shave." But so it was. Taking the piece of fat with which he had greased his boots, Good washed it thoroughly in the stream. Then diving again into the bag he brought out a little pocket razor with a guard to it, such as are bought by people who are afraid of cutting themselves, or by those about to undertake a sea voyage. Then he rubbed his face and chin vigorously with the fat and began. Evidently it proved a painful process, for he groaned very much over it, and I was convulsed with inward laughter as I watched him struggling with that stubbly beard. It seemed so very odd that a man should take the trouble to shave himself with a piece of fat in such a place and in our circumstances. At last he succeeded in getting the hair off the right side of his face and chin, when suddenly I, who was watching, became conscious of a flash of light that passed just by his head.

Good sprang up with a profane exclamation (if it had not been a safety razor he would certainly have cut his throat), and so did I, without the exclamation, and this was what I saw. Standing not more than twenty paces from where I was, and ten from Good, were a group of men. They were very tall and copper-coloured, and some of them wore great plumes of black feathers and short cloaks of leopard skins; this was all I noticed at the moment. In front of them stood a youth of about seventeen, his hand still raised and his body bent forward in the attitude of a Grecian statue of a spear-thrower. Evidently the flash of light had been caused by a weapon which he had hurled.

As I looked an old soldier-like man stepped forward out of the group, and catching the youth by the arm said something to him. Then they advanced upon us.

Sir Henry, Good, and Umbopa by this time had seized their rifles and lifted them threateningly. The party of natives still came on. It struck me that they could not know what rifles were, or they would not have treated them with such contempt.

"Put down your guns!" I hallooed to the others, seeing that our only chance of safety lay in conciliation. They obeyed, and walking to the front I addressed the elderly man who had checked the youth.

"Greeting," I said in Zulu, not knowing what language to use. To my surprise I was understood.

"Greeting," answered the old man, not, indeed, in the same tongue, but in a dialect so closely allied to it that neither Umbopa nor myself had any difficulty in understanding him. Indeed, as we afterwards found out, the language spoken by this people is an old-fashioned form of the Zulu tongue, bearing about the same relationship to it that the English of Chaucer does to the English of the nineteenth century.

"Whence come you?" he went on, "who are you? and why are the faces of three of you white, and the face of the fourth as the face of our mother's sons?" and he pointed to Umbopa. I looked at Umbopa as he said it, and it flashed across me that he was right. The face of Umbopa was like the faces of the men before me, and so was his great form like their forms. But I had not time to reflect on this coincidence.

"We are strangers, and come in peace," I answered, speaking very slowly, so that he might understand me, "and this man is our servant."

"You lie," he answered; "no strangers can cross the mountains where all things perish. But what do your lies matter?—if ye are strangers then ye must die, for no strangers may live in the land of the Kukuanas. It is the king's law. Prepare then to die, O strangers!"

I was slightly staggered at this, more especially as I saw the hands of some of the men steal down to their sides, where hung on each what looked to me like a large and heavy knife.

"What does that beggar say?" asked Good.

"He says we are going to be killed," I answered grimly.

"Oh, Lord!" groaned Good; and, as was his way when perplexed, he put his hand to his false teeth, dragging the top set down and allowing them to fly back to his jaw with a snap. It was a most fortunate move, for next second the dignified crowd of Kukuanas uttered a simultaneous yell of horror, and bolted back some yards.

"What's up?" said I.

"It's his teeth," whispered Sir Henry excitely. "He moved them. Take them out, Good, take them out!"

He obeyed, slipping the set into the sleeve of his flannel shirt.

In another second curiosity had overcome fear, and the men advanced slowly. Apparently they had now forgotten their amiable intention of killing us.

"How is it, O strangers," asked the old man solemnly, "that this fat man (pointing to Good, who was clad in nothing but boots and a flannel shirt, and had only half finished his shaving), whose body is clothed, and whose legs are bare, who grows hair on one side of his sickly face and not on the other, and who wears one shining and transparent eye—how is it, I ask, that he has teeth which move of themselves, coming away from the jaws and returning of their own will?"

"Open your mouth," I said to Good, who promptly curled up his lips and grinned at the old gentleman like an angry dog, revealing to his astonished gaze two thin red lines of gum as utterly innocent of ivories as a new-born elephant. The audience gasped.

"Where are his teeth?" they shouted; "with our eyes we saw them."

Turning his head slowly and with a gesture of ineffable contempt, Good swept his hand across his mouth. Then he grinned again, and lo, there were two rows of lovely teeth.

Now the young man who had flung the knife threw himself down on the grass and gave vent to a prolonged howl of terror; and as for the old gentleman, his knees knocked together with fear.

"I see that ye are spirits," he said falteringly; "did ever man born of woman have hair on one side of his face and not on the other, or a round and transparent eye, or teeth which moved and melted away and grew again? Pardon us, O my lords."

Here was luck indeed, and, needless to say, I jumped at the chance.

"It is granted," I said with an imperial smile. "Nay, ye shall know the truth. We come from another world, though we are men such as ye; we come," I went on, "from the biggest star that shines at night."

"Oh! oh!" groaned the chorus of astonished aborigines.

"Yes," I went on, "we do, indeed"; and again I smiled benignly, as I uttered that amazing lie. "We come to stay with you a little while, and to bless you by our sojourn. Ye will see, O friends, that I have prepared myself for this visit by the learning of your language."

"It is so, it is so," said the chorus.

"Only, my lord," put in the old gentleman, "thou hast learnt it very badly."

I cast an indignant glance at him, and he quailed.

"Now friends," I continued, "ye might think that after so long a journey we should find it in our hearts to avenge such a reception, mayhap to strike cold in death the imperious hand that—that, in short—threw a knife at the head of him whose teeth come and go."

"Spare him, my lords," said the old man in supplication; "he is the king's son, and I am his uncle. If anything befalls him his blood will be required at my hands."

"Yes, that is certainly so," put in the young man with great emphasis.

"Ye may perhaps doubt our power to avenge," I went on, heedless of this by-play. "Stay, I will show you. Here, thou dog and slave (addressing Umbopa in a savage tone), give me the magic tube that speaks"; and I tipped a wink towards my express rifle.

Umbopa rose to the occasion, and with something as nearly resembling a grin as I have ever seen on his dignified face he handed me the gun.

"It is here, O Lord of Lords," he said with a deep obeisance.

Now just before I had asked for the rifle I had perceived a little *klipspringer* antelope standing on a mass of rock about seventy yards away, and determined to risk a shot at it.

"Ye see that buck," I said, pointing the animal out to the party before me. "Tell me, is it possible for man born of woman to kill it from here with a noise?"

"It is not possible, my lord," answered the old man.

"Yet shall I kill it," I said quietly.

The old man smiled. "That my lord cannot do," he answered.

I raised the rifle and covered the buck. It was a small animal, and one which a man might well be excused for missing, but I knew that it would not do to miss.

I drew a deep breath, and slowly pressed on the trigger. The buck stood still as a stone.

"Bang! thud!" The antelope sprang into the air and fell on the rock dead as a door nail.

A groan of simultaneous terror burst from the group before us.

"If ye want meat," I remarked coolly, "go fetch that buck."

The old man made a sign, and one of his followers departed, and presently returned bearing the *klipspringer*. I noticed with satisfaction that I had hit it fairly behind the shoulder. They gathered round the poor creature's body, gazing at the bullet-hole in consternation.

"Ye see," I said, "I do not speak empty words."

There was no answer.

"If ye yet doubt our power," I went on, "let one of you go stand upon that rock that I may make him as this buck."

None of them seemed at all inclined to take the hint, till at last the king's son spoke.

"It is well said. Do thou, my uncle, go stand upon the rock. It is but a buck that the magic has killed. Surely it cannot kill a man."

The old gentleman did not take the suggestion in good part. Indeed, he seemed hurt.

"No! no!" he ejaculated hastily, "my old eyes have seen enough. These are wizards, indeed. Let us bring them to the king. Yet if any should wish a further proof, let *him* stand upon the rock, that the magic tube may speak with him."

There was a most general and hasty expression of dissent.

"Let not good magic be wasted on our poor bodies," said one; "we are satisfied. All the witchcraft of our people cannot show the like of this."

"It is so," remarked the old gentleman, in a tone of intense relief; "without any doubt it is so. Listen, children of the Stars, children of the shining Eye and the movable Teeth, who roar out in thunder, and slay from afar. I am Infadoos, son of Kafa, once king of the Kukuana people. This youth is Scragga."

"He nearly scragged me," murmured Good.

"Scragga, son of Twala, the great king—Twala, husband of a thousand wives, chief and lord paramount of the Kukuanas, keeper of the great Road, terror of his enemies, student of the Black Arts, leader of a hundred thousand warriors, Twala the One-eyed, the Black, the Terrible."

"So," said I superciliously, "lead us then to Twala. We do not talk with low people and underlings."

"It is well, my lords, we will lead you; but the way is long. We are hunting three days' journey from the place of the king. But let my lords have patience, and we will lead them."

"So be it," I said carelessly; "all time is before us, for we do not die. We are ready, lead on. But Infadoos, and thou Scragga, beware! Play us no monkey tricks, set for us no foxes' snares, for before your brains of mud have thought of them we shall know and avenge. The light of the transparent eye of him with the bare legs and the half-haired face shall destroy you, and go through your land; his vanishing teeth shall affix themselves fast in you and eat you up, you and your wives and children; the magic tubes shall argue with you loudly, and make you as sieves. Beware!"

This magnificent address did not fail of its effect; indeed, it might almost have been spared, so deeply were our friends already impressed with our powers.

The old man made a deep obeisance, and murmured the words, "*Koom Koom*," which I afterwards discovered was their royal salute, corresponding to the *Bayéte* of the Zulus, and turning, addressed his followers. These at once proceeded to lay hold of all our goods and chattels, in order to bear them for us, excepting only the guns, which they would on no account touch. They even seized Good's clothes, that, as the reader may remember, were neatly folded up beside him.

He saw and made a dive for them, and a loud altercation ensued.

"Let not my lord of the transparent Eye and the melting Teeth touch them," said the old man. "Surely his slave shall carry the things."

"But I want to put 'em on!" roared Good, in nervous English.

Umbopa translated.

"Nay, my lord," answered Infadoos, "would my lord cover up his beautiful white legs (although he is so dark Good has a singularly white skin) from the eyes of his servants? Have we offended my lord that he should do such a thing?"

Here I nearly exploded with laughing; and meanwhile one of the men started on with the garments.

"Damn it!" roared Good, "that black villain has got my trousers."

"Look here, Good," said Sir Henry; "you have appeared in this country in a certain character, and you must live up to it. It will never do for you to put on trousers again. Henceforth you must exist in a flannel shirt, a pair of boots, and an eye-glass."

"Yes," I said, "and with whiskers on one side of your face and not on the other. If you change any of these things the people will think that we are impostors. I am very sorry for you, but, seriously, you must. If once they begin to suspect us our lives will not be worth a brass farthing."

"Do you really think so?" said Good gloomily.

"I do, indeed. Your 'beautiful white legs' and your eye-glass are now *the* features of our party, and as Sir Henry says, you must live up to them. Be thankful that you have got your boots on, and that the air is warm."

Good sighed, and said no more, but it took him a fortnight to become accustomed to his new and scant attire.

VIII. We Enter Kukuanaland

All that afternoon we travelled along the magnificent roadway, which trended steadily in a north-westerly direction. Infadoos and Scragga walked with us, but their followers marched about one hundred paces ahead.

"Infadoos," I said at length, "who made this road?"

"It was made, my lord, of old time, none know how or when, not even the wise woman Gagool, who has lived for generations. We are not old enough to remember its making. None can fashion such roads now, but the king suffers no grass to grow upon it."

"And whose are the writings on the wall of the caves through which we have passed on the road?" I asked, referring to the Egyptian-like sculptures that we had seen.

"My lord, the hands that made the road wrote the wonderful writings. We know not who wrote them."

"When did the Kukuana people come into this country?"

"My lord, the race came down here like the breath of a storm ten thousand thousand moons ago, from the great lands which lie there beyond," and he pointed to the north. "They could travel no further because of the high mountains which ring in the land, so say the old voices of our fathers that have descended to us the children, and so says Gagool, the wise woman, the smeller out of witches," and again he pointed to the snow-clad peaks. "The country, too, was good, so they settled here and grew strong and powerful, and now our numbers are like the sea sand, and when Twala the king calls up his regiments their plumes cover the plain so far as the eye of man can reach."

"And if the land is walled in with mountains, who is there for the regiments to fight with?"

"Nay, my lord, the country is open there towards the north, and now and again warriors sweep down upon us in clouds from a land we know not, and we slay them. It is the third part of the life of a man since there was a war. Many thousands died in it, but we destroyed those who came to eat us up. So since then there has been no war."

"Your warriors must grow weary of resting on their spears, Infadoos."

"My lord, there was one war, just after we destroyed the people that came down upon us, but it was a civil war; dog ate dog."

"How was that?"

"My lord the king, my half-brother, had a brother born at the same birth, and of the same woman. It is not our custom, my lord, to suffer twins to live; the weaker must always die. But the mother of the king hid away the feebler child, which was born the last, for her heart yearned over it, and that child is Twala the king. I am his younger brother, born of another wife."

"Well?"

"My lord, Kafa, our father, died when we came to manhood, and my brother Imotu was made king in his place, and for a space reigned and had a son by his favourite wife. When the babe was three years old, just after the great war, during which no man could sow or reap, a famine came upon the land, and the people murmured because of the famine, and looked round like a starved lion for something to rend. Then it was that Gagool, the wise and terrible woman, who does not die, made a proclamation to the people, saying, 'The king Imotu is no king.' And at the time Imotu was sick with a wound, and lay in his kraal not able to move.

"Then Gagool went into a hut and led out Twala, my half-brother, and twin brother to the king, whom she had hidden among the caves and rocks since he was born, and stripping the 'moocha' (waist-cloth) off his loins, showed the people of the Kukuanas the mark of the sacred snake coiled round his middle, wherewith the eldest son of the king is marked at birth, and cried out loud, 'Behold your king whom I have saved for you even to this day!'

"Now the people being mad with hunger, and altogether bereft of reason and the knowledge of truth, cried out—'The king! The king!' but I knew that it was not so, for Imotu my brother was the elder of the twins, and our lawful king. Then just as the tumult was at its height Imotu the king, though he was very sick, crawled from his hut holding his wife by the hand, and followed by his little son Ignosi—that is, by interpretation, the lightning.

" 'What is this noise?' he asked. 'Why cry ye *The king! The king!*'

"Then Twala, his twin brother, born of the same woman, and in the same hour, ran to him, and taking him by the hair, stabbed him through the heart with his knife. And the people being fickle, and ever ready to worship the rising sun, clapped their hands and cried, *'Twala is king!* Now we know that Twala is king!' "

"And what became of Imotu's wife and her son Ignosi? Did Twala kill them too?"

"Nay, my lord. When she saw that her lord was dead the queen seized the child with a cry and ran away. Two days afterward she came to a kraal very hungry, and none would give her milk or food, now that her lord the king was dead, for all men hate the unfortunate. But at nightfall a little child, a girl, crept out and brought her corn to eat, and she blessed the child, and went on towards the mountains with her boy before the sun rose again, and there she must have perished, for none have seen her since, nor the child Ignosi."

"Then if this child Ignosi had lived he would be the true king of the Kukuana people?"

"That is so, my lord; the sacred snake is round his middle. If he lives he is king; but, alas! he is long dead."

"See, my lord," and Infadoos pointed to a vast collection of huts surrounded by a fence, which was in its turn encircled by a great ditch, that lay on the plain beneath us. "That is the kraal where the wife of Imotu was last seen with the child Ignosi. It is there that we shall sleep to-night, if, indeed," he added doubtfully, "my lords sleep at all upon this earth."

"When we are among the Kukuanas, my good friend Infadoos, we do as the Kukuanas do," I said majestically, and turned round quickly to address Good, who was tramping along sullenly behind, his mind fully occupied with unsatisfactory attempts to prevent his flannel shirt from flapping in the evening breeze. To my astonishment I butted into Umbopa, who was walking along immediately behind me, and very evidently had been listening with the greatest interest to my conversation with Infadoos. The expression on his face was most curious, and gave me the idea of a man who was struggling with partial success to bring something long ago forgotten back into his mind.

All this while we had been pressing on at a good rate towards the undulating plain beneath us. The mountains we had crossed now loomed high above our heads, and Sheba's Breasts were veiled modestly in diaphanous wreaths of mist. As we went the country grew more and more lovely. The vegetation was luxuriant, without being tropical; the sun was bright and warm, but not burning; and a gracious breeze blew softly along the odorous slopes of the mountains. Indeed, this new land was little less than an earthly paradise; in beauty, in natural wealth, and in climate I have never seen its like. The Transvaal is a fine country, but it is nothing to Kukuanaland.

So soon as we started Infadoos had despatched a runner to warn the people of the kraal, which, by the way, was in his military command, of our arrival. This man had departed at an extraordinary speed, which Infadoos informed me he would keep up all the way, as running was an exercise much practised among his people.

The result of this message now became apparent. When we arrived within two miles of the kraal we could see that company after company of men were issuing from its gates and marching towards us.

Sir Henry laid his hand upon my arm, and remarked that it looked as though we were going to meet with a warm reception. Something in his tone attracted Infadoos' attention.

"Let not my lords be afraid," he said hastily, "for in my breast there dwells no guile. This regiment is one under my command, and comes out by my orders to greet you."

I nodded easily, though I was not quite easy in my mind.

About half a mile from the gates of this kraal is a long stretch of rising ground sloping gently upwards from the road, and here the companies formed. It was a splendid sight to see them, each company about three hundred strong, charging swiftly up the rise, with flashing spears and waving plumes, to take their appointed place. By the time we reached the slope twelve such companies, or in all three thousand six hundred men, had passed out and taken up their positions along the road.

Presently we came to the first company, and were able to gaze in astonishment on the most magnificent set of warriors that I have ever seen. They were all men of mature age, mostly veterans of about forty, and not one of them was under six feet in height, whilst many stood six feet three or four. They wore upon their heads heavy black plumes of Sakaboola feathers, like those which adorned our guides. About their waists and beneath the right knees were bound circlets of white ox tails, while in their left hands they carried round shields measuring about twenty inches across. These shields are very curious. The framework is made of an iron plate beaten out thin, over which is stretched milk-white ox-hide. The weapons that each man bore were simple, but most effective, consisting of a short and very heavy two-edged spear with a wooden shaft, the blade being about six inches across at the widest part. These spears are not used for throwing, but like the Zulu "*bangwan*," or stabbing assegai, are for close quarters only, when the wound inflicted by them is terrible. In addition to his *bangwan* every man carried three large and heavy knives, each knife weighing about two pounds. One knife was fixed in the ox-tail girdle, and the other two at the back of the round shield. These knives, which are called "*tollas*" by the Kukuanas, take the place of the throwing assegai of the Zulus. The Kukuana warriors can cast them with great accuracy to a distance of fifty yards, and it is their custom on charging to hurl a volley of them at the enemy as they come to close quarters.

Each company remained still as a collection of bronze statues till we were opposite to it, when at a signal given by its commanding officer, who, distinguished by a leopard skin cloak, stood some paces in front, every spear was raised into the air, and from three hundred throats sprang forth with a sudden roar the royal salute of "*Koom*." Then, so soon as we had passed, the company formed up behind us and followed us towards the kraal, till at last the whole regiment of the "Greys"—so called from their white shields—the crack corps of the Kukuana people, was marching in our rear with a tread that shook the ground.

At length, branching off from Solomon's Great Road, we came to the wide fosse surrounding the kraal, which is at least a mile round, and fenced with a strong palisade of piles formed of the trunks of trees. At the gateway this fosse is spanned by a primitive drawbridge, which was let down by the guard to allow us to pass in. The kraal is exceedingly well laid out. Through the centre runs a wide pathway intersected at right angles by other pathways so arranged as to cut the huts into square blocks, each block being the quarters of a company. The huts are dome-shaped, and built, like those of the Zulus, of a framework of wattle, beautifully thatched with grass; but, unlike the Zulu huts, they have doorways through which men could walk. Also they are much larger, and surrounded by a verandah about six feet wide, beautifully paved with powdered lime trodden hard.

All along each side of this wide pathway that pierces the kraal were ranged hundreds of women, brought out by curiosity to look at us. These women, for a native race, are exceedingly handsome. They are tall and graceful, and their figures are wonderfully fine. The hair, though short, is rather curly than woolly, the features are frequently aquiline, and the lips are not unpleasantly thick, as is the case among most African races. But what struck us most was their exceedingly quiet and dignified air. They were as well-bred in their way as the habituées of a fashionable drawing-room, and in this respect they differ from Zulu women and their cousins the Masai who inhabit the district beyond Zanzibar. Their curiosity had brought them out to see us, but they allowed no rude expressions of astonishment or savage criticism to pass their lips as we trudged wearily in front of them. Not even when old Infadoos with a surreptitious motion of the hand pointed out the crowning wonder of poor Good's "beautiful white legs," did they suffer the feeling of intense admiration which evidently mastered their minds to find expression. They fixed their dark eyes upon this new and snowy loveliness, for, as I think I have said, Good's skin is exceedingly white, and that was all. But it was quite enough for Good, who is modest by nature.

When we reached the centre of the kraal, Infadoos halted at the door of a large hut, which was surrounded at a distance by a circle of smaller ones.

"Enter, Sons of the Stars," he said, in a magniloquent voice, "and deign to rest a while in our humble habitations. A little food shall be brought to you, so that ye may have no need to draw your belts tight from hunger; some honey and some milk, and an ox or two, and a few sheep; not much, my lords, but still a little food."

"It is good," said I. "Infadoos; we are weary with travelling through realms of air; now let us rest."

Accordingly we entered the hut, which we found amply prepared for our comfort. Couches of tanned skins were spread for us to lie on, and water was placed for us to wash in.

Presently we heard a shouting outside, and stepping to the door, saw a line of damsels bearing milk and roasted mealies, and honey in a pot. Behind these were some youths driving a fat young ox. We received the gifts, and then one of the young men drew the knife from his girdle and dexterously cut the ox's throat. In ten minutes it was dead, skinned, and jointed. The best of the meat was then cut off for us, and the rest, in the name of our party, I presented to the warriors round us, who took it and distributed the "white lords' gift."

Umbopa set to work, with the assistance of an extremely prepossessing young woman, to boil our portion in a large earthenware pot over a fire which was built outside the hut, and when it was nearly ready we sent a message to Infadoos, and asked him and Scragga, the king's son, to join us.

Presently they came, and sitting down upon little stools, of which there were several about the hut, for the Kukuanas do not in general squat upon their haunches like the Zulus, they helped us to get through our dinner. The old gentleman was most affable and polite, but it struck me that the young one regarded us with doubt. Together with the rest of the party, he had been overawed by our white appearance and by our magic properties; but it seemed to me that, on discovering that we ate, drank, and slept like other mortals, his awe was beginning to wear off, and to be replaced by a sullen suspicion—which made me feel rather uncomfortable.

In the course of our meal Sir Henry suggested to me that it might be well to try to discover if our hosts knew anything of his brother's fate, or if they had ever seen or heard of him; but, on the whole, I thought that it would be wiser to say nothing of the matter at this time. It was difficult to explain a relative lost from "the Stars."

After supper we filled our pipes and lit them; a proceeding which filled Infadoos and Scragga with astonishment. The Kukuanas were evidently unacquainted with the divine uses of tobacco-smoke. The herb is grown among them extensively; but, like the Zulus, they only use it for snuff, and quite failed to identify it in its new form.

Presently I asked Infadoos when we were to proceed on our journey, and was delighted to learn that preparations had been made for us to leave on the following morning, messengers having already left to inform Twala the king of our coming. It appeared that Twala was at his principal place, known as Loo, making ready for the great annual feast which was to be held in the first week of June. At this gathering all the regiments, with the exception of certain detachments left behind for garrison purposes, are brought up and paraded before the king; and the great annual witch-hunt, of which more by-and-by, is held.

We were to start at dawn; and Infadoos, who was to accompany us, expected that we should reach Loo on the night of the second day, unless we were detained by accident or by swollen rivers.

When they had given us this information our visitors bade us good-night; and, having arranged to watch turn and turn about, three of us flung ourselves down and slept the sweet sleep of the weary, whilst the fourth sat up on the look-out for possible treachery.

IX. TWALE THE KING

It will not be necessary for me to detail at length the incidents of our journey to Loo. It took two full days' travelling along Solomon's Great Road, which pursued its even course right into the heart of Kukuanaland. Suffice it to say that as we went the country seemed to grow richer and richer, and the kraals, with their wide surrounding belts of cultivation, more and more numerous. They were all built upon the same principles as the first camp which we had reached, and were guarded by ample garrisons of troops. Indeed, in Kukuanaland, as among the Germans, the Zulus, and the Masai, every able-bodied man is a soldier, so that the whole force of the nation is available for its wars, offensive or defensive. As we travelled we were overtaken by thousands of warriors hurrying up to Loo to be present at the great annual review and festival, and more splendid troops I never saw.

At sunset on the second day, we stopped to rest awhile upon the summit of some heights over which the road ran, and there on a beautiful and fertile plain before us lay Loo itself. For a native town it is an enormous place, quite five miles round, I should say, with outlying kraals projecting from it, that serve on grand occasions as cantonments for the regiments, and a curious horseshoe-shaped hill, with which we were destined to become better acquainted, about two miles to the north. It is beautifully situated, and through the centre of the kraal, dividing it into two portions, runs a river, which appeared to be bridged in several places, the same indeed that we had seen from the slopes of Sheba's Breasts. Sixty or seventy miles away three great snow-capped mountains, placed at the points of a triangle, started out of the level plain. The conformation of these mountains is unlike that of Sheba's Breasts, being sheer and precipitous, instead of smooth and rounded.

Infadoos saw us looking at them, and volunteered a remark.

"The road ends there," he said, pointing to the mountains known among the Kukuanas as the "Three Witches."

"Why does it end?" I asked.

"Who knows?" he answered with a shrug; "the mountains are full of caves, and there is a great pit between them. It is there that the wise men of old time used to go to get whatever it was they came for to this country, and it is there now that our kings are buried in the Place of Death."

"What was it they came for?" I asked eagerly.

"Nay, I know not. My lords who have dropped from the Stars should know," he answered with a quick look. Evidently he knew more than he chose to say.

"Yes," I went on, "you are right, in the Stars we learn many things. I have heard, for instance, that the wise men of old came to these mountains to find bright stones, pretty playthings, and yellow iron."

"My lord is wise," he answered coldly; "I am but a child and cannot talk with my lord on such matters. My lord must speak with Gagool the old, at the king's place, who is wise even as my lord," and he went away.

So soon as he was gone I turned to the others, and pointed out the mountains. "There are Solomon's diamond mines," I said.

Umbopa was standing with them, apparently plunged in one of the fits of abstraction which were common to him, and caught my words.

"Yes, Macumazahn," he put in, in Zulu, "the diamonds are surely there, and you shall have them, since you white men are so fond of toys and money."

"How dost thou know that, Umbopa?" I asked sharply, for I did not like his mysterious ways.

He laughed. "I dreamed it in the night, white men"; then he too turned on his heel and went.

"Now what," said Sir Henry, "is our black friend driving at? He knows more than he chooses to say, that is clear. By the way, Quatermain, has he heard anything of—of my brother?"

"Nothing; he has asked everyone he has become friendly with, but they all declare that no white man has ever been seen in the country before."

"Do you suppose that he got here at all?" suggested Good; "we have only reached the place by a miracle; is it likely he could have reached it without the map?"

"I don't know," said Sir Henry gloomily, "but somehow I think that I shall find him."

Slowly the sun sank, then suddenly darkness rushed down on the land like a tangible thing. There was no breathing-space between the day and night, no soft transformation scene, for in these latitudes twilight does not exist. The change from day to night is as quick and as absolute as the change from life to death. The sun sank and the world was wreathed in shadows. But not for long, for see in the west there is a glow, then come rays of silver light, and at last the full and glorious moon lights up the plain and shoots its gleaming arrows far and wide, filling the earth with a faint refulgence.

We stood and watched the lovely sight, whilst the stars grew pale before this chastened majesty, and felt our hearts lifted up in the presence of a beauty that I cannot describe. Mine has been a rough life, but there are a few things I am thankful to have lived for, and one of them is to have seen that moon shine over Kukuanaland.

Presently our meditations were broken in upon by our polite friend Infadoos.

"If my lords are rested we will journey on to Loo, where a hut is made ready for my lords to-night. The moon is now bright, so that we shall not fall by the way."

We assented, and in an hour's time were at the outskirts of the town, of which the extent, mapped out as it was by thousands of camp fires, appeared absolutely endless. Indeed, Good, who is always fond of a bad joke, christened it "Unlimited Loo." Soon we came to a moat with a drawbridge, where we were met by the rattling of arms and the hoarse challenge of a sentry. Infadoos gave some password that I could not catch, which was met with a salute, and we passed on through the central street of the great grass city. After nearly half an hour's tramp, past endless lines of huts, Infadoos halted at last by the gate of a little group of huts which surrounded a small courtyard of powdered limestone, and informed us that these were to be our "poor" quarters.

We entered, and found that a hut had been assigned to each of us. These huts were superior to any that we had yet seen, and in each was a most comfortable bed made of tanned skins, spread upon mattresses of aromatic grass. Food too was ready for us, and so soon as we had washed ourselves with water, which stood ready in earthenware jars, some young women of handsome appearance brought us roasted meats, and mealie cobs daintily served on wooden platters, and presented them to us with deep obeisances.

We ate and drank, and then, the beds having been all moved into one hut by our request, a precaution at which the amiable young ladies smiled, we flung ourselves down to sleep, thoroughly wearied with our long journey.

When we woke it was to find the sun high in the heavens, and the female attendants, who did not seem to be troubled by any false shame, already standing inside the hut, having been ordered to attend and help us to "make ready."

"Make ready, indeed," growled Good; "when one has only a flannel shirt and a pair of boots, that does not take long. I wish you would ask them for my trousers, Quatermain."

I asked accordingly, but was informed that these sacred relics had already been taken to the king, who would see us in the forenoon.

Somewhat to their astonishment and disappointment, having requested the young ladies to step outside, we proceeded to make the best toilet of which the circumstances admitted. Good even went the length of again shaving the right side of his face; the left, on which now appeared a very fair crop of whiskers, we impressed upon him he must on no account touch. As for ourselves, we were contented with a good wash and combing our hair. Sir Henry's yellow locks were now almost upon his shoulders, and he looked more like an ancient Dane than ever, while my grizzled scrub was fully an inch long, instead of half an inch, which in a general way I considered my maximum length.

By the time that we had eaten our breakfasts, and smoked a pipe, a message was brought to us by no less a personage than Infadoos himself that Twala the king was ready to see us, if we would be pleased to come.

We remarked in reply that we should prefer to wait till the sun was a little higher, we were yet weary with our journey, etc., etc. It is always well, when dealing with uncivilised people, not to be in too great a hurry. They are apt to mistake politeness for awe or servility. So, although we were quite as anxious to see Twala as Twala could be to see us, we sat down and waited for an hour, employing the interval in preparing such presents as our slender stock of goods permitted—namely, the Winchester rifle which had been used by poor Ventvögel, and some beads. The rifle and ammunition we determined to present to his royal highness, and the beads were for his wives and courtiers. We had already given a few to Infadoos and Scragga, and found that they were delighted with them, never having seen anything like them before. At length we declared that we were ready, and guided by Infadoos, started off to the audience, Umbopa carrying the rifle and beads.

After walking a few hundred yards we came to an enclosure, something like that surrounding the huts which had been allotted to us, only fifty times as big, for it could not have covered less than six or seven acres of ground. All round the outside fence stood a row of huts, which were the habitations of the king's wives. Exactly opposite the gateway, on the further side of the open space, was a very large hut, built by itself, in which his majesty resided. All the rest was open ground; that is to say, it would have been open had it not been filled by company after company of warriors, who were mustered there to the number of seven or eight thousand. These men stood still as statues as we advanced through them, and it would be impossible to give an adequate idea of the grandeur of the spectacle which they presented, with their waving plumes, their glancing spears, and iron-backed ox-hide shields.

The space in front of the large hut was empty, but before it were placed several stools. On three of these, at a sign from Infadoos, we seated ourselves, Umbopa standing behind us. As for Infadoos, he took up a position by the door of the hut. So we waited for ten minutes or more in the midst of a dead silence, but conscious that we were the object of the concentrated gaze of some eight thousand pairs of eyes. It was a somewhat trying ordeal, but we carried it off as best we could. At length the door of the hut opened, and a gigantic figure, with a splendid tiger-skin karross flung over its shoulders, stepped out, followed by the boy Scragga, and what appeared to us to be a withered-up monkey, wrapped in a fur cloak. The figure seated itself upon a stool, Scragga took his stand behind it, and the withered-up monkey crept on all fours into the shade of the hut and squatted down.

Still there was silence.

Then the gigantic figure slipped off the karross and stood up before us, a truly alarming spectacle. It was that of an enormous man with the most entirely repulsive countenance we had ever beheld. This man's lips were as thick as a Negro's, the nose was flat, he had but one gleaming black eye, for the other was represented by a hollow in the face, and his whole expression was cruel and sensual to a degree. From the large head rose a magnificent plume of white ostrich feathers, his body was clad in a shirt of shining chain armour, whilst round the waist and right knee were the usual garnishes of white ox-tail. In his right hand was a huge spear, about the neck a thick torque of gold, and bound on the forehead shone dully a single and enormous uncut diamond.

Still there was silence; but not for long. Presently the man, whom we rightly guessed to be the king, raised the great javelin in his hand. Instantly eight thousand spears were lifted in answer, and from eight thousand throats rang out the royal salute of "*Koom.*" Three times this was repeated, and each time the earth shook with the noise, that can only be compared to the deepest notes of thunder.

"Be humble, O people," piped out a thin voice which seemed to come from the monkey in the shade, "it is the king."

"*It is the king,*" boomed out the eight thousand throats in answer. "*Be humble, O people, it is the king.*"

Then there was dead silence again—dead silence. Presently, however, it was broken. A soldier on our left dropped his shield, which fell with a clatter on to the limestone flooring.

Twala turned his one cold eye in the direction of the noise.

"Come hither, thou," he said, in a cold voice.

A fine young man stepped out of the ranks, and stood before him.

"It was thy shield that fell, thou awkward dog. Wilt thou make me a reproach in the eyes of these strangers from the Stars? What hast thou to say for thyself?"

We saw the poor fellow turn pale under his dusky skin.

"It was by chance, O Calf of the Black Cow," he murmured.

"Then it is a chance for which thou must pay. Thou hast made me foolish; prepare for death."

"I am the king's ox," was the low answer.

"Scragga," roared the king, "let me see how thou canst use thy spear. Kill me this awkward dog."

Scragga stepped forward with an ill-favoured grin, and lifted his spear. The poor victim covered his eyes with his hand and stood still. As for us, we were petrified with horror.

"Once, twice," he waved the spear, and then struck, ah! right home—the spear stood out a foot behind the soldier's back. He flung up his hands and dropped dead. From the multitude about us rose something like a murmur, it rolled round and round, and died away. The tragedy was finished; there lay the corpse, and we had not yet realised that it had been enacted. Sir Henry sprang up and swore a great oath, then, overpowered by the sense of silence, sat down again.

"The thrust was a good one," said the king; "take him away."

Four men stepped out of the ranks, and lifting the body of the murdered man, carried it thence.

"Cover up the blood-stains, cover them up," piped out the thin voice that proceeded from the monkey-like figure; "the king's word is spoken, the king's doom is done!"

Thereupon a girl came forward from behind the hut, bearing a jar filled with powdered lime, which she scattered over the red mark, blotting it from sight.

Sir Henry meanwhile was boiling with rage at what had happened; indeed, it was with difficulty that we could keep him still.

"Sit down, for heaven's sake," I whispered; "our lives depend on it."

He yielded and remained quiet.

Twala sat silent until the traces of the tragedy had been removed, then he addressed us.

"White people," he said, "who come hither, whence I know not, and why I know not, greeting."

"Greeting, Twala, King of the Kukuanas," I answered.

"White people, whence come ye, and what seek ye?"

"We come from the Stars, ask us not how. We come to see this land."

"Ye journey from far to see a little thing. And that man with you," pointing to Umbopa, "does he also come from the Stars?"

"Even so; there are people of thy colour in the heavens above; but ask not of matters too high for thee, Twala the king."

"Ye speak with a loud voice, people of the Stars," Twala answered in a tone which I scarcely liked. "Remember that the Stars are far off, and ye are here. How if I make you as him whom they bore away?"

I laughed out loud, though there was little laughter in my heart.

"O king," I said, "be careful, walk warily over hot stones, lest thou shouldst burn thy feet; hold the spear by the handle, lest thou should cut thy hands. Touch but one hair of our heads, and destruction shall come upon thee. What, have not these"—pointing to Infadoos and Scragga, who, young villain that he was, was employed in cleaning the blood of the soldier off his spear— "told thee what manner of men we are? Hast thou seen the like of us?" and I pointed to Good, feeling quite sure that he had never seen anybody before who looked in the least like *him* as he then appeared.

"It is true, I have not," said the king, surveying Good.

"Have they not told thee how we strike with death from afar?" I went on.

"They have told me, but I believe them not. Let me see you kill. Kill me a man among those who stand yonder"—and he pointed to the opposite side of the kraal— "and I will believe."

"Nay," I answered; "we shed no blood of men except in just punishment; but if thou wilt see, bid thy servants drive in an ox through the kraal gates, and before he has run twenty paces I will strike him dead."

"Nay," laughed the king, "kill me a man and I will believe."

"Good, O king, so be it," I answered coolly; "do thou walk across the open space, and before thy feet reach the gate thou shalt be dead; or if thou wilt not, send thy son Scragga" (whom at that moment it would have given me much pleasure to shoot).

On hearing this suggestion Scragga uttered a sort of howl, and bolted into the hut.

Twala frowned majestically; the suggestion did not please him.

"Let a young ox be driven in," he said.

Two men at once departed, running swiftly.

"Now, Sir Henry," said I, "do you shoot. I want to show this ruffian that I am not the only magician of the party."

Sir Henry accordingly took his "express," and made ready.

"I hope I shall make a good shot," he groaned.

"You must," I answered. "If you miss with the first barrel, let him have the second. Sight for 150 yards, and wait till the beast turns broadside on."

Then came a pause, until presently we caught sight of an ox running straight for the kraal gate. It came on through the gate, then, catching sight of the vast concourse of people, stopped stupidly, turned round, and bellowed.

"Now's your time," I whispered.

Up went the rifle.

Bang! *thud*! and the ox was kicking on his back, shot in the ribs. The semi-hollow bullet had done its work well, and a sigh of astonishment went up from the assembled thousands.

I turned round coolly—

"Have I lied, O king?"

"Nay, white man, it is the truth," was the somewhat awed answer.

"Listen, Twala," I went on. "Thou hast seen. Now know we come in peace, not in war. See," and I held up the Winchester repeater; "here is a hollow staff that shall enable thee to kill even as we kill, only I lay this charm upon it, thou shalt kill no man with it. If thou liftest it against a man, it shall kill thee. Stay, I will show thee. Bid a soldier step forty paces and place the shaft of a spear in the ground so that the flat blade looks towards us."

In a few seconds it was done.

"Now, see, I will break yonder spear."

Taking a careful sight I fired. The bullet struck the flat of the spear, and shattered the blade into fragments.

Again the sigh of astonishment went up.

"Now, Twala, we give this magic tube to thee, and by-and-by I will show thee how to use it; but beware how thou turnest the magic of the Stars against a man of earth," and I handed him the rifle.

The king took it very gingerly, and laid it down at his feet. As he did so I observed the wizened monkey-like figure creeping from the shadow of the hut. It crept on all fours, but when it reached the place where the king sat it rose upon its feet, and throwing the furry covering from its face, revealed a most extraordinary and weird countenance. Apparently it was that of a woman of great age so shrunken that in size it seemed no larger than the face of a year-old child, although made up of a number of deep and yellow wrinkles. Set in these wrinkles was a sunken slit, that represented the mouth, beneath which the chin curved outwards to a point. There was no nose to speak of; indeed, the visage might have been taken for that of a sun-dried corpse had it not been for a pair of large black eyes, still full of fire and intelligence, which gleamed and played under the snow-white eyebrows, and the projecting parchment-coloured skull, like jewels in a charnel-house. As for the head itself, it was perfectly bare, and yellow in hue, while its wrinkled scalp moved and contracted like the hood of a cobra.

The figure to which this fearful countenance belonged, a countenance so fearful indeed that it caused a shiver of fear to pass through us as we gazed on it, stood still for a moment. Then suddenly it projected a skinny claw armed with nails nearly an inch long, and laying it on the shoulder of Twala the king, began to speak in a thin and piercing voice—

"Listen, O king! Listen, O warriors! Listen, O mountains and plains and rivers, home of the Kukuana race! Listen, O skies and sun, O rain and storm and mist! Listen, O men and women, O youths and maidens, and O ye babes unborn! Listen, all things that live and must die! Listen, all dead things that shall live again—again to die! Listen, the spirit of life is in me and I prophesy. I prophesy! I prophesy!"

The words died away in a faint wail, and dread seemed to seize upon the hearts of all who heard them, including our own. This old woman was very terrible.

"*Blood! blood! blood!* rivers of blood; blood everywhere. I see it, I smell it, I taste it—it is salt! it runs red upon the ground, it rains down from the skies.

"*Footsteps! footsteps! footsteps!* the tread of the white man coming from afar. It shakes the earth; the earth trembles before her master.

"Blood is good, the red blood is bright; there is no smell like the smell of new-shed blood. The lions shall lap it and roar, the vultures shall wash their wings in it and shriek with joy.

"I am old! I am old! I have seen much blood; *ha, ha!* but I shall see more ere I die, and be merry. How old am I, think ye? Your fathers knew me, and *their* fathers knew me, and *their* fathers' fathers' fathers. I have seen the white man and know his desires. I am old, but the mountains are older than I. Who made the great road, tell me? Who wrote the pictures on the rocks, tell me? Who reared up the three Silent Ones yonder, that gaze across the pit, tell me?" and she pointed towards the three precipitous mountains which we had noticed on the previous night.

"Ye know not, but I know. It was a white people who were before ye are, who shall be when ye are not, who shall eat you up and destroy you. *Yea! yea! yea!*

"And what came they for, the White Ones, the Terrible Ones, the skilled in magic and all learning, the strong, the unswerving? What is that bright stone upon thy forehead, O king? Whose hands made the iron garments upon thy breast, O king? Ye know not, but I know. I the Old One, I the Wise One, I the *Isanusi*, the witch doctress!"

Then she turned her bald vulture-head towards us.

"What seek ye, white men of the Stars—ah, yes, of the Stars? Do ye seek a lost one? Ye shall not find him here. He is not here. Never for ages upon ages has a white foot pressed this land; never except once, and I remember that he left it but to die. Ye come for bright stones; I know it—I know it; ye shall find them when the blood is dry; but shall ye return whence ye came, or shall ye stop with me? *Ha! ha! ha!*

"And thou, thou with the dark skin and the proud bearing," and she pointed her skinny finger at Umbopa, "who art *thou*, and what seekest *thou*? Not stones that shine, not yellow metal that gleams, these thou leavest to 'white men from the Stars.' Methinks I know thee; methinks I can smell the smell of the blood in thy heart. Strip off the girdle—"

Here the features of this extraordinary creature became convulsed, and she fell to the ground foaming in an epileptic fit, and was carried into the hut.

The king rose up trembling, and waved his hand. Instantly the regiments began to file off, and in ten minutes, save for ourselves, the king, and a few attendants, the great space was left empty.

"White people," he said, "it passes in my mind to kill you. Gagool has spoken strange words. What say ye?"

I laughed. "Be careful, O king, we are not easy to slay. Thou hast seen the fate of the ox; wouldst thou be as the ox is?"

The king frowned. "It is not well to threaten a king."

"We threaten not, we speak what is true. Try to kill us, O king, and learn."

The great savage put his hand to his forehead and thought.

"Go in peace," he said at length. "To-night is the great dance. Ye shall see it. Fear not that I shall set a snare for you. To-morrow I will think."

"It is well, O king," I answered unconcernedly, and then, accompanied by Infadoos, we rose and went back to our kraal.

X. The Witch-Hunt

On reaching our hut I motioned to Infadoos to enter with us.

"Now, Infadoos," I said, "we would speak with thee."

"Let my lords say on."

"It seems to us, Infadoos, that Twala the king is a cruel man."

"It is so, my lords. Alas! the land cries out because of his cruelties. To-night ye shall see. It is the great witch-hunt, and many will be smelt out as wizards and slain.

No man's life is safe. If the king covets a man's cattle, or a man's wife, or if he fears a man that he should excite a rebellion against him, then Gagool, whom ye saw, or some of the witch-finding women whom she has taught, will smell that man out as a wizard, and he will be killed. Many must die before the moon grows pale to-night. It is ever so. Perhaps I too shall be killed. As yet I have been spared because I am skilled in war, and am beloved by the soldiers; but I know not how long I have to live. The land groans at the cruelties of Twala the king; it is wearied of him and his red ways."

"Then why is it, Infadoos, that the people do not cast him down?"

"Nay, my lords, he is the king, and if he were killed Scragga would reign in his place, and the heart of Scragga is blacker than the heart of Twala his father. If Scragga were king his yoke upon our neck would be heavier than the yoke of Twala. If Imotu had never been slain, or if Ignosi his son had lived, it might have been otherwise; but they are both dead."

"How knowest thou that Ignosi is dead?" said a voice behind us. We looked round astonished to see who spoke. It was Umbopa.

"What meanest thou, boy?" asked Infadoos; "who told thee to speak?"

"Listen, Infadoos," was the answer, "and I will tell thee a story. Years ago the king Imotu was killed in this country and his wife fled with the boy Ignosi. Is it not so?"

"It is so."

"It was said that the woman and her son died upon the mountains. Is it not so?"

"It is even so."

"Well, it came to pass that the mother and the boy Ignosi did not die. They crossed the mountains and were led by a tribe of wandering desert men across the sands beyond, till at last they came to water and grass and trees again."

"How knowest thou this?"

"Listen. They travelled on and on, many months' journey, till they reached a land where a people called the Amazulu, who also are of the Kukuana stock, live by war, and with them they tarried many years, till at length the mother died. Then the son Ignosi became a wanderer again, and journeyed into a land of wonders, where white people live, and for many more years he learned the wisdom of the white people."

"It is a pretty story," said Infadoos incredulously.

"For years he lived there working as a servant and a soldier, but holding in his heart all that his mother had told him of his own place, and casting about in his mind to find how he might journey thither to see his people and his father's house before he died. For long years he lived and waited, and at last the time came, as it ever comes to him who can wait for it, and he met some white men who would seek this unknown land, and joined himself to them. The white men started and travelled on and on, seeking for one who is lost. They crossed the burning desert, they crossed the snow-clad mountains, and at last reached the land of the Kukuanas, and there they found *thee*, O Infadoos."

"Surely thou art mad to talk thus," said the astonished old soldier.

"Thou thinkest so; see, I will show thee, O my uncle.

"*I am Ignosi, rightful king of the Kukuanas!*"

Then with a single movement Umbopa slipped off his "moocha" or girdle, and stood naked before us.

"Look," he said; "what is this?" and he pointed to the picture of a great snake tattooed in blue round his middle, its tail disappearing into its open mouth just above where the thighs are set into the body.

Infadoos looked, his eyes starting nearly out of his head. Then he fell upon his knees.

"*Koom! Koom!*" he ejaculated; "it is my brother's son; it is the king."

"Did I not tell thee so, my uncle? Rise; I am not yet the king, but with thy help, and with the help of these brave white men, who are my friends, I shall be. Yet the old witch Gagool was right, the land shall run with blood first, and hers shall run with it, if she has any and can die, for she killed my father with her words, and drove my mother forth. And now, Infadoos, choose thou. Wilt thou put thy hands between my hands and be my man? Wilt thou share the dangers that lie before me, and help me to overthrow this tyrant and murderer, or wilt thou not? Choose thou."

The old man put his hand to his head and thought. Then he rose, and advancing to where Umbopa, or rather Ignosi, stood, he knelt before him, and took his hand.

"Ignosi, rightful king of the Kukuanas, I put my hand between thy hands, and am thy man till death. When thou wast a babe I dandled thee upon my knees, now shall my old arm strike for thee and freedom."

"It is well, Infadoos; if I conquer, thou shalt be the greatest man in the kingdom after its king. If I fail, thou canst only die, and death is not far off from thee. Rise, my uncle."

"And ye, white men, will ye help me? What have I to offer you! The white stones! If I conquer and can find them, ye shall have as many as ye can carry hence. Will that suffice you?"

I translated this remark.

"Tell him," answered Sir Henry, "that he mistakes an Englishman. Wealth is good, and if it comes in our way we will take it; but a gentleman does not sell himself for wealth. Still, speaking for myself, I say this. I have always liked Umbopa, and so far as lies in me I will stand by him in this business. It will be very pleasant to me to try to square matters with that cruel devil Twala. What do you say, Good, and you, Quatermain?"

"Well," said Good, "to adopt the language of hyperbole, in which all these people seem to indulge, you can tell him that a row is surely good, and warms the cockles of the heart, and that so far as I am concerned I'm his boy. My only stipulation is that he allows me to wear trousers."

I translated the substance of these answers.

"It is well, my friends," said Ignosi, late Umbopa; "and what sayest thou, Macumazahn, art thou also with me, old hunter, cleverer than a wounded buffalo?"

I thought awhile and scratched my head.

"Umbopa, or Ignosi," I said, "I don't like revolutions. I am a man of peace and a bit of a coward"—here Umbopa smiled—"but, on the other hand, I stick up for my friends, Ignosi. You have stuck to us and played the part of a man, and I will stick by you. But mind you, I am a trader, and have to make my living, so I accept your offer about those diamonds in case we should ever be in a position to avail ourselves of it. Another thing: we came, as you know, to look for Incubu's (Sir Henry's) lost brother. You must help us to find him."

"That I will do," answered Ignosi. "Stay, Infadoos, by the sign of the snake about my middle, tell me the truth. Has any white man to thy knowledge set his foot within the land?"

"None, O Ignosi."

"If any white man had been seen or heard of, wouldst thou have known?"

"I should certainly have known."

"Thou hearest, Incubu," said Ignosi to Sir Henry; "he has not been here."

"Well, well," said Sir Henry, with a sigh; "there it is; I suppose that he never got so far. Poor fellow, poor fellow! So it has all been for nothing. God's will be done."

"Now for business," I put in, anxious to escape from a painful subject. "It is very well to be a king by right divine, Ignosi, but how dost thou propose to become a king indeed?"

"Nay, I know not. Infadoos, hast thou a plan?"

"Ignosi, Son of the Lightning," answered his uncle, "to-night is the great dance and witch-hunt. Many shall be smelt out and perish, and in the hearts of many others there will be grief and anguish and fury against the king Twala. When the dance is over, then I will speak to some of the great chiefs, who in turn, if I can win them over, will speak to their regiments. I shall speak to the chiefs softly at first, and bring them to see that thou art indeed the king, and I think that by to-morrow's light thou shalt have twenty thousand spears at thy command. And now I must go and think, and hear, and make ready. After the dance is done, if I am yet alive, and we are all alive, I will meet thee here, and we can talk. At the best there must be war."

At this moment our conference was interrupted by the cry that messengers had come from the king. Advancing to the door of the hut we ordered that they should be admitted, and presently three men entered, each bearing a shining shirt of chain armour, and a magnificent battle-axe.

"The gifts of my lord the king to the white men from the Stars!" said a herald who came with them.

"We thank the king," I answered; "withdraw."

The men went, and we examined the armour with great interest. It was the most wonderful chain work that either of us had ever seen. A whole coat fell together so closely that it formed a mass of links scarcely too big to be covered with both hands.

"Do you make these things in this country, Infadoos?" I asked; "they are very beautiful."

"Nay, my lord, they came down to us from our forefathers. We know not who made them, and there are but few left.* None but those of royal blood may be clad in them. They are magic coats through which no spear can pass, and those who wear them are well-nigh safe in the battle. The king is well pleased or much afraid, or he would not have sent these garments of steel. Clothe yourselves in them to-night, my lords."

The rest of that day we spent quietly, resting and talking over the situation, which was sufficiently exciting. At last the sun went down, the thousand watch fires glowed out, and through the darkness we heard the tramp of many feet and the clashing of hundreds of spears, as the regiments passed to their appointed places to be ready for the great dance. Then the full moon shone out in splendour, and as we stood watching her rays, Infadoos arrived, clad in his war dress, and accompanied by a guard of twenty men to escort us to the dance. As he recommended, we had already donned the shirts of chain armour which the king had sent us, putting them on under our ordinary clothing, and finding to our surprise that they were neither very heavy nor uncomfortable. These steel shirts, which evidently had been made for men of a very large stature, hung somewhat loosely upon Good and myself, but Sir Henry's fitted his magnificent frame like a glove. Then strapping our revolvers round our waists, and taking in our hands the battle-axes which the king had sent with the armour, we started.

On arriving at the great kraal, where we had that morning been received by the king, we found that it was closely packed with some twenty thousand men arranged round it in regiments. These regiments were in turn divided into companies, and between each company ran a little path to allow space for the witch-finders to pass up

---

*In the Soudan swords and coats of mail are still worn by Arabs, whose ancestors must have stripped them from the bodies of Crusaders.—EDITOR

and down. Anything more imposing than the sight that was presented by this vast and orderly concourse of armed men it is impossible to conceive. There they stood perfectly silent, and the moon poured her light upon the forest of their raised spears, upon their majestic forms, waving plumes, and the harmonious shading of their various-coloured shields. Wherever we looked were line upon line of dim faces surmounted by range upon range of shimmering spears.

"Surely," I said to Infadoos, "the whole army is here?"

"Nay, Macumazahn," he answered, "but a third of it. One third is present at this dance each year, another third is mustered outside in case there should be trouble when the killing begins, ten thousand more garrison the outposts round Loo, and the rest watch at the kraals in the country. Thou seest it is a great people."

"They are very silent," said Good; and indeed the intense stillness among such a vast concourse of living men was almost overpowering.

"What says Bougwan?" asked Infadoos.

I translated.

"Those over whom the shadow of Death is hovering are silent," he answered grimly.

"Will many be killed?"

"Very many."

"It seems," I said to the others, "that we are going to assist at a gladiatorial show arranged regardless of expense."

Sir Henry shivered, and Good said he wished that we could get out of it.

"Tell me," I asked Infadoos, "are we in danger?"

"I know not, my lords, I trust not; but do not seem afraid. If ye live through the night all may go well with you. The soldiers murmur against the king."

All this while we had been advancing steadily towards the centre of the open space, in the midst of which were placed some stools. As we proceeded we perceived another small party coming from the direction of the royal hut.

"It is the king Twala, Scragga his son, and Gagool the old; and see, with them are those who slay," said Infadoos, pointing to a little group of about a dozen gigantic and savage-looking men, armed with spears in one hand and heavy kerries in the other.

The king seated himself upon the centre stool, Gagool crouched at his feet, and the others stood behind him.

"Greeting, white lords," Twala cried, as we came up; "be seated, waste not precious time—the night is all too short for the deeds that must be done. Ye come in a good hour, and shall see a glorious show. Look round, white lords; look round," and he rolled his one wicked eye from regiment to regiment. "Can the Stars show you such a sight as this? See how they shake in their wickedness, all those who have evil in their hearts and fear the judgment of 'Heaven above.'"

"*Begin! begin!*" piped Gagool, in her thin piercing voice; "the hyænas are hungry, they howl for food. *Begin! begin!*"

Then for a moment there was intense stillness, made horrible by a presage of what was to come.

The king lifted his spear, and suddenly twenty thousand feet were raised, as though they belonged to one man, and brought down with a stamp upon the earth. This was repeated three times, causing the solid ground to shake and tremble. Then from a far point of the circle a solitary voice began a wailing song, of which the refrain ran something as follows:—

"*What is the lot of man born of woman?*"

Back came the answer rolling out from every throat in that vast company—

"*Death!*"

Gradually, however, the song was taken up by company after company, till the whole armed multitude were singing it, and I could no longer follow the words, except in so far as they appeared to represent various phases of human passions, fears, and joys. Now it seemed to be a love song, now a majestic swelling war chant, and last of all a death dirge ending suddenly in one heart-breaking wail that went echoing and rolling away in a volume of blood-curdling sound.

Again silence fell upon the place, and again it was broken by the king lifting his hand. Instantly we heard a pattering of feet, and from out of the masses of warriors strange and awful figures appeared running towards us. As they drew near we saw that these were women, most of them aged, for their white hair, ornamented with small bladders taken from fish, streamed out behind them. Their faces were painted in stripes of white and yellow; down their backs hung snake-skins, and round their waists rattled circlets of human bones, while each held a small forked wand in her shrivelled hand. In all there were ten of them. When they arrived in front of us they halted, and one of them, pointing with her wand towards the crouching figure of Gagool, cried out—

"Mother, old mother, we are here."

"*Good! good! good!*" answered that aged Iniquity. "Are your eyes keen, *Isanusis* [witch doctresses], ye seers in dark places?"

"Mother, they are keen."

"*Good! good! good!* Are your ears open, *Isanusis*, ye who hear words that come not from the tongue?"

"Mother, they are open."

"*Good! good! good!* Are your senses awake, *Isanusis*—can ye smell blood, can ye purge the land of the wicked ones who compass evil against the king and against their neighbours? Are ye ready to do the justice of 'Heaven above,' ye whom I have taught, who have eaten of the bread of my wisdom, and drunk of the water of my magic?"

"Mother, we can."

"Then go! Tarry not, ye vultures; see, the slayers"—pointing to the ominous group of executioners behind—"make sharp their spears; the white men from afar are hungry to see. *Go!*"

With a wild yell Gagool's horrid ministers broke away in every direction, like fragments from a shell, the dry bones round their waists rattling as they ran, and headed for various points of the dense human circle. We could not watch them all, so we fixed our eyes upon the *Isanusi* nearest to us. When she came to within a few paces of the warriors she halted and began to dance wildly, turning round and round with an almost incredible rapidity, and shrieking out sentences such as "I smell him, the evil-doer!" "He is near, he who poisoned his mother!" "I hear the thoughts of him who thought evil of the king!"

Quicker and quicker she danced, till she lashed herself into such a frenzy of excitement that the foam flew in specks from her gnashing jaws, till her eyes seemed to start from her head, and her flesh to quiver visibly. Suddenly she stopped dead and stiffened all over, like a pointer dog when he scents game, and then with outstretched wand she began to creep stealthily towards the soldiers before her. It seemed to us that as she came their stoicism gave way, and that they shrank from her. As for ourselves, we followed her movements with a horrible fascination. Presently, still creeping and crouching like a dog, the *Isanusi* was before them. Then she halted and pointed, and again crept on a pace or two.

Suddenly the end came. With a shriek she sprang in and touched a tall warrior with her forked wand. Instantly two of his comrades, those standing immediately next to him, seized the doomed man, each by one arm, and advanced with him towards the king.

He did not resist, but we saw that he dragged his limbs as though they were paralysed, and that his fingers, from which the spear had fallen, were limp like those of a man newly dead.

As he came, two of the villainous executioners stepped forward to meet him. Presently they met, and the executioners turned round, looking towards the king as though for orders.

"*Kill!*" said the king.

"*Kill!*" squeaked Gagool.

"*Kill!*" re-echoed Scragga, with a hollow chuckle.

Almost before the words were uttered the horrible dead was done. One man had driven his spear into the victim's heart, and to make assurance double sure, the other had dashed out his brains with a great club.

"*One*," counted Twala the king, just like a black Madame Defarge, as Good said, and the body was dragged a few paces away and stretched out.

Hardly was the thing done before another poor wretch was brought up, like an ox to the slaughter. This time we could see, from the leopard-skin cloak which he wore, that the man was a person of rank. Again the awful syllables were spoken, and the victim fell dead.

"*Two*," counted the king.

And so the deadly game went on, till about a hundred bodies were stretched in rows behind us. I have heard of the gladiatorial shows of the Cæsars, and of the Spanish bull-fights, but I take the liberty of doubting if either of them could be half so horrible as this Kukuana witch-hunt. Gladiatorial shows and Spanish bull-fights at any rate contributed to the public amusement, which certainly was not the case here. The most confirmed sensation-monger would fight shy of sensation if he knew that it was well on the cards that he would, in his own proper person, be the subject of the next "event."

Once we rose and tried to remonstrate, but were sternly repressed by Twala.

"Let the law take its course, white men. These dogs are magicians and evil-doers; it is well that they should die," was the only answer vouchsafed to us.

About half-past ten there was a pause. The witch-finders gathered themselves together, apparently exhausted with their bloody work, and we thought that the performance was done with. But it was not so, for presently, to our surprise, the ancient woman, Gagool, rose from her crouching position, and supporting herself with a stick, staggered off into the open space. It was an extraordinary sight to see this frightful vulture-headed old creature, bent nearly double with extreme age, gather strength by degrees, until at last she rushed about almost as actively as her ill-omened pupils. To and fro she ran, chanting to herself, till suddenly she made a dash at a tall man standing in front of one of the regiments, and touched him. As she did this a sort of groan went up from the regiment which evidently he commanded. But two of its officers seized him all the same, and brought him up for execution. We learned afterwards that he was a man of great wealth and importance, being indeed a cousin of the king's.

He was slain, and Twala counted one hundred and three. Then Gagool again sprang to and fro, gradually drawing nearer and nearer to ourselves.

"Hang me if I don't believe she is going to try her games on us," ejaculated Good in horror.

"Nonsense!" said Sir Henry.

As for myself, when I saw that old fiend dancing nearer and nearer, my heart positively sank into my boots. I glanced behind us at the long rows of corpses, and shivered.

Nearer and nearer waltzed Gagool, looking for all the world like an animated crooked stick or comma, her horrid eyes gleaming and glowing with a most unholy lustre.

Nearer she came, and yet nearer, every creature in that vast assemblage watching her movements with intense anxiety. At last she stood still and pointed.

"Which is it to be?" asked Sir Henry to himself.

In a moment all doubts were at rest, for the old hag had rushed in and touched Umbopa, alias Ignosi, on the shoulder.

"I smell him out," she shrieked. "Kill him, kill him, he is full of evil; kill him, the stranger, before blood flows from him. Slay him, O king."

There was a pause, which I instantly took advantage of.

"O king," I called out, rising from my seat, "this man is the servant of thy guests, he is their dog; whosoever sheds the blood of our dog sheds our blood. By the sacred law of hospitality I claim protection for him."

"Gagool, mother of the witch-finders, has smelt him out; he must die, white men," was the sullen answer.

"Nay, he shall not die," I replied; "he who tries to touch him shall die indeed."

"Seize him!" roared Twala to the executioners; who stood around red to the eyes with the blood of their victims.

They advanced towards us, and then hesitated. As for Ignosi, he clutched his spear, and raised it as though determined to sell his life dearly.

"Stand back, ye dogs!" I shouted, "if ye would see to-morrow's light. Touch one hair of his head and your king dies," and I covered Twala with my revolver. Sir Henry and Good also drew their pistols, Sir Henry pointing his at the leading executioner, who was advancing to carry out the sentence, and Good taking a deliberate aim at Gagool.

Twala winced perceptibly as my barrel came in a line with his broad chest.

"Well," I said, "what is it to be, Twala?"

Then he spoke.

"Put away your magic tubes," he said; "ye have adjured me in the name of hospitality, and for that reason, but not from fear of what ye can do, I spare him. Go in peace."

"It is well," I answered unconcernedly; "we are weary of slaughter, and would sleep. Is the dance ended?"

"It is ended," Twala answered sulkily. "Let these dead dogs," pointing to the long rows of corpses, "be flung out to the hyænas and the vultures," and he lifted his spear.

Instantly the regiments began to defile through the kraal gateway in perfect silence, a fatigue party only remaining behind to drag away the corpses of those who had been sacrificed.

Then we rose also, and making our salaam to his majesty, which he hardly deigned to acknowledge, we departed to our huts.

"Well," said Sir Henry, as we sat down, having first lit a lamp of the sort used by the Kukuanas, of which the wick is made from the fibre of a species of palm leaf, and the oil from clarified hippopotamus fat, "well, I feel uncommonly inclined to be sick."

"If I had any doubts about helping Umbopa to rebel against that infernal blackguard," put in Good, "they are gone now. It was as much as I could do to sit still while that slaughter was going on. I tried to keep my eyes shut, but they would open just at the wrong time. I wonder where Infadoos is. Umbopa, my friend, you ought to be grateful to us; your skin came near to having an air-hole made in it."

"I am grateful, Bougwan," was Umbopa's answer, when I had translated, "and I shall not forget. As for Infadoos, he will be here by-and-by. We must wait."

So we lit our pipes and waited.

XI. WE GIVE A SIGN

For a long while—two hours, I should think—we sat there in silence, being too much overwhelmed by the recollection of the horrors we had seen to talk. At last, just as we were thinking of turning in—for the night drew nigh to dawn—we heard a sound of steps. Then came the challenge of a sentry posted at the kraal gate, which apparently was answered, though not in an audible tone, for the steps still advanced; and in another second Infadoos had entered the hut, followed by some half-dozen stately-looking chiefs.

"My lords," he said, "I have come according to my word. My lords and Ignosi, rightful king of the Kukuanas, I have brought with me these men," pointing to the row of chiefs, "who are great men among us, having each one of them the command of three thousand soldiers, that live but to do their bidding, under the king's. I have told them of what I have seen, and what my ears have heard. Now let them also behold the sacred snake around thee, and hear thy story, Ignosi, that they may say whether or no they will make cause with thee against Twala the king."

By way of answer Ignosi again stripped off his girdle, and exhibited the snake tattooed about him. Each chief in turn drew near and examined the sign by the dim light of the lamp, and without saying a word passed on to the other side.

Then Ignosi resumed his moocha, and addressing them, repeated the history he had detailed in the morning.

"Now ye have heard, chiefs," said Infadoos, when he had done, "what say ye; will ye stand by this man and help him to his father's throne, or will ye not? The land cries out against Twala, and the blood of the people flows like the waters in spring. Ye have seen to-night. Two other chiefs there were with whom I had it in my mind to speak, and where are they now? The hyænas howl over their corpses. Soon shall ye be as they are if ye strike not. Choose then, my brothers."

The eldest of the six men, a short, thick-set warrior, with white hair, stepped forward a pace and answered—

"Thy words are true, Infadoos; the land cries out. My own brother is among those who died to-night; but this is a great matter, and the thing is hard to believe. How know we that if we lift our spears it may not be for a thief and a liar? It is a great matter, I say, and none can see the end of it. For of this be sure, blood will flow in rivers before the deed is done; many will still cleave to the king, for men worship the sun that still shines bright in the heavens, rather than that which has not risen. These white men from the Stars, their magic is great, and Ignosi is under the cover of their wing. If he be indeed the rightful king, let them give us a sign, and let the people have a sign, that all may see. So shall men cleave to us, knowing of a truth that the white man's magic is with them."

"Ye have the sign of the snake," I answered.

"My lord, it is not enough. The snake may have been placed there since the man's childhood. Show us the sign. We will not move without a sign."

The others gave a decided assent, and I turned in perplexity to Sir Henry and Good, and explained the situation.

"I think that I have it," said Good exultingly; "ask them to give us a moment to think."

I did so, and the chiefs withdrew. So soon as they had gone Good went to the little box where he kept his medicines, unlocked it, and took out a note-book, in the fly-leaves of which was an almanack. "Now look here, you fellows, isn't to-morrow the 4th of June?" he said.

We had kept a careful note of the days, so were able to answer that it was.

"Very good; then here we have it—'4 June, total eclipse of the moon commences at 8:15 Greenwich time, visible in Teneriffe—*South Africa*, etc.' There's a sign for you. Tell them we will darken the moon to-morrow night."

The idea was a splendid one; indeed, the only weak spot about it was a fear lest Good's almanack might be incorrect. If we made a false prophecy on such a subject, our prestige would be gone for ever, and so would Ignosi's chance of the throne of the Kukuanas.

"Suppose that the almanack is wrong," suggested Sir Henry to Good, who was busily employed in working out something on a blank page of the book.

"I see no reason to suppose anything of the sort," was his answer. "Eclipses always come up to time; at least that is my experience of them, and it especially states that this one will be visible in South Africa. I have worked out the reckonings as well as I can, without knowing our exact position; and I make out that the eclipse should begin here about ten o'clock tomorrow night, and last till half-past twelve. For an hour and a half or so there should be almost total darkness."

"Well," said Sir Henry, "I suppose we had better risk it."

I acquiesced, though doubtfully, for eclipses are queer cattle to deal with—it might be a cloudy night, for instance, or our dates might be wrong—and sent Umbopa to summon the chiefs back. Presently they came, and I addressed them thus—

"Great men of the Kukuanas, and thou, Infadoos, listen. We love not to show our powers, for to do so is to interfere with the course of nature, and to plunge the world into fear and confusion. But since this matter is a great one, and as we are angered against the king because of the slaughter we have seen, and because of the act of the *Isanusi* Gagool, who would have put our friend Ignosi to death, we have determined to break a rule, and to give such a sign as all men may see. Come hither"; and I led them to the door of the hut and pointed to the red ball of the moon. "What see ye there?"

"We see the dying moon," answered the spokesman of the party.

"It is so. Now tell me, can any mortal man put out that moon before her hour of setting, and bring the curtain of black night down upon the land?"

The chief laughed a little at the question. "No, my lord, that no man can do. The moon is stronger than man who looks on her, nor can she vary in her courses."

"Ye say so. Yet I tell you that to-morrow night, about two hours before midnight, we will cause the moon to be eaten up for a space of an hour and half an hour. Yes, deep darkness shall cover the earth, and it shall be for a sign that Ignosi is indeed king of the Kukuanas. If we do this thing, will ye be satisfied?"

"Yea, my lords," answered the old chief with a smile, which was reflected on the faces of his companions; "*if* ye do this thing, we will be satisfied indeed."

"It shall be done; we three, Incubu, Bougwan, and Macumazahn, have said it, and it shall be done. Dost thou hear, Infadoos?"

"I hear, my lord, but it is a wonderful thing that ye promise, to put out the moon, the mother of the world, when she is at her full."

"Yet shall we do it, Infadoos."

"It is well, my lords. To-day, two hours after sunset, Twala will send for my lords to witness the girls dance, and one hour after the dance begins the girl whom Twala thinks the fairest shall be killed by Scragga, the king's son, as a sacrifice to the Silent Ones, who sit and keep watch by the mountains yonder," and he pointed towards the three strange-looking peaks where Solomon's road was supposed to end. "Then let my lords darken the moon, and save the maiden's life, and the people will believe indeed."

"Ay," said the old chief, still smiling a little, "the people will believe indeed."

"Two miles from Loo," went on Infadoos, "there is a hill curved like a new moon, a stronghold, where my regiment, and three other regiments which these chiefs command, are stationed. This morning we will make a plan whereby two or three other regiments may be moved there also. Then, if in truth my lords can darken the moon, in the darkness I will take my lords by the hand and lead them out of Loo to this place, where they shall be safe, and thence we can make war upon Twala the king."

"It is good," said I. "Let leave us to sleep awhile and to make ready our magic."

Infadoos rose, and, having saluted us, departed with the chiefs.

"My friends," said Ignosi, so soon as they were gone, "can ye do this wonderful thing, or were ye speaking empty words to the men?"

"We believe that we can do it, Umbopa—Ignosi, I mean."

"It is strange," he answered, "and had ye not been Englishmen I would not have believed it; but I have learned that English 'gentlemen' tell no lies. If we live through the matter, be sure that I will repay you."

"Ignosi," said Sir Henry, "promise me one thing."

"I will promise, Incubu, my friend, even before I hear it," answered the big man with a smile. "What is it?"

"This: that if ever you come to be king of this people you will do away with the smelling out of wizards such as we saw last night; and that the killing of men without trial shall no longer take place in the land."

Ignosi thought for a moment after I had translated this request, and then answered—

"The ways of black people are not as the ways of white men, Incubu, nor do we value life so highly. Yet I will promise. If it be in my power to hold them back, the witch-finders shall hunt no more, nor shall any man die the death without trial or judgment."

"That's a bargain, then," said Sir Henry; "and now let us get a little rest."

Thoroughly wearied out, we were soon sound asleep, and slept till Ignosi woke us about eleven o'clock. Then we rose, washed, and ate a hearty breakfast. After that we went outside the hut and walked about, amusing ourselves with examining the structure of the Kukuana huts and observing the customs of the women.

"I hope that eclipse will come off," said Sir Henry presently.

"If it does not it will soon be all up with us," I answered mournfully; "for so sure as we are living men some of those chiefs will tell the whole story to the king, and then there will be another sort of eclipse, and one that we shall certainly not like."

Returning to the hut we ate some dinner, and passed the rest of the day in receiving visits of ceremony and curiosity. At length the sun set, and we enjoyed a couple of hours of such quiet as our melancholy forebodings would allow to us. Finally, about half-past eight, a messenger came from Twala to bid us to the great annual "dance of girls" which was about to be celebrated.

Hastily we put on the chain shirts that the king had sent us, and taking our rifles and ammunition with us, so as to have them handy in case we had to fly, as suggested by Infadoos, we started boldly enough, though with inward fear and trembling. The great space in front of the king's kraal bore a very different appearance from that which it had presented on the previous evening. In place of the grim ranks of serried warriors were company after company of Kukuana girls, not over-dressed, so far as clothing went, but each crowned with a wreath of flowers, and holding a palm leaf in one hand and a white arum lily in the other. In the centre of the open moonlit space sat Twala the king, with old Gagool at his feet, attended by Infadoos, the boy Scragga, and twelve guards. There were also present about a score of chiefs, amongst whom I recognised most of our friends of the night before.

Twala greeted us with much apparent cordiality, though I saw him fix his one eye viciously on Umbopa.

"Welcome, white men from the Stars," he said; "this is another sight from that which your eyes gazed on by the light of last night's moon, but it is not so good a sight. Girls are pleasant, and were it not for such as these," and he pointed round him, "we should none of us be here this day; but men are better. Kisses and the tender words of women are sweet, but the sound of the clashing of the spears of warriors, and the smell of men's blood, are sweeter far! Would ye have wives from among our people, white men? If so, choose the fairest here, and ye shall have them, as many as ye will," and he paused for an answer.

As the prospect did not seem to be without attractions for Good, who, like most sailors, is of a susceptible nature, being elderly and wise, foreseeing the endless complications that anything of the sort would involve, for women bring trouble so surely as the night follows the day, I put in a hasty answer—

"Thanks to thee, O king, but we white men wed only with white women like ourselves. Your maidens are fair, but they are not for us!"

The king laughed. "It is well. In our land there is a proverb which runs, 'Women's eyes are always bright, whatever the colour,' and another that says, 'Love her who is present, for be sure she who is absent is false to thee'; but perhaps these things are not so in the Stars. In a land where men are white all things are possible. So be it, white men; the girls will not go begging! Welcome again; and welcome, too, thou black one; if Gagool here had won her way, thou wouldst have been stiff and cold by now. It is lucky for thee that thou too camest from the Stars; ha! ha!"

"I can kill thee before thou killest me, O king," was Ignosi's calm answer, "and thou shalt be stiff before my limbs cease to bend."

Twala started. "Thou speakest boldly, boy," he replied angrily; "presume not too far."

"He may well be bold in whose lips are truth. The truth is a sharp spear which flies home and misses not. It is a message from 'the Stars,' O king."

Twala scowled, and his one eye gleamed fiercely, but he said nothing more.

"Let the dance begin," he cried, and then the flower-crowned girls sprang forward in companies, singing a sweet song and waving the delicate palms and white lilies. On they danced, looking faint and spiritual in the soft, sad light of the risen moon; now whirling round and round, now meeting in mimic warfare, swaying, eddying here and there, coming forward, falling back in an ordered confusion delightful to witness. At last they paused, and a beautiful young woman sprang out of the ranks and began to pirouette in front of us with a grace and vigour which would have put most ballet girls to shame. At length she retired exhausted, and another took her place, then another and another, but none of them, either in grace, skill, or personal attractions, came up to the first.

When the chosen girls had all danced, the king lifted his hand.

"Which deem ye the fairest, white men?" he asked.

"The first," said I unthinkingly. Next second I regretted it, for I remembered that Infadoos had told us that the fairest woman must be offered up as a sacrifice.

"Then is my mind as your minds, and my eyes are your eyes. She is the fairest! and a sorry thing it is for her, for she must die!"

"*Ay, must die!*" piped out Gagool, casting a glance of her quick eyes in the direction of the poor girl, who, as yet ignorant of the awful fate in store for her, was standing some ten yards off in front of a company of maidens, engaged in nervously picking a flower from her wreath to pieces, petal by petal.

"Why, O king?" said I, restraining my indignation with difficulty; "the girl has danced well, and pleased us; she is fair too; it would be hard to reward her with death."

Twala laughed as he answered—

"It is our custom, and the figures who sit in stone yonder," and he pointed towards the three distant peaks, "must have their due. Did I fail to put the fairest girl to death to-day, misfortune would fall upon me and my house. Thus runs the prophecy of my people: 'If the king offer not a sacrifice of a fair girl, on the day of the dance of maidens, to the Old Ones who sit and watch on the mountains, then shall he fall, and his house.' Look ye, white men, my brother who reigned before me offered not the sacrifice, because of the tears of the woman, and he fell, and his house, and I reign in his stead. It is finished; she must die!" Then turning to the guards—"Bring her hither; Scragga, make sharp thy spear."

Two of the men stepped forward, and as they advanced, the girl, for the first time realising her impending fate, screamed aloud and turned to fly. But the strong hands caught her fast, and brought her, struggling and weeping, before us.

"What is thy name, girl?" piped Gagool. "What! wilt thou not answer? Shall the king's son do his work at once?"

At this hint, Scragga, looking more evil than ever, advanced a step and lifted his great spear, and at that moment I saw Good's hand creep to his revolver. The poor girl caught the faint glint of steel through her tears, and it sobered her anguish. She ceased struggling, and clasping her hands convulsively, stood shuddering from head to foot.

"See," cried Scragga in high glee, "she shrinks from the sight of my little plaything even before she has tasted it," and he tapped the broad blade of his spear.

"If ever I get the chance you shall pay for that, you young hound!" I heard Good mutter beneath his breath.

"Now that thou art quiet, give us thy name, my dear. Come, speak out, and fear not," said Gagool in mockery.

"Oh, mother," answered the girl, in trembling accents, "my name is Foulata, of the house of Suko. Oh, mother, why must I die? I have done no wrong!"

"Be comforted," went on the old woman in her hateful tone of mockery. "Thou must die, indeed, as a sacrifice to the Old Ones who sit yonder," and she pointed to the peaks; "but it is better to sleep in the night than to toil in the daytime; it is better to die than to live, and thou shalt die by the royal hand of the king's own son."

The girl Foulata wrung her hands in anguish, and cried out aloud, "Oh, cruel! and I so young! What have I done that I should never again see the sun rise out of the night, or the stars come following on his track in the evening, that I may no more gather the flowers when the dew is heavy, or listen to the laughing of the waters? Woe is me, that I shall never see my father's hut again, nor feel my mother's kiss, nor tend the lamb that is sick! Woe is me, that no lover shall put his arm around me and look into my eyes, nor shall men children be born of me! Oh, cruel, cruel!"

And again she wrung her hands and turned her tear-stained flower-crowned face to Heaven, looking so lovely in her despair—for she was indeed a beautiful woman—

that assuredly the sight of her would have melted the hearts of any less cruel than were the three fiends before us. Prince Arthur's appeal to the ruffians who came to blind him was not more touching than that of this savage girl.

But it did not move Gagool or Gagool's master, though I saw signs of pity among the guards behind, and on the faces of the chiefs; and as for Good, he gave a fierce snort of indignation, and made a motion as though to go to her assistance. With all a woman's quickness, the doomed girl interpreted what was passing in his mind, and by a sudden movement flung herself before him, and clasped his "beautiful white legs" with her hands.

"Oh, white father from the Stars!" she cried, "throw over me the mantle of thy protection; let me creep into the shadow of thy strength, that I may be saved. Oh, keep me from these cruel men and from the mercies of Gagool!"

"All right, my hearty, I'll look after you," sang out Good in nervous Saxon. "Come, get up, there's a good girl," and he stooped and caught her hand.

Twala turned and motioned to his son, who advanced with his spear lifted.

"Now's your time," whispered Sir Henry to me; "what are you waiting for?"

"I am waiting for that eclipse," I answered; "I have had my eye on the moon for the last half-hour, and I never saw it look healthier."

"Well, you must risk it now, or the girl will be killed. Twala is losing patience."

Recognising the force of the argument, and having cast one more despairing look at the bright face of the moon, for never did the most ardent astronomer with a theory to prove await a celestial event with such anxiety, I stepped with all the dignity that I could command between the prostrate girl and the advancing spear of Scragga.

"King," I said, "it shall not be; we will not endure this thing; let the girl go in safety."

Twala rose from his seat in wrath and astonishment, and from the chiefs and serried ranks of maidens who had closed in slowly upon us in anticipation of the tragedy came a murmur of amazement.

"*Shall not be!* thou white dog, that yappest at the lion in his cave; *shall not be!* art thou mad? Be careful, lest this chicken's fate overtake thee, and those with thee. How canst thou save her or thyself? Who art thou that thou settest thyself between me and my will? Back, I say. Scragga, kill her! Ho, guards! seize these men."

At his cry armed men ran swiftly from behind the hut, where they had evidently been placed beforehand.

Sir Henry, Good, and Umbopa ranged themselves alongside of me, and lifted their rifles.

"Stop!" I shouted boldly, though at the moment my heart was in my boots. "Stop! we, the white men from the Stars, say that it shall not be. Come but one pace nearer, and we will put out the moon like a wind-blown lamp, as we who dwell in her House can do, and plunge the land in darkness. Dare to disobey, and ye shall taste of our magic."

My threat produced an effect; the men halted, and Scragga stood still before us, his spear lifted.

"Hear him! hear him!" piped Gagool; "hear the liar who says that he will put out the moon like a lamp. Let him do it, and the girl shall be spared. Yes, let him do it, or die by the girl, he and those with him."

I glanced up at the moon despairingly, and now to my intense joy and relief saw that we—or rather the almanack—had made no mistake. On the edge of the great orb lay a faint rim of shadow, while a smoky hue grew and gathered upon its bright surface. Never shall I forget that supreme, that superb moment of relief.

Then I lifted my hand solemnly towards the sky, an example which Sir Henry and Good followed, and quoted a line or two from the "Ingoldsby Legends" at it in the most impressive tones that I could command. Sir Henry followed suit with a verse out of the Old Testament, and something about Balbus building a wall, in Latin, whilst Good addressed the Queen of Night in a volume of the most classical bad language which he could think of.

Slowly the penumbra, the shadow of a shadow, crept on over the bright surface, and as it crept I heard deep gasps of fear rising from the multitude around.

"Look, O king!" I cried; "look, Gagool! Look, chiefs and people and women, and see if the white men from the Stars keep their word, or if they be but empty liars!

"The moon grows black before your eyes; soon there will be darkness—ay, darkness in the hour of the full moon. Ye have asked for a sign; it is given to you. Grow dark, O Moon! withdraw thy light, thou pure and holy One; bring the proud heart of usurping murderers to the dust, and eat up the world with shadows."

A groan of terror burst from the onlookers. Some stood petrified with dread, others threw themselves upon their knees and cried aloud. As for the king, he sat still and turned pale beneath his dusky skin. Only Gagool kept her courage.

"It will pass," she cried; "I have often seen the like before; no man can put out the moon; lose not heart; sit still—the shadow will pass."

"Wait, and ye shall see," I replied, hopping with excitement. "O Moon! Moon! Moon! wherefore art thou so cold and fickle?" This appropriate quotation was from the pages of a popular romance that I chanced to have read recently, though now I come to think of it, it was ungrateful of me to abuse the Lady of the Heavens, who was showing herself to be the truest of friends to us, however she may have behaved to the impassioned lover in the novel. Then I added: "Keep it up, Good, I can't remember any more poetry. Curse away, there's a good fellow."

Good responded nobly to this tax upon his inventive faculties. Never before had I the faintest conception of the breadth and depth and height of a naval officer's objurgatory powers. For ten minutes he went on in several languages without stopping, and he scarcely ever repeated himself.

Meanwhile the dark ring crept on, while all that great assembly fixed their eyes upon the sky and stared and stared in fascinated silence. Strange and unholy shadows encroached upon the moonlight, an ominous quiet filled the place. Everything grew still as death. Slowly and in the midst of this most solemn silence the minutes sped away, and while they sped the full moon passed deeper and deeper into the shadow of the earth, as the inky segment of its circle slid in awful majesty across the lunar craters. The great pale orb seemed to draw near and to grow in size. She turned a coppery hue, then that portion of her surface which was unobscured as yet grew grey and ashen, and at length, as totality approached, her mountains and her plains were to be seen glowing luridly through a crimson gloom.

On, yet on, crept the ring of darkness; it was now more than half across the blood-red orb. The air grew thick, and still more deeply tinged with dusky crimson. On, yet on, till we could scarcely see the fierce faces of the group before us. No sound rose now from the spectators, and at last Good stopped swearing.

"The moon is dying—the white wizards have killed the moon," yelled the prince Scragga at last. "We shall all perish in the dark," and animated by fear or fury, or by both, he lifted his spear and drove it with all his force at Sir Henry's breast. But he forgot the mail shirts that the king had given us, and which we wore beneath our clothing. The steel rebounded harmless, and before he could repeat the blow Curtis had snatched the spear from his hand and sent it straight through him.

Scragga dropped dead.

At the sight, and driven mad with fear of the gathering darkness, and of the unholy shadow which, as they believed, was swallowing the moon, the companies of girls broke up in wild confusion, and ran screeching for the gateways. Nor did the panic stop there. The king himself, followed by his guards, some of the chiefs, and Gagool, who hobbled away after them with marvellous alacrity, fled for the huts, so that in another minute we ourselves, the would-be victim Foulata, Infadoos, and most of the chiefs who had interviewed us on the previous night, were left alone upon the scene, together with the dead body of Scragga, Twala's son.

"Chiefs," I said, "we have given you the sign. If ye are satisfied, let us fly swiftly to the place of which ye spoke. The charm cannot now be stopped. It will work for an hour and the half of an hour. Let us cover ourselves in the darkness."

"Come," said Infadoos, turning to go, an example which was followed by the awed captains, ourselves, and the girl Foulata, whom Good took by the arm.

Before we reached the gate of the kraal the moon went out utterly, and from every quarter of the firmament the stars rushed forth into the inky sky.

Holding each other by the hand we stumbled on through the darkness.

XII. Before the Battle

Luckily for us, Infadoos and the chiefs knew all the paths of the great town perfectly, so that we passed by side-ways unmolested, and notwithstanding the gloom we made fair progress.

For an hour or more we journeyed on, till at length the eclipse began to pass, and that edge of the moon which had disappeared the first became again visible. Suddenly, as we watched, there burst from it a silver streak of light, accompanied by a wondrous ruddy glow, which hung upon the blackness of the sky like a celestial lamp, and a wild and lovely sight it was. In another five minutes the stars began to fade, and there was sufficient light to see our whereabouts. We then discovered that we were clear of the town of Loo, and approaching a large flat-topped hill, measuring some two miles in circumference. This hill, which is of a formation common in South Africa, is not very high; indeed, its greatest elevation is scarcely more than 200 feet, but it is shaped like a horseshoe, and its sides are rather precipitous and strewn with boulders. On the grass table-land at its summit is ample camping-ground, which had been utilised as a military cantonment of no mean strength. Its ordinary garrison was one regiment of three thousand men, but as we toiled up the steep side of the mountain in the returning moonlight we perceived that there were several of such regiments upon it.

Reaching the table-land at last, we found crowds of men roused from their sleep, shivering with fear and huddled up together in the utmost consternation at the natural phenomenon which they were witnessing. Passing through these without a word, we gained a hut in the centre of the ground, where we were astonished to find two men waiting, laden with our few goods and chattels, which of course we had been obliged to leave behind in our hasty flight.

"I sent for them," explained Infadoos; "and also for these," and he lifted up Good's long-lost trousers.

With an exclamation of rapturous delight Good sprang at them, and instantly proceeded to put them on.

"Surely my lord will not hide his beautiful white legs!" exclaimed Infadoos regretfully.

But Good persisted, and once only did the Kukuana people get the chance of seeing his beautiful legs again. Good is a very modest man. Henceforward they had to satisfy their æsthetic longings with his one whisker, his transparent eye, and his movable teeth.

Still gazing with fond remembrance at Good's trousers, Infadoos next informed us that he had commanded the regiments to muster so soon as the day broke, in order to explain to them fully the origin and circumstances of the rebellion which was decided on by the chiefs, and to introduce to them the rightful heir to the throne, Ignosi.

Accordingly, when the sun was up, the troops—in all some twenty thousand men, and the flower of the Kukuana army—were mustered on a large open space, to which we went. The men were drawn up in three sides of a dense square, and presented a magnificent spectacle. We took our station on the open side of the square, and were speedily surrounded by all the principal chiefs and officers.

These, after silence had been proclaimed, Infadoos proceeded to address. He narrated to them in vigorous and graceful language—for, like most Kukuanas of high rank, he was a born orator—the history of Ignosi's father, and of how he had been basely murdered by Twala the king, and his wife and child driven out to starve. Then he pointed out that the people suffered and groaned under Twala's cruel rule, instancing the proceedings of the previous night, when, under pretence of their being evil-doers, many of the noblest in the land had been dragged forth and wickedly done to death. Next he went on to say that the white lords from the Stars, looking down upon their country, had perceived its trouble, and determined, at great personal inconvenience, to alleviate its lot: That they had accordingly taken the real king of the Kukuanas, Ignosi, who was languishing in exile, by the hand, and led him over the mountains: That they had seen the wickedness of Twala's doings, and for a sign to the wavering, and to save the life of the girl Foulata, actually, by the exercise of their high magic, had put out the moon and slain the young fiend Scragga; and that they were prepared to stand by them, and assist them to overthrow Twala, and set up the rightful king, Ignosi, in his place.

He finished his discourse amidst a murmur of approbation. Then Ignosi stepped forward and began to speak. Having reiterated all that Infadoos his uncle had said, he concluded a powerful speech in these words:—

"O chiefs, captains, soldiers, and people, ye have heard my words. Now must ye make choice between me and him who sits upon my throne, the uncle who killed his brother, and hunted his brother's child forth to die in the cold and the night. That I am indeed the king these"—pointing to the chiefs—"can tell you, for they have seen the snake about my middle. If I were not the king, would these white men be on my side with all their magic? Tremble, chiefs, captains, soldiers, and people! Is not the darkness they have brought upon the land to confound Twala and cover our flight, darkness even in the hour of the full moon, yet before your eyes?"

"It is," answered the soldiers.

"I am the king; I say to you, I am the king," went on Ignosi, drawing up his great stature to its full, and lifting his broad-bladed battle-axe above his head. "If there be any man among you who says that it is not so, let him stand forth and I will fight him now, and his blood shall be a red token that I tell you true. Let him stand forth, I say"; and he shook the great axe till it flashed in the sunlight.

As nobody seemed inclined to respond to this heroic version of "Dilly, Dilly, come and be killed," our late henchman proceeded with his address.

"I am indeed the king, and should ye stand by my side in the battle, if I win the day ye shall go with me to victory and honour. I will give you oxen and wives, and ye shall take place of all the regiments; and if ye fall, I will fall with you.

"And behold, I give you this promise, that when I sit upon the seat of my fathers, bloodshed shall cease in the land. No longer shall ye cry for justice to find slaughter, no longer shall the witch-finder hunt you out so that ye may be slain without a cause. No man shall die save he who offends against the laws. The 'eating up' of your kraals shall cease; each one of you shall sleep secure in his own hut and fear naught, and justice shall walk blindfold throughout the land. Have ye chosen, chiefs, captains, soldiers, and people?"

"We have chosen, O king," came back the answer.

"It is well. Turn your heads and see how Twala's messengers go forth from the great town, east and west, and north and south, to gather a mighty army to slay me and you, and these my friends and protectors. To-morrow, or perchance the next day, he will come against us with all who are faithful to him. Then I shall see the man who is indeed my man, the man who fears not to die for his cause; and I tell you that he shall not be forgotten in the time of spoil. I have spoken, O chiefs, captains, soldiers, and people. Now go to your huts and make you ready for war."

There was a pause, till presently one of the chiefs lifted his hand, and out rolled the royal salute, "*Koom.*" It was a sign that the soldiers accepted Ignosi as their king. Then they marched off in battalions.

Half an hour afterwards we held a council of war, at which all the commanders of regiments were present. It was evident to us that before very long we should be attacked in overwhelming force. Indeed, from our point of vantage on the hill we could see troops mustering, and runners going forth from Loo in every direction, doubtless to summon soldiers to the king's assistance. We had on our side about twenty thousand

men, composed of seven of the best regiments in the country. Twala, so Infadoos and
the chiefs calculated, had at least thirty to thirty-five thousand on whom he could rely
at present assembled in Loo, and they thought that by midday on the morrow he would
be able to gather another five thousand or more to his aid. It was, of course, possible
that some of his troops would desert and come over to us, but it was not a contingency
which could be reckoned on. Meanwhile, it was clear that active preparations were
being made to subdue us. Already strong bodies of armed men were patrolling round
and round the foot of the hill, and there were other signs of coming assault.

Infadoos and the chiefs, however, were of opinion that no attack would take place
that day, which would be devoted to preparation and to the removal of every available
means of the moral effect produced upon the minds of the soldiery by the supposed
magical darkening of the moon. The onslaught would be on the morrow, they said,
and they proved to be right.

Meanwhile, we set to work to strengthen the position in all ways possible. Almost
every man was turned out, and in the course of the day, which seemed far too short,
much was done. The paths up the hill—that was rather a sanatorium than a fortress,
being used generally as the camping place of regiments suffering from recent service in
unhealthy portions of the country—were carefully blocked with masses of stones, and
every other approach was made as impregnable as time would allow. Piles of boulders
were collected at various spots to be rolled down upon an advancing enemy, stations
were appointed to the different regiments, and all preparation was made which our
joint ingenuity could suggest.

Just before sundown, as we rested after our toil, we perceived a small company of
men advancing towards us from the direction of Loo, one of whom bore a palm leaf in
his hand for a sign that he came as a herald.

As he drew near, Ignosi, Infadoos, one or two chiefs and ourselves, went down
to the foot of the mountain to meet him. He was a gallant-looking fellow, wearing the
regulation leopard-skin cloak.

"Greeting!" he cried, as he came; "the king's greeting to those who make unholy
war against the king; the lion's greeting to the jackals that snarl around his heels."

"Speak," I said.

"These are the king's words. Surrender to the king's mercy ere a worse thing
befall you. Already the shoulder has been torn from the black bull, and the king drives
him bleeding about the camp."*

---

* This cruel custom is not confined to the Kukuanas, but is by no means uncommon amongst African
tribes on the occasion of the outbreak of war or any other important public event.—A.Q.

"What are Twala's terms?" I asked from curiosity.

"His terms are merciful, worthy of a great king. These are the words of Twala, the one-eyed, the mighty, the husband of a thousand wives, lord of the Kukuanas, keeper of the Great Road (Solomon's Road), beloved of the Strange Ones who sit in silence at the mountains yonder (the Three Witches), Calf of the Black Cow, Elephant whose tread shakes the earth, Terror of the evil-doer, Ostrich whose feet devour the desert, huge One, black One, wise One, king from generation to generation! these are the words of Twala: 'I will have mercy and be satisfied with a little blood. One in every ten shall die, the rest shall go free; but the white man Incubu, who slew Scragga my son, and the black man his servant, who pretends to my throne, and Infadoos my brother, who brews rebellion against me, these shall die by torture as an offering to the Silent Ones.' Such are the merciful words of Twala."

After consulting with the others a little, I answered him in a loud voice, so that the soldiers might hear, thus—

"Go back, thou dog, to Twala, who sent thee, and say that we, Ignosi, veritable king of the Kukuanas, Incubu, Bougwan, and Macumazahn, the wise ones from the Stars, who make dark the moon, Infadoos, of the royal house, and the chiefs, captains, and people here gathered, make answer and say, 'That we will not surrender; that before the sun has gone down twice, Twala's corpse shall stiffen at Twala's gate, and Ignosi, whose father Twala slew, shall reign in his stead.' Now go, ere we whip thee away, and beware how thou dost lift a hand against such as we are."

The herald laughed loudly. "Ye frighten not men with such swelling words," he cried out. "Show yourselves as bold to-morrow, O ye who darken the moon. Be bold, fight, and be merry, before the crows pick your bones till they are whiter than your faces. Farewell; perhaps we may meet in the fight; fly not to the Stars, but wait for me, I pray, white men." With this shaft of sarcasm he retired, and almost immediately the sun sank.

That night was a busy one, for weary as we were, so far as was possible by the moonlight all preparations for the morrow's fight were continued, and messengers were constantly coming and going from the place where we sat in council. At last, about an hour after midnight, everything that could be done was done, and the camp, save for the occasional challenge of a sentry, sank into silence. Sir Henry and I, accompanied by Ignosi and one of the chiefs, descended the hill and made a round of the outposts. As we went, suddenly, from all sorts of unexpected places, spears gleamed out in the moonlight, only to vanish again when we uttered the password. It was clear to us that none were sleeping at their posts. Then we returned, picking our way through thousands of sleeping warriors, many of whom were taking their last earthly rest.

The moonlight flickering along their spears, played upon their features and made them ghastly; the chilly night wind tossed their tall and hearse-like plumes. There they lay in wild confusion, with arms outstretched and twisted limbs; their stern, stalwart forms looking weird and unhuman in the moonlight.

"How many of these do you suppose will be alive at this time to-morrow?" asked Sir Henry.

I shook my head and looked again at the sleeping men, and to my tired and yet excited imagination it seemed as though Death had already touched them. My mind's eye singled out those who were sealed to slaughter, and there rushed in upon my heart a great sense of the mystery of human life, and an overwhelming sorrow at its futility and sadness. To-night these thousands slept their healthy sleep, to-morrow they, and many others with them, ourselves perhaps among them, would be stiffening in the cold; their wives would be widows, their children fatherless, and their place know them no more for ever. Only the old moon would shine on serenely, the night wind would stir the grasses, and the wide earth would take its rest, even as it did æons before we were, and will do æons after we have been forgotten.

Yet man dies not whilst the world, at once his mother and his monument, remains. His name is lost, indeed, but the breath he breathed still stirs the pine-tops on the mountains, the sound of the words he spoke yet echoes on through space; the thoughts his brain gave birth to we have inherited to-day; his passions are our cause of life; the joys and sorrows that he knew are our familiar friends—the end from which he fled aghast will surely overtake us also!

Truly the universe is full of ghosts, not sheeted churchyard spectres, but the inextinguishable elements of individual life, which having once been, can never *die*, though they blend and change, and change again for ever.

All sorts of reflections of this nature passed through my mind—for as I grow older I regret to say that a detestable habit of thinking seems to be getting a hold of me—while I stood and stared at those grim yet fantastic lines of warriors, sleeping, as their saying goes, "upon their spears."

"Curtis," I said, "I am in a condition of pitiable fear."

Sir Henry stroked his yellow beard and laughed, as he answered—

"I have heard you make that sort of remark before, Quatermain."

"Well, I mean it now. Do you know, I very much doubt if one of us will be alive to-morrow night. We shall be attacked in overwhelming force, and it is quite a chance if we can hold this place."

"We'll give a good account of some of them, at any rate. Look here, Quatermain, this business is nasty, and one with which, properly speaking, we ought not to be mixed up, but we are in for it, so we must make the best of our job. Speaking personally, I had rather be killed fighting than any other way, and now that there seems little chance of our finding my poor brother, it makes the idea easier to me. But fortune favours the brave, and we may succeed. Anyway, the battle will be awful, and having a reputation to keep up, we shall need to be in the thick of it."

He made this last remark in a mournful voice, but there was a gleam in his eye which belied its melancholy. I have an idea Sir Henry Curtis actually likes fighting.

After this we went to sleep for a couple of hours.

Just about dawn we were awakened by Infadoos, who came to say that great activity was to be observed in Loo, and that parties of the king's skirmishers were driving in our outposts.

We got up and dressed ourselves for the fray, each putting on his chain armour shirt, for which garments at the present juncture we felt exceedingly thankful. Sir Henry went the whole length about the matter, and dressed himself like a native warrior. "When you are in Kukuanaland, do as the Kukuanas do," he remarked, as he drew the shining steel over his broad breast, which it fitted like a glove. Nor did he stop there. At his request Infadoos had provided him with a complete set of native war uniform. Round his throat he fastened the leopard-skin cloak of a commanding officer, on his brows he bound the plume of black ostrich feathers worn only by generals of high rank, and about his middle a magnificent moocha of white ox-tails. A pair of sandals, a leglet of goat's hair, a heavy battle-axe with a rhinoceros-horn handle, a round iron shield covered with white ox-hide, and the regulation number of *tollas*, or throwing-knives, made up his equipment, to which, however, he added his revolver. The dress was, no doubt, a savage one, but I am bound to say that I seldom saw a finer sight than Sir Henry Curtis presented in this guise. It showed off his magnificent physique to the greatest advantage, and when Ignosi arrived presently, arrayed in a similar costume, I thought to myself that I had never before seen two such splendid men.

As for Good and myself, the armour did not suit us nearly so well. To begin with, Good insisted upon keeping on his new-found trousers, and a stout, short gentleman with an eye-glass, and one half of his face shaved, arrayed in a mail shirt, carefully tucked into a very seedy pair of corduroys, looks more remarkable than imposing. In my case, the chain shirt being too big for me, I put it on over all my clothes, which caused it to bulge in a somewhat ungainly fashion. I discarded my trousers, however, retaining only my veldtschoons, having determined to go into battle with bare legs, in order to be the lighter for running, in case it became necessary to retire quickly.

The mail coat, a spear, a shield, that I did not know how to use, a couple of *tollas*, a revolver, and a huge plume, which I pinned into the top of my shooting hat, in order to give a bloodthirsty finish to my appearance, completed my modest equipment. In addition to all these articles, of course we had our rifles, but as ammunition was scarce, and as they would be useless in case of a charge, we arranged that they should be carried behind us by bearers.

When at length we had equipped ourselves, we swallowed some food hastily, and then started out to see how things were going on. At one point in the table-land of the mountain, there was a little koppie of brown stone, which served the double purpose of head-quarters and of a conning tower. Here we found Infadoos surrounded by his own regiment, the Greys, which was undoubtedly the finest in the Kukuana army, and the same that we had first seen at the outlying kraal. This regiment, now three thousand five hundred strong, was being held in reserve, and the men were lying down on the grass in companies, and watching the king's forces creep out of Loo in long ant-like columns. There seemed to be no end to the length of these columns—three in all, and each of them numbering, as we judged, at least eleven or twelve thousand men.

As soon as they were clear of the town the regiments formed up. Then one body marched off to the right, one to the left, and the third came on slowly towards us.

"Ah," said Infadoos, "they are going to attack us on three sides at once."

This seemed rather serious news, for our position on the top of the mountain, which measured a mile and a half in circumference, being an extended one, it was important to us to concentrate our comparatively small defending force as much as possible. But since it was impossible for us to dictate in what way we should be attacked, we had to make the best of it, and accordingly sent orders to the various regiments to prepare to receive the separate onslaughts.

XIII. THE ATTACK

Slowly, and without the slightest appearance of haste or excitement, the three columns crept on. When within about five hundred yards of us, the main or centre column halted at the root of a tongue of open plain which ran up into the hill, to give time to the other divisions to circumvent our position, which was shaped more or less in the form of a horse-shoe, with its two points facing towards the town of Loo. The object of this manoeuvre was that the threefold assault should be delivered simultaneously.

"Oh, for a gatling!" groaned Good, as he contemplated the serried phalanxes beneath us. "I would clear that plain in twenty minutes."

"We have not got one, so it is no use yearning for it; but suppose you try a shot, Quatermain," said Sir Henry. "See how near you can go to that tall fellow who appears to be in command. Two to one you miss him, and an even sovereign, to be honestly paid if ever we get out of this, that you don't drop the bullet within five yards."

This piqued me, so, loading the express with solid ball, I waited till my friend walked some ten yards out from his force, in order to get a better view of our position, accompanied only by an orderly; then, lying down and resting the express on a rock, I covered him. The rifle, like all expresses, was only sighted to three hundred and fifty yards, so to allow for the drop in trajectory I took him half-way down the neck, which ought, I calculated, to find him in the chest. He stood quite still and gave me every opportunity, but whether it was the excitement or the wind, or the fact of the man being a long shot, I don't know, but this was what happened. Getting dead on, as I thought, a fine sight, I pressed, and when the puff of smoke had cleared away, to my disgust, I saw my man standing there unharmed, whilst his orderly, who was at least three paces to the left, was stretched upon the ground apparently dead. Turning swiftly, the officer I had aimed at began to run towards his men in evident alarm.

"Bravo, Quatermain!" sang out Good; "you've frightened him."

This made me very angry, for, if possible to avoid it, I hate to miss in public. When a man is master of only one art he likes to keep up his reputation in that art. Moved quite out of myself at my failure, I did a rash thing. Rapidly covering the general as he ran, I let drive with the second barrel. Instantly the poor man threw up his arms, and fell forward on to his face. This time I had made no mistake; and—I say it as a proof of how little we think of others when our own safety, pride, or reputation is in question—I was brute enough to feel delighted at the sight.

The regiments who had seen the feat cheered wildly at this exhibition of the white man's magic, which they took as an omen of success, while the force the general had belonged to—which, indeed, as we ascertained afterwards, he had commanded—fell back in confusion. Sir Henry and Good now took up their rifles and began to fire, the latter industriously "browning" the dense mass before him with another Winchester repeater, and I also had another shot or two, with the result, so far as we could judge, that we put some six or eight men *hors de combat* before they were out of range.

Just as we stopped firing there came an ominous roar from our far right, then a similar roar rose on our left. The two other divisions were engaging us.

At the sound, the mass of men before us opened out a little, and advanced towards the hill and up the spit of bare grass land at a slow trot, singing a deep-throated song as they ran. We kept up a steady fire from our rifles as they came, Ignosi joining in occasionally, and accounted for several men, but of course we produced no more effect upon that mighty rush of armed humanity than he who throws pebbles does on the breaking wave.

On they came, with a shout and the clashing of spears; now they were driving in the pickets we had placed among the rocks at the foot of the hill. After that the advance was a little slower, for though as yet we had offered no serious opposition, the attacking forces must climb up hill, and they came slowly to save their breath. Our first line of defence was about half-way down the side of the slope, our second fifty yards further back, while our third occupied the edge of the plateau.

On they stormed, shouting their war-cry, "*Twala! Twala! Chiele! Chiele!*" (Twala! Twala! Smite! Smite!) "*Ignosi! Ignosi! Chiele! Chiele!*" answered our people. They were quite close now, and the *tollas*, or throwing-knives, began to flash backwards and forwards, and now with an awful yell the battle closed in.

To and fro swayed the mass of struggling warriors, men falling fast as leaves in an autumn wind; but before long the superior weight of the attacking force began to tell, and our first line of defence was slowly pressed back till it merged into the second. Here the struggle was very fierce, but again our people were driven back and up, till at length, within twenty minutes of the commencement of the fight, our third line came into action.

But by this time the assailants were much exhausted, and besides had lost many men killed and wounded, and to break through that third impenetrable hedge of spears proved beyond their powers. For a while the seething lines of savages swung backwards and forwards, in the fierce ebb and flow of battle, and the issue was doubtful. Sir Henry watched the desperate struggle with a kindling eye, and then without a word he rushed off, followed by Good, and flung himself into the hottest of the fray. As for myself, I stopped where I was.

The soldiers caught sight of his tall form as he plunged into battle, and there rose a cry of—

"*Nanzia Incubu! Nanzia Unkungunklovo!*" (Here is the Elephant!) "*Chiele! Chiele!*"

From that moment the end was no longer in doubt. Inch by inch, fighting with splendid gallantry, the attacking force was pressed back down the hillside, till at last it retreated upon its reserves in something like confusion. At that instant, too, a messenger arrived to say that the left attack had been repulsed; and I was just beginning to congratulate myself, believing that the affair was over for the present, when, to our horror, we perceived our men who had been engaged in the right defence being driven towards us across the plain, followed by swarms of the enemy, who had evidently succeeded at this point.

Ignosi, who was standing by me, took in the situation at a glance, and issued a rapid order. Instantly the reserve regiment around us, the Greys, extended itself.

Again Ignosi gave a word of command, which was taken up and repeated by the captains, and in another second, to my intense disgust, I found myself involved in a furious onslaught upon the advancing foe. Getting as much as I could behind Ignosi's huge frame, I made the best of a bad job, and toddled along to be killed as though I liked it. In a minute or two—the time seemed all too short to me—we were plunging through the flying groups of our men, who at once began to re-form behind us, and then I am sure I do not know what happened. All I can remember is a dreadful rolling noise of the meeting of shields, and the sudden apparition of a huge ruffian, whose eyes seemed literally to be starting out of his head, making straight at me with a bloody spear. But—I say it with pride—I rose—or rather sank—to the occasion. It was one before which most people would have collapsed once and for all. Seeing that if I stood where I was I must be killed, as the horrid apparition came I flung myself down in front of him so cleverly that, being unable to stop himself, he took a header right over my prostrate form. Before he could rise again, I had risen and settled the matter from behind with my revolver.

Shortly after this somebody knocked me down, and I remember no more of that charge.

When I came to I found myself back at the koppie, with Good bending over me holding some water in a gourd.

"How do you feel, old fellow?" he asked anxiously.

I got up and shook myself before replying.

"Pretty well, thank you," I answered.

"Thank Heaven! When I saw them carry you in, I felt quite sick; I thought you were done for."

"Not this time, my boy. I fancy I only got a rap on the head, which knocked me stupid. How has it ended?"

"They are repulsed at every point for a while. The loss is dreadfully heavy; we have quite two thousand killed and wounded, and they must have lost three. Look, there's a sight!" and he pointed to long lines of men advancing by fours.

In the centre of every group of four, and being borne by it, was a kind of hide tray, of which a Kukuana force always carries a quantity, with a loop for a handle at each corner. On these trays—and their number seemed endless—lay wounded men, who as they arrived were hastily examined by the medicine men, of whom ten were attached to a regiment. If the wound was not of a fatal character the sufferer was taken away and attended to as carefully as circumstances would allow. But if, on the other hand, the injured man's condition proved hopeless, what followed was very dreadful, though doubtless it may have been the truest mercy. One of the doctors, under pretence of carrying out an examination, swiftly opened an artery with a sharp knife, and in a minute or two the sufferer expired painlessly. There were many cases that day in which this was done. In fact, it was done in the majority of cases when the wound was in the body, for the gash made by the entry of the enormously broad spears used by the Kukuanas generally rendered recovery impossible. In most instances the poor sufferers were already unconscious, and in others the fatal "nick" of the artery was inflicted so swiftly and painlessly that they did not seem to notice it. Still it was a ghastly sight, and one from which we were glad to escape; indeed, I never remember anything of the kind that affected me more than seeing those gallant soldiers thus put out of pain by the red-handed medicine men, except, indeed, on one occasion when, after an attack, I saw a force of Swazis burying their hopelessly wounded *alive*.

Hurrying from this dreadful scene to the further side of the koppie, we found Sir Henry, who still held a battle-axe in his hand, Ignosi, Infadoos, and one or two of the chiefs in deep consultation.

"Thank Heaven, here you are, Quatermain! I can't quite make out what Ignosi wants to do. It seems that though we have beaten off the attack, Twala is now receiving large reinforcements, and is showing a disposition to invest us, with the view of starving us out."

"That's awkward."

"Yes; especially as Infadoos says that the water supply has given out."

"My lord, that is so," said Infadoos; "the spring cannot supply the wants of so great a multitude, and it is failing rapidly. Before night we shall all be thirsty. Listen, Macumazahn. Thou art wise, and hast doubtless seen many wars in the lands from whence thou camest—that is if indeed they make wars in the Stars. Now tell us, what shall we do? Twala has brought up many fresh men to take the place of those who have fallen. Yet Twala has learnt his lesson; the hawk did not think to find the heron ready; but our beak has pierced his breast; he fears to strike at us again. We too are wounded, and he will wait for us to die; he will wind himself round us like a snake round a buck, and fight the fight of 'sit down.'"

"I hear thee," I said.

"So, Macumazahn, thou seest we have no water here, and but a little food, and we must choose between these three things—to languish like a starving lion in his den, or to strive to break away towards the north, or"—and here he rose and pointed towards the dense mass of our foes—"to launch ourselves straight at Twala's throat. Incubu, the great warrior—for to-day he fought like a buffalo in a net, and Twala's soldiers went down before his axe like young corn before the hail; with these eyes I saw it—Incubu says 'Charge'; but the Elephant is ever prone to charge. Now what says Macumazahn, the wily old fox, who has seen much, and loves to bite his enemy from behind? The last word is in Ignosi the king, for it is a king's right to speak of war; but let us hear thy voice, O Macumazahn, who watchest by night, and the voice too of him of the transparent eye."

"What sayest thou, Ignosi," I asked.

"Nay, my father," answered our quondam servant, who now, clad as he was in the full panoply of savage war, looked every inch a warrior king, "do thou speak, and let me, who am but a child in wisdom beside thee, hearken to thy words."

Thus adjured, after taking hasty counsel with Good and Sir Henry, I delivered my opinion briefly to the effect that, being trapped, our best chance, especially in view of the failure of our water supply, was to initiate an attack upon Twala's forces. Then I recommended that the attack should be delivered at once, "before our wounds grew stiff," and also before the sight of Twala's overpowering force caused the hearts of our soldiers "to wax small like fat before a fire." Otherwise, I pointed out, some of the captains might change their minds, and, making peace with Twala, desert to him, or even betray us into his hands.

This expression of opinion seemed, on the whole, to be favourably received; indeed, among the Kukuanas my utterances met with a respect which has never been accorded to them before or since. But the real decision as to our plans lay with Ignosi, who, since he had been recognised as rightful king, could exercise the almost unbounded rights of sovereignty, including, of course, the final decision on matters of generalship, and it was to him that all eyes were now turned.

At length, after a pause, during which he appeared to be thinking deeply, he spoke.

"Incubu, Macumazahn, and Bougwan, brave white men, and my friends; Infadoos, my uncle, and chiefs; my heart is fixed. I will strike at Twala this day, and set my fortunes on the blow, ay, and my life—my life and your lives also. Listen; thus will I strike. Ye see how the hill curves round like the half-moon, and how the plain runs like a green tongue towards us within the curve?"

"We see," I answered.

"Good; it is now mid-day, and the men eat and rest after the toil of battle. When the sun has turned and travelled a little way towards the darkness, let thy regiment, my uncle, advance with one other down to the green tongue, and it shall be that when Twala sees it he will hurl his force at it to crush it. But the spot is narrow, and the regiments can come against thee one at a time only; so may they be destroyed one by one, and the eyes of all Twala's army shall be fixed upon a struggle the like of which has not been seen by living man. And with thee, my uncle, shall go Incubu my friend, that when Twala sees his battle-axe flashing in the first rank of the Greys his heart may grow faint. And I will come with the second regiment, that which follows thee, so that if ye are destroyed, as it might happen, there may yet be a king left to fight for; and with me shall come Macumazahn the wise."

"It is well, O king," said Infadoos, apparently contemplating the certainty of the complete annihilation of his regiment with perfect calmness. Truly, these Kukuanas are a wonderful people. Death has no terrors for them when it is incurred in the course of duty.

"And whilst the eyes of the multitude of Twala's soldiers are thus fixed upon the fight," went on Ignosi, "behold, one-third of the men who are left alive to us (*i.e.*, about 6,000) shall creep along the right horn of the hill and fall upon the left flank of Twala's force, and one-third shall creep along the left horn and fall upon Twala's right flank. And when I see that the horns are ready to toss Twala, then will I, with the men who remain to me, charge home in Twala's face, and if fortune goes with us the day will be ours, and before Night drives her black oxen from the mountains to the mountains we shall sit in peace at Loo. And now let us eat and make ready; and, Infadoos, do thou prepare, that the plan be carried out without fail; and stay, let my white father Bougwan go with the right horn, that his shining eye may give courage to the captains."

The arrangements for attack thus briefly indicated were set in motion with a rapidity that spoke well for the perfection of the Kukuana military system. Within little more than an hour rations had been served out and devoured, the divisions were formed, the scheme of onslaught was explained to the leaders, and the whole force, numbering about 18,000 men, was ready to move, with the exception of a guard left in charge of the wounded.

Presently Good came up to Sir Henry and myself.

"Good-bye, you fellows," he said; "I am off with the right wing according to orders; and so I have come to shake hands, in case we should not meet again, you know," he added significantly.

We shook hands in silence, and not without the exhibition of as much emotion as Englishmen wont to show.

"It is a queer business," said Sir Henry, his deep voice shaking a little, "and I confess I never expect to see to-morrow's sun. So far as I can make out, the Greys, with whom I am to go, are to fight until they are wiped out in order to enable the wings to slip round unawares and outflank Twala. Well, so be it; at any rate, it will be a man's death. Good-bye, old fellow. God bless you! I hope you will pull through and live to collar the diamonds; but if you do, take my advice and don't have anything more to do with Pretenders!"

In another second Good had wrung us both by the hand and gone; and then Infadoos came up and led off Sir Henry to his place in the forefront of the Greys, whilst, with many misgivings, I departed with Ignosi to my station in the second attacking regiment.

XIV. The Last Stand of the Greys

In a few more minutes the regiments destined to carry out the flanking movements had tramped off in silence, keeping carefully to the lee of the rising ground in order to conceal their advance from the keen eyes of Twala's scouts.

Half an hour or more was allowed to elapse between the setting out of the horns or wings of the army before any stir was made by the Greys and their supporting regiment, known as the Buffaloes, which formed its chest, and were destined to bear the brunt of the battle.

Both of these regiments were almost perfectly fresh, and of full strength, the Greys having been in reserve in the morning, and having lost but a small number of men in sweeping back that part of the attack which had proved successful in breaking the line of defence, on the occasion when I charged with them and was stunned for my pains. As for the Buffaloes, they had formed the third line of defence on the left, and since the attacking force at that point had not succeeded in breaking through the second, they had scarcely come into action at all.

Infadoos, who was a wary old general, and knew the absolute importance of keeping up the spirits of his men on the eve of such a desperate encounter, employed the pause in addressing his own regiment, the Greys, in poetical language: explaining to them the honour that they were receiving in being put thus in the forefront of the battle, and in having the great white warrior from the Stars to fight with them in their ranks; and promising large rewards of cattle and promotion to all who survived in the event of Ignosi's arms being successful.

I looked down the long lines of waving black plumes and stern faces beneath them, and sighed to think that within one short hour most, if not all, of those magnificent veteran warriors, not a man of whom was under forty years of age, would be laid dead or dying in the dust. It could not be otherwise; they were being condemned, with that wise recklessness of human life which marks the great general, and often saves his forces and attains his ends, to certain slaughter, in order to give their cause and the remainder of the army a chance of success. They were foredoomed to die, and they knew it. It was to be their task to engage regiment after regiment of Twala's army on the narrow strip of green beneath us, till they were exterminated or till the wings found a favourable opportunity for their onslaught. And yet they never hesitated, nor could I detect a sign of fear upon the face of a single warrior. There they were—going to certain death, about to quit the blessed light of day for ever, and yet able to contemplate their doom without a tremor. Even at that moment I could not help contrasting their state of mind with my own, which was far from comfortable, and breathing a sigh of envy and admiration. Never before had I seen such an absolute devotion to the idea of duty, and such a complete indifference to its bitter fruits.

"Behold your king!" ended old Infadoos, pointing to Ignosi; "go fight and fall for him, as is the duty of brave men, and cursed and shameful for ever be the name of him who shrinks from death for his king, or who turns his back from the foe. Behold your king, chiefs, captains, and soldiers! Now do your homage to the sacred Snake, and then follow on, that Incubu and I may show you a road to the heart of Twala's forces."

There was a moment's pause, then suddenly a murmur arose from the serried phalanxes before us, a sound like the distant whisper of the sea, caused by the gentle tapping of the handles of six thousand spears against their holders' shields. Slowly it swelled, till its growing volume deepened and widened into a roar of rolling noise, that echoed like thunder against the mountains, and filled the air with heavy waves of sound. Then it decreased, and by faint degrees died away into nothing, and suddenly out crashed the royal salute.

Ignosi, I thought to myself, might well be a proud man that day, for no Roman emperor ever had such a salutation from gladiators "about to die."

Ignosi acknowledged this magnificent act of homage by lifting his battle-axe, and then the Greys filed off in a triple-line formation, each line containing about one thousand fighting men, exclusive of officers. When the last companies had advanced some five hundred yards, Ignosi put himself at the head of the Buffaloes, which regiment was drawn up in a similar three-fold formation, and gave the word to march, and off we went, I, needless to say, uttering the most heartfelt prayers that I might emerge from that entertainment with a whole skin. Many a queer position have I found myself in, but never before in one quite so unpleasant as the present, or one in which my chance of coming off safe was smaller.

By the time that we reached the edge of the plateau the Greys were already half-way down the slope ending in the tongue of grass land that ran up into the bend of the mountain, something as the frog of a horse's foot runs up into the shoe. The excitement in Twala's camp on the plain beyond was very great, and regiment after regiment was starting forward at a long swinging trot in order to reach the root of the tongue of land before the attacking force could emerge into the plain of Loo.

This tongue, which was some three hundred yards in depth, even at its root or widest part was not more than six hundred and fifty paces across, while at its tip it scarcely measured ninety. The Greys, who, in passing down the side of the hill and on to the tip of the tongue, had formed into a column, on reaching the spot where it broadened out again, reassumed their triple-line formation, and halted dead.

Then we—that is, the Buffaloes—moved down the tip of the tongue and took our stand in reserve, about one hundred yards behind the last line of the Greys, and on slightly higher ground. Meanwhile we had leisure to observe Twala's entire force, which evidently had been reinforced since the morning attack, and could not now, notwithstanding their losses, number less than forty thousand, moving swiftly up towards us. But as they drew near the root of the tongue they hesitated, having discovered that only one regiment could advance into the gorge at a time, and that there, some seventy yards from the mouth of it, unassailable except in front, on account of the high walls of boulder-strewn ground on each side, stood the famous regiment of Greys, the pride and glory of the Kukuana army, ready to hold the way against their power as the three Romans once held the bridge against thousands.

They hesitated, and finally stopped their advance; there was no eagerness to cross spears with these three grim ranks of warriors who stood so firm and ready. Presently, however, a tall general, wearing the customary head-dress of nodding ostrich plumes, appeared, attended by a group of chiefs and orderlies, being, I thought, none other than Twala himself. He gave an order, and the first regiment, raising a shout, charged up towards the Greys, who remained perfectly still and silent till the attacking troops were within forty yards, and a volley of *tollas*, or throwing-knives, came rattling among their ranks.

Then suddenly with a bound and a roar, they sprang forward with uplifted spears, and the regiment met in deadly strife. Next second the roll of the meeting shields came to our ears like the sound of thunder, and the plain seemed to be alive with flashes of light reflected from the shimmering spears. To and fro swung the surging mass of struggling, stabbing humanity, but not for long. Suddenly the attacking lines began to grow thinner, and then with a slow, long heave the Greys passed over them, just as a great wave heaves up its bulk and passes over a sunken ridge. It was done; that regiment was completely destroyed, but the Greys had but two lines left now; a third of their number were dead.

Closing up shoulder to shoulder, once more they halted in silence and awaited attack; and I was rejoiced to catch sight of Sir Henry's yellow beard as he moved to and fro arranging the ranks. So he was yet alive!

Meanwhile we moved on to the ground of the encounter, which was cumbered by about four thousand prostrate human beings, dead, dying, and wounded, and literally stained red with blood. Ignosi issued an order, which was rapidly passed down the ranks, to the effect that none of the enemy's wounded were to be killed, and so far as we could see this command was scrupulously carried out. It would have been a shocking sight, if we had found time to think of it.

But now a second regiment, distinguished by white plumes, kilts, and shields, was moving to the attack of the two thousand remaining Greys, who stood waiting in the same ominous silence as before, till the foe was within forty yards or so, when they hurled themselves with irresistible force upon them. Again there came the awful roll of the meeting shields, and as we watched the tragedy repeated itself.

But this time the issue was left longer in doubt; indeed, it seemed for awhile almost impossible that the Greys should again prevail. The attacking regiment, which was formed of young men, fought with the utmost fury, and at first seemed by sheer weight to be driving the veterans back. The slaughter was truly awful, hundreds falling every minute; and from among the shouts of the warriors and the groans of the dying, set to the music of clashing spears, came a continuous hissing undertone of "*S'gee, s'gee,*" the note of triumph of each victor as he passed his assegai through and through the body of his fallen foe.

But perfect discipline and steady and unchanging valour can do wonders, and one veteran soldier is worth two young ones, as soon became apparent in the present case. For just when we thought that it was all over with the Greys, and were preparing to take their place so soon as they made room by being destroyed, I heard Sir Henry's deep voice ringing out through the din, and caught a glimpse of his circling battle-axe as he waved it high above his plumes. Then came a change; the Greys ceased to give; they stood still as a rock, against which the furious waves of spearmen broke again and again, only to recoil. Presently they began to move once more—forward this time; as they had no firearms there was no smoke, so we could see it all. Another minute and the onslaught grew fainter.

"Ah, these are *men*, indeed; they will conquer again," called out Ignosi, who was grinding his teeth with excitement at my side. "See, it is done!"

Suddenly, like puffs of smoke from the mouth of a cannon, the attacking regiment broke away in flying groups, their white head-dresses streaming behind them in the wind, and left their opponents victors, indeed, but, alas! no more a regiment. Of the gallant triple line, which forty minutes before had gone into action three thousand strong, there remained at most some six hundred blood-spattered men; the rest were under foot. And yet they cheered and waved their spears in triumph, and then, instead of falling back upon us as we expected, they ran forward, for a hundred yards or so, after the flying groups of foemen, took possession of a rising knoll of ground, and, resuming their triple formation, formed a threefold ring around it. And there, thanks be to Heaven, standing on the top of the mound for a minute, I saw Sir Henry, apparently unharmed, and with him our old friend Infadoos. Then Twala's regiments rolled down upon the doomed band, and once more the battle closed in.

As those who read this history will probably long ago have gathered, I am, to be honest, a bit of a coward, and certainly in no way given to fighting, though somehow it has often been my lot to get into unpleasant positions, and to be obliged to shed man's blood. But I have always hated it, and kept my own blood as undiminished in quantity as possible, sometimes by a judicious use of my heels. At this moment, however, for the first time in my life, I felt my bosom burn with martial ardour. Warlike fragments from the "Ingoldsby Legends," together with numbers of sanguinary verses in the Old Testament, sprang up in my brain like mushrooms in the dark; my blood, which hitherto had been half-frozen with horror, went beating through my veins, and there came upon me a savage desire to kill and spare not. I glanced round at the serried ranks of warriors behind us, and somehow, all in an instant, I began to wonder if my face looked like theirs. There they stood, their heads craned forward over their shields, the hands twitching, the lips apart, the fierce features instinct with the hungry lust of battle, and in the eyes a look like the glare of a bloodhound when he sights his quarry.

Only Ignosi's heart, to judge from his comparative self-possession, seemed, to all appearance, to beat as calmly as ever beneath his leopard-skin cloak, though even *he* still ground his teeth. I could bear it no longer.

"Are we to stand here till we put out roots, Umbopa—Ignosi, I mean—while Twala swallows our brothers yonder?" I asked.

"Nay, Macumazahn," was the answer; "see, now is the ripe moment: let us pluck it."

As he spoke a fresh regiment rushed past the ring upon the little mound, and wheeling round, attacked it from the hither side.

Then, lifting his battle-axe, Ignosi gave the signal to advance, and, raising the Kukuana war-cry, the Buffaloes charged home with a rush like the rush of the sea.

What followed immediately on this it is out of my power to tell. All I can remember is a wild yet ordered advance, that seemed to shake the ground; a sudden change of front and forming up on the part of the regiment against which the charge was directed; then an awful shock, a dull roar of voices, and a continuous flashing of spears, seen through a red mist of blood.

When my mind cleared I found myself standing inside the remnant of the Greys near the top of the mound, and just behind no less a person than Sir Henry himself. How I got there I had at the moment no idea, but Sir Henry afterwards told me that I was borne up by the first furious charge of the Buffaloes almost to his feet, and then left, as they in turn were pressed back. Thereon he dashed out of the circle and dragged me into it.

As for the fight that followed, who can describe it? Again and again the multitudes surged against our momentarily lessening circle, and again and again we beat them back.

> The stubborn spearmen still made good
> The dark impenetrable wood,
> Each stepping where his comrade stood
> The instant that he fell,

as someone or other beautifully says.

It was a splendid thing to see those brave battalions come on time after time over the barriers of their dead, sometimes lifting corpses before them to receive our spear-thrusts, only to leave their own corpses to swell the rising piles. It was a gallant sight to see that old warrior, Infadoos, as cool as though he were on parade, shouting out orders, taunts, and even jests, to keep up the spirit of his few remaining men, and then, as each charge rolled on, stepping forward to wherever the fighting was thickest, to bear his share in repelling it. And yet more gallant was the vision of Sir Henry, whose ostrich plumes had been shorn off by a spear stroke, so that his long yellow hair streamed out in the breeze behind him. There he stood, the great Dane, for he was nothing else, his hands, his axe, and his armour all red with blood, and none could live before his stroke. Time after time I saw it sweeping down, as some great warrior ventured to give him battle, and as he struck he shouted "*O-hoy! O-hoy!*" like his Berserkir forefathers, and the blow went crashing through shield and spear, through head-dress, hair, and skull, till at last none would of their own will come near the great white "*umtagati*," the wizard, who killed and failed not.

But suddenly there rose a cry of "*Twala, y' Twala*," and out of the press sprang forward none other than the gigantic one-eyed king himself, also armed with battle-axe and shield, and clad in chain armour.

"Where art thou, Incubu, thou white man, who slewest Scragga my son—see if thou canst slay me!" he shouted, and at the same time hurled a *tolla* straight at Sir Henry, who fortunately saw it coming, and caught it on his shield, which it transfixed, remaining wedged in the iron plate behind the hide.

Then, with a cry, Twala sprang forward straight at him, and with his battle-axe struck him such a blow upon the shield that the mere force and shock of it brought Sir Henry, strong man as he is, down upon his knees.

But at this time the matter went no further, for that instant there rose from the regiments pressing round us something like a shout of dismay, and on looking up I saw the cause.

To the right and to the left the plain was alive with the plumes of charging warriors. The outflanking squadrons had come to our relief. The time could not have been better chosen. All Twala's army, as Ignosi predicted would be the case, had fixed their attention on the bloody struggle which was raging round the remnant of the Greys and that of the Buffaloes, who were now carrying on a battle of their own at a little distance, which two regiments had formed the chest of our army. It was not until our horns were about to close upon them that they had dreamed of their approach, for they believed these forces to be hidden in reserve upon the crest of the moon-shaped hill. And now, before they could even assume a proper formation for defence, the outflanking *Impis* had leapt, like greyhounds, on their flanks.

In five minutes the fate of the battle was decided. Taken on both flanks, and dismayed at the awful slaughter inflicted upon them by the Greys and Buffaloes, Twala's regiments broke into flight, and soon the whole plain between us and Loo was scattered with groups of running soldiers making good their retreat. As for the hosts that had so recently surrounded us and the Buffaloes, they melted away as though by magic, and presently we were left standing there like a rock from which the sea has retreated. But what a sight it was! Around us the dead and dying lay in heaped-up masses, and of the gallant Greys there remained but ninety-five men upon their feet. More than three thousand four hundred had fallen in this one regiment, most of them never to rise again.

"Men," said Infadoos calmly, as between the intervals of binding a wound on his arm he surveyed what remained to him of his corps, "ye have kept up the reputation of your regiment, and this day's fighting will be well spoken of by your children's children." Then he turned round and shook Sir Henry Curtis by the hand. "Thou art a great captain, Incubu," he said simply; "I have lived a long life among warriors, and have known many a brave one, yet have I never seen a man like unto thee."

At this moment the Buffaloes began to march past our position on the road to Loo, and as they went a message was brought to us from Ignosi requesting Infadoos, Sir Henry, and myself to join them. Accordingly, orders having been issued to the remaining ninety men of the Greys to employ themselves in collecting the wounded, we joined Ignosi, who informed us that he was pressing on to Loo to complete the victory by capturing Twala, if that should be possible. Before we had gone far, suddenly we discovered the figure of Good sitting on an ant-heap about one hundred paces from us. Close beside him was the body of a Kukuana.

"He must be wounded," said Sir Henry anxiously. As he made the remark, an untoward thing happened. The dead body of the Kukuana soldier, or rather what had appeared to be his dead body, suddenly sprang up, knocked Good head over heels off the ant-heap, and began to spear him. We rushed forward in terror, and as we drew near we saw the brawny warrior making dig after dig at the prostrate Good, who at each prod jerked all his limbs into the air. Seeing us coming, the Kukuana gave one final and most vicious dig, and with a shout of "Take that, wizard!" bolted away. Good did not move, and we concluded that our poor comrade was done for. Sadly we came towards him, and were astonished to find him pale and faint indeed, but with a serene smile upon his face, and his eyeglass still fixed in his eye.

"Capital armour this," he murmured, on catching sight of our faces bending over him. "How sold that beggar must have been," and then he fainted. On examination we discovered that he had been seriously wounded in the leg by a *tolla* in the course of the pursuit, but that the chain armour had prevented his last assailant's spear from doing anything more than bruise him badly. It was a merciful escape. As nothing could be done for him at the moment, he was placed on one of the wicker shields used for the wounded, and carried along with us.

On arriving before the nearest gate of Loo we found one of our regiments watching it in obedience to orders received from Ignosi. The other regiments were in the same way guarding the different exits to the town. The officer in command of this regiment saluted Ignosi as king, and informed him that Twala's army had taken refuge in the town, whither Twala himself had also escaped, but he thought that they were thoroughly demoralised, and would surrender. Thereupon Ignosi, after taking counsel with us, sent forward heralds to each gate ordering the defenders to open, and promising on his royal word life and forgiveness to every soldier who laid down his arms, but saying that if they did not do so before nightfall he would certainly burn the town and all within its gates. This message was not without its effect. Half an hour later, amid the shouts and cheers of the Buffaloes, the bridge was dropped across the fosse, and the gates upon the further side were flung open.

Taking due precautions against treachery, we marched on into the town. All along the roadways stood thousands of dejected warriors, their heads drooping, and their shields and spears at their feet, who, headed by their officers, saluted Ignosi as king as he passed. On we marched, straight to Twala's kraal. When we reached the great space, where a day or two previously we had seen the review and the witch hunt, we found it deserted. No, not quite deserted, for there, on the further side, in front of his hut, sat Twala himself, with but one attendant—Gagool.

It was a melancholy sight to see him seated, his battle-axe and shield by his side, his chin upon his mailed breast, with but one old crone for companion, and notwithstanding his crimes and misdeeds, a pang of compassion shot through me as I looked upon Twala thus "fallen from his high estate." Not a soldier of all his armies, not a courtier out of the hundreds who had cringed round him, not even a solitary wife, remained to share his fate or halve the bitterness of his fall. Poor savage! he was learning the lesson which Fate teaches to most of us who live long enough, that the eyes of mankind are blind to the discredited, and that he who is defenceless and fallen finds few friends and little mercy. Nor, indeed, in this case did he deserve any.

Filing through the kraal gate, we marched across the open space to where the ex-king sat. When within about fifty yards of him the regiment was halted, and accompanied only by a small guard we advanced towards him, Gagool reviling us bitterly as we came. As we drew near, Twala, for the first time, lifted his plumed head, and fixed his one eye, which seemed to flash with suppressed fury almost as brightly as the great diamond bound round his forehead, upon his successful rival—Ignosi.

"Hail, O king!" he said, with bitter mockery; "thou who hast eaten of my bread, and now by the aid of the white man's magic hast seduced my regiments and defeated mine army, hail! What fate hast thou in store for me, O king?"

"The fate thou gavest to my father, whose throne thou hast sat on these many years!" was the stern answer.

"It is good. I will show thee how to die, that thou mayest remember it against thine own time. See, the sun sinks in blood," and he pointed with his battle-axe towards the setting orb; "it is well that my sun should go down in its company. And now, O king! I am ready to die, but I crave the boon of the Kukuana royal House* to die fighting. Thou canst not refuse it, or even those cowards who fled to-day will hold thee shamed."

"It is granted. Choose—with whom wilt thou fight? Myself I cannot fight with thee, for the king fights not except in war."

Twala's sombre eye ran up and down our ranks, and I felt, as for a moment it rested on myself, that the position had developed a new horror. What if he chose to begin by fighting *me*? What chance should I have against a desperate savage six feet five high, and broad in proportion? I might as well commit suicide at once. Hastily I made up my mind to decline the combat, even if I were hooted out of Kukuanaland as a consequence. It is, I think, better to be hooted than to be quartered with a battle-axe.

Presently Twala spoke.

"Incubu, what sayest thou, shall we end what we began to-day, or shall I call thee coward, white—even to the liver?"

"Nay," interposed Ignosi hastily; "thou shalt not fight with Incubu."

"Not if he is afraid," said Twala.

Unfortunately Sir Henry understood this remark, and the blood flamed up into his cheeks.

"I will fight him," he said; "he shall see if I am afraid."

* It is a law amongst the Kukuanas that no man of the direct royal blood can be put to death, unless by his own consent, which is, however, never refused. He is allowed to choose a succession of antagonists, to be approved by the king, with whom he fights, till one of them kills him.—A.Q.

"For Heaven's sake," I entreated, "don't risk your life against that of a desperate man. Anybody who saw you to-day will know that you are not a coward."

"I will fight him," was the sullen answer. "No living man shall call me a coward. I am ready now!" and he stepped forward and lifted his axe.

I wrung my hands over this absurd piece of Quixotism; but if he was determined on this deed, of course I could not stop him.

"Fight not, my white brother," said Ignosi, laying his hand affectionately on Sir Henry's arm; "thou hast fought enough, and if aught befell thee at his hands it would cut my heart in twain."

"I will fight, Ignosi," was Sir Henry's answer.

"It is well, Incubu; thou art a brave man. It will be a good fray. Behold, Twala, the Elephant is ready for thee."

The ex-king laughed savagely, and stepping forward faced Curtis. For a moment they stood thus, and the light of the sinking sun caught their stalwart frames and clothed them both in fire. They were a well-matched pair.

Then they began to circle round each other, their battle-axes raised.

Suddenly Sir Henry sprang forward and struck a fearful blow at Twala, who stepped to one side. So heavy was the stroke that the striker half overbalanced himself, a circumstance of which his antagonist took a prompt advantage. Circling his massive battle-axe round his head, he brought it down with tremendous force. My heart jumped into my mouth; I thought that the affair was already finished. But no; with a quick upward movement of the left arm Sir Henry interposed his shield between himself and the axe, with the result that its outer edge was shorn away, the axe falling on his left shoulder, but not heavily enough to do any serious damage. In another moment Sir Henry got in a second blow, which was also received by Twala upon his shield. Then followed blow upon blow, that were, in turn, either received upon the shields or avoided. The excitement grew intense; the regiment which was watching the encounter forgot its discipline, and, drawing near, shouted and groaned at every stroke. Just at this time, too, Good, who had been laid upon the ground by me, recovered from his faint, and, sitting up, perceived what was going on. In an instant he was up, and catching hold of my arm, hopped about from place to place on one leg, dragging me after him, and yelling encouragements to Sir Henry—

"Go it, old fellow!" he hallooed. "That was a good one! Give it him amidships," and so on.

Presently Sir Henry, having caught a fresh stroke upon his shield, hit out with all his force. The blow cut through Twala's shield and through the tough chain armour behind it, gashing him in the shoulder. With a yell of pain and fury Twala returned the blow with interest, and, such was his strength, shore right through the rhinoceros' horn handle of his antagonists battle-axe, strengthened as it was with bands of steel, wounding Curtis in the face.

A cry of dismay rose from the Buffaloes as our hero's broad axe-head fell to the ground; and Twala, again raising his weapon, flew at him with a shout. I shut my eyes. When I opened them again it was to see Sir Henry's shield lying on the ground, and Sir Henry himself with his great arms twined round Twala's middle. To and fro they swung, hugging each other like bears, straining with all their mighty muscles for dear life, and dearer honour. With a supreme effort Twala swung the Englishman clean off his feet, and down they came together, rolling over and over on the lime paving, Twala striking out at Curtis' head with the battle-axe, and Sir Henry trying to drive the *tolla* he had drawn from his belt through Twala's armour.

It was a mighty struggle, and an awful thing to see.

"Get his axe!" yelled Good; and perhaps our champion heard him.

At any rate, dropping the *tolla*, he snatched at the axe, which was fastened to Twala's wrist by a strip of buffalo hide, and still rolling over and over, they fought for it like wild cats, drawing their breath in heavy gasps. Suddenly the hide string burst, and then, with a great effort, Sir Henry freed himself, the weapon remaining in his hand. Another second and he was upon his feet, the red blood streaming from the wound in his face, and so was Twala. Drawing the heavy *tolla* from his belt, he reeled straight at Curtis and struck him in the breast. The stab came home true and strong, but whoever it was who made that chain armour, he understood his art, for it withstood the steel. Again Twala struck out with a savage yell, and again the sharp knife rebounded, and Sir Henry went staggering back. Once more Twala came on, and as he came our great Englishman gathered himself together, and swinging the big axe round his head with both hands, hit at him with all his force. There was a shriek of excitement from a thousand throats, and, behold! Twala's head seemed to spring from his shoulders: then it fell and came rolling and bounding along the ground towards Ignosi, stopping just at his feet. For a second the corpse stood upright; then with a dull crash it came to the earth, and the gold torque from its neck rolled away across the pavement. As it did so Sir Henry, overpowered by faintness and loss of blood, fell heavily across the body of the dead king.

In a second he was lifted up, and eager hands were pouring water on his face. Another minute, and the grey eyes opened wide.

He was not dead.

Then I, just as the sun sank, stepping to where Twala's head lay in the dust, unloosed the diamond from the dead brows, and handed it to Ignosi.

"Take it," I said, "lawful king of the Kukuanas—king by birth and victory."

Ignosi bound the diadem upon his brows. Then advancing, he placed his foot upon the broad chest of his headless foe and broke out into a chant, or rather a pæan of triumph, so beautiful, and yet so utterly savage, that I despair of being able to give an adequate idea of it. Once I heard a scholar with a fine voice read aloud from the Greek poet Homer, and I remember that the sound of the rolling lines seemed to make my blood stand still. Ignosi's chant, uttered as it was in a language as beautiful and sonorous as the old Greek, produced exactly the same effect on me, although I was exhausted with toil and many emotions.

"Now," he began, "now our rebellion is swallowed up in victory, and our evil-
doing is justified by strength.

    In the morning the oppressors arose and stretched themselves; they bound
on their harness and made them ready to war.

    They rose up and tossed their spears: the soldiers called to the captains,
'Come, lead us'—and the captains cried to the king, 'Direct thou the battle.'

    They arose in their pride, twenty thousand men, and yet a twenty
thousand.

    Their plumes covered the earth as the plumes of a bird cover her nest;
they shook their spears and shouted, yea, they shook their spears in the
sunlight; they lusted for battle and were glad.

    They came up against me; their strong ones ran swiftly to slay me; they
cried, 'Ha! ha! he is as one already dead.'

"Then breathed I on them, and my breath was as the breath of a storm,
and lo! they were not.

    My lightnings pierced them; I licked up their strength with the lightning
of my spears; I shook them to the earth with the thunder of my shoutings.

    They broke—they scattered—they were gone as the mists of the morning.

    They are food for the crows and the foxes, and the place of battle is fat with
their blood.

    Where are the mighty ones who rose up in the morning?

"Where are the proud ones who tossed their plumes and cried, 'He is as a man
already dead'?

    They bow their heads, but not in sleep; they are stretched out, but not
in sleep.

They are forgotten; they have gone into the blackness; and will not return; yea, others shall lead away their wives, and their children shall remember them no more.

"And I—! the king—like an eagle I have found my eyrie.

Behold! far have I wandered in the night time, yet have I returned to my young at the daybreak.

Creep ye under the shadow of my wings, O people, and I will comfort you, and ye shall not be dismayed.

Now is the good time, the time of spoil.

Mine are the cattle on the mountains, mine also are the virgins in the kraals.

The winter is overpast, the summer is come.

Now shall Evil cover up her face, now Mercy and Joy shall dwell in the land.

Rejoice, rejoice, my people!

Let all the stars rejoice in that the tyranny is trodden down, in that I am the king."

Ignosi ceased, and out of the gathering gloom came back the deep reply—

"Thou art the king!"

Thus was my prophecy to the herald fulfilled, and within the forty-eight hours Twala's headless corpse was stiffening at Twala's gate.

XV. Good Falls Sick

After the fight was ended, Sir Henry and Good were carried into Twala's hut, where I joined them. They were both utterly exhausted by exertion and loss of blood, and, indeed, my own condition was little better. I am very wiry, and can stand more fatigue than most men, probably on account of my light weight and long training; but that night I was quite done up, and, as is always the case with me when exhausted, that old wound which the lion gave me began to pain me. Also my head was aching violently from the blow I had received in the morning, when I was knocked senseless. Altogether, a more miserable trio than we were that evening it would have been difficult to discover; and our only comfort lay in the reflection that we were exceedingly fortunate to be there to feel miserable, instead of being stretched dead upon the plain, as so many thousands of brave men were that night, who had risen well and strong in the morning.

Somehow, with the assistance of the beautiful Foulata, who, since we had been the means of saving her life, had constituted herself our handmaiden, and especially Good's, we managed to get off the chain shirts, which had certainly saved the lives of two of us that day. As I expected, we found that the flesh underneath was terribly contused, for though the steel links had kept the weapons from entering, they had not prevented them from bruising. Both Sir Henry and Good were a mass of contusions, and I was by no means free. As a remedy Foulata brought us some pounded green leaves, with an aromatic odour, which, when applied as a plaster, gave us considerable relief.

But though the bruises were painful, they did not give us such anxiety as Sir Henry's and Good's wounds. Good had a hole right through the fleshy part of his "beautiful white leg," from which he had lost a great deal of blood; and Sir Henry, with other hurts, had a deep cut over the jaw, inflicted by Twala's battle-axe. Luckily Good is a very decent surgeon, and so soon as his small box of medicines was forthcoming, having thoroughly cleansed the wounds, he managed to stitch up first Sir Henry's and then his own pretty satisfactorily, considering the imperfect light given by the primitive Kukuana lamp in the hut. Afterwards he plentifully smeared the injured places with some antiseptic ointment, of which there was a pot in the little box, and we covered them with the remains of a pocket-handkerchief which we possessed.

Meanwhile Foulata had prepared us some strong broth, for we were too weary to eat. This we swallowed, and then threw ourselves down on the piles of magnificent karrosses, or fur rugs, which were scattered about the dead king's great hut. By a very strange instance of the irony of fate, it was on Twala's own couch, and wrapped in Twala's own particular karross, that Sir Henry, the man who had slain him, slept that night.

I say slept; but after that day's work, sleep was indeed difficult. To begin with, in very truth the air was full

> Of farewells to the dying
> And mournings for the dead.

From every direction came the sound of the wailing of women whose husbands, sons, and brothers had perished in the battle. No wonder that they wailed, for over twelve thousand men, or nearly a fifth of the Kukuana army, had been destroyed in that awful struggle. It was heart-rending to lie and listen to their cries for those who never would return; and it made me understand the full horror of the work done that day to further man's ambition. Towards midnight, however, the ceaseless crying of the women grew less frequent, till at length the silence was only broken at intervals of a few minutes by a long piercing howl that came from a hut in our immediate rear, which, as I afterwards discovered, proceeded from Gagool "keening" over the dead king Twala.

After that I got a little fitful sleep, only to wake from time to time with a start, thinking that I was once more an actor in the terrible events of the last twenty-four hours. Now I seemed to see that warrior whom my hand had sent to his last account charging at me on the mountain-top; now I was once more in that glorious ring of Greys, which made its immortal stand against all Twala's regiments upon the little mound; and now again I saw Twala's plumed and gory head roll past my feet with gnashing teeth and glaring eye.

At last, somehow or other, the night passed away; but when dawn broke I found that my companions had slept no better than myself. Good, indeed, was in a high fever, and very soon afterwards began to grow light-headed, and also, to my alarm, to spit blood, the result, no doubt, of some internal injury, inflicted during the desperate efforts made by the Kukuana warrior on the previous day to force his big spear through the chain armour. Sir Henry, however, seemed pretty fresh, notwithstanding his wound on the face, which made eating difficult and laughter an impossibility, though he was so sore and stiff that he could scarcely stir.

About eight o'clock we had a visit from Infadoos, who appeared but little the worse—tough old warrior that he was—for his exertions in the battle, although he informed us that he had been up all night. He was delighted to see us, but much grieved at Good's condition, and shook our hands cordially. I noticed, however, that he addressed Sir Henry with a kind of reverence, as though he were something more than man; and, indeed, as we afterwards found out, the great Englishman was looked on throughout Kukuanaland as a supernatural being. No man, the soldiers said, could have fought as he fought or, at the end of a day of such toil and bloodshed, could have slain Twala, who, in addition to being the king, was supposed to be the strongest warrior in the country, in single combat, shearing through his bull-neck at a stroke. Indeed, that stroke became proverbial in Kukuanaland, and any extraordinary blow or feat of strength was henceforth known as "Incubu's blow."

Infadoos told us also that all Twala's regiments had submitted to Ignosi, and that like submissions were beginning to arrive from chiefs in the outlying country. Twala's death at the hands of Sir Henry had put an end to all further chance of disturbance; for Scragga had been his only legitimate son, so there was no rival claimant to the throne left alive.

I remarked that Ignosi had swum to power through blood. The old chief shrugged his shoulders. "Yes," he answered; "but the Kukuana people can only be kept cool by letting their blood flow sometimes. Many are killed, indeed, but the women are left, and others must soon grow up to take the places of the fallen. After this the land would be quiet for a while."

Afterwards, in the course of the morning, we had a short visit from Ignosi, on whose brows the royal diadem was now bound. As I contemplated him advancing with kingly dignity, an obsequious guard following his steps, I could not help recalling to my mind the tall Zulu who had presented himself to us at Durban some few months back, asking to be taken into our service, and reflecting on the strange revolutions of the wheel of fortune.

"Hail, O king!" I said, rising.

"Yes, Macumazahn. King at last, by the might of your three right hands," was the ready answer.

All was, he said, going well; and he hoped to arrange a great feast in two weeks' time in order to show himself to the people.

I asked him what he had settled to do with Gagool.

"She is the evil genius of the land," he answered, "and I shall kill her, and all the witch doctors with her! She has lived so long that none can remember when she was not very old, and she it is who has always trained the witch-hunters, and made the land wicked in the sight of the heavens above."

"Yet she knows much," I replied; "it is easier to destroy knowledge, Ignosi, than to gather it."

"That is so," he said thoughtfully. "She, and she only, knows the secret of the 'Three Witches,' yonder, whither the great road runs, where the kings are buried, and the Silent Ones sit."

"Yes, and the diamonds are. Forget not thy promise, Ignosi; thou must lead us to the mines, even if thou hast to spare Gagool alive to show the way."

"I will not forget, Macumazahn, and I will think on what thou sayest."

After Ignosi's visit I went to see Good, and found him quite delirious. The fever set up by his wound seemed to have taken a firm hold of his system, and to be complicated with an internal injury. For four or five days his condition was most critical; indeed, I believe firmly that had it not been for Foulata's indefatigable nursing he must have died.

Women are women, all the world over, whatever their colour. Yet somehow it seemed curious to watch this dusky beauty bending night and day over the fevered man's couch, and performing all the merciful errands of a sick-room swiftly, gently, and with as fine an instinct as that of a trained hospital nurse. For the first night or two I tried to help her, and so did Sir Henry as soon as his stiffness allowed him to move, but Foulata bore our interference with impatience, and finally insisted upon our leaving him to her, saying that our movements made him restless, which I think was true. Day and night she watched him and tended him, giving him his only medicine, a native cooling drink made of milk, in which was infused juice from the bulb of a species of tulip, and keeping the flies from settling on him. I can see the whole picture now as it appeared night after night by the light of our primitive lamp; Good tossing to and fro, his features emaciated, his eyes shining large and luminous, and jabbering nonsense by the yard; and seated on the ground by his side, her back resting against the wall of the hut, the soft-eyed, shapely Kukuana beauty, her face, weary as it was with her long vigil, animated by a look of infinite compassion—or was it something more than compassion?

For two days we thought that he must die, and crept about with heavy hearts.

Only Foulata would not believe it.

"He will live," she said.

For three hundred yards or more around Twala's chief hut, where the sufferer lay, there was silence; for by the king's order all who lived in the habitations behind it, except Sir Henry and myself, had been removed, lest any noise should come to the sick man's ears. One night, it was the fifth of Good's illness, as was my habit, I went across to see how he was doing before turning in for a few hours.

I entered the hut carefully. The lamp placed upon the floor showed the figure of Good tossing no more, but lying quite still.

So it had come at last! In the bitterness of my heart I gave something like a sob.

"Hush—h—h!" came from the patch of dark shadow behind Good's head.

Then, creeping closer, I saw that he was not dead, but sleeping soundly, with Foulata's taper fingers clasped tightly in his poor white hand. The crisis had passed, and he would live. He slept like that for eighteen hours; and I scarcely like to say it, for fear I should not be believed, but during the entire period did this devoted girl sit by him, fearing that if she moved and drew away her hand it would wake him. What she must have suffered from cramp and weariness, to say nothing of want of food, nobody will ever know; but it is the fact that, when at last he woke, she had to be carried away—her limbs were so stiff that she could not move them.

After the turn had once been taken, Good's recovery was rapid and complete. It was not till he was nearly well that Sir Henry told him of all he owed to Foulata; and when he came to the story of how she sat by his side for eighteen hours, fearing lest by moving she should wake him, the honest sailor's eyes filled with tears. He turned and went straight to the hut where Foulata was preparing the mid-day meal, for we were back in our old quarters now, taking me with him to interpret in case he could not make his meaning clear to her, though I am bound to say that she understood him marvellously as a rule, considering how extremely limited was his foreign vocabulary.

"Tell her," said Good, "that I owe her my life, and that I will never forget her kindness."

I interpreted, and under her dark skin she actually seemed to blush.

Turning to him with one of those swift and graceful motions that in her always reminded me of the flight of a wild bird, Foulata answered softly, glancing at him with her large brown eyes—

"Nay, my lord; my lord forgets! Did he not save *my* life, and am I not my lord's handmaiden?"

It will be observed that the young lady appeared entirely to have forgotten the share which Sir Henry and myself had taken in her preservation from Twala's clutches. But that is the way of women! I remember my dear wife was just the same. Well, I retired from that little interview sad at heart. I did not like Miss Foulata's soft glances, for I knew the fatal amorous propensities of sailors in general, and of Good in particular.

There are two things in the world, as I have found out, which cannot be prevented: you cannot keep a Zulu from fighting, or a sailor from falling in love upon the slightest provocation!

It was a few days after this last occurrence that Ignosi held his great "indaba," or council, and was formally recognised as king by the "indunas," or head men, of Kukuanaland. The spectacle was a most imposing one, including as it did a grand review of troops. On this day the remaining fragments of the Greys were formally paraded, and in the face of the army thanked for their splendid conduct in the battle. To each man the king made a large present of cattle, promoting them one and all to the rank of officers in the new corps of Greys which was in process of formation. An order was also promulgated throughout the length and breadth of Kukuanaland that, whilst we honoured the country by our presence, we three were to be greeted with the royal salute, and to be treated with the same ceremony and respect that was by custom accorded to the king. Also the power of life and death was publicly conferred upon us. Ignosi, too, in the presence of his people, reaffirmed the promises which he had made, to the effect that no man's blood should be shed without trial, and that witch-hunting should cease in the land.

When the ceremony was over we waited upon Ignosi, and informed him that we were now anxious to investigate the mystery of the mines to which Solomon's Road ran, asking him if he had discovered anything about them.

"My friends," he answered, "I have discovered this. It is there that the three great figures sit, who here are called the 'Silent Ones,' and to whom Twala would have offered the girl Foulata as a sacrifice. It is there, too, in a great cave deep in the mountain, that the kings of the land are buried; there ye shall find Twala's body, sitting with those who went before him. There, also, is a deep pit, which, at some time, long-dead men dug out, mayhap for the stones ye speak of, such as I have heard men in Natal tell of at Kimberley. There, too, in the Place of Death is a secret chamber, known to none but the king and Gagool. But Twala, who knew it, is dead, and I know it not, nor know I what is in it. Yet there is a legend in the land that once, many generations gone, a white man crossed the mountains, and was led by a woman to the secret chamber and shown the wealth hidden in it. But before he could take it she betrayed him, and he was driven by the king of that day back to the mountains, and since then no man has entered the place."

"The story is surely true, Ignosi, for on the mountains we found the white man," I said.

"Yes, we found him. And now I have promised you that if ye can come to that chamber, and the stones are there—"

"The gem upon thy forehead proves that they are there," I put in, pointing to the great diamond I had taken from Twala's dead brows.

"Mayhap; if they are there," he said, "ye shall have as many as ye can take hence—if indeed ye would leave me, my brothers."

"First we must find the chamber," said I.

"There is but one who can show it to thee—Gagool."

"And if she will not?"

"Then she must die," said Ignosi sternly. "I have saved her alive but for this. Stay, she shall choose," and calling to a messenger he ordered Gagool to be brought before him.

In a few minutes she came, hurried along by two guards, whom she was cursing as she walked.

"Leave her," said the king to the guards.

So soon as their support was withdrawn, the withered old bundle—for she looked more like a bundle than anything else, out of which her two bright and wicked eyes gleamed like those of a snake—sank in a heap on to the floor.

"What will ye with me, Ignosi?" she piped. "Ye dare not touch me. If ye touch me I will slay you as ye sit. Beware of my magic."

"Thy magic could not save Twala, old she-wolf, and it cannot hurt me," was the answer. "Listen; I will this of thee, that thou reveal to us the chamber where are the shining stones."

"Ha! ha!" she piped, "none know its secret but I, and I will never tell thee. The white devils shall go hence empty-handed."

"Thou shalt tell me. I will make thee tell me."

"How, O king? Thou art great, but can thy power wring the truth from a woman?"

"It is difficult, yet will I do it."

"How, O king?"

"Nay, thus; if thou tellest not thou shalt slowly die."

"Die!" she shrieked in terror and fury; "ye dare not touch me—man, ye know not who I am. How old think ye am I? I knew your fathers, and your fathers' fathers' fathers. When the country was young I was here; when the country grows old I shall still be here. I cannot die unless I be killed by chance, for none dare slay me."

"Yet will I slay thee. See, Gagool, mother of evil, thou art so old that thou canst no longer love thy life. What can life be to such a hag as thou, who hast no shape, nor form, nor hair, nor teeth—hast naught, save wickedness and evil eyes? It will be mercy to make an end of thee, Gagool."

"Thou fool," shrieked the old fiend, "thou accursed fool, deemest thou that life is sweet only to the young? It is not so, and naught thou knowest of the heart of man to think it. To the young, indeed, death is sometimes welcome, for the young can feel. They love and suffer, and it wrings them to see their beloved pass to the land of shadows. But the old feel not, they love not, and, *ha! ha!* they laugh to see another go out into the dark; *ha! ha!* they laugh to see the evil that is done under the stars. All they love is life, the warm, warm sun, and the sweet, sweet air. They are afraid of the cold, afraid of the cold and the dark, *ha! ha! ha!*" and the old hag writhed in ghastly merriment on the ground.

"Cease thine evil talk and answer me," said Ignosi angrily. "Wilt thou show the place where the stones are, or wilt thou not? If thou wilt not thou diest, even now," and he seized a spear and held it over her.

"I will not show it; thou darest not kill me, darest not! He who slays me will be accursed for ever."

Slowly Ignosi brought down the spear till it pricked the prostrate heap of rags.

With a wild yell Gagool sprang to her feet, then fell again and rolled upon the floor.

"Nay, I will show it. Only let me live, let me sit in the sun and have a bit of meat to suck, and I will show thee."

"It is well. I thought that I should find a way to reason with thee. To-morrow shalt thou go with Infadoos and my white brothers to the place, and beware how thou failest, for if thou showest it not, then thou shalt slowly die. I have spoken."

"I will not fail, Ignosi. I always keep my word—*ha! ha! ha!* Once before a woman showed the chamber to a white man, and behold! evil befell him," and here her wicked eyes glinted. "Her name was Gagool also. Perchance I was that woman."

"Thou liest," I said, "that was ten generations gone."

"Mayhap, mayhap; when one lives long one forgets. Perhaps it was my mother's mother who told me; surely her name was Gagool also. But mark, ye will find in the place where the bright things are a bag of hide full of stones. The man filled that bag, but he never took it away. Evil befell him, I say, evil befell him! Perhaps it was my mother's mother who told me. It will be a merry journey—we can see the bodies of those who died in the battle as we go. Their eyes will be gone by now, and their ribs will be hollow. *Ha! ha! ha!*"

XVI. THE PLACE OF DEATH

It was already dark on the third day after the scene described in the previous chapter when we camped in some huts at the foot of the "Three Witches," as the triangle of mountains is called to which Solomon's Great Road ran. Our party consisted of our three selves and Foulata, who waited on us—especially on Good—Infadoos, Gagool, who was borne along in a litter, inside which she could be heard muttering and cursing all day long, and a party of guards and attendants. The mountains, or rather the three peaks of the mountain, for the mass was evidently the result of a solitary upheaval, were, as I have said, in the form of a triangle, of which the base was towards us, one peak being on our right, one on our left, and one straight in front of us. Never shall I forget the sight afforded by those three towering peaks in the early sunlight of the following morning. High, high above us, up into the blue air, soared their twisted snow-wreaths. Beneath the snow-line the peaks were purple with heaths, and so were the wild moors that ran up the slopes towards them. Straight before us the white ribbon of Solomon's Great Road stretched away uphill to the foot of the centre peak, about five miles from us, and there stopped. It was its terminus.

I had better leave the feelings of intense excitement with which we set out on our march that morning to the imagination of those who read this history. At last we were drawing near to the wonderful mines that had been the cause of the miserable death of the old Portuguese Dom three centuries ago, of my poor friend, his ill-starred descendant, and also, as we feared, of George Curtis, Sir Henry's brother. Were we destined, after all that we had gone through, to fare any better? Evil befell them, as that old fiend Gagool said; would it also befall us? Somehow, as we were marching up that last stretch of beautiful road, I could not help feeling a little superstitious about the matter, and so I think did Good and Sir Henry.

For an hour and a half or more we tramped on up the heather-fringed way, going so fast in our excitement that the bearers of Gagool's hammock could scarcely keep pace with us, and its occupant piped out to us to stop.

"Walk more slowly, white men," she said, projecting her hideous shrivelled countenance between the grass curtains, and fixing her gleaming eyes upon us; "why will ye run to meet the evil that shall befall you, ye seekers after treasure?" and she laughed that horrible laugh which always sent a cold shiver down my back, and for a while quite took the enthusiasm out of us.

However, on we went, till we saw before us, and between ourselves and the peak, a vast circular hole with sloping sides, three hundred feet or more in depth, and quite half a mile round.

"Can't you guess what this is?" I said to Sir Henry and Good, who were staring in astonishment at the awful pit before us.

They shook their heads.

"Then it is clear that you have never seen the diamond diggings at Kimberley. You may depend on it that this is Solomon's Diamond Mine. Look there," I said, pointing to the strata of stiff blue clay which were yet to be seen among the grass and bushes that clothed the sides of the pit, "the formation is the same. I'll be bound that if we went down there we should find 'pipes' of soapy brecciated rock. Look, too," and I pointed to a series of worn flat slabs of stone that were placed on a gentle slope below the level of a watercourse which in some past age had been cut out of the solid rock; "if those are not tables once used to wash the 'stuff,' I'm a Dutchman."

At the edge of this vast hole, which was none other than the pit marked on the old Dom's map, the Great Road branched into two and circumvented it. In many places, by the way, this surrounding road was built entirely out of blocks of stone, apparently with the object of supporting the edges of the pit and preventing falls of reef. Along this path we pressed, driven by curiosity to see what were the three towering objects which we could discern from the hither side of the great gulf. As we drew near we perceived that they were Colossi of some sort or another, and rightly conjectured that before us sat the three "Silent Ones" that are held in such awe by the Kukuana people. But it was not until we were quite close to them that we recognised the full majesty of these "Silent Ones."

There, upon huge pedestals of dark rock, sculptured with rude emblems of the Phallic worship, separated from each other by a distance of forty paces, and looking down the road which crossed some sixty miles of plain to Loo, were three colossal seated forms—two male and one female—each measuring about thirty feet from the crown of its head to the pedestal.

The female form, which was nude, was of great though severe beauty, but unfortunately the features had been injured by centuries of exposure to the weather. Rising from either side of her head were the points of a crescent. The two male

Colossi, on the contrary, were draped, and presented a terrifying cast of features, especially the one to our right, which had the face of a devil. That to our left was serene in countenance, but the calm upon it seemed dreadful. It was the calm of that inhuman cruelty, Sir Henry remarked, which the ancients attributed to beings potent for good, who could yet watch the sufferings of humanity, if not without rejoicing, at least without sorrow. These three statues form a most awe-inspiring trinity, as they sit there in their solitude, and gaze out across the plain for ever.

Contemplating these "Silent Ones," as the Kukuanas call them, an intense curiosity again seized us to know whose were the hands which had shaped them, who it was that had dug the pit and made the road. Whilst I was gazing and wondering, suddenly it occurred to me—being familiar with the Old Testament—that Solomon went astray after strange gods, the names of three of whom I remembered—"Ashtoreth, the goddess of the Zidonians, Chemosh, the god of the Moabites, and Milcom, the god of the children of Ammon"—and I suggested to my companions that the figures before us might represent these false and exploded divinities.

"Hum," said Sir Henry, who is a scholar, having taken a high degree in classics at college, "there may be something in that; Ashtoreth of the Hebrews was the Astarte of the Phoenicians, who were the great traders of Solomon's time. Astarte, who afterwards became the Aphrodite of the Greeks, was represented with horns like the half-moon, and there on the brow of the female figure are distinct horns. Perhaps these Colossi were designed by some Phœnician official who managed the mines. Who can say?"*

Before we had finished examining these extraordinary relics of remote antiquity, Infadoos came up, and having saluted the "Silent Ones" by lifting his spear, asked us if we intended entering the "Place of Death" at once, or if we would wait till after we had taken food at mid-day. If we were ready to go at once, Gagool had announced her willingness to guide us. As it was not later than eleven o'clock—driven to it by a burning curiosity—we announced our intention of proceeding instantly, and I suggested that, in case we should be detained in the cave, we should take some food with us. Accordingly Gagool's litter was brought up, and that lady herself assisted out of it. Meanwhile Foulata, at my request, stored some "biltong," or dried game-flesh, together with a couple of gourds of water, in a reed basket with a hinged cover.

---

* Compare Milton, *Paradise Lost*, Book i.:—

> With these in troop
> Came Ashtoreth, whom the Phoenicians called
> Astarté, Queen of Heaven, with crescent horns;
> To whose bright image nightly by the moon
> Sidonian virgins paid their vows and songs.

Straight in front of us, at a distance of some fifty paces from the backs of the Colossi, rose a sheer wall of rock, eighty feet or more in height, that gradually sloped upwards till it formed the base of the lofty snow-wreathed peak, which soared into the air three thousand feet above us. As soon as she was clear of her hammock, Gagool cast one evil grin upon us, and then, leaning on a stick, hobbled off towards the face of this wall. We followed her till we came to a narrow portal solidly arched that looked like the opening of a gallery of a mine.

Here Gagool was waiting for us, still with that evil grin upon her horrid face.

"Now, white men from the Stars," she piped; "great warriors, Incubu, Bougwan, and Macumazahn the wise, are ye ready? Behold, I am here to do the bidding of my lord the king, and to show you the store of bright stones. *Ha! ha! ha!*"

"We are ready," I said.

"Good, good! Make strong your hearts to bear what ye shall see. Comest thou too, Infadoos, thou who didst betray thy master?"

Infadoos frowned as he answered—

"Nay, I come not; it is not for me to enter there. But thou, Gagool, curb thy tongue, and beware how thou dealest with my lords. At thy hands will I require them, and if a hair of them be hurt, Gagool, be'st thou fifty times a witch, thou shalt die. Hearest thou?"

"I hear Infadoos; I know thee, thou didst ever love big words; when thou wast a babe I remember thou didst threaten thine own mother. That was but the other day. But, fear not, fear not, I live only to do the bidding of the king. I have done the bidding of many kings, Infadoos, till in the end they did mine. *Ha! ha!* I go to look upon their faces once more, and Twala's also! Come on, come on, here is the lamp," and she drew a large gourd full of oil, and fitted with a rush wick, from under her fur cloak.

"Art thou coming, Foulata?" asked Good in his villainous Kitchen Kukuana, in which he had been improving himself under that young lady's tuition.

"I fear, my lord," the girl answered timidly.

"Then give me the basket."

"Nay, my lord, whither thou goest there I go also."

"The deuce you will!" thought I to myself; "that may be rather awkward if we ever get out of this."

Without further ado Gagool plunged into the passage, which was wide enough to admit of two walking abreast, and quite dark. We followed the sound of her voice as she piped to us to come on, in some fear and trembling, which was not allayed by the flutter of a sudden rush of wings.

"Hullo! what's that?" halloed Good; "somebody hit me in the face."

"Bats," said I; "on you go."

When, so far as we could judge, we had gone some fifty paces, we perceived that the passage was growing faintly light. Another minute, and we were in perhaps the most wonderful place that the eyes of living man have beheld.

Let the reader picture to himself the hall of the vastest cathedral he ever stood in, windowless indeed, but dimly lighted from above, presumably by shafts connected with the outer air and driven in the roof, which arched away a hundred feet above our heads, and he will get some idea of the size of the enormous cave in which we found ourselves, with the difference that this cathedral designed by nature was loftier and wider than any built by man. But its stupendous size was the least of the wonders of the place, for running in rows adown its length were gigantic pillars of what looked like ice, but were, in reality, huge stalactites. It is impossible for me to convey any idea of the overpowering beauty and grandeur of these pillars of white spar, some of which were not less than twenty feet in diameter at the base, and sprang up in lofty and yet delicate beauty sheer to the distant roof. Others again were in process of formation. On the rock floor there was in these cases what looked, Sir Henry said, exactly like a broken column in an old Grecian temple, whilst high above, depending from the roof, the point of a huge icicle could be dimly seen.

Even as we gazed we could hear the process going on, for presently with a tiny splash a drop of water would fall from the far-off icicle on to the column below. On some columns the drops only fell once in two or three minutes, and in these cases it would be an interesting calculation to discover how long, at that rate of dripping, it would take to form a pillar, say eighty feet by ten in diameter. That the process, in at least one instance, was incalculably slow, the following example will suffice to show. Cut on one of these pillars we discovered the crude likeness of a mummy, by the head of which sat what appeared to be the figure of an Egyptian god, doubtless the handiwork of some old-world labourer in the mine. This work of art was executed at the natural height at which an idle fellow, be he Phoenician workman or British cad, is in the habit of trying to immortalise himself at the expense of nature's masterpieces, namely, about five feet from the ground. Yet at the time that we saw it, which *must* have been nearly three thousand years after the date of the execution of the carving, the column was only eight feet high, and was still in process of formation, which gives a rate of growth of a foot to a thousand years, or an inch and a fraction to a century. This we knew because, as we were standing by it, we heard a drop of water fall.

Sometimes the stalagmites took strange forms, presumably where the dropping of the water had not always been on the same spot. Thus, one huge mass, which must have weighed a hundred tons or so, was in the shape of a pulpit, beautifully fretted over outside with a design that looked like lace. Others resembled strange beasts, and on the sides of the cave were fanlike ivory tracings, such as the frost leaves upon a pane.

Out of the vast main aisle there opened here and there smaller caves, exactly, Sir Henry said, as chapels open out of great cathedrals. Some were large, but one or two—and this is a wonderful instance of how nature carries out her handiwork by the same unvarying laws, utterly irrespective of size—were tiny. One little nook, for instance, was no larger than an unusually big doll's house, and yet it might have been a model for the whole place, for the water dropped, tiny icicles hung, and spar columns were forming in just the same way.

We had not, however, enough time to examine this beautiful cavern so thoroughly as we should have liked to do, since unfortunately, Gagool seemed to be indifferent as to stalactites, and only anxious to get her business over. This annoyed me the more, as I was particularly anxious to discover, if possible, by what system the light was admitted into the cave, and whether it was by the hand of man or by that of nature that this was done; also if the place had been used in any way in ancient times, as seemed probable. However, we consoled ourselves with the idea that we would investigate it thoroughly on our way back, and followed on at the heels of our uncanny guide.

On she led us, straight to the top of the vast and silent cave, where we found another doorway, not arched as the first was, but square at the top, something like the doorways of Egyptian temples.

"Are ye prepared to enter the Place of Death, white men?" asked Gagool, evidently with a view to making us feel uncomfortable.

"Lead on, Macduff," said Good solemnly, trying to look as though he was not at all alarmed, as indeed we all did except Foulata, who caught Good by the arm for protection.

"This is getting rather ghastly," said Sir Henry, peeping into the dark passageway. "Come on, Quatermain—*seniores priores*. We mustn't keep the old lady waiting!" and he politely made way for me to lead the van, for which inwardly I did not bless him.

Tap, tap, went old Gagool's stick down the passage, as she trotted along, chuckling hideously; and still overcome by some unaccountable presentiment of evil, I hung back.

"Come, get on, old fellow," said Good, "or we shall lose our fair guide."

Thus adjured, I started down the passage, and after about twenty paces found myself in a gloomy apartment some forty feet long, by thirty broad, and thirty high, which in some past age evidently had been hollowed, by hand-labour, out of the mountain. This apartment was not nearly so well lighted as the vast stalactite ante-cave, and at the first glance all I could discern was a massive stone table running down its length, with a colossal white figure at its head, and life-sized white figures all round it. Next I discovered a brown thing, seated on the table in the centre, and in another moment my eyes grew accustomed to the light, and I saw what all these things were, and was tailing out of the place as hard as my legs could carry me.

I am not a nervous man in a general way, and very little troubled with superstitions, of which I have lived to see the folly; but I am free to own that this sight quite upset me, and had it not been that Sir Henry caught me by the collar and held me, I do honestly believe that in another five minutes I should have been outside the stalactite cave, and that a promise of all the diamonds in Kimberley would not have induced me to enter it again. But he held me tight, so I stopped because I could not help myself. Next second, however, *his* eyes became accustomed to the light, and he let go of me, and began to mop the perspiration off his forehead. As for Good, he swore feebly, while Foulata threw her arms round his neck and shrieked.

Only Gagool chuckled loud and long.

It *was* a ghastly sight. There at the end of the long stone table, holding in his skeleton fingers a great white spear, sat *Death* himself, shaped in the form of a colossal human skeleton, fifteen feet or more in height. High above his head he held the spear, as though in the act to strike; one bony hand rested on the stone table before him, in the position a man assumes on rising from his seat, whilst his frame was bent forward so that the vertebræ of the neck and the grinning, gleaming skull projected towards us, and fixed its hollow eye-places upon us, the jaws a little open, as though it were about to speak.

"Great heavens!" said I faintly, at last, "what can it be?"

"And what are *those things*?" asked Good, pointing to the white company round the table.

"And what on earth is *that thing*?" said Sir Henry, pointing to the brown creature seated on the table.

"*Hee! hee! hee!*" laughed Gagool. "To those who enter the Hall of the Dead, evil comes. *Hee! hee! hee! ha! ha!*"

"Come, Incubu, brave in battle, come and see him thou slewest"; and the old creature caught Curtis' coat in her skinny fingers, and led him away towards the table. We followed.

Presently she stopped and pointed at the brown object seated on the table. Sir Henry looked, and started back with an exclamation; and no wonder, for there, quite naked, the head which Curtis' battle-axe had shorn from the body resting on its knees, was the gaunt corpse of Twala, the last king of the Kukuanas. Yes, there, the head perched upon the knees, it sat in all its ugliness, the vertebræ projecting a full inch above the level of the shrunken flesh of the neck, for all the world like a black double of Hamilton Tighe.* Over the surface of the corpse there was gathered a thin glassy film, that made its appearance yet more appalling, for which we were, at the moment, quite unable to account, till presently we observed that from the roof of the chamber the water fell steadily, *drip! drop! drip!* on to the neck of the corpse, whence it ran down over the entire surface, and finally escaped into the rock through a tiny hole in the table. Then I guessed what the film was—*Twala's body was being transformed into a stalactite.*

A look at the white forms seated on the stone bench which ran round that ghastly board confirmed this view. They were human bodies indeed, or rather they had been human; now they were *stalactites*. This was the way in which the Kukuana people had from time immemorial preserved their royal dead. They petrified them. What the exact system might be, if there was any, beyond the placing of them for a long period of years under the drip, I never discovered, but there they sat, iced over and preserved for ever by the silicious fluid.

Anything more awe-inspiring than the spectacle of this long line of departed royalties (there were twenty-seven of them, the last being Ignosi's father), wrapped, each of them, in a shroud of ice-like spar, through which the features could be dimly made out, and seated round that inhospitable board, with Death himself for a host, it is impossible to imagine. That the practice of thus preserving their kings must have been an ancient one is evident from the number, which, allowing for an average reign of fifteen years, supposing that every king who reigned was placed here—an improbable thing, as some are sure to have perished in battle far from home—would fix the date of its commencement at four and a quarter centuries back.

But the colossal Death, who sits at the head of the board, is far older than that, and, unless I am much mistaken, owes his origin to the same artist who designed the three Colossi. He is hewn out of a single stalactite, and, looked at as a work of art, is most admirably conceived and executed. Good, who understands such things, declared that, so far as he could see, the anatomical design of the skeleton is perfect down to the smallest bones.

My own idea is, that this terrific object was a freak of fancy on the part of some old-world sculptor, and that its presence had suggested to the Kukuanas the idea of placing their royal dead under its awful presidency. Or perhaps it was set there to frighten away any marauders who might have designs upon the treasure chamber beyond. I cannot say. All I can do is to describe it as it is, and the reader must form his own conclusion.

Such, at any rate, was the White Death and such were the White Dead!

---

*Now haste ye, my handmaidens, haste and see
How he sits there and glowers with his head on his knee.

XVII. Solomon's Treasure Chamber

While we were engaged in recovering from our fright, and in examining the grisly wonders of the Place of Death, Gagool had been differently occupied. Somehow or other—for she was marvellously active when she chose—she had scrambled on to the great table, and made her way to where our departed friend Twala was placed, under the drip, to see, suggested Good, how he was "pickling," or for some dark purpose of her own. Then, she hobbled back, stopping now and again to address the remark, the tenor of which I could not catch, to one or other of the shrouded forms, just as you or I might greet an old acquaintance. Having gone through this mysterious and horrible ceremony, she squatted herself down on the table immediately under the White Death, and began, so far as I could make out, to offer up prayers to it. The spectacle of this wicked creature pouring out supplications, evil ones no doubt, to the arch enemy of mankind, was so uncanny that it caused us to hasten our inspection.

"Now, Gagool," said I, in a low voice—somehow one did not dare to speak above a whisper in that place—"lead us to the chamber."

The old witch promptly scrambled down off the table.

"My lords are not afraid?" she said, leering up into my face.

"Lead on."

"Good, my lords;" and she hobbled round to the back of the great Death. "Here is the chamber; let my lords light the lamp, and enter," and she placed the gourd full of oil upon the floor, and leaned herself against the side of the cave. I took out a match, of which we had still a few in a box, and lit a rush wick, and then looked for the doorway, but there was nothing before us except the solid rock. Gagool grinned. "The way is there, my lords. *Ha! ha! ha!*"

"Do not jest with us," I said sternly.

"I jest not, my lords. See!" and she pointed at the rock.

As she did so, on holding up the lamp we perceived that a mass of stone was rising slowly from the floor and vanishing into the rock above, where doubtless there is a cavity prepared to receive it. The mass was of the width of a good-sized door, about ten feet high and not less than five feet thick. It must have weighed at least twenty or thirty tons, and was clearly moved upon some simple balance principle of counter-weights, probably the same as that by which the opening and shutting of an ordinary modern window is arranged. How the principle was set in motion, of course none of us saw; Gagool was careful to avoid this; but I have little doubt that there was some very simple lever, which was moved ever so little by pressure at a secret spot, thereby throwing additional weight on to the hidden counter-balances, and causing the monolith to be lifted from the ground.

Very slowly and gently the great stone raised itself, till at last it had vanished altogether, and a dark hole presented itself to us in the place which the door had filled.

Our excitement was so intense, as we saw the way to Solomon's treasure chamber thrown open at last, that I for one began to tremble and shake. Would it prove a hoax after all, I wondered, or was old Da Silvestra right? And were there vast hoards of wealth hidden in that dark place, hoards which would make us the richest men in the whole world? We should know in a minute or two.

"Enter, white men from the Stars," said Gagool, advancing into the doorway; "but first hear your servant, Gagool the old. The bright stones that ye will see were dug out of the pit over which the Silent Ones are set, and stored here, I know not by whom. But once has this place been entered since the time that those who hid the stones departed in haste, leaving them behind. The report of the treasure went down indeed among the people who lived in the country from age to age, but none knew where the chamber was, nor the secret of the door. But it happened that a white man reached this country from over the mountains—perchance he too came 'from the Stars'—and was well received by the king of that day. He it is who sits yonder," and she pointed to the fifth king at the table of the Dead. "And it came to pass that he and a woman of the country who was with him journeyed to this place, and that by chance the woman learnt the secret of the door—a thousand years might ye search, but ye should never find it. Then the white man entered with the woman, and found the stones, and filled with stones the skin of a small goat, which the woman had with her to hold food. And as he was going from the chamber he took up one more stone, a large one, and held it in his hand." Here she paused.

"Well," I asked, breathless with interest as we all were, "what happened to Da Silvestra?"

The old hag started at the mention of the name.

"How knowest thou the dead man's name?" she asked sharply; and then, without waiting for an answer, went on—

"None know what happened; but it came about that the white man was frightened, for he flung down the goat-skin, with the stones, and fled out with only the one stone in his hand, and that the king took, and it is the stone which thou, Macumazahn, didst take from Twala's brow."

"Have none entered here since?" I asked, peering again down the dark passage.

"None, my lords. Only the secret of the door has been kept, and every king has opened it, though he has not entered. There is a saying, that those who enter there will die within a moon, even as the white man died in the cave upon the mountain, where ye found him, Macumazahn, and therefore the kings do not enter. *Ha! ha!* mine are true words."

Our eyes met as she said it, and I turned sick and cold. How did the old hag know all these things?

"Enter, my lords. If I speak truth, the goat-skin with the stones will lie upon the floor; and if there is truth as to whether it is death to enter here, that ye will learn afterwards. *Ha! ha! ha!*" and she hobbled through the doorway, bearing the light with her; but I confess that once more I hesitated about following.

"Oh, confound it all!" said Good; "here goes. I am not going to be frightened by that old devil"; and followed by Foulata, who, however, evidently did not at all like the business, for she was shivering with fear, he plunged into the passage after Gagool— an example which we quickly followed.

A few yards down the passage, in the narrow way hewn out of the living rock, Gagool had paused, and was waiting for us.

"See, my lords," she said, holding the light before her, "those who stored the treasure here fled in haste, and bethought them to guard against any who should find the secret of the door, but had not the time," and she pointed to large square blocks of stone, which, to the height of two courses (about two feet three), had been placed across the passage with a view to walling it up. Along the side of the passage were similar blocks ready for use, and, most curious of all, a heap of mortar and a couple of trowels, which tools, so far as we had time to examine them, appeared to be of a similar shape and make to those used by workmen to this day.

Here Foulata, who had been in a state of great fear and agitation throughout, said that she felt faint and could go no farther, but would wait there. Accordingly we set her down on the unfinished wall, placing the basket of provisions by her side, and left her to recover.

Following the passage for about fifteen paces farther, we came suddenly to an elaborately painted wooden door. It was standing wide open. Whoever was last there had either not found the time to shut it, or had forgotten, to shut it.

Across the threshold of this door lay a skin bag, formed of a goat-skin, that appeared to be full of pebbles.

"*Hee! hee!* white men," sniggered Gagool, as the light from the lamp fell upon it. "What did I tell you, that the white man who came here fled in haste, and dropped the woman's bag—behold it!"

Good stooped down and lifted it. It was heavy and jingled.

"By Jove! I believe it's full of diamonds," he said, in an awed whisper; and, indeed, the idea of a small goat-skin full of diamonds is enough to awe anybody.

"Go on," said Sir Henry impatiently. "Here, old lady, give me the lamp," and taking it from Gagool's hand, he stepped through the doorway and held it high above his head.

We pressed in after him, forgetful for the moment of the bag of diamonds, and found ourselves in King Solomon's treasure chamber.

At first, all that the somewhat faint light given by the lamp revealed was a room hewn out of the living rock, and apparently not more than ten feet square. Next there came into sight, stored one on the other to the arch of the roof, a splendid collection of elephant-tusks. How many of them there were we did not know, for of course we could not see to what depth they went back, but there could not have been less than the ends of four or five hundred tusks of the first quality visible to our eyes. There, alone, was enough ivory to make a man wealthy for life. Perhaps, I thought, it was from this very store that Solomon drew the raw material for his "great throne of ivory," of which "there was not the like made in any kingdom."

On the opposite side of the chamber were about a score of wooden boxes, something like Martini-Henry ammunition boxes, only rather larger, and painted red.

"There are the diamonds," cried I; "bring the light."

Sir Henry did so, holding it close to the top box, of which the lid, rendered rotten by time even in that dry place, appeared to have been smashed in, probably by Da Silvestra himself. Pushing my hand through the hole in the lid I drew it out full, not of diamonds, but of gold pieces, of a shape that none of us had seen before, and with what looked like Hebrew characters stamped upon them.

"Ah!" I said, replacing the coin, "we shan't go back empty-handed, anyhow. There must be a couple of thousand pieces in each box, and there are eighteen boxes. I suppose this was the money to pay the workmen and merchants."

"Well," put in Good, "I think that is the lot; I don't see any diamonds, unless the old Portuguese put them all into his bag."

"Let my lords look yonder where it is darkest, if they would find the stones," said Gagool, interpreting our looks. "There my lords will find a nook, and three stone chests in the nook, two sealed and one open."

Before translating this to Sir Henry, who carried the light, I could not resist asking how she knew these things, if no one had entered the place since the white man, generations ago.

"Ah, Macumazahn, the watcher by night," was the mocking answer, "ye who dwell in the stars, do ye not know that some live long, and that some have eyes which can see through rock? *Ha! ha! ha!*"

"Look in that corner, Curtis," I said, indicating the spot Gagool had pointed out.

"Hullo, you fellows," he cried, "here's a recess. Great heavens! see here."

We hurried up to where he was standing in a nook, shaped something like a small bow window. Against the wall of this recess were placed three stone chests, each about two feet square. Two were fitted with stone lids, the lid of the third rested against the side of the chest, which was open.

"*See!*" he repeated hoarsely, holding the lamp over the open chest. We looked, and for a moment could make nothing out, on account of a silvery sheen which dazzled us. When our eyes grew used to it we saw that the chest was three-parts full of uncut diamonds, most of them of considerable size. Stooping, I picked some up. Yes, there was no doubt of it, there was the unmistakable soapy feel about them.

I fairly gasped as I dropped them.

"We are the richest men in the whole world," I said. "Monte Christo was a fool to us."

"We shall flood the market with diamonds," said Good.

"Got to get them there first," suggested Sir Henry.

We stood still with pale faces and stared at each other, the lantern in the middle and the glimmering gems below, as though we were conspirators about to commit a crime, instead of being, as we thought, the most fortunate men on earth.

"*Hee! hee! hee!*" cackled old Gagool behind us, as she flitted about like a vampire bat. "There are the bright stones ye love, white men, as many as ye will; take them, run them through your fingers, *eat* of them, *hee! hee! drink* of them, *ha! ha!*"

At that moment there was something so ridiculous to my mind at the idea of eating and drinking diamonds, that I began to laugh outrageously, an example which the others followed, without knowing why. There we stood and shrieked with laughter over the gems that were ours, which had been found for *us* thousands of years ago by the patient delvers in the great hole yonder, and stored for *us* by Solomon's long-dead overseer, whose name, perchance, was written in the characters stamped on the faded wax that yet adhered to the lids of the chest. Solomon never got them, nor David, or Da Silvestra, nor anybody else. *We* had got them: there before us were millions of pounds' worth of diamonds, and thousands of pounds' worth of gold and ivory only waiting to be taken away.

Suddenly the fit passed off, and we stopped laughing.

"Open the other chests, white men," croaked Gagool, "there are surely more therein. Take your fill, white lords! *Ha! ha!* take your fill."

Thus adjured, we set to work to pull up the stone lids on the other two, first—not without a feeling of sacrilege—breaking the seals that fastened them.

Hoorah! they were full too, full to the brim; at least, the second one was; no wretched burglarious Da Silvestra had been filling goat-skins out of that. As for the third chest, it was only about a fourth full, but the stones were all picked ones; none less than twenty carats, and some of them as large as pigeon-eggs. A good many of these bigger ones, however, we could see by holding them up to the light, were a little yellow, "off coloured," as they call it at Kimberley.

What we did *not* see, however, was the look of fearful malevolence that old Gagool favoured us with as she crept, crept like a snake, out of the treasure chamber and down the passage towards the door of solid rock.

Hark! Cry upon cry comes ringing up the vaulted path. It is Foulata's voice!

"*Oh, Bougwan! help! help! the stone falls!*"

"Leave go, girl! Then—"

"*Help! help! she has stabbed me!*"

By now we are running down the passage, and this is what the light from the lamp shows us. The door of the rock is closing down slowly; it is not three feet from the floor. Near it struggle Foulata and Gagool. The red blood of the former runs to her knee, but still the brave girl holds the old witch, who fights like a wild cat. Ah! she is free! Foulata falls, and Gagool throws herself on the ground, to twist like a snake through the crack of the closing stone. She is under—ah! god! too late! too late! The stone nips her, and she yells in agony. Down, down it comes, all the thirty tons of it, slowly pressing her old body against the rock below. Shriek upon shriek, such as we have never heard, then a long sickening *crunch*, and the door was shut just as, rushing down the passage, we hurled ourselves against it.

It was all done in four seconds.

Then we turned to Foulata. The poor girl was stabbed in the body, and I saw that she could not live long.

"Ah! Bougwan, I die!" gasped the beautiful creature. "She crept out—Gagool; I did not see her, I was faint—and the door began to fall; then she came back, and was looking up the path—I saw her come in through the slowly falling door, and caught her and held her, and she stabbed me, and *I die*, Bougwan!"

"Poor girl! poor girl!" Good cried in his distress; and then, as he could do nothing else, he fell to kissing her.

"Bougwan," she said, after a pause, "is Macumazahn there? It grows so dark, I cannot see."

"Here I am, Foulata."

"Macumazahn, be my tongue for a moment, I pray thee, for Bougwan cannot understand me, and before I go into the darkness I would speak to him a word."

"Say on, Foulata, I will render it."

"Say to my lord, Bougwan, that—I love him, and that I am glad to die because I know that he cannot cumber his life with such as I am, for the sun may not mate with the darkness, nor the white with the black.

"Say that, since I saw him, at times I have felt as though there were a bird in my bosom, which would one day fly hence and sing elsewhere. Even now, though I cannot lift my hand, and my brain grows cold, I do not feel as though my heart were dying; it is so full of love that it could live ten thousand years, and yet be young. Say that if I live again, mayhap I shall see him in the Stars, and that—I will search them all, though perchance there I should still be black and he would—still be white. Say—nay, Macumazahn, say no more, save that I love—Oh, hold me closer, Bougwan, I cannot feel thine arms—*oh! oh!*"

"She is dead—she is dead!" muttered Good, rising in grief, the tears running down his honest face.

"You need not let that trouble you, old fellow," said Sir Henry.

"Eh!" exclaimed Good; "what do you mean?"

"I mean that you will soon be in a position to join her. *Man, don't you see that we are buried alive?*"

Until Sir Henry uttered these words I do not think that the full horror of what had happened had come home to us, preoccupied as we were with the sight of poor Foulata's end. But now we understood. The ponderous mass of rock had closed, probably for ever, for the only brain which knew its secret was crushed to powder beneath its weight. This was a door that none could hope to force with anything short of dynamite in large quantities. And we were on the wrong side!

For a few minutes we stood horrified, there over the corpse of Foulata. All the manhood seemed to have gone out of us. The first shock of this idea of the slow and miserable end that awaited us was overpowering. We saw it all now; that fiend Gagool had planned this snare for us from the first. It would have been just the jest that her evil mind would have rejoiced in, the idea of the three white men, whom, for some reason of her own, she had always hated, slowly perishing of thirst and hunger in the company of the treasure they had coveted. Now I saw the point of that sneer of hers about eating and drinking the diamonds. Probably somebody had tried to serve the poor old Dom in the same way, when he abandoned the skin full of jewels.

"This will never do," said Sir Henry hoarsely; "the lamp will soon go out. Let us see if we can't find the spring that works the rock."

We sprang forward with desperate energy, and, standing in a bloody ooze, began to feel up and down the door and the sides of the passage. But no knob or spring could we discover.

"Depend on it," I said, "it does not work from the inside; if it did Gagool would not have risked trying to crawl underneath the stone. It was the knowledge of this that made her try to escape at all hazards, curse her."

"At all events," said Sir Henry, with a hard little laugh, "retribution was swift; hers was almost as awful an end as ours is likely to be. We can do nothing with the door; let us go back to the treasure room."

We turned and went, and as we passed it I perceived by the unfinished wall across the passage the basket of food which poor Foulata had carried. I took it up, and brought it with me to the accursed treasure chamber that was to be our grave. Then we returned and reverently bore in Foulata's corpse, laying it on the floor by the boxes of coin.

Next we seated ourselves, leaning our backs against the three stone chests which contained the priceless treasure.

"Let us divide the food," said Sir Henry, "so as to make it last as long as possible." Accordingly we did so. It would, we reckoned, make four infinitesimally small meals for each of us, enough, say, to support life for a couple of days. Besides the "biltong," or dried game-flesh, there were two gourds of water, each of which held not more than a quart.

"Now," said Sir Henry grimly, "let us eat and drink, for to-morrow we die."

We each ate a small portion of the "biltong," and drank a sip of water. Needless to say, we had but little appetite, though we were sadly in need of food, and felt better after swallowing it. Then we got up and made a systematic examination of the walls of our prison-house, in the faint hope of finding some means of exit, sounding them and the floor carefully.

There was none. It was not probable that there would be any to a treasure chamber.

The lamp began to burn dim. The fat was nearly exhausted.

"Quatermain," said Sir Henry, "what is the time—your watch goes?"

I drew it out, and looked at it. It was six o'clock; we had entered the cave at eleven.

"Infadoos will miss us," I suggested. "If we do not return to-night he will search for us in the morning, Curtis."

"He may search in vain. He does not know the secret of the door, nor even where it is. No living person knew it yesterday, except Gagool. To-day no one knows it. Even if he found the door he could not break it down. All the Kukuana army could not break through five feet of living rock. My friends, I see nothing for it but to bow ourselves to the will of the Almighty. The search for treasure has brought many to a bad end; we shall go to swell their number."

The lamp grew dimmer yet.

Presently it flared up and showed the whole scene in strong relief, the great mass of white tusks, the boxes of gold, the corpse of the poor Foulata stretched before them, the goat-skin full of treasure, the dim glimmer of the diamonds, and the wild, wan faces of us three white men seated there awaiting death by starvation.

Then the flame sank and expired.

XVIII. WE ABANDON HOPE

I can give no adequate description of the horrors of the night which followed. Mercifully they were to some extent mitigated by sleep, for even in such a position as ours wearied nature will sometimes assert itself. But I, at any rate, found it impossible to sleep much. Putting aside the terrifying thought of our impending doom—for the bravest man on earth might well quail from such a fate as awaited us, and I never made any pretensions to be brave—the *silence* itself was too great to allow of it. Reader, you may have lain awake at night and thought the quiet oppressive, but I say with confidence that you can have no idea what a vivid, tangible thing is perfect stillness. On the surface of the earth there is always some sound or motion, and though it may in itself be imperceptible, yet it deadens the sharp edge of absolute silence. But here there was none. We were buried in the bowels of a huge snow-clad peak. Thousands of feet above us the fresh air rushed over the white snow, but no sound of it reached us. We were separated by a long tunnel and five feet of rock even from the awful chamber of the Dead; and the dead make no noise. Did we not know it who lay by poor Foulata's side? The crashing of all the artillery of earth and heaven could not have come to our ears in our living tomb. We were cut off from every echo of the world—we were as men already dead.

And then the irony of the situation forced itself upon me. There around us lay treasures enough to pay off a moderate national debt, or to build a fleet of ironclads, and yet we would have bartered them all gladly for the faintest chance of escape. Soon, doubtless, we should be rejoiced to exchange them for a bit of food or a cup of water, and, after that, even for the privilege of a speedy close to our sufferings. Truly wealth, which men spend their lives in acquiring, is a valueless thing at the last.

And so the night wore on.

"Good," said Sir Henry's voice at last, and it sounded awful in the intense stillness, "how many matches have you in the box?"

"Eight, Curtis."

"Strike one and let us see the time."

He did so, and in contrast to the dense darkness the flame nearly blinded us. It was five o'clock by my watch. The beautiful dawn was now blushing on the snow-wreaths far over our heads, and the breeze would be stirring the night mists in the hollows.

"We had better eat something and keep up our strength," I suggested.

"What is the good of eating?" answered Good; "the sooner we die and get it over the better."

"While there is life there is hope," said Sir Henry.

Accordingly we ate and sipped some water, and another period of time passed. Then Sir Henry suggested that it might be well to get as near the door as possible and halloa, on the faint chance of somebody catching a sound outside. Accordingly Good, who, from long practice at sea, has a fine piercing note, groped his way down the passage and set to work. I must say that he made a most diabolical noise. I never heard such yells; but it might have been a mosquito buzzing for all the effect they produced.

After a while he gave it up and came back very thirsty, and had to drink. Then we stopped yelling, as it encroached on the supply of water.

So we sat down once more against the chests of useless diamonds in that dreadful inaction which was one of the hardest circumstances of our fate; and I am bound to say that, for my part, I gave way in despair. Laying my head against Sir Henry's broad shoulder I burst into tears; and I think that I heard Good gulping away on the other side, and swearing hoarsely at himself for doing so.

Ah, how good and brave that great man was! Had we been two frightened children, and he our nurse, he could not have treated us more tenderly. Forgetting his own share of miseries, he did all he could to soothe our broken nerves, telling stories of men who had been in somewhat similar circumstances, and miraculously escaped; and when these failed to cheer us, pointing out how, after all, it was only anticipating an end which must come to us all, that it would soon be over, and that death from exhaustion was a merciful one (which is not true). Then, in a diffident sort of way, as once before I had heard him do, he suggested that we should throw ourselves on the mercy of a higher Power, which for my part I did with great vigour.

His is a beautiful character, very quiet, but very strong.

And so somehow the day went as the night had gone, if, indeed, one can use these terms where all was densest night, and when I lit a match to see the time it was seven o'clock.

Once more we ate and drank, and as we did so an idea occurred to me.

"How is it," said I, "that the air in this place keeps fresh? It is thick and heavy, but it is perfectly fresh."

"Great heavens!" said Good, starting up, "I never thought of that. It can't come through the stone door, for it's air-tight, if ever a door was. It must come from somewhere. If there were no current of air in the place we should have been stifled or poisoned when we first came in. Let us have a look."

It was wonderful what a change this mere spark of hope wrought in us. In a moment we were all three groping about on our hands and knees, feeling for the slightest indication of a draught. Presently my ardour received a check. I put my hand on something cold. It was poor Foulata's dead face.

For an hour or more we went on feeling about, till at last Sir Henry and I gave it up in despair, having been considerably hurt by constantly knocking our heads against tusks, chests, and the sides of the chamber. But Good still persevered, saying, with an approach to cheerfulness, that it was better than doing nothing.

"I say, you fellows," he said presently, in a constrained sort of voice, "come here." Needless to say we scrambled towards him quickly enough.

"Quatermain, put your hand here where mine is. Now, do you feel anything?"

"I *think* I feel air coming up."

"Now listen." He rose and stamped upon the place, and a flame of hope shot up in our hearts. *It rang hollow.*

With trembling hands I lit a match. I had only three left, and we saw that we were in the angle of the far corner of the chamber, a fact that accounted for our not having noticed the hollow sound of the place during our former exhaustive examination. As the match burnt we scrutinised the spot. There was a join in the solid rock floor, and, great heavens! there, let in level with the rock, was a stone ring. We said no word, we were too excited, and our hearts beat too wildly with hope to allow us to speak. Good had a knife, at the back of which was one of those hooks that are made to extract stones from horses' hoofs. He opened it, and scratched round the ring with it. Finally he worked it under, and levered away gently for fear of breaking the hook. The ring began to move. Being of stone it had not got set fast in all the centuries it had lain there, as would have been the case had it been of iron. Presently it was upright. Then he thrust his hands into it and tugged with all his force, but nothing budged.

"Let me try," I said impatiently, for the situation of the stone, right in the angle of the corner, was such that it was impossible for two to pull at once. I took hold and strained away, but no results.

Then Sir Henry tried and failed.

Taking the hook again, Good scratched all round the crack where we felt the air coming up.

"Now, Curtis," he said, "tackle on, and put your back into it; you are as strong as two. Stop," and he took off a stout black silk handkerchief, which, true to his habits of neatness, he still wore, and ran it through the ring. "Quatermain, get Curtis round the middle and pull for dear life when I give the word. *Now.*"

Sir Henry put out all his enormous strength, and Good and I did the same, with such power as nature had given us.

"Heave! heave! it's giving," gasped Sir Henry; and I heard the muscles of his great back cracking. Suddenly there was a grating sound, then a rush of air, and we were all on our backs on the floor with a heavy flag-stone upon the top of us. Sir Henry's strength had done it, and never did muscular power stand a man in better stead.

"Light a match, Quatermain," he said, so soon as we had picked ourselves up and got our breath; "carefully, now."

I did so, and there before us, Heaven be praised! was the *first step of a stone stair.*

"Now what is to be done?" asked Good.

"Follow the stair, of course, and trust to Providence."

"Stop!" said Sir Henry; "Quatermain, get the bit of biltong and the water that are left; we may want them."

I went, creeping back to our place by the chests for that purpose, and as I was coming away an idea struck me. We had not thought much of the diamonds for the last twenty-four hours or so; indeed, the very idea of diamonds was nauseous, seeing what they had entailed upon us; but, reflected I, I may as well pocket a few in case we ever should get out of this ghastly hole. So I just put my fist into the first chest and filled all the available pockets of my old shooting-coat and trousers, topping up—this was a happy thought—with a few handfuls of big ones from the third chest. Also, by an afterthought, I stuffed Foulata's basket, which, except for one water-gourd and a little biltong, was empty now, with great quantities of the stones.

"I say, you fellows," I sang out, "won't you take some diamonds with you? I've filled my pockets."

"Oh, come on, Quatermain! and hang the diamonds!" said Sir Henry. "I hope that I may never see another."

As for Good, he made no answer. He was, I think, taking his last farewell of all that was left of the poor girl who had loved him so well. And curious as it may seem to you, my reader, sitting at home at ease and reflecting on the vast, indeed the immeasurable, wealth which we were thus abandoning, I can assure you that if you had passed some twenty-eight hours with next to nothing to eat and drink in that place, you would not have cared to cumber yourself with diamonds whilst plunging down into the unknown bowels of the earth, in the wild hope of escape from an agonising death. If from the habits of a lifetime, it had not become a sort of second nature with me never to leave anything worth having behind if there was the slightest chance of my being able to carry it away, I am sure that I should not have bothered to fill my pockets.

"Come on, Quatermain," repeated Sir Henry, who was already standing on the first step of the stone stair. "Steady, I will go first."

"Mind where you put your feet, there may be some awful hole underneath," I answered.

"Much more likely to be another room," said Sir Henry, while he descended slowly, counting the steps as he went.

When he got to "fifteen" he stopped. "Here's the bottom," he said. "Thank goodness! I think it's a passage. Come on down."

Good went next, and I came last, carrying the basket, and on reaching the bottom lit one of the two remaining matches. By its light we could just see that we were standing in a narrow tunnel, which ran right and left at right angles to the staircase we had descended. Before we could make out any more, the match burnt my fingers and went out. Then arose the delicate question of which way to go. Of course, it was impossible to know what the tunnel was, or where it led to, and yet to turn one way might lead us to safety, and the other to destruction. We were utterly perplexed, till suddenly it struck Good that when I had lit the match the draught of the passage blew the flame to the left.

"Let us go against the draught," he said; "air draws inwards, not outwards."

We took this suggestion, and feeling along the wall with the hand, whilst trying the ground before us at every step, we departed from that accursed treasure chamber on our terrible quest for life. If ever it should be entered again by living man, which I do not think probable, he will find tokens of our visit in the open chests of jewels, the empty lamp, and the white bones of poor Foulata.

When we had groped our way for about a quarter of an hour along the passage, suddenly it took a sharp turn, or else was bisected by another, which we followed, only in course of time to be led into a third. And so it went on for some hours. We seemed to be in a stone labyrinth that led nowhere. What all these passages are, of course I cannot say, but we thought that they must be the ancient workings of a mine, of which the various shafts and adits travelled hither and thither as the ore led them. This is the only way in which we could account for such a multitude of galleries.

At length we halted, thoroughly worn out with fatigue and with that hope deferred which maketh the heart sick, and ate up our poor remaining piece of biltong and drank our last sup of water, for our throats were like lime-kilns. It seemed to us that we had escaped Death in the darkness of the treasure chamber only to meet him in the darkness of the tunnels. As we stood, once more utterly depressed, I thought that I caught a sound, to which I called the attention of the others. It was very faint and very far off, but it *was* a sound, a faint, murmuring sound, for the others heard it too, and no words can describe the blessedness of it after all those hours of utter, awful stillness.

"By heaven! it's running water," said Good. "Come on."

Off we started again in the direction from which the faint murmur seemed to come, groping our way as before along the rocky walls. I remember that I laid down the basket full of diamonds, wishing to be rid of its weight, but on second thoughts took it up again. One might as well die rich as poor, I reflected. As we went the sound became more and more audible, till at last it seemed quite loud in the quiet. On, yet on; now we could distinctly make out the unmistakable swirl of rushing water. And yet how could there be running water in the bowels of the earth? Now we were quite near it, and Good, who was leading, swore that he could smell it.

"Go gently, Good," said Sir Henry, "we must be close." *Splash!* and a cry from Good.

He had fallen in.

"Good! Good! where are you?" we shouted, in terrified distress. To our intense relief an answer came back in a choky voice.

"All right; I've got hold of a rock. Strike a light to show me where you are."

Hastily I lit the last remaining match. Its faint gleam discovered to us a dark mass of water running at our feet. How wide it was we could not see, but there, some way out, was the dark form of our companion hanging on to a projecting rock.

"Stand clear to catch me," sung out Good. "I must swim for it."

Then we heard a splash, and a great struggle. Another minute and he had grabbed at and caught Sir Henry's outstretched hand, and we had pulled him up high and dry into the tunnel.

"My word!" he said, between his gasps, "that was touch and go. If I hadn't managed to catch that rock, and known how to swim, I should have been done. It runs like a mill-race, and I could feel no bottom."

We dared not follow the banks of the subterranean river for fear lest we should fall into it again in the darkness. So after Good had rested a while, and we had drunk our fill of the water, which was sweet and fresh, and washed our faces, that needed it sadly, as well as we could, we started from the banks of this African Styx, and began to retrace our steps along the tunnel, Good dripping unpleasantly in front of us. At length we came to another gallery leading to our right.

"We may as well take it," said Sir Henry wearily; "all roads are alike here; we can only go on till we drop."

Slowly, for a long, long while, we stumbled, utterly exhausted, along this new tunnel, Sir Henry now leading the way.

Suddenly he stopped, and we bumped up against him.

"Look!" he whispered, "is my brain going, or is that light?"

We stared with all our eyes, and there, yes, there, far ahead of us, was a faint, glimmering spot, no larger than a cottage window pane. It was so faint that I doubt if any eyes, except those which, like ours, had for days seen nothing but blackness, could have perceived it at all.

With a gasp of hope we pushed on. In five minutes there was no longer any doubt; it *was* a patch of faint light. A minute more and a breath of real live air was fanning us. On we struggled. All at once the tunnel narrowed. Sir Henry went on his knees. Smaller yet it grew, till it was only the size of a large fox's earth—it was *earth* now, mind you; the rock had ceased.

A squeeze, a struggle, and Sir Henry was out, and so was Good, and so was I, and there above us were the blessed stars, and in our nostrils was the sweet air. Then suddenly something gave, and we were all rolling over and over and over through grass and bushes and soft, wet soil.

I caught at something and stopped. Sitting up I halloed lustily. An answering shout came from just below, where Sir Henry's wild career had been stopped by some level ground. I scrambled to him, and found him unhurt, though breathless. Then we looked for Good. A little way off we discovered him also, hammed in a forked root. He was a good deal knocked about, but soon came to himself.

We sat down together, there on the grass, and the revulsion of feeling was so great that really I think we cried for joy. We had escaped from that awful dungeon, which was so near to becoming our grave. Surely some merciful Power guided our footsteps to the jackal hole, for that is what it must have been, at the termination of the tunnel. And see, yonder on the mountains the dawn we had never thought to look upon again was blushing rosy red.

Presently the grey light stole down the slopes, and we saw that we were at the bottom, or rather, nearly at the bottom, of the vast pit in front of the entrance to the cave. Now we could make out the dim forms of the three Colossi who sat upon its verge. Doubtless those awful passages, along which we had wandered the livelong night, had been originally in some way connected with the great diamond mine. As for the subterranean river in the bowels of the mountain, Heaven only knows what it is, or whence it flows, or whither it goes. I, for one, have no anxiety to trace its course.

Lighter it grew, and lighter yet. We could see each other now, and such a spectacle as we presented I have never set eyes on before or since. Gaunt-cheeked, hollow-eyed wretches, smeared all over with dust and mud, bruised, bleeding, the long fear of imminent death yet written on our countenances, we were, indeed, a sight to frighten the daylight. And yet it is a solemn fact that Good's eye-glass was still fixed in Good's eye. I doubt whether he had ever taken it out at all. Neither the darkness, nor the plunge in the subterranean river, nor the roll down the slope, had been able to separate Good and his eye-glass.

Presently we rose, fearing that our limbs would stiffen if we stopped there longer, and commenced with slow and painful steps to struggle up the sloping sides of the great pit. For an hour or more we toiled steadfastly up the blue clay, dragging ourselves on by the help of the roots and grasses with which it was clothed.

At last it was done, and we stood by the great road, on that side of the pit opposite to the Colossi.

At the side of the road, a hundred yards off, a fire was burning in front of some huts, and round the fire were figures. We staggered towards them, supporting one another, and halting every few paces. Presently one of the figures rose, saw us and fell on to the ground, crying out for fear.

"Infadoos, Infadoos! it is we, thy friends."

He rose; he ran to us, staring wildly, and still shaking with fear.

"Oh, my lords, my lords, it is indeed you come back from the dead!—come back from the dead!"

And the old warrior flung himself down before us, and clasping Sir Henry's knees, he wept aloud for joy.

XIX. Ignosi's Farewell

Ten days from that eventful morning found us once more in our old quarters at Loo; and, strange to say, but little the worse for our terrible experience, except that my stubbly hair came out of the treasure cave about three shades greyer than it went in, and that Good never was quite the same after Foulata's death, which seemed to move him very greatly. I am bound to say, looking at the thing from the point of view of an oldish man of the world, that I consider her removal was a fortunate occurrence, since, otherwise, complications would have been sure to ensue. The poor creature was no ordinary native girl, but a person of great, I had almost said stately, beauty, and of considerable refinement of mind. But no amount of beauty or refinement could have made an entanglement between Good and herself a desirable occurrence; for, as she herself put it, "Can the sun mate with the darkness, or the white with the black?"

I need hardly state that we never again penetrated into Solomon's treasure chamber. After we had recovered from our fatigues, a process which took us forty-eight hours, we descended into the great pit in the hope of finding the hole by which we had crept out of the mountain, but with no success. To begin with, rain had fallen, and obliterated our spoor; and what is more, the sides of the vast pit were full of ant-bear and other holes. It was impossible to say to which of these we owed our salvation. Also, on the day before we started back to Loo, we made a further examination of the wonders of the stalactite cave, and, drawn by a kind of restless feeling, even penetrated once more into the Chamber of the Dead. Passing beneath the spear of the White Death we gazed, with sensations which it would be quite impossible for me to describe, at the mass of rock that had shut us off from escape, thinking the while of priceless treasures beyond, of the mysterious old hag whose flattened fragments lay crushed beneath it, and of the fair girl of whose tomb it was the portal. I say gazed at the "rock," for, examine as we could, we could find no traces of the join of the sliding door; nor, indeed, could we hit upon the secret, now utterly lost, that worked it, though we tried for an hour or more. It is certainly a marvellous bit of mechanism, characteristic, in its massive and yet inscrutable simplicity, of the age which produced it; and I doubt if the world has such another to show.

At last we gave it up in disgust; though, if the mass had suddenly risen before our eyes, I doubt if we should have screwed up courage to step over Gagool's mangled remains, and once more enter the treasure chamber, even in the sure and certain hope of unlimited diamonds. And yet I could have cried at the idea of leaving all that treasure, the biggest treasure probably that in the world's history has ever been accumulated in one spot. But there was no help for it. Only dynamite could force its way through five feet of solid rock. and so we left it. Perhaps, in some remote unborn century, a more fortunate explorer may hit upon the "Open Sesame," and flood the world with gems. But, myself, I doubt it. Somehow, I seem to feel that the tens of millions of pounds' worth of jewels which lie in the three stone coffers will never shine round the neck of an earthly beauty. They and Foulata's bones will keep cold company till the end of all things.

With a sigh of disappointment we made our way back, and next day started for Loo. And yet it was really very ungrateful of us to be disappointed; for, as the reader will remember, by a lucky thought, I had taken the precaution to fill the wide pockets of my old shooting coat with gems before we left our prison-house. A good many of these fell out in the course of our roll down the side of the pit, including several of the big ones, which I had crammed in on the top. But, comparatively speaking, an enormous quantity still remained, including ninety-three large stones ranging from about one hundred to thirty carats in weight. My old shooting coat and the basket still held sufficient treasure to make us all, if not millionaires as the term is understood in America, at least exceedingly wealthy men, and yet to keep enough stones each to make the three finest sets of gems in Europe. So we had not done so badly.

On arriving at Loo we were most cordially received by Ignosi, whom we found well, and busily engaged in consolidating his power, and reorganising the regiments which had suffered most in the great struggle with Twala.

He listened with intense interest to our wonderful story; but when we told him of old Gagool's frightful end he grew thoughtful.

"Come hither," he called, to a very old Induna or councillor, who was sitting with others in a circle round the king, but out of ear-shot. The ancient man rose, approached, saluted, and seated himself.

"Thou art aged," said Ignosi.

"Ay, my lord the king! Thy father's father and I were born on the same day."

"Tell me, when thou wast little, didst thou know Gagaoola the witch doctress?"

"Ay, my lord the king!"

"How was she then—young, like thee?"

"Not so, my lord the king! She was even as she is now and as she was in the days of my great grandfather before me; old and dried, very ugly, and full of wickedness."

"She is no more; she is dead."

"So, O king! then is an ancient curse taken from the land."

"Go!"

"*Koom!* I go, Black Puppy, who tore out the old dog's throat. *Koom!*"

"Ye see, my brothers," said Ignosi, "this was a strange woman, and I rejoice that she is dead. She would have let you die in the dark place, and mayhap afterwards she had found a way to slay me, as she found a way to slay my father, and set up Twala, whom her heart loved, in his place. Now go on with the tale; surely there never was its like!"

After I had narrated all the story of our escape, as we had agreed between ourselves that I should, I took the opportunity to address Ignosi as to our departure from Kukuanaland.

"And now, Ignosi," I said, "the time has come for us to bid thee farewell, and start to see our own land once more. Behold, Ignosi, thou camest with us a servant, and now we leave thee a mighty king. If thou art grateful to us, remember to do even as thou didst promise: to rule justly, to respect the law, and to put none to death without a cause. So shalt thou prosper. To-morrow, at break of day, Ignosi, thou wilt give us an escort who shall lead us across the mountains. Is it not so, O king?"

Ignosi covered his face with his hands for a while before answering.

"My heart is sore," he said at last; "your words split my heart in twain. What have I done to you, Incubu, Macumazahn, and Bougwan, that ye should leave me desolate? Ye who stood by me in rebellion and in battle, will ye leave me in the day of peace and victory? What will ye—wives? Choose from among the maidens! A place to live in? Behold, the land is yours as far as ye can see. The white man's houses? Ye shall teach my people how to build them. Cattle for beef and milk? Every married man shall bring you an ox or a cow. Wild game to hunt? Does not the elephant walk through my forests, and the river-horse sleep in the reeds? Would ye make war? My Impis wait your word. If there is anything more which I can give, that will I give you."

"Nay, Ignosi, we want none of these things," I answered; "we would seek our own place."

"Now do I learn," said Ignosi bitterly, and with flashing eyes, "that ye love the bright stones more than me, your friend. Ye have the stones; now ye would go to Natal and across the moving black water and sell them, and be rich, as it is the desire of a white man's heart to be. Cursed for your sake be the white stones, and cursed he who seeks them. Death shall it be to him who sets foot in the place of Death to find them. I have spoken. White men, ye can go."

I laid my hand upon his arm. "Ignosi," I said, "tell us, when thou didst wander in Zululand, and among the white people of Natal, did not thine heart turn to the land thy mother told thee of, thy native land where thou didst see the light, and play when thou wast little, the land where thy place was?"

"It was even so, Macumazahn."

"In like manner, Ignosi, do our hearts turn to our land and to our own place."

Then came a silence. When Ignosi broke it, it was in a different voice.

"I do perceive that now as ever thy words are wise and full of reason, Macumazahn; that which flies in the air loves not to run along the ground; the white man loves not to live on the level of the black. Well, ye must go, and leave my heart sore, because ye will be as dead to me, since from where ye are no tidings can come to me.

"But listen, and let all your brothers know my words. No other white man shall cross the mountains, even if any man live to come so far. I will see no traders with their guns and gin. My people shall fight with the spear, and drink water, like their forefathers before them. I will have no praying-men to put a fear of death into men's hearts, to stir them up against the law of the king, and make a path for the white folk who follow to run on. If a white man comes to my gates I will send him back; if a hundred come I will push them back; if armies come, I will make war on them with all my strength, and they shall not prevail against me. None shall ever seek for the shining stones: no, not an army, for if they come I will send a regiment and fill up the pit, and break down the white columns in the caves and choke them with rocks, so that none can reach even to that door of which ye speak, and whereof the way to move it is lost. But for you three, Incubu, Macumazahn, and Bougwan, the path is always open; for, behold, ye are dearer to me than aught that breathes.

"And ye would go. Infadoos, my uncle, and my Induna, shall take you by the hand and guide you with a regiment. There is, as I have learned, another way across the mountains that he shall show you. Farewell, my brothers, brave white men. See me no more, for I have no heart to bear it. Behold! I make a decree, and it shall be published from the mountains to the mountains; your names, Incubu, Macumazahn, and Bougwan, shall be 'hlonipa' even as the names of dead kings, and he who speaks them shall die.* So shall your memory be preserved in the land for ever.

"Go now, ere my eyes rain tears like a woman's. At times as ye look back down the path of life, or when ye are old and gather yourselves together to crouch before the fire, because for you the sun has no more heat, ye will think of how we stood shoulder to shoulder, in that great battle which thy wise words planned, Macumazahn; of how thou wast the point of the horn that galled Twala's flank, Bougwan; whilst thou stood in the ring of the Greys, Incubu, and men went down before thine axe like corn before a sickle; ay, and of how thou didst break that wild bull Twala's strength, and bring his pride to dust. Fare ye well for ever, Incubu, Macumazahn, and Bougwan, my lords and my friends."

Ignosi rose and looked earnestly at us for a few seconds. Then he threw the corner of his karross over his head, so as to cover his face from us.

We went in silence.

Next day at dawn we left Loo, escorted by our old friend Infadoos, who was heart-broken at our departure, and by the regiment of Buffaloes. Early as was the hour, all the main street of the town was lined with multitudes of people, who gave us the royal salute as we passed at the head of the regiment, while the women blessed us for having rid the land of Twala, throwing flowers before us as we went. It was really very affect-ing, and not the sort of thing one is accustomed to meet with from natives.

One ludicrous incident occurred, however, which I rather welcomed, as it gave us something to laugh at.

---

*This extraordinary and negative way of showing intense respect is by no means unknown among African people, and the result is that if, as is usual, the name in question has a significance, the meaning must be expressed by an idiom or other word. In this way a memory is preserved for generations, or until the new word utterly supplants the old one.

Just before we reached the confines of the town, a pretty young girl, with some lovely lilies in her hand, ran forward and presented them to Good—somehow they all seemed to like Good; I think his eye-glass and solitary whisker gave him a fictitious value—and then said that she had a boon to ask.

"Speak on," he answered.

"Let my lord show his servant his beautiful white legs, that his servant may look upon them, and remember them all her days, and tell of them to her children; his servant has travelled four days' journey to see them, for the fame of them has gone throughout the land."

"I'll be hanged if I do!" exclaimed Good excitedly.

"Come, come, my dear fellow," said Sir Henry, "you can't refuse to oblige a lady."

"I won't," replied Good obstinately; "it is positively indecent."

However, in the end he consented to draw up his trousers to the knee, amidst notes of rapturous admiration from all the women present, especially the gratified young lady, and in this guise he had to walk till we got clear of the town.

Good's legs, I fear, will never be so greatly admired again. Of his melting teeth, and even of his "transparent eye," the Kukuanas wearied more or less, but of his legs never.

As we travelled, Infadoos told us that there was another pass over the mountains to the north of the one followed by Solomon's Great Road, or rather that there was a place where it is possible to climb down the wall of cliff which separates Kukuanaland from the desert, and is broken by the towering shapes of Sheba's Breasts. It appeared, also, that rather more than two years previously a party of Kukuana hunters had descended this path into the desert in search of ostriches, whose plumes are much prized among them for war head-dresses, and that in the course of their hunt they had been led far from the mountains and were much troubled by thirst. Seeing trees on the horizon, however, they walked towards them, and discovered a large and fertile oasis some miles in extent, and plentifully watered. It was by way of this oasis that Infadoos suggested we should return, and the idea seemed to us a good one, for it appeared that we should thus escape the rigours of the mountain pass. Also some of the hunters were in attendance to guide us to the oasis, from which, they stated, they could perceive other fertile spots far away in the desert.*

---

*It often puzzled all of us to understand how it was possible that Ignosi's mother, bearing the child with her, should have survived the dangers of her journey across the mountains and the desert, dangers which so nearly proved fatal to ourselves. It has since occurred to me, and I give the idea to the reader for what it is worth, that she must have taken this second route, and wandered out like Hagar into the wilderness. If she did so, there is no longer anything inexplicable about the story, since, as Ignosi himself related, she may well have been picked up by some ostrich hunters before she or the child was exhausted, was led by them to the oasis, and thence by stages to the fertile country, and so on by slow degrees southwards to Zululand.—A.Q.

Travelling easily, on the night of the fourth day's journey we found ourselves once more on the crest of the mountains that separate Kukuanaland from the desert, which rolled away in sandy billows at our feet, and about twenty-five miles to the north of Sheba's Breasts.

At dawn on the following day, we were led to the edge of a very precipitous chasm, by which we were to descend the precipice, and gain the plain two thousand and more feet below.

Here we bade farewell to that true friend and sturdy old warrior, Infadoos, who solemnly wished all good upon us, and nearly wept with grief. "Never, my lords," he said, "shall mine old eyes see the like of you again. Ah! the way that Incubu cut his men down in the battle! Ah! for the sight of that stroke with which he swept off my brother Twala's head! It was beautiful—beautiful! I may never hope to see such another, except perchance in happy dreams."

We were very sorry to part from him; indeed, Good was so moved that he gave him as a souvenir—what do you think?—an *eye-glass*; afterwards we discovered that it was a spare one. Infadoos was delighted, foreseeing that the possession of such an article would increase his prestige enormously, and after several vain attempts he actually succeeded in screwing it into his own eye. Anything more incongruous than the old warrior looked with an eye-glass I never saw. Eye-glasses do not go well with leopard-skin cloaks and black ostrich plumes.

Then, after seeing that our guides were well laden with water and provisions, and having received a thundering farewell salute from the Buffaloes, we wrung Infadoos by the hand, and began our downward climb. A very arduous business it proved to be, but somehow that evening we found ourselves at the bottom without accident.

"Do you know," said Sir Henry that night, as we sat by our fire and gazed up at the beetling cliffs above us, "I think that there are worse places than Kukuanaland in the world, and that I have known unhappier times than the last month or two, though I have never spent such queer ones. Eh! you fellows?"

"I almost wish I were back," said Good, with a sigh.

As for myself, I reflected that all's well that ends well; but in the course of a long life of shaves, I never had such shaves as those which I had recently experienced. The thought of that battle makes me feel cold all over, and as for our experience in the treasure chamber—!

Next morning we started on a toilsome trudge across the desert, having with us a good supply of water carried by our five guides, and camped that night in the open, marching again at dawn on the morrow.

By noon of the third day's journey we could see the trees of the oasis of which the guides spoke, and within an hour of sundown we were walking once more upon grass and listening to the sound of running water.

XX. FOUND

And now I come to perhaps the strangest adventure that happened to us in all this strange business, and one which shows how wonderfully things are brought about.

I was walking along quietly, some way in front of the other two, down the banks of the stream which runs from the oasis till it is swallowed up in the hungry desert sands, when suddenly I stopped and rubbed my eyes, as well I might. There, not twenty yards in front of me, placed in a charming situation, under the shade of a species of fig-tree, and facing to the stream, was a cosy hut, built more or less on the Kafir principle with grass and withes, but having a full-length door instead of a bee-hole.

"What the dickens," said I to myself, "can a hut be doing here?" Even as I said it the door of the hut opened, and there limped out of it a *white man* clothed in skins, and with an enormous black beard. I thought that I must have got a touch of the sun. It was impossible. No hunter ever came to such a place as this. Certainly no hunter would ever settle in it. I stared and stared, and so did the other man, and just at that juncture Sir Henry and Good walked up.

"Look here, you fellows," I said, "is that a white man, or am I mad?"

Sir Henry looked, and Good looked, and then all of a sudden the lame white man with a black beard uttered a great cry, and began hobbling towards us. When he was close he fell down in a sort of faint.

With a spring Sir Henry was by his side.

"Great Powers!" he cried, "*it is my brother George!*"

At the sound of this disturbance, another figure, also clad in skins, emerged from the hut, a gun in his hand, and ran towards us. On seeing me he too gave a cry.

"Macumazahn," he hallooed, "don't you know me, Baas? I'm Jim the hunter. I lost the note you gave me to give to the Baas, and we have been here nearly two years." And the fellow fell at my feet, and rolled over and over, weeping for joy.

"You careless scoundrel!" I said; "you ought to be well hided."

Meanwhile the man with the black beard had recovered and risen, and he and Sir Henry were pump-handling away at each other, apparently without a word to say. But whatever they had quarrelled about in the past—I suspect it was a lady, though I never asked—it was evidently forgotten now.

"My dear old fellow," burst out Sir Henry at last, "I thought you were dead. I have been over Solomon's Mountains to find you. I had given up all hope of ever seeing you again, and now I come across you perched in the desert, like an old *assvögel*."*

"I tried to cross Solomon's Mountains nearly two years ago," was the answer, spoken in the hesitating voice of a man who has had little recent opportunity of using his tongue, "but when I reached here a boulder fell on my leg and crushed it, and I have been able to go neither forward nor back."

Then I came up. "How do you do, Mr. Neville?" I said; "do you remember me?"

"Why," he said, "isn't it Hunter Quatermain, eh, and Good too? Hold on a minute, you fellows, I am getting dizzy again. It is all so very strange, and, when a man has ceased to hope, so very happy!"

That evening, over the camp fire, George Curtis told us his story, which, in its way, was almost as eventful as our own, and, put shortly, amounted to this. A little less than two years before, he had started from Sitanda's Kraal, to try to reach Suliman's Berg. As for the note I had sent him by Jim, that worthy lost it, and he had never heard of it till to-day. But, acting upon information he had received from the natives, he headed not for Sheba's Breasts, but for the ladder-like descent of the mountains down which we had just come, which is clearly a better route than that marked out in old Dom Silvestra's plan. In the desert he and Jim had suffered great hardships, but finally they reached this oasis, where a terrible accident befell George Curtis. On the day of their arrival he was sitting by the stream, and Jim was extracting the honey from the nest of a stingless bee which is to be found in the desert, on the top of a bank immediately above him. In so doing he loosened a great boulder of rock, which fell upon George Curtis's right leg, crushing it frightfully. From that day he had been so lame that he found it impossible to go either forward or back, and had preferred to take the chances of dying in the oasis to the certainty of perishing in the desert.

As for food, however, they got on pretty well, for they had a good supply of ammunition, and the oasis was frequented, especially at night, by large quantities of game, which came thither for water. These they shot, or trapped in pitfalls, using the flesh for food, and, after their clothes wore out, the hides for clothing.

"And so," George Curtis ended, "we have lived for nearly two years, like a second Robinson Crusoe and his man Friday, hoping against hope that some natives might come here to help us away, but none have come. Only last night we settled that Jim should leave me, and try to reach Sitanda's Kraal to get assistance. He was to go to-morrow, but I had little hope of ever seeing him back again. And now *you*, of all people in the world,

---

* Vulture.

you, who, as I fancied, had long ago forgotten all about me, and were living comfortably in old England, turn up in a promiscuous way and find me where you least expected. It is the most wonderful thing that I have ever heard of, and the most merciful too."

Then Sir Henry set to work, and told him the main facts of our adventures, sitting till late into the night to do it.

"By Jove!" he said, when I showed him some of the diamonds: "well, at least you have got something for your pains, besides my worthless self."

Sir Henry laughed. "They belong to Quatermain and Good. It was a part of the bargain that they should divide any spoils there might be."

This remark set me thinking, and having spoken to Good, I told Sir Henry that it was our joint wish that he should take a third portion of the diamonds, or, if he would not, that his share should be handed to his brother, who had suffered even more than ourselves on the chance of getting them. Finally, we prevailed upon him to consent to this arrangement, but George Curtis did not know of it until some time afterwards.

Here, at this point, I think that I shall end my history. Our journey across the desert back to Sitanda's Kraal was most arduous, especially as we had to support George Curtis, whose right leg was very weak indeed, and continually threw out splinters of bone. But we did accomplish it somehow, and to give its details would only be to reproduce much of what happened to us on the former occasion.

Six months from the date of our re-arrival at Sitanda's, where we found our guns and other goods quite safe, though the old rascal in charge was much disgusted at our surviving to claim them, saw us all once more safe and sound at my little place on the Berea, near Durban, where I am now writing. Thence I bid farewell to all who have accompanied me through the strangest trip I ever made in the course of a long and varied experience.

P.S.—Just as I had written the last word, a Kafir came up my avenue of orange trees, carrying a letter in a cleft stick, which he had brought from the post. It turned out to be from Sir Henry, and as it speaks for itself I give it in full.

> October 1, 1884
> BRAYLEY HALL, YORKSHIRE

MY DEAR QUATERMAIN,

I send you a line a few mails back to say that the three of us, George, Good, and myself, fetched up all right in England. We got off the boat at Southampton, and went up to town. You should have seen what a swell Good turned out the very next day, beautifully shaved, frock coat fitting like a glove, brand new eye-glass, etc., etc. I went and walked in the park with him, where I met some people I know, and at once told them the story of his "beautiful white legs."

He is furious, especially as some ill-natured person has printed it in a Society paper.

To come to business, Good and I took the diamonds to Streeter's to be valued, as we arranged, and really I am afraid to tell you what they put them at, it seems so enormous. They say that of course it is more or less guess-work, as such stones have never to their knowledge been put on the market in anything like such quantities. It appears that (with the exception of one or two of the largest) they are of the finest water, and equal in every way to the best Brazilian stones. I asked them if they would buy them, but they said that it was beyond their power to do so, and recommended us to sell by degrees, over a period of years indeed, for fear lest we should flood the market. They offer, however, a hundred and eighty thousand for a very small portion of them.

You must come home, Quatermain, and see about these things, especially if you insist upon making the magnificent present of the third share, which does *not* belong to me, to my brother George. As for Good, he is *no good*. His time is too much occupied in shaving, and other matters connected with the vain adorning of the body. But I think he is still down on his luck about Foulata. He told me that since he had been home he hadn't seen a woman to touch her, either as regards her figure or the sweetness of her expression.

I want you to come home, my dear old comrade, and to buy a house near here. You have done your day's work, and have lots of money now, and there is a place for sale quite close which would suit you admirably. Do come; the sooner the better; you can finish writing the story of our adventures on board ship. We have refused to tell the tale till it is written by you, for fear lest we shall not be believed. If you start on receipt of this you will reach here by Christmas, and I book you to stay with me for that. Good is coming, and George; and so, by the way, is your boy Harry (there's a bribe for you). I have had him down for a week's shooting, and like him. He is a cool young hand; he shot me in the leg, cut out the pellets, and then remarked upon the advantages of having a medical student with every shooting party!

Good-bye, old boy; I can't say any more, but I know that you will come, if it is only to oblige

Your sincere friend,

HENRY CURTIS

P.S.—The tusks of the great bull that killed poor Khiva have now been put up in the hall here, over the pair of buffalo horns you gave me, and look magnificent; and the axe with which I chopped off Twala's head is fixed above my writing-table. I wish that we could have managed to bring away the coats of chain armour.

H.C.

To-day is Tuesday. There is a steamer going on Friday, and I really think that I must take Curtis at his word, and sail by her for England, if it is only to see you, Harry, my boy, and to look after the printing of this history, which is a task that I do not like to trust to anybody else.

ALLAN QUATERMAIN

ORIGINAL SOURCES

Bierce, Ambrose. "The Secret of Macarger's Gulch," *Can Such Things Be?* New York: Cassell Publishing Co., 1893.

Burroughs, Edgar Rice. "The Capture of Tarzan," *Jungle Tales of Tarzan*. Chicago: A. C. McClurg & Co., 1919.

Clifford, Sir Hugh. "The Quest of the Golden Fleece," *Blackwood's Edinburgh Magazine*, January 1903.

Conrad, Joseph. "The Brute," *A Set of Six*. New York: Doubleday, Page & Co., 1908.

Crane, Stephen. "One Dash—Horses," *The Open Boat and Other Tales of Adventure*. New York: Doubleday & McClure Co., 1898.

Doyle, Arthur Conan. "The Green Flag," *The Green Flag and Other Stories*. New York: P. F. Collier & Son, 1900.

Greene, L. Patrick. "Tools," *Adventure*, August 1, 1921.

Haggard, H. Rider. *King Solomon's Mines*. London: Cassell and Company, Ltd., 1907.

Henry, O. "The Caballero's Way," *Heart of the West*. New York: Doubleday, Page & Co., 1904.

Hodgson, William Hope. "The Albatross," *Adventure*, July 1911.

Kipling, Rudyard. *The Man Who Would Be King*. New York: Doubleday & McClure Co., 1899.

London, Jack. "The Heathen," *South Sea Tales*. New York: Macmillan, 1911.

Mason, Elmer Brown. "The Golden Anaconda," *The Popular Magazine*, February 20, 1916.

Maugham, W. Somerset. "Mackintosh," *The Trembling of a Leaf*. London: Heinemann, 1921.

McCulley, Johnston. *The Mark of Zorro*. New York: Grosset & Dunlap, 1920.

Montross, Lynn. "A Gulp of Water," *Adventure*, November 18, 1920.

Mundy, Talbot. "For the Salt Which He Had Eaten," *Told in the East*. Indianapolis: The Bobbs Merrill Company, 1920.

Musgrave, Joseph W. "Sword of Gimshai," *Jungle Stories*, Spring 1954.

O'Brien, David Wright. "Even the Worm Turns," *South Sea Stories*, December 1939.

Poe, Edgar Allan. "A Descent into the Maelström," *Tales*. New York: Wiley and Putnam, 1845.

Rohmer, Sax. "Lord of the Jackals," *Tales of Secret Egypt*. New York: Robert McBride & Company, 1919.

Stevenson, Robert Louis. "The Beach of Falesá," *Island Nights' Entertainments*. London: Cassell & Co., 1893.

Wallace, Edgar. "The Wood of Devils," *Sanders of the River*. London: Ward, Lock & Co., Limited, 1911.

Wister, Owen. "A Kinsman of Red Cloud," *The Jimmyjohn Boss and Other Stories*. New York: Harper & Brothers Publishers, 1902.

Wren, P. C. "Ten Little Legionaries," *Stepsons of France*. London: John Murray, 1917.